ECOLOGISTS

A Novel

William Dritschilo

This book is a work of fiction. All characters in this book are fictional, including the real ones. Historical events and personalities have been modified for dramatic purposes.

Samizdat

Created using OpenOffice Writer 4.1.1

Cover design and photography: Jamie Dritschilo

2015

Printed by CreateSpace, An Amazon.com Company

"... If you want to become a man of letters and perhaps write some History some day, you must also lie and invent tales, otherwise your History would become monotonous. But you must act with restraint. The world condemns liars who do nothing but lie, even about the most trivial things, and it rewards poets, who lie only about the greatest things."

Niketas had some trouble following Baudolino's story, year by year. Not only did it seem to him that his narrator was a bit confused about what had happened before and what had happened after, but he also found that Frederick's exploits were repeated, always the same, and he could no longer understand when the Milanese had taken up arms again, when they had threatened Lodi, or when the emperor had come down again to Italy.

— Umberto Ecco
Baudolino

Chicago

I

BEING late to class is straight out of a nightmare. Being late to its first meeting makes it even worse.

As much as she tries, she cannot nudge those ahead of her to move any faster or to let her pass. So she grabs her hat with one hand, jumps a low cordon, and plunges into the quadrangle and the wind off the lake that whistles through the campus. She draws several disapproving looks for violating the spring grass, and a few admiring ones for the graceful way she does it.

These slow pokes shall not make me late, she says to herself. This class, in which her uncle insisted she enroll, to her perplexity, took too much trouble to get into. As a freshman, she was low on its waiting list. It took Uncle George's intercession by telephone with Cowles to finally—just that morning—get her into it. She can not now be late.

She makes it to the class just in the nick of time, sliding into an empty place at the back of the room. She flashes a quick smile at the only other person in her row. As he returns her silent greeting with his own, she takes note of how handsome he might be but for the thick glasses he wears.

The man at the front of the room turns out not to be the famous "Doctor Coals," as the name is pronounced, but a lesser personage by the name of Fuller. Undaunted, she writes this new name out as the first entry in her notebook. "Ecology is the study of mutual relationships between plants and their environment," she then adds.

Stealing quick glances at the other students, she can find not one familiar face. A frightening realization sneaks up on her: she is the only freshman in the class, and she is a tenuous one, at that, barely sixteen, coming to the college straight from eleventh grade. Taking their measure, she notes glumly that the women's faces are all in lipstick and mascara and their dress hems reach their ankles, very unlike her own freshly scrubbed face and outmoded hemline.

"Why did sweet old Uncle George put me in this course?" she groans to herself at class's end as she rushes out ahead of the others. "And why now? In the third quarter? I have to prepare for comprehensive exams. I'm not ready for this."In fact, she feels generally not ready, and it is not just because of her age. The "New Plan" is just too new. She is in the first group subject to it. There is little guidance and no past practice to rely on. She feels a pressing need, now in the final quarter of her biology and sociology courses, to revisit, if not reread, the entire year's assignments for both, all while continuing to assimilate—No! she interrupts herself. Not assimilate!—MASTER new material. She thanks God for the review sessions just scheduled in bio. But they take time too! How can she now take on a new course? Especially an upper level one!

But that boy in the same row with her ... well, man, really. Did he sneak glances at her? Could she hope for that? Could it be that he followed her out?

She stops and looks behind her. Disappointment. Among all the faces heading in her direction, not one is his.

Cowles does not do much teaching. Why is obvious to all. He suffers from palsy in speech and movement. There are no tremors, just slow motion in everything. His writing, perhaps to conserve energy, Jewel speculates, produces minute scrawls on the backboard. His mumbles are little more comprehensible. In secretive giggles, he is unkindly described as having a pig face and his mumbles, pig grunts.

Tears well up in Jewel's eyes from frustration at not being able to follow his words. Sympathetic to her distress, the young man in the back row gives her a glance at his own notes. She cannot decipher his handwriting either, with its curlicues and unnecessary flourishes, but her tears do stop.

Fuller, who taught the first class, fortunately takes on the responsibility of interpreting Cowles' scrawls and words for those—most in attendance—who wish to stay after class to have him repeat the old professor's lantern slides. Many more days than not, though, it is Fuller who gives the class lectures, with Cowles missing or, more rarely, nodding in agreement beside him. Although it is Cowles for whom they signed up, the students appreciate not having to sit through the class twice. They brighten when it is Fuller who greets them from the front of the room.

Neither does Cowles go on the field trips for which the course is famous. The one to the dunes is an exception, however. He spends the week before the trip anticipating for them with his old lantern slides what they will find in that very special place.

"What should I wear should the weather be unpropitious or unclement that day?" Jewel writes in her notebook.

That day starts out as anything but clement. Rain descends on the group as they cross the border into Indiana. Complaining moans emerge ahead of the students from the motor cars as they assemble around Cowles and Fuller. They are damp in spirit and person. Lake Michigan is gray. But Cowles cackles cheerfully.

"This is the world that plants live in!" he admonishes the groaners in a voice that is surprisingly loud and clear. "It's not always sunshine and flowers, and there is no heading for shelter. We are lucky to have this rain. Wouldn't be much plant life without it! Would there?"

The rain does not concern Jewel as much as what people are wearing. At the last minute, she decided on a riding outfit, complete with boots and jodhpurs. It was all that she had specifically bought for her school wardrobe, the rest of which was mostly outmoded hand-me-downs from her flapper mother, who had argued against the purchase. Jewel then never found a need for the outfit. There are slaughterhouses still in Chicago, Jewel learned, but no riding stables. Now, seeing that she is not the only one so attired, she is pleased to be finally wearing the riding outfit. In fact, Jewel is surprised to be in the height of style. Other women, mostly in dresses and knickers, the latter stuffed into calf-high boots, voice their envy. Some have no boots. It is the middle of the Great Depression.

"Do you ride?" Jewel hears a high-pitched, but male voice behind her.

"Miss, uh—"

It is the young man with the thick glasses.

"I've ridden a few horses myself," he continues when she does not offer her name.

She is struck by his accent. Unlike the nasal twang of the Midwesterners in the class, his nasality resonates with the modulating tones of Eastern prep schools, although not the New England ones, she guesses, but those of Manhattan. He is clearly Upper West Side, or Scarsdale, perhaps, in origin.

"Fairfax," she finally decides to introduce herself, controlling the frog in her throat. "Jewel Fairfax. Pleased to meet you."

"Like the Fairfaxes of Virginia?"

"Well, yes," she says, pleasingly noting that she is looking up at him slightly, rather than down, "but my roots are all in New England, even though there is some sort of genealogical connection with the Fairfaxes of Virginia. It must be strictly on paper, though, for none of my family in New London, Old Lyme, or even New Haven can claim having any Virginia Fairfax ever acknowledge a kinship."

"I too am from Connecticut in a way," the young man responds.

Their conversation is interrupted by Fuller and Cowles rapidly lobbing bits of information at them. The reverential way the young man tries to catch every word the old man launches impresses Jewel. She will never again think of his utterances as grunts.

"No plants on beach b/c wave action but at back edge grass roots stabilize sand," Jewel scribbles furiously in her field book as Fuller and Cowles lead the group inland. "Grasses add humus to sand making soil so other plants thrive displacing grass," she adds as she goes up the trail. Even with his obvious health issues, it is difficult to keep up both physically and intellectually with the short, rather paunchy Cowles as he leads everyone at a steady pace through the sequence being described.

Jewel looks back to check if the young man is still close behind her. He is, very close. And—another surprise—he is taking no notes.

"A new dune offers plants a world to conquer," Cowles expounds from atop a sandy bluff as others struggle up it. "And each conquest is subject almost entirely to the existing physical conditions. Do you all see that?"

Jewel does see it, but does not write it down. Too big an idea for so few words, she decides, giving up her desperate attempt to write down the great man's words, most of which are being conveyed through echoes from Fuller. Besides, the old man is already leading the group down off the dune and into a bog. Jewel's boots turn out to be of no help in traversing it, a quaking one she realizes as she steps out onto it, marveling at the trampoline feel she experiences.

"Stay away from the water lilies," Jewel hears Fuller behind her, the advice already too late. "They have roots that go down into deeper water."

The young man, on firmer ground, is about to repeat the admonition, but thinks better of it on seeing the look on her face. One of her boots has broken through the matted surface. Reacting instantly, he reaches out and pulls her toward firmer footing.

"My goodness," he says, smiling, as he sets her atop a solid surface. "You don't want to get bogged down in that."

Embarrassed by the girlish shriek she let out, Jewel tries to hurry away before he can even let go of her hand. But his grip is too tight. She has to turn and face him.

"Thank you," she says breathlessly before he lets go, taking away the electricity of his touch.

The boots make for slow going in the steep sandy sides of the blowout enclosing the bog. Still, she is better off than those without boots, who have to wear heavy socks up to their knees.

"Their poor dogs!" she silently sympathizes as she watches a pair of classmates slog along in what have to be cold, wet feet. "They'll be that way for the rest of the day."

Her own feet still feel dry. And the difficult scrambles up the sand are eased by having the young man pull her along.

Like the other men students, he displays the usual male oblivion to the elements. Doctor Cowles, Jewel notes, has on the same white shirt and not very fashionable tie that he wears invariably to class. A floppy hat, instead of a bowler is his only concession to the elements. Her young man with the Upper West Side accent is bareheaded. All others in the group, women included, wear large, shady hats. There are none of the helmet-shaped bonnets that are still in style among the women, who outnumber the men on the trip by a wide margin. Sleeves are long, even though, once the sun comes out, it is a warm and very humid day. And all reek from citronella except for Cowles, who lights a cigar against the omnipresent mosquitoes.

They are at the Indiana Dunes, where Cowles made his reputation. What they are seeing, Fuller, repeats what has been drummed into them all week as he counts heads, is what Doctor

Cowles was the first to see with his geologically trained eyes some forty years before.

Cowles is waiting for them atop a dune that is invaded by shrubs and trees. "Ecology is a study in dynamics," he announces for all to hear as they assemble around him, his words finally slowing to a slur. "This flora is not changeless. It is rather a panorama. Never twice alike. All flora is dynamic."

It is the highest dune in the area. On this day it is a mountain.

"From up here, the dunes look like Connecticut snow drifts after a Nor'easter," Jewel says, looking back toward the lake.

"Yes they do," her young man agrees. "Precisely so."

"Tolleson Dune is four thousand years old," Fuller announces. "As you can see, it is covered with vegetation, but it, too, started as a bare dune."

Then, to general consternation, Cowles recites something in Greek. Many assume he has merely fallen back into mumbled grunts.

"And thou are one," the young man beside her translates. "One with the eternal hills."

Then he adds in a whisper meant for her alone: "It's from the bible, but in Greek."

"Yes, thank you, Mr. Küchler," Cowles says, having overheard. His mumble is definitely back, but he is easily understood. The years of repeating each phrase that he now says allow it to form itself on his lips and slide off his tongue. "However, the hills aren't eternal. They are changing. Even mountains change. The normal primitive formation here, as Professor Fuller has told you, is the beach. Then, in order, the stationary beach dunes, the wandering dunes, the transitional dunes, and the established dunes. Oak forest is the end of succession here, its climax. After it comes only disturbance and a regression to a former stage and the process starts all over again."

"How can we know?" someone asks.

"That is why you must look with the eye of a geologist," Fuller jumps in loudly. "Glaciers, winds, and waves move the dunes. The lake was much bigger in the past. And smaller."

The group had been instructed before setting off on the trip to take notes on whatever plant or formation Fuller or Cowles or someone in the group found interesting. However, the specimens are small, too many observers crowd around for all to get a good look, and the transitions from stopping to examine a plant and then hurtling forward again are too abrupt. The students turn to teamwork. Jewel instantly joins Küchler. She takes on the responsibility of trying to get a view of the specimen at issue and make a quick sketch. Küchler notes the Latin and common name, while a third member takes notes on soil and microclimate.

"Hectic," Jewel says, thinking aloud, "but better by far than the lab in my biology course. The specimens in Dr. Coulter's demonstrations are strictly hands-off to students. Why—"

But it is time to move on.

"Why aren't you writing down the name like the others, Mr. Küchler?" Cowles chuckles on seeing the slim young man grinning at him at one of the stops.

"I am very familiar with Ignotus damnifiknow, sir." Küchler answers, his eyes sending a return twinkle Cowles' way.

II

"MY goodness! The entire credit hinges on one six-hour exam! Nothing else counts! How does one survive?" Liza despairs. "I'm supposed to learn all the forces that are supposed to be the Industrial Revolution. I don't think there's an F=ma for it. How can a revolution be forces? How can industry be a revolution? Where are the Bolsheviks?"

"Oh, they're coming, believe me," Jewel answers.

The two are in Jewel's Spartan dormitory room. A wind-up Victrola on a shabby, small table tucked into a corner is the only concession to luxury. A shellac disk recording of Stardust by Louis Armstrong lies on its turntable. It is the only "jigaboo" music the Victrola's owner will tolerate. The dark-spined albums leaning haphazardly against each other on the bare floor beneath are all classical music. Jewel is sprawled surrounded by books and papers on her bed, while Liza sits at the room's single desk. Earlier increases in enrollment converted the room from a double to a triple; more recent decreases failed to return it to its intended occupancy. Jewel is trying to write a paper for her botany class, carrying on an audible conversation with herself as she does so. Liza is silently cramming for an exam, all the while watching the clock in order not to miss her train home. Actually, her eyes flit from one to another of the three alarm clocks in the room that bedevil in orderly succession whomever is the last to arise each morning, usually Jewel. This afternoon is a far cry from the more leisurely park-to-park expeditions they sometimes take together on Saturdays along the Midway Plaisance, drawn to museums, which is Jewel's pleasure, or the observatory, which is Liza's.

"Did you know what Doctor Cowles once said when someone asked him how long a paper should be?" Jewel asks, breaking Liza's concentration. "He said it should be like a skirt. It should be long enough to cover the subject, but short enough to keep things interesting."

Liza fends off the distraction with a weak laugh. "And how do these forces affect our economic, social and political institutions?" she asks without looking up from her notes. "Someone tell me what they are first! The only one I know is socialism. I read about it in Norman Thomas's book."

Jewel suddenly pops upright. "Oh, you should have been here last year!" she almost shrieks. "What a scandal! The editor of the Maroon waged a campaign against the core courses."

"?"

"He kept writing editorials—I swear there was a new one each day—and commissioned critiques that said all they did was cram facts into students."

"I'd like some facts for sociology right now."

"My friend, Marie Berger," Jewel begins, then thinks to add, "She graduated already." After pausing to make sure she really had Liza's attention, she continues, "She gathered together hundreds of signatures on a petition to show that this Braden fellow was all wet."

"So, what did this Braden person want?"

"They wanted a Great Books curriculum!"

"I thought that was what we had."

"So did I."

"Then what about this Walgreen affair?"

This time, it is Jewel who replies, "?"

"Charles Walgreen claims the core courses inculcated his niece with Communism, is how I think he said it. It was in all the papers"

"Oh, I think that's just a Hearst provocation, like Sacco and Vanzetti. There are no Communists teaching the core courses. Gideonse and Wirth? Communists? Never! Don't trust everything you read in the paper. A lot of it is all wet. Just a bunch of baloney. In fact, don't keep your nose in the paper so much."

"They do teach the Communist Manifesto," Liza retorts. "Here." She passes a sheet of paper to Jewel. "See? It's on the reading list."

"I know. I know," Jewel says. "Well, I think you should just get into the discussion section led by this young man from Montana. Maclean, his name is. Norman, I think. Very engaging. Very energetic. The cat's pajama's, really. He makes the material not just understandable, but fun!"

Liza's nose is back into her sociology reading.

Good, thinks Jewel, seeing that Liza is no longer listening. She starts scribbling furiously in her small, black, hardbound notebook, hoping to make some progress on her paper before the next interruption.

Jewel first met Liza on a day she overslept. Both her roommates were already gone when she awoke too late to even venture out for class. She had lazed in bed looking at their unmade beds until she was certain that sleep would no longer return, so she threw the covers over her own bed, wrapped a raincoat tightly around her pajamas, and headed out for the cafeteria. And there, sitting alone at a table near the back, she spied what she took to be a schoolgirl. She even imagined her in pigtails and pinafores, playing at the table with dolls. She was so sweet looking. She was furtively reading about Wally and Edward in the paper, having folded the tabloid awkwardly to hide its headline. When Jewel thought to sit down at her table—the only one empty in the cafeteria, which was already mobbed by the lunch crowd—the girl looked up with a startle and pushed the paper away.

Jewel asked if she was waiting for someone. A brother or sister perhaps? Or even mother maybe, she wondered to herself.

She was Liza Woods, the girl announced, smiling brightly. "Lee-za," she pronounced it. Then there was silence. Jewel sipped her coffee. The little girl watched wordlessly, cocking her head in a way that made Jewel think a parrot was examining her.

Well, Jewel thought, maybe I said something to put her off—or maybe there is just not that much in common between us, given the difference in ages. She smiled back and prepared to leave.

That was when the girl finally spoke up.

"You're nice," she said. "When you smile, your entire face curls into it. Thank you for sitting next to me. I thought no one here ever would."

What a pill she would have been to leave just then, Jewel now proudly thinks, looking at Liza once more before forcing her attention back on her paper.

"I see it and I love it and I write it," she says aloud, almost as a chant.

"What?"

"It's Gertrude Stein."

"Who?"

"A poetess."

"What's it mean?"

"Exactly what it says, I guess."

"Oh. You have to get back to your paper?"

A few minutes later, Liza, now from behind her Chicago Tribune interrupts with: "Why don't they just get married?"

"Maclean?"

"No, Wally and Edward."

"Hmm," is Jewel's response. At it again, she says to herself. How distracted by simple human foibles are the "fish," as freshmen are called by upperclassmen. Especially of movie stars and kings! No wonder Liza is having trouble with sociology.

"I wish I could explain it to you simply," she finally says in frustration, "but maybe there is no reason why they can't just get married, but they can't."

Liza returns a perplexed expression. Jewel reciprocates.

"How did you get from sociology to that?"

"Isn't it sociology?"

"More to the point is this Maclean guy. Switch into his section. You won't worry so much about the course with him. He makes you learn the stuff without realizing it."

"Babe Ruth hit three home runs yesterday," Liza says, emerging from behind her paper. "Can you imagine that?"

"How can that be sociology?"

Liza shrugs her shoulders. "I got bored with sociology, I guess."

"Here's some sociology for you," Jewel offers moments later. "Education, crime control, and religion."

"What is it?"

"Wildflowers. I just found the notes I was looking for. On the value of wildflowers. All are sociological values."

"You left out esthetics," Liza says, now looking over Jewel's shoulder. "But when did you ever write like that? Look at all those crazy curlicues. I can hardly make it out."

"They're another student's notes from a class we took together. He left them for me."

Jewel tries to pretend a blush is not forming on her cheeks.

"Esthetics?" Liza asks.

"Beauty."

"Ah! Of course. Must have been too obvious for this friend of yours to write down. But how do wildflowers promote education?" Liza asks.

"He wrote, they stimulate investigation, foster studies indispensable to science and the world at large," Jewel reads in a firm, slow voice, hoping with her words to push away the red that is still on her cheeks.

"Meaning?"

Jewel shrugs her shoulders. "People like to study them?"

"Because they're pretty?"

"I would guess."

"Don't people study things that aren't attractive?"

"Not botanists. Not Küchler, for example." She stops for a second, as if making some decision, then continues matter-of-factly, "He started college at Syracuse Forestry in order to beautify the world."

"Was that out of religious feeling?"

"You ask difficult questions. Is beautifying the world spiritual? Hmm. If so, then Cookie has dedicated his life to the study of God. Now that's a stretch."

"Cookie?"

"KOOCHler," Jewel enunciated.

"Ah! So is that thing about appreciating flowers reducing crime also a stretch."

"Well, people sniffing flowers are hardly able to rob banks at the same time!"

Liza laughs. "I bet your Küchler said that." Then she asks again, "Cookie?"

Jewel's face is a deep red. Liza's, however, has turned pale. She is looking at a clock. She quickly gathers her things together and bolts from the room with just an "Oh dear!" in farewell. As soon as she is gone, Jewel puts down her notebook and takes out a packet of blue stationary decorated with the stylized dark silhouette of a cat.

"Dear Frederick," she begins in bold script. "You would really REALLY love to meet my friend Liza! She really is one of a kind. I met her one day when I had overslept—I seem to be doing a lot of that these days, what with having passed all my comprehensives. How Great Books fill my head now! Shakespeare discourses with Darwin. Dante with Rousseau."

But it seems somehow not good enough. She crumples the page in her hand.

"You would really LOVE to meet my friend Liza" she begins anew. "She is a chemistry major, a hard science. Can you imagine? She took calculus in high school. She can barely imagine what a social science is. She lives close by—LaGrange—and comes to school each day on the train, but she is practically living with us now in the dorm."

That too is not good enough. Another crumpled blue paper. She bounces it off her roommate's Victrola into a wastebasket.

"You should meet my best friend, Liza," she begins her next effort. "She looked like she was twelve when I first met her, but she turned out to be fifteen. And she was enrolled at Chicago. And she felt awkwardly out of place. And she was friendless, she confided to me. And thought she would remain so."

How quickly Liza made those years between them melt away, it suddenly strikes Jewel. She stops her pen. An idea, explanation perhaps, is floating invisibly above her in the room. Why did she look for her again in the cafeteria? Why does she now treat the younger Liza as an equal? Her delicate, dark features suddenly dominate Jewel's attention. Someone else comes to mind. Yes, of course, Woods Hole. Liza's name being Woods must have effected the connection. Rachel even has the same features, but for

Liza's heavier brow line, which nonetheless has Liza as the prettier one, in Jewel's opinion.

Jewel too had been feeling alone and unwanted then. She too had felt out of place, too young to be friends with anyone. The Marine Biological Laboratories, she had started to fear, was just another of Uncle George's failed experiments. And then Rachel called her over to her table at the mess. She had arrived as part of a covey, it seemed to Jewel, of women—all graduate students—from Johns Hopkins. They had their own research table at the laboratories. Jewel had assumed the same exclusivity extended to the mess—but they had taken her in with a single, simple gesture from Rachel. And like her, Rachel was queasy on the water and preferred research along the shoreline of that beautiful seaside village. She and Jewel were perfect companions. True, Jewel admits, she became little more than a low-level unpaid assistant to them at best and a hanger-on at worst—but it was all that she needed to get her through three lonely weeks.

So she must have decided to be Liza's Rachel, Jewel now concludes.

She writes none of that in her letter.

"When will you ever return to Chicago?" she writes instead. "Don't you miss walking along the Midway and the parks? Stock is back for another season at the Symphony. Don't you need a respite from that violinist, Ormandy? I understand that he is moving to Philadelphia. That means an even more inexperienced conductor for you to tolerate. Why not come back and enjoy an old pro?

"Hope your thesis will work out. I mentioned what you were doing to Uncle George. He was very interested."

She wanted to sign it, "with love," but signed, "yours," instead.

III

THE sea was what she missed most of home when she was at Chicago. Lake Michigan was a poor substitute. As much as Liza tried, she could not touch Jewel with her infectious zest for it. Liza would swim in Lake Michigan every morning if she could, winter or summer. But without waves and rip currents doing their best to drown the unwary, the lake seemed but a large, dull swimming hole that gave no excuse for Jewel to shy away from full immersion. And what is the shore, after all, without the sound of sheets clanging against masts, their rhythm entirely dependent on wave actions, or without the smell of salt in the air? What would a clambake have been like at the Indiana Dunes? Probably chicken salad.

Jewel takes refuge this August day along a long arm of the Atlantic. Driven away by the chaos at her house, she walks down Maple Avenue to Willard Bay, where she can step into the waters of the sound. She does not, however, join the bathers, mostly vacationers who are playing in its calm waves. Finding suitable driftwood away from them, she plunks herself down on the sand and props her back against a large, smooth-surfaced log.

What she has brought with her to be enjoyed out of earshot of the angry voices in her home is a single letter, tucked away against a still-girlish breast inside her summer blouse. She has tied that garment daringly high, revealing a narrow strip of flat, white tummy.

He has finally answered her letter. It is months late, but still, it is a letter. It is a long letter, pages full of details from his new life. There are his new friends. Murray and Helen Buell, names she commits to memory, are foremost among them. They must be truly marvelous, she thinks. He describes them with so much enthusiasm. And how romantic to be working together on the same little lake for their PhD projects? How she would love to meet them!

The letter is full of ecology, especially of his misgivings about the science. He does not think that the quadrat method is in any way better than simply choosing samples based on experienced professional judgment. Bold that, she thinks, in this modern era of mathematical analysis. Heretical, even. She does not have to wonder what Uncle George might think of it. Clements's quadrat method, she knows, is standard in plant ecology. It allows reproducible estimates of what plants make up what forest or meadow, and in what amounts, without poking into every square inch. Even Liza commends the method, although only with the caveat that the world should be as regular and predictable above the molecular level as it is below it. Why should there be sampling issues? Liza challenges. Why can't everything be resolved uniformly on some lower level?

Now here is Fred, not only doubting Clements's method, but also belittling his theory, the only general theory that Jewel could point to in ecological science for Liza. It was brilliant, she and Liza agreed, that plant communities, such as the various formations through which she had trudged with Cowles, grow and develop into a creature-like thing at climax, the individual plants like the cells of what is normally thought to be organisms. Of course, it was not as brilliant to Liza as the theory of the atom.

Fred, Jewel can tell from his letter, has a new champion: his esteemed "Dr. Cooper," who seems to take issue both with Clements and with her Uncle George. Cooper does not subscribe to Clements's theory of the climax community functioning as an individual organism, Küchler reports. Vegetational succession should be thought of as something more like a "flowing, braided stream." That isn't all, Küchler further reports. Unlike Clements, who discounts it, the influence of fire and man on succession should not be ignored according to Cooper. And, vegetation dynamics cannot be understood without taking past climate changes into consideration.

That last idea makes Jewel look away toward the sea. Uncle George, she knows, is trying to understand the vegetation of New England as it is at present, with little regard for what might have happened in the distant past, which he insists can be known only imperfectly. She should pop over to New Haven, Jewel thinks, make use of Uncle George's library, and read some of "Dr. Cooper's" writings. She might even catch Uncle George with time to sit down to talk at some length about all of this. How they both love such talks! But mother would no doubt call the trip an extravagant waste of money. Everything to her these days is a waste of money. They seem to have so little of it, hardly enough for an occasional train fare. How will they ever afford her last year at Chicago?

She shifts her attention from Küchler's words to those she intends to put down on the folded sheet of blue paper that she now takes from its resting-place beside her other breast. All that about ecology, she says almost aloud, is well and good, but what about me? Us, she adds more tentatively. How can we be living in the same state without having somehow met up with each other? It is downright embarrassing!

I did so enjoy your letter from Arden Forest, she thinks to write as she ponders the name—meant to invoke Eden? Particularly your marvelous description of the doings of its wildlife. How I would love to see it. I looked it up on the map. Cole Brook is so close to here.

No. Not right. She rethinks her thoughts, starts over.

I guess it is time to be thinking of returning to the Midwest! I am looking forward to seeing my friend Liza again and I am sure that you have missed your …

No. How trite, clichéd, even.

But wait! She has an idea! Why can't we take the train out together? At least arrange to be on the same train part of the way out to Chicago? We will be traveling over the same paths. Better yet, why couldn't I go with him to Minneapolis? Is there a spare couch in that rooming house of his that he described so fondly? I could be back at Chicago the next day!

How brazen! What will he think of her?

And why not?

PS, she decides she will write, do you know that before I set these words on it, this piece of paper journeyed out to a beach on Long Island Sound caressing the skin of my virginal breast?

Then she realizes she has brought nothing with which to write.

A sailboat out on the sound catches her attention for a few moments, then a voice does. It is her younger sister, looking for her. She will want to cry on her shoulder, Jewel knows. She is desperate enough for Jewel's support that she has ventured out in daylight with her black eye and bruises. Why are some people such monsters?

IV

"LIZA, look."

Jewel's face is pressed against the train window. Liza, who took the train almost daily, had gladly conceded the window seat to her. They are passing by a collection of tin-roofed shacks.

"A Hooverville," Liza says nonchalantly after shifting herself awkwardly to look over her friend's shoulders through the window. "All the shacks seem well on the way to falling in on themselves and becoming anonymous track-side rubble. Some of them, I think, had signs of still being occupied."

"Occupied?" Jewel made a face. "You mean like by the Bonus Marchers in Washington? I thought Mrs. Roosevelt took care of all that by going out and having tea with them, then giving them all jobs building roads in the swamps of Florida."

"Where did you learn that? Not from the newspapers."

"Radio? All the newspapers have these days is whether Bruno Hauptmann is guilty or not."

"Of, course he is. It's just awful what he's done to the Lindberg family. That flyboy was one of my heroes. Spirit of St. Louis. Wasn't that the bee's knees?"

"My hero, too. Lucky Lindy. His flight to France was on my tenth birthday. How we all celebrated then!"

"Ireland," Liza interrupts.

"Ireland?"

"I'm pretty sure."

"Anyway, the important thing was how happy we all were. It was like a spontaneous birthday party." She pauses as happiness drains from her face. "Everything was so better then. My father smiled all the time. Tar paper and tin dwellings didn't litter the landscape."

"I know what you mean. We had tough times, too. I most remember being afraid to answer a knock on the door. When once I flew to it, expecting to greet some friend, I started to let my mother answer it."

"I know what you mean. It seemed that only beggars knocked on our doors, too, going from house to house in search of a meal or a handout and we had nothing for them."

"But we should have had nothing to fear but fear itself."

Jewel looks at her crossly, wondering if her friend's Midwestern Republicanism was surfacing to belittle Eastern Democrats.

"But what do you think about Vickie Sharp?" Liza changes the subject.

"What can I think? She was involved somehow. In fact, my guess was that she might have had an affair with Lindy and it went bad."

"Jeepers!"

Liza's scatter-shot chatter is a needed distraction for Jewel. For the moment, she would rather be on a train to Minneapolis, not LaGrange, and in the company of Fred Küchler, not Liza. Jewel did manage to connect with him on the train west, but their trip together ended in Chicago. Once back at school, Jewel seemed so despondent, so rarely did her face light up with a smile, that Liza attributed the mood to Jewel's unsympathetic new roommates. That compelled her to invite Jewel home for a weekend and away from them. She even paid Jewel's fare out of her own pocket money, insisting over Jewel's protest that she had to, as it was her invitation.

"Here we are," Liza announces to Jewel's surprise. It seemed that not enough time had passed for the train to get out of Chicago.

There is no lighthouse, there are no boat harbors, and the stately mansions of La Grange have no sea to face, but the place has very much the feeling Old Saybrook to Jewel. Same size. Same makes of automobiles. Same men's and women's fashions. And although a suburb of a giant city, La Grange is far enough into the country to, like Old Saybrook, still have horses stabled within its city limits.

Oh, how she wishes she could mount up on the chestnut stallion she spies in a paddock within sight of the station. What a ride that would be! But will she ever ride again, she wonders, losing herself once more in gloominess, or is that all part of her lost childhood? Just memories?

The Woods turn out not to be horse people, to her disappointment. Still, the family greets her so warmly that, from her first minute with them, she is glad to be there and not in her dorm room—or home.

When, exactly, Jewel now asks herself, did things start falling apart? Black Tuesday presents itself as a convenient date, but she really cannot connect any of the events around the stock market crash to memories of goings on in her family. Her father must have hushed everything up back then, she realizes now. There had also been times before the crash when her father seemed not to be her father, when he acted like some stranger. Had he already been hiding the truth?

How unlike the warmth exuded by Liza's father!

"You know, Liza, I feel wrapped in an aura of belonging here" she confides when the two are once more alone with each other. "I no longer have that feeling in Old Saybrook. My father's drinking, his and my mother's withdrawals into their moods, my sister's problems—fights is what they are—with her husband— It all seems off in another world."

They are enjoying lemonade in her family's back yard in what Liza calls her secret garden. House and yard are appropriately spacious for a lawyer. They proudly fit Liza, or Eliza, as her mother still calls her, her two brothers and two sisters as children. Jewel finds few luxuries in it, however. There is nothing equivalent to even the plainest of family antiques that still fill Fairfax homes.

The power of old money, Jewel thinks. It explains why Liza needs a scholarship and a part-time job to be able to attend Chicago, while Jewel still has her tuition paid by her father.

"So that's what has had you moping around!" Liza breaks into Jewel's thoughts. "All families have their problems. But you have a duty to yourself, too. You have to just get on with your own life."

There is a pause, then Jewel confides, "Getting on with my life is exactly my problem." And she bursts into tears.

Liza manages to quell the heaving sobs with her soothing touches, but only momentarily.

"I love him, Liza," Jewel gasps. "I love him so much it hurts."

Sobs rack Jewel's body once more.

"Who?" Liza asks.

"And it all turns out to have been my Uncle George's fault," comes out of Jewel when her sobs subside. "Sweet old Uncle George. I can't even get angry with him. Ha! He is the only one in my family who seems to have any sanity left. And he married into it!"

"Huh?"

Jewel wants to say that it was Uncle George who had insisted that she take Cowles' class. Had he not, she never would have met Küchler and she never would have told Uncle George about him and Uncle George would not have lured him away from his precious "Dr. Cooper" with the offer of a fellowship at Yale. But it seems pointless.

Liza, meanwhile, puzzles out that it is not Jewel's Uncle George who is the object of painful love. Instantly, she forms a hypothesis about who it is.

"I can see you and Küchler making a handsome couple together, Scott and Zelda perhaps," Liza guesses, having little more notion of Scott Fitzgerald's looks than what she took from a grainy newspaper photo and none at all of Küchler's. "You're so stylishly thin, so beautiful, a flapper. You're so attractive. How could anyone not fall for you?"

"Really? Am I attractive?"

"Gorgeous! I wish I had half your looks. You look like Merle Oberon."

"Who?"

"I just saw her in Dark Angel. You have her cheek bones. I don't know how she could have fallen for that Alan character, though. I—"

"But then, shouldn't all the boys be swooning over me? It's what an attractive woman deserves, don't you think? But the boys back home certainly did not."

"What? High school boys? Those children? They still think the way to charm a woman is to dip her pigtails into an inkwell. If you no longer have pigtails, they no longer have any way of showing you."

"Hmm," Jewel says, lost in thought, "but flappers, my dear Liza, are no longer stylish. I guess."

Something resembling that playful, all-over-her-face smile begins to appear.

"I hate current fashions," Jewel says, "even if I could afford all the clothes I imagine other women must have. I like the persona of a flapper. I read somewhere that it might become chic again."

"It will! It will! I have no love for current fashions either. Skirts down to the ankle again. How can a woman catch a man's eye?"

"Or even run after him!" Jewel laughs.

"And those plunging necklines!"

"Not for us, Liza. And imagine those expensive stoles they wrap their bosoms in. That fox would have a hard time finding a tit to bite on us!"

"And how! You and me both. But still, your figure is ideal for the flapper silhouette. Scott and Zelda, remember?

"Or how about the ridiculous hats that women are wearing" Jewel asks. "They can't make up their minds what they should be. Some are cowboy-ish, others just seem to be tiny hat boxes or sailor's hats, the silly things that hotel bellboys wear. And those equally silly black veils that they have taken to wearing—with plumes and costume jewelry on them! It has to be costume jewelry—who these days can afford those things otherwise? And are there that many widows these days? Even black evening dresses are being given dark bridal veils. The widow at her wedding."

"And never could I succumb to a permanent wave. No ma'am."

"Yes! Our boyish cuts are the only way to have our hair. And cut by a sister or brother, not some fancy hairdresser."

"So, what happened between you two?" Liza suddenly asks.

"Oh, Liza! Nothing! Nothing happened! I offered myself to him, Liza. I dolled myself up in my mother's most vampy old clothes, what little bubs I have almost hanging out for him to pick like apples. I was willing to let him play with my body like it was a toy, if he wanted to!"

"And nothing? No nookie?"

"Nothing, Liza. How could he have resisted, if I'm as gorgeous as you say? Not even any necking. And I would have done anything for him that he wanted, whatever a man might need, short of nookie, as you put it."

"Anything?" this gave Liza pause. "Did you—"

"Liza," Jewel interrupted, "I pressed my hand on it in his pants on the train in a car full of people. I told him I would go with him to Minneapolis. And nothing."

"Nothing?"

"Nothing. Like he didn't notice. He didn't even swell. I could feel it with my fingers through the linen of his pants. It wasn't at all hard. I could tell that much. He said he did not feel that way about me. I was so ashamed! So embarrassed! He said he valued my friendship too much."

"I think it's a good thing that you did not go off to Minneapolis with your Frederick," Liza says, taking on a serious tone. "A very good thing. You know, I just read—have you ever heard of the Mann Act? There was a case right here in Chicago of a college girl visiting her beau. And Jack Johnson, the boxer, had to leave the country to avoid being sent to prison for the same offense. And Frank Lloyd Wright was threatened with arrest right in Minnesota."

"What offense?'

"Transporting a female—especially an underage one—across state lines for ... for ... nefarious purposes."

"Illicit purposes?'

"Maybe."

"Underage? I'm almost eighteen."

"Under twenty-one."

"Do you think that was why?"

"Could be."

And suddenly, they are on the New Deal—is it really working?—and the rise of a funny-looking man with a tiny brush of a mustache in Germany. Then they are laughing about Jewel's advice the previous term to switch sociology sections. It had taken Liza two sessions to realize that Maclean led a humanities section. Then they are at the piano. Jewel tries to teach Liza the sonata form. Liza proudly brings out her set of molecular models and tries to teach Jewel about atomic structure. Jewel counters with an exposition on vampires.

"I like the way your mind can jump from one thing to another," Liza tells Jewel. "Most of my classmates seem to badger an idea or subject to death before letting it go. You leave it with something interesting still in it and open up another, even more interesting thing."

"And you," responds Jewel, "might be able to charm Edward away from Wally."

"Fat chance. As if I would want to!"

Then Liza asks, "What would you have done for Küchler, if things had gone differently?"

"Whatever he wanted me to."

Liza is left to imagine what "whatever" is.

V

"I can't see myself doing anything but trying to find out what makes matter the way it is, even if I have to mash it into atoms. I intend to start taking graduate courses as soon as I can fit them into my schedule. I already have my way planned to a doctoral degree here. If things work out, the two of us might march together at graduation, even given your head start"

"That would be great!" Jewel marvels. "But, Jeepers, I don't think I have the same commitment to the study of botany. Flowers are pretty, but boring, unless they're outdoors. Once you've seen them in a herbarium and named them, what else is there?"

They are in Liza's room. Weekends now find them more often at La Grange than Chicago. A small bed, once occupied by a sister, has been restored to her room to welcome Jewel's visits. The bathroom at the end of the hall is in permanent possession of a toothbrush belonging to Jewel and often displays her various soaps and lotions. Jewel has even mastered the vagaries of the pull cord for the toilet.

"There's only one thing that I think struck me in any way like the mysteries of the atom have you in their grip," Jewel announces. "That's a single, simple phrase in one of Cowles' lectures. He called the process of succession a variable tracking a variable. That's as deep to me as what is going on inside an atom. Maybe that's what life is like. We chase something only to find it has changed on us, that it's not the same thing we started after. Maybe not just life, but everything, even science, is like that."

"The things that science studies are determinate," Liza says with pomposity. "Or else you can't study them—or shouldn't. You can only truly learn the meaning of life by examining smaller and smaller pieces of it, delving way down into the molecular level, even into the atom. The ecological level is so vast. Where do you even start?"

"I can start by learning the names of things, at least, and where they live and how. That will give me access to the knowledge I'll need to understand life. Meaning will eventually come to me."

"Maybe, but you'll need more schooling for that. Lots more. There are an awful lot of critters out there to learn. In physics, we have less than a hundred things that are equivalent to species, and they only have three basic building blocks. Then there's the problem that ecologists seem to be defining what they are studying as they study it. Talk about a moving target!"

"I imagine myself finishing with my classes and looking for a teaching position," Jewel answers, "hopefully at a high school. Even though Uncle George is a professor at Yale, none of the Fairfax women have aspired to much in the way of higher education. Connecticut College and marriage were sufficient for them. I'm the exception. Enrolling here was looked at by all in my family as just another of Uncle George's experiments, and I think he expects me to go further than I am capable."

"Don't be silly! I think I see in you exactly what your Uncle George sees. Of course, you're capable of a PhD."

"Well, thank you," Jewel says ending the conversation by heading for the bathroom.

"Why don't you try animal ecology?" Liza asks when Jewel returns in her nightgown. It has become routine for Liza to change into nightclothes while Jewel is at her evening ablutions.

"Huh?" Jewel asks, having already forgotten the previous conversation.

"Animal ecology. There are a lot fewer animals than there are plants, aren't there? We had a lecture on it by someone—Oh what was his name? Wally something. Ward, maybe? Of course, that was his first name. He was interesting. He even tied the subject to wars and Nazism. I think maybe you just haven't found the right subject."

Liza jumps out of bed to look through an old notebook while Jewel impatiently waits for the lights to be turned off.

"Allee," Liza finally announces, bouncing back onto her bed. "But all I have is initials. No first name. He is an interesting man is the full lowdown. And he gave his entire lecture seated before the blackboard. Didn't write a thing on it."

The light goes off.

"Liza, there are a lot more insects, I think, than there are plants."

"Insects aren't animals, are they?"

"Do you mean mammals?"

"Oh. Of course."

"Have you ever—" Liza asks awkwardly later in the night. "You know—with a man?"

"Hmm?" Jewel murmurs sleepily.

"With a man. Like what you told me you did with Küchler. Have you had other—"

"Not really," Jewel answers, giving up on sleep. "Not that I haven't wondered about it or thought about doing it. Not that I haven't hoped for it, hoped for being simply swept off my feet."

"Really?"

There is silence. Neither one sleeps, however.

"You think it's good?" Liza finally breaks the silence. "Does it feel good? I thought it was just painful."

"It has to feel good," Jewel answers. "Even if painful, there has to be pleasure to it. Has to be, or else my sister would never stay with her lout of a husband. They fight all the time, but after every fight there is a creaky bed in their room rapidly creaking faster and faster. It might be like childbirth. Exquisite pain that in the end is worth it. It has to be a pleasure or neither of us would be here. Nor would our species. Natural selection has to make procreation pleasurable. Who would want to make children otherwise?"

"I thought it was only the men who enjoyed it. I thought we had to submit to it, just to keep them happy. They're stronger than we are anyway."

"Liza," Jewel says, getting up to turn on the light, as if for emphasis. "When I had my hand on Küchler, I felt myself go weak. It was good that I was sitting down, for I would have collapsed on the floor with my legs opened up to him. Listen—my underpants were wet somehow. I felt a fuzzy, warm feeling there, like an itch that would be oh so pleasant to scratch."

Liza makes no reply. Jewel returns to bed, forgetting to turn out the light. Maybe it was too much to share, Jewel wonders.

"Have you ever touched yourself?" Jewel asks.

"No! Where? I mean why? Well, my breasts, as they became impossible to ignore. And sometimes—"

"Let me show you," Jewel says, moving to Liza's bed. "Pull up your nightie."

Liza cautiously reaches under the covers, then quickly lifts her wool nightgown up over her shoulders and slides it gracefully off her head. For some reason, she hands the garment to Jewel, now beside her in bed. Jewel holds it absent-mindedly as she compares what she sees to her image of herself.

Her breasts are small but tipped with tiny dark nipples, no bigger than a shirt button. They must be puckered from the cold, Jewel thinks, comparing them mentally to her own wide, pinkish-brown aureoles.

"Should we turn off the light?" Liza asks.

"No. Leave it on. How will you be able to see?"

Jewel's nightgown is pulled up on her belly. "Look," she says, her hand settling into the light fuzz at the bottom of her abdomen. "I do this a lot," Jewel says without a hint of embarrassment. "Hmm," she cannot avoid comparing, "yours is thicker than my fuzz and jet black. Another example of biological variability for the books."

"I don't think I have it right."

"Put your finger right here," Jewel demonstrates, "at the top of the fold."

"I wonder if it feels the same with a man?"

It is another night. The lights are off. They are bundled against the winter cold in their separate beds. But their thoughts are in synchrony. Each can tell what the other is surreptitiously doing.

"How can it?" Jewel answers in a whisper. "He has his penis inside you."

"We could try something, I suppose," Liza suggests, sitting up in bed. "An experiment, one might think, with a banana maybe. Or a cucumber? A small cucumber? Hot dog?"

"How do we know how hard it should be? Or long? Or fat? And I don't think it would be the same, even if we did get all that right. Not without real a male organ. And not without a real male attached. I almost can't wait to find out what it really feels like. And as soon as I do, I'll let you know all about it."

"There must be no lack of college boys who would be willing to do that for you. I've noticed how they look at you, believe me. Men love blondes. You just seemed to have bad luck with your Mr. Küchler."

"Calling it Mr. Küchler is funny," Jewel laughs. "Do you think they will always be Mr. Küchler to us from now on?"

Liza, too, laughs out loud. "Why not?" she says, her voice no longer lowered. "That's as good as anything else we call it."

"But listen," Jewel says in almost a whisper. "Do you want to try something?"

"Hmm?"

"The vampire way. Dracula satisfies his women without a working penis. His teeth are scary, I know, but it could be the touch of his lips that conquer their defenses. And when they too become vampires, could he keep them under control that way? Lips—or tongue?"

Liza says nothing. She listens to Jewel cross the room. Then she feels her presence in her bed.

"There is an older vampire story, even, than Bram Stoker's," Jewel says in her ear. "It is about a female vampire. Carmilla."

Jewel lips finds Liza's cheek, then her mouth. Then she moves her lips down her neck and shoulders, across her chest and to her nipples. She takes those in her mouth and softly sucks.

"Ohh!" Liza whispers. "Like a baby. That's good."

"There's more." Jewel moves down Liza's abdomen and into her dark bush, taking playful bites of its wiry hair. "I caught my old roommates doing this one night," she whispers. "They woke me up. I said nothing."

"Oh, my God," Liza squeaks when Jewel's tongue finds the right spot. It feels nothing at all like that other night to Liza, when Jewel showed her that secret place women have.

Somehow, Jewel knows when to reach out with a hand and smother Liza's appreciative cry.

VI

INDEED, Jewel learns at registration, there is someone named Allee teaching animal ecology at Chicago, and it is from a wheel chair. His name is Warder Clyde Allee. A spinal tumor put him in the chair. Its surgical removal left him in it permanently. And as Liza promised, he gives Jewel a different idea of what ecology is. Instead of animals simply being found in communities of plants—or formations or whatever—that necessitate knowing dozens of obscure terms, Jewel excitedly tells Liza, animals are actual, important parts of communities in ways that are so familiar as to need no new terms. And you can get right to counting animals for your data, instead of first having to master Latin names and Latinized terms.

"Listen to this, Liza" Jewel reads from her notes. "Animal aggregations. Cooperation. I remember the terms from my bio core in a lecture by Professor Emerson, the young prof I liked so very much. He was such a relief from that Professor Carlson. Carlson was a sweet man, but he was so much like Küchler—always asking, What's the evidence? Scientific method this and scientific method that all over the place."

"Do you hear much from him?' Liza interrupts. "Mr. Küchler?"

They are at one of the smaller tables under the Gothic arches and dangerously pendant chandeliers of the Harper Library reading room. Its arched windows cry out for stained glass scenes of saintly doings. Even lacking such, they invite a beatific quiet. It is a weekend. Liza does not resent that weekends together outside of the library have become rarities. She sees that Jewel has caught the same fire for her new interest that Liza has always been blessed with about her own.

"Cards," Jewel answers, a slight smirk on her lips, acknowledging the private joke. "A birthday card. I know more about his doings from Uncle George than from him."

"Still hope, you think?"

"There's always hope, Liza, but listen to these ecologists. Empedocles. Spencer. Kropotkin. Allee's lectures are Great Books in themselves. I've had to reread Origin of Species to realize—that even to Darwin—not all interactions between animals are aggressive. And there was that folksy lecture on ecological methods in which the class was asked to pretend to sample the university with quadrats. That really opened my eyes. Jeepers, can we be getting it all wrong that way? Especially for animals?

"Kropotkin, Liza, is Prince Kropotkin. That glamorous hint of Russian royalty made me go right to the library and find his book. It's called Mutual Aid, and it's full of examples of animals helping other animals.

"And are there principles beyond Clements's superorganism, you ask? You bet, Liza! How about the Law of the Minimum and the Law of Toleration? And listen to this. There is Bergman's rule and

Gloger's rule and the age and area principle and that there's a biotic balance and something called the logistic curve to describe it. Some of those, Allee admits were not discovered by what he calls self-conscious ecologists, meaning those who used the term to describe themselves, but they are ecological principles, nevertheless, even if their discoverers didn't know they were discovering ecological principles. The community concept is still the central concept to animal ecology, I think, but it unfolds through examples of cooperation and symbiosis in the web of life, instead of competition for space, like it is in the plant world alone. And there is a food pyramid, something suggested by a young English ecologist. Plants form its base, but animals are just as important, and oh, so much more interesting. Sometimes, with a hint of sarcasm, I think, Allee calls his science bioecology. That's because so many plant scientists use ecology to mean only their own field."

"Jeepers," Liza whispers back to her friend. Jewel's monologue is drawing annoyed looks, especially from the librarian's table. "You've definitely found your atom. And I'm glad. It sounds to me as if you've got the football in your hands now. Go run with it. Run with it as if you were Red Grange!"

Jewel does well in Allee's course, very well. The week after term papers are submitted, Allee asks her to stay after class. She waits nervously while he tends to the concerns of several stragglers as the rest of the class files out. She wonders if there might not be some difficulty with her paper.

He does want to see her about the paper, he tells her. Her heart stops.

"I read yours first," he says as her heart sinks in her chest. "What a bold title. It was what attracted me. What a bold premise."

Her heart, she is certain, is collapsing into itself.

"You certainly have the vagaries of the quadrat method well analyzed," he says, handing back her hand-written manuscript, "even as it is used in plant biology. I congratulate you."

A large, red "A" is conspicuous on its cover page. Not only that, but as she glances through it, she finds a number of lengthy marginal comments, some adorned with exclamation points.

"They are mostly questions about alternatives to quadrats," Allee explains on noticing her eying them uncertainly.

Jewel hesitates before cautiously saying, "I am not always sure what quadrats really show for animal communities. Sometimes I am not even sure what they show for plants. I think quadrats may be missing the main point of animal ecology, and that is how the animal associations evolved to be what they are."

"So you are suggesting laboratory studies to tease out evolutionary processes?"

"Oh no! I would think something like a field experiment might do better. Put out two quadrats in similar habitats, or whatever number of pairs is required. Fence the sides some way. Do something to one, such as maybe pluck all the tallest plants. See what happens. Ecological principles need to have ecologists confirming them in the field before they can be accepted. And that takes experimentation."

"Precisely, young lady. Now you were in a version of our University High School program, were you not? Skipped your last year to enroll here?"

She wonders how he could know that. Her resuscitated heart threatens relapse.

"Do you have time to come into my office for a bit?" Allee asks when a new instructor and new students fill the classroom. Jewel automatically positions herself behind his wheeled chair in order to push it out the room, but he refuses her help with a wave of his hand.

"If I don't do these things myself," he says, wheeling himself around, "I'll get too lazy to ever do them."

"How did—" she begins to ask as she follows him out into the hallway.

"A spinal problem," he anticipates the question. "Only surgery can correct it. I keep putting it off, though, hoping I'll wake up one day and be able to walk the way I did before I was afflicted by this tumor. Spinal surgery is risky. The nerves involved are very complicated."

His office is almost across the hall from the classroom.

"Your uncle is George Nichols, I understand," Allee asks after offering her a chair.

Now how does he know that? Jewel wonders.

Allee smiles before saying, "I've checked up on you. You'll be graduating soon. What are your plans?"

"I— I hadn't thought—" she stutters. "I didn't— I thought maybe—"

"Teaching?"

"Yes!" erupts from her in relief.

"Have you thought of pursuing ecology further before embarking on a teaching career? I have a position open. I was thinking about it for you, even before reading your paper. I've found some queer things about the logistic curve in my laboratory work. Undercrowding can be as bad for a population as high numbers. Loneliness might be as detrimental as overcrowding. You know of the logistic equation, don't you?"

"Of course! I paid attention to every word of your lecture on it. It was so exciting to learn that something as complicated as population growth can be explained by so elegant an equation. My friend Liza—she's a physics major—she says if you can't describe something in science with an equation, then you really don't understand it."

"Elegant?" he asks, puzzled.

"Simple," she answers, equally puzzled by his puzzlement. "Precise. That's what Liza likes about the logistic. I told her about that Russian's experiments you told about in class, how he tested the logistic—"

"Gause," Allee affably interrupts her, "but he actually tested something else. He tested the Lotka equation."

"They're pretty much the same equation, aren't they?"

"I am afraid I'm not much of a mathematician. Most of us biologists aren't. You, however, seem to have a good head for math. Passed calculus with flying colors, I assume."

Jewel blushes.

"I thought so. That's why I think you should pursue a career in ecology. You are perfectly suited for this work I am doing with flatworms in lab. They seem able to condition their water to make it favorable for others of their species. How would you like to give things a try?"

She is caught entirely by surprise. Yes, yes, she thinks, I will pursue! But something in Jewel has her say, "I don't know. There's so much to consider. I need time to think." How can she tell him?

"Yes," he says, seeming to understand, "there is the matter of prestige. Robert Hutchins recently said to me that ecology seemed to be the study of a pig sty with the pig let out."

"Oh, no no no!" she blurts out. "I have great respect for ecology. Why, Mr. Friedrich Küchler says it is the only area of biology for the thinking person. No, it's not that. I just need to think about it."

"Küchler," he repeats and is suddenly lost in thought.

"Why don't you give it a try?" he breaks his silence gently enough not to have his suggestion frighten her.

The very next afternoon, she is in Allee's cramped laboratory. She is led to a counter with dozens of Petri dishes arrayed on it. Some are empty. Some are filled half way with a clear fluid, water, Jewel guesses. Others are filled with what she recognizes as the flatworms of the experiment. She can make out individuals cruising around the crowded Petri plates and performing various slow-motion feats of flatworm acrobatics.

"I've already shown that Planaria, through death," he begins in a lecturing tone, "through an act of altruism, if you will, can protect the remaining others from the various toxic chemicals that kill it. There is even a suggestion of a chemical mechanism for it. Flatworms must deal physiologically with a variety of chemical insults, much as we do through our livers with what we ingest. However, I've only recently become interested in whether the same holds true for purely physical factors."

He rises unsteadily from his chair. Propping himself on one arm on the too-tall-to-use-from-a-wheelchair counter, he picks up a small pipette from a sterile Petri dish and expertly extracts some fluid from a small beaker that swarms with flatworms.

"There," he says, holding the pipette up triumphantly. "Exactly ten."

He then releases the pipette's contents into a waiting Petri dish beneath a fluorescent lamp.

"Let's see what happens when we give them a shot of UV light," he says, turning on the lamp.

The twin tubes glow purple. It is not the color of ultraviolet light, Jewel knows. Ultraviolet is not visible to the human eye, although speculation has it that it may be visible to certain insects.

"They clump together," Jewel announces.

"Yes," Allee says as he turns off the light. "The exposure they just received should make them all die within twelve hours."

"But the ones on the inside will not get the same same exposure as those on the outside."

"Very acute," Allee says, smiling at her. "And that is exactly what most simply explains why, when separated one to a dish, these worms will survive significantly longer than those that received the same dosage singly from the same lamp for the same duration."

"Fascinating."

"I hoped you would find it so. Your task, should you accept it, will be to see if you can keep them from clumping somehow, so that it is just the numbers, not the aggregation, that differ between the crowded plates and those with just single individuals. I've tried gently stirring the clumps apart. Like this."

He demonstrates on a second Petri dish into which he has just released ten.

"Perhaps you will find some better way after you've done a few trials."

Jewel wants to. She leaps into the task wholeheartedly. As time passes, as the number of trials increases, she becomes aware that she has not moved from her place by the counter. The same dull walls close her in. The same drab, institutional gray hems her in. Only electric light illuminates the room, she realizes. The window shades are down to keep sunshine from interfering with the experiments. When she looks up from her specimen dish, her view is that of a flat, gray plaster wall. Chipped areas here and there mark some long forgotten collision with something. She compares that view to that she imagines was seen by Cowles in the Indiana dunes as he was discovering the stages in their succession.

Oh, what have I done? How can I tell Professor Allee? Jewel wonders glumly, her head in hands.

She suddenly notices his presence at her side. How long had he been watching her?

"Is your preference still strictly for field work?" he asks.

"Dr. Allee," she says, letting out a sigh of relief. "I thrive in the field. Ever since I took Dr. Cowles' class. I want to study nature out in nature. I positively wilted during my hours in the herbarium."

Allee is pensive for a moment.

"I admire that and support it wholeheartedly," he finally says. "About field work, I mean, not your abhorrence of herbariums or that you might wilt in a laboratory. Still, you can see for yourself the way I am. There is some work possible with marine worms in the field, but I would not be able to supervise you, not with my infirmity. I can no longer stray very far from my laboratory for research, I am afraid. Let me have some time to think, too. Maybe something can be worked out. Perhaps Emerson can use someone. Do you like ants?"

Jewel's face is blank. She does like Emerson, but is afraid to admit to any fondness for six-legged creatures that she knows mainly as pantry raiders and picnic spoilers.

"Pity."

Allee then suggests that she might choose to study instead under his old professor at Chicago, Victor Shelford, he of the Law of Tolerance. On Allee's recommendation, Jewel is accepted at the University of Illinois, where Shelford is now. It does not bring her joy, however.

"How can I?" she cries to Liza. "Money is so scarce. My family can no longer pay for my education. That's why I had to take a campus job this year like you. It wasn't at all that I should have enough money of my own to pay the train fare to La Grange, like I told you. When my father died last fall, we all found out that he had left us penniless. How can I tell that to Shelford or Allee?"

"How can you not tell them, Jewel?" Liza answers simply. Then she returns to her newest distraction. She has abandoned tabloids in favor of a magazine. "Betty Jaynes has made Life magazine," she announces. "It says that her debut with the Opera was sensational and that she's planning on becoming a movie star next. But what does n-e-e mean?"

"Maiden name, usually."

"Fifteen and she's married?"

"And a sensation. We better get a move on it. But maybe Jaynes is a stage name?"

"There's also a picture in here of a girl with every part of her body tattooed, at least every part that would not show with her clothes on."

"They can't show a naked woman, can they?"

"She has what looks like underwear on. Very vampy black, too. It also says one in ten Americans is tattooed."

VII

ONE month in Hawaii now; finally time to write. Getting here was more of an adventure than I had anticipated. It was a gigantic experience. I feel incapable of singling out any experiences to mention and still keep this letter within normal size.

The letter is not normal size, Jewel notes with pleasure. Küchler goes on to relate having his pocket picked of a wallet, passport, money, and papers inside, within fifteen minutes of landing at Java. It takes him much longer that fifteen minutes to write about the incident, Jewel thinks, lovingly lingering over his every excessive word. He has adopted volcanoes, he expounds over another two pages. Batavia-Hong Kong steamship line, Dr. Dakkus, Buitenzorg Gardens, Holland, Tjibodas, Gedeh and Pangrango Malay, Hong Kong and the University of Hong Kong, Canton and Lingnan University, Kobe, Tokyo, Yokohama bloom more dominantly in his prose than the plants he is there to study.

Three pages without a single word to her personally. The last page, she is certain, is where that will be found. He has saved the best for last, reserved that page for her. It trembles like a leaf in her fingers.

My first month in Hawaii I have been debunked and reconditioned. It seems that the Hawaii Tourist Bureau is a most active and potent affair and that they have slightly overexaggerated the heavenly qualities of this Paradise by the Pacific. Omnis Hawaii in tres partes divisus est: Honolulu, the Army and the Navy, and the pineapple and sugar and other lands and activities of a small group of millionaire descendents of the old missionary families, who are not exactly chips off the old cross.

But for all that, I have really become quite satisfactorily established here, have enjoyed the first month, and look keenly forward to the rest of the time. I have decided to work on Oahu – as being most practical – and am beginning on the arid southeast part of the island. How far I get, I have no idea at all, for I do not know what complexities may turn up. I suspect I shall do very little with ecology, for climate and soil vary tremendously in time and space and I could not lay much importance on what little data I could gather in a few months. Vegetation studies, however, of an introduced flora – that should be quite interesting.

My PhD manuscript of the Berkshire region is going on the same boat. I have not heard from your uncle since I left America, so I was under some uncertainty in rewriting it. I grant one thing, the paper is not written up in a conventional style. And I do feel that there is not a single new idea in the whole thing, so something in the point of view must be different to have given great difficulty in getting Dr. Nichols to understand – through the maze of bad English and poor construction. I hope this new version will meet with his acceptance, at least, if not complete approval.

VIII

LIZA trudges across campus to Stagg Field, leaving firm tracks in the snow. One who takes an interest in such things can judge from them that she is neither hurrying nor dawdling. Each step is made with measured determination.

Who really understands what is going on? Liza wonders. Then she tries to answer her own question.

Fermi, certainly. He always needs to swim farther, bike farther, walk farther. He must be seeing farther into the atom than the rest of us.

Hans Bethe and his apprentice from Cornell. They probably know more than the rest of us, but their minds move so fast, who can tell?

Then she is distracted by a memory lapse. What was that name again? Fineburg? Dick, I think Bethe called him.

Oppie, hopefully.

Teller, maybe.

Mullikan?

He is her PhD advisor.

She didn't think so. That's probably why he lent her to Fermi before her dissertation was finished. It was right after she tried to catch the eye of the young physicist smelting metal bricks in the hallway of the Met Lab. "You guys have discovered how the chain reaction works," she joked, and the next day Fermi insisted she join his team.

She stops on arriving at the recently abandoned football stadium, looking for some sign that today would be different from all others. She is standing beneath stone turrets before the Gothic-style portal that is the entrance to the Met Lab. The entrance so often makes her think that some monster is lurking within it. Today, though, she feels as if she is stepping forward in time into a Buck Rogers serial, rather than backward into some Gothic horror.

She is one of the first in, but for Fermi, who is too engrossed in his own preparations to do more than nod to her in greeting. She goes directly to her post and turns on the power to the radiation counter that she has constructed. As it warms up, human activity increases all around her, but other than taking note of the steady background count, a need for her expertise does not arise. She falls back on musings over the universe she has entered, so foreign to even the imaginings of all ordinary people, and to trying to spot the young metallurgist, who, she has learned, came over from Columbia with Fermi.

Then she is pressed into action. Everything is ready. The control rod is removed from the pile. The clicks from her instrument increase in frequency from countable to a steady, rasping burr. She can only estimate from the recording pen on her instrument, which is on a path to the top of the paper. Liza periodically calls out the counts to a member of the team in the middle of the lab, who conveys them to Fermi, whose eyes dart from one dial before him to another. Every so often, he runs off a quick pencil-and-paper calculation.

Finally, he ceases his frantic observations. His face breaks into a broad smile.

"The reactor is self-sustaining," he announces. "The curve is exponential!"

Liza does not hear. Her ears are filled with what seems to her the ever-louder growl from her radiation counter. She checks the time. It has been over twenty minutes since the room began to fill with more radiation than she has ever recorded.

She abandons her post and walks across the lab to Fermi.

"When do we become scared?" she whispers, not an iota of fear detectable either in her voice or demeanor.

Fermi laughs.

"OK. Zip in," he announces.

The control rod is reinserted. The radiation counter subsides. The universe is once more as it had been, but the same cannot be said for those who are in the room. They have looked into a universe that is unimaginable to others.

Someone produces a bottle of Chianti. Paper cups appear. All share in a toast to the day and the discovery. Someone asks Fermi to sign the bottle. He agrees on the condition that everyone else does so also. Liza signs in an available space, wondering how Liza Sheriff would look in her handwriting, instead of Liza Woods.

Arden Forest

WHAT a lonely road, he thought, navigating it through patchy fog. And in what a seemingly forgotten part of the world. It was barely paved. Potholes were untended and large patches of macadam disintegrated noticeably with each passing auto. Fortunately they were few. Tourists that flooded nearby areas were not apt to wander down this road. It served only the very few who lived along it.

How different, he mused, from the hustle and bustle of aging, well-heeled Baby Boomers to the north, come for the music of Tanglewood or in search of the remnants of Alice's Restaurant. Few of them would by any stretch of imagination need to put their autos on the road cutting through Arden Forest. Here and there along it was a house, its white clapboards and simple proportions suggesting farmland. Here and there was a massive stone gate, guarding wealth, he imagined.

A metal gate, the functional kind the Forest Service used, marked his destination. It was unlocked in anticipation of his arrival.

The Dutch Colonial house within was not visible from the road. It was not even visible from the beginning of the circular drive that once must have enclosed grassy lawn and well-tended flowers. And the house seemed out of place to him in its disheveled surroundings. It would look stately on a main street in any of the small towns and villages nearby, but it was nothing at all like the white clapboard capes and saltboxes he knew as New England farmhouses. The remains of a farm—if not of farmland—surrounded the unlikely house. A former chicken coop beside it now held books, papers, and correspondence. Much correspondence. It—rather than the haunts of his fellow Baby Boomers—was what had drawn the bespectacled driver.

The farmhouse was locked and unattended. So much the better, he decided. It would give him a chance to look about the grounds in solitude.

Fields that once yielded hay were now hard to perceive, although the back of the house, sitting lower on the hillside than the front, still looked like the hay barn it once had been. He understood it was now more museum than home, this house, left exactly as it was when the owner was still whiling away his final days. Through its the window the visitor could see to the cozy sitting room of a porch that overlooked what once were fields and gardens. The gardens, once arranged in neat experimental squares, were now unrecognizable. Weeds had invaded. Plot boundaries were no longer visible. Yet here and there, the mark of the gardener remained. Sunflowers planted by him in one plot were escaping. Having jumped the gardener's path, they were now heading into surrounding shrubbery. It was entirely probable that the gardener would have approved.

Stones marked some forgotten intention along a path through the one remaining open field. They were set out singly at irregular intervals, but not, perhaps, without purpose. Hay and its harvester had long been gone from the field. Goldenrod and blueberries now marched through it. In the distance was a view of the southernmost Berkshires.

He suddenly felt strangely in the presence of ghosts—in the field and around it. There were little stumpy ghosts. Small tree and shrub stumps had been cut and left for sure death after being doused, no doubt, with weed killer. It had been pichloram, he knew, for recent ghosts, 2,4-D for older ones. And there were larger ghosts around the field, pale, leafless, phantom trees. On approach, they showed their manner of death. They were girdled at chest height. Bark and cambium had been stripped all the way around the trunk, as if by some crazed band of beavers with stepladders. It had not been the forester's hand that girdled these standing ghosts, but it had been as he wished. The forest, in all of its oddities, was the manifestation of his wishes.

It is a strange monument the gardener has left, the visitor thought, if monument it was meant to be, for it is disappearing from sight in the overgrowth, much as the Dutch Colonial house is. The ghostly signs are but hints of things the gardener, farmer, forester, wanted to create.

A patch of hay-scented fern suddenly caught the visitor's eye. It was obvious to him it had once been scientifically tended, and that it, too, represented some idea.

Letters locked within the one remaining farm building told the story. The gardener had been a scientist and a not insignificant one. He also had been a man with dreams, passions, successes, and frustrations.

Arden Forest

Finally, the visitor was greeted by the estate's attendant and shown the letters. Water, mold, insects, and mice had had their way with them. They would reveal the designs of the ghost's life in partial and peculiar ways.

Some things about him will forever remain beyond our understanding, the visitor thought. That is as it should be. Ghosts in ghost stories should reveal themselves slowly, if it all.

He got to work.

It was a haphazard collection, this trove of letters boxed on shelves in a former chicken coop. He set to mining the papers for correspondence with the greats. He expected to find Cowles, Clements, Shelford, Whittaker, MacArthur, Carson. He found few letters with those names, but by skipping over names unfamiliar to him he discovered some under-appreciated names, whose letters would be of use to him. Cooper, Buell, Buechner, Fosberg. The cramped quarters in the narrow aisles made it uncomfortable to write, and the single bulb hanging from the ceiling barely produced enough light to penetrate his cataract-clouded vision unless he was directly under it. What few notes he took were little more than reminders for future reference. But as he pulled down one of the boxes, stretching fully to reach it on a top shelf and settling it unsteadily on the floor to the accompaniment of twinges in his lower back, he found a remarkable surprise, a gem, he thought, or jewel, perhaps. It was a stack of letters between Küchler and one Jewel Fairfax. Hers were originals, handwritten in a feminine script on elegant stationary. His were typewritten carbon copies on onion paper. Many, pressed together for over half a century, were imprinted with the contents of their neighbors and almost impossible to decipher. He knew he had to try. Taking advantage now of the attendant's offer of lodging at the estate's lakeside cabin, which he had before declined politely, he cleared his schedule for the following day.

He picked up beer and a sandwich in Winsted, driving a distance that dissuaded a return for breakfast. The cabin overlooked not the lake he expected, but a shallow beaver pond. Still, it was relaxing to sit briefly in front of a large window looking out on the water's shore. The cabin's cupboard was hardly bare, but disappointingly contained only condiments. Still, he thought, turning on an elaborate stereo system, he had the letters, his stomach was full, and he had a comfortable place in which to peruse them.

He set to organizing by date the letters in the thick file he had discovered, those between Jewel Fairfax and Fred Küchler. He put hers in one pile, his in another. He had known of their acquaintance and had expected to find some such correspondence—as he had with George Nichols, although for some reason he could not. The lack of that correspondence surprised him as much as the multitude currently before him did. So did its starting date. It was 1942, a letter from Jewel.

Fred, my lad,

The fountains of sumac leaves against the blue of the sky suggested palms so insistently – that I promptly coiled the hose, left my shoes discretely on the basement floor, - and now having removed the blue overalls – and considerable of the good earth I shall project myself to your private paradise. For such, I've a sneaking suspicion, it is.

Since your airmail letter took 4 weeks to reach me, I'd better hustle this one, or it will have to follow you home. Of course some of the delay might have been due to the dilemma of the censor. You really should use a typewriter. Think of the poor guy going home each night to toss in sleepless agitation wondering if those little curlicues had a sinister meaning.

♣

Detroit has had one partial practice black-out. Having learned from the experiences of other cities the danger of John Q. Public's falling off roofs or into excavation in his enthusiasm for first nights at these affairs - we had ours with the street lights burning. We behaved very well, thank you. We are busy and orderly. It is <u>simply impossible</u> to realize – as one rubs the last tires of this era out upon the pavements – in the accustomed pursuits – that there is nothing predictable in the years ahead save the astronomical framework of our existence. Thank God no meddlesome ape has yet learned how to release sub-atomic energy – large scale - or we might find even that wobbling.

My brother-in-law, who was in Manila in Dec is still unheard from, of course. My sister is distraught. A cable in March said none of the missionaries or transients had been killed in the initial bombing – and that they were carrying on hospital services etc. So the family hopes on.

Since my latest transfer – in February – I have non-college prep students only in a course called "General Biology." When I have acquired some of this thing called seniority, I hope to be able to see students with brains part of the time. You complain about college students – You should see what the other 90% of the human race is like: unresponsive, uncurious, lacking in either imagination or sense of responsibility! Unless society gets a chance to settle down for a few generations to give the right people time to rediscover the old interest in survival – thru families — we won't need colleges. You might suggest ways and means of motivating <u>that</u> sort of improvement of human society. Mr. Hitler seems bent on trying — using something like the methods of a stone breaker attempting to repair a watch.

In a shady corner of our tidy back yard the spring progresses at a great rate. The blood root leaves are huge – the trilliums almost gone, buttercups rampant threaten to crowd out everything else. Delicate hislops cap and Jack in the pulpit fraternise incongruously. Cornus stolonifera – has grown to be a tree. Even the ferns are bigger than they usually grow in the woods. Crazy weather this spring – the yellow trumpets of jonquils were visible above 3 inches of snow; then a dry month very hot – and tulips and lilacs came – and went too soon.

I'd really like to know more about this chicle business – are they selecting stocks for raising on plantations or merely surveying jungle for new trees, or what?

As ever
Jewel

The chill he felt on his spine could not have come from a draft blowing through the cabin. It was a balmy August night. He cautiously picked up another letter from the same pile, sticking with his decision to read the letters chronologically.

9-1-43

Dear Fred,

Ecologists

Mother and I have been taking turns carrying each other's meals down on a tray during the August heat. How we both miss our old house in Connecticut! Still, the total meals in bed is much in my favor. Now that's over – to get started on the hundred little jobs that wait for me – as handy-man. You wouldn't know about such things.

What a whirlwind trip it was with Shelford! What a treat! Tenn, Ark, No Ala & Miss, Duke forest – Georg – then home by way of Va, Wva & Kentuck. Deciduous forests all the way. You might be interested in our data. It was such a surprise – Not a class – the war, you know – It was just me and Drew Sparkman — she had been Shelford's "best ever" field assistance when he used to take entire classes on the summer trips — also another HS teacher, the war, you know. And no "Billy Buick" or bus and commissary truck – but there were gas ration stamps. Every stop, we'd make insect sweeps, beating the bushes, so to speak. Easier was cruising for birds and animals in the Ford wagon. Hardest was trapping mammals. I caught pitiably few. Mostly I ID'd and collected plants, while Drew took care of ground invertebrates. And we took notes! Did we take notes!

My eleven tomato plants are my pride and joy. Did you ever experience the uncertain joys of farming – all this thrill of being hand-in-glove with <u>Nature</u>? "S wonderful!" Tho beset by aphis – green, black, & red, and 2 or 3 species of fungi – yet they struggle on – almost – now at the top of their 5 foot stakes. Of course I "control aphis" as the book says – but a species with such birth rates is unconquerable.

♥

Please give my regards to your father and mother.
I'd give a lot to know what's on your mind these days. Yes – I know its none of my damned business – but still I'm curious.

As ever
Jewel

He knew of that summer trip. She had often described it, but why no mention of Mexico? And that incident with the border agents? That had been the highlight of the oft-repeated story.

December 11, 1943

Dear Jewel,

After Pearl Harbor I was really 100% enthusiastic in applying my botany to war problems, and altho I had just contracted to go to Guatemala for C.D.C., I was able to get various unofficial commissions for reports on certain botanical matters for Washington agencies for the regions I was going to – things I could not speak of at the time. Back in the States, I began to sort my way out of chewing gum. I may have written to you that I approached the forestry college to let me start some greenhouse quinine root-cutting studies, but they actually laughed at the idea. I did a large amount of work in organizing an antimalarial drug project for Guatemala, which the coordinator's office was to sponsor (I, on expenses only – one of my silly ideas of war service that I do not mind talking about now). But Washington delay was getting me no where, so when the Forest Service offered me the status of Senior Dendrologist, to go to Costa Rica as botanist on the Latin American Forest Resources Survey, I jumped at the chance, and told Chicle to "go to". It was an all-out war job, in connection with an Army project. Mebbe I told you last Christmas that I was leaving on it. I was called back to Washington the day after Christmas.

Three months later I left Washington for Syracuse, fired from the Forest Service, and with a charge lodged against me in the State Dept. that carries a prison sentence with it, and with an order from my Draft Board to report for immediate induction! It may sound melodramatic and mysterious. At least it was mysterious and still is. When I arrived in Washington, I was told not to unpack my suitcase, that I would leave in a few days. So for three months, I lived a day by day existence. Washington red tape is a phenomenon known only to God and those who suffer it. Eventually I had all papers signed, countersigned, passed and repassed, and waited only for my passport. But that wait finally became embarrassing. Eventually, it appeared that a passport had been refused, with absolutely no comments. I felt sure that had been a clerical error. There was absolutely nothing in my history that could have accounted for the refusal, but reconsideration brought a final NO. After three months of enforced idleness, and in wartime, I was put in no particularly happy frame of mind.

I determined to do <u>some</u> botanical war work, even if on no salary – or should I say on the salary I had been receiving for doing nothing. So I cooked up an agreement with the federal rubber research people to be guest investigator at the station in southern Florida. Then I returned to Syracuse to get plans reorganized. My statement for my draft board was met with a letter, already sealed and ready to mail to me, supposedly still in Washington: orders to report for induction. It seems that they knew about my being fired, even before I had word of my official release from the Forest Service- and what else they knew was beyond me. The Board considered my rubber proposal, and turned it down. It seems that if Uncle Sam had given me $6000.00 a year for such work, I would have been deferred, but to do it gratis, as one's personal contribution to the war, that would be impossible. And I was told that if I could find an essential occupation in the next few days, my case would be reconsidered.

In a matter of hours, I had been offered a position teaching geography to aviation students on this campus. But the Vice-Chancellor of the University, a Draft Board member, said that if I wanted to be where most needed, I should be teaching physics. "Did I know any physics?" How I regret my answer. A half hour later, I had applied for, and had accepted a position in the Physics Dept. for teaching aviation physics to aviation students in the 65th C.T.D. If I had been just a decent narrow-minded botanist, I never would have done it. For nine months, I have tried to distill the principles of a marvelous mechanical universe into men who see no greater connection between such knowledge and piloting a plane than does the proverbial woman driver see between what-is-under-the-hood and driving a car. At least, I have taught myself much.

My relations with the college have gone from bad to worse. A war certainly brings things out of people. Dr. Meier, perhaps through age, perhaps with more open eyes on my part, is one whom I no longer would think of as friend. Indeed, so very much in the professional university world has shown itself to be jealousy, selfishness, egotism, with so little of the social consciousness, altruism and enthusiasm that I mistakenly believed, that I look forward to changes. Altho I am still on leave from the forestry college, I am resigning at the expiration of that leave, in March. I suppose it was "success" to become a professor at the age of 26, and a Director of the Experiment Station last year. I have a much clearer idea now just what attributes of indifference, disinterest and sheer laziness are necessary to get along in this high and mighty brotherhood of "companions in jealous research" (to paraphrase Sigma Xi's motto). I prefer to get away from it, and keep a few ideals of what some universities and some scientists, may be, somewhere. I may be teaching physics for the Duration. I keep an affiliation with Chicle, and they plan on using me full time as soon as I can get away, but I do not particularly care. I am toying with a rubber position in Liberia, not only for its war importance, but because I'll be working with plants. I have bought 250 more acres in NW Connecticut, and really look forward to living there, growing most of my own food, and reading and writing.

I chased down to Washington about 2 months ago, to see if there could be any clarification of the charge against me. The matter remains a mystery. There is much evidence that I was only the goat in an interdepartmental feud (the entire project cracked 2 months later). At least the charge has apparently never been investigated or referred to any other agency for consideration: it just stays there, and prevents me from getting a passport. This is hardly Christmas cheer; my apologies. Do you ever get East, I would very much enjoy seeing you again.

"... told you last Christmas" stayed in his head. He reread that part again, then shuffled through the piles of letters once more. Nothing. No sign of the conversation other than that off-hand remark. Lost? Not copied? Could it have been a phone call? After all, it had hardly been the Stone Age. Long distance may have been tedious and expensive, but it was available. Could they have met?

He turned the stereo down and read on.

Same place
January 1, 1944

Dear Fred

So you're offering your dear Aunt Jewel another chance to scold you? She really couldn't – not on this nice new Christmas stationary – besides it would seem to be that first aid is indicated – rather than admonitions. A detective story, with which I whiled *away the ghastly hours of getting a "permanent" last month, stipulated – "Seek the motive of the crime in the character of the victim." I seriously doubt that <u>you</u> have any, since you did <u>not</u> write last Christmas.*

I hope you are going to be objective enough not to become cynical over the events of 1943. Can't you try – on every other Thursday, at least - to see life and the world and yourself through the eyes of someone else? You should take up novel reading - or accept Adler's notes on psychiatry and social interest – his advice to others – not his feud with Freud.

You once remarked on your lack of faith, or any religious sense – yet you do seem to expect the descendants of cave men to be so very <u>very</u> little lower than the angels!

You are hurt because your very hard work has been resented by older professors. Can't you see that with your intense application you make them look old and tired back numbers even to themselves. When you were a student they beamed with pride. Your progress reflected a glow upon them. Now you are a rather obstreperous competitor – admit it! Since you are too young to be utterly altruistic you want credit for everything you do. Result – resentment. Your parents with their blindly adoring & quite uncritical attitude did not prepare you for jealousy and unreasonable criticism from older people.

One value you can salvage out of an apparently wasted year – when – thirty years from now – you are head of a department – or a foundation, and have acquired a paunch – a goatee – or a helicopter – depending on how your personal vanities lead – and you are beginning to lean a little too heavily upon "my researches in in Timbuktu" — and into your department come the brash youths who consider you secretly a lazy old bore – while fearfully checking the spelling in all reports presented to you – You will know how to be tolerant – generous – and to begin to move with dignity from the center of the stage ...

Yes?

I'm not worrying that you will hermit long in Connecticut – if ever you have time to get there. You need solitude among your woods and rolling acres just long enough to recharge your batteries – then you will be back again – lecturing with the usual verve and sparkle.

I'd like to hear those physics lectures. Sometimes when I'm swamped with routine paper marking, I have a nostalgic notion I'd like to get some more physics – sometimes biology seems a little cluttered – creative evolution a bit too prolific – and oh for the wings of an hypothesis!

Though I must sound like a harpy I'm truly sorry that the war has you in such a tangle, Fred. It has its frustrating effect – even upon those of us who are not directly or personally involved. To teach civilized ideals today - to boys who must tomorrow be stripped of them and trained as commandos – is sickening. It begins to look as though everyone with the capacity for thinking at all must be trained to <u>think</u> and <u>act</u> politically. We must not allow our young people to go off in their own little special services and resign the matters of human organization to those who think they want to manage them for us. No group is qualified and perhaps never will be. May 1944 be a <u>much</u> happier year for you.

Sincerely,

"Aunt Jewel?" he wondered aloud. She was younger than Küchler by a number of years.

Having finished transcribing the letter into his laptop, he ran a spell check, consulting with the original document on each highlighted error, and realized that he might have to stay up late into the night. He would also have to return for another visit, and it would have to be with a scanner. The Arden Forest copier was unavailable to him outside of office hours and unreliable when it was available, especially with the attendant constantly distracting him with conversation.

He read on.

My dear Jewel,

Do you recall that you wrote to me just about a year ago? (Jan. 1) A letter with amazingly fine thoughts. Indeed, to have hit the truth so often about myself I found, strangely, rather embarrassing – not objectionably so, but in the manner of one caught in the ole swimming hole.

I am wondering how you yourself are weathering the times. Admitting that cynicism is in the character of the "victim", we might go one step farther and correlate it with the <u>diffe</u>rence between the *world as it is, and the world as we th<u>ou</u>ght it was. There are some that grow cynical with relatively slight cause from current events, but as current events continue to get worse, that "threshold difference" hits more and more people. Then again, some are so fortunately constituted that they are optimists in any situation. I never fail to admire the typical Negro, and part-Negro, for a good humor, which is not apparently downed by adversity. I am sure I would not last long in the work you are doing – if indeed it has any resemblance to the New York City school system. I have one cousin and one friend in that system, and their tales are amazing.*

Another year has passed and several new chapters have been written in my history. The Army teaching program was discontinued, so I took to fishing, and landed an Associate Professorship at Knox College, Galesburg, Illinois. Grantedly, it was a relief to leave the bickerings between military and academic at Syracuse Physics, the inefficiency and the "damned if I'll learn anything" attitude of our then-future pilots. The three months at Knox were relatively pleasant. The military program was organized far more effectively, the attitude of the aviation students was better, and the faculty seemed to have a bit of interest in the work. Cannot say I enjoyed the town: 30,000 people embedded in a cloud of soft coal smoke and colorless architecture, dropped into a flat flat country covered with dead cornstalks. When there are so many landscapes that are a pleasure to the eye and mind, it is amazing that so many are thus content.

But the Knox program was also discontinued. They were getting an ASTR program, and wanted me to stay, but I had the chance to do what was obviously more important work, that I then thought should keep me more busy. We are working on a project requested by the Bureau of Ships of the U. S. Navy, through Division 6 of the National Defense Research Committee, of the Office of Scientific Research and Development, of the Office of Emergency Management, of the Executive Office of the President of the U. S. A., and being carried out by the New York office, of the San Diego Sound Laboratory, of the Division of War Research, of the University of California. And each such office has a boss or bosses which sticks a finger in the pie. It is a pleasure to be home again, for the first time since Freshman college days. And it is a pleasure to watch the city each day from an altitude of some 700 (?) feet above the street. *Visibility and color and atmospheric conditions are never the same. But it is a world of man that we look out upon; I should like to have had the view 300 years ago. There are 70 in the office. From typists to tops. The work involves technical writing in electrical and mechanical engineering. They took me on the basis of my botanical writings and physics teachings. Background of the others are varied. It cannot be said that we have worked efficiently. Sociably, I have liked the people unusually well. But I never dreamed it possible, that talent and ability could be so <u>mis</u>used, <u>mis</u>placed, that organization could be so bad even when controlled by people without previous administrative experience, and that draft-dodging and salary-grabbing could be so indifferent not only to the welfare of the project, but to the wasting of their lives as well.*

I resigned from Syracuse forestry in March. Conditions there are not improving by any means, and I would never enjoy it again.

I resigned from the Chicle Development Company after a series of meetings that opened my eyes to the situation there. Apparently I was a better salesman than adult educator, and sold my research program without their knowing what they were getting. I finally realized that they hired me in 1941 to give scientific bolstering to what they had already decided: that the industry could be converted to a plantation basis without delay. They looked upon my research program as a very small scale commercial venture: and told me that I would have impressed them more by asking for 500 thousand dollars than 50 thousand. In addition, they never quite made the mental change from considering me not as a consultant, but as a director of research. I found them making all sorts of decisions by themselves, some of which were not at all sound from any forestry viewpoint. I was in that work with a 20-year point of view, so I admit I was much disappointed to realize that nothing remained of my three years with them except some salary and experience.

Then, back in July, I opened the State Department matter again in reference to the passport refusal. It seems that while I was in Central American in 1942, they received information that I was staying down there to avoid the draft!! It is known of course that the State Department is not concerned with the enforcement of the Selective Service Act, so I do not know what intra-State activity caused them to act on the information that they apparently did receive. But that time, July, I received permission to give them a full statement of my connections and interests, which should, without any trouble whatever, have clarified the issue and cleared me. The matter, actually, became ridiculous. They held firm, however: "no reconsideration without a 4F status". About that time, my patriotism weakened and I decided that I'd get some excitement, and let the country get no more out of me than the services of an Army private. I enlisted – and was turned down because of near-sightedness. I notified State of the change in my status, and refrained from adding my personal opinion on the matter.

But now, our U of Cal project will be over in a month. I am being considered for a professional position with the Navy Dept, and will take it if offered – or any other professional war job. But a post-war position, either in a university or industry just has no appeal. I am much interested in the writing of some books, both in physics and in botany. My interest in teaching is as strong as ever – but I guess I am through in doing it by the spoken word. It will be by proxy from now on. Colebrook, Connecticut will be my home, at least for the summer months. Whether or not I will like winter months remains to be seen. Thus, 1944.

All my best wishes to you for a merry Christmas and a grand New Year.
Sincerely,

1 – 1 – 45

Dear Fred,

The last departing guest is sped, I found it simpler to escort the aged aunt to her car thru the blizzard than to get the ice off the walks. The last dish is washed – and it's still – for a little while – January one. How better start the new year than by a very appropriate expression of repentance for past sins – Something like – "My patient friend, I have no advice to give you" – Imagine that!

If in a class of 35 students there are one or two really interested and curious intelligent students it seems worth while – if by good luck there are 4 or 5, that class is an exhilaration and a delight. I'm afraid I don't worry as much as I should about the other duffers who also sit. You see we have no state board examinations – hence no rigid standards. On a good day we may start off with a sane review of adaptations of plants to various environments and wind up in a tangle of birth rate and population problems in India. It's still biology.

Last summer's victory garden was quite satisfying – both in process and product. We are still passing out pepper squashes to anyone who will take them. Did you ever have to figure out what to do with the fruits of 18 tomato plants? Since these grew on the vacant lot I bought next door, I should walk in the garden in the cool of the evening like the Lord in Genesis, admiring the mysterious shapes and their shadows and the white cosmos and gladiolus, and the sweet delicious smell of the corn. Did the Lord deal with that other matter of hoeing and spraying in the heat of the morning? Although I am as thankful to my mother, who watched over the garden while I was away on another excursion with Shelford – not enough space on this paper to tell about that! - as I am to the Lord.

So boast not overmuch of your hundred acres. I, too, am a land holder to the extent of 35 feet of clay loam. My strawberry plants with their prodigious families, my raspberry bushes – my Stanley prunes and Bartlett pear may make me an independent farmer before you are yet.

ω

At Chicago at 16 I was racking my brain trying to understand Mr. Einstein's theories of relativity. Months closeted with Liza were no help. – Did you know she is now a mother! A son! She kept on working almost to his birth! She disguised the impending motherhood with very very baggy overalls. – She stuffed her pockets with various bulky tools that completely hid her shape! Now, a decade later, I pick up Einstein's 'World as I see it' – and discover I can skip the technical chapters without a question – that I am only interested in how the world looks to him – as a human being – and have to react to its terrible problems – as a human being. So do our planes of interest shift. I suppose it's those endocrines.

I should <u>like</u> to do something to reduce the stupid prejudices that make life miserable for members of various minority groups – but actually I talk a little – send 'Common Ground' to the friends who don't need it – and realize how foolishly ineffective mere good wishes are – etc – etc.

Ecologists 54

Please tell me what happens – and what you think of it – in the next chapter. Don't you ever get inspired to write letters – around April 1 – or the 4th of July?

As ever
Jewel

"Of course!" he exclaimed aloud, setting his laptop aside to find the charger. There had been a second summer. That had been the one with the border incident.

14760 Holmur Ave
Detroit, 21, Mich
8 – 10 – 45

Dear Fred,
The watched mailbox, having as yet yielded no further details, I suspect you're having a painful week – with possibly more of that ocular surgery. – Maybe someone should send me a card – if you are unable to write ... I was relieved to know you arrived, since I was regretting having failed to attach a tag to your coat tails: "IF LOST – FINDER PLEASE FURNISH FOOD AND <u>WATER</u> – AND NOTIFY ——— AT ONCE."
The world's news of terror and hope and relief has been thundering from every radio this week – All in all – in the long view, anything but reassuring.
I'm glad you are a biologist rather than a research physicist. After the next desert-making war those of us having respect for life – who have survived may have to form a posse – round up these cosmic smart alecs and firmly if regretfully seal them with their notes within their laboratories – and drop upon them the last atomic bombs.
You mentioned being disturbed by the rapid industrialization of backward populations. – I am incapable even of contact with Liza. 'Nough said - The whole experiment of modern society is a failure - let the earth start the drama over again with a few savages.
This week I forwarded – under new cover, a letter from the War Dept. Yes – I know how to forward letters – but the probabilities of its being 'official business' seemed low, and the "penalty for private use to avoid postage" appalling – and keeping people out of jail is my special forte in life.

You left our city a day too soon. Had you waited you might have enjoyed luscious freshly pulled ears of Mays hybrid "4th of July" corn. What's a mere month of waiting – for such delight! Sunday also was the occasion of the premier appearance of the slick blue suit I've been making in odd moments. Paradoxically – its sleek Vogue-ish lines will always remind me of that last hectic week of July.

My arm is a little lame but the porch glistens – within and without. I hope the inventor of rick-rack under porches is still in purgatory – applying white paint to miles of the stuff – even until now!

Good night, mon ami, - and if dreams must come – may they be the sort in which your jaguar and panther shall lie down together.

Sincerely,

"Ocular surgery?"

His mind snapped away from its rote transcribing. Was that the result of the horse riding incident mentioned in a letter to Cooper? And the hint of a police matter in the—who was it? Buechner? Fosberg? How had she been involved in that? Where was it in his notes? Not there. And not among the copied pages.

He kept reading.

The traumatic cataract is apparently a very real thing. Altho Dr. Castroviejo, who is famous for inventing the surgical instrument used in corneal transplants, had said earlier that he might operate this week, his last reply to my question was "not now – might endanger the eye at this time." You see, while at Presbyterian, this glaucoma developed. ...

Altho I did not have a tag on my coattails, I did have a card in my pocket, with an "in case of accident, please notify ...." And I had the audacity to use a Holmur Ave. address, until well out of Detroit. There were times I was not too sure of myself, and the pounds of cherries were very reassuring

Yes, I listened to the radio for hours on end, during the atomic bomb droppings – and I had many a chill ... Those bombs did upset my equilibrium, and I am far more desirous of retiring to

Arden Forest and enjoying that society for what few years of peace may remain.

On the other hand ... I confess that I should like to prevent you from atomizing the research physicists. ... Especially not your best friend.

I may be wrong, but I believe that the spirit which moves our researchers is a sheer intellectual curiosity, the satisfaction of which is the noblest thing in life. The discoveries are completely unmoral. They become moral only when others use them for better or worse. ...

And did I tell you that when I left Knox College and came to New York it was for an expense-paid interview with Union Carbide, for a position at Oak Ridge, Tennessee, on what now we know to be an atomic bomb factory. I did not take the position, for the University of California work sounded much more interesting. What a lucky break.

I still shudder at what it all would have been without you. So sorry I missed the corn and the blue suit: one on the other – a good color combination.

The next item was a postcard.

Sat A.M. 8-18-45

Dear Fred –

I'm sure someone will read this to you – while sealed letters may get stacked up for your recovery.

It is difficult to forgive Uncle Sam for delaying your Sunday note until Friday afternoon. Naturally the poor guy was preoccupied with getting a war over – but such things can wreck a nervous system.

It is wonderful to know you have such fine prospects of recovery of sight. Keep up the good work! – I hope you got my letter last week – even though I did address it to the wrong zone.

Mother is all becurled and manicured and packed off with Sis and husband for Grand Rapids for a week.

I'm on emergency call if young Danny should do anything that his mother deems irregular. He is driving Chez moi tomorrow. In his first 200 mile trip he has already proved himself an excellent *if unconscious traveler. He'd better enjoy it if he stays with this family. From his great-grandmother down – they have itchy feet.*

Wish I might pop in this afternoon – with a pound of cherries. In lieu of that – my sincere best wishes.

"There I am."

Wed. nite

Greetings!

The convalescence should be well advanced by now. – Due to a brainstorm (maybe like lead poisoning or house maids' knee) I have a plane reservation for Washington – Aug 24. Be seeing you maybe Monday – so be prepared to give an account of yourself. Business as usual begins 2 weeks from today, so this is my last splurge

Best wishes

Jewel

9-4-45

Dear Fred,

It was nice to find your note as I started off for our advance pep-meeting this P.M. It was a subtle and pleasant intimation that I'd been forgiven for all that poking and prying and pecking that I'd done. I guess when that shabby-disguise of yours was snatched away by the course of events and sir-knight-in-shining-armor met my dazzled gaze – each splash of mud or speck of rust drove me frantic till I could spit on my hanky and rub and rub and rub. It's just beginning to get through my thick head that, as cynic and pessimist, you are an impious old humbug.

One last word on the atomic subject — I have the utmost respect for those unpublicized British physicists who refused to have anything to do with translating their knowledge of the mysteries of the atom into an instrument of destruction. I am rapidly losing my respect for Liza for doing the opposite, though. And just think — she has no qualms at all about having contributed to the construction of that horrible monstrosity. — "Oh," she dismissed my concerns, "but Oppie" — she pronounces it "Opie," claiming the nickname was originally Dutch. How does someone born in New York City get a Dutch nickname? — *"Oppie said we had to do it and Oppie"* — *and here, it was as if she were pulling rank on me* — *"is such a sweet man and a liberal and has such gentle friends and he quotes from the Bhagavad Gita." I find irritation building up inside me until I just want to whack her across the face with a loaded pocketbook to stop her. My pocketbook!* — *You know how loaded that is!*

<u>*Finis!*</u>

There were some high points of my trip after New York by Greyhound. Had hardening of the arteries and was coaxed into Albany an hour and a half late. Helen (Late of Santo Thomas – Manila – you remember) was delightful – I confess I'd been fearful as to what 3 years under Jap rule might have done to her. She's the same charming, sane, poised, and frequently gay, person she always was. Almost ten years ago when I last saw her at Chicago she was trying to reduce. As she puts it the Japs took care of that. As a result she really looks no older than then – and a lot better than I do right now. She's hoping to take her Master's at Columbia this year. She was so excited that I would be going back to Urbana as soon as I can figure out what to do with my house and my mother. It occurs to me your mother might know some one who would like to rent a room to a person of that sort – You might ask her if you think she might help. You must meet her. You'd like her contralto – as much as her objets d'art – Japanese Chinese and Korean.

The midnight hour approaches – and I must be passing out schedules at 8 AM – seven miles from here.

Yours

625 West 156 Street
New York 32, NY
October 13, 1945

Dear Jewel,

Was it intentional of you to write almost one month to the day after your previous letter? It is a very effective reminder of one's neglect of correspondence.

And now that I look once more at the earlier letter I realize that you might have been waiting for some word from me in the event that your roomless old roommate Helen might be able to find *no room at all in New York. Neither I nor my mother know of anyone at that time. It is quite true that we have an unused bedroom and bath (one of the two maid's rooms and bath of this apartment), which mother would never forgive any friend of a friend of a friend of mine for not using in an emergency. The idea of renting is alien to our family. Altho I myself think it would be well for my parents to have someone else in the house, we have such a host of strange customs and mannerisms and interests that it would take a most understanding creature to feel at ease for any length of time.*

I suppose I should take advantage of the first page of that letter, and rest on the laurels and compliments it contains. But honestly, Jewel, you make me feel like more of a hypocrite than ever. There was some quotation of Santayana in a copy of Time some months ago that struck accord, a comment of his being able to love humanity only when he was far away from it. Let time tell as to who is right, you or me – if you will give time a chance.

My good eye has risen to the occasion in grand style and I can spend a whole work day at a desk with no concern, I first read up on back issues of Science. What glorious and grandiose lectures and essays our scientists can deliver. I wonder if they believe all their beautiful bosh. It certainly makes an impression on the public, but I should think it would bother their consciences. Or maybe they are like a Sunday-church-going unscrupulous lawyer; or like Patton praying to his Protestant Pater?

I went to Syracuse for a week, primarily to get my car out of storage. What a grand and glorious feeling to get her going again. All the pleasant memories of 70,000 miles brought back. I was amazed at the number of friends I had in town. It looks as tho the activities of the few "agin" me had dominated the scenes of the last few years. And all that gossip and lowdown on college activities – an organization replete with all the human frailties. There was no sense of regret at having resigned: I'd go back only if my clothes were holy and my stomach empty, and there was nothing else.

So I finally drove to Arden Forest, for the first time in three years, the end of a 16-year odyssey that leaves me very much where I was at the beginning. But ye gawds what a mess of family problems I plunked myself into. Entire indifference to the most basic principles of landscaping, architecture, and interiors, a sense of housekeeping fit for the slums, has left a place where there is not a single respectable room in the house, certainly none to which I would bring any friend. And I am not the only loose screw in the family. The others are exceedingly nervous, blindly kind, and repeatedly creating the most monstrous situation. I find entire evenings taken up with me acting as arbiter and protestant and straightener and assuming a role that now makes it difficult or impossible to leave home again for any length of time. A 9-room apartment, a huge house on 350 acres, and I do not have a single room equipped for being surrounded by books and papers and long enough stretches of uninterrupted time to really write.

But in most of those two weeks at Colebrook I have escaped to the fields, and did more honest physical work than in the last five years put together. Cutting brush where it had invaded fields, building stone walls, cutting trails, just wandering about – autumn colored the land while I was there, and humanless nature seemed at peace. There seemed an infinite satisfaction in adding a touch to the naturalistic landscaping that I never obtained from driving facts into unwilling students. For the first time since I had my cabin in British Honduras did the day seem too short, and the night just an unpleasant interlude that one had to admit. I am not sure how much I'll plant next spring – if I am there – for I find canned beans very cheap, and there are other things to be done, but physical work and writing will vie with each other. I shall probably have to lay down a schedule so that one does not intrude on the other. Life may seem too short again.

The big house is still a problem. It has been a source of infinite dissension in the past 11 years among the rest of the family. Maybe I'll get onto my high horse; either I'll cut myself loose from it entirely, or take over the charge completely. It seems treason and blasphemy to fill a few acres with such eyesores and live in the midst of them when all around is beauty. My present plan is to go into the hospital October 15th for the traumatic cataract operation (the high tension is still present, and Dr. C. says only that "we are still trying to save the shape of the eye", and thus, I suppose, the eye). When I come out, I either settle at Colebrook even for the winter, or I drive south and search for adventure. Maybe the next time you drive or come East I'll have the Forest to show you. It may not be the most beautiful place in the world, but it has a type of beauty that makes it a gem among gems.

Arden Forest

Best to you,

The next few came in rapid succession. First from Jewel.

I hope its not too soon for visitors. One feels a bit apologetic as a visitor-without-benefit-of-Prunus serotina. Try to overlook the omission.

You should have reached the squinting Cyclops stage by now, but I suppose it's too soon to predict much about the success of the surgery. So glad you managed to get to Arden forest and cut brush – I'm certain that the maldistribution of manual labor, like that of wealth, is one of the ugly maggots at the root of our civilization. With two days in the dark – you probably have the place landscaped to your heart's desire.

A few snow flakes fluttered down yesterday – and I gathered the russet chrysanthemums and the last carnation with regret. A little more fall spading and the garden with its earthy smells and sumac leaves against blue sky – and straightening up to find oneself surrounded by quiet and a mother of pearl sunset must exist only in memory for too many months. I really need a moral equivalent for gardening – one that makes use of the larger muscles.

The pretty nurse is coming with a thermometer I suppose. I hope to hear, soon, that you have been a model patient. I hope Dr. C. has made the most of my moral support.

Then from Küchler.

I was one small jump ahead of you this time, for your letter arrived on my first day <u>out</u> of the hospital. I did miss all the Prunus (plural) during this siege. Yet the stay was by no means unpleasant. My M.D. uncle, Herbert Wilshusen, was prominent during the operation. I am not sure whether his chief interest was medical, or for my moral support. He is grand at the latter anyway. The operation was much shorter than the first. Locally anaesthetized as before. My good eye was uncovered 24 hours after; I was out of bed 48 hours after the operation. Friends dropped in often; the Eye Institute Librarian turned out to be one with interesting experiences and a readiness to make them sound interesting; codeine made life practically painless, WQXR supplied good music all the time; and a *mystery story in Braille gave me no end of puzzling. I can't say that my Braille reading ability has arrived at the "useful" stage yet for reading, but at least each day I noticed the tempo increased. And so 11 days passed. It was far easier to take than my recent Army job, where coffee and tobacco vied with each other, in contest with phenobarbitol to put me off balance. Kindly friends still occasionally pass a comment about the lightness with which I have accepted the whole matter. Some day one will say that to me after a cocktail or two and I will guarantee that I shall not retort with a "Pal! You ain't heard the half of it yet!"*

Apropos of tales of woe: I was talking to an ex-student of mine recently, and he spoke with great indignation of the humiliation and mistreatment that some fellow officers of his had received in Jap internment camps under conditions that were generally recognized as very good. I sorely wanted to vie with him with an all-American story, of an arrest that resembled a mugging job, where the fellow never knew he was being arrested, where the crime was a thought supposed to exist in the accused's mind, with "medical treatment" an hour later that was a complete farce, with a legal trial where the accused was not given a chance to defend himself, and where 24 hours passed with an eye hanging wide open before a surgeon could be had – and how much longer than 24 hours it would have been had not a ray of humanity intervened, I hate to think. Oh well, this is the first time the situation has so come to mind in weeks.

I managed 2 more weeks at Norfolk and had another grand time. The weather was even warmer and Indianer than before, and I basked in it like a snake in the sun. A can of Kemtone and Kemtone border strips hid the continuous stream of grease and stains around the lower three feet of the small living room walls. And plans for removing other eyesores were made, which made said eyesores easier to bear. Altho wildlife is by no means of the Everglades variety there, an occasional deer, fox, skunk, woodchuck, winter birds, are ample for sociability. The extraordinary wealth of a non-human environment makes it a most exciting place to live. The land was an abundance of mountain laurel, white pine, and hemlock, so that I may even find myself liking the landscape. The matter of the house has been settled, in a way surprising even to me. I have bought the whole darn outfit from my mother, the remaining 47 acres, house and all it contains. I suddenly find myself among the landed gentry, far from having the wee hut I had planned. Not at all sure how I'm going to use it all, or even how I am going to finance its maintenance. The move, however, seemed the best from several points of view, and the purchase solved a very great number of family problems for my parents. So Jewel, if you and your mother, or friends, drive East next summer, I'll expect you to make a stop, and use it as if it were your own.

All of which makes my retirement one step closer. I admit I am slow getting started. Some day I hope to win you over to the idea that life begins at retirement – the time when one can cease to bow and kowtow to his superiors, always forsaking truth and integrity and honesty for the sake of the security of his position, and for professional advancement and social climbing. I grant that I was a bit shocked when one recently forced me to admit I had received my Ph.D only 9 years ago, and that I left to start college as a freshmen 16 years ago. It seems like many more years than that number. And now I am back just where I started, at Norfolk. If another war does not interfere, I hope to get the next 16 out of books rather than travel. Sounds tame, no?

Until again,
Always,

From Jewel, again, only a few days later.

Congratulations on being landed gentry. Somehow I fancy that the adventitious roots will be very becoming. Seriously – I think you have something there. The responsibility for some 400 acres of the earth – and the improvement of house and grounds are likely to be as deeply satisfying an experience as you have ever indulged in.

Uncle George was a dear – and a rare judge of people. His comment "Fred's a good man, a very good man, but you can't tell him anything; he has to learn everything for himself" – should rank as one of the best thumbnail sketches of the century.

I had to smile at the bowing and kowtowing my profession is supposed to require. Hitherto I have been as brutally frank with my superiors as – for example – with you. Horrid of me isn't it? Since I have no talent for administrative work – I have not sought "advancement" here. My 4 or 5 hours a week with 160 kids is a big enough job to use the energy I feel that I am generating. Should I not return to Urbana – it is not at all clear to me how my careeer in ecology fell away from me or can be restored - and should I put on the best show I can in those 4-5 hours daily for another dozen years I shall have earned the right really *to retire – and boon doggle any way I chose. I know several teachers who are doing a very honest day's work – I must frequently remind myself that the few who are plain damned lazy are not my responsibility.*

Be sure to let me know if the kind invitation to visit Arden forest is hearby forfeit for that faulty kow tow, for I really intend to take you up on it some day. I like the idea of being the Eve of your forest. There wouldn't be a little sphagnum somewhere would there? – or wintergreen? – Are you lucky enough to have a fire place? – How far is the purling brook from the house? Is there, by chance, a flowering dogwood at the edge of a clearing against a background of green – or an old pasture overgrown with hawthorns with warblers (in May) in the branches? - ??

Should business call you west again it would be nice if it were during Xmas holidays. I shall have time to play and argue then.

Two days of midsemesters – and five Sunday guests add up to little leisure for a while. Try to behave my lad, even if Auntie can't keep an eye on you. Remember – no *more horse back riding! Best wishes for full recovery of the eye.*

And, chronologically on its heels, from Küchler.

So how are the 160 youngsters developing? I suppose they are not old enough to have been impressed either by the war or the atom bomb, so that a decade hence they will be all too eager to march, and once more to save the world for democracy. Honestly – I am truly amazed – to get back to the kids – that your position has not required the hypocritical kowtowing, which amused you so. I have friends in the Chicago, N.Y., and Frisco school systems, and sundry friends in other teaching work. They are all exceedingly critical of various educational procedures, and claim to various degrees that they never say what they think, could not, and hold their jobs. Is it the hope of another stint at Urbana that has given such a pleasant optimism to your situation?

For two weeks now the radio has been my only contact with current events. I came up just before the snow storm, intending to make several trips to N.Y. to bring up books and papers. Fortunately filled up with furnace oil, and had furnace stove and hotwater heater cleaned out a matter of hours before the snows came. It was a week later that the town road was plowed out. The town plow took half a day to open up half of our 300 feet of private drive, and got stuck. So Fred has decided to put up his car for the winter. It may give one a sense of power to drive out every day; but the plow made things look as tho a Sherman tank went thru. The hours spent and the hours to be spent in putting the road back in shape next spring: I'd rather walk a mile and a half to the state road every two weeks or so, and keep all my beautiful snowdrifts untouched.

I am always decidedly interested in your analyses of some of my maze-wanderings. So often you hit right down on a point that I had not quite seen before. But you know, it was not until this last letter that I realized clearly that we are oceans apart in regard to our overall evaluation of the human species. Needless to go into details. You would say of one that his social interest is not strong enough to stand the strain of cooperation of people. Santayana, I believe, would say of the same person that the stupidities of the people are so great as to discourage him, despite his social interests.

It was interesting to have Dr. Nichol's comment recalled to me, for it gains new perspective. Obviously, you accept your uncle's very words. But there may be more to the story. I do not recall any particular incident, not one, to which that would apply. I do remember several discussions on ecological thought, in which I did not agree with him, and I was quite unable to make him justify himself. I am inclined to think the question reflects back on him. Such a statement is a defence statement, by many people, to "explain" a situation where someone disagrees, and will not accept his word. I liked Dr. Nichols, but frankly Jewel, I do not place him on the pedestal that you do. As a person, he was extremely likeable. As a teacher, I found him quite indifferent. And, quite frankly, I had little respect for his knowledge of the ecological literature. I do not consider that he was a clear thinker, anything of a philosopher, or had the ability to think clearly, logically, and without prejudice, or the favoring of personal likes. He may have sensed that I did not respect his thinking ability. On such matters, I did choose to learn by myself. The harshest statement he ever used on me, was used on three occasions. Then disgusted with certain ideas in ecology I wanted to try out, his comment was "That is what Stanley Cain does. Would you want to be like Stanley Cain?" In his mind, it was like being compared with Mephisto, or with Huey Long. Today Stanley Cain is a greater ecologist than Nichols ever was. He is probably the leading active American ecologist of the time!

You are directly invited to visit Arden Forest next summer, if not earlier. It may not be what you expect. The house annoys me vastly. Our family will spend money for heat and light and water. But we have no more taste in certain things than an Australian aborigine. A fireplace!! Never, never, a most inefficient way of heating. Only the three winter rooms are papered; the rest of the house is still with bare plasterboard, plaster seams and nail holes and all. Etc. No sphagnum around, but we do have wintergreen. No dogwood (it's too far "north"). No hawthorn pastures for the same reason. The small brook is 100 feet behind the house, in a ravine. I own for half a mile along a much larger one back in the woods. But if you have seen no laurel in blossom, you cannot understand where some people consider hawthorn and dogwood something to look at if there is no laurel. Laurel is one of our commonest shrubs. And highbush blueberries are all through the pastures and forest edges. I will not be able to entertain you with the services of cook, butler, chauffeur, maids, etc. But I'll have one or two rooms fixed up by then, and the house will be yours to use as your own as long as you are here. Thanks SO much for suggesting I stay with you if I get again to Detroit during the holidays. I seem quite content to stay right here at the moment and "work". Take a quick trip to N.Y. every 15 days for a Dr. checkup. Eye coming along. Glaucoma apparently disappeared. Getting used to using one eye now. I doubt if my desk work will suffer too much.

The next is from Jewel. He rereads the first two pages twice.

Christmas Day – in the evening.
I thought of you today as we held the usual festivities – beginning with clan assembled in front of the lighted tree at Marjories – Danny gurgling and wobbling in his high chair – his

great grandmother very excited and erect beside him. The cards were read by Jimmy from his wheelchair as the gay packages piled up on the assembled circle of laps. Then its opening – one at a time around the circle. For the men the gifts run to ties and mechanical gadgets – since neither smoke or use liquor or play cards. The feminine 2/3 gathered loot in the form of gay & foolish items tending to tickle the vanity. Where I was concerned both friends and family seemed to be in some sort of conspiracy to make a lady of me. Not a pair of overalls in the lot and you should see how badly I need overalls! The second feature was an invasion of the privacy of Danny's bath to watch him making an aquatic whirling dervish of himself. What a joy to behold is his perfection!

Then we picked up most of the clutter and moved to have dinner at my aunt's. Extra guest for the sixth year, he reminds us, was a charming and fragile-looking gentleman of 76 – a bachelor without relatives in the city, living in a rooming house, and still earning his living at some clerkly job. He is at once pious and gay – fastidious and pleasant.

Danny was unusually well behaved. He has passed – as you have reason to know – his fifth month – a perfectly cared for but not coddled infant. Talk about conditioning! When he has kicked and chattered until he is bored and peevish – you just turn him on his tummy – and he promptly puts his thumb in his mouth and goes to sleep. It is as simple as turning on a faucet.

✧

So you don't really mind my poking and prying – and spying upon your "maze wanderings"? Then let me express my idea of your most often repeated error – cynicism. I can claim no "religion" in the usually accepted sense – only a profound sense of law – the inevitability of certain discoverable patterns in relationships of all levels from those of physical bodies —atomic or planetary – all the way up thru organic life – and including the delicate relationships that constitute human society. Such laws as "Thou shalt love they neighbor as thyself" – "Share ye one another's burdens and so fulfill the law of life" – are the formula for the sweat which holds together human society. – Amazing speculations of that group mind which has evolved out of mud and is – to use J. B. Cabell's phrase – merely the "ape bereft of his tail and grown rusty at climbing!" I do not believe that – even with the formula for the chain reaction in his clumsy hands – that he will quite eliminate himself as a species of social animal. Some sort of world organization will be settled on to muddle along even should half the world's population be destroyed.

—— "One another's burdens" – that involves a personal challenge – so let's look at yours. - The big one that eclipses all the others in my view – that attitude of disgust and loathing for the human species. But Fred, that burden is so ugly – and so non-essential – as it contains neither tools for work nor objets d'art. Now since mutuality – symbiosis – is essential to sound society – you'll have to take some responsibility for my burden. – It being a dearth of intellectually stimulating companionship – of persons with a little time to spare from their other duties – it's practically made to order for you!

I wonder if it's wise to allow considerations of your parents' worry to bear too heavily on the direction of your future course. Worry by now is so fixed in habit with them that – did you live across the street they would daily be haunted by the fear that you'd be run down by a truck some day when you came to see them.

The savory woods — and getting that accumulation of data in shape for publication – or Guatemala – sunshine – and a new job – fascinating choice! I wonder which it would be if you used the test of the greatest good to the greatest number, and count Freddie only once?

◊

Be a gentleman and burn this now. For if you should run across it months after the Christmas tree has gone up in smoke, it would seem even more impossibly bold and badly expressed than it does now.

Please, convey my best wishes to your parents. Good night, mon ami, and may the new year bring you much joy.

***

*Norfolk, Connecticut
February 8, 1946*

Your Christmas Day letter has continued to be enjoyed, and has continued to afford meet for chewing. I doubly appreciate the honor of having Christmas evening devoted to a monologue for me – for I am sure that the largest share of the evening was so devoted.

I accept the rebukes, mild as they are: this time; and cannot take credit for the opening compliment for, alas the species of brick referred to, eludes my memory at the moment. I seem to have infinite faith in my being a rational being. On the basis of probability, I should some time surprise you and act rationally.

I am sure you remember Miss Prigge. A comment of hers needs repeating, even tho by doing so, I open myself to the reproof of an arched eyebrow. Let it be said that in the course of the past decade or so a variety of friends and acquaintances have had occasion to pass through New York, and some have stopped at #625. Miss Prigge is an observing person, although as silent as the sphinx. I may have told you that she has little formal education, comes from a very successful farm family on the outskirts of Hamburg, Germany. Her tastes are spontaneous, refined, cultivated... While talking to her one evening in the kitchen, she asked how you were, and added: She is the finest girl, Fred, the f-I-nest girl of all your friends. Take it as you wish. But among many other angles, I think you can consider it an opinion quite independent of your education and intelligence (rather, obvious evidence of those) for such would have little effect on Miss Prigge.

Report on the eye: no change. I've all but forgotten about it. As for the other little matter out in your town: I am frank to say that R. never replied, assuming he did receive my letter. In the meantime, I obtained a copy of the Record. Weeell, it is best left unsaid. It threw me pretty well off balance. I did not get back to writing for an entire week. The entire first half of the Record was entirely new to me: I had never heard it before! You see at the time I did not know where I was; I thought I was standing in line waiting for something and I remember now I sort of woke up, when it was half over, I realize now. The information in it: the fact that I was halted just when I was ready to give <u>my</u> account; the fact that my final words "not guilty" were entirely overridden; the fact that I was medically unfit for any such affair – it gripped me all over again. Some of the information was unqualifiedly false, as when it was said that he took off my glasses <u>before</u> the accident occurred (if so, his concern before the emergency doctor, to see whether any glass was in my eye, sounds strange). And all that was left <u>out</u> of the evidence....Oh well. I was told that I did not have much chance, that it would be my word against <u>three</u> others, that I would be fighting a magistrate, a dept., *and a city. It is quite clear to me that there is nothing to be done. To try to <u>disprove</u> someone else's word is next to impossible. What is <u>my</u> word against that array? It still surprises me that it <u>all</u> hinges on <u>words</u>, absolutely nothing else. Excuse all these details. I have not blown off this much about it for weeks and weeks. I am taking my licking, and it is not all bad. I confess that had such a thing happened six or seven years ago I would have rebelled to an extraordinary degree, but a person only rebels once against downright injustice, and thereafter he knows that there is no such thing as justice.*

And when am I going to get this visit from you? In case you are not driving, a bus goes from Albany to Norfolk. My own car is still snowed in, but I can get you a taxi if you brave this season.

A friend wrote recently commenting on my being a snowed-in recluse. Bigosh, I suppose he is right in a way. However strange the life may be to others, it is being one of the most magnificent experiences I have ever enjoyed. From now on I shall recommend to everyone who really wants to be thrilled with life in all its ways, to live alone in the country for a time! So many of my theories and opinions on human nature are being tossed aside that I shall have far less respect for myself than ever before. It reminds me of my recent attempts to distinguish the plant community from the human community. It is conventional, and expected, to say that they differ completely in the absence, in plants, of altruism and self-sacrificing behavior for the good of the community. Conversely, in a human community there are certain activities carried on for the good of the whole, even tho individuals may suffer in the process. I wonder whether our crediting the human community with such noble self-sacrificing individuals is not a little bit like putting earth at the center of the universe, like making God in man's image, or like the male toad claiming that the quintessence of beauty lay within the warthy hide and the blobby abdomen of his lady toad. And then I found that the definition of the <u>pla</u>nt community could very well fit the <u>hu</u>man community: each individual for himself, no altruism; if any activities resulted in the good of the community, it was purely coincidental, and would be continued just as strongly by the individual even if they were resulting in harm to the community.

And so life goes on. I make no promises about the future, but up to the present I have no idea of changing. And if I do more than set an example for other people, and thus lend them to partake of the same pleasure, I might be accomplishing as much as by spending a life time expounding a poorly written text book. (My own book is still going on, top speed). I have none of the moments of idleness, the waits, the futile arguments with prejudiced and opinionated pseudo-intelligentsia. Life really tears along, a continuous string of rich experiences. I am no longer a big fish in a small pond: I am picking up crumbs from the tables of the world's mightiest. Tango-bastante salud, y bastante pesetas, y – for the first time – el tiempo para gozarias. It is no sin to enjoy life so: I am depriving no one of the same opportunity. The blank walls, and the blanker conversation of city life is a prison by comparison: I prefer my forests and my books. How soon can I give you a look at them?

And it was morning. He had fallen asleep in the armchair, letter in his lap. He might as well go home. He can and will come back with a scanner.

Urbana

I

JEWEL has to keep from shouting that today's guest speaker at Vivarium 203 is—of all things— Surprise!—a woman! A woman and an ecologist and a professor!

Vivarium 203 is headquarters for the animal ecologists at the university and where the Animal Ecology Club meets every Wednesday, promptly at five o'clock. Usually they assemble to hear one of their own, either a new grad student interpreting a paper assigned to him or her (for there is a healthy proportion of women) or an older one presenting dissertation research. Sometimes it is to hear Shelford or Kendeigh or, more rarely, some other Illinois professor. Guest speakers are unusual.

Having just caught a glimpse of the speaker, Jewel now wishes she had read the papers that Shelford put out the day before. Often, he spread reprints of papers relevant to a talk over the long table in the department's seminar room. His reason for leaving them lying about is attributed to professorial forgetfulness, but Jewel knows that nothing works quite so well in getting a student's attention—from grammar school to grad school—as what appears to be a carelessly left document that is glimpsed in transit. Jewel glances at the pale blue cover of one such without touching it. It is a reprint of a recent paper. Its title, Glacial and post-glacial plant migrations indicated by relic colonies of southern Ohio, impresses her. The blue cover identifies it as from *Ecology*. Its author is given as E. L. Braun.

It is past five. Shelford has already taken his usual position at the end of the table nearest his office door. Afraid to appear not to have read the paper, Jewel reaches for a cookie instead. Cookies and tea are always provided. Jewel is certain they are sops for having to postpone supper. In her case, it means missing supper. To make it worse, her duties at the herbarium, where she prepares specimens for lab courses, kept her working through lunch. It is her second missed meal in a row, no matter how far what is served at her boarding house stretches the meaning of a meal. And it is included in the cost of her room, whether eaten or not. She reaches for a second cookie and uses that to cover the third that she takes.

She can go to bed without supper tonight. The fifty dollars she can expect from her stipend and herbarium work combined, she knows, will barely match her living expenses. She needs every penny she can earn. The extra work she has just taken on she hopes will keep her from dipping too far into her meager savings—or going hat in hand once more to her Uncle George.

That additional work is proofreading the book that Shelford is furiously trying to finish up. His co-author is Frederic Clements. It is a project that has been in gestation for a decade. It has finally reached the galley-proof stage. But for the pocket money, she will not miss its coming to an end. She works not with the actual galley proofs but with negative photocopies. Having to slave laboriously over page after page of white-on-black letters and looking for errors to circle in red pencil by checking against an original draft—and that marked with numerous hand-written revisions—it can't end soon enough for her. Not that she exactly checks word-for-word with the original, which is itself not free of errors. Jewel has quickly managed to develop a reader's eye for something that does not look correct, which she can then catch and bring to Shelford's attention.

"My, how did you get through that so fast," Shelford marvels every time she brings him a section. She knows better than to tell him her technique, even though it yields results in accord with his own proofreading.

Scientific names, however, the bane of typesetters and proofreaders, slow her down. Most are unfamiliar to her. Slow, methodical inspection cannot be avoided. Not only does each name —and there are entire lists of them—have to be checked against the original, but too often for her taste, the spelling of the original requires verification by a search through musty old documents in archives spread over the campus.

Jewel's efficiency pleases Shelford. His smile turns to a frown, however, when she brings him any more substantive suggestion than a misspelling or a needless comma.

"Coactions and reactions?" Jewel asked the first time she dropped off a set of proofed pages. "Why not just symbiosis?"

"Yes, an interesting suggestion," Shelford politely fended her off, "but I am afraid that you might not have quite a clear enough grasp of the specific meanings and uses of each term."

Obviously not, she told herself then, indignant over what she saw as condescension. She stifled the urge to quote from Charles Elton's *Animal Ecology* about how ecology should not consist of saying what everyone knows in ways that no one can understand, but could not remember if she had the quote right or whether it was Elton's own. Maybe if she had a chance to read the first two chapters, she later punctuated her petulance, maybe those terms would make more sense. However, she now keeps her editorial comments to herself.

A woman speaker, Jewel marvels again, looking at Lucy Braun at the far side of the table from Shelford and Kendeigh. She is the first working woman ecologist Jewel has come across. She will have to write to Liza about it, Jewel decides. Liza's graduate professor has just warned her that, as a woman, she might starve to death if she continues in her quest of a career in physics.

Of course, Edith Clements, who is sitting beside Braun, is a PhD ecologist, also, but Jewel can personally testify that the wife of Frederic Clements is no longer a practicing scientist. She admitted as much to Jewel, describing herself on the first day of their acquaintance as "chauffeur, typist, photographer, mechanic, commissary general, and second field assistant" on her travels with her husband in Billie Buick, the large vehicle they purchased especially for their long field trips. Jewel would like to add cook, nursemaid, secretary, and intellectual slave to her husband and his career to that admission. It is as if Mrs. Clements never stopped being her husband's graduate assistant when she became his wife. She merely added the other roles after completing her degree under him. Both are presently at Urbana for their semi-yearly fall visit to Shelford, this time in the company of John Phillips, the South African ecologist who is traveling with them. And this time there is a tension about the Vivarium that is obvious to all of its denizens. The book is having a difficult birth.

Jewel decides against taking the remaining two cookies before she slips into a seat next to Reggie Parker.

"Where is Clements?" she whispers.

"Talk to me later," he shushes her.

With warmth that suggests long acquaintance, Shelford is already introducing their guest speaker. At Shelford's left, as always, is Charles Kendeigh, his former student and now his newest and closest colleague, so close that their respective stables of graduate students are beginning to think of the two as a single mentor. The students do everything together. "Sheldeigh," or more often "Kenford," is being heard out of either professor's earshot. Next to Kendeigh today is the tall, gangly graduate student he brought with him from Western Reserve. Jewel calls him "Odum the Okie." Sometimes she calls him "yokel" or "Rube." Less often, it is "the hillbilly." Other students around the table, Jewel categorizes as boringly "Illini," meaning born, bred, and destined to live and die in the state, and—stranger still to Jewel—liking it all. There are exceptions. Frank Pitelka is one, although an Illini. He is a sparkly-eyed undergraduate who for some reason shares an office with the Okie and dreams of California. Reggie Parker is another. He caught her attention at once with his New England accent.

"If you're not a Downeaster," she said to him on overhearing him call someone in the Registrar's Office a "dumb bastid," "then you must be a Gloucesterman!"

She was right. He had just completed research on marine communities at Cape Ann, Massachusetts, where, like Küchler at his still-unseen-by-her Arden Forest, he lived essentially at home. Back at Urbana to write his dissertation, Parker has already taken a position at Kent State and now returns only to visit his Illini fiancee, a union that seems like a waste of an interesting man to Jewel. There is allegedly an Oregonian and a Ute in Shelford's stable, but they are off doing research in—can she guess?—Oregon and Utah!

Lucy Braun is a handsome woman about the same age as her mother, Jewel judges. From Shelford's introduction, it seems as if she has spent her entire life in Cincinnati, managing from that base to study almost everything possible about the deciduous forests of the eastern United States.

Among Braun's many accomplishments, Shelford continues his introduction, is being a recent Vice President of the Ecological Society of America, founding the Wildflower Preservation Society of North America, and having a contribution enthusiastically included by him in his *Naturalist's Guide to the Americas*. She has come to Urbana to give a more formal talk at noon the next day.

"What a treat it is to have Dr. Braun to ourselves before then in this intimate setting," Shelford ends his introduction.

After thanking Shelford and the Animal Ecology Club with self-effacement that charms Jewel, Braun launches into a discussion of her research. Issues of terminology quickly take on significance by their inadequacy for her data. Her beeches, sugar maples, tulip poplars, buckeyes, basswoods, and white ashes seemed not to fit any of the categories of climax forests. What Jewel is hearing she has also heard from Küchler. (How every thought of him sends a cold sliver of ice, tiny though it now might be, through her heart.) Küchler's red spruces, yellow birches, balsam firs, beeches, hemlocks, white pines, sugar maples, and oaks in the Berkshires fit no better than Braun's Appalachian trees. He complained to Jewel at their last meeting of an inability to get across to Uncle George that the categories he was supposed to study might not exist. He has gone off to Hawaii with the task undone.

Braun is no longer self-effacing in closing her talk. Her solution for the predicament is to offer a term of her own, association-segregate.

That'll never stick, Jewel decides, as she fills out the three-by-five card that each student must turn in for course credit. She needs to share that thought with someone, but Parker, on one side, has his attention elsewhere, while tall, elegantly attractive Jane Dirks, on the other, she hardly knows.

"What impresses me most," Shelford rises first to speak, "is that you braved moonshiners in the back woods of the Appalachians. I know the type well. They all have guns and dogs and don't cotton to strangers. The sites you studied are not for the faint-hearted. I salute you for even entering those woods."

"My older sister Annette was with me on almost all my trips," Braun answers hesitantly. "She's an entomologist. We live together, so that it is convenient for us to work together."

She appears relieved when the next question is on technical issues.

Jewel would rather the subject not have been changed. She waits quietly for a chance to bring it up again as others file out. When only Edith Clements is beside Braun, she shyly approaches to introduce herself.

"How is it for a woman?" Jewel asks, her directness surprising her into incoherence. "That is, in making a career in ecology?"

Dr. Braun understands at once.

"Why, there are a number of women in ecology," she replies. "Beside Edith here," she nods at Mrs. Clements, "there is another Edith at the Desert Laboratory, Edith Shreve."

"And Frances Long," Edith Clements puts in. "Like me, she also obtained her PhD under Frederic. Frances Louise is a research associate with us now. Of course, a mere wife, such as myself, would not have been hired as Frederic's assistant at the Desert Laboratory. Why should she? A mere wife will work just as hard for nothing. I am sure that is why I was never given a formal position."

"Married women have a hard go at getting academic positions," Lucy says somewhat gravely. "It is much easier for me being unmarried. Some academic positions are purposefully filled only by unmarried women. And then, there is often the stipulation that they stay unmarried."

The conversation has caught the attention of two students in a tiny room off Vivarium 203. One is Marie Ostendorf, who Jewel knows only as an Illini. The other is Jane Dirks.

"But you know," Edith fends off any questions they may have by addressing Jewel, "Mrs. Shreve never did get her PhD. She had trained at Chicago in chemistry and physics. No wonder she is doing so well with her physiology studies."

"And have any of you come across Minna Jewell, at Wisconsin?" Lucy asks, stepping closer to Marie and Jane. "She received her PhD with Dr. Shelford, too. It looks like Dr. Shelford will have trained two jewels."

She flashes Jewel a smile, then turns back to the others.

"Dr. Jewell publishes a lot of very good work on lakes," she continues, "most of it in Ecology and Ecological Monographs. So it is possible in this field, if not in physics or chemistry. Marie, is it?"

There is a nod in affirmation. Jewel is surprised to be jealous that Lucy knows Marie's name. All three students started graduate school just months ago. It must be an advantage of having an office so close to Shelford's, Jewel guesses, and thus dismisses her jealousy.

"I'm glad that my parents were both schoolteachers, very much equals," Lucy continues. "They encouraged both myself and my sister to study nature and to take our studies as far as we could. They were unusual for those days, I should think."

"These days, too," Marie picks up the thought with an animation Jewel has not yet witnessed in her. "Everyone at home called me a kind of oddball, because I was the valedictorian of my high school. No one understood why I put my time into studies instead of just looking out for a husband. Fortunately, my parents let me come here. Clarence and I—"

"But it is time," Edith Clement interrupts, ushering the speaker away. The two girls disappear back into their little office.

"Nothing could suit me better than returning to Linfield College to teach," is heard from inside. "I won't need a husband."

Like mice, Jewel thinks, looking wistfully at their open door. But what a location for their hole! She starts to follow Lucy and Edith at a polite distance out into the Vivarium's central hallway, but another open door, the one to Reggie's office, distracts her. He shares it with the other two students who are finishing their theses. Neither has been seen in months. She pokes her head in.

"I know why Clements wasn't at the talk," Reggie says in invitation. "An emergency! A crisis! He was still closeted with John Phillips. Those first two chapters you asked me about earlier seem to be the subject of special attention. There was much huddling going on today between Clements and Shelford —and John Phillips."

"What do you think?"

"What else? Ego, as always."

Jewel gives him a shocked expression.

"No not Shelford," Reggie corrects her, "not that he doesn't have a healthy dose, but Clements. I was sitting in the seminar room this afternoon reading Lucy Braun's paper, and I could hear them in Shelford's office. You know how his door is always open? Phillips seemed to be bragging that he had managed to talk Clements into participating in a symposium—for the first time in twenty years. Supposedly he had convinced Clements that he needed to show that he was neither unapproachable nor superior. The way Phillips said it, he put the word in quotes, superior. With a capital S, maybe. Other, lesser scientists, he said, thought that was why Clements won't mingle at their meetings. Phillips said they all think he refuses to descend from his high eminence—I think was his word—to meet with them—or even call on them when he and Edith pass through their towns on their many journeys."

Jewel waits for more. This is juicy.

"I have always been intellectually arrogant," Reggie tries to imitate Clements's haughty manner. "That is all that Clements said to that. And then I heard, And why not? It was a female voice. Must have been Edith. John, here, she said, openly calls you on all occasions as the greatest living ecologist.

"But that's peripheral," Reggie says, finally having relieved himself of his gossip. "What will interest you is what the issue is with the first two chapters."

"That's why I didn't get to proof them?"

"Absolutely. Both are what Shelford calls Clements's philosophizing about ecology. They're being revised furiously. He is still insisting on his complex organism, but what the first chapter is really stuck on seems to be priority for the idea. It is a crisis, in fact. The publisher sent the chapters out for review and the reviewer recommended the entire first chapter be rewritten. I heard Shelford say he thought the reviewer was Allee. He didn't seem to agree with Clements's history of how the idea came about. My God! Biocoenosis, ecosystem, community, the idea must have been in the air! But in Bio-Ecology, they claim that Mobius's biocenose, as Clements has it, had to do only with animals. Cut the chapter, they will not, but there is agony over how to revise it. The current version has Clements's first using his term, biome, in 1917. And now Arthur Vestal—do you know him?"

"How could I not? I prepare specimens for his botany lab. He calls me a fellow student of Cowles."

"Well, he had the biome idea a few years before Clements, I think, but not a good term for it. He talked of associations, terrestrial associations, biotic associations, biotic community, everything that is a biome, except the word itself."

"Ecosystem," Jewel fills Reggie's pause, "isn't anywhere in the text. Neither have I heard it yet in Shelford's class. Now there must be some story to that."

"Which class? Climatic ecology?"

"Animal geography. And I don't remember it in Elton's book, either."

"Hmm. No reason to bring it up, I guess. Anyway, I doubt you'll find ecosystem in either of those two chapters. Elton's book, by the way, was before Tansley's paper. And I can assure you that

that paper was never a subject of discussion at the Animal Ecology Club. I even—"

The thought goes unsaid. Reggie has popped out of his chair. "I've got to go!" he says reaching for hat and coat. "I'm already late."

His Jean, Jewel thinks, walking with him out of his office, through the seminar room, and out into the hallway. She decides to accompany him as far as the stone pillar outside the entrance to the Vivarium.

"Get your coat, dear," he says, giving her a hug. For warmth, she supposes. Each has a last look at the other from opposite sides of the pillar. Coatless, but not cold, she watches him disappear down a row of successively smaller elms. Like a figure in a perspective drawing, she fancies the image. Then she turns back toward the building.

The Vivarium struck her as a rather plain building after the Gothic exuberance of Chicago. Given her preference for fieldwork, it seemed more of a prison to her than the respected laboratory that it was. She now grants that the tolerances of animals to environmental conditions that was being studied with experimental precision within it is important to ecology. However, that respect has not changed her opinion of it. The building remains every bit the long, squat, functional two-story building that disappointed her on first sight. The wrought iron fence, with its corner pillars, and the attached greenhouses are its only points of interest. Add to that, she now thinks, the shrinking elms.

Re-emerging from the building with coat, hat, and light scarf, it strikes her that the entire campus suffers in comparison to Chicago. Ivy on walls can't hide that it is too rural, she thinks, its open spaces too many and too open. The Armory and Kinley Hall dominate their huge spaces. Even somehow moving closer together, though, she judges as she passes by, would not be that much of an improvement. To her, their style is still too much of a compromise between Gothic and Classical.

Jewel prefers the drug store on the unfashionably wrong side of the tracks past which she walks to and from campus. It was once a bank, the Cattle Bank. She stops before it to imagine the skinny bovines of Illinois not being able to keep the bank solvent, even before the crash. Then she decides to go in and splurge on a malted milk. Extravagant, yes, but not when making up for two separate meals, she rationalizes.

The seedy looking drug store was where she took refuge with her bags on getting off the Illinois Central at the station nearby. She sat in it that night reading a book and wondering if she might not be making a mistake. The book was *Animal Ecology*. It then comprised her entire library. It had been a going away gift from Ward Allee. It was a strange gift, in that Elton is British and in it called for animal ecology to be studied in the field. Ecology "simply means scientific natural history" Elton defined it, but what of Allee's lab work? Wasn't that ecology? And those words by Gilbert White that Elton quoted that she read that night?

"Faunists are too apt to acquiesce in bare descriptions and a few synonyms. The reasons for it are plain. All that can be done at home in a man's study, but investigation of the life of animals is much more difficult and is not to be attained but by the active and inquisitive who reside in the country."

She remembers those words from that night still. The drug store and the book, which she keeps at her bedside, are still refuges for her, and she still wonders if she has made the right decision.

Then she wonders, "Did he just call me dear?"

II

JEWEL has lost her roommate, or lab mate, or office mate, or whatever her situation with Edith Clements was. Even though they were to share Jewel's space only temporarily, it still comes as a surprise when Jewel returns from her mammalogy class to find Edith and her trappings gone. It is a pleasant surprise. Jewel pulls over a vacant chair to enjoy the luxury of putting her tired feet up. That however is short-lived. Shelford pops in almost at once, a sheepishly apologetic grin on his face. It is what passes as a smile for him. It is the same kindly half-smile Shelford gave when he popped in a week before to ask if she could fit a temporary guest.

"Apparently," he now explains, smile still on face, "it is because of your having smoked a cigarette in here the other day."

Jewel pretends not to be offended or disappointed. That is easy. Harder is not turning cartwheels of joy in front of her professor.

"They're rather puritanical, you know, the Clementses," Shelford continues in his usual, deliberate way. Jewel can see that he is trying to ease the disappointment he thinks she must feel. "Frederic's disdain for smoking and drinking is why he always stays with the Wards instead of with Mabel and me when they visit."

"But you don't smoke!" Jewel protests.

"Not much. I really don't have the habit. I just smoke sometimes to make smokers on field trips feel more comfortable. In fact," he says, pointing to the pack of ivory-tipped Marlboros on Jewel's desk, "I wouldn't mind having a smoke right now."

Would he have made the same request, Jewel wonders as he lights up, had the pack been the more feminine red-tipped version she usually smoked? Or would he not notice?

Jewel knows it was not that one cigarette she lit in front of Edith Clements that drove the woman off, but she keeps that to herself. She does not tell Shelford that Mrs. Clements is the most self-important person Jewel has ever met. Even Fred Küchler comes in a very very distant second, Jewel smirks to herself, and Fred, at least, exudes a certain charm while running roughshod over you intellectually.

Nobody has ever talked down to Jewel the way Mrs. Clements has. No one has ever managed to show off their erudition, their talents, and their many important acquaintances so soon on meeting. And no one has ever displayed so few of her own ideas in doing so. The only seemingly independent idea to come out of her mouth is her hatred for Urbana.

"Don't you think this the most abominable climate in the country?' she asked Jewel on learning of her Connecticut roots.

"The fall days are so gloomy here," Mrs. Clements explained in what Jewel supposed was an apology for imposing on her. "It makes it very difficult to get proper lighting for my painting."

Shelford commandeered for her the space that Jewel had been allotted for her proofreading work. Students who were finishing up had not managed to move out before those replacing them moved in. Office space was limited. Jewel had been given a desk in a corner of the laboratory across the hall from the seminar room. It had suited her fine, but the photocopies and dog-eared originals of *Bio-Ecology* that once were spread over all the lab benches became a crowded pile of clutter on Jewel's desk.

Shelford had Jewel clear everything away to make a studio for Edith Clements's wildflower painting. Then he set up a huge grow lamp he borrowed from the botany department.

"This may allow us to draw Edith out so that you all can benefit from her first-rate mind," he explained. "Edith tends to spend most of her time with the same small circle of friends when away from her husband on these visits."

Jewel witnessed little drawing out and no benefits. Mrs. Clements's morning routine was invariant. Both Colorado and California, where the Clementses spent summers and winters, she had to announce, have much more suitable natural light for her drawing. Those two marvelous places were so unlike "the Midwestern gloom" she had to deal with at Urbana. In fact, they were in all respects far superior to "this sad little place out on the edge of a prairie that names itself a city." Then she turned to her painting. She was less a roommate than a giant blazing lamp that irritated Jewel not just by its light, but also by constant throat-clearing and snuffing into a handkerchief kept in a sleeve.

And she was an inveterate eavesdropper.

"Oh my dear," Edith launched into a litany on overhearing Jewel's plans to study how mammals affect succession, "you simply MUST visit our laboratories! They encompass entire mountains. We have quadrats and transects for just the sort of studies you envision. At Pike's Peak, we have areas fenced off against rodents at three different altitudes. Short-grass, chaparral, pine, and Douglas fir habitats. There is even a transect that has been in place for almost twenty years, spanning habitats from gravel slide to Douglas fir forests. It is like Professor Cowles' dunes encompassed in one two-meter strip that runs for over half a mile. My goodness, just imagine what you can do there that you cannot on a mere sixty acres at University Wood! And the indoor laboratories take up acres of space!"

Jewel did the math in her head. Six-and-a-half feet times three thousand was only half an acre.

"I really haven't decided which mammals I should study yet," Jewel answered without sharing her calculation.

Edith's entreaties were more like commands. Jewel could well imagine what working under Clements, instead of Shelford, would be like, especially if Edith was as meddlesome as Jewel suspected she would be. In addition, the expense and logistic difficulties of getting to the Rocky Mountain Laboratories compared poorly to the six-mile ride out to University Wood on a borrowed bicycle.

Frederic and Edith Clements were a matching pair, Jewel is convinced, even after hearing from Reggie how charming Clements had been when he and Shelford sat down with the ecology club during a previous visit. Both men had let their hair down in a very informal discussion of the prospects and limitations of ecology as they saw it. Everybody, according to Reggie, had been charmed.

Jewel believes not a word of that. She finds the husband as haughty as the wife.

"Mrs. Clements would hold a position near the top of the world's ecologists had she not devoted herself to furthering my career instead of winning recognition in her own right," Clements had the need to announce to Jewel apropos of nothing on coming for Edith one day.

Now lamp and artist have disappeared into the Clementses' usual rooms in the house of the former zoology chairman. As she has in the past, Edith can now emerge only for meals, which the couple eat out. To Jewel, it does not seem like a loss either to the ecologists or the greater university community.

The last straw for Jewel, her final abandonment of hope that Mrs. Clements's presence might in any way be salutary, was the woman's thoughtless meddling into a conversation she was pretending not to be overhearing between Jewel and Reggie Parker. Reggie was worried over his fiancee's predilection for living in Danville and her disappointment at having to move to Ohio after their wedding.

"Jean can always go back for extended visits if homesick," Jewel suggested.

That had Edith Clements bursting in.

"I have never been separated from my husband for more than twenty-four hours," she pronounced, haughtily emphasizing "never."

It made Jewel reach for the cigarette. But it did not make Edith leave, no matter how much Jewel might have wished it. That came later. The cigarette and Edith's snide objection to it were only preludes. The cigarette was put out.

With Shelford back in his office, Jewel rushes directly to Reggie Parker's room to share her own version of the events.

"She noticed me reading Tansley's article in Ecology," she tells Reggie in answer to his unvoiced question.

"Good, you should read it," he says, "if only to fully understand the opposition."

"Not at all," Jewel disagrees. "I think Tansley is right. I think the ecosystem point of view makes the most sense. Somehow, Clements and Shelford aren't making the connection. They're using biome exclusively in Bio-Ecology. I know that biome is Clements's own term, but it is for an idea that is positively inferior to ecosystem."

"You told her that?"

"Every bit—when I could get a word in edgewise. She launched into me like I was a schoolgirl. She went on and on, repeating things I already knew. Biome, don't you know, stands for the regional outcome of succession to climax, she lectured. With the role of animals included, she needed to emphasize for some reason. She even thought she had to defend Shelford against me. Cowles in his Indiana Dunes took no note of how the grasses or shrubs or trees got to their places on the dunes, she said, looked down her nose at me from her easel as she spoke, which is hard to do. And why should he? she asked. Seeds, after all, she kept on lecturing without letting me get a word in, can certainly blow wherever before a wind. What Shelford realized is that birds and mammals carried seeds, too. A sumac seed or plum pit dropped into a gopher hole in prairie sod has a better chance to thrive than numberless seeds dropped randomly on its surface by the wind."

"That's right out of his paper in Ecology," Reggie noted.

"Of course. How could I argue with that?"

"I don't see the problem then."

"Why doesn't your husband just drop his fight over the priority for biome? I finally asked in frustration. It's just a term, I said. It just obscures the fact that no one—not even Shelford—is buying his superorganism idea. And don't you see? I asked her. Cowles may have downplayed or missed the animal influences, but he certainly had us thinking like a geologist about succession. That's ecosystem, I said, not biome.'"

"Actually," Reggie corrects, "complex organism is the term Clements uses to mean biome. But you said that, too?"

"What?"

"About Shelford not buying the biome idea?"

"Worse."

"Worse? That's when Mrs. Clements left?"

"I said Tansley had it right. You can't find the boundaries to biomes and they make no sense without the physical environment. That was the whole point of Cowles' analysis of the dunes."

"What did Mrs. Clements say about that?"

"Left. That was it. Haven't seen her since. Probably never will. You think I'll get in trouble if Shelford finds out? I need every penny he has been sparing me."

"I wouldn't worry. That's not like Shelford. He's had years of experience dealing with wise-acre students like you."

Then he added, "and me."

III

MABEL Shelford is right. He is happy to see her. That funny half smile of his, seemingly using only his upper lip, lights up when she walks into his room. It is almost Christmas. Jane Dirks is working full time on preparing her trip home to Oregon for the holiday. So is Reed Fautin, the bird guy from Utah. Jewel marvels at the two having the financial wherewithal to take their journeys. She can't even afford a visit to relatives in Michigan, let alone her Mom and Sis in Connecticut.

Shelford has been hospitalized since November. He blames it on the usual suspect: the university heating plant, which has distinguished itself according to him by delivering no heat at all on the coldest winter day and steaming up his office on mild spring and fall days. No wonder his sinus condition never goes away—not to mention that his chronic indigestion is not helped by tussles with the rapscallions in charge of the physical plant.

His students suspect that what is at fault is exhaustion from the pressure of completing *Bio-Ecology*. It weakened his system, they hypothesize, so that it could not fend off the viral infection that made its way harmlessly through the rest of them. Mabel Shelford says it is simply overwork.

All believe that getting away from ecology for a while might be good for him. Still, Jewel can think of nothing to bring to the hospital that he might want but the latest ecology journals, fresh from the mailroom.

"You can keep your glasses off," she tells him. "I'll read to you. I'm a good reader. I was a schoolteacher, don't you know. And don't worry about your mussed hair and three-day growth. Schoolteachers are like nurses."

"That they are," he says and settles into his pillow.

They put *Ecological Monographs* aside for later. Although the titles of all three articles in it interest him very much, all are very long. They decide to start with *Ecology*'s shorter articles. Jewel assumes that they will be cherry picking, reading just the articles having direct interest, but Shelford insists that they go through it paper by paper, including a rather lengthy one on seasonal changes in light intensity in waters off Woods Hole. The only title in the table of contents that holds no interest for him is his own note, a historical point about the formation of the Ecological Society. According to him it had been formed for the purpose of protecting the habitats that ecologists study.

"I thought you didn't think much of research coming out of Woods Hole?" Jewel asks when she finishes reading that paper. "Remember how you frightened me by your reaction to my having spent a summer session there? I thought you would never take me on after that."

"Did you?" Shelford asks with genuine surprise. Seemingly not remembering the incident, he falls back into silence, his signal for her to resume reading.

It is a particularly meaty paper by Arthur Vestal that is next. Jewel has trouble keeping her mind on it. Her thoughts wander back to that first meeting she had with Shelford and the kindness he showed her. It was just after her father's death. Shelford was so sympathetic when he apologized for only being able to offer her partial funding. Where she could get the rest, he could only despair along with her. She was already sending money to her mother periodically.

Maybe, she confessed, almost in tears, a career in science was just never meant to be for her. Maybe her father was right, she was about to concede.

Shelford gave her a look that was almost a hug and took out his watch.

"This had been my father's watch," he said with his usual, measured tone. "It is an Eglin National. How proud he had been of it. I never remember him being without it. He used to wind it every morning at breakfast and hold it against my ear. Still running, he waited for me to announce before he would go off for the day. Sometimes I pretended not to hear. I wanted to see if he would keep waiting. He always did. It was as hard for me to wait him out as it was to hold my breath. I always gave up in less than a minute, even though it seemed forever. The watch is the most precious thing to come down from my father aside from fond memories. It's never left my side, just as it never left my father's side, except it has traveled so much farther in my pocket than his."

The sad look on his face was so sweet. What he had shared with her was so precious. At that moment, she was willing to place her life in his hands.

"Of course, you can take a year off to prop up your mother," he told her. "You will have a place waiting here for you when you want it.

"I was lucky, you know," he continued, sensing her acquiescence. "When my bank here in Urbana closed, I lost no money at all, in actuality. It turned out I had as much of their money, that I owed them in loans, as they had of mine. I know so many others were not as lucky."

Vestal's paper is not finished. Shelford has fallen asleep.

How peacefully he sleeps, she thinks. So unlike her father the last time she saw him, also in a hospital. He had not wanted her to read to him or talk to him or even be in his presence. She could tell that he was just holding on from the massive coronary that would take his life, but seemed not to want to say goodbye. Neither did he seem to want to return to the life he had been living. He had not particularly wanted to see his wife and daughters. That had been obvious. Had his life with them been that bad?

Jewel wipes a tear. He had always shown no interest in what his two girls did, she now accuses. That was true as far back as she can remember, she is certain. He never really talked to them. A nod and dismissal was all Jewel ever remembers from him when she came to him excited over something. In fact, not caring, probably is why he let her take Uncle George's suggestion to go to Chicago. Maybe he only cared for his friends and his liquor bottles.

How cruel of me, she then thinks and rushes out of the room for fear the sobs she feels coming on will wake Shelford. The sobs come outdoors, out in those indifferent, pompous spaces she so ridicules. She sobs her heart and guts out. Strangers passing by stop to offer help, but she refuses them. Her tears are cathartic in some way she does not understand. When they subside, there is no pain. There is no joy, either.

The Vivarium seems empty when she returns to it. Almost everyone is gone already, although the Illini, Jewel thinks contemptuously, should be able to keep on working right up to Christmas Eve and still make it to all their family festivities.

Rather than catching up on a paper she still has to write—postponed due to the professor's illness—Jewel sits down to write a letter to Liza to follow up the embarrassingly plain card she just mailed. Oh, how she would love to talk to Liza! But the long-distance charges would break her budget, she is sure. Why didn't Liza call her?

She decides not to suggest that in her letter and looks up from her writing, hoping to find something else to say. What she finds is Reggie Parker standing before her. Both hands are raised toward her. He holds a milk bottle with one hand and a smile, seemingly, with the other.

"Eggnog," he announces, pouring some into a lab beaker. "Christmas cheer, you know. From the chemistry department. They throw quite a party. Like we would have, had Dr. Shelford not been well."

He has partaken already, Jewel notes. "Unwell," she corrects.

"Where is everyone?" Reggie asks, slurring his words.

"Merry Christmas," she says, taking the beaker. Two hundred and fifty milliliters, she notes, just about the size of a drinking glass. She drinks half of it quickly, then puts it down with a confused look.

"It's made with lab alcohol. Be careful."

"Now you tell me," she says. Then she giggles suddenly and takes another drink.

Her mirth is infectious. Parker is soon giggling along with her.

"Moose-spruce forests," comes to his mind, and he voices it. It is a name Shelford likes to use for the northern forests that abound with moose. It emphasizes that dominant mammals are equal in importance to dominant plants.

"Pheasant-desert," Jewel tries.

"Nooo," Reggie giggles. "That neither rhymes nor is biologically correct."

"Hickory-dickory-chicory."

"No! No! No!"

What happens next surprises both. Verbal play progresses to physical play until they are entangled, mentally and physically, in each other's silliness. Both realize, too, that it has become something more than just silliness. And both find it to be perfectly natural—and welcome.

"The door," Jewel gasps as soon as she can free her lips.

Door closed, both know what is about to happen. They can see it in each other's eyes as Reggie strides back unsteadily from the door. Clothes do not come off, but are violated. Her breasts swell as his hands find them beneath her flimsy white slip.

"Should the lights be off?" she whispers, but it no longer matters. Jewel is not sure if her underwear is damp when she helps him slip it off, but she is sure that she wants it off. Unlike Küchler, Reggie is very ready for her.

"Hurry," is all she can say from her desktop perch as he fumbles with his fly until his penis pokes out. Is it an angry red—or a shameful red? She giggles at the question as he pushes her down toward the floor, then pushes into her.

She feels pain more than anything else, yet it is a pleasurable pain. It builds in time with his thrusts until she can't stand it, then subsides with his throbs. She thinks she may have screamed, but she is not certain. His penis, she noticed before he put it away, was bloody

"I'm sorry," he says. "I didn't. I mean, I didn't know. I wouldn't have—"

Nothing to be sorry about, thinks Jewel. Nothing to be ashamed of. Not for me or him. But she can say nothing. All she can do is shake her head.

"I think I had better go," he says.

She still says nothing, thinks nothing. She watches him go out the door, where he bumps into Jane Dirks, who glances quickly in at Jewel before Reggie can shut the door again. Jewel's skirt is down, but she is still on the floor with her underpants beside her and her blouse half-buttoned. And her face, she is sure, has betrayed everything.

How unexpected, she thinks. How different from what she anticipated. How delicious is this quiet burning between her legs, neither painful nor annoying. Just delicious.

IV

HE is southern-born, it is true, but Gene Odum is hardly an Okie or yokel, even Jewel now admits. She has been listening in on his conversation with Jane Dirks in the seat behind her on the bus. He is from an academic family, she learns. He is telling Jane that when the family moved from Athens to Chapel Hill, there were no paved streets.

"Fessor—that's what Charlie called my father," Odum continues. "Fessor, is this where you brung us to, he said on seeing a rat jump off the back porch of the house we were moving into."

"Charlie?" Jane asks.

Odum has to stop his forced laughter to explain.

"Charlie is our black hired hand," he says. "He came along with us from Georgia to North Carolina. Don't remember if the others did. We had a whole retinue of black servants."

Ha! Probably descended from slave owners, Jewel fusses triumphantly in her seat.

Then he adds that their house was one of the few in Chapel Hill to welcome "Negroes."

"Many who could not find accommodations," he explains proudly, "were taken in by us."

His dad might have been a great scholar, Jewel continues to fuss, but his yokel son is not one of the great minds of the university. Or any university. Gossip has it that Kendeigh had to go to special lengths with the registrar to admit him to Illinois. His undergraduate grades were that bad. Finally, they fixed the problem by using only the grades he earned at Western Reserve.

His brain seems to be stuck in second gear, thinks Jewel. In conversations, his mental horse is stuck pulling a plow while other grad students race around him in sulkies. Ha again! It pleases her to recognize that last thought as a mixed metaphor, very much like the phrases Küchler uses, that he describes as "complex metaphors."

Hmm. She suddenly is in deep thought. Maybe that's the meaning of Clements's complex organism. Hmm. A metaphor. Not so dumb.

Now Odum is describing his thesis work. It has nothing to do with ecology as far as Jewel can tell. He has cobbled together some Rube Goldberg device, no doubt, to measure heart rate in birds. Cardio-vibrometer, he calls it.

What the heck? "Piezo-electric?" Is that what she hears? It sounds like the sort of thing Liza is working on. What on earth is he doing with us ecologists? He should be in the engineering school.

Finally, after stops along the Mississippi River bluffs in southern Illinois, the long bus trip is over. They have arrived at Reelfoot Lake. It was either formed or greatly enlarged by the New Madrid quake, which Jewel now knows was actually a series of large earthquakes in the winter of eighteen eleven to eighteen twelve. All that she remembers from her geology class, taken under Cowles' inspiration at Chicago, is that the main tremor was so strong that it threw cows into the air and made the Mississippi River run backwards. And a little corner of northwestern Tennessee, she now can add, dropped some twenty-five feet and flooded.

The trip has become a yearly tradition. Shelford specifically wanted Jewel to be on the bus this year, for she has to miss the more extensive summer field trip. Shelford expects ecology students at Illinois to see all the major biomes, running field trips for them on weekends and holidays like clockwork, but a day's drive will only get them so far. The big expedition he has already organized for the upcoming summer will take them beyond prairies and deciduous forests. But it takes Jewel beyond her pocketbook. She needs to return to Connecticut to try to get more money into it.

"Jewel, I think this trip will be a great benefit to you in becoming the ecologist I expect of you," Shelford entreated her.

She finally broke down and agreed to go on the Easter trip without any idea of how she would get the eight dollars and forty-five cents that covered each participant's expenses, but Shelford already knew even that amount was a hardship for her. So he appointed her as an assistant. The university graduate alumnus association picked up her expenses. Shelford and Jewel worked together on bus, tent, and food arrangements. Another assistant was in charge of scientific equipment.

"You know, Dr. Shelford," Jewel joked as he bustled about excitedly with preparations, "Reelfoot Lake must be your Indiana Dunes."

He laughed heartily. "Yes, Miss Fairfax," he agreed, wiping the round lenses of his glasses with his large, white pocket-handkerchief. "More than you know, perhaps. It was by a field trip with Cowles to the dunes that I was won over to ecology at Chicago."

Then he took a good owl-like look at her through those glasses. "You are a bright thing," he said. "No wonder Ward sent you to me. You know, at your age—what are you? Twenty two? At your age, I was still in high school."

That brought a vow to be the best assistant he has ever had.

As that assistant, Jewel feels she should be next to Shelford at all times on the trip, in case he needs anything done. This is apparently not possible with Gene Odum present. He is right there next to Shelford as tents are set up along the side of a rolling meadow. They are six tents, each theoretically fitting as many as four persons. Rain flies are pulled taut against anticipated April showers. A flap suspended by two poles shelters the entrance to each. The tents are better in the rain than most motor court cabins, Shelford insists, almost into Odum's ear, as one goes up.

Odum is right between Shelford and Kendeigh at the evening meal. Jewel wonders where his bed will be.

Bus and commissary truck are by the side of the road next to a small canvas shelter for meals. The vehicles complete the circle formed by the tents.

The Okie gets more and more on Jewel's nerves. What raises her ire the most is his pushiness. He is very pushy with that hawk-like nose. In the field, he uses it as his instrument of entrée, opening up like a can of sardines any tightly packed group of people around Shelford. Then he keeps so close to him that no one else can get near.

Even though Shelford is now past sixty, like his old professor, Cowles, before him, he sets a pace that tasks the younger students. Odum is always right next to him, though, enjoying Shelford's sarcastic remarks about "reductionist biologists" and "eastern establishment ecologists." When they return from the field and Shelford is off enjoying an end-of-the-day beer with Kendeigh, Odum lords it over the others by repeating the comments with special pleasure.

Strangely so, thinks Jewel. His dissertation research is exactly reductionist. It borders on Liza's submolecular level.

Next she hears Odum repeat Shelford's remark that the "Woods Hole establishment is anti-ecological." The lingering embarrassment it makes her feel is one more annoyance Jewel charges against him.

Then Odum is on to another story. This one everyone already knows. It is about how a professor at Chicago told Shelford he should get out of ecology because it was "ignis fatuus," and that the true purpose of biology is to "reduce the organism in terms of physics and chemistry."

"And that was nineteen oh two!" the yokel adds with aplomb as the others try to disguise groans.

"Haw haw!" is shouted sarcastically above the groans before everyone disperses in exhaustion to their tents.

Jane Dirks shares a tent with Marie Ostendorf. The yokel is in a tent with Clarence Goodnight, who has been at Marie's side every bit as much as Odum has been at Shelford's. Jewel wonders if there might not be some bed hopping in the night and what Dr. Shelford would make of it.

She need not worry. Shelford runs a tight ship. He is the last to go to bed and the first up every morning. Besides, thinks Jewel, these are University of Illinois students, not the Godless types found at Chicago or Yale. And the expedition is run like an Indian camp—everyone has enough assigned tasks to keep them too tired to cause trouble.

Jewel is up and out before the others the next morning. She is checking snap traps, the "museum specials" of rodent nightmares, that she put out the previous night before dinner. It was already getting dark but she thought she noticed vole runs near her tent. As she looks back from atop the meadow now in dawn light, the tents strike her as resembling an Indian encampment. And there is Shelford, already dressed for the field. He has a walking stick in his hand. He is beating the side of a tent with it like the tent was a drum —and making as much noise. Odum and Clarence crawl out with sheepish grins on their faces.

"Up! Up!" she hears. "It is six o'clock!"

Shelford is already in his field dress, which includes a white shirt and tie. A felt hat protects his head. He is armed for battle. Binoculars are around his neck and a shoulder strap of a belt holds his weapons. They consist of a magnifying glass, forceps, buck knife, etc., and two whistles. One has a soft warble to move people along. The other is a loud, shrill whistle to get them to assemble. And he runs things by the clock. There will be no breakfast for her today, she thinks as she hurries down the hill.

He's an even a harder taskmaster in the field than Cowles, Jewel decides, but also just as fair. The only time he lost his temper on the trip was when Jewel put into practice an idea put into her head by Reggie Parker. She convinced Odum to take a photo of Shelford napping on the bus on the way back from the field. What a scene! The Okie had to surrender his half-exposed film before Shelford took him back into his good graces.

Deciduous forests, caves, streams, and cypress swamps have them jumping off the bus today. Jewel sees her first tree with "knees," the above-ground projections that some trees in wet places produce. It is as surprising to her as turning a corner and coming upon a dinosaur, even a small one. She wants desperately to hear Shelford's interpretation of what their purpose is, but she can't get close enough past the Okie. Then they are already striding through the next item of interest, a successional sequence of cottonwood-willow to beech-maple along old Mississippi River channels.

Then, Kendeigh and his crew, the yokel with them, split off for bird studies. Jewel teams with Arthur Twomey to study "the rest of the vertebrates," as the task is described to them. To Jewel, that means muskrat, all she will have time for. To Arthur, it means snakes. Reelfoot Lake holds many diverse assemblages of animals, especially water moccasins and copperheads, he gaily warns her.

There is a mid-afternoon stop at the house of a local. Ostensibly, it is to replenish drinking water supplies, but actually, it is to let the ladies use the conveniences there. Shelford loves to talk to locals. He has a whole porch full of men, cousins and brothers, to talk to at this house. One brags from his perch on a wooden rocker about a large snake he has seen. While he continues pulling remarks from his bag of exaggerations, Arthur stealthily retrieves his sack of snakes from the bus through its back door. None are poisonous, but when he opens the sack and lets them out, the locals scatter faster than the snakes can spread over the porch. A few get away before they can be gathered back.

"Perhaps we will need to find a different stopping place in the future," Shelford laughs heartily.

"Or we can say that we have come back for the snakes next time," Kendeigh suggests.

"At least Ole' Claude might not be so eager to court me anymore, if that's what he thinks he's doing," Jewel adds.

Claude, one of the cousins, has become so enamored with Jewel that he has asked Kendeigh for permission to see Jewel with the intent of matrimony, a matter that leaves Odum speechless.

"She is the purt'est gal I ever seen," he said to them. "Ah jes' have to make her mah fifth wife."

Odum fled the scene after Claude added, "And the las'," as more inducement

So it is back to work.

Jewel learns through her trapping experience that *how* to study the community ecology of mammals is as much a question as *what* to study about them. Community analysis, plant or animal, is nothing without numbers. Locating more than a few specimens outside of herds of range animals, however, seems impossible to Jewel. Unlike plants, mammals run and hide. But locate large numbers she must, if she wants to establish dominance, confluence, or any of those other community terms dreamed up by Clements that she can never keep straight.

Many mammals are small or secretive or both. And nocturnal. And live under ground or seemingly under water. How will she find them to study them? There is no agreement on methods.

"Throwing a quadrat out in a field," Jewel complains to Jane Dirks, "is about as futile for mammals as expecting to find them in your bedroll—although some do so appear! Walk the woods in search of them? Forget it."

Then she turns to Odum, who has finally been shaken off by Shelford.

"That can work with your birds," she says to him. "Birds are conspicuous. Living mostly in trees, like squirrels, they are totally unconcerned about humans. A set of field glasses and a pair of ears that can tell one song apart from another is all the equipment you need to identify just about every bird in an area. Mammals? Good luck! Even large, fierce creatures like wolves or cougars are secretive—and nocturnal. All you can do is look for traces. So, it is footprints, fur, and feces—the three F's—that make up my data points."

Dirks and Odum are helping her retrieve a trap she hopes has caught a muskrat. It takes three of them because Jewel cannot find—or perhaps forgot to put up—a little red flag she uses to mark trap locations. It surprises her to feel sympathy for Odum as he slogs through the marshy ground beside her, dead set on the task at hand. Maybe guilt from the incident on the bus with the camera and the sleeping professor has changed her attitude. And that he seems to hold no grudge about it that she can notice. Jane Dirks seems colder to her than Gene Odum.

"Of course," she goes on, talking to him more than her, "mammals can be trapped. Trappers do it every day for their livelihoods. But their traps kill and mutilate. Not always good for studies, especially mark-recapture. I might as well just pick up road kill. Beside, trappers only put their traps where the easiest success is assured. They already know what places are thick with the creatures and easy to get to. Sometimes right by the side of the road."

"Is there nothing equivalent to a mist net?" Gene asks.

"Hmm, you can sink a fence for digging animals with pitfalls on each end. That's for a long term commitment."

Then she turns to Jane.

"But quadrats!" Jewel complains again. "Forget it. I could hear little feet skittering away before the quadrat frame hit the ground."

Earlier in the day, the two had set quadrats together in forest understory, Jane for plants, Jewel animals.

"Snap traps seem the way to go," Odum offers.

"They work so much better than any of the live traps," Jewel agrees, "cage or box, especially if peanut butter is used for bait instead of cheese. None of the live traps that have good trap doors seems to be the right size for microtines. You know, those little mice-like creatures, whose family name tells it all?"

She added the last to show off her cleverness, but it gets a cool reception from Jane.

"I know what a Microtus is," she cuts Jewel off.

"And too many perish in the traps to allow for mark-recapture techniques, anyway," Jewel says, turning back to Gene. "There just is no agreement on any of the trapping methods being at all superior to the three Fs."

She suddenly realizes that she has not been in as bubbly a mood since her last visit with Liza—or with Reggie, before then.

"Maybe you should invent a better mousetrap," Gene suggests.

The trap is never found. It was one of those larger live traps and not inexpensive. Jewel is disconsolate and retires to her tent early. Soon there is a voice whispering "Jewel? Are you alone in there?" It is the yokel and he must know that she has the tent to herself that night. It has been part of discussions most of the day that one of her tentmates has been taken to a nearby hospital with possible appendicitis and the other one went along for moral support.

She wonders what he could want as she silently lets him in. He has come to cheer her up, he announces. His smile is so bright and genuine in the light of her lamp. His eyes implore like a puppy's. He has brought her chocolates. How can you be annoyed with a puppy?

"You're not the first to have lost or ruined a piece of equipment," he tells her. "I can guarantee that."

Then he starts whispering a story—hilariously funny in parts —of a professor who is now famous and the boners he was responsible for as a grad student. The need to whisper requires him to come closer to her until there is accidental body contact. Jewel is immediately suspicious.

Oh, he is not going to get what he expects, she decides in advance. Her brief coupling with Reggie had her worrying for two full weeks before her period came. She and Liza hypothesized that virgins might be induced to ovulate in response to intercourse, much like cats. The statistics they needed were all there in a book Jewel ferreted out from the university library at Chicago. They put their combined mathematical abilities into analyzing them. Their conclusion was undeniable: the day of the month hardly mattered.

Even though no longer a virgin, she is not about to risk going through that agony with the calendar again, but it feels good to be wanted. And his breath on her ear is exciting. And his arms around her feel strong and raise warm feelings. And he asks her to marry him. And it makes her giggle. And the puppy looks hurt.

"I can't marry you," she gently tells him, looking soulfully into his eyes, her giggle stifled. "I am already meant for another. But oh, if I could ..."

The lamp goes off. It is still off when he leaves only moments later. She squirms down into her sleeping bag, alone with her thoughts.

What new she can report to Liza beyond what she already has after the quick and furtive episode with Reggie and that debacle with the boy physicist? She and Reggie were fully dressed. Well, kind of. Liza's friend had undressed beneath the bedsheets. Tonight it was too dark to see anything.

Then she goes over in her mind the checklist Liza sent her after Jewel's tryst with her boy-physicist friend. Volume? Mass? Degrees Celsius?

Yes, heat. There was that this time. It surprised her, although it should not have, given that it was filled with 37° C blood.

Length? Of course, length. No clue. What is the variation?

Shape? What she saw on Reggie. What she assumed on the boy physicist. What both Liza and she already knew from books: it is pileus and stape, with hairy volva at its base, exactly a large mushroom.

Taste? Don't, she decides. Bitter? But also salty like potato chips.

Now how can I put all that in a letter?

Odum avoids her eyes when they return to Urbana. She expected as much, but not how soon it is that he begins to parade Martha Ann Huff through the vivarium, announcing her as his one true love. Each of the couple's tours takes them past Jewel.

"Martha Ann rooms with my sister, Mary Francis, in the Delta Gama sorority house," Odum offers on introduction.

"Mary Francis enrolled here the year Gene's father, Howard W., taught here," Martha Ann announces. "Isn't that a grand coincidence?"

Spotting a length of twine on Jewel's desktop, she startles the other two by picking it up and tying a knot into it.

"This is a bowline," she says. Then she unravels it and ties another.

"Do you sail?" she asks, leaving Jewel bewildered.

"I acquired this skill sailing in Wisconsin," she says when Jewel does not respond.

"I have," Jewel answers noncommittally.

"I grew up in Wilmette on Chicago's North Shore," Martha Ann then feels free to add. "My family traveled and camped out West many summers."

Jewel is less bewildered, but no more enthusiastic in carrying on the conversation.

"My father also lost money in the stock market crash," Martha Ann then reveals to Jewel, as if under some obligation to do so. "It forced me to come to Illinois, instead of Northwestern. More expensive, you know."

The last is a whisper, almost in Jewel's ear. She s reaching out to her, Jewel realizes, and lets her silence be its rebuff.

Reggie Parker does not quite take back his invitation, but it is clear to Jewel that she is not welcome at his wedding. Then he is gone and Odum is gone and she is gone.

The unexpected death of Uncle George reveals how much her family had depended on his generosity. The Nicholses had never seemed as well off as the Fairfaxes. It had been a real conquest for Jewel's midwestern mom to snare a New England scion. It had been thought a much better match than that of her older sisters to impoverished college professors. By the time her father died, however, a wildflower-collecting college professor was supporting her mother almost in full. Only the house was left of the Fairfax legacy. When George Nichols died, it was discovered that not even the house was theirs. Jewel's mother was truly penniless. She was truly destitute. Jewel's sister, with her rocky marriage, could not be looked to for much help. When Jimmy was not away at sea, they fought and made up constantly under her mother's roof. It fell to Jewel, the scholar, the impractical one, to assume the duties of head of the family.

V

"QUITE a difference from the University Wood, don't you think? You're going to make great progress on this trip, Jewel. We'll be going through desert, chaparral, and several of the coniferous forest group. And you won't just be looking out of a car window. You'll be out there taking data. You will have to get to taiga and tundra on your own, though. I've made my last trip to the Great North, I think."

They are standing on a low bluff somewhere in Oklahoma. It was easily scaled, but it nonetheless provides a spectacularly panoramic view—horizon to horizon in all directions. They are studying biomes with the intention of collecting data that will help to determine how faithful various animals are to specific biomes. With the help of his vivarium studies, the field work will contribute to Shelford's three-decade quest to determine what limits animals to the places in which they are found and how many of them there are. It is his Law of Tolerance being applied on the grand scale of an entire continent.

"If we knew the physiological life histories of most of the animals, then most of the other ecological problems would almost solve themselves," he likes to repeat in various forms to his students.

"As far as I am concerned," he now says, "this endless grassland is the best-studied of all the biotic communities, the only one yet that can be used to illustrate general principles."

"Biomes, do you mean?" Jewel asks, still not comfortable with what exactly the various terms are supposed to represent.

"Biotic community, biotic formation, biome, they are all very much synonymous in use, even if there are slight differences in connotation," Shelford answers her with great patience. He has heard variants on this question before from her.

"I think ecosystem is a better term than biome," Jewel counters mischievously.

"I should say that they are very much synonymous," Shelford replies without a hint of annoyance, "but biome is more convenient to use."

"So, what do all of you think of this little stop?" he then asks. "Worth it? I wanted you to experience in this way the peculiar physiognomy of grassland that you see around you. So different, isn't, it from the little relict tall-grass prairies closer to home?"

Unexpectedly, he takes on a lecturing tone. He is normally not a good lecturer. His words do not come smoothly when he is in front of a class of any size. Too often, he stumbles in search of the right thought or phrasing. There is none of his characteristic hesitancy now, however. He treats them to a perfect guided tour of a gigantic, living lantern slide. Words flow as if read from a book.

"As you can see, the vegetation itself offers little or no obstruction to vision," his lecture begins. "Large areas of the central portion of our North American grasslands, green in summer and brown in autumn and winter, stretch away as far as the eye can reach. Generally, however, slopes, rolling ground, small hills, like this one, and ravines and valleys, relieve the uniformity. The depressions often hold relict or seral communities of trees or shrubs. I think I see a good example off to the north there."

"I see it," Drew Sparkman answers first. "Willows, are they?"

"Don't, uh, jump to conclusions, Drew," Shelford continues, suddenly reverting to his normal, stumbling lecture style. "Consequently, strong delimitation, uh, contrast—that is, sharp break—of valley and plain are among the, um, striking features. Near the grassland margins—where the contacts are with tree or shrub communities—there are small groups of shrubs that break the monotony and afford shelter or perching places for various animals. The sort of habitat you might want to sample, Jewel."

"Not the grassland, itself?"

"Of course," Shelford says, shifting back to normal conversation, "the grassland, even though it has been so well studied already. Expect to find surprises. I just think the various seres and ecotones can always benefit from additional, serious, quantitative study. Too many investigators, it seems to me, look at nothing but climax. And look *for* nothing but climax."

Jewel is on her second summer field trip. The war has made it impossible for Shelford to take the usual caravan of students. Before that had been Mabel's death from malaria in Central America, a great blow. It deprived him not only of a life companion, but also his favorite traveling companion. Without her or travel, his life became listless. Afternoons at the local pub soon followed mornings there. Only by immersion in field research could he escape the loss of his wife. He simply could not be kept home. So, he bought a not-particularly-large Ford wagon, acquired the needed gas stamps, strapped extra tires (all retreads, new rubber being unobtainable), and—so as not to be alone—recruited three traveling assistants. Verna Johnston, a schoolteacher from Berwyn, Illinois, from the first year, has been replaced this trip by Marie Tucker, a schoolteacher from Alton, as fourth member and third woman in the group.

"I know that if I took only two women on the trip," he explained, with emphasis on the numbers, the previous year, "they might vote me down on a decision such as whether we should stop for a beer or how far we drive in a day. But I know that three women can never agree on anything, so I have a chance."

None took offense. Shelford endeared his many women students by often telling them that he was certain that "Women can have babies and do science too." Many simply wished they had met him when he was younger.

The trip started in Arkansas and continued to Oklahoma, where there was a relaxing stay with Drew's relatives. Then it was to be on to California, southern Texas, and northern Mexico.

"In conformity with the biome concept," Shelford continues from the Oklahoma bluff, with almost a bow toward Jewel, and back in lecture mode, "animals have a distinct role in the—oh—what is it?—physiognomy of grassland, but this was naturally much more evident before the period of settlement. Hmmh. At that time, an ecologist standing on a small rise such as this on a July morning might well have seen a large herd of bison grazing to the right. A smaller herd of antelope might be to the left. Nearer at hand, a coyote or wolf would be seen slipping away to its den."

A jackrabbit, its large ears characteristic of dry habitats, suddenly bounds up and gallops away, startling birds from their shelters behind rocks and tufts of plants as it goes.

"Horned lark," Shelford identifies one.
"Lark bunting," Drew calls out.
"Sprague's pipit!"
"Lark sparrow!"

They sing on the wing as they fly past. The mid-day heat brings out bee flies and robber flies that are as rapid and conspicuous in flight as the birds. Grasshoppers are everywhere.

VI

"I like you Jewel," Drew Sparkman says one day as she helps Jewel retrieve the large traps set out for jackrabbits, of which they capture all of one (1). It is a major and unexpected success. There is discussion about what to do with the creature—as a trophy to parade before Dr. Shelford is considered briefly—but it soon bolts from the cage and is bounding away in full view of the world.

"He is flaunting his freedom at us, isn't he?" Jewel says.
"You know it's a he?"
"Actually, no. I didn't check. I just assumed."

Of the four traps, two held roadrunners. Jewels guessed they must have either decided on the traps as nesting sites, even though she knows they are not ground nesters, or, more likely, she joked, ate whatever creature had been in the trap and decided on a nap. The birds were more fun to come across unexpectedly than the tarantulas that liked to hide in pitfall traps. She wondered why the roadrunners didn't eat those. Tarantula was supposed to be one of their food favorites. And why, she wonders, do they stick their abdomens up in the air at you like stink beetles when encountered in the open? Their business end is elsewhere.

"I hope you won't hold it against me if I tell you something," Drew nervously resumes what the jackrabbit interrupted. "I do really like you, so don't think it is my opinion."

They are either in California, Mexico, or Arizona, possibly Texas. All have similarly long-eared jackrabbits cruising through similar vegetation. Jewel will not long remember where, but she will never forget the conversation.

"Of course," Jewel answers, having no idea what is coming. Why shouldn't Drew like her?

"It has to do with—" Drew has to pause. "Well, it's delicate."

Jewel waits.

Finally, Drew blurts it out. "You have a bad reputation," she says dispassionately. "You are seen to be something of a loose woman. Some in the Vivarium even took to calling you Jewel Harlot."

"Who called me that?" Her voice is sharply defensive, but she is hurt.

Drew does not answer. "There's the Ford," she says. "It's right on time and so are we."

Jewel wonders why anyone might think that of her. There was just Reggie Parker. Gene Odum, well, she thinks, that can't have counted. Liza's friends? How could anyone at the university know anything about that? Or that sweet young teacher in Detroit? She has to admit that she has come to like men's cocks. She especially likes the way they look and feel—erect, of course, not those silly little squishy Mr. Küchlers they usually have between their legs. Does that make her a harlot?

It is a question she lives with for the rest of the trip as she traps jackrabbits in mixed prairie in Texas. She wonders who knows what—or thinks they know— as she samples rodents in hard and soft chaparral in California. She wonders who is spreading what rumor as she walks desert grassland and oak-juniper savanna and forest in Arizona and Mexico in search of mammal signs. A badger in California, however, startles her off the topic momentarily. It arrogantly takes its time in putting distant between them. A thin, bedraggled coyote, tail between its legs, draws out her sympathy in Mexico. Normally, they are heard, not seen. Dragging itself back no doubt, she thinks, to some canine version of a Hooverville. A rock squirrel whistles at her in Arizona. Then it frustrates her by allowing only fleeting partial glimpses in a hide-and-seek game they carry on for the good part of an hour. Pocket mice and kangaroo rats everywhere have her wishing she could bring them back to Detroit to keep in her classroom, not only for the pleasure and education of the students, but also for the sheer joy that gazing on their beauty gives her.

Pinyon-pine woodland in Colorado and the cold desert of the Great Basin are yet to come. Jewel may get to see all the major biomes on the continent, she thinks, but she will never understand what Drew has told her. Drew politely refuses to be drawn into any further conversation on the matter. Jewel stops pressing her. She loses herself in the mundane minutia of her science. She sees the pinyon-pine biome through its cones, labeled and boxed, and twigs with needles attached to cardboard and pressed by being weighted down by whatever is handy. Labeled cardboard, of course. The Great Basin is for her a pocket mouse captured in the Mojave. It is sacrificed and skinned for preservation. That requires a deft, swift maneuver to sever its neck vertebrae with her fingers. The she spends an evening slicing the tiny pelt open from chin to tail and to the extremities, then slowly peeling away the skin with a very dull scalpel and the liberal use of corn meal. Eventually, skeleton, muscle and viscera are discarded, leaving a mouse-sized rug missing only forepaws, which were clipped off with scissors to facilitate skinning. It is stuffed with cotton and sewn up to look like a little ball of fur with ears and tail and white, cotton eyes. A labeled tag is attached to its hind foot.

Everywhere there are the contents of killing jars upended onto motel room tables, open newspaper pages, or bed sheets. The insects are picked through with soft forceps, pinned through the appropriate anatomical part, thorax or elytron, but always on the right side, then labeled, and affixed in rows to the cardboard bottom of black specimen boxes. Specimens too fine for even the narrowest pins are glued, always on their right sides, to paper points with a drop of clear nail polish. Labels are pinned beneath each specimen. Fragile, soft-bodied specimens are stored in alcohol in small vials, labels inside. Butterflies and moths, more often than not, are stored with their wings folded up in envelopes, labeled on their outsides.

Killing jars are thick-glassed and cork-stoppered. Beneath a hard plaster layer at their bottoms is potassium cyanide. A drop of water releases the very poisonous gas from its salt, which Jewel can smell as a hint of almond. She knows that cyanide is odorless, but there is that hint of almonds for her, always, on taking out the stopper, even before charging with water. Somehow, something must have gotten mixed up in her physiology, she explains to the others, for she can smell cyanide, while the sweetness of ozone is a mystery to her.

Grasses and herbs provide the safest and most pleasant duty. They use quadrats for sampling. Even though Cowles never used quadrats, Jewel falls into their use without qualms.

"After all," she remembers his slurred slow speech in a class, "one must select one's quadrats, and that brings in the subjective element."

Küchler is violently anti-quadrat, perhaps in homage to his idol. Jewel has learned not to discuss the subject with him.

Reference samples of the appropriate parts (stems, leaves, flowers, hopefully all together) of plants are collected and pressed between blotting paper in a sophisticated plant press, with wing nuts to tighten that increase the pressure between wooden end plates, when such is available. When not available, because someone else in the team has filled them up, plants are placed between the pages of a telephone book, often purloined from a motel room. Always, there are labels specifying genus and species, if known, date collected, location, and habitat type.

Then, some time before midnight, some rest. No, she does not sleep. She picks up the heavy tome that Shelford has lent her for the journey. It is *Voles, Mice, and Lemmings* by Charles Elton, almost new. It begins with a historical section that is prefaced by an untranslated quote in French. The author names the field mouse in several languages, including Russian. In Cyrillic letters.

"To comprehend the history of European mouse plagues," she reads, "one has to read, among other and less peculiar works, a fauna of Alsace by a French notary; a vole plague report by a learned Indian civil servant and oriental scholar who retired to become a landowner in Scotland; a folk-lore essay written by a classical scholar and head of an Oxford college; a painstaking collection of classical references about animals by a school-teacher in Germany; and part of the works of Aristotle."

She is instantly hooked. Its stories of rodent "irruptions," as Elton calls them, hold her more strongly than do Scarlett O'Hara's emotional eruptions over Rhett Butler, the subject of Drew Sparkman's reading, inspired by having recently seen the movie.

Out in the field, where specimens are collected, is the only fun part. That is, if the mosquitoes, chiggers, and black flies are ignored or forgotten. And the scorpions in boots (or the other various insects in boots that make Jewel fear they are scorpions) and the tarantulas in live traps. Or the kissing bugs in the California deserts that can end a field trip by transmitting Valley Fever. Or the squirrels, which still carry plague.

VII

SHELFORD is as hot and tired at the end of the day as the rest, but instead of a beer, he brings out a bottle of tequila from the cantina at which they stop. Jewel follows him out with bottles of Coca-Cola. Its owner must remember him from some past trip, she suspects. "Buenas dias" and "Como esta?" were all that Shelford needed of his small stock of Spanish phrases, honed through the use of a tutor in anticipation of the trip, before the bottle appeared. She had to point and pantomime to get what she wanted.

"Here is a little something I have learned to like," Shelford announces, offering the bottle around.

Drew and Marie turn their noses up immediately in refusal. Jewel pours a bit into her metal cup and has a sip. The face she makes draws immediate laughter.

"Mexican food has been a revelation," she manages to say, "but tequila might as well stay south of the border."

"Hah!" Shelford trumpets, taking the bottle back and pouring himself a healthy swig. "You really shouldn't dismiss it like that."

He passes the bottle once more. It comes back untouched.

"As far as I am concerned," he says, trying to sound superior to the women, "there are only three things in this world that are undrinkable. They are tea, tomato juice, and kerosene. Kerosene, at least, has the benefit of being sterile, unlike the other two."

"Just like tequila, I bet," Drew says. "Is that all it has to recommend it?"

Shelford's spirits are too good for him to take offense. The mealtime conversation he normally orchestrates tightly now wanders where it may.

"Why would anyone not vote for Roosevelt again?" he demands to know while failing to bring in a radio station on the Motorola he has had installed in the Ford. "A hundred and thirty dollars for the thing just to get static instead of news."

"It would be like throwing your vote away, I imagine," Drew offers. "Voting for Wilkie again would be a courtesy only. Roosevelt wins no matter what."

"No. No. No. No," Shelford chides. "Being in the minority is not throwing your vote away. Never. You know, I voted for Eugene

V. Debs pretty much every time he ran, even the year he campaigned from prison. Besides being a neighboring Indianan, I believe in everything he stood for—but where have you been, Drew? Wilkie didn't get nominated!"

"You know very well, where I've been, and the outcome of the Republican Convention seems not to be of any significance this year. That's exactly my point."

"I think I agree with you. Just look at what FDR has done. He's put in place the programs that Debs and Norman Thomas ran on all those years. How about you, Jewel? With your pedigree, I imagine you're a good Republican."

"Of course," Jewel answers with a trace of embarrassment.

"What about that tailor he's running with? What do you make of him?"

"Tailor?"

"Haberdasher, I think."

"He's from Missouri. That's in his favor."

"Kansas City doesn't count as Missouri."

Jewel, Shelford notices, is uncharacteristically quiet.

"Jewel?" he asks. "Everything OK?"

"Hmm?"

"You're looking glum."

"Oh, it's nothing," she says after a moment's thought. "I guess I'm just concerned about the data I'm getting. I know it will be useful to you, but I don't see a dissertation in it."

"Of course there is," he reassures her, taking another swig. "Let me tell you, when Frederic Clements and I sat down to see if we could merge animal ecology into the only true ecology—that of Cowles and Clements, of course, plant ecology..."

He stops, then starts again with, "You know how irritated I get when plant ecologists talk about ECOLOGY and all they are talking about is vegetation? Well, we set out to change that—although I would have preferred calling it general ecology, rather than bio-ecology. But what was I talking about?"

Jewel laughs. How many sips of that bottle had he taken?

"Bio-ecology," she answers. "Did you know I finally got a chance to read the first two chapters?"

"And?" Shelford asks expectantly.

"I found two typos!"

"Bah! Yes, those were difficult chapters. More difficult was trying to fit animal communities to Frederic's system. My tiger beetles were such a good fit to the stages of oak-maple forests. I thought other animals would fit as well."

"But they wander too much?"

"Right on the nose! The dominants do. Although mussel and barnacle communities I studied around Puget Sound seem to fit the same kind of community patterns that vegetation does."

"Because they're sessile?"

"Yeah," Drew puts in. "Mussels and barnacles might as well be plants!"

"Probably true."

Then Shelford turns back to Jewel.

"But what were the typos?" he asks.

"Ceology, instead of ecology, I think, and somebody really murdered the spelling of Mt. Katahdin in Maine."

"I noticed that! Too late, I'm afraid. But getting back to the point. Which was…Oh?"

"A dissertation!" Drew reminds.

"Yes. The reason why we could only go into detail on grasslands and those Puget Sound communities in the book is there is so little information on the animals of other biomes that is at all useful. The trapping you are doing in these deserts will be a real contribution, believe me. I have seen too many studies that record nothing more than in which state an animal was found or on what mountain—without even any hint as to altitude."

Jewel is less confident. She is unimpressed with her data. She has lists to show for her efforts instead of tables of numbers. All that she needs to show with her mammals, she supposes, is what Shelford did with his tiger beetles. But that is not going to happen, she knows. How can she tell from her census methods if an animal is really missing from a habitat, or only not found by her?

"And don't forget University Wood," Shelford suddenly remembers. "You've got some good data there."

"Maybe. The University Wood, at least, is set up for it. Still, what I have from it looks puny compared to the kind of data Charles Elton has. University Wood is only one spot. One data point, so to speak. It would be great if I could keep coming back to it for fifty years or so, but what an age that would take for a dissertation!"

"Elton is doing population studies, not community studies. Of course, he needs more numbers. I gather you've been reading his new book."

"Voles, Mice and Lemmings," Jewel recites for the benefit of the others. "Well, you gave it to me."

"So, what do you make of it?"

"I'm shocked by how gracefully he writes," Jewel answers. "I wish I could write with equal talent."

"No typos, huh?"

"He stopped me cold with esquimeaux."

"Oh?"

"I don't know if it should have the second e. But don't you think there is an awful lot of ecology going on in Europe? And isn't there more to ecology than classifying biomes? Plagues of voles, for example. Cats and kestrels eating them."

"That's population ecology," Shelford says almost dismissively. "Raymond Pearl at Hopkins pretty much has that sewed up."

"But it sounds like so much fun," Jewel counters. "It is solving puzzles. Clearly, foxes depend to a large extent on the mice. What causes the mice to fluctuate? It's like a detective story. A novel, really. But Elton is not just about populations. What about food chains and pyramids?"

"Yes, well," Shelford hems and haws, "but what is at the bottom of a food pyramid?"

"Plants?" Drew offers.

"Plants! And before you think about changing professions, Jewel, you should take a look at what Hutchinson at Yale wrote in his review of this latest book by Elton. It had a Latin title, the review, Nati Sunt Mures et Facta Est Confusio."

"How precious!" Jewel almost squeals as if she is suddenly ten years younger.

"Mice are born and all is confusion," Drew translates for the benefit of the others, although Marie is the only one whose Latin is rusty.

"But about dissertations," Shelford says, making it sound as if he is taking the group into his confidence on another subject, one of more interest. "In the end, a dissertation is as adequate as the doctoral committee declares it to be, and that reflects more on the doctoral candidate than on the dissertation. Your committee is?"

"Kendeigh and Vestal. And you, of course. At least, when last I was enrolled."

Shelford then lets that conversation drop.

"Which way tomorrow?" he asks the entire group as he gets to his feet.

He gets three different suggestions. Essentially, they are east, west, and south.

"I have a different idea," he says, "so I guess that is where we will go."

There is little opposition beyond a few half-hearted groans, before the trio of assistants realize they are going homeward. It is the end of July. The halfway point in the trip has been passed without their noticing. Groans turn to cheers.

They re-cross the border at Laredo, where they find they are not the only contingent from the University of Illinois. Ed Baylor, a graduate student, is at the border station a few lanes from them. With him is his wife Martha, an alumna. Baylor is overjoyed to recognize Shelford. They are travelers in an exotic land coming upon not only fellow countrymen but fellow Illini. Ed immediately gets out of his car and walks over to Shelford.

"Hello, you old spy!" he jokes loudly. "What are you smuggling in your station wagon?"

And he leaves.

Customs agents immediately descend on Shelford and his wagon. Many things draw their suspicion, but the field notes are what hold their attention. They are confiscated under suspicion of being some sort of indecipherable code.

"They are being sent to Washington DC for cryptoanalysis," Shelford announces apologetically after having tried at length to retrieve them. "They say we can get them back as soon as the war is over. I think they are being used as little more than justification for their search, but once they get into that war bureaucracy, who knows when we may ever get them back

"There goes my dissertation," Jewel cries out, only half in jest.

VIII

JOAN Hinton was beginning to think it was not such a great idea, after all. As much as she wants to witness it along with the others, she wishes she hadn't suggested the motorcycle to Liza. She did not feel that way, however, until they got past Santa Fe. That was when Liza, hitting the straight, flat highway south, began to feel comfortable on the seat of the borrowed motorcycle and let the throttle out.

"My God, Liza!" Joan shouts futilely into the wind. "We won't have to worry about the radiation, if we wind up spread all over the pavement."

Liza would not worry, even if she could hear me, Joan thinks. She was never one to be shy around radiation. And she clearly is not worrying about anything else now.

Hundreds of people were involved in various testing duties that day. Vehicles were scarce. She and Liza, physicists though they are, did not rate the limited transportation available. But there was that motorcycle. Joan suggested it as a joke. Liza was feeling free of motherhood duties by having left Peter, her barely-year-old son back in Hanford under the care of husband John's mother. She was not about to be left behind, not as long as there was even one mode of transport left to her.

"Of course, I can drive that thing," she said confidently after Joan had explained the clutch and throttle controls.

They were off, after one false start, a little after midnight, Joan clinging for life to Liza's back.

Four hours later, Liza pulls off onto a dirt road that climbs a butte.

"This should give us a pretty good view," she says, pulling off by the edge of a bluff.

She is right, Joan thinks as she looks out on the landscape. She is relieved to be off the bike, and not just to be able to get the stiffness out of her legs. The desert stars give enough light for them to see the white sands spread out below them.

"How far is it?" she asks. "That was Alamogordo we passed down there, wasn't it?"

"We're maybe 25 miles from Trinity," Liza replies. "Close enough to get a good view, but far enough not to get ourselves in trouble. There's a seismology lab somewhere near here. What time is it?"

"I think we still have almost a half an hour. Will we need sunglasses?"

"I didn't bring any. Well, I'm not taking my eyes away from that direction."

Without the benefit of an official countdown, it comes sooner than they expect. They are suddenly bathed in light from all directions.

"It's like being at the bottom of an ocean of light," Joan whispers. "Look! It's withdrawn back into the bomb as if the bomb sucked it up. Now it's turned purple and blue."

"I saw purple and green before that bright white light," Liza whispers back.

"Whew!" Joan says, still in a whisper. "The mountains all around are lit as if it's daylight."

They are still whispering as the cloud changes from a huge white puffball to become more mushroom-shaped. The bottom—stape, Jewel would call it, Liza thinks with amusement—is dark and red. The top— Liza cannot remember what Jewel would have called it—is lit by the rising sun. Then the sound surprises them.

"Shock wave," Liza announces as it rumbles around the mountains.

They are no longer whispering.

Nearer the test site, Kenneth Bainbridge, test director, says to Robert Oppenheimer, "Now we are all sons of bitches."

Oppenheimer's mind is searching for a line from the Bhagavad Gita. Yes. That's it, he thinks.

"Now I am become Death, the destroyer of worlds."

IX

THE Vivarium is not the same. The stone pot in Vivarium 200 is still heating a concoction that must be a whole can of coffee in an equal volume of water, but by the afternoon, Shelford is more apt to be found discussing politics over beer and peanuts at Bidwell's Tavern than minding the pot.

It is her office, but it is no longer her office. A strange fellow named Robert Whittaker is in possession of her desk. He is Kendeigh's student. Strange indeed. Slow to speak, with beady, frightened grey eyes, his intention is to be a plant ecologist, Jewel dragged out of him. The botany department refused to admit him to graduate standing, however, due to his poor college preparation. Then Kendeigh, who seems willing to pick up all stray graduate students, took him on. Now, Whittaker told her in their brief conversation, he feels himself to be a student of Arthur Vestal, who is in the department that turned him down. What a glutton for punishment, Jewel thinks. What an imbecile, she adds.

She had not bothered to ask for his rationale for all that maneuvering. What would be the point, even were he capable of putting more than three words together in answer to any of her questions? Are they all like him, she asks herself, our war veterans? Hiding from those of us who did not share that experience with them?

Then her thoughts turn back to herself. It is all so futile, this wait, she fears. Shelford has officially retired. He can no longer be her professor. She cannot go back to things the way they were. The stone pot and Shelford will be gone by the fall. Kendeigh is a possibility—that much seems evident. If he is willing to take on someone like Whittaker, why not her, too? But is that what she really wants?

She has brought nothing to read, not expecting such a long wait. She has nothing with which to pass the time but memories that have been dredged up, most pleasant, but not all. There is no one at her old desk at the moment. She crosses the lab and sits down at it. She has the feeling that it is the returning GI and not herself who is trespassing. She resents the new neatness of her old desktop. A single notebook is centered on it. Stapled stacks of white, typed papers are arranged around its periphery. There being no free space on the desk, she puts her own notebook and papers on one of the piles. His notebook draws her stare. She turns a few of its pages. He was enrolled in Shelford's climatic ecology course, she can tell with a few quick glances.

Then her eye drifts to the paper stacks. Dissertation perhaps? She picks one up.

RELEASE is its title, but it has been crossed off and under it, in pencil, is written Enfranchisement. She starts reading.

"They almost always talked of their adventures going into town and coming back. They did not even stop to damn the army while they were on pass."

The manuscript has nothing to do with ecology or botany or even biology. It is about soldiers in England going into town to look for Land Army girls, whatever they were. Memoir? Fiction?

Jewel reads on.

Fiction, she concludes. There is a lot of dialog, too much for a memoir. Holding a page in her hand, its look and feel are oddly familiar to her. Then it suddenly strikes her that the type face is the same as Fred's. No doubt made by the same model prewar Remington.

"Of course they would have been faithful to each other," catches her eye, as does, "go steady and "marriage delayed." She stops skimming and starts reading.

Not too bad, she thinks, putting the manuscript back on top of its pile, but not very good either. Very modern, perhaps. Lots of dialog that goes nowhere. Hemingway-esque, but not Hemingway. When the young woman takes home the soldier who "picks her up" at a dance, then starts unbuttoning his blouse, "blood pounded in his temples" and he "felt unbearable pressure as if it would explode." But "he could not spend the night with her," the reader is told in the next sentence. A portrait of the woman's husband is watching them. The soldier then goes off to wonder what his parents would think of him. No, Jewel corrects herself. He knows exactly what form their reaction to the episode will take. It would be silent disappointment.

Strange.

She takes up another. LEADERSHIP is its title. Jewel reads as far as "Captain Henry walked down the corridor of the headquarters." It is not the complete first line, only the first line of type, but she abandons it to take a quick glance at the rest of the page. She notes a heavy use of the word, sir, and various ranks. She puts it aside casually and reaches for another.

VICTORY IN THE NEW INN is the next. Her eye catches, "White Cliffs of Dover" and "English soldier" and "Canadians and Americans" after "Scotch" and "unattached women," all on its first page. She passes the rest by.

Next is a poem, VILLANELLE TRISTE.

All joy is brief and shadowed, tinged with grief,
For man and all man's joys will perish fast;
And shadowed joy and grief alike are brief.

The sunlight joy and moonlit mood are brief;
The pleasures we would hold cannot be grasped,
All joy is brief and shadowed, tinged with grief.

Relentless, thoughtless time, as might a thief,
Steals off with what we treasure or would ask;
And shadowed joy and grief alike are brief.

We might be tranquil, sure in some belief,
But faith is lost in reason's searing blast.
All joy is brief and shadowed, tinged with grief.

Our joy-filled hours, and those of pressing grief
Are gone, like flowers fade, like clouds are past;
And shadowed joy and grief alike are brief.

From knowing this, why should we not as lief
Each transitory pleasure be our last?
All joy is brief and shadowed. Tinged with grief;
And shadowed joy and grief alike are brief.

    What is a villanelle? Jewel wonders. Something having to do the rhyme scheme? She tries hard to remember. Something about how "joy," "grief," and "brief" chase each other around the stanzas, she thinks. She likes that. But what does "triste" mean?
    Then there is THE PHOTOGRAPH. "College Inn" catches her eye in the first line. She reads on. The soldier is now back from the war and in Emporia. Illinois? Nope, he refers to Wichita on the next page. That suggests Kansas. The soldier has reunited with his old girlfriend. Something romantic, perhaps? Jewel anticipates. But no. Meaningless conversation alternates with just as meaningless silences between the pair. The main character suffers an inability to express himself to others except through words having little

meaning. The only meaningful exchange he has with his fiancee in the story is "slipping his hand around under her breast." But "her pleasure in his embrace" seems to kill the relationship. Thoughts of "fornication and adultery" drive him to take refuge with a pinball machine. A proper relationship for the character, Jewel thinks. Then she thinks, he is writing about himself. He is writing about personal torments.

Next is THE CRIPPLE, labeled "first draft" and decorated with many penciled corrections. Is he taking a creative writing course? Jewel wonders. In graduate school? For a PhD in ecology?

As the title suggests, it is not a happy story. It starts with the hero in the throes of a massive hangover, three full pages worth. He is a man brilliantly skilled for success, but trapped by lack of "force and persuasion, unable to influence" people by his speech. How, he wonders, "his brother, a polished mediocrity, could mix well with others, when he could not?" He finds an answer in their childhood. Then he loses his true love by an inability to set a wedding date, possibly because he is unable to come to terms with her sexuality—a recurring theme, thinks Jewel. That leads to psychological perishment over the final five pages.

Weird!

The next is titled NOTES – STOICS, and it appears to be just that, notes. The philosophy of Epictetus is followed by that of Marcus Aurelius. Stoics are followed by Epicureans. A class? Must be. Does that mean that the stories were written for a class?

Attached to the notes, handwritten, is "The story of my father." Jewel immediately recognizes it as notes for a novel. One of the characters is "Robert, viewed by everyone as sane, normal, hard-headed, & good-natured. But, married to a tramp & brought her to farm, found her in bed with hired hand. Later took common law wife in town nearby, never brought her to the farm. Father thinks he may have been overcoming fears of 1st marriage, or may have felt he would not be so well able to take care of his mother. Brainy for a farmer, a good talker, radio ham, scientifically inquisitive."

She grabs her purse and notebook, gathering together as she does so the papers under it, not caring that the desk is obviously disarranged. Then, almost tiptoeing, she leaves her old office and walks past Vivarium 203 without even glancing within. She no longer wishes to wait until Kendeigh is free to see her. She no longer wants to worry whether the data she obtained on those two summer field trips will be sufficient for a dissertation. She no longer feels a need to redeem her anguish over the set of data in the notebook she did not get back after the war or whether the hemlines of her skirts were too slow to descend from their Flapper levels, as Drew Sparkman once delicately put it, or her necklines too low. She no longer wants to worry about Kendeigh's reasons for making her wait so long. She no longer wants to worry about what will be done about Danny if she comes back to Urbana. She is shutting the door on Urbana and that part of her life and vows never to look back.

Middlebury

"OH, don't read those," Jewel said in a matter-of-fact tone. "Did he really keep them?"

"Every one, apparently."

They were in Danny's apartment in an old Victorian within easy bicycling of campus. As a bachelor, and without tenure, it met all his needs. Yet the advantage of home ownership—especially with Aunt Jewel as part of the household—was becoming clearer and clearer each time he made the almost three-hour trip to Ames Hill. It was one of those situations to which the old Yankee saying, "You cahn't git theah from heah," applied.

"Hmm. It must mean something," Jewel said, still dead pan.

She did not like the idea of Danny digging into her past and did not want to encourage him by overreacting. She was afraid she knew what he would find there.

"He kept everything," Dan elaborated, "all his correspondence, even all his own letters."

Jewel mostly dwelled on the more recent past. It presented her with an endless series of puzzles. She rummaged through it like she did the old chests and dressers she had brought from Ames Hill, never finding what she was looking for and being distracted by clothing that she could not remember as ever having been hers.

"How could he—?"

"Typewriters used to make carbon copies very handily, remember?"

Her future held little more for Jewel than the insults of old age. Friends died or moved away or became distant in other ways. Vision and hearing faded. Muscles and joints no longer did her will. Most insulting was having the functioning of her bowel become the most important item of her day. She did not need a crisis from the past. Having Danny trying to uproot her from Ames Hill was crisis enough.

"Well, don't read them."

It was the last word she would say on the subject. Danny closed the file and put away his laptop.

"How do you want to go back?" he asked.

The route south, to Bennington, was fast and easy, even with the congestion there sometimes was in Rutland. Once there, however, they had to cross the southern spine of the Green Mountains to get to the dirt road to Ames Hill. One alternative was to go over Middlebury Gap to Route 100, then cut across to the Interstate and go by superhighway to Brattleboro. It saved some time, but it seemed somehow unlike a Vermont way to travel. To stay on 100 to Wilmington could be torture, however. One had to be in a tourist mood to enjoy it. Snowstorms, of course, really did make all routes between Dan and Jewel impossible.

"It doesn't matter to me," Jewel said, having gotten her things together. "Pick whichever you like."

He wished she hadn't said that. The more often he had to take any of the routes, the less charming they became to him. And he had to take them often. Sometimes, it was every week.

There was always some sort of crisis needing his attention. A bat could be in her bedroom or a window too drafty. She could not go to sleep in the room under either condition. One time it was a kitten marooned atop the old oak tree. Her car needed repair. Her heart was suddenly fluttering wildly. A shutter had blown off in a windstorm. Suspicious noises from her furnace needed his immediate attention. The smoke detector was beeping in the night and keeping her awake. More commonly, she was feeling dizzy and feared she had mixed up her medicines or forgotten them or they were no longer working and what was she to do?

Each answered summons rewarded him with an eager greeting and fawning attention. She never failed to make hot cross buns, his favorite for breakfast ever since Jonathan had introduced him to them. But there were just far too many summonses.

Although she insisted that she intended to die and be buried on Ames Hill, next to Jonathan, they had spent the weekend scouting houses for sale. Even as Jewel was saying how much she might enjoy reading on the porch at one place—or would never live in a place that required crossing through the kitchen to get to the bathroom—neither said a word as to who was to be the occupant.

Rejecting housing in Middlebury as too expensive, they had similarly rejected the Champlain-side villages of Cornwall and Bridport and Shoreham, popular as they were with faculty. Then they similarly rejected the similarly popular mountain-side villages of East Middlebury and Ripton. That meant having to look farther into the mountains, to Bristol, perhaps. Or south to Brandon, which was suddenly popular with the upscale crowd for its art galleries and first-class French restaurant. Or in another direction, to Vergennes, which was becoming popular with the same upscale crowd for no reason that Dan could discover,

Then the fall semester began—too soon. He was overwhelmed with academic duties. Research at Middlebury, an essentially undergraduate institution, necessitated waiting for holidays and vacations. So did house hunting.

He did not purposefully stay away from the letters. Jewel's proscription had seemed more advice than demand, but as digital files tucked away in a folder in another folder in "My documents," they did not draw him the way the stack of his aunt's letters had at Arden Forest.

Then ski season came. It was a good year, lots of snow, lots of sunny days, lots of incentive to get in as much skiing as he could before arthritis took him off the slopes. Ripton, with its proximity to Rickert and the Snow Bowl, began to look better and better as a domicile, even with the brutal commutes it could necessitate in winter.

Then Jean Thomson Black at Yale Press encouraged him to go ahead with the book he had been wanting to write. He returned in earnest to his books and notes and reprints and scans, looking for material on how ecology and ecologists had influenced Rachel Carson—and she them.

Instead, inexplicably, his thinking drifted toward something like a biography of Fred Küchler.

"Fred Küchler," Jean Black responded to that idea. "What a figure he cut across ecology!"

Then she gave her estimate of the market potential of the proposed biography. Nil is how Dan interpreted it.

He went back to his original idea. It meant digging further into Küchler's letters, each time skipping by the file with Jewel's correspondence.

Before the editor's encouragement could lead to a book contract, he had to submit a proposal. That required almost writing a book in advance, then condensing it to some twenty pages, but as the summer wore on, he could not find a shape for the book.

It was not until a rainy August morning the next summer, after some more house hunting, this time on his own, that he stumbled upon Jewel's letters once more. Maybe, he thought facetiously, there was a book in them. He knew he should be reading the other letters from Arden Forest, instead of eavesdropping on his aunt, but her last letter was dated 1953, post nightmare. By then, he remembered, they had been in New Haven.

Jewel was so remarkably tight-lipped with everyone about that time. Could she have opened up to Küchler? Could that be why she did not want him to read the letters?

Instead of sitting down in an easy chair with originals to read, as he had at Arden Forest, he sat down in his office desk chair with scanned images on his computer screen. And, instead of going right to the end and reading backwards, he compulsively sought out the first letter he had scanned. It was Jewel's. Lines of poetry caught his eye. They were by Robert Frost and were inspired somehow by Küchler's last letter to her.

> *But so with all, from babes that play*
> *At hide and seek, to God afar*
> *So all who hide too well away*
> *Must speak and tell us where they are.*

Whatever it was in the correspondence that had inspired the lines had been left at Arden Forest. Still, it tweaked his curiosity. It was like having an interesting puzzle to solve.

"Thanks for reporting Miss Prigge's nice compliment," caught his eye next. "I do so remember her well – liked her on first sight." He did remember a Miss Prigge from the last letter he had read at Arden Forest, but not the part she had in Jewel's story. Where could she have met Jewel? At the hospital, concerning Küchler's eye? Was there some other meeting, long before? He read on.

> *Your mother is unique in my experience. Only in certain case histories have I glimpsed elements of her problem. Try to forgive the intrusion of this comment, Fred, and realize how deeply she is to be pitied. For she has endured the pain and endless tedium of rearing children, has suffered – in exaggerated form the fear for their safety which stems from the primitive protective instinct of every mammal,*

and in the end has failed utterly to achieve the joy of their growing —and mature companionship. One would like to know what fear of what responsibility, what dread of moving forward into full maturity arrested her development, prohibited her giving to her children that basic pre-verbal foundation assurance that life is good, and that it is just a question of trying again – to find the right paths to make it so.

Be assured, tho, that my interest in the subject is merely academic. I once found the writings of psychiatrists and mental hygienists a sort of jungle knife by which I was enabled to hack my way out of a horrible tangle having to do with Danny and my sister.

He rushed through the rest, looking for more. He came quickly to her last line.

Do I have to buy a Spanish-English Dictionary or will you do your rhapsodizing in French hereafter?

Nothing more on that "horrible tangle," he thought disappointedly, but another puzzle, at least. He did remember a Spanish quote in Küchler's previous letter. Maybe if he read further, he thought, all the mysteries would converge on—

On what?

The next letter was Küchler's. Like most of his letters, it needed enlarging to read. The onion skin paper used for carbon copies was so transparent that what was on the page at issue and what had been imprinted from another carbon could only be deciphered by examining a magnified image. Tedious though it was, he had to admit that being able to enlarge an image with the facility a computer allowed was a big plus on the side of technology. The few Xeroxes of the old carbons he had made with Arden Forest's copying machine were worthless in comparison. The scans let him read on, even if in fits and starts.

I wish you could be here now. The weather has been grand for several days. As the sun rises higher and higher, along with the thermometer and my own feelings, the desire to return to city life recedes at the same rate. With some presumption, I might quote: "I have not only retired from all public employments, but I am retiring within myself ...Envious of none, I am determined to be pleased by all; and this, my dear friend, being the order of my march, I will move gently down the stream of life until I sleep with my fathers." Its author wrote so, to Lafayette, on retiring to Mt. Vernon after the Revolutionary War. True, he left to become President. My own stay here can be said to have passed the experimental stage. I chose Adam, at least until Wall Street, our democratic government, or the next war uses me as a pawn again.

Our porch-nesting phoebe is back; bluebirds and robins have been seen. The owls (?) are hooting again at night. Bats are around. Six deer browsed 100 feet from the house the other evening. Squirrels and chipmunks are tearing about. Rhubarb and iris on the sunny side of the house are up an inch. My outdoor time is all too short.

My interlinear translation of Carmen finally received the shock that had been destined for it. I finally found out in trying to pursue a certain edition of Carmen, that the Translational Publishing Co., N.Y., has put out a few in Latin, Greek, German and Hebrew. But I still think my system is better. How about coming here some time and looking at some of the manuscript? All jokes aside, will you please tell me when you next write whether (1) you wish a special invitation here, in respect to date, or (2) you will choose the time most convenient to you, and tell me you are coming?

The botany text marches ahead a bit every day. Very soon now I will be going to Yale for library work occasionally. I've often had the idea of visiting various universities, getting others' ideas of what is wanted in an ecology text, and, admittedly, doing a bit of spreading my own gospel. But I should know better than to try to convince anyone over 30 of ideas which differ from those which he accepted before 30. (I know, even though just 30, you'd have some good comebacks for those ideas. Why not come out and give them to me?) Within a week the town road should be dried out sufficiently for driving, and then I can meet bus and rail visitors – just in case you want to check out of Detroit for Easter or spring vacations.

My outside reading at the moment is Plutarch, a volume of which I have found here in the house. One must be a downright escapist to know the history of mankind, and still have that faith in human nature which allows him to strive for a social Utopia. "Faith" is the correct word in the previous sentence. If there are a few men and times that stand out as being good, noble, etc. etc., it is conspicuous, indeed, that man has never preserved such conditions, or learned by them. They have come and gone with even less frequency than the Neros and the Borgias. Juan Valer's Pepita Jiménez is taking another goodly chunk of my time.

Which reminds me: Salud, pesetas, y el tiempo para gozarias is a common Spanish toast. Literally, "Health, dollars, and the time for to-enjoy-them." It is oft quoted in contrast to our "health, wealth, and happiness", The Latin is more concerned with "the time to enjoy them" rather than with the American standard of material possession. "Bastante" is a word used idiomatically to carry the idea of sufficiently, enough, not too much.

I've found some Crataegus for you, but they amount to nothing in this region. Despite their beauty, I still think that you should not die without seeing mountain laurel in bloom.

The next in sequence was also Küchler's, and in the middle of it, Danny was pleased to discover a new trick. He had been clicking on the arrow on the side bar of the window in order to move down the enlarged page. Each click, however, necessitated a reconstituted image that, although rapid, as compared to a photographic print having to be developed, was not instant enough for his patience. What he accidentally discovered was that he could drag the scroll bar down half a page or more and save time. Flush with his victory over technology, he read on.

March has been a glorious month. The season is striding forward like some glorious pageant. I am more excited than a child at its first circus – and me, a Ph.D and an ex-professor of the natural sciences! I have always wanted to live thru a spring out in the woods. And now that I am doing it, I want little else. The woodcocks have arrived, Two phoebes have found the porch nest, and I hope will settle there. My kitchen-door chipmunk is getting tamer. The lilac bushes have a feint green cast of bursting buds. Rhubarb's up 6 inches; chives most ready to pick; asparagus earnestly awaited. The few seeds I bought from Macy's basement, where I save a cent or so on each package – so I guess I do not rate as landed gentry. The seeds are Burpee's though.

The eye is but little thought of those days. I am due to see Dr. C. the middle of April. Is it really 8 months ago that the light went

*out! I can still make my heart pump loudly when I think of what might have happened had a friend failed that Saturday morning.
June is the month of mountain laurel. Don't forget.*

Burpee seeds, Macy's, he really should, he decided, not waste his time eavesdropping on Aunt Jewel, when he had a pressing project that could cap his career, or, at the minimum, bring him back into the big time. "Horrible tangle" seemed unlikely to reappear, while the new way of scrolling he had at his command cried out to be used on other files. He navigated to Küchler's correspondence with Ray Fosberg. It went from pre-war, pre-Rachel Carson to post-Earth Day. In his dotage, Fosberg claimed a close mentoring relationship to Carson and long friendship with her through the Washington chapter of the Audubon Society.

Much of the correspondence was drearily specific to particular projects, but now and then, there was a nugget to be found. Küchler had pioneered an area, Dan realized, the ecology of invasive species, that later became very "hot." No one in it, however, referred to Küchler. The ecology of invasive species, the dogma went, started with Charles Elton's book two decades later.

Küchler and Fosberg's view of the "balance of nature" was refreshingly level headed for 1939, more modern, in fact, than the version Eugene Odum propounded well into the 1980s. Küchler also had his own logic. Another surprise was Küchler's willingness to examine a disturbed habitat. Harold St. John of the Bishop Museum, a legend in Hawaiian botany, had warned Küchler not to study the arid vegetation on Oahu. It was an area that St. John thought had no plant communities, Küchler wrote to Fosberg. It was nothing more than a mess of introduced weeds, Küchler reported St. John saying, to which no self-respecting botanist would give anything but a passing glance. Küchler's study on those weeds was one of three papers, he now remembers, that Dan Simberloff credited with putting the final nails on Clements's superorganism.

Then there were letters concerning a paper that Fred wrote that on the surface seemed to try to apply philosophical principals to ecology well before Karl Popper had turned his full attention to science. It was not exactly what he could use for his proposed book, but it did interest him. He read on, but then, suddenly, war broke out. Letters were few and light.

I am back for a short visit, leaving again for Columbia on June 23 or thereabouts. Hear you had bad luck with your passport. I wish I could get you pried loose down to Columbia. Never did I see a country that more urgently needed ecologists, especially of your kind. Most of the inhabited part of the country is on at least a 45° slope. They have butchered their forests beyond all imagination. I am sure that the phenomenon of a "wet desert" will be an actuality in Columbia in a few years. Their soil is very rapidly being conveyed to the lower Magdalena river, which is out of it's banks and all over the place. The Columbians hate trees worse than our own Middle Westerners did a hundred years ago.

I asked one man why he planted his potatoes straight up and down a 60° slope. He said because the water collected behind them if they were any other way.

By the way, we had a young man from Uruguay accompanying us part of the way, collecting butterflies. He could not have been more than 15. He still didn't shave. I don't know what nationality he was. His name was Eisner and English was obviously not his first language. He had the most intense curiosity, poked into everything, not just butterflies. It was a pleasure to have him along.

That had been it for Fosberg's next letter, and Dan was surprised that censors had even allowed that. Fosberg was in South America on a secret botanical mission. The letters that followed came by way of transcriptions from Fosberg's wife, Violet. They, too, had been subject to censorship.

He read on. He might be able to use how ecologists had served in wartime. Carson had wanted to write an article about the misuse of DDT during World War Two. Reader's Digest magazine's rejection of it resulted in its stillbirth.

The next two letters were hurried one-paragraph notes from Vi.

It was thoughtful of you to write your letter on airmail paper. I usually write Ray three pages. That leaves the weight of a fourth sheet for enclosures of various kinds—clippings, pictures, or a letter like yours. You might be interested in knowing what has happened to our friend, Satsui Fujii. She was studying laboratory technique in

California at the time of Pearl Harbor and got thrown in an internment camp in Arizona.

I copied parts of your letter to send to Ray. I deliberately avoided mentioning your name. For several reasons I thot it best not to send the entire letter.

Then next was in similarly hurried handwriting.

I had Camp signed up to come down and do a job, an exploration of the Uribe region, Meta, which includes the north end of the mysterious Cordillera Macarena. Somehow or other he got shunted off to Ecuador. The job is still to be done if our program here continues. I am in charge of Cinchona exploration here in Columbia, and am also working toward a monograph of the genus.

So much for being classified, Dan thought with amusement.

The next was a long letter in Ray Fosberg's handwriting. The war had ended. Its discussion of "Gleasonian indeterminism" was of interest to Dan, but again, nothing to a reader of a book about Rachel Carson.

Then the following paragraph captured his attention.

Fred Hermann came down to South America to work with me, leaving his wife at home, near Beltsville. I took him and a forester off up into the northern part of Colombia and, after showing them what the work was all about, left them there to carry out a two months' exploration. Then I came back here to the states for a few weeks. After I had been here a couple of weeks, Violet told me one evening that Dory Hermann had called up and that all sorts of things had happened to Fred—she had got a letter from Fred in Bogota written about ten days after I had left him four hundred miles from there and that they had run out of food, gotten lost for several days, that I hadn't given them enough blankets or pills to disinfect their water, that they had run out of money (though I had left them with more than I had ever been able to spend in two months), Fred had a heart attack, he had walked out and returned to Bogota to get more money, leaving the forester there, that the doctor had told Fred that he should not go back into such strenuous work, and that he had resigned. (There were many more misfortunes that I cannot recall.) I waited for some letters from others there, and when I got them they said nothing except that Fred had had a slight heart flutter and that he had returned to Bogota and got himself transferred to some other work in the lowlands. Dory had given the letter to Erlanson to read, so I couldn't see it. A couple of weeks later she called again and told Violet that she had got the letter back from Erlanson and had looked at it again, and that, much to her surprise and embarrassment, all the letter said was that Fred had had a heart attack and had returned to Bogota and had got transferred to barbasco work in the llanos. She had imagined or made up all the rest! She couldn't understand why she had said such things!

What an interesting bit of history, he thought, rereading it a third time. Then again, what could he make of it? He had to somehow concoct a book about Rachel Carson's ecology, not Fosberg's or Küchler's. He saw no way to tie the wartime material, interesting as it was to him, to Silent Spring. He could find no word in it about any pesticide, not even DDT.

Bereft of ideas, he turned back to Aunt Jewel in frustration.

The 'day before April' - 1946
My dear, you'll be making a philosopher of me yet, much as I deplore the thought for thought's sake school of inaction.

Your negative attitudes, your refusal to have part or lot in this nasty thing called human society – your refusal to have any share in the common responsibility either for its sins or the modification thereof challenges me.

I am surrounded by people who <u>think</u> as you do, but because they go on playing their useful roles as mothers & fathers, teachers and friends – bringing lots of order out of chaos – they do not disturb me. True – their actions belie their words – but actions being more important – and theirs being in full accord with the essentials of human survival – the contradiction does not seriously distress them – or worry me.

With you – I sense the capacity for a very high order of productivity – held in check by nameless inner confusions &

conflicts. Confess you spend nearly as much mental energy raging against the things you hate as cultivating the qualities you love.

The framework has been laid of the science of the study of man – Freud & Jung & Adler – like the opposing sides of a triangle contribute to its finding. Only the last, I think, has written things of use to the layman – in seeking to solve his own personal problems. Without a basic understanding of the physiology of the human nervous and endocrine system, the amazing interaction of "mind" and "body" [as though there were such entities!] the effects of various experiences upon emotional & intellectual growth of multifarious tricks of the perfectly normal mind to escape the unpleasant – projections, identification, substitutions – without these basic concepts – your introspections are about as reliable as the separate dissertations of the blind men on the anatomy of the elephant!

Listen, Brother, I spent years reading & thinking and trying to understand this confusing world and my place in it – and the ignominious contradictions of our own nature. Whatever it was that you seemed somehow grateful for in my being around last August – you may credit to those women-years of searching and effort (and being of feminine gender – not a few tears in the night.)

Could you please tell me something definite about the eye? – When mother remarks – "I see you got a letter from the Lone Ranger today. How is the eye?" – I'd like something sensible to say.

No – I'm staying put – doing some sewing and gardening during the holiday week after Easter. I'm only a working girl, you know – and may not even be that if I take Professor Shelford's offer to come back. It's very kind of your landed-gentryship to offer us shelter tho. How about the last of June or the first week in July? There is a biological station in West Virginia I'd like to revisit. If she stands that much and gets rested up at your place – I hope to go a little ways into the Maine woods – and the Mount Washington area. After you show me the glories of Arden – maybe we could induce you to join us. We may camp out a few times – even to visit the old homestead, alas! Perhaps your books could spare you for a few days.

♥

Really Fred – I'm rather proud of you – tho I won't admit it. There's so much more to you than the usual spoiled child I was prepared for. You changed a lot since Chicago – and not – I think – for the worse.

Really – I must write those midsemesters now – you shouldn't be so distracting.

Please forgive me if I've erred – but I practically promised Helen (Albany, late of Chicago, Manila, Nagasaki – etc) that you'd call next time you go to see the MD. Like Miss Prigge she is one of the world's treasures. If you can explain to her the beauties of nature as a scientist sees them you'll do better than I ever could. Tell me how you like her. Copy this down <u>NOW</u> 435 W 119th St. Apt 3C, New York 27, N.Y.

A student interrupted his reading. This one was a pleasure. Bill McKibben was busily writing another book, mostly at his home in Ripton, on what was once part of the Robert Frost homestead, and couldn't spare him the time to advise him on his particular independent study. McKibben's position as resident scholar allowed, but did not require, supervision of undergraduates on their flights of fancy, so he had sent him instead to Dan. Dan had piled enough suggestions on the student, he thought, to keep him busy to the end of the semester, but he had come back the next week with all the information digested and organized, with copies of especially relevant articles on hand. Dan had then suggested a computer program, "app" as the student called it, to work out green trade-offs that had Dan thinking for certain that he would never see him again. And here he was, back with something that worked.

It made Dan realize how lucky he was to have landed where he was after a succession of semi-employments as researcher or adjunct or administrator. All were temporary. Many were at places he never would have once considered. Somebody had definitely smiled down at him and he did not care who it had been, although he greatly suspected that the hikes he took with McKibben in the Adirondacks and the Long Trail may have had something to do with it. Strange, how that had come about. Someone Dan did not know had recommended him to McKibben as someone who could help him with a book he was considering. The book never happened, but a friendship blossomed. Now they were colleagues. At any rate, luck or whatever had plucked him from the intellectual wasteland of Green Mountain College and deposited him where an undergraduate could take an idea from him and run with it past where Dan could have taken it himself.

With a great sense of smugness, Dan abandoned his office in what was officially Bicentennial Hall, but was soon to become McArdle Hall, and was referred to by all as the Science Building. He favored the library. His was a comfortable office, impressive even, with its third-floor view of the hills to the north of campus, but it was, after all, an office, a place of work. He did not go downstairs to the science library, however, but took his laptop all the way across campus to the brand new Main Library. Where his office was comfortable, the upstairs reading area in the library to which he headed was luxurious, especially when he sunk into a soft, new chair in front of the tall picture windows that looked out at the hills to the south. He imagined he could see into the mountains above Bristol to where there was a farmhouse that he might make an offer on. It was in Lincoln, another quaint, tiny town full of charm—and potters and artists and writers and, soon maybe, an ecologist.

And where both office and library in the Science Building cried "Work!" in his mind, his sanctuary here whispered "relax." He quickly found the next letter from Küchler in the chronology of the correspondence and enlarged it almost before looking at it.

I went for the mail today – the first time in perhaps over a week. Though I was very glad to get a letter from you, my conscience bothered me: I trust this note may make a bit of amend. In brief, I did not go back to the hospital (tho recommended to do so by Dr. C.); and I am in the fourth week of having men working through the house on a ceiling and wall-papering job.

Your letter of the last day of March has been picked up many a time for answering. I confess very frankly that it had me buffaloed in several ways. Plainly, I was stumped to answer it; and each time put it aside waiting for a more inspired moment – which such moment never arrived. I certainly look forward to discussing several points in that letter, personally, not by correspondence. I am quite sure there is much room for agreement where we appear to disagree; and I am equally sure that my command of quality and quantity in the English language, and my foresight of your reactions to it, are not sufficient to ward off further inappropriate connotations.

Apparently my "escape" to the woods, away from society, you take to be a sort of flight from reality. Am I not correct in believing that the life that you value is that of being a daily-acting cog in a daily-acting social mechanism, regardless of whether you fully believe in the principle of that mechanism? I grant that that is one kind of good life. At the end of each and every day one feels that he has ground through so many useful coggy revolutions. I have chosen to take a gamble on the whole (rest) of my life. This time it is to win all or lose all. Would mankind not have lost some of its finest contributions if it had forced Thoreau into schoolroom teaching, instead of letting him live his two years at Walden Pond? Would you have preferred Donald Culross Peattie to be confined to a botany lectureship instead of expanding into what may be a literary immortality of far greater value than the endless array of formas and varietate of a Fernald or a Merrill, or routine administrative duties of deans and chancellors? And, to complete the proposition, would you not prefer to lose to obscurity 49 mediocre ex-professors in order to have one Peattie? Whether or not something comes of my life here is not for you or me to say, or even this generation. I will gladly take my place with 49 others of similar status, if I believe one of us will contribute to our cultural heritage.

As for the eye, I feel no handicap with my present cyclopean existence, the thought of another hospital and post-hospital-N.Y. siege at this season is unpleasant, and since such an operation can be done at any time, I am postponing the matter indefinitely. The first anniversary of the affair will soon be around, and when I think what it might have been without you, I still react almost as violently as I did ten months ago.

I felt pleased and honored that you should ask me to go up into the White Mts. with you and your mother. I assume the trip is postponed for the time now, but I will say, Jewel, that I probably would have begged off with a reasonable excuse. It is time for another confession: while a professor I always had an answer of too much professional duty. Perhaps you will understand when I say that I have taken no "vacation" since receiving my first degree, and perhaps earlier. Tho I have traveled muchly, each trip had definite value, towards, some book, some research paper or in some other professional obligation. I have been "working" at least 8 hours a day and will continue to do so. If I am prevented from doing so, I have a strong feeling of not having lived socially worthily and constructively that day. I hope you understand.

I h<u>ave</u> taken down Helen Moore's address, and I <u>will</u> look her up on the first occasion. I have been to N.Y. twice since receiving that letter: each time for overnight only. Since all my business correspondence still goes to 625, those evenings are very full.

News of your mother was so very disheartening – for her and for you. Please give her my best wishes for recovery I do hope she makes a better and better patient.

But please tell me more of your auto accident. Since you say the family do not know about it, I assume you are not the party to be bashed up. I do hope you did not suffer too much, nor that the matter is too heavy on the purse. I assure you that one's first escapade is the hardest to bear in secret (tho perhaps you know that).

I'll be waiting for information about the bail. No joking: phone me if I can be of any help.

I still hope you can get to Arden Forest, early. Do you want a special invitation, by date and time?

The house is giving me a job and a half, for all rooms were stripped of all furnishings, curtains, shades, and even doors. I will certainly qualify as charwoman after this experience. The writing of course has dropped out entirely for the time being. What few free minutes I have have been spent outside, on a very small garden, and on my brush-killing project with 2-4-D (2-4-dichlorohydroxy-acetic acid), a really miraculous chemical.

The events of the world after VJ day have been far different from what I hoped and anticipated. I was slightly pessimistic at the end of the war; but the way the nations have acted since then can only give reason for hope to those pathetic escaping individuals who, mounting the scaffold, look forward to life, even if it is in death. Perhaps that is the best way after all.

The lilies are now in full bloom. Try to get here for the laurel.

He had been too long away from the letters, Dan realized. Much confused him now. His conjecture that—telephones having long before been invented—he was not getting the whole story of the two from letters might explain some of the confusion. And somehow, the letters seemed not so interesting any more. That about 2-4-D he already knew from other correspondence. What, he wondered had so interested him originally? Was it only that they were from his Aunt Jewel? Was that still reason enough to plod through them?

Yes, he answered the question and went on to the next letter.

Our Sabbath peace here, with the family out of town for the day, is probably exceeded only by your own. It's a beautiful sunny day – cool indoors, brilliantly green outside - thanks to the ample water supply our city affords. Things were so dry when I arrived – I ran the hose pretty much steadily for 3 or 4 days. A family of killdeer adopted our lawn – and were pretty outspoken in their resentment of my daily intrusions to weed and cultivate. It seemed strange to see them teetering about this tiny patch of grass on their high heels – or walking up and down the sidewalk scolding.

But – to go back a week – Perhaps it was la tristesse occasioned by necessity for leaving your lovely hills too soon – but it took only the glimpse of Gus the Ghost – drifting across my path – to throw me into such panic – and me scuttling backward like a frightened crayfish to your door. I knew that every instruction regarding the roads dropped from my mind. I visualized myself – turning endless corners – cloaked by Gus'es myriad misty fellow wraiths – till my graham crackers and gasoline gave out – the map was very reassuring.

Did I thank you for your perfect hospitality? – You have that rare gift of making people feel at home – on the instant – I know I shall be grateful to you a thousand times in the cluttered days to come for the memory of those lovely spots – your trail – the view from the top of the field – the waterfall – the Stephen Foster melodies – Yet undoubtedly the things which give me most delight of all – are those qualities in you – which you permitted me to sense clearly the first time. Oui – je suis tres content de vous – mon ami.

My usual luck was with me - all the way home. When my fan belt broke – it was the top of a ½ mile down grade – and I coasted down to a little garage that had one then right size in stock After spending Mon. night by Momma Atkins' waterfall in Ithaca I drove straight home – The roads through Canada are so straight & empty

I didn't mind the 550 miles at all – It was broken by dinner – an hour off for a quiet little man to listen to my tale of the gearshift that refused to go into anything but reverse – took out a worn rubber ring from the clutch housing, that resembled a stepped on doughnut – and replaced it with a piece of rubber heel or something – and lo – all was smooth – and forward again - At sunset I turned up a nearly vertical driveway into a stony little graveyard – completely hidden from the road by pines – and munched cheese and crackers – and drank tea – and watched the goldfinches and swallows – and felt very mellow indeed. Yes it was a good trip – one of the very best — One thing tho – please promise me if any unpleasant comment threatens to reach your parents regarding my visit that you will let me know. I think I could so word a note of apology – as to give them a few rebuttal points – facts you would probably be too chivalrous to use. They certainly do not deserve to be annoyed by that sort of thing.

I found Mother stronger than when I left – She now sits in a chair a few minutes each morning and afternoon – Today I pulled her on a little rocker into the living room – for the first time in four weeks. You would be appalled at the dishes we accumulated in a day – and weeds – This rich loam grows Portulaca olearacea with a three-foot wing spread. I've chopped out bushels and bushels with a dull hoe. – But Sis canned my raspberries – and the tomatoes will soon be ripening

Strange to have Momma Atkins pop up like that, he thought, looking away to a storm building over the mountains. She was the grandmother he had longed for throughout most of his childhood. Then she had disappointed him painfully. That had not been until he was at Cornell and could trudge on foot to that Tioga Street house of hers. He found more welcome on its front doormat than within. She introduced herself as if to a stranger. She called him Daniel, rather than Danny. Six years almost he had spent at Ithaca, yet that uncomfortable twenty minutes had been their only meeting. Nothing could be learned from her—or Aunt Jewel, later—about why there had not been cards or visits, especially in the days when he had only his Aunt Jewel for family. Jimmy, as she referred to him, rather than "your father," had learned to sail on Cayuga with friends who were faculty brats, she had been willing to reveal. After that, there was no way he was going to work at Ithaca Guns, alongside her and his dad. He decided to become a fisherman, instead, and moved away. Nothing could be drawn out of her beyond that.

But things look up for Jewel back there in 1946, Daniel decided. Even though he had difficulty reading between the lines, his overall impression of the signs was good. A visit was a visit. But what could have gone on?

"Tres content?" Formal.
"Unpleasant comments?" Over what?
"Word a note of apology?" Difficult to make that out.
What did Küchler have to be chivalrous about?
Why not just read on?

However strong your thoughts about my silence, I accept them all without rebuttal. I ain't got no apology. In whatever shape fate decides to mold me, I am sure it will not be in such a form. (Time out to try to identify a ladybug: no go.) Many times all summer and fall I ask myself "Shall I write a letter? Or shall I read Plato, Confucius, Plutarch, or a science text?" Reading always wins out, after a one-sided argument. I have been most shamefully negligent in letting you know that your visit was a bright spot in the summer, all too small and that the volume of poetry was extremely appreciated and much used – and is being used.

Lest my thoughtfulness go on and on – I hereby ask that you pay Arden a visit come next July – or earlier – and let it be more than a spot. As to whether my parents would mind, or the townspeople. The former do not and the latter do not know since I have no neighbors within earshot or eyeshot. Mother and Dad acquiesce in everything I do. Tho they must require some conceptual distortions, apparently their own moral standards, and my actions, somehow get harnessed together, and trot off as a reasonably unskilled sully. As I look back now, I fear I was ungratefully inarticulate in recalling the events of which that time was the first anniversary. Your daily moral support, supplemented by cherries and all other sorts of good things, during that hospital siege – darn it, it still leaves me inarticulate...And I wish words could come to me about those times past you forced me to remember.

As to the Verse – the volume has stayed in my car. My education in poetry is sadly deficient. Influenced by the little music I know, I look for rhythm, rhyme, and architectural structure. The babblings of Gertrude Stein, and the spatterings of recent art are perfectly interesting as a babble and a spatter – but life can be richer.

I wonder how this fall at school has treated you. With what little I know of the group of teachers you must be with, I admire your ability to fit in with a crowd over whom you certainly must tower.

I'll hope to hear that your Mother has been well – not only for her sake – but for that of the daughter.

November 24th marked the close of my first year in the woods. As for my previous colleagues, I see them in quite a new light. Plant taxonomists in particular are a strange breed of psychologic abnormality, pigeon-holing themselves in a dark corner, which I do not find good company. I react most strongly to the two-facedness which I see my ex-colleagues practicing all the time; I react not definitely to inefficiency, and the lack of a wish to rectify it, I must believe in the job I am doing. Call it intolerance if you wish. Yet I guess I am not wholly immune to the praises I've left behind. I am not quite yet big enough to accept being a "nobody", without position, title, standing. Several times I've considered taking a position. Fortunately, I get back my senses in time.

With it all, I am actually being considered for a part-time (2-day) teaching position at the Univ. of Connecticut, Waterbury branch, to which I could commute. In visiting that Univ., in connection with a state Vegetation Bibliography, they jumped me with the offer. I thought it over. I do like to teach, but the motives are vastly different than those which incent my old forestry students. There the values were solely in the form of producing more trees, to produce more lumber, to produce more houses and more pulp magazines, to make living more comfortable, to produce more children, who would demand more lumber and start the blasted process again. Such material wants, under the guise of "standard of living" get us nowhere. Wanting is a psychological problem, not a physiological necessity. But with a liberal arts background, teaching might be different. Let those who wish teach knowledge for its practical value and use. The pleasure of knowledge for its own sake, in this age or in ancient Greece, can solve more of the practical problems of humanity than the development of atomic power for industry. But I turned the job down, on the excuse of salary and title.

Now they are reconsidering. My uppermost hope is that they do not come through with another offer; I would not know how to turn it down. The idea of getting up early on a winter morning, walking to the state road (eastwards, not westwards), taxi to Winsted, bus to Waterbury; overnight in a hotel; city clothes and all the time and money that go into them; to rant before a group of "students" undoubtedly incapable of grasping the value of knowledge other than its relation to grades, courses, and degrees, it all has little appeal, other than that shameful desire, which I hope to outgrow, of again having a recognized standing among people whose values I do not too well respect anyway. And so life goes on. I admit that in winter the hills of New England are a far cry from the Everglade and the bird islands of the Pacific. At the same time, there is a wealth of mosses, fungi algae, insects, other invertebrate, minerals which are crying to be known. Would you not care to live with some of it for several days? I'm quite sure you would fit in to my routine of: desk work until 1; afternoons out and on maintenance; evenings with non-botanical books."

Since Küchler did not answer her letter right away, then nothing untoward probably took place, Daniel decided. All that circumspection in Aunt Jewel's letter must have been about appearances only. Sexual mores were so different back then. Not that people were not having sex. Somehow, though, Dan expected that flowers and a note or letter would have been almost waiting for Jewel on her return to Detroit had there been something between them.

Or had there been? Would they have written about it? Possibilities drew him to the next letter in the sequence.

He had named the files badly, he realized to his chagrin. Instead of being arranged chronologically, as the originals had been, the file names appeared on his screen in alphabetical order. The letter from Küchler he had just read, "K to F 3 Dec 46," was followed "K to F 7 Apr 50." It had made sense at the time he was doing his scans, but now he had to look through all the files to pick out which letter in 1946—or maybe 1947— followed that one.

Surprise! Not even time for a semi-annual report! This time, I can thank you for a gift within a socially respectable period of time. *I am really pleased, Jewel, not only for the chance to get to know Frost, but to have the volume from you, and to have your guiding check-marks as a personal steer. I received recently a copy of Mark Van Doren, by one who perhaps also thought I had, or should have, a bit of poetry in my life. My present premature reaction to some of the poems is that they are rather beautifully worded prose, about ideas as light and significant as a summer breeze.*

Before I forget again: Stanley Cain is now botanist at Cranbrook. By all means introduce yourself when you get out there again. I shall probably have occasion to write him in the near future, and shall say that you may stop in. I do not know what he thinks of me, if anything at all – but his comments should interest you, against the background of your better knowledge of me.

Let me assure you that there is only one true science of ecology in the US – the study of communities (ecosystems). Animals too, as in Shelford's studies, but plants are what determine where animals will be. C. C. Adams rote a book he called Animal Ecology before either of us were born – but it had to do mainly with sampling methods. Adams was trained as a plant ecologist.

Darn it – you speak so convincingly of the kick one can get out of teaching, you almost make me wish I was back in the field – that is – until the train of thought leads back to the enjoyment I received out of catalyzing certain graduate students, and then leads on for them to a destination I had not anticipated. Unlike you I cannot comfortably enjoy the activities of a nest of fledglings in a hay field, knowing the mowing machine will destroy them tomorrow.

The winter so far has been quite successful. Rather a lively place. Deer track all over the land. My porcupine (down by the ledges I took you to is thoroly wrecking a tall hemlock tree – but that is his privilege. A fox walked past the other day. An ermine was in front of the kitchen door when I walked in this morning. A mouse insists on eating all the bird seed I put out in the shelter – even in broad daylight. So now I have some hanging gadgets for the chickadees. White-winged crossbills are rather frequent at the forest edge. And desk work has finally worked up speed. I usually start in the morning while it is still pitch dark. A short 2,4-D article is out looking for a publisher; the Conn. Veg. Bibliogr. is finished; the long

Oahu ms. is all done (on the fire for 10 years); the Chile article is almost finished; I start very soon on the Martinique article.

But perhaps Martinique will not go so quickly. The Univ of Conn job is maturing. They have come through with practically all my requests. The only bug now is that the offer is contingent on my accepting the same work for Hartford also (originally for the Waterbury college). But the Botany Dept. head in the same letter indicates his dislike of the request, as it would be too expensive of my time. And the contingency only indicates that they have no one else for that Hartford job. The text book is stymied. I seem to have stepped quite out of the contemporary ecologic picture; feel entirely independent of the impressions or reactions of those contemporaries (there are only a <u>small</u> handful, whose opinions I would respect and would be of concern to me). My field is the next century. I am more concerned in constructing something that will be serviceable in <u>that</u> period, than in using the well-known and easily-applied techniques for impressing the living.

Mebbe Rogers had the same thing in mind when he wrote the music for the Warrior – world premier on the Met radio broadcast today. It did not strike home here. Sounded like melodically pitched recitative, with a thin dissonant musical background. Time will tell.

Stanley Cain? That was a name not on Dan's radar. He was only vaguely familiar with it. In what context, he could not remember. He googled Cain and found out from an obituary that he had been Assistant Secretary of the Interior for Fish, Wildlife, and Parks in the Johnson administration. There was also a short list of references to his botanical studies. *Foundations of Geography* caught his eye. He made a mental note to see if he could find it on campus. That Cain had obtained his PhD from Chicago made Dan suspect that he had come upon another student of Henry Cowles of one sort or another.

Then he realized that, right in his hands, he had the tool to see if the library had a copy of Cain's book. He clicked to the MIDCAT and discovered that yes, they did. A sixty-year-old textbook and it was still in the library, in the Science Building.

Never did I more thoroly welcome a quiet Sunday afternoon. Following the January thaw came a series of northers that dumped snow on us. Before we got that disposed of it alternately rained + sleeted all night. The resulting porrige consisting of ice pellets – from 6 in to 2 ft. thick was the last word in friction elimination. A shovel – buckets of ashes – rag rugs are now standard equipment. Next night the crust froze so hard I can now drive + park on top of it.

New term starts tomorrow. How hopefully we scan the new faces each first day – searching for the gleam of intelligence and flash of wit - yea – even for the eager beaver who will cheerfully keep our attendance records – and keep the goldfish from starving.

We may have some excitement before spring. The local A.F.L-affiliated Teachers union is suggesting a strike vote. So you may next hear of me impaled upon a picket line. They have cause for grouching of course – a promised raise failed to come thru – married men are all working at outside jobs – inc. G.I. night classes. While I want to strike – I'll refuse to sign a contract in the spring – if that is decided upon as appropriate action.

This is the season for gazing at the glorious exaggerations in the garden catalogues. This has turned me against a floribunda (rose) called summer snow – by another name it would to me be sweeter.

I hope I shall have occasion to meet your friend Dr. Cain. I'm curious to know what he has that, alone of all men in the world, has caused my modest friend Freddie to say of him "He's a better man than I am" – only ecologically speaking, of course. The two mentions in the Cranbrook bulletin he's had – tell of his making amusing animal forms out of leaves – (for kindergarten supervisors) – and some adventure in numerology – in spacing leaf buds on stems. Sounds like a very versatile genius. Hope I meet him.

I wonder if you are still companion to the porcupine and ermine, or do the bobbysoxers and boyfriends sit in rapt attention at your feet; or in spite of your loathing for human society would you be filling your pockets with the resulting green husks said to be the fare of the bureaucrats in the far country of Washington.

Would you like to see your Aunt Jewel in greasepaint - behind footlights? In mid March – she flutters on and off stage as the Grand Duchess Katrina – late of Russia – now Childs Restaurant – waitress. The more frivolous of our faculty are rehearsing for 2 nights of "You can't take it with you" – an escapist plot - in which everyone indulges in his hobby with religious zeal.

Had to smile at your phrase (re S. Cain) – "Your better knowledge of me." My curious anomaly, you might be one of H.G. Wells "selenites" for all I comprehend of what makes you tick. You should never stir outside your door unaccompanied by explanatory notes in 3 languages.

Good night, my dear, and pleasant dreams to you, and thoroly astounding relatives.

The next time he came back to Jewel's letters was unintentional. It was J-Term, Middlebury's academic solution to an economic problem. Normal winter break left dorms and classrooms empty, but heating systems continued to operate through the coldest weeks of the year. Way back in the nineteen-sixties, someone had a brilliant idea. Have a January term. Ski-Term, it quickly came to be called by many, though not unkindly. Everyone was happy. Dollars were not wasted to heat empty buildings. Students could go to class in the morning, ski in the afternoon, and study at night. Much drunken (and herbal) revelry was avoided. And that had been at the height of the protest era. All manner of brief academic flights of fancy were launched. Useful investigations of racism, colonialism, feminism, and other –isms were carried out alongside those of ancient tapestries, wool making and weaving, and the theory and practice of living in a yurt.

This year, Dan loved the concept—he had no teaching duties. There was an overabundance of faculty willing to lead students through photography, writing, music, or some work a professor had been meaning to read. Skiing, meanwhile, had become institutionalized as a physical education credit.

Dan plunged deeply into the letters between Küchler and one Helmut K. Buechner. Hal Buechner was a one-time student of Küchler at Syracuse forestry who became a lifelong friend to him. (Dan was surprised that there had been so many such friends for the cantankerous old windbag: Fosberg, Buechner, Murray Buell, Bill Niering, Mason Hale, to name only the ecologists. Unsurprising, except for viciousness, were some of the attacks on him that Küchler shared with his friends. On finding the following, Dan printed it out to share with friends.

"I was not at all surprised to find that your letter to Dr. Parr was written in your usual inimitable style," the letter to Küchler began, innocently enough, "that is, without reference to thought, accuracy, facts, understanding or any indication of many traits inherent in the average analytical, objective, scientific mind.

"In my humble opinion your letter does, however, serve admirably in two respects. First and foremost it tenders your resignation from the Museum. Secondly it verifies my opinion of you personally and your published works, both of which I have had an opportunity to scrutinize first hand.

"I find nothing that is either thought provoking or savory in your communication to Dr. Parr and in my opinion your behavior, lack of understanding and insight is as much to be pitied as censured."

Küchler, it was clear, kept copies of it to share with his friends. It was from Mont Cazier, who will be remembered longer, perhaps, for tolerating the bite of a brown recluse spider in order to then report on the progress of symptoms. Brown recluse bites result in a disfiguring ulceration that can last for months. Occasionally, renal failure can occur. Apparently, the spider was intimidated by Cazier and had first to be "restrained" then "prodded" repeatedly to get it to bite.

And in those Buechner letters, Dan made a shockingly surprising discovery about an ecological icon. It was shocking, because he should not have been surprised. Hal Buechner and Robert Whittaker had been colleagues at the State College of Washington at Pullman, Washington. Both came in as brand new faculty members.

You pictured Bob alright! He has a brilliant mind and he is a cultured person. Likes good music and often came over for an evening of records. His overbearing conceit got him in trouble around Pullman repeatedly. Hatch thinks well of him. Bob gave the zoology lectures in the integrated course before I took over. We still recognize his difficulties in getting along with people.

Strangely enough, Bob, despite his brilliant mind, is not getting along too well with the faculty. He is too dogmatic and radical in his thinking. He has done some fine work, but he sets himself up as a dogmatic authority in the field of ecology. His attitude is not appreciated. I probably understand him better than any other member of our staff, yet even I cannot tolerate too much of him.

He suffers some psychological difficulties stemming from recognition of his superior intelligence, and he has been taking psychiatric advice. Bob feels he is a top man in his field and that he does not receive sufficient recognition. He certainly needs some help, and I believe he will respond well if he gets the right kind of encouragement. He has adjusted himself to society with remarkable improvement since I first knew him.

Lots of fireworks between Bob and Daubie over Bob's brilliant abstract work on gradient analysis showing that populations of plants are distributed independently. He does not throw out the community concept but objects violently to what he calls the 'association-unit' concept. He says ecologists have focused too much attention on the center of the community and overlooked (for convenience) the things that they do not wish to see in the transitions or ecotones. You will be much interested in the paper when it comes out. He has made a splash that Daubie and others turn their cheeks away from.

They were not colleagues for long. Whittaker was fired from what Dan imagined must have been an inconsequential little institution. The wildlife ecologists had gathered to it only for the opportunity to study western wildlife and rangeland that it presented.

Bob is and always will be a good friend of mine – one whom I will always admire. But I had developed such awe for his brilliance that it had resulted in adding considerably to my inferiority complex. I felt very insignificant and lost confidence in my own ideas. He told me repeatedly that he had accomplished more in one summer of his research in the Smokies than most ecologists could accomplish in 10 years. He was at his worst when he first came – blunt, overbearing, overly self-confident, rude, glorying in his wonderful ability to debate and make Daubie look silly. Eastlick welcomed the opportunity to get rid of him when the staff cut came in 1951.

That letter had marginal notations in blue ink: "He improved considerably before he left," and "Married at Xmas time."

Dan realized from the letters that both thought that having been fired from Pullman so that he had to find work with GE in nearby Richland, where he was little more tolerated, Whittaker had then buried himself forever at Brooklyn College. Küchler thought it "quite appropriate. Those city colleges seem to favor intellectual misfits."

Little did they know.

Then there was a jolt in a letter to Buechner in 1946.

"Strangely," Küchler wrote, "the gentle sex is the one to have first invaded these precincts of Adam."

Jewel? Dan wondered. "Several hundred miles" in the next sentence could be the right distance for Jewel. But no. The dates were close, but not properly aligned. Küchler's letter to Beuchner preceded Jewel's visit. Unless he meant her visit to the hospital. But no. That did not jibe with remarks about "Norfolk" and "same taxi man" that followed. Sorting all that out, however, brought him back to Jewel's letters, which he started to read once more, still very compulsively in chronological order.

It's Easter Sunday – floods are receding, the sun is a miracle after the months we've been through. I'm watching wind ripples race across the temporary lake that was strawberry bed and corn patch, - and nibbling at custard for my innards' sake.

I'm writing to you for conscience's sake about my last epistle to you. I'm not going to take the easy way of hoping you were too busy or engrossed in new activities to absorb or notice its venom. I hereby apologize, unconditionally.

It was Walt Whitman who shouted "I got a zoo – I got a menagerie underneath my ribs!" Who hasn't? Most of us have a sufficiently hard time keeping the animals in some semblance of order without interference from outside. Maybe one of the beasts does get out of line sometimes, but it doesn't help to have some nincompoop heave a brick at him. I hereby forswear meddling. Kick me next time I forget.

Poor Mom – another Easter – and no chance to wear the bonnet intended for last year. She was on her feet after a Penicillin checked chest infection – when I brought home a new bug.

After reading a very asinine French 'roman', and a mystery tale of international intrigue I got into a good book. Have you read any of Oliver LeFarge's stuff? Of course I don't know his technical work in anthropology and ethnology, but he is a rare raconteur. This "Raw Material" – Houghton-Mifflin – '45 is snatches of autobiography –stuff that can't be fitted into his fiction frames. It has the authentic ring of the honest reporter of his own adolescence and later struggles with childhood inspired fears. I liked his lines —

"Art is the expression of something one has seen that is bigger then oneself. ... — ... The thing seen is bigger than the man – and the intention to communicate is more important than himself. The result is that the artist becomes – if he is an artist – bigger than himself and his work outshines his own small fallible being. – So we come back again to character, in this case, the ability to devote oneself to something sincerely felt to be more important than oneself. ..." And I found myself thinking that Fred – more than anyone else I know has that kind of character – that ability to discipline himself to devote himself. I feel that he is not yet sure of the thing seen which is – etc ... Someday soon- I hope – he will see clearly the channel his energies must take.

Then I was deeply ashamed of that vicious verbal kick in the shins. It was inexcusable – and quite incomprehensible – except in terms of vengeance for a very old hurt. I've traced it back to correspondence of several years ago. Your criticism of Dr. Nichols cut me – unreasonably. You see, Uncle George had become for me a symbol (sentimental of course) But after my father's death in '36 – I began to realize how his affection for and pride in me had been an unrecognized cement in the security of the foundations of my life. Dr. Nichols was so kindly, I hung the frame of the Benevolent Fatherly Person about him – and venerate him.

When people do inexplicable things, Fred, it is nearly always from deeply buried emotional motivations. Be generous with me and tell me what goes on with you. I'm collecting geological information about our newest National Park – Isle Royale. Four of us have acquired army sleeping bags and are preparing to camp out in the wilderness for a week next summer. I hope a moose doesn't step on us.

Did everything get published? – Are you a college professor or a bureaucrat – or a woman hating hermit in April 1947 –

> *Your*
> *Jewel*
> *In the very rough*

"Conscience sake?" The "last epistle" was harmless, Danny was certain on reading it. There was nothing that needed apology for.

Was there a letter missing? Not saved on purpose? Several letters? What else might not have been saved?

"Vengeance for a very old hurt?" Dr. Nichols?

Well, it's not like he was writing a biography of Aunt Jewel, after all, Dan thought. Maybe he should not be wasting his time with these letters. Maybe he should use the time for his book project.

But how many times had he already decided that? Besides, he was curious about Küchler's reply.

> *I'll start writing to the strains of a Hayden symphony and the NBC Symphony- but I am sure I will finish in silence, after several vain whirlings of the radio dial. Six o'clock marks the end of good radio music, except for WQXR which today is not coming in well.*
>
> *I really sh<u>ou</u>ld be writing you, even without the added incentive of your two letters. You see, this is the time you are planning your summer sojourning. I'd like to put in a plug boosting this corner of the country. I do wish you would pay a visit to Norfolk this summer. There are several places in the state I need to visit; perhaps you would do so with me. And if you could stay several days, or weeks, I can assure you that I would not bother you too much: the books and the Forest and the country-side are eager to play host to you.*
>
> *I am very glad you told me, Jewel, about Dr. Nichols. I should have had wits enough to guess as such, for I certainly sensed that you were not telling me everything. An apology now would sound false. May I say however that I can well sympathize with the trouble I caused; Dr. Meier (Syracuse forestry botany head) was all that to me, and perhaps more. But in this case, Dr. Meier was not the man I thought he was. To this day I cannot forgive him for – and actively resent him for – not living up to my ideal also. And I hate*

myself for being the last one in the college to see thru his sham. It is strange how I cling to that ideal of what I thought he was and only censure him for not fulfilling it.

Yes, I took the Univ of Connecticut position. Suddenly I find myself professor again. Twice a week I commute to Waterbury, for a "day" which often lasted overnight. Transportation was often rather rugged. I left my car in Norfolk village, so as always to have it available for inter-city transportation on the state highways. That meant 11 miles of walking each day (5.5 miles to Norfolk), and some of those days were the kind that a hoimnut like myself likes to stay home with his slippers on. I am not sure why I like the work. It would be easy to say that it allows me to do my share in society – or some such. Or perhaps I find it valuable as practice speaking English. But like most professors, I probably find a glory in the title, in the prestige it gives among laymen, in the self-assurance it gives to handle a class, and other such egotistic factors. Despite our agreement at the beginning they now want me for next year, one or both semesters. Of course, I'd be hurt if they did not; but still, I want to go south for part of the next winter; and winter is the only time I can do so.

No, I've missed all of Oliver Le Farge – would not even have known he was an anthropologist. I'll see what the library has of his books.

Your Easter apology for the venom of your earlier letter had me absorbed all day – until I could get out that earlier letter. Alas, I could remember no venom, just some good cracks which were perfectly applicable. And now that I've checked for venom, I really cannot see anything that is not deserved. I much fear that, any day you really want to cut deep, the blade must be handled with evil intent. And even then, if you hit a vulnerable spot, I'd blame it on the vulnerability. I'd feel no worse than those times when people (in China, C.A., and other places) took me for Russian, mulatto, or what-not. If I look that way, then I do; and so what?

I've had a good chance since February to get a look at the profession I left. Not only in actual teaching. I've had reason to contact most universities within two hundred miles, including Yale and Harvard; and I've had first hand contacts with Presidents and Provosts and other such pedestaled personages. No, I'll stick to active retirement. So you do not think that is the proper chance for *my energies? Perhaps I am n<u>o</u>t energetic. And what is to be considered "proper"? I am reasonably sure that you judge in conventional accepted statuses in society. But I am not at all concerned with such a status: it involves too many concessions and would put me on a diet of skimmed milk, instead of this country dream. During the past 12 months I have begun to grow again. It seems I've left my professor days far behind. And as I visit my professional confreres, I feel quite alien to them. Each day is a pleasure: each witnesses some forward steps. What will come of it all? I do not know; I care less; I'll gamble on some result, rather than take the sterile drudgery of a routine existence. I have enough to write right now for the next five years - tho to get them published will be another problem. How much easier it would be if I'd learn more and more about less and less, and become an authoritative specialist, and write in the expected idiom.*

Word of your mother's illness I was sorry to have. Please give her my best wishes, and say that I shall hope that she can be here too this summer for a visit.

Baked potatoes should be ready now. Time for dinner. And then to some Hindu scriptures for the evening (when I should be studying my botany for class tomorrow).

The letters, Dan noted, once frequent, had become yearly affairs. Only a few were left for him to read. Even Jewel was tardy with her replies.

It's Friday night, and I've retired – before sunset, to p.j.s and peace. Trouble with a typewriter is – you can not know the luxury of writing letters in bed. I've been looking forward all week to time for a chat with you.

Such a busy month it is. Last weekend – 200 miles north to Hazel's cottage on Higgins Lake – 8 inches of snow marked the former huge drifts. Trailing arbutus in the bog woods – black and white warblers – an evening grosbeak (first I ever saw) thousands of juncos giving our weeds a farewell peck.

This weekend – report cards and a family conclave – next – taking 10 youngsters to the student campout at Walden – some 50 miles away.

☼

Who said I didn't approve of the way you're spending your energies? <u>Will</u> you stop putting words into my mouth? Your present regimen sounds perfect – making the best of both worlds. So it's Hindu scriptures now. I recall being vastly if not vaguely thrilled by them – as interpreted by the poems of Tagore. "— For I know that my heart would open like a flower — That my life has filled itself at a hidden fountain." If only we could implement oriental thought with the firm vitamin-rich actualities of occidental action.

Happiness becomes you, my dear. Fortunately it's contagious. Thanks for passing it on.

Thank you, too, for the invitation to sojourn in Norfolk. I really couldn't – though it sounds delightful. I'd not take the risk again – even though you supplied an ever-so-starchy-and-respectable chaperone. Perhaps I shall shock you once more, my friend, - you have such weird artificial notions about ♀. To you they are either barmaids – or ladies. Too bad you always emphasize in human relations the differences between people rather than seeking the generic similarities. [Adler should say that this is the curse of every 2nd child – who must measure himself anxiously against an elder brother – it becomes an idée fixe.] Be assured that the face you sound so glumly resigned about is quite adequate. This spinster was startled once more, on more than one occasion, by certain cardiac manifestations directly traceable to awareness of it elements of beauty. – Most recently when she should have been keeping her mind on applying properly – a bandage to a damaged optic.

No, no, me lad. It's school mar'm I am now. And I'll not be reduced again to a palpitating mass of quivering jelly by graceful hands, and suave voices, or even young men who stride up and down interminable hills like pagan gods. Be off with ye!

My small (26) Biol. (1) class was in fine form yesterday – watching protozoa for the first time. You'd like Duane – a little fellow – who always reminds me of a new-hatched chick. He's all golden fuzz and blue-eyed wonder. There's a marvelous satisfaction in just being there to meet those eyes when they lift in entranced excitement from first views of that micro-world.

In another class is Jane – who's going to be a <u>really</u> good biology teacher – and Jack. Jack's parents were divorced – and Jack lived with his Dad. He came home one night + discovered him dead – of coronary thrombosis. Now he's living with his mother –

and easing the pain of 2 so recent upheavals of his life's foundations by writing bad verse – and vivid stories – all full of intimate home life, and family loyalty + adoration of wives by husbands. These he diffidently tosses on my desk – and retrieves a day later.

It's a three ring intellectual circus, too. Today Aristotle's errors on spontaneous generation led to the untrustworthiness of scientists opinions outside their specialty – to a dissertation on overspecialization in modern life. Then an hour of volcanoes, and the life cycle of the malarial protozoan – and the use of hypnosis in psychiatry. The kids always get interested when the topic is drifting out of my reach.

For the "free" periods when the deadly clerical work must be done – there are the good moments of understanding chatter - with the professional conferes. The last years have taught me to make friends of people, same techniques used on birds and squirrels. You go into a new group, sit quietly, make no sudden sound or motion, do your share of the dirty work – seek no distinctions – and honestly want to understand the world as seen through their eyes. Gradually the ice thaws – the delightful quick thought is expressed by the fellow who looked like an underfed hillbilly – the atmosphere of friendly warmth repays the cautious waiting.

You were saying something about escaping the sterile drudgery of a routine existence. Isn't it largely feeling + imagination that enables us to thrill to the life beneath our fingertips?

How I do ramble. Try to find a moment to return the visit. Come to think of it – you owe me three (3) visits – in the flesh. Four times I've hunted the Küchler to his lair. And you've the promised Cranbrook tour still coming. Don't be like the Boston matron – who – when asked by a Chicago acquaintance if she had ever ridden on the new Pullman cars replied "<u>Of course not</u>, I <u>live</u> here!"

Another year, another letter, Dan thought, almost speed-reading them now like he did with technical writing. Küchler's was next.

What more fitting way to celebrate a Second Anniversary than to get in trouble with the police, and appear in court! Aye, verily, that is what I did this day. The matter was more one of coincidence than planning however. At 5:30 one morning two weeks ago I drove around the wrong side of a rotary in a small town; in the interests of safe driving, as the rotary was wholly in my lane, the streets were wet, and I had swung left to be clear of a state trooper who was standing in the road giving a ticket to some other unfortunate individual. Perhaps said state trooper was annoyed by the argument of his first victim. I was his second victim. This matter was only a six dollar affair, and I came to the court well heeled with cash. Past experiences have their values, and this injustice was no worse than a mosquito bite.

It was way back in May that you wrote. I wonder how the summer has turned out for you. East, west, north, or south this time? I am sorry you have not sent a telegram so far: "Arriving Monday, staying one week". It would be grandly pleasant to see your smiles around again, which one can see even in the darkness.

My teaching was over in June – and mighty glad I was. But it was a profitable semester in many ways. 24 students, all vets, except the four women, three of which latter were caricatures of talkingness, that is, until I told them so, and then smiled at them each time they began talking in class. They all took botany in a fairly welcome stride. I found out too late that I had to give an Elem. Bot. which was designed as the first of a Bot sequence, whereas my interest lies in giving a survey of the entire field for ones who will never take another botany course. The faculty at Waterbury (branch of the Univ of Conn) were mostly young and pleasingly inexperienced, or elder ex-high school teachers getting less in return from the doubtful halo of a faculty rating. Such ranks ran from Asst. Instr. to Assoc. Prof. The life of many was a dismal routine of all day and most evenings in a dilapidated, barely renovated school bldg in a decrepit part of town, meals in greasy-spoon restaurants, nights in worn rooms of the local Y. If I felt they were doing it for some noble humanitarian purpose.... But it was all too obvious that they were just making a living, in a manner decided by coincidence, than by their own particular brand of being important – at least to themselves. Technically, I am still on the faculty. I "postponed" accepting the teaching in Waterbury, or Hartford, or both, for next fall, asking them to consider various points (changes in the textbook, course content, etc.), and so far no decision has been reached. If they do not offer me the job, I shall be saved one difficult decision.

My 2,4-D research was about 5 times as extensive as last year, which means that I lugged about 5 times as many gallons about the fields. The Grassland Project is taking definitely a shape of some kind – all in that nebulous realm of "basic and fundamental research", which is what the ivory-tower-er now calls his speculative musings. After all, this is an age when wisdom is not loved for its own sake, when philo-sophy is out of style, and even the concepts of theoretical physics are transmuted by modern war-riers into bombs and rockets. Alas, even my seminatural grasslands may have a practical value. I am being thrown a hook by one corporation which seems to think that my 2,4-D work has some connection with the growing of peppermint, to flavor the gum that works the jaws of our jittery, jumpy, juke-box jive-hounds. I won't leave the Forest, and I won't change my project. If the Co. will pay me for what I am doing, and would do, anyway, my morals are low enough to take their money. We shall see

I really would enjoy a trip to Holmur Avenue – but I fear the summer is, or will be, the poorest time for me to travel. Besides, I no longer have the several-thousand-a year which used to help me in my travel. Perhaps if I had sense enough to take a job winters, I could travel summers; but then I would not be here at all. You know, there was a time not so far past when I lived only for the summers, surviving in suspended animation, or at least with held breath, from one summer to the next. But now, each season seems to hold so much that I am only half-way thru one before I start anticipating the next. After all, how many seasons remain to us before humanity sears the earth again? The past two years have been a most pitiful expression of man's irrational vagaries. Up here they seem more distant and unreal: like any other organism, I escape from the undesirable environment

The length of the next letter shocked Daniel. It ran to twelve pages of lady-like stationary. And he thought he made out a pattern. Aunt Jewel ever seemed to try to draw Küchler into something that Küchler so easily sidestepped. But was he really sidestepping? Could she have been so enamored of him that she was blind to his parries? Küchler? The Küchler he knew as an old curmudgeon, too reclusive to build on a promising career in ecology.

Ah, good old precious Aunt Jewel, Dan thought. Poor old spinster, he added.

But it was so hard to read between the lines. Could he have missed something?

Then he doubted that he would find any such thing in any of the letters. Or that it really mattered if he did. And it was late. It was no use to read further.

New Haven

I

WHO is this person? Rachel wonders. "Department of Biology, Kent State University, Kent, Ohio," she reads.

He's a long way from the sea, she thinks. She is right by the sea. Not that it's doing her any good. She should be out on Penzance Point, looking back at the ferries shuttling through the harbor, or out to sea—or even just by the Eel Pond—instead of being tucked away in this little reading alcove.

He credits a "Prof. Victor E. Shelford," along with two other professors and a number of other people she's never heard of, including two members of the clergy, for some reason. Still, there's information in the article of value for her. Notebook open, the small, three-ringed one she's labeled "Ecology," she writes:

"Parker, Reginald W. 1947 Ecol. Monographs, Vol. 17, no. 3 pp. 261-294. Marine Communities of a Tidal Inlet at Cape Ann, Mass."

She skips over the "Methods" section. She starts copying into her notebook with "Laminaria holdfasts," which she underlines. "... .The deepest portions of the channel are populated by <u>Laminaria digitata</u> and <u>L. saccharina</u>. In the holdfasts of these algae are found aggregations of small animals which occupy this microhabitat."

She decides not to make the effort of writing "Sea Squirts." She knows perfectly well that they are Molgula and Botryllus. Then she loses her concentration.

Things are not turning out the way she thought they would, now that she's finally able to devote herself fully to writing. She never thought in her wildest dreams that she'd have a book on the best-seller charts for over a year, almost half of that time at the top. Neither could she have imagined that her first book would join it in the top ten on reissue. She's a success as a writer. Even before publication, she has a TV deal, a film deal (netting her twenty thousand dollars), and a request to write jacket notes for a recording of La Mer. Boy is she successful!

So why was she resenting her time in the library?

It's always been such an attractive spot in which to while away a rainy afternoon. But maybe that's exactly it. It's not raining.

The weather's as good as it gets. Woods Hole's been a draw since her youth, but not for this sort of thing, she moans to herself, suddenly a resentful adolescent. She didn't come here to suffer through boring scholarly theses. First hand is how to learn. The facts are presented in some of these articles can be so boring that they could kill anyone's love for the subject.

But wait. This could be useful.

Her attention is back on the journal. She reads on to the bottom of the paragraph and labels her next section as "Laminaria stipa," underlined, as are all genus and species names, the handwritten substitute for italicization. An MS biologist, she is careful to observe that convention, even though she is often puzzled over names such as Molgula and Botryllis, in which the genus name is used informally. Why not still underline? And why not always capitalized?

After copying some scientific and informal names of varying levels, she gets to what she really needs. "Laminaria produces important reactions by slowing the current of water, reducing light intensity," she copies, "and serving to catch and hold sediment, as well as serving as a place for attachment or refuge for many animals."

Now that's ecology. But what can he possibly mean by "reactions?"

Paid researchers assist her now. Her mother answers fan mail and screens requests for appearances. Still, Rachel only has time, it seems, for this kind of reading and laboratory work, very little laboratory work, at that. Well, she did rent lab space, so she might as well use it, even if it means sitting with her eyes glued to the powerful binocular 'scope she has purchased, studying creatures brought in by others, instead of studying them out in their habitats.

She skips over the next few paragraphs of the paper, especially those besotted with numbers and terms. "Permeant influents?" she asks out loud. Then she copies, "The algae (Laminaria, Chaetomorpha, Ulva, Chrondus, etc.) of the river bottom are the basic foods for many snails (Littorina, Lacuna), crustaceans (Crago, Cancer, Pagarus, Carcinides, etc.) and fishes," peculiarly capitalizing all leading "T's", all the way up the food chain. Then there is more boring stuff. "The system of Lindeman 1942" draws a yawn and frown. A very confusing diagram and sections headed "Annuation and Succession," "Faciations," and "Zonation and Coactions" she skips over.

Now, habitat, there is a good ecological word, she thinks. She would rather be wandering along the tide pool and sand dune habitats of St. Simon's Island or wading through mangrove swamps in the Florida Keys or searching for specimens in the coral coves of the Keys, studying habitats, than wondering what a "faciation" was. Has it only been weeks ago that she had indeed been doing just that?

When she and her mother settled in Paul Galtzoff's house, it had been like coming to a sanctuary. Her old friend's house, which they have rented through September, is right across the street from MBL.

But there must be no haven from fame, she thinks. Not, at least, a stationary one. It'll find you anywhere you settle.

There should be more that's useful in the article, she knows, and forces her attention back to it. She accuses herself of having daydreamed past useful information and goes back to underline "L. littorina and Onoba continue to feed to some extent. Anurida ... surface invertebrate ... is at its peak of activity ... hunting dead bodies of fishes, mollusks, crustaceans, etc. on which it feeds."

Her publisher wants her to make appearances she has had to turn down.

"All these requests for personal appearances here and there are getting me down," she had to explain to Oxford's publicity director. "To do even half the things people want, I'd have to be a sort of Alice in Wonderland character, rushing madly in all directions at once."

Still, the longer The Sea Around Us stays at the top of the lists, she knows, the greater will be the pressure of correspondence, telephone calls, and interruptions of all sorts. Even just the labor of saying "No!" in a way that doesn't make people mad takes a good deal of nervous energy—and one cannot say no to everything.

And she has a bigger problem, which she bears in secret. Her brother's erratic behavior makes him unfit to head the family. Caring for her octogenarian mother has fallen to Rachel. So too did caring for a niece from a marriage that her brother has never told his second wife about—and never intends to. The girl needed care and protection through a very risky secret pregnancy. Now there is an added member, Roger, in her household.

"Each fortnight as the spring tides spread over the high marsh communities," she forces herself to copy, "the spiders and insects are floated and driven off." She underlines that sentence for future reference.

Other than the trips she and her mother managed to take to Booth Bay, she muses, this stay at Woods Hole has been more pressure than pleasure. What a marvelous place, the Booth Bay area! Maybe she could buy that land on Southport Island. Maybe that might make the fame and money as worthwhile as she once imagined. Could she hope for so much?

But it's clear to her, she glumly acknowledges, the thought bursting the happy balloon she just launched, that she'll never meet her spring deadline for this new book. She's not yet come up with a working title. Guide to Seashore Life on the Atlantic Coast has evolved into Rock, Sand, and Coral, a Beachcomber's Guide to Atlantic Coast. Neither is suitable.

Why, if she's acknowledged to be such a good writer, can't she do something as simple as come up with a good title?

That's it for this paper, she decides. Who eats whom and is eaten by whom and where, that's all the ecology she needs to know.

II

"NO," he says to Jewel in his very British mumble, "I am sorry to say that I did not know George Nichols at all well, other than from chance meetings, even though he was the only professed ecologist when I came here. Botanists, don't you know, rarely wander into the Osborn Zoological Laboratories. Although we share a common library and contribute to the elementary course in biology, there is a great gulf artificially fixed between the two disciplines of botany and zoology. It cannot be crossed officially during working hours. Strange, is it not?"

Jewel has no response. In death, she fears, Uncle George is letting her down. He was such a solid personage at Yale. Now, after just a decade, all trace of him has disappeared.

"I have heard from a number of colleagues," the Englishman fills the silence, "about what a fine man he was and what a loss his death had been to the university. Paul Sears, I believe, knew him well. Perhaps you should try him."

He leaned forward in his leather chair just then, as if to add the next in confidence.

"He is in the School of Forestry."

She already has seen Sears, Jewel is tempted to say, and without much promise. This interview, she frets, is going no better than it started out.

"Chicago," he had read from her resume almost before she seated herself. "Great books and what. You don't by chance read Greek?"

"No," was all she could answer.

"Do you know Hebrew?"

"No."

"I don't suppose you read Sanskrit or Chinese?"

"No."

"In that case all the classical languages are closed to you, aren't they?"

"I know French and Latin."

"Well, that is a start," he said, looking intently at her with his droopy eyes.

Then in what must have been as close to a drawl as possible for an Englishman he added, "However, I would no more call French a classical language than I would the brand of English spoken on my old side of the Atlantic."

Jewel had a notion to say that the Latin she knew was sufficient for the library research and "mild," as he had described it, editing he needed done. She also had a notion to complain that his inquisition was becoming excessive for a part-time position. But she bit her tongue.

A younger man in an almost identical herringbone now interrupts their embarrassed silence with a quick question that sounds like some sort of code to Jewel.

"I will see you in a few minutes, Ed," the older tweed jacket dismisses the younger affably and turns his attention back to Jewel.

"You seem to have some three or four years at the University of Illinois with Victor Shelford," he says articulating the names carefully, as if they were for the first time on his lips. "No degree?"

"No."

"Not even a Master's?"

"I was a PhD student. I never got far enough on my dissertation for a Master's."

"Hmmph. Yes. A rather barbaric custom on this side of the Atlantic. Cambridge conferred a Master's degree merely for my having sent in the appropriate fee."

Jewel wants to tell him about the missing notebook, her years teaching in order to support her mother and sister, Shelford's retirement, and more, but she fears losing her composure. Instead, she looks back for Danny, who is in the laboratory, for which Hutchinson's office is only an alcove. The tiny office is crammed with books, papers, specimen boxes, and whatever. There is room for the two currently in it. A third, Jewel imagines, would burst it like an overfilled balloon. A soapstone sink with obligatory dirty lab glassware cluttering the lab and clean glassware on a wooden pegboard above testify it to being more than a naturalist's grand closet. It is a working wet lab in every sense. Jewel can see heavy glass bottles, the kind used for storing strong acids, on its shelves.

To her chagrin, she had to bring Danny along to New Haven. Bored now with examining the giant stuffed tortoise, Tibetan prayer wheels and mask, or the various dusty bones in the lab, he has taken to spinning a swivel chair. Another nail in her job-hunting coffin, Jewel thinks.

"Why does it keep spinning when you are not pushing it?" the Englishman calls out.

He too has turned his attention to him. He had made no inquiries about the boy when the two came into his office, other than name and age, but let Danny wander where his inquisitiveness took him.

"Does that not seem odd?" he now asks him.

"Because I pushed it once," Danny answers. "I push it and it spins."

"Yes. Indeed," is the reply, delivered beneath a drooping squint that stops the boy's investigation.

Then the squint returns to the single-sheet resume in his hands. Then again to Jewel. Her attention, while under this scrutiny, is on a motto obviously cut from a magazine and taped to the wall behind her. Had she not turned to look for Danny, she would not have noticed it. It stares down continually at whoever is at the desk, a constant reminder. "Never try to discourage a student for you will almost certainly succeed" are its words.

"Schools all about here, I understand, are bursting at the seams with all the children being born after the war," he says very seriously. "Why don't you apply for a teaching position? A science degree is de rigueur for a successful applicant these days. I have a student just now on a leave to teach at a high school. He tells me he has every intention to take such a position on completing his degree. I should think that your lack of an advanced degree is suitably trumped by your graduate transcript."

"Those children born to soldiers can hardly be of high school age yet." Jewel counters.

She considers, then rejects, explanations having to do with licensing requirements and other prevarications she has rehearsed just for that question. The answer that she can no longer expect to be allowed to teach anywhere, given her notoriety, is too close to her tongue.

"I suppose not."

The sleepy eyes drift back to the boy, who is once more spinning the chair. Jewel suddenly realizes why the eyes have held her attention. They are the eyes of British film star James Mason. With their sleepy, vaguely Asiatic slant, they are at once sinister and captivating. Is he in the role of hero or villain? Jewel wonders. James Mason's eyes are the same in either case. And the interview is over, she realizes.

"Danny? Can you wait out by the front door?" she calls to the boy. "You know, where we came in? Not by the street, though. In the courtyard. I'll just be a minute."

After Danny leaves, the Englishman smiles shyly and says, "He must be a treasure to you."

Then, hesitantly, with the same smile, he says, "Do you know, I was fired from my first teaching job?"

His accent is thick enough to make Jewel strain to understand him. The sudden warmth to his speech, however, makes her want to.

"It had been at the University of the Witwatersrand in South Africa," he continues, sure of her attention. "Incompetence in teaching was the reason given. I fought the dismissal only to hold on and try to salvage what little pension money was due me, and also not to have to remit the price of my passage from England, which had been quite dear. Meanwhile, a friend most kindly wrote a very laudable letter to Professor Ross G. Harrison here, recommending me for anything that happened to be available. Harrison was in Naples on sabbatical leave, but the letter ultimately reached a Professor Woodruff, who was acting chairman of the zoology department, and from him I received a fellowship application form. The deadline for the fellowship had already passed, but I decided, nevertheless to cable my qualifications to Woodruff. I used the numbers of the application form to save on words, but the overseas telegraph still cost five pounds. I felt rather as though I had placed a large bet on an improbable horse, but it was in fact the only thing I could do. To my surprise, Woodruff cabled me mid-May offering me not a fellowship, but an instructorship, and I immediately accepted. It happened that a Professor Kirby—well, you need not know about him but that he received an excellent offer from the University of California late in the academic year and so was leaving Yale rather unexpectedly. I later learned that the sheer improbability of receiving an application by transatlantic cable from the Southern Hemisphere shortly after Kirby's resignation had worked strongly in my favor."

It's the kind of monologue one makes, Jewel thinks, in the false hope of easing rejection for an applicant, but is instead, she suspects, a show of compassion for the benefit only of the person about to wield the ax. She cannot let go of the knowledge that this shabbily dressed—his jacket's elbow is in need of a leather patch—avuncular man, who offered her tea and Bourdeaux cookies, is the same man who wrote a scathing review of Bio-Ecology. Untroubled by the cynicism of her thoughts, she uses Danny as an excuse to free herself from the interview.

The boy is, as instructed, in the central courtyard of the Osborn Memorial Laboratories, which is what the combined wings of the building are collectively and officially called, one housing zoology, the other botany. She wonders what the botanists call their wing as she ushers Danny through the building's corner entrance arch. Once a covered entry for carriages, it connects the two wings through the library atop it. Two Gothic turrets defend the entrance. Other turrets rise in pairs at other corners. She hurries Danny past medieval gables before realizing she has turned the wrong way on

Prospect Street. Having to retrace her steps adds to her feeling of trespass. She prods Danny to go faster. They are barely away from Osborn's castle-like, impregnable fortress, when they find themselves beneath the gargoyles of Harkness Tower. Its carillon bells toll defeat in her ears all the way back to where she parked. There is no sigh of relief on getting into the familiar pre-war Hudson that she could barely then afford to buy and barely now afford to keep in repair. She and Danny are not heading homeward away from Yale's malevolent shadows to Old Saybrook—or home anywhere—but to quarters tenuously borrowed from a childhood friend in East Lyme. And it is not a homey cape or saltbox to which they are going, but a new ranch house. And not to a bedroom in it, but to a basement sofa-bed.

Jewel's friend has settled into a small house in a neighborhood of identical houses. Jewel imagines identical couples with identical children within each. It is a long way from her old neighborhood in Detroit or some of the parts of New Haven she passes through on her way out of the city, and not just in distance. Negroes come up from the south for wartime jobs will soon overrun both, she fears. Would she have chosen to stay in her house, if she could have stayed in Detroit? Flowers, summer vegetables, and bird life will follow her anywhere, she knows. The lead-lined corner in the basement she designed for that house, where the four people closest to her were to huddle in safety from a radioactive cloud, is one more thing she must drive from memory, she knows. Let that coffin fade in concert with the small bundle of cash she exchanged it for.

New Haven might well have been safe haven, Jewell thinks with finality and regret. Perhaps like Uncle George fading away for Yale, memories of that awful night might have faded there for her and Danny, not even ghosts haunting their dreams.

What now though? Going back to Urbana went out the door with Victor Shelford. And Fred Küchler showed his clay feet. Now there is no hope, nothing to do but hurry through Route One traffic before being too late for a promised dinner.

But when she and Danny arrive at the small house, there is someone on the telephone for her. It is G. Evelyn Hutchinson, she is told as she grabs the earpiece. From Yale.

"On an hunch," he says, "I telephoned Victor Shelford, who praised to the skies both your work on Bio-Ecology and your research skills."

He certainly made her sound, Hutchinson tells her with lengthy asides, like exactly the right person to help him with his own opus, his Treatise on Limnology, the first volume of which was nearing completion. And he apologizes that he might have to upset her child-caring duties with Danny, for he also has a need at the moment for a lab technician, one with the management skills to ride herd over some strong-willed graduate students. If she could do so with thirty teenagers at a time, he suggests, she should be able to manage that.

"Could you work for me full time?" he asks. "It might mean moving to New Haven."

III

ED is Ed Deevey. His office is down the hall. He was the second of Hutchinson's doctoral students. After a first academic job and a stint at Woods Hole doing research for the Navy during World War II, he came back to Yale.

Jewel suspects another Shelford-Kendeigh situation has arisen. She wonders if their students will start to call their mentor "Deevinson" or "Hutcheevey."

Ed and Evelyn, as they call each other, are closeted together when Jewel, barely having settled into her job, bursts into the office without ceremony.

"I have to go," she announces. "They just called from school. Danny had a sore throat this morning. Now he has a headache and fever. The teacher said he vomited all over his desk."

Ed has children of his own at a similarly susceptible age. He can read on Jewel's face the horrifying thought that crosses his own mind.

"Stiff neck?" he asks. "Has he his tonsils?"

"Removed this summer," Jewel says. "Just before we left Detroit. Why?"

"Come."

Deevey takes her by the elbow and swiftly walks her out of the office.

"We need to get him to the Polio Unit."

Hutchinson follows, promising to "prepare the way" for them. He corrals Tom Goreau, his senior graduate student.

"Tom," he tells him, "you are by far the most brilliant student I have ever had, much more so than these youngsters cluttering up our laboratory this fall. Let's see what you can do to help me deal with the intransigence of medical bureaucracy."

There is another polio epidemic under way. It started more slowly than the previous year and gave rise to false hopes, but it accelerated with the opening of school. Ed and Jewel take Danny, not to the Polio Study Unit at the School of Medicine, where Hutchinson and Goreau find little in the way of bureaucracy with which to deal, but to Grace-New Haven Hospital.

"Can you swallow for me?" the attending physician asks, feeling Danny's head and neck. "No? Trouble speaking, too?"

Then he turns to the grownups.

"How long has he been slurring his words like that?" he asks.

When Jewel shakes her head, he whisks Danny away immediately.

"Aunt Jewel, please don't leave me here," he cries out weakly as he is hustled away.

He had been silent until that outburst. Barely audible, barely intelligible, his plaintiff cry resounds in both Ed and Jewel. Neither says a word as they search for seats in the crowded waiting room. They find only a seat for Jewel.

Some die within hours of being admitted to a hospital, both know, their symptoms no more than a headache and fever—and a stiff neck. For some there is not even enough time to say goodbye.

"I can't help picturing Danny among rows and rows of children in wheelchairs or iron lungs," she finally breaks their silence. "Have you ever seen those pictures in Life magazine?

"And in my nightmares," Ed says, standing above her.

"Most will recover in a few days, though," he adds after summoning a smile to his face. "The great majority, in fact. Although that never gives me much confidence when my children come down with fevers."

"How many?" she asks, eager to change the subject. "Your children, I mean."

"Three. Ruth, Brian and Kevin. Edward Brian, actually, but Brian works better in our household. He keeps my wife the busiest. He also gave us the biggest scare of our lives last year. What an awful, awful summer that was!"

"Polio?"

"No. Fortunately, it turned out not. Just influenza. I don't know how we could have been so lucky. At any rate, it made my wife read all the literature she could get her hands on."

Then his face lights up.

"I know you!" he says in almost a shout. "I mean, I know of you!"

A cold paralysis instantly sweeps through Jewel. What can he know? From whom?

"I've finally placed why you look so familiar," he explains. "George Nichols had your picture on his desk. You're some sort of relative, aren't you?"

"Niece," Jewel says in relief.

"He was so kind to me when I was doing my thesis work. He loaned me his peat corer and spent hours going over how to classify the forests represented by the cores. I think he would have taken me on as a student, had Evelyn not already done so. He took on someone else, instead."

"Fred Küchler?"

"Why, yes. That was his name. He kept your uncle's head spinning, I'll tell you. Just analyze the vegetation, please, I remember overhearing him say once when—Fred is it?—blew in from the field, full of ideas."

"Mrs. Atkins?" a loud voice interrupts.

It comes from a tall, elegantly professional woman, who is scanning the room, her neck moving swanlike. Jewel startles on realizing that it is she being called and catches the woman's eye.

"Fairfax," she corrects. "I'm Danny's— Daniel Atkins is my nephew."

The woman gives Ed a puzzled look.

"Friend," he answers.

"Where are the parents?"

"Deceased," Jewel says. "I have custody."

"I'm Dorothy Horstmann," she finally introduces herself. "I'm with the Yale Polio Unit. We do not normally get directly involved in treatment of cases, but you have a persuasive friend."

"Dr. Horstmann here has just wrapped up research that according to Georgiana," Ed says to Jewel, "will allow Jonas Salk to go ahead with an idea he has had that will eliminate polio forever."

"You are too kind," Dr. Horstmann replies.

A faint blush is visible on her cheeks. It momentarily takes Jewel's attention off the woman's bright blue eye shadow.

"Let us all hope that dead polio virus cells actually will immunize children against live ones," Dr. Horstmann adds. "Our research results certainly point to the possibility. But who is Georgiana?"

"My wife. I'm Ed Deevey."

When she looks at him inquiringly, he adds, "A zoologist."

Dr. Horstmann then pivots her lovely neck back toward Jewel. Jewel steels herself for what she knows is to come.

"Danny, we think, has bulbar poliomyelitis," Dr. Horstmann says. "We usually test spinal fluid for a definitive diagnosis, but I think we know what the result will be. You may want to spare him the procedure. Bulbar polio affects the region in the brain controlling cranial nerves. That is what is making it difficult for him to swallow, and that is the greatest danger to him at the moment. He might choke to death or get aspiration pneumonia. The disease can affect his breathing, too. He will have to be watched carefully in case it progresses further. He is fortunate, though, to be at Yale and to have Evelyn for a friend, for I came here bearing an ample supply of gamma globulin. Actually, you should thank the young man who came with him. Evelyn seemed too shy to get the point of the visit. Had it not been for—Tom, was it?"

"Tom Goreau."

"He deserves the credit for asking me to intervene in this case. The gamma globulin should slow down the progress of Danny's disease. Still, guard your hopes. We know so little about its course."

"Can I—?"

"See him? You can, if you wish, come with me for a look at him from the corridor, but through a window only. No contact, please. Polio patients are no longer quarantined as rigidly as before, but isolation is still necessary for your own protection—and those with whom you may come in contact."

"How long?"

"That depends. He may be asymptomatic in seven to ten days. Then there will be another week until we are certain he is no longer infectious."

Jewel declines Ed's offer to accompany them for what both fear might be her last look at Danny. She lets Dr. Horstmann, moments ago a stranger, lead her down a corridor to the door of the isolation ward. A nurse is blocking it. She is copying notations on a chart taped to the window, Dr. Horstmann explains. The chart itself is not allowed through the door for fear of contamination, so the attending nurse tapes it where she can copy it from the corridor for use in the world outside. Nothing that goes into the room is allowed to come out without special handling.

When Jewel can look in, it is not quite the crowded image in her mind from the magazine, but it is no less heart wrenching to her. Everyone on the room is masked, gloved, and gowned but the children. Black and white, they lay in a long row of beds, each naked but for a single diaper, their knees raised identically by some sort of leather pad.

"Why are they—?"

"Toronto splints, they are called," Dr. Horstmann explains. "It is hoped the flat-footed position will slow down the progress of the paralysis."

"But where is—?"

Dr. Horstmann points Jewel to the far corner of the room at Danny, also naked, also in a diaper, also probably barely conscious of his surroundings.

"The headache at this stage can be very severe, I am afraid," Dr. Horstmann says. "How I wish we could do something for their pain."

Then she abruptly leads Jewel away.

"I am truly sorry," she says in handing her back to Ed. "You have my complete sympathy. Anything more I can do—?"

"Thank you," Jewel interrupts.

"Can I take you home?" Ed asks.

She shakes her head.

More people are added to the waiting room than leave it, Jewel notices. She wanders away in search of the hospital cafeteria, not so much out of hunger or the knowledge that the sun is setting outdoors, but in hope of escaping the heartbreak on the faces of parents adrift in the same hopeless shock as she is. She finds an empty table off in a corner of the sparsely appointed cafeteria. It is next to one with a trio of young nurses.

One of the nurses, a very natural blonde, Jewel decides, in comparison to her own sun-aided color, must be new to the hospital. She speaks by accenting the ends and middles of sentences in a way that is somehow familiar to Jewel. It is not a Chicago way of speech, but one that she thinks she might have heard there.

"That was very sad," Jewel overhears the nurse saying. "It was weird, because it was just a young girl. She must have been six or seven. And before we were going off for supper, she wanted—she was in the lung, and she was talking to somebody, and she had—I don't know if it was a doll or a toy, and she wanted to give it away. And it was kind of weird because we went for supper and there were other people on, and we came back and she had died in the —at that —I think before we got back. And it was sad because you had to, you know, have her parents come in to see her—that type thing— and it was tough, you know. But we didn't—there weren't a lot of deaths, you know, when we were there. I think the main epidemic may have been over already in Minneapolis, to tell the truth."

Runny noses, fevers, upset stomach, how Jewel had wanted to nurse Danny through those little ills of childhood, but could not, because Marjorie insisted on doing all of the mothering. How jealous Jewel was over those daily baths, hugs, and kisses that were Marjorie's alone.

"Something with his leg," Jewel overhears the same voice. "I started working on it right away. I didn't wait for the doctors."

Jewel stares at her tuna sandwich. Not hungry, she decides.
No tears.
No pain.
Numbness.
"My perfect child," she sobbed. "My poor child."

IV

SHE is now Aunt Jewel to them. It happened instantly. "This is your Aunt Jewel," Robert MacArthur heard her say into the telephone. MacArthur, a Canadian, is handsome, fresh-faced, always smiling. A mathematician by training, his research consists of reading and scribbling pages that are mostly white space, sparsely spotted with concise, mathematical expressions. He needs no lab. An easy chair is sufficient for his pursuit of some elusive thing he calls a "lemma." His Ontario diction sounds very British, even compared to Hutchinson's, although some of his fellow students believe it to be a New England accent. It is a misconception he allows. He loves Vermont and has a wife from the state. Robert always looks like he has come in from a sail or a set of tennis and is searching for someone to share further play. It is never for tennis, his invitation, but it is never turned down. The others follow him intellectually anywhere he leads. When he started to call her "my Aunt Jewel," she became everyone's Aunt Jewel.

She intended to stay at the hospital around the clock, but that proved futile. She could not sit at Danny's bedside. She could not tend to his needs. She could not guard him against his fears or comfort him in his pain. All she could do was sit and wait out of sight of him and think dark thoughts. Being in the lab helped take her mind off them.

Hutchinson first assigned her to help Henry Werntz in his basement lab. His dissertation topic was on how a small group of crustaceans adapted to the differing amounts of salt in their waters. Collecting specimens from various streams around New Haven was a treat to Jewel. She suspected it was Hutchinson's way of getting her outdoors, into fresh air and sunshine. But what really helped take her mind off her troubles were the precise measurements needed on the concentration of salts in the blood and urine of the shrimp-like creatures. That required determining the freezing point of a frozen sample of blood or urine as it slowly warmed. This, in turn, required watching the frozen crystals as they melted, using a horizontally mounted microscope to look through the front glass wall of a specially constructed aquarium. The microscope has a Polaroid analyzer. By using polarized light, the crystals were seen as brilliant white objects against a dark background. They otherwise would be barely visible. Henry filled the aquarium with an ethyl alcohol solution and mounted it in the front wall of an insulated box. The box was in a continuously stirred, constant-temperature bath. The bath was simultaneously heated by an immersion heater and cooled by a pack of crushed dry ice that was pressed against the back of the aquarium using a spring-driven plunger. Keeping all that running properly turned out to be a cinch. The hard part was getting blood samples from the less-than-inch-long creatures. Jewel or Henry, but usually Jewel, first dried the animal gently between layers of absorbent paper toweling, then wiped its back with moist filter paper. Then Henry took over. With the still-live animal held under paraffin oil, he punctured the exoskeleton over the heart with a fine needle. If lucky, a tiny drop of blood appeared. This he took into a fine capillary tube, which had been cleaned by Jewel in hot nitric acid. Capillary action first drew paraffin oil into the capillary, then a tiny blood sample, and finally more paraffin oil. Henry then broke off the bit of capillary that contained the sample, sealed its ends with sealing wax, and passed it on for Jewel to affix a label. If all went well—and it did not always—the sample then went into a freezer, there to await the less demanding chores of determining its freezing point and from that calculating freezing point depression and salt concentration.

  Urine samples gave them more trouble. The creatures had no bladders. Miraculously to Jewel, Henry did manage to draw drops of urine from what passed as a kidney for the little critters, using a similar technique to that for blood, but the animals died before he could estimate flow rate. Soon, Henry was totally absorbed in perfecting a better technique.

  Hutchinson has graduate students spread over three floors of Osborn. Labs are mostly separate from offices and often on different floors. Some grad students, barely weeks newer to Yale than Jewel, assume on seeing the deference given her that she is a long-time fixture in his lab. She is not unhappy with that. Her hair, now straight and bobbed because she can no longer afford visits to hairdressers, is seen by them as Bohemian. She is not unhappy with that either, always having fancied herself as a non-conformist. But she fends off their mock flirtations amid fleeting thoughts of wrapping her head in her favorite European scarf and revisiting some of the Columbia dropouts she had met at an old friend's

Greenwich Village apartment. That had been on her first, giddy attempt at flight from the horror in Detroit. Although she is now within easy drive of New York City, they are all gone, her friend tells her, all off writing poetry in San Francisco.

Being cast by the students into an older generation catches her by surprise. She does not mind it though, not so long as the younger ones are ready to help her with the needs of a "single mother whose child is in the hospital with polio," as they describe her situation.

"I really appreciate all these young men helping me out," she mentions to Hutchinson as he hunches over his binocular microscope. "How did you ever gather so many of them together?"

"Interesting question," Hutchinson answers, slowly straightening his back. "Before the war, most biology professors at Yale had no more than one student at a time. Many had none. I rather imagine it has to do with the need for new faculty due to all the war veterans, including now from this new war in Korea, that are on the GI Bill and crowding colleges and universities. I imagine it also has to do with that report by Vannevar Bush, The Endless Frontier, I believe was its title, which called for more and better training in science. It may also have to do with the Russians blowing up their own atom bombs. All those three-initialed agencies, NIH and NSF and AEC and their ilk, that were set up to promote research in science, applied and basic, although mostly basic, are finally getting around to funding it in response to the Vannevar Bush report. Henry has an NSF Graduate Fellowship, you know.

"But it is truly curious," he continues after a moment's thought, "that so many have decided to choose me. There should be some explanation for it."

Jewel thinks she sees a twinkle in his eye. She tries to twinkle back.

"Could it be," Hutchinson wonders aloud, "that my being Director of Graduate Studies allows me to skim off the best applicants?"

"Well, I think it's on good advice they're coming here," Jewel says.

"I do hope so. Do you know that I was strongly advised by my father not to take that position in South Africa?"

A smile fills his face.

"My uncle, in particular warned me that Professor H. B. Fantham was an extremely difficult man, whom I should avoid. But I was young enough to be extremely pig-headed about other people's opinions. My wife tells me I still am."

He motions to her to come closer.

"But on to another matter," he says. "This may interest you."

It is a pinned specimen of a water boatman, a taxonomic specialty of his. The microscope is focused on its abdomen.

"Why, that is strange." Jewel focuses up and down on it. "It's abdomen is asymmetrical."

"Yes." Hutchinson says, pleased with her observation. "It is a male. The modified parts are used to hold the female in mating. Now look at this one."

He replaces that specimen with another.

"Same species," she says.

"Jolly good. What else?"

She can find nothing.

"Maybe if you hold them side by side," he suggests.

"They're reversed!"

"Spot on! In some species the asymmetry has the female held left-to-right, while in others, it is right-to-left, but this species has it both ways. My Jesuit friend, Father Walter Peters, has shown that the left-handed male is usually due to a dominant gene that is lethal when homozygous, so that the heterozygotes, which are sinistral, must have some enormous advantage over the dextral individuals. The whole story is very odd."

"Evelyn, I just suddenly realized that you are at heart nothing more than a butterfly-collecting child, plagued, I think, with a classical education."

"What a delightful observation! I did, you know, in childhood, collect butterflies. Then at thirteen, I believe it had been, I decided somewhat snobbishly that Lepidoptera were too much collected, by too uninteresting people, to be worthy of my attention."

"You're a zoologist and taxonomist to the bone, then, almost from birth," Jewel ventures. "How ever did you become an ecologist?"

"Another interesting question, my dear. Well, I suppose it was all due to the same friend who helped get me this position at

Yale. Lancelot Hogben is his name. In the throes of my difficulties at Witwatersrand, when I had been relieved of all teaching duties, he suggested I look at the chemistry of some South African lakes. I did, and realized I had found what I wanted to do. My father, you see, was a chemist. It was only fate, wasn't it? I sat down with Standard Methods, the fat handbook the American Public Health Association puts out on water testing, and I found myself to be a limnologist."

"But ecology? You didn't study with any of the names I was taught started the field, and that all American ecologists seem to derive from—or any ecologist for that matter!"

"Oh blast! As if that would have helped me in any way! What did help, however, was reading Charles Elton's thin volume on animal ecology. It was at just about the same time. It let me see how all the ways of looking at nature that I had acquired in my random, disorganized way, could be focused together on lakes as microcosms. I very much thought of myself as an ecologist of lakes on coming to Yale."

Thank God for his stories, she thinks, and thank God for his students. Almost as soon as they learned that she was only able to communicate between the hours of six and seven PM with Danny or the hospital, MacArthur set off with skinny Joe Shapiro to make the university switchboard operator keep a clear line to their laboratory telephone. They kept a vigil at that phone for her, making and taking their own calls elsewhere.

Ruth Beloff, a physiology student who shares a room with Peter Klopfer, twinned her up in her own small daughter's bedroom, on discovering Jewel asleep in the lab one morning, so that she would not have to drive back and forth to East Lyme. Alan Kohn did even better. He gave Jewel the first chance at an apartment close to campus and at a reasonable rent that he had just found. It was a tiny third-floor walk-up, but it had some charming touches and was within walking distance of both campus and hospital. She would be able to leave the Hudson idle as it concluded its battle with rust. Klopfer volunteered to help her move her things.

"You're fortunate to have this car," he told her as the Hudson rattled its way down Highway One. "Movers can cost a pretty penny, and they don't really take care of your things. Things get lost."

"You get along without an automobile?"

Unlike in rural Urbana, the idea is odd to Jewel in New Haven, except for dormitory-fettered undergraduates. Most professors seem to live outside New Haven. Some are rumored to have apartments in Manhattan.

"I can't afford anything more than a bicycle."

"That should slow you down in the winters."

"Not at all."

He punctuated it with a hoarse, "Heh heh heh," before continuing.

"Where I live there is neither electricity nor heat. Hitting the streets on a bicycle is less harsh if you are not leaving a warm bed to do it. Heh heh heh."

Jewel was flabbergasted into silence. There was more to this soft-spoken, long-boned, athletic young man than first met her eye.

"It's part of the Oak Street Christian Parish," Klopfer continued. "Everyone else there is a divinity student. I think there are ten of 'em. It's free. In exchange for rent, I am responsible for weekend workouts, fixing up places that do have heat. Maybe I'll schedule the Parish next. The nights are getting chilly and it's getting dark sooner."

"What faith is that?" Jewel asked, more out of politeness than curiosity.

"I'm maybe no faith."

Again, the self-effacing little laugh.

"I guess I'm actually a Quaker. At least I believe in their principles."

"Such as?"

"Such as being thrown out of UCLA after my freshman year for rabble rousing and other subversive acts, as they were called."

He laughed again as he studied her face for a reaction.

"It had to do with ROTC and the loyalty oath entering males had to give. Quakers believe neither in war nor in oaths. I had to transfer to LA City College before I could get back into UCLA for my junior and senior years. But that wasn't the end."

"You were thrown out again?"

"Worse. I sent back my draft card as a CO. Conscientious objector. That got me arrested and sentenced to three years, but the sentence got postponed until after commencement. A number of my teachers made entreaties on my behalf, especially George

Bartholomew at UCLA. An absolutely charismatic teacher and just a great person. But his help was a mixed blessing. I'd stopped attending classes after my arrest. So I had to make up three months of class work in only a week. It was sleepless night after sleepless night, but with class notes borrowed from friends, I passed my exams. Then the judge that sentenced me died. He was definitely a hanging judge. He would have thrown me into prison. The one who replaced him was more humane. He released me on probation, as long as I obeyed all laws as far as conscience allows. I think those were his exact words."

"Your parents were Quakers?"

"The folks I grew up with were. My father died when I was young. With her family money tied up in Germany, my mother could not cope with my brother and me or the German refugee children we had taken in. I was farmed out to a Quaker couple outside of Philadelphia. Aunt Alice and Uncle Thomas. They turned out to be a God send."

"Your parents were German? I don't detect an accent."

"I was born on a trip to Germany. My mother insisted on it. But no, we all spoke English to each other."

Time went by quickly. The Hudson was already rolling across the Connecticut.

"Pretty, isn't it?" Jewel could not help saying about the countryside in which she grew up.

"I understand you taught high school," was Klopfer's attempt to get Jewel into conversation on the way back.

The trunk and back seat of the Hudson were stuffed full of all of Jewel and Danny's worldly goods, except for the carton of paper-backed books on Peter's lap. Packing was the easy part of their task. Both dreaded hauling everything up two flights of Victorian staircase at first, but it got done.

"The market crash was not good for my family," Jewel told him. "I couldn't afford to start at Illinois without earning some money. Then I couldn't afford to finish. My father died and I had to take care of the family, it turned out."

"That's why Danny is with you?"

"It became harder and harder for me to return to grad school, even with Shelford being so encouraging. It surprises me that you came back from a year of teaching."

"I have a little money put away. I may not have to eat spaghetti sandwiches for dinner this year. But I want to know more about you. You see, my plan is to go back to teaching high school after I get my degree. Heck, the job market in academics is abysmal, and the salaries of assistant professors at a lot of colleges hardly match what an advanced degree can earn teaching high school in a city. A lot of young faculty at Yale have to take on summer duties just to make ends meet."

"You may be right about pay. I certainly miss the salary I got from the Detroit school system."

"Yeah. But there is another reason to teach high school. After UCLA, I joined something called a technical assistance training program at Haverford College. It had to do with my probation. I discovered a lot of things there about myself and science. I got to read Tinbergen's 1952 Quarterly Review of Biology paper, for example. That led me to a paper by Ramsey and Hess. Hess was a professor of psychology at the University of Chicago, but A.O. Ramsey, I found out, was a high school science teacher. So, I can teach high school after grad school AND do science. Perfect! Job security. Good pay. And summers off for research!"

V

HER name was Georgiana. She had trained as a nurse in Minnesota, then married a doctor and moved with him to New Haven. They both worked at the hospital. She too had fears, she told him, vigorously working his lower leg.

"I came home many times at the end of the day with an ache or a pain in the leg and wondered if I had caught the disease, too. But I never had. I'm immune to it now, I guess, but so will you be when you are sent home."

She was beautiful he knew. He suspected he would fall in love with her every bit as much as—

That thought stopped him cold. He had to force himself to enunciate the rest of its words, even if only in his head.

Every…bit…as…much…as…Rufus…did…before…before

The next thought he knew he would not be able to put into even silent words. First the pretty blonde nurse, and then …Things he once thought were gone were back in his world again. There were things like that night—

Things he should never tell anyone, not even Aunt Jewel. She called him every night now with questions that he did not want to answer, even if they didn't have anything to do with Rufus or the —

Why can't she just take me home?

Danny was intubated to be fed, then needed a tracheotomy. It was performed without anesthetic.

"I could see it all," he finally said to his Aunt Jewel when they were face to face with each other, instead of disembodied voices within phone lines. "The doctor wore glasses. I could see the —how do you say it? Like in a mirror?"

"Reflection?"

"Yeah, a reflection, in his glasses. I could see the knife cutting my neck. And all the time he had this smile on his face. A funny one, like he had just done something bad. Then the tube went into my neck. I saw it all on the doctor's glasses."

"Oh, Danny. I am very sorry."

And he stopped talking. Memories of that night were intruding. Each ghost found a spot in the room. A knife slashed into flesh beside him. He began to shiver.

"Are you OK, Danny?" Jewel asked, concern clear to him on her face, although she tried not to show it.

That, too, was the same. Then, slowly, he tried once more to disconnect the separate incidents.

Except this time, as he came back from wherever the ghosts took him, it was children dying, rather than grownups. Rufus, the black boy in the bed next to him. Dead. They were instant friends. Rufus did all the talking and Danny the listening. He died and was taken away. Danny was just warming to the friendship, his first since…

"He is recovering," Jewel is told, "but there is some question about his leg. We want to keep him for a while."

Panic.

"What's wrong with his leg?"

"Probably nothing. We just want to make certain."

"**Inexplicably** for the bulbar form of polio," Jewel is told by another physician, "his right leg seems to have been affected. The weakness is barely perceptible, but it is real."

The rest is a pastiche to her of words and thoughts, but not always meanings. She hears "Sister Kenny." Rosalind Russell and hope come to mind. Then she hears "lag" and "months" and "brace" and can only wonder how she and Danny can long survive without each other. Then something snaps her to attention.

"We don't know everything we wish about the disease," she hears.

VI

JEWEL'S main duty at Osborn, more important than helping Henry and more important than the minor editing that she does, is to return Hutchinson's things to their proper places. This involves books, journals, and other documents to libraries, shelves, and drawers. Other things, specimens, instruments, or the funny finger-bowl-like specimen dishes, she realizes early on are in their right place wherever they happen to be. First thing in the morning, before graduate students and others arrive to distract her from the task, and immediately after tending to glassware, she cruises the lab and Hutchinson's office in search of misplaced items. Then she searches for a home for them. Glassware, especially broken and in need of replacement, is less a problem now that Hutchinson is no longer directly involved with lake chemistry, although students working in the lab—male all—too often need tidying after.

"At least you don't have to clean up after Hutchinson's clumsiness," Larry Slobodkin tells her by way of apology, although none of the mess is his own. "It was most acute during the days of radioactive tracer studies. Not coincidentally, they were initiated when someone—name always withheld—ACCIDENTALLY spilled some radioactive phosphorus into Linsley Pond."

Many items seem to move on their own from lab bench or chair to Hutchinson's desk and back again. She lets them do so. Anything that does have a place, however, is relentlessly returned to it.

Recent issues of *Ecology* are stacked on a bookshelf behind Hutchinson's desk chair. Others are archived in a book closet off the lab. "Recent," however, means recently used, not recently published. What goes where is never clear, even to Hutchinson.

The issue in Jewel's hands is several years out of date, but ecology research ages slowly, she knows. She scans the titles to see if any might be relevant to the chapter Hutchinson is currently writing. Something with a penciled check mark next to it having to do with the total mineral content of lakes catches her eye, but what is below it immediately rivets her attention. The title, "A Commentary on American Plant Ecology, Based on the Textbooks of 1947-1949," is not worth a second glance to her, but the author is.

Friedrick V. Küchler, she reads, shuddering as from cold. It is not some sort of book review, she realizes as she settles into Hutchinson's chair to read. It is something like a call to arms.

"If it is to be thought of as an indictment," she reads, "then it is an indictment of the era—but not of individuals. I have been accused, in this manuscript, both of being holier-than-thou, and of being satanic. With either accusation, I plead that to be both forceful and modest at the same time is a difficult task."

One phrase in it catches her eye as being quintessentially Küchlerian.

"This paper was not intended," it reads, "for those men not yet dead."

It is the most unusual thing Jewel has ever read in *Ecology*. And it is as if Küchler is in the room with her, sharing the thoughts, using exactly the words she would expect from him, complete with the metaphors that he called complex, but grammatically might best be deemed mangled.

Americans, she reads, have not "advanced beyond a 'natural history' stage of development" in ecological science, according to Küchler. Perhaps, he suggested, they should take to calling themselves naturalists, instead of ecologists.

His comments on the four books, therefore, were "in the nature of a critical analysis of certain methodologic and epistemologic foundations of American Ecology." The problems were not with the books, but with the foundations upon which they stood.

"The immaturity and artlessness of some of these foundations deserve serious scrutiny in these times that have seen the rise of Nazi physics and Soviet genetics," Jewel reads further into the article, which runs to twenty-three pages. "As Americans, we bugle our claim that totalitarian straight-jacketing of the scientific intellect destroys science. It follows as a corollary that freedom of the scientific intellect is a precious privilege, and those who possess it have a deep obligation to exercise it for the advance of science. It comes as a curious anomaly to find evidence of a self-imposed imprisonment on the part of some scientific workers, with apparent contentment on their part. If such scientists can accept so placidly the control of their thoughts by traditional dogma, one wonders whether they might not accept with equal placidity the control of their thoughts by governmental decree."

That mouthful was crammed into one of two paragraphs with quotations from John Locke, Albert Einstein, and James B. Conant. It is all so like Fred, Jewel thinks. There also was the claim that he was not trying to "impose a Küchlerian opinion upon those who are in the field of ecology."

Küchler called Clements, a "speculative philosopher" who had the "extraordinary ability to take an idea, organize it, break it down, classify it to a degree of minutiae that not only leaves nothing for anyone else to do but defeats its very purpose by giving us ultimate particles which are identical with those we already know." Clements's "pseudo-theological system" interfered with common sense in practical matters, Küchler continued, such as restoring an eroded hillside or managing rangeland. Then Küchler spread his litany of complaints onto Clements's "harem of adherents," as he called them.

Ecology at the moment, according to Küchler, was innocent "of the principles of scientific methodology," insidiously so. American ecologists had a "pathic fear" of using their minds, he wrote, so as not to be wrong. Ecological theories were not proposed and tested. They were simply accepted.

So this was what Fred was working on when ...

She lets the thought drop. She gets up and takes the journal out into the laboratory. It is now mid-morning, but Peter Wangersky, unmistakable in his dark-rimmed glasses, is the only one there. Peter started with Hutchinson at the same time as MacArthur and Werntz, but he is older, having served in the military during the war, then taken advantage of the GI Bill. He is down in Hutchinson's lab instead of the spacious third-floor room he shares with the other two. He claims he can think better away from that facility. According to him, it has too much the ambiance of a fraternity living room for him, with its easy chair, sofa, and rickety chairs.

"Have you read this?" Jewel asks, handing him the journal, open to the appropriate page. "Küchler's commentary on ecology?"

"Oh yes. That," Peter answers with something of a sneer on his face. "No, I didn't, but there was some discussion soon after it came out. Quite a few laughs, too, about it, as I recall. There is really nothing new to it, though."

"Nothing new? He paints a rather dire picture of ecology."

"Who does?"

Larry Slobodkin has just wandered back in. A former student between jobs and now a postdoc, he is temporarily Jewel's roommate in the lab, "Hutch's" lab, as he calls it. Since Slobodkin's arrival, all the students have taken to calling Hutchinson that nickname. Evelyn, which Hutchinson claims to prefer, seems too informal for students, even grad students. "Dr." is inappropriate for someone without a doctoral degree, Hutchinson insists, while "Professor" is rarely used in formal address in American universities. "Mr." is almost pejorative in American academic spaces. "Hutch" feels perfect on their tongues.

"It's plant ecology," Peter continues.

"That's old ecology," Slobodkin says on looking at Küchler's article, his face taking on a dismissive expression. "That stuff went out with nineteenth century geography. It's really only good for getting elderly botanists out in the field for fresh air and exercise. I really don't keep up with plant ecologists."

"What? Life zones and such?"

It is Dick Benoit, speaking just as dismissively. He has just come into the room with Hutchinson.

"Population and community ecology are now hot, Jewel," he says. "Although, there are some interesting things coming out of Wisconsin. Interesting methods of analysis."

"But isn't that exactly what bio-ecology is?" she asks.

"Hardly."

Hutchinson now adds his opinion as he hangs his winter overcoat on a wooden peg beside his office door. In the wintertime, at least, it is as much a sign as is the door being open that he is there for the business of having students pop in on him without appointment.

"That all depends on climax and the climax concept is dead," he explains. "I always said that if an ecosystem is like an organism, then we should be measuring its metabolism. Mathematics was the language I thought was missing from bio-ecology, Jewel. And have you read Gleason? Or Whittaker? And there is someone else, whose name does not come to mind. At Wisconsin, I believe. I am afraid that plant ecology has otherwise been very arthritic."

"Curtis," someone offers.

"Whittaker?" Jewel repeats.

She recognizes Hutchinson's remarks as coming from his review of *Bio-Ecology*. She chooses to let them pass. But that name jars her as much as having stumbled onto Küchler's article had.

"Robert H. Whittaker. A brilliant person. Keep your eye on him," Hutchinson announces before he and Benoit disappear into his office and the door is closed, something that usually only indicates his absence.

Jewel turns to Larry. Once he heard that she was a mother—an impression that Jewel chose not to clear up—Slobodkin adopted Jewel as a "sort of Jewish grandmother," as he put it, for his newborn. MacArthur had already adopted her as a "Waspish" grandmother for the same purpose. In return for her advice on babies, both took her instantly into their confidence.

"So, what could have riled Küchler so much about these textbooks?" Jewel asks. "It had to have been something more than just their Clementsian point of view."

"I don't know. It's all plant stuff. Maybe he was just ticked that his own textbook wasn't getting published. He's still passing it around publishers, I understand."

"Both Oosting and Daubenmire were at Wisconsin around the time Küchler was there," Jewel ponders aloud.

"You know," Slobodkin says to her as he glances at the closed office door, "I can see that Hutch thinks very highly of you. It must be something he sees in your face. Did you know that I was admitted to Yale based on his belief that he can recognize scientific talent from facial appearance? In my case, it was from a photograph. I should have bought that photographer a present! Although my high GREs maybe didn't hurt."

"He hired me after speaking to Shelford on the phone," Jewel says.

"Shelford? Never happened!" Larry counters animatedly. "If he told you that, he made it up."

"But why don't you go on for a PhD?" Wangersky asks.

Jewel's red face makes him wish he could be somewhere else.

"Why not?" Slobodkin persists after Wangersky finds a reason to go elsewhere.

Larry has been letting his hair grow. Jewel is suddenly struck by its resemblance to Little Orphan Annie's. She stifles a giggle.

"Somehow," he continues, "Hutch gets the best out of everyone. His teaching policy is nothing more than the careful avoidance of any teaching, I think. And it works just great. It fits his philosophy of science. Nothing is outside his field. That's how Gordon Riley became an oceanographer and Tom Odum a systems scientist. That's why he is letting Klopfer do a dissertation on animal behavior, even though Hutch knows less about it than Peter."

"They're learning together," Jewel suggests, putting down the manuscript pages she picked up, but still avoiding Larry's question.

"Absolutely! Although that has drawbacks too. Did I ever tell you that he assigned me to enroll in a class on symbolic logic? I did but I was drowning in it and wanted out. I asked him if it was really that important to know symbolic logic, thinking I had him cornered. Without batting an eye, he said, Perhaps not, but it is certainly important to know how it feels to be doing symbolic logic. Then he smiled at me."

"Was it?"

"Hmm. Yeah. Maybe. I don't know!"

Hutchinson and his students, postdocs, and hangers-on have been leading Jewel through snatches of overheard conversations into a totally different kind of ecology from that of Cowles and Clements —or even Allee or Shelford. New names slowly force their way into her pantheon of scientists: Forbes, Grinnel, Pearl, Lindeman, and Lack. Some are exotic: Lotka, Verlhurst, Gause, and Vernadsky. Some are the former Hutchinson students that are well known to her: Riley, Smith, Slobodkin. Ed Deevey and Raymond Lindeman, she overhears, shared a sandwich lunch in the fourth floor attic at Osborn and out of it came a totally abstract new way of looking at ecosystems: through its energy pathways. It is now part of the Lindeman legend, along with the steps Hutchinson had to take after Lindeman's untimely death to get the paper published that launched the study of ecosystem metabolism. That Allee had been dismissive of the paper was one of the few parts of the legend that Jewel already knew.

And Lindeman, Jewel overheard, came to Yale to be Hutchinson's postdoc fresh from his dissertation work rowing a boat on a boggy lake in Minnesota with Helen and Murray Buell. They were Fred Küchler's good friends, she knew, when he was with his beloved Dr. Cooper. Why, she wondered, did Küchler seem to know nothing about ecosystems, then? She also learned that Oosting and Daubenmire were Cooper's grad students at the same time. And yet Küchler had taken them to task as authors of two of the books he criticized in his Commentary.

Why, she wondered, the lack of loyalty? Add Humphries, Cooper's other PhD student, and Lindeman, virtually his student, to that all-star group of students and it compared favorably with any of Hutchinson's. But Hutchinson's intellectual offspring were building each other—and Hutch—up. Why didn't Cooper's students do the same? Was it that Cooper was retired? Was it a peculiarity of the particular students? Was it Eastern—and British—erudition versus Midwestern pragmatism? Or was it the subject? Plant ecology dying and being replaced by whatever was fermenting around Jewel— population biology? All were difficult questions for her, but wasn't that what Küchler predicted in his Commentary?

And there are old names in new settings: Odum—or the Odums, for there are two of them. Younger brother Tom, this legend

Ecologists   188

goes, abandoned an engineering career in order to teach his doctoral professor—Hutchinson—about cybernetics, the science of the control of systems. Or is it the other way around? Legends can be so murky. Howard T., as the younger brother is known in print, then convinces the Okie to drop his studies of birds and look at the big picture. "Put away your microscope," he urges (in the legend), "and look through a macroscope!" and off they go to study the ecology of an island before it is blown up by an H-bomb, with all the financial support they need gratis the Atomic Energy Commission. It is all enough to make a soon-to-be middle-aged pretend beatnik and ecologist's head spin.

Larry Slobodkin proves to be right about Hutchinson's intentions for Jewel.

"When you finally decide to go on with your PhD, Jewel," Hutch says to her one day, "I must warn you to curb your compulsive tendency to gather information to no particular purpose, as that Midwestern exposure may have created in you. I must tell you a little story that may be amusing, or at least informative. When I decided I should be a limnologist, I decided to get some direction from the best. They were, of course—?"

Jewel shrugs her shoulders.

"E. A. Birge and Chancy Juday. You might look into their work. They were kind enough to let me spend a week at the Trout Lake Laboratory in Wisconsin. I learned a fabulous amount about limnological technique but came away with two feelings of dissatisfaction. One was that it would be nice to know how to put all their mass of data into some sort of informative scheme of general significance. The other was that it would be nice to have either tea or coffee, without seeming decadent, for breakfast. I now suspect a connection between the two. I think Ray Lindeman had trouble getting that paper accepted because he and I had been suffering some sort of commonsense backlash generated all the way back at the Reformation by the ultra-intellectual and anti-empirical aspects of medieval scholasticism, which backlash flourished in America wherever a Puritanical attitude was still strong. My first student, Gordon Riley, suffered similarly with his excellent dissertation. Now you, Jewel, I've noticed are definitely not opposed to tea or coffee—or even stronger stimulants?"

VII

THE lab is locked. Danny has been put to bed, always a trial. He complained again about not being able to sleep. No matter how he tried he could not remember his mother, what she looked like, how her voice sounded. Jewel's usual words that she is his mother now only partially soothed. Still, it was the last of her daily duties, sad as it was. She is free for the night.

Jewel is also restless. The radio has no appeal for her. She wishes she had indulged in a television set, even though she believes it would be bad for Danny. She needs the kind of mindless oblivion she knows watching those singers and comedians on the grainy little screen would give her. Somehow, unlike the same tunes on the radio, the inane dramatizations she watched on Your Hit Parade with her downstairs neighbor sucked all thoughts out of her mind. And that was not a bad feeling. They were mostly thoughts about having nothing to her life but days in the lab and evenings and weekends with Danny.

Ten North Frederick lies beside The Courage to Be. The O'Hara novel she finished the night before. The Paul Tillich book has remained half read on her bedside table for years, more reminder of an obligation than invitation to finish. She found more to ponder in The Screwtape Letters. Twain and Dickens have no appeal this night. They remain on the shelf next to the Nearings' Living the Good Life and Margaret Mead's Coming of Age in Samoa, both also only partially read. After pacing back and forth and rejecting The Organization Man and an overdue library copy of Michener's Tales of the South Pacific, she takes out a piece of paper and starts to write.

"Life has so caught and held me to its rhythm," is the first line. She rewrites it, splitting it at "me." The rest of the poem goes quickly. She sits down at her typewriter and transcribes it on a blue sheet of stationary as,

>Life has so caught and held me
>to its rhythm
>Thru all my daily acts I feel
>its beat,

> And order groceries and meat
> in metric feet.

That about sums me up, she thinks. There is no room anywhere in the trap of this little apartment in this once-grand house in this rapidly deteriorating neighborhood to plant even a single tomato.

She wishes she could find for Danny the kind of life she had at Old Saybrook when she was his age. The beach and the fields, a different class of children, it could not but work to bring him out of his shell. But that was a world of money.

But should it be? Robert MacArthur keeps telling her that he intends to somehow or other raise his children in Vermont. She picks up Living the Good Life but puts it down when she realizes she had not bookmarked where she had left off. Reading it again from the beginning seemed too ambitious for the evening.

She takes a small box off a bookshelf, instead, and sets it on her desk. After a second to admire the tiny cat images that decorate the box, she folds her poem in half and drops it inside. Then she picks out a similar folded sheet of paper from the box. Frowning, she puts it back. Rummaging further, she comes upon another poem. "Cloak" is its title.

"What does this say about me before?" she asks aloud. Then she reads,

> Oh! Surely those eyes held love;
> Else were I naked in an unfriendly place.
> That quickened step, that quick averted
> > look
> Were but the effort to hide tenderness
> Which, like a fragrant rose, you would
> > withhold
> Because you deemed its thorns too dangerous
>
> Say it was thus!
> Leave me not standing, shivring in
> > suspense
> But draw your cloak of gentleness about

>   me
> And lead me hence.

"I should have sent it," she thinks aloud. "And this one."
She is looking at a poem titled "Two Functions."

> In our partnership leave to me the
>   domestic function,
> And tho the hearth be warm, be not
>   chained to the hearth
> But come and go, to carry its glowing
>   warmth
> To a world where faith in creative love
> Is all but dead.

"Did I send that one?" she wonders, still aloud.
She hopes not, but she knows she did. It is a carbon copy.
She certainly would not write something like that now. So ladylike. So spinsterish. "I think I did send it," she decides. "Why did I ever save it?" She pulls out another. "But did I send this one?"

> And I love you, and I shall not mock my
>   truth
> With travestying caution. Let none
>   say
> 'She played her cards right well'.
>
> True loving is no game of cheap
>   advantage
> One on a side. I say again
>
> You have stirred depths in me I did
>   not know;
> I can repay you only in sharing their
>   beauty;
> Enter my life and see if it
>   be not so…

"So strange not to remember," she says with tired finality.

She should write more, she decides. She should write long discursive poems, built with powerful phrases, full of American life. She wants to write, she realizes like Neal and Jack. Maybe she should get a roll of adding-machine tape and see if she can find a way to feed it through her typewriter and just fire away. But how can she? She is so mentally stuck in a New Haven apartment and her academic corridors that her words will never break free of those bounds. Could she write poetry like theirs about the logistic equation?

She would much rather write a letter, she thinks as she looks at the bundles of letters that are in the box. The ribbons with which she had tied them together when she left Detroit have stayed undisturbed. Küchler's and Liza's are the largest.

Liza and she have parted company, even epistolary, over their incompatible views on atom bombs and nuclear power. Küchler ... well, better not go there.

Maybe it is time to throw them away, she thinks. Then she wonders who might be keeping her letters.

She should write a letter every night, she decides, instead of the poems that she begins then abandons. To whom?

Hutchinson, who dearly loves children, but has none of his own, has adopted Danny in the same sense that he and Margaret adopted Yemaiel when they sheltered her during the bleak days of the war, when London was not a fit place for children. Danny appears every day after school in Hutch's lab, where Jewel can keep an eye on him while he does his homework. Evelyn watches the clock as anxiously as she does until he arrives safely.

"What are you afraid of?" he first persisted with Danny. "Your mom tells me you are having nightmares."

When Danny said nothing, he suggested counseling, as had the doctor who released the boy from the polio ward. A devout Freudian, Evelyn steered Jewel to an analyst on the Yale faculty.

"Maybe Freudian analysis is not meant for children," Jewel told him when they quit after a few sessions.

His surprise invitation to them to accompany him to New Haven's Christ Church for Easter services had similar lack of success. Its ritualistic High Episcopalian service, heavy with incense, so cherished by both Hutchinsons, at first intrigued Danny and Jewel. After several visits, though, they found other things to do Sunday mornings, more often than not, simply staying in bed.

Danny does take an interest in the older man's usual invitation of "You might find this interesting." But to his disappointment, Danny is more interested in watching a live daphnia than learning its scientific name or how it differs from others having other names.

"Would you like to study lakes?" Evelyn, which is how he insisted Danny call him, tried a different tack.
"Would I have to go out in them or on them?"
"Indeed."
Danny was aghast at the thought.
"I will only if I can study them from shore," he said with finality.
And they did, on certain Saturdays at Linsley Pond.

Danny's nightmare wakes Jewel before it does him.
"I want my mother," he says as she cradles his head in her arms.
"You have a mother," she says. "I'm your mother."
"I can't see my father any more."

VIII

UNUSUALLY warm weather for December has brought students out of their dorm rooms like rabbits in search of grass after a thaw. Footballs fly across the quad. Brown loafers splash through puddles. Someone in an Argyle sweater is practicing his putting. Caught in the sun, Sterling Library's sternly Gothic tower looks proudly modern to Jewel, an absolutely joyous skyscraper. Even the carillon in Harkness Tower is buoying her mood by playing "Jingle Bells."

Jewel is on a quest to find a paper on some African lakes in the Proceedings of the Royal Society of Tanzania. That and the date, 1923, was all Evelyn, as she now consistently calls him, could give her as guidance. It had come up in her reading of a passage in the massive first volume of his *Treatise* manuscript, *Geography, Physics and Chemistry*, which nearing a thousand pages, Jewel thinks should itself be broken into smaller volumes. The subject matter had been a surprise to her from the first, being so far removed from biology, but from the first, he had assured her that she was exactly the reader the material needed. Well, she could make no sense of the passage. How, she complained to Evelyn, could she offer any suggestions on rewriting it?

"Yes, I think I can see your difficulty," he told her, almost indifferently, an unusual mood for him. "Perhaps if you read the paper cited, you might see the passage more clearly."

Jewel, expecting more guidance, made no sign of leaving.

"I must confess at the moment to be in a quandary over this Wenner-Bren invitation," he said in an explanation of sorts. "I don't see how I can possibly have the time for it. I believe it is the same week I have accepted an invitation to give a talk at Woods Hole this summer. Unless I have my years confused."

Then, after stopping to rummage through papers on his desk, he suddenly announced triumphantly, "Ah, not at all!"

"Do what you think you will enjoy more," Jewel suggested, still awaiting guidance. "Woods Hole is gorgeous in summer."

"Yes, of course. You've been there."

"Where is this, uh—?"

"Wenner-Bren. It is a philanthropic institution of some sort. I think they may have funded some of Margaret Mead's work."

"Well?" Jewel asked, still waiting for an answer.

"Oh dear," Evelyn said, finally putting aside the invitations, "of course. I thought you'd be off to the library already. I have no idea where the foundation is, but the conference is to be held at Princeton."

So it was off to the library.

Jewel likes visits to Sterling Library almost as much as she does the departmental library, with its ceiling painted in clouds and blue sky. Trips Evelyn asks her to make to the Peabody Museum are also more treat than errand. Dillon Ripley is always so kind to her, even inviting her to his up-coming holiday dinner party. She has been particularly buoyed by it ever since. Surrounded almost constantly by young men, Jewel feels isolated in New Haven from women, especially ones with children. Unlike at Illinois, laboratory assistants, librarians, and secretarial workers are what seem to represent women to Yale men. There are few women graduate students and even fewer women professors. Faculty wives are almost invisible. She knows Georgiana by name only. That Evelyn even has a wife is a surprise. Former students tell her that, although she shares a deep interest in art, music, and religion with Evelyn, she does not share his interest in science or its students. According to Larry Slobodkin, the only time she tolerated students in her home was when Hutch invited them to hear her sing. Fortunately, that painful tradition seems to have been forgotten.

Evelyn is tight-lipped about his private life. Rumor has it that there have been other wives, one possibly on the faculty at Yale. Rumor also has it that houseguests are not tolerated at the Hutchinson's, but for Margaret Mead and Rebecca West. Even Hutch's relatives are directed to the local YMCA when visiting from England.

Still, according to Evelyn, it was his Margaret who insisted that Danny be included in Ripley's invitation when Jewel voiced her doubts about bringing him. It was she, he had also assured Jewel, whose idea it had been to throw a little party for Danny at their house. That had been when Danny had been released from the polio rehab wing of the hospital two Christmases before. The first Christmas had not been a happy holiday. He was alternately, and unpredictably, listless and defiant, more so than since the death of his parents. Fears of all kinds seemed to occupy him fully in both moods. School held no interest for him. Friends he had not had time to make.

That had given the Hutchinsons reason to throw a small dinner party in the boy's honor. There was not much dinner to it, only cold meats and snacks from a deli. Neither Hutchinson cooked anything more complicated than a boiled egg. That evening had not cheered the boy. Unfortunately, in an attempt to talk through Danny's fears, Hutch had launched into a discourse on Italian werewolves. Then he reminisced about how frightened he had been by the ghosts he imagined in the wine cellar of his childhood home. He also told a story of the phantasm of his grandmother, as seen walking past the tenants of her former room on the very night that she suffered a fatal stroke miles away. The Bach requiem on the record-playerwas no help, either, to the boy, who was becoming used to the sounds of Dizzy Gillespie and Charlie Parker coming from Jewel's record-player.

Jewel thought Margaret Hutchinson dowdy and overly feminine. She was unable to drive from her mind her hostess's resemblance to a Victorian armchair, especially one draped in too many lace doilies. Margaret said not a word for the several minutes she stood awkwardly next to Jewel. When she finally did speak to Jewel, it was to excuse herself to look into some mischief "My Sambo," as she called the cat, was causing at the buffet.

"Siamese cats and no sex, I imagine," Larry Slobodkin whispered in Jewel's ear, "but doesn't Hutch seem to adore her?"

"There is, of course," Hutchinson was apparently instructing the boy, "an enormous literature on such phantasms, which are hard to treat statistically, though they are very convincing when one is brought up against a case personally."

The genealogy of the de Mezzis, from whom his mother descended, Hutchnson's next topic, merely bored Danny. Hutch then switched to experiments in mental telepathy that had been performed during the London blitz.

"I am prepared to take psychical phenomena seriously, however," he said, still thinking he was addressing Danny, "even after the curious suggestions of fraud in Soal's experiments that is occupying the pages of Science and Nature at this moment, I still feel the history of the experiments strongly suggests real parapsychological phenomena…"

That was when MacArthur and Slobodkin gently ushered Danny and aunt out.

Alas, Jewel fails to find the journal in any library on campus, even though Jewel insists on having a memory of handling a copy of it recently. There is no library in the country, apparently, that subscribed to the journal, except for the one Jewel should have looked through first, but did not. The volume at issue is in Evelyn's personal library. Jewel finds it under some reprints of papers and speeches by Margaret Mead, who had just been through Yale on a visit to Evelyn, it seemed to Jewel. So had Rebecca West. Both gave ample indications that they were personal friends.

Anthropologists, writers, geochemists, even a historian of Russia, are all claimed by Hutchinson as colleagues and all become friends, it seems to Jewel. His reputation for erudition is such that he is one of the few scientists accepted into Yale's Elizabethan Club, which Jewel heard him describe to Rebecca West, as "dedicated to drinking tea and discussing literature beneath a likeness of that queen and a folio edition of Shakespeare." She, of course, was disappointed that their next meeting would not fit her schedule, but Evelyn gallantly offered and succeeded at rearranging the organization's meeting times to suit the author.

It was a heady world that was unfolding for Jewel outside Hutchinson's little office with its always ready boiled eggs and Bunsen burner set up to offer tea to anyone who should drop in. And people did. Stuart Little, come to consult with Ed Deevey on radiocarbon dating of lake sediments, stopped by to let Evelyn uncork two bottles of claret, labels covered, to test whether Little's tritium dating method was truly superior to an educated palate.

"Next time," he promised as he ushered Little out, "it will be Champagne to celebrate the Nobel Prize you are certain to win for your carbon-dating discovery."

"You flatter me," Little remarked. Jewel was impressed at it being without a hint of inebriation, for she could see that both bottles were empty. "However, the only work that could ever earn me that kind of honor is the still-classified work I did for the Manhattan Project."

With that pronouncement, he opened the door and walked straight into the closet. Dignity somehow still intact, he then turned and exited through the door on the other side of the lab.

Konrad Lorenz, a legend literally and figuratively and another recent visitor, was, of course, monopolized by Peter Klopfer, as was only just, especially since Peter had not been invited to the small dinner the Hutchinson's gave for the great man. Lorenz was.

How like Santa Claus, Jewel had been struck. His white beard was thick. His cheeks were rosy. And eyes were twinkly, of course.

His lecture was a sack full of presents to Jewel. There were the concepts of imprinting, internalization, aggressive drive, and overflow, all totally new to her. And he brought animals that seemed somehow inappropriate to bring up in a room full of ecologists. Graylag goose, jackdaw, and stickleback, Jewel had never heard the names spoken before.

Jewel purposefully missed Gene Odum, but she did read the paper he presented. To Jewel, it was clear that the Odum brothers looked at the atoll they studied in the same way that Hutchinson and Deevey and Lindeman looked at lakes, only in reverse. Transformed by his brother Tom into an ecosystem scientist, the Okie wrote a textbook popular for its ecosystem point of view and the brevity of its prose. Gene Odum's name was now formidable in ecology.

Hutchinson finds himself unusually at a loss for words at Dillon Ripley's party. The topic of discussion has turned to politics. He can merely mumble that he believes only in "something like guild socialism" when Jewel confesses that she likes Ike in the up-coming election.

Others, liberal academics all, Jewel thinks without derision, remembering Shelford's politics fondly, vigorously return the conversation to the merits of the "egghead" Stevenson over the soldier that Winston Churchill had called a "clerk."

"The really important human problems," Evelyn in frustration says to stop the conversation, "I believe, cannot be stated in any clear way, much less can any formal solution be offered."

Jewel wanders away to track down Danny. He is with other children, but rather than joining them in a game of Monopoly, he is watching "I Love Lucy" on an expensive-looking television in one corner of the large room.

"…aspect of the goddess does not appear on the cimurata," she hears Evelyn holding sway in another room. "The mano a fico, an obviously phallic gesture, was part of an ancient Roman charm, the res turpicula, or shameful thing, of which it formed one end…"

He can certainly change a topic, Jewel thinks, and his fiasco at the dedication of the Laboratory of Oceanography at Woods Hole has had no impact on him at all. There, with an audience expecting a lecture on oceanography, he made an intellectual leap from cowry shells to the history and sexual connotations of their land equivalent, the mandrake root.

"A vocal minority," he had reported afterwards to Jewel, "believed that sex and religion were immiscible with seawater and complained to the management."

Dillon Ripley's wife has a giant friend from their days working together at the OSS during the war. She is a "full one meter ninety, in height," Jewel hears someone remark. Her large, fully filled frame towers over her husband when they are together, even as his sharp itellect towers over hers in conversation. She is currently in the kitchen preparing something French, demonstrating techniques learned at Le Cordon Bleu in Paris. Her sing-song voice rings out pleasantly above the din of the party, although not enough to be understood by Jewel. Whatever she is making, Jewel will have to miss out on. Danny has capriciously decided he cannot stay another minute at the party.

"...horn as indicator of sexual infidelity is," Evelyn holds forth as Jewel and Danny leave, "of course, very widespread. In Naples cornuto or cornuta meant not only the husband or wife of an unfaithful spouse, but also the brother or sister of someone so misbehaving. Saint Martin was regarded as…"

Hutch has exchanged his first audience for another, Jewel thinks, but the subject is exactly the same.

IX

JEWEL feels it an honor when she is invited to share the excitement of Hutchinson's ecology seminars. Up to now, she has felt like an intellectual outsider when ideas spilled out of classes and seminars and into the lab. She listened avidly as one line of reasoning was countered by another. Envious of the speakers, she was tempted to insert ideas of her own into the fray, but she stayed silent, convinced that it was not her place to do so. Now she will no longer need to.

"Are you going?" she asks a student who has newly appeared in the lab. He is sharing space with her, doing whatever it is there that he is doing until allotted a more permanent space. Mostly he appears to Jewel to be trying to settle things regarding his apartment.

"Vas?" he asks.

"The seminar?"

He shakes his head and shrugs his shoulders.

"German?" she asks. "Your accent?"

"I was born in Germany, it is true, but my accent," he answers, speaking slowly, enunciating clearly, "I do not think it is German, by any means."

And she has to go. She does not want to be late, not to the seminar's first meeting.

Slipping into a seat in the back row of the large lecture hall, Jewel notices Wangersky, Kohn, Klopfer, and MacArthur, all sitting together near the front. There are others spread about the room. There is Gordon Riley, now a professor in the department. There are also a few faces grouped together that she does not recognize. Rows of empty seats surround them.

Farther back is an attractive young couple, Jane and Lincoln Brower, whose study of butterflies is technically supervised by entomologist Charles Remington, but who have been taken under Hutch's wing. Each is so interested in the other's thesis work, that each is the other's assistant, he on her monarchs and viceroys and she on his swallowtails.

Ed Deevey, just back from a Fulbright year in Denmark, stands at the podium beside Hutchinson. There has been drama building concerning Ed's return. In his absence, Dan Livingstone was shooting down a major part of Ed's research oeuvre. Data that Dan gathered and analyzed on the development of Linsley Pond is in direct contradiction to Ed's published description. Dan fears his professor was a bit too impressed by the beauty of the s-shaped sigmoid curve and had relied on it too heavily in the paper he wrote about the pond. Dan fretted interminably about it with others, afraid of what would happen when Deevey learned of his results.

"Attempted professoricide," he once muttered in Jewel's hearing, "is not a recommended way to launch a career."

To no surprise to anyone but Livingstone, the drama resolved itself happily. Deevey took the research setback in stride. Livingstone's feared "Et tu, Brute" moment never came to pass. He is now joking with his professor from the front row.

"You're not gonna show us your uncanny ability to go right to the periphery of an issue, are you?" Jewel can hear Dan, even from the back of the room, as Ed begins his talk.

"I guess I should start with the Leslie matrix," he says, staring at the large, newly washed blackboard.

He speaks hesitantly, in a quiet voice. Some sentences simply trail away. It makes Jewel wish she had sat closer or could now muster enough courage to move to a seat up front. Fortunately, the math he writes out with elegant precision and the explanatory sketches he makes help to keep her involved.

Informality runs rampant. Hutchinson soon makes the kind of interjection that only he is capable of making. He tells about a tree in Tenerif that blew down the previous century at an age of six thousand. That leads to a report about sea anemones living in captivity for sixty-five years. He gives both items appropriate citations.

When the sigmoid curve comes up, Deevey's lecture totally falls apart from the crush of all the informality. The point of the vital statistics Deevey has been presenting, Hutch interrupts, is that from them can be calculated "the intrinsic rate of increase" for a population. In its various aspects and consequences, it is what the seminar will be about.

Ed then goes is off on a tangent about black widow spiders. It requires a quote from Cicero: "grow old early if you would be old long." Jewel strongly suspects it and its original Latin were fed to him by Hutchinson.

Population terms are flying about Jewel's head. They are interspersed with names that are conjoined by hyphens apparently into perpetuity, "Lotka-Volterra" and "Pearl-Verlhurst." Much of it is surprisingly familiar to her. She can see it coming to her with less mathematical precision, single page by single page, from Elton's book on rodent cycles.

The lemming crashes and the predators crash and migrate, she reads in her mind's eye. The lemming begins to recover before the slower-breeding predator can catch up. This is a rough description, Elton had emphasized, of just a part of a phenomenon that is usually referred to as Lotka-Volterra oscillation.

She wants to recite Elton aloud to the group, but there is a digression by Hutchinson on William of "Ockham," or "Ockam," or "Occam." He writes out all three spellings on the blackboard. Then there is something that she is sure she remembers from Voles, Mice and Lemings that she tries without success to get properly into her notes. She variously hears it as "Gause's hypothesis," "Gause's postulate," and "Gause's axiom." Which is it?

"It's not an axiom," Robert MacArthur corrects someone.

"What exactly is an axiom?" the someone asks.

"Not that," says MacArthur, and the matter is dropped by those in front.

"Gause's Law?" someone from the center seats suggests tentatively.

"Yes," Hutch says. "There could well be some sort of law there. We will decide on that at the end, perhaps. Next time, Robert will guide us through all the mathematical formalism in Leslie's paper. I certainly am not capable of it."

Hutchinson is capable, however, of providing the group with the words of the epitaph on the monument for Malthus at his grave at Bath Abbey. And Condorcet's views, in the original French, on birth control. Both fall on what Jewel thinks must be ears like hers: deaf, but appreciative.

Jewel remembers, however, the experiments Elton described Gause doing and the mathematics they tested. They appeared in Elton's tome right after Robert Flaherty's *Nanook of the North* made an appearance. They had to do with mite predators and prey going extinct together in lab vessels. That is, unless the prey found a refuge. The sigmoid curve, or logistic, as it is more often called, however, was robustly supported, Jewel knew well, in Gause's single-species experiments.

What is it about the logistic curve that is so attractive to theoreticians? Is it because it carries with it the marvelous musical symbol that is also the mathematical sign for integration? Is there some universal harmony that it symbolizes? But then, why calculus was needed at all for the work discussed is a question that bothers Jewel as she walks back from that seminar. The mathematics to do the actual calculations for life tables are no more than sixth-grade arithmetic, nothing beyond addition, multiplication, and division.

"Right!" Jewel suddenly blurts out, more to herself than the seminar at their next meeting. She has just put together the life table Deevey reproduced at the previous seminar that was based on work by Leslie and Ransom that Elton gave in his book that MacArthur is analyzing with that of a problem she struggled through in a matrix algebra class she took at Chicago on Liza's prodding. She was the only female in the class of mostly graduate students trying to figure out what Einstein, who at least she had heard of, and Dirac, who might as well have been a French novelist to her, and others were about in describing their universe. Then she realizes that no one in the room is speaking

MacArthur is silent before the large blackboard. He had been pontificating on how to solve for the stability characteristics of a Leslie matrix when he became befuddled by the sudden misbehavior of his own chalk marks. Everyone in the room is uncomfortably waiting for him to figure his way out of whatever has brought his thinking to a halt. Meanwhile, accusatory glances are sent Jewel's way.

"Shouldn't that be one minus lambda X?" she says casually. "You forgot the lambda."

MacArthur looks at her. Then he looks at what he has just written. Now red faced, he looks at her again. The others look around in confused embarrassment.

After years of skepticism, Jewel is now grateful that Liza had prodded her into taking that math course. And for the A's she earned in calculus in high school. Others in the room likely never had more than a smidgen of stats after their high school algebra. Biology, even ecology was not drawing in math whizzes. That was why they needed MacArthur.

"Thank you, Jewel," he finally says, having convinced himself that she is correct. Then he goes on with the solution.

"The one problem I see with Elton's data," Jewel is emboldened to say after MacArthur finishes, "is simply that he has no real definition of what a peak year is. Just looking at numbers go up and down within a local time period should result in some sort of small-term cycle, if only coincidentally. After all, in any three numbers, one has to be bigger than the other two. How much bigger? When I looked at those trapping numbers, I saw peaks in 1873, 1876, 1879, and then nothing until 1901, and not much of a peak at that. Then what? 1910. 1917. What four-year cycle? What is the year-to-year variation one can expect? Why is there no estimate of that? Isn't this like the random walk you get from coin flipping? And where does your equation show that a predator can actually help a prey increase?"

"It doesn't," a flustered MacArthur answers. "It can't. That doesn't happen."

"You might want to look at some work that an insect ecologist at Cornell has recent published," Hutchinson rises from his seat to suggest to Jewel. "He has ideas very much like yours. I think you will find them very interesting. LaMont Cole is his name. I believe I have a copy."

Along with the new reading material and a feeling of annoyance over this new ecology, more mathematics than biology, she also brings back from this seminar a useful name: Michael Warburg. He is from Israel, Hutchinson tells her after the seminar. His parents had migrated there when he was three.

She is pleased to find him in the lab.

"Israeli!" she startles him to attention. "You must have been in—?"

"The war," he interrupts wearily. "Yes. I joined the Haganah in Haifa at sixteen years. Then I became a commando in the Palmach. I was trained in guerrilla tactics and sabotage."

What can one say to that? Jewel thinks, as Warburg turns back to the papers he is filling out. No wonder he feels no need to talk about himself.

When Ruth Patrick comes from Philadelphia to give a talk, Hutchinson introduces her as "my good friend." The talk is on a paper in which she proposes a biological measure for pollution in streams. It is buried in a publication put out by the Philadelphia Academy of Science, at which she works.

She strikes Jewel as a not very good representative for her sex. She and the work she presents are dullness integrated from zero to infinity, dullness of vision, dullness of intellect, and dullness of appearance. Yet the men give her their full respect, Jewel notices. There is no breakdown into the chaos of informality.

Her talk does not take up the time allotted for it. Unlike at other seminars, Jewel does not rush to be the first to raise a hand for a question. No one raises a hand. Instead, Hutchinson has to take over the floor in order not to have the meeting adjourn embarrassingly early.

"I find very interesting that there are such a large number of species in your stream communities," he begins, "and that they represent so many phylogenetic groups. It has me thinking about something I observed when I was in Sicily recently. I was driven up Monte Pellegrino, the hill that rises above Palermo, to admire the view. A little below the summit, there is a church with a simple baroque façade that stands in front of a cave in the limestone of the hill. There, in the sixteenth century, a stalactite-encrusted skeleton was discovered, along with a cross and twelve beads. Of this skeleton nothing is certainly known save that it is of Santa Rosalia, a saint of whom little is reliably reported, save that she seems to have lived in the twelfth century and that her skeleton was found in this cave. She has been the chief patroness of Palermo ever since. But just beyond the sanctuary, fed no doubt by the water that percolates through the limestone cracks of the mountain, and which formed the sacred cave, was a small artificial pond."

No one dares interrupt him, not even those like Jewel who have heard it all before.

"Vast numbers of Corixidae were living in its water. At first I was rather disappointed because every specimen of the larger of the two species present was a female, and so lacking in most critical diagnostic features, while both sexes of the second slightly smaller species were present in about equal number. Examination of the material at leisure, and of the relevant literature, has convinced me that the two species are the common European C. punctata and C. affinis, and that the peculiar Mediterranean species are illusionary. The large C. punctata was clearly at the end of its breeding season, the smaller C. affini was probably just beginning to breed. Now what does this assemblage of promising ecologists make of that?"

Silence.

Then a brave voice rings out with, "I think it's an example of Poulson's Principle."

"Poulson's Principle?" Patrick asks. "I don't think I know that one."

"It states that the day after you give a lecture on some topic an important publication on the same topic arrives in the mail," is the answer.

"Then there's Deevey's corollary," another voice from the back of the room adds. "That states that the next year when you try to get it from the library, it is at the bindery."

"No. No. No. That's not Deevey's corollary," Jewel recognizes Dan Livingstone's voice. "Deevey's corollary is that, if you see on a restaurant menu, One egg fifty cents, second egg twenty-five cents, you order the second egg, and save twenty-five cents."

"Did he REALLY get away with that?"

"Accompanied by giggles from the waitress."

"It is the sort of observation that any naturalist can and does make all the time," Hutchinson resumes when the giggling has died down. "I don't mean about the eggs."

Guffaws, this time.

"It was not until I asked myself why the larger species should breed first, and then I asked the more general question as to why there were two and not twenty or two hundred species of the genus in the pond, that finally prompted the very general question as to why there are such an enormous number of animal species," Hutchinson continues, his bearing recovered. "Well, if each predator in a chain had twice the mass—that would be one point two six in linear dimensions—and assuming in general that twenty percent—as Lindeman showed—of the energy goes to the next level—although Larry Slobodkin found that thirteen percent was pretty much a limit—we get about the five-member maximum chains that are found."

"Are you suggesting that competition maintains that one-point-three size difference?" Jewel suddenly perks up to ask.

"Precisely! That is, approximately one point three. In theory."

Hutchinson starts writing data on the board, as the others watch in silence.

"See?" he turns to his audience after putting up data for a half-dozen pairs of species, ranging from weasels and mice to nuthatches and finches. "When species co-occur, the ratio of the larger to the small form varies from one point one to one point four. The mean is one point two eight, or roughly one point three."

He pauses for dramatic effect.

"There are at present time supposed to be about one million described species of animals. Of these, about three-quarters are insects, of which a quite disproportionately large number are members of a single order, the Coleoptera," he continues.

"By the way, there is a story, possibly apocryphal, of J. B. S. Haldane, who found himself in the company of a group of theologians. On being asked what one could conclude as to the nature of the Creator from a study of his creation, Haldane is said to have answered, An inordinate fondness for beetles."

"Well, there is your answer," Jewel offers. "Haldane seems to have hit the nail right on the head."

Her comment draws not laughs, but a mass exodus.

"This one," Hutchinson opens the next meeting, "you may like, Jewel."

And she does. It is a paper by Fred Smith. It is a critique of the experimental methods used to test the fine, exact differential equations that are purported to describe population growth and that so annoy Jewel. Random events, or stochastic events, as they are called, need to be incorporated somehow in those lovely equations before they can reflect reality, according to Smith. Hutchinson, who takes upon himself the role of presenting the paper to the Ecology Seminar, makes certain in a preamble to it that everyone knows that Smith studied under him for his PhD. He was at Yale after Deevey and at about the same time as Slobodkin.

"The degree of acceptance of such concepts as, for example, the Verlhulst-Pearl Logistic," Hutchinson reads directly from the paper, pausing to note that "Logistic" is capitalized, "and the Lotka-Volterra equation is astonishing."

In some way missed by Jewel, MacArthur takes over the discussion from Hutchinson at this point. He emphatically tries to impress on them the utility and the divine significance, as Jewel sees it, of the logistic equation and the biological consequences that can be drawn from it. He is becoming more and more frustrated by the arguments of previous years against it, he tells them, and against the idea of equilibrium in nature.

"Sure, populations Andrewartha and Birch studied fluctuated wildly from year to year, in response, I guess, to unpredictable weather, or whatever," he says in a rare display of annoyance. "Still, there are other populations, birds, my warblers, for example, that are fairly stable. Why not use all this great math on them?"

He has been looking deeply into system science, he tells them. He thinks he might have found something in information theory.

"It may be sort of a first principle" he explains. "Like Lotka was looking for with his thermodynamic idea that evolution has to proceed so as to make the total energy flux through the system a maximum. A principal such as that should explain species diversity and niche breadth and the lognormal distribution."

"That book," Hutch says authoritatively, "is really the birth of systems analysis. And his central equation is just the logistic, is it not?"

Lotka's book, long forgotten, has recently been reprinted, its title changed from Elements of Physical Biology to Elements of Mathematical Biology. The name change and publication information are duly recorded on the syllabus prepared by Hutchinson for the course.

"Yes," MacArthur answers Hutchinson's question, "essentially, but he came to it in his own way. What he borrowed from Pearl was… What was original was…"

Jewel's attention lags on both points. Mathematicians are so like boys playing games she thinks. Let's build an equation! Just for the heck of it. Then they gather together their tools and materials: numbers and operators, LaPlace transforms and chain rules. Let's start with this and do this and that to it. Not for her!

"The Lotka-Volterra equations have not the testable cause and effect of Newton's Second Law," she says aloud, "or the utilitarian mass-action predictions of reaction kinetics, or even Hardy-Weinberg equilibrium. What are they then?"

"I'm not sure I understand your point," comes from the back of the room.

"Did you ever—?" she starts to ask Warburg on getting back to her lab.

"Burn villages, shoot Arabs, rape women?"

It is not what she was going to ask, but she realizes it is what she wanted to ask had she the courage.

"Some of those things," he tells her without looking up from what he is doing. "We did level several villages. But what has you feeling so worked up that I could find that question on your face? Who do YOU want to kill?"

He is right, Jewel thinks. I am ready for violence.

"But you know," Warburg says, looking up and adopting a friendlier tone, "the Palmach also had great influence over our Israeli Tzabar culture. Take, for example, our tradition of the

Kumzitz, sitting around a fire at night, eating, talking, and having fun. We also gave public singing performances and took cross-country walking trips, some of mythical proportions."

Then as curtly as ever, he says, "But after the forty-seven Jews were killed at the Haifa oil refinery, we destroyed dozen of houses and left sixty villagers for dead. And in the northern Negev, my unit—two armored cars—destroyed nine bedouin lay-bys and one mud hut. That's how I put it in my report. Four April, nineteen forty-eight. I can still remember exactly what I wrote. It was after a mine attack on one of our patrols. My orders were to cause deaths, to blow up houses, and to burn everything possible.

"So, my dear Jewel, I suggest you take a camping trip with Danny. Sit around a fire. Roast marshmallows. Sing! Sing all those cowboy songs that Americans like to sing when camping. It's very therapeutic. Life will look better to you."

She should, she thinks. What, after all, is Danny's life with her, feeling trapped in his own body, even on outings with Evelyn? They should go camping. Vermont is but a morning's drive away.

"Hutch, sometimes I think you must look at science as some kind of an artistic achievement," Gordon Riley says at one seminar. "Do you think scientific ideas must be perceived in the same way as are paintings or poems or a string quartet? Should they be judged by their beauty?"

"Why, of course," Hutchinson answers. "Small, logical deductions from hard facts are to me what brushstrokes are to a painter."

"I absolutely agree," MacArthur adds. "That's very much like what G. H. Hardy, of the Hardy-Weinberg Law, said. That's the way math is. Some results are just beautiful. A mathematician is a maker of patterns, I think the exact quote is, and beauty the criterion by which the patterns should be judged."

"Thank you," says Hutchinson. "But if I can continue the analogy, if you follow the brushstrokes without visualizing the larger structure, what do you have?"

"Abstract expressionism?" Jewel ventures. "Jackson Pollock?"

"Delightful!"

"But I like Picasso," someone says. "He said, Art is a lie that helps show the truth. Mathematical models are very much like art."

"Picasso is Cubism," comes from the back of the room.

"Abstract expressionism is exactly it," Hutchinson brings them back on track, and with more than a hint of derision. "But, more to the point, it is not necessary in any empirical science to keep an elaborate logicomathematical system always apparent, any more than it is necessary to keep a vacuum cleaner conspicuously in the middle of the room at all times. When a lot of relevant litter has accumulated, the machine must be brought out, used, then put away."

"Thank you, Dr. Hutchinson," Jewel blurts out. "Absolutely. But only if you have a working vacuum cleaner, not some sort of abstraction of it."

"What do you mean?" MacArthur asks.

"Interesting point," Hutchinson says.

"What I mean is what am I to make of a half individual, for example?" Jewel blurts out. "That's what your vacuum cleaner picks up, Robert. Fractional individuals of all sorts. Rational, real, and irrational parts. I know that time is continuous, but what is zero point two eight three seven—or whatever— of an individual?"

The silence that follows is thick enough to be opaque. Jewel can crawl away in it, if she wishes.

"It's calculus," from Peter Klopfer diffuses things.

"You would not have Newton retract F equals m a, would you?" MacArthur asks.

"Neither would I have him live in a world without seasons or bright days and dark nights. Look, according to Elton, all kinds of trapping phenomena can bias that predator-prey cycle data you just showed. Hungry foxes, for example, are easier to catch than foxes that are eating well. That has to all be taken into account. Elton did. He looked at disease in the trappers and not just at foxes. He considered Eskimos"—Esquimaux in her mind still—"and Indians and how they trapped, and ... and ... and the taste of lemmings!"

When they get to Gause's principal, it is Georgi Gause himself who presents it. He calls it "Competitive Exclusion," the term the seminar group has settled on for it.

Gause is on his first and only visit to America. Although, his research is now in other areas, here he is in New Haven, Jewel notes, stopping in to meet Hutchinson. Not a coincidence, she thinks.

George Vernadsky, whose Russian history text is in its fifth edition and passes through the hands of many Yale students, is the other Russian at the seminar. Vernadsky's father, a Russian geochemist invented that field and the concept of biosphere, which Hutchinson has popularized, as he has the elder Vernadsky's work. But for a difference in age, the two Russians, ecologist and historian, with their Slavic features, are indistinguishable to Jewel.

Gause's is the most formal of all the presentations, even Ruth Patrick's. Like her, he reads from a prepared text. His accent is thick. Jewel supposes that Vernadsky is there in case of a need for translation. Still, the lecture is riveting for all. The experiments that Gause describes—all done in his youth, his early twenties—are now classics. And they should be, thinks Jewel. They are so clearly thought out and so well done. There is no room at all for uncertainty about their results, even if there is room for questions about the logistic-based equations they test.

"Competition for the same resource will cause species to use different niches," he concludes.

"But isn't that coexistence?" Jewel anxiously asks the first question.

"You don't understand..."

Lincoln Brower has answered her before Gause can collect his thoughts—or words, maybe. Immediately, Jewel loses interest in what Brower has to say and the argument that follows. Those three words of his did it. She does understand. The men are not listening to her. So she stops listening to them. But that they listen politely to Jane Brower the very few times she has an opinion, has Jewel fuming inside.

Maybe, Jewel thinks, it is because I am just the lab tech. No PhD. No prospect for one. Not a graduate student, so no longer a colleague. Why should she be listened to? I will never become someone they will need to deal with professionally, like Jane might.

Or is she just on the wrong wavelength for them? Cowles, they hardly know. Shelford is something of a living fossil. The only time she hears his name come up is in regard to his having had something to do with the Ecologists Union, which is now to become the Nature Conservancy.

"Do men take women for granted?" she asks Michael Warburg.

She had to track him down in his basement office. They no longer share a space together and she misses him. He is the only one she can trust to give her an honest answer.

"Take women for granted? Not in Israel."

"No. I mean intellectually."

"Intellectually? Not in Israel. I take nothing for granted about women. I had women fighting with me in my unit during the war."

Somehow, Jewel decides, Michael is not the right person for her question, after all. Then she realizes that he is the only one she has for such a question. Liza, who to the best of her knowledge is now an assistant professor at Chicago, she has not spoken to in years.

There is much inscrutable discussion the next session over an old article by a physicist, Frank Preston, who specializes in glass technology, Hutchinson tells them. He is also a birder. Preston has turned his mathematical abilities to a regularity he sees in the relationship between the number of species found in a sampling regime and their abundances. If he arranges the data on graph paper ruled off by eights, instead of tens, with each "octave," as he calls it, on the graph represented by one-eighth the space of the previous, he thinks he sees most of the bell-shaped curve that statisticians call a "normal" curve. Jewel is struck by the realization that this is the lognormal distribution in which Hutchinson and MacArthur have been seeing evidence for competition between species. It is as if she was learning a foreign language and suddenly discovered that the meaning of a word she had taken for granted actually was something opposite.

"What if this interesting mathematical relationship I just found explains it all," Robert MacArthur interjects.

He is always trying out playful "what ifs." Any idea in his opinion is worth arguing for, even if only briefly, and even if only to have it be discredited before going on to another.

"Think of this. What if a slender stick represented the resource axis for a species. Food, shelter, whatever. Then think of breaking it as representing two species dividing that resource. Odds are, it will not break exactly in half. Each successive break of course, will also be a random length. The first break will leave the largest piece, the most abundant species, and so on, for a lognormal distribution."

The last paper, again presented by Hutchinson, is a delight. It is by two young Harvard scholars, Bill Brown and Ed Wilson. Most in the group call them by those nicknames, instead of William L., Jr., and Edward O. They must know them personally, Jewel thinks, based on that informality. One, Ed, a young man with a thin nose and thinning hair, had visited Hutchinson recently, Jewel knew. The paper presents evidence for closely related species differing more in the sizes of their beaks when found together than apart. They claim it to be a general phenomenon that evolves to reduce competition, which they call "character displacement."

What a breath of fresh air to Jewel.

"Clearly these are cases of competition for the same niche," Robert MacArthur excitedly concludes.

"Character displacement does, I think, give us a mechanism to study it. It is much like the species per genus ratio," Hutchinson adds, somewhat less excitedly.

Niche has already been thrown around in what seemed to Jewel very much a common sense meaning. Niche is what Elton called the "role" that an animal plays in a community, much like the vicar, Elton's example, or teacher or greengrocer plays in a human community. Now, with MacArthur's help, Hutch is transforming a perfectly clear concept into something he describes as an "n-dimensional hyperspace" representing the role and place and resource needs, in every sense possible, for a species.

And Jewel has a revelation—two, in fact. The first is that she is in a room full of ecologists and the topic now under argumentation is their research and ideas on evolution. That is so different from the ecology she has learned until coming to Yale. The seminar has exposed her to a huge body of research and thinking about the process of evolution. More than she is capable of mastering now.

The other revelation comes to her as she listens with bemusement to these young scientists argue more and more heatedly. The only contributions that come from the old British gentleman, she realizes, who has gathered them together, is to praise whatever he can find in any argument. She realizes that she has never heard him criticize any of the younger men's ideas in the time she has worked for him. Apparently he has left it for them to criticize each other, which they are amply doing now.

Then she has another realization. Hutchinson's hypervolume niche axes are nothing more than Shelford's Law of Tolerance put into confusingly mathematical and unmeasurable form. There is nothing new in it, really.

X

EVELYN was there to greet him when Danny was sent home from school for locking a little girl into a coatroom. She had been mean to him.

"I was responsible for a similar incident, don't you know," he told the boy. "It was not a closet, however. It was a lovely room in which to lock someone in. The house had been built for my parents by an architect called Alan Mumby, who was an old friend of my father, don't you know. He had spent most of his professional life designing laboratories, so he must have decided to do something less utilitarian for us. He secured from somewhere a set of plaster zodiacal signs that he set, to my brother's and mine great delight, in a circle in the ceiling of the dining room."

"Zodiac signs?"

"Yes. They had significance at one time. At present they are just in horoscopes. Let me show you."

He sat down beside the boy and took out his pen.

"My parents must have become rather sick of hearing us chant at mealtimes," he said, reciting from memory the following, as he drew the signs,

> The Ram, the Bull, the Heavenly Twin
> And next the Crab, the Lion shine
> The Virgin and the Scale
> The Scorpion, Archer and He goat

The Man who holds the watering pot
And the Fish with glittering tales

"One for each month?" Danny asked.

"Yes, but not in synchrony."

That brought a puzzled look to Danny's face, which Evelyn ignored.

"This room was the scene of a disgraceful incident," he resumed his story. "It was one time reliably reported to us that Sir George and Lady Darwin had come to dinner. Two small boys waited at the top of the stairs watching the guests go in to dine. Lady Darwin, presumably the female guest of honor, was in a magnificent cerise dress. In a few minutes the party was locked in the dining room and the lights turned out at the main switch. Being presumably the only living person to have incarcerated one of Charles Darwin's sons has often provided a useful link with the past, particularly when I give a class on evolution."

"What happened then?" Danny wanted to know.

"I'll leave that to your imagination."

"Evelyn sounds too much like a woman's name," Danny suddenly noted. "Isn't that a girl's name?"

"Not if pronounced the proper way, with a long e."

"Even if pronounced with a long e. Why don't you just call yourself George?"

"Your hair is the same color of gold as your mother's," Evelyn once more ignored the boy's question. "And your skin is as white. Do you know that you remind me ever so much of a boy I went to school with at Gresham's. I came to admire him very much, and not just for his physical beauty, which, I must say, you match completely. He always got the part of the heroine in any performance we put on. He simply looked like such a beautiful young girl with a wig on. You are almost the age at which I remember him, too. Not quite still a boy, but not quite a man yet."

Lame, teased in school as a "Mama's boy," Danny finally warmed up to the older man, who, outside of trips to Linsely Pond, had until just that moment been merely a disruption of concentration on his homework.

As she reaches the laboratory, stopping to look in for Danny, who seems elsewhere, probably on an expedition with Evelyn, she thinks, she hears "Jewel?" coming from behind her. She turns, and there is Gene Odum, smile on his face.

"Jewel Fairfax, how are you?"

His smile has turned into a grin. She cautiously offers a hand, which he pumps eagerly and squeezes with a manly firmness.

"I heard there was an Aunt Jewel working here," he says, not letting go of her hand. I thought it might be you."

"So it is."

"You look different," he says after looking her over from top to bottom. "I like your hair like that. You look like a blonde Audrey Hepburn."

He looks different, too, not as tall, somehow, less gangly. His face is fuller, more handsome than it had been. But she refuses to say so.

"I've been hearing so much about you," she says instead, taking back her hand. "Your atoll study is being well received."

"We're getting the Mercer Prize for it, my brother Tom and I. It never would have happened had Tom not gotten me away from studying the heart rates of birds. Now I study the circulatory system of entire ecosystems."

He pauses to wait for a comment.

"Let me tell you," hearing none, he goes on, "there is no better way to become impressed with the functional operation of a community than to put on a face mask and explore a coral reef. Tom and I had a marvelous summer together. We just looked at it like a black box. The flow was all in one direction, so we just measured what went in and what went out. We got helicopter rides out to it whenever we wanted. Nighttime was the most fun. We could swim through the canyons of the reef with our flashlights and see coral polyps waving their tentacles like people with handkerchiefs waving out of city windows. Beautiful! But you had to watch out for sharks and moray eels. None of it would have happened, you know, if Tom had not gotten his degree here under Evelyn."

He pauses, as if expecting a comment. Hearing none, he continues.

"You know, Jewel, there is not just one kind of ecology. Ecology has many roots. One deep root is natural philosophy, what we call natural history. Another important root starts with Liebig's limiting factors. Still another begins with Malthus. Another root may be found in the studies of Mobius, Warming, Cowles, Elton, Clements, and Shelford at the community level. But a very important root comes from aquatic ecology, springing from the thinking of Forbes, Thienemann, Hutchinson, Lindeman, and many others, leading up to studies of tropho-dynamics, bioenergetics, and biogeochemical cycles."

He pauses again. He continues again.

"The ecosystem concept brings together all ecologists, from all those roots, because the ecosystem is the basic unit of structure and function with which we must ultimately deal. So the new ecology, Jewel, is systems ecology."

"And how is that reef now?" Jewel finally speaks up.

"It's still there," he answers, totally oblivious to any derision in her voice. "Someone else is studying it now."

"The radiation you mean."

There is an awkward silence.

"Some very reputable ecologists are studying the atolls," he volunteers. "Ray Fosberg has a very promising young plant ecologist named Bill Niering working with him. He's with Connecticut College. He's doing some very good work with Robert Whittaker, I hear."

"And you've written a book," Jewel says, deciding to try to atone for her previous remarks.

"Working on a second edition," Gene answers, smile back on his face. "Dad encouraged me. He wrote lots of books. I asked him, What if I don't know enough yet? You'll learn as you write, he told me. Well, what if I make mistakes? I asked him. You correct them in the second edition, he said."

"And you're working for the Atomic Energy Commission."

"University of Georgia. I'm a professor of biology."

"But I thought—"

"Oh, I get government grants to do some work. My dad encouraged that too. He was always getting funding from various agencies. I use the money to pay PhD students. It's a sad situation when the University of Georgia, a relatively small university and only a recent entry into graduate training, turns out to have a larger program in ecology than is supported by many of our finest prestige universities that traditionally attract the best brains. We have more staff, graduate students, and field facilities, I think, than Harvard and Princeton put together. You could throw in Yale, too, if not for Evelyn."

"And you're married?" Jewel surprises him by asking.

Jewel suddenly wants to take that back. She did not—absolutely did not—want the conversation to go to anything personal.

"Yep. Two sons. And you?"

"No," she says. Too late, she thinks. "I'm Aunt Jewel the spinster to my orphaned nephew."

He gives her a look that is genuinely sympathetic.

"Life can be hard on us sometimes," he says. "My younger son was born severely retarded. We had to ... He no longer lives with ..."

He obviously does not want to continue what he was saying. Jewel does nothing to relieve the awkwardness.

"But I have to let you know," he finally says, brightening again. "I'm teaching next summer at Woods Hole, taking the whole family. I know how excited you were at being there."

He pauses again for Jewel, only to continue when she says nothing.

"And I'm just back from seeing the damnedest thing. I've been on a fellowship, you know. Worked with Charles Elton—but that's not what I wanted to tell you. I just got back from UCLA. They took me out to the Nevada Proving Grounds. They is a group that calls itself Warren Hall for some reason. This lizard guy, Fred Turner, showed me around. Nice guy. We all took this three-hour train ride from Los Angeles to Las Vegas. You know, full of gamblers and midnight ramblers. We had to wait around to see if conditions were right for a blast. They weren't always. The wind has to blow a certain way. Blue lights indicated they would go ahead with a dawn blast, red if it was canceled, which could be in the middle of the night. If it was on, everyone went out to Yucca Flats in trucks and buses. Everyone who can wants to see one. There is a kind of inner excitement each time, because each is different and anything can happen."

He is totally oblivious to Jewel's lack of interest and goes on to describe the blast and the shock and the boom in detail. Not even his vivid description of the little rockets that sample the radioactive cloud and the airplanes that chase the rockets to their landing places can get her attention.

XI

"THANK God, that's done. With the money now safely under Bill Niering's control, I can get on with life, whatever that might now be."

They were out under power lines with packs on their backs. One was an Osmose employee, a company originally formed to treat wood. The other was a consultant. They behaved toward each other like nephew and uncle.

"Niering is a good man," the older one continued. "You should meet him. A Murray Buell PhD. A steady WQXR listener. I once, almost jokingly asked him to come along on a trip south, to visit the experimental herbicide plots I had down there in national forests. He took me up on it! We were together for two full weeks, on a high speed trip, as far as northern Florida."

The backpacks supported metal cylinders rather than hiking or camping supplies. Rubber hoses connected the cylinders to nozzles from which they sprayed a liquid that smelled like used motor oil.

"He is the only one who has been able to keep with me for two full weeks—and still end up a friend. Hah! He even seems able to get along with Robert Whittaker."

"Who's he?" the younger one asked.

"Bah! Whittaker! He is one of the reasons I no longer wish to be considered an ecologist. Why should I? They stopped publishing my research on herbicides. That was not Whittaker, I know, but he is still part of THEM. THEY in their ivy towers. They don't have enough backbone to get into the public arena."

"If what we're doing isn't ecology," the younger said, "well, what is it then?"

"Ah, they're all—! Oops! Have to break that habit of talking as loud as I want, so I don't talk so loud in the house. As I have to break my habit of doing my writing in my little sitting room. Now, if I have any serious work to do, I have to take refuge in the chicken coop you helped me fix up. Ever since mother moved in with me, the house is no longer mine. And, yes, I do think it was my trip to Bangkok that put her in the hospital."

They were treating the vegetation under the powerlines but emphatically avoiding spraying the shrubbery. Only tree saplings were being sprayed. The treatment was in line with Küchler's research on succession. Trees, according to Küchler, do not sprout through dense shrubbery. By not spraying the shrubs, vegetation could be kept from threatening the powerlines with less use of herbicide, at a saving in cost. Unknown to them, however, the mixture they were spraying would, in a somewhat different formulation, soon be put to use across the globe as something called Agent Orange.

"I had it all so well worked out, Dick. You know that scientists are judged not so much by what they do, but by what they are and where, don't you?"

"Sure do. That's why I helped get Mason out of Wichita. Osmose sent me out to demonstrate our electrical brush-killing devise. It failed miserably."

"Four thousand volts. I'm surprised you didn't electrocute yourself."

"So am I."

"So, what did this have to do with Mason?"

A tall oak sapling took over their attention as Dick sprayed it.

"Maybe I should chop it down?" Dick then asked.

"No. Just leave it."

"Girdle it maybe?"

"No, put away your hatchet. I think it will die."

"Well, I guess I impressed the head of the Botany Department at West Virginia," Dick continued, putting the nozzle and hatchet back into their holsters. "With my knowledge of the flora, not the device. He probably felt sorry for me about that. Anyway, he invited me to see their new herbarium. After a while, he said to me, It's odd, but you have the same name as lichenologist Mason Hale in Wichita. I replied, Yup, he's my twin brother! Then he said, Boy, we would do anything to get him into our department. I called him that night. He got the job two days later."

"He's still not happy though."

"Nah! Same old stuff! The students are all stupid and boring, he says."

An entire copse of saplings then curtailed their conversation. They wore no special protective clothing. They feared only bramble bushes and dirty clothes. The chemicals they used were known to be safe to humans.

"But I found a way around those ivy towers!" Küchler resumed as they resumed walking. "My affiliation with the Museum of Natural History was perfect, even if with no office or salary. That was OK. I made my own salary. Everyone came out better that way, museum, Osmose, and me. And you! It was an ideal setup, finally. The Museum's location was convenient by car and was close to mother and father's apartment, not to mention the New York Botanical Garden, where I could talk vegetation with Gleason. Then, of course, there was the New York City Opera."

"You and opera! Mason told me that if you hadn't played that opera for him when he first met you, he might not have gone into botany."

"Walkurie does have that effect. What does it for you?"

There was no response from Dick.

"Well, then, let me go on. The museum let me present myself as Friedrick V. Küchler, American Museum of Natural History, New York 24 New York, on papers and at conferences. Not exactly Yale, but quantum levels better than Waterbury. No more having to explain Arden Forest. The prestige and dignity of the world's largest museum now backed the stands I took. Maybe better than Yale. It was as if a soapbox orator with a cardboard megaphone were transferred to TV and a dignified podium. That's how I felt it was like. My words may be the same. But how different their effect! I kept my fingers crossed. I needed to. Things soon became sticky at the Museum."

The young man and his brother are part of a succession of younger men mentored and succored, even almost adopted, by the older man. Knowing Küchler well, he stayed silent.

"Strange, how it all started out. It was just a trivial item, in some newsletter put out by the American Chemical Paint Company. It quoted from another item, just as obscure. Brush Killers Benefit Wildlife was the title and just about all the content. Of course, the American Museum of Natural History just happened to have the world's leading expert in managing brush and in the successional changes that result, Dr. Friedrick V. Küchler. And, of course, you know what my research showed. Goodness! My method was being marketed very successfully as the American Museum System of Rightofway Vegetation Management. The Museum even cosponsored that twenty-three-minute film for it that you were in— with sound and in color. I had to speak out."

"You didn't say anything that wasn't true."

"No, I did not. But that Dick Pough! I know it was through his efforts that Pennsylvania's Hawk Mountain became a hawk-watching rather than hawk-shooting station. I also know all about his warning of the dangers of DDT to birds, even back then during the war, and that he helped to ban the sale of feathers from wild birds. I give him credit for all that. But! He has made some incredible blunders! He just charges in like a bull in a china shop. You see all these house finches ruining our rafters? Thank Dick Pough. When he got Macy's to stop illegally selling them in New York City, the dealers were left with no place to sell their birds, so they simply let them escape into the great outdoors. They didn't want to pay fines for harboring them."

"He did that?"

"He was my direct boss at the museum, and the one who brought me in. What else could I do when he brought me the item in the Arborist's News? I was already locked in battle with Dow and DuPont with my own short articles. Have you seen them? Dow's Death to Game Habitat was one title. The DuPont Desert was another. I sent over a dozen copies to the vippiest VIP's in each company. Their fury was interesting."

"Actually, I don't think I have."

"I'll have to show them to you when we get back. They were what may have led to my being set up at the Northeast Weed Control Conference. That was an ambush by McMahon Brothers protecting their lucrative contracts from me. I just wish I knew who it was that had warned them, although I have a suspicion."

"What now?" Dick asked at the crest of a ridge.

It looked a long way down and a longer way back up. The trail under the powerlines fell almost straight down away from them. And they had an even longer walk back to their vehicle just from where they were.

"We're almost out of herbicide," Dick added.

"This is a good place to stop, then," Küchler decided. "Make a note of it, so I know where it is next year. What we do now is go back."

"I like that."

Both took off their packs for a rest. Dick made some notations in a pocket notebook. Trailing arbutus had somehow established itself against the bank of the trail where they were sitting. Dick made a note of that, too.

"You have to admit that your words on subjects on which you are passionate can be bullets and grenades," Dick said.

"I admit it. Word got back to the Museum, with assistance, I am certain, from McMahon Brothers and their little stooge at the museum."

"And?"

"That was when I noted a new zephyr blowing in Museum policy. Staff scientists were suddenly told not to proffer advice unless called upon for it. That included everyone, even Dick Pough. The heat on the Museum became so bad that Pough had to ask for my resignation. My outspoken obstinacy was making things difficult, he said. Oh, I gave Pough a resignation, all right, but one he was certain not to pass on, since it was essentially a criticism of Dick Pough! He used me like the goats in India that are tied to trees to attract tigers, then are sacrificed without a backward thought when the tiger strikes."

Dick Hale let out a hardy laugh.

"But then word came down that the entire Department of Conservation and General Ecology was to be phased out. Dick Pough himself was looking for a job."

"Wow!"

"That was when my problems started with the Nature Conservancy. The museum still had some of my money. I thought it would be a simple thing to set up the same financial arrangement with the Nature Conservancy that I had with the Museum. It was a matter of justice, you have to understand. Unlike Ray Fosberg and Dick Pough, who are on salary, and for whom the matter of personal professional deductions has been a well exploited ground, I have to scrape together my own support. Then I have to pay for every pencil and postage stamp with my own money. You can appreciate that, I know. They, meantime, knock off as much as they can legally, and only pay income tax on the remainder. I was trying to do nothing less."

"This ground's cold."

Dick stood up. Both put their gear back on.

"The matter SHOULD have been pro forma," Küchler said as they resumed walking. "Pough was President of the Conservancy's Board of Governors. Ray Fosberg was Vice President. I myself was a Board Member."

"So?"

"So I forgot about the accursed George B. Fell. We must steer clear of any situation that would lead us into difficulty with Section 503c of the Internal Revenue Code, is how Fell put it to me. I tried to counter that I had already set several tax precedents with the IRS. I just could not understand Fell's delicate delays."

"And?"

"But thank God for the Wenner-Gren Conference. I don't know how I would have survived without it. What a magnificent intellectual experience! Man's Role in Changing the Face of the Earth, the affair was called. There were only seventy participants. Chairing it were Carl Sauer, Marston Bates, and Lewis Mumford, all top men in their field. Lots of heavyweight participants, too. There was Frasier Darling, Kenneth Boulding—you know, of Spaceship Earth?—and Sir Charles Darwin. Not the ghost, of course, but the physicist descendant of THE Charles Darwin, although Teilhard de Chardin did show up as a ghost. He wrote his paper then died. Rachel Carson, my favorite author ever, was invited but did not attend. Neither did someone at Yale. Hutchinson, I think his name was. It was heady company. Fairfield Osborn and I had several occasions to talk together. I think I taught him a few things about land misuse that weren't in Our Plundered Planet. He really appreciated it."

"What was your paper on?"

"What? Oh Yes. Not everyone at the conference was asked to write a paper. I was, but I just could not find the time. I think they might have asked Curtis to present some of his witchcraft statistics instead, but I'm not sure—you should ask your brother."

"Mason is not a big fan of Curtis."

"You know you really should consider Murray Buell's offer. Frankly, it's a very brilliant opportunity to author, maybe co-author, a very sizable project that could be the turning point, one way or another, of the whole massive Curtis School. And you will be treading some of the paths your brother has trod, but with different intent and in a different region."

"Vegetation analysis."

"Yes."

"Northern New Jersey."

"Yes."

"What exactly is it you mean when you say Curtis School?"

"Didn't you pay attention to what your twin brother was doing? Multi-variate analysis, principal components, ordination!"

"Well, there was a war in Korea, if you remember."

"Of course. So, instead of trying to identify communities by just throwing down quadrats and sampling fauna, you sample along a gradient."

"Like altitude?"

"Yeah, low to high. Or dry to wet. Or soil type. Sometimes in the Curtis method, your gradient is just community."

"Communities? Isn't that circular?"

"Might have been, if there really were communities."

"So, that's what I would be doing with Dr. Buell?"

"Just vegetation analysis, but what they do is apply this crazy geometry: multidimensional—"

"X, y, z?"

"Yes. X could be moisture, etc. The idea is to see if communities fall out as such or whether species just track environmental conditions, or even if it is all just random."

"But I thought that was what ecologists believe now, that there are no communities."

"Yes, not in the sense of Clements. I showed all that way back when with my Hawaiian data and my Berkshire studies. But people tend to keep worshiping their sacred cows, I guess. What Curtis and Whittaker are doing is putting the final nail in the coffin of Clements's biome idea."

"I thought Mason's cryptogam species did fall out into distinct communities."

"That's what he was afraid of telling Curtis. Curtis wanted answers only one way. Mason's data was a little ambiguous and Curtis was a real son of a bitch about it coming out his way. Murray Buell, though, is one hell of a nice guy."

"I feel bad about turning him down. He made the best offer he could, but I couldn't live on it. Not with a family. And following Mason's path is exactly why I don't want to go to grad school. Four years or more of living in poverty and no good jobs when you do get done."

Dick stopped for a break. He took off his pack again and planted his rear on a boulder that had been warmed by the sun. With no more spraying to be done, it seemed to him that Küchler might never stop talking.

"Of course, I made my ideas known in discussions at the conference," Küchler said, pointedly ignoring Dick's last comment, "especially my views on climax vegetation. And I promoted the importance of rightofway vegetation, of course. I also took on the human population problem. It can never be solved, I realized at the conference, as long as organized industry continues to need more people as a market for its products."

Dick offered Fred his canteen then stood up and put his pack back on.

"Now this is the good part," Küchler returned the canteen after a long, slow sip and picked up where he had left off. "I made sure the gathering knew that ecology was on the skids—and I wasn't the only one to say so. Ecology drew pity at the conference for lacking experimental methods, and it was accused of neglecting man as an ecological agent. Just the sort of thing I wanted to say. Someone simply called ecology archaic and sterile, useless to man's problems. I couldn't agree more."

"You really think so? Ecology should no longer be the study of communities?"

"It's the study of NATURAL communities. Only natural communities. Hell, we humans are the driving force of much succession!"

"So Cowles' discovery that communities evolve with his dune studies is worthless?"

"Not evolve! Change!"

"Right. Develop, as in succession."

"Clements is the one who claimed they developed."

"As his superorganism!"

Dick set off again. It was downhill now and the mostly empty cylinders made for easy walking. Küchler resumed his monologue, staying pace for pace with Hale.

"But then it was back to that business with the museum money at the Conservancy. I have to live without a salaried position, as you know. And my total interest from all sources is a darn sight less than what my colleagues receive from their salaries. George Fell should have understood. He was the first and only one on salary in the Nature Conservancy."

Küchler really needs students to be lecturing to, Dick thought in deciding not to offer any more interjections. Maybe he'll just talk himself out. But why isn't he as tired as I am?

"Now Fell, I was given to understand, had taken courses in ecology from Shelford, who started the Ecologist's Union, and his student, Charles Kendeigh, the organization's Vice-President, so he should have been OK. And it was Fell who teamed up with Pough to push the Ecologist's Union to enlarge its membership and expand its activities. Pough's prodding is what caused the Nature Conservancy to be born out of it, with Stanley Cain as President and Fell as Vice-President. Soon, though, the salaried Fell was running the Conservancy as its Executive Director, with his wife as his assistant and Pough its unpaid President. And that was the problem. The Conservancy could not get along the way it was being run. George Fell was a most dangerous man to have at the head of an organization, dangerous because of his fanciful fears, his fussiness in the office, and his fanaticism in following out his fancies.

"Now, it wasn't just his stupidity in making a big deal out of my Vegetation Studies Fund that I brought to the Board of Governors. That was second after nepotism in my list of seven charges. Maybe I shouldn't have brought up their absurd criticism concerning my typing and their urging me to buy an electric one, after making fun of my perfectly serviceable one. But I make no apologies for my complaint about the new stationary—blue!—with the legend changed from The Conservation Society of America to A Conservation Society of America. You can't do a thing like that on your own!"

Dick stopped and shook his head before walking on.

"Ray was somewhere in the Pacific at the time, probably still doing classified work on atolls and atomic bomb tests. I had to work through Marie-Héléne Sachet. She's Ray's mouthpiece when he's gone. Now she is something, let me tell you! We both paid calls on the Fells. I could only report from mine that George Fell was one of the most annoying, unattackable dictators I have ever know. It was time, I decided to tell the Governors, to investigate their Executive Secretary.

"Marie-Héléne and I went together to Storrs for that. She wanted nothing more to do with Conservancy business, after that, she was so disgusted by it. I had my list of charges in hand, but events, I am afraid, did not unfold as I had expected. Fell had a mole on the Board of Governors who tipped him off to what was coming down. I was broadsided. It was the McMahon Brothers all over again."

"The McMahon Brothers leaned on the Nature Conservancy?"

"No. No. No. You're not listening. The story that was spread at the Storrs meeting was that I had lost my temper on my visit to the Fells' earlier that summer. It grew in the retelling until I had come so close to violence that they had to call the police. Can you imagine that? Me? Violent?"

"Never."

"What really happened was the three of us talked for a couple of hours. Nothing really important. I was guarded, tactful. I made no direct charges. I do recollect mentioning something about his salary increase. To this comment, Barbara Fell rose in most self-righteous defiance to tell me that George was a magnificent administrator, and certainly worth not only seven thousand five, but easily worth ten thousand. And so it went. There was no talking too strongly on my part. Apparently it takes little crossing of Barbara to cause tearful hysterics, and I was in no mood to get so drowned.

"There was only one course of action, as far as I was concerned. George Fell had to be fired, but Ray thought that was too strong. I told Ray and the others that they could continue to be unpaid stooges for the Fells. If he could draw ten thousand a year, grinding out mimeographed material, and get people like Ray and Goodwin to do the real work, then, clearly, it was Küchler who was all wrong. Ray said he had George pretty well in hand, however. The new management committee snubbed him pretty hard, he said, then Dick Goodwin had a heart-to-heart talk with him about some of the facts of life. Well, I warned them. George Fell had some tricks up his sleeve. He almost took over the leadership of the Conservancy. By then, I was watching from the sidelines, working on my book on plant ecology for the Guggenheim fellowship that friends I made at the conference helped me get."

Finally, they arrived back at their vehicle. As he put their gear away, Dick hoped that Fred would forget to restart his monologue on the drive back. It would be some three hours getting to the Hudson and crossing it, then making their way back to Norfolk.

"Meanwhile," Küchler started up again on the other side of Poughkeepsie, however, "things came to a head at the Nature Conservancy. It was a convoluted chain of events, but the gist of it is that the Conservancy, Richard Goodwin now President, demoted both Fell and his wife in the hope that they would either leave or remain in new, powerless positions. The Fells were not like minded, to say the least. They first worked quietly under the new man hired to manage the Conservancy's affairs. Then Fell announced he was running for President, and at the head of a slate of candidates for Board of Governors who were all sympathetic to him. The election was to be at the Conservancy's meeting in Bloomington, Indiana, not someplace that most of us here in the East could get to. He was gathering proxy votes to overwhelm those able to come to Bloomington and vote in person. I would have cast a proxy, believe me, but I could not pay them my three-dollar membership fee before the meeting started."

Dick drove on in silence.

"That meeting would make a good book for someone. There were personal attacks, testimonials, parliamentary procedures and tricks, and an appeal from Victor Shelford. At the end, Richard Goodwin's efforts—he was the outgoing President—held the day. Goodwin's and Fosberg's and Pough's candidates garnered the most votes. The Fells resigned.

"But my attempts to retrieve the money in my vegetation fund had Fell screaming at Fosberg over the phone and then ordering his new superior, who was supposed to be keeping him in check, out of his office.

"So, my position at the Museum is long gone. My Guggenheim is ending. My book is making no progress.

"Nineteen fifty-eight, so far, I tell you, has been the lowest in my career.

"But I got my money back. George Fell was happy to get that hot potato out of his hands."

"How much was it?" Dick finally spoke up, hesitantly, as if trodding on forbidden ground.

"What? Oh, it was a thousand dollars."

Marlboro

I

A 1949 Buick carrying five students is put into neutral and given a push in front of Dalrymple Hall, Marlboro College's main building. Engine off, it starts to roll downhill in the general direction of Brattleboro. There is not an ounce of gasoline in its tank.

"Do you think they'll make it?" Jewel asks, looking out the window.

"I-uh ca-hn't see why not. I-uh've done myself one time or t'other."

"But do you think they'll have enough money left to buy gas after a Saturday night in town? Marlboro is uphill all the way."

"Mawl-bro," Luke Dalrymple corrects Jewel's pronunciation, as the Buick disappears down the country road. "Now Brattlebuh IS a city, but I-uh expect they-ll still have a few pennies left in they-uh pockets."

A century before, the hillside in which the tiny college is tucked abounded in sheep. Wool then could be sold for enough to mills along the river valleys below to keep farms, if not prosperous, at least profitable. Then the market for wool crashed. Dairy cows replaced the sheep. Some meadows now have been abandoned long enough, even by cows, for pines, hemlocks, and maples to follow the blueberry shrubs, pin cherry, and birch that colonized first. On Potash Hill, however, returning GIs have replaced the mostly forgotten merino sheep.

"Situated on a bluff and runnin' on the same principle, is how one of the fust students described it," Luke proudly shared on first meeting Jewel. "Dave Hertzbrun was his name. A city boy-uh. Almost didn't last tha-aht fust winter."

Luke Dalrymple is neither student nor GI. He is the head of the makeshift construction team that is renovating a corner of his family's former barn. The upstairs space is about to become the Culbertson Room, suitable for use as the school's library. Most of his construction team has left in the Buick. Even Don Woodard, the school's only maintenance person, has deserted him, as has Don's dog, Babe, for whom the daytime safety of the campus is a sacred canine trust. Luke stays late, as he always does when on a project. There is one bookshelf left to put up.

Marlboro College was created out of two adjoining farmsteads by a genius whose philosophy of higher education was to have a professor on one end of a log and a student on the other. This was not his particular genius. It was borrowed from an early president of nearby Williams College. What was original to Walter Henricks's genius was his realization at the end of the war that the newly enacted GI Bill would send a torrent of government-guaranteed, tuition-paying freshmen at established colleges. Many would have to be turned away for lack of space. Returning students seeking readmission should, Hendricks reasoned, take up all the available spaces at the best New England colleges.

"Hendricks seems to have had the theory that the key to education for the student and professor on that log of his," Jewel says as she shelves copy after copy of the same book, "was the study of Henry James's The Wings of the Dove."

"They were all scrounged from post-war Army stores," Olive MacArthur explains.

Jewel is at Marlboro assisting Olive, who is Dean of Women, Professor of Biology, and mother of Robert MacArthur. Jewel was lured to Marlboro by Robert to spell Olive while she recovered from unspecified surgery.

Robert is a Marlboro College alumnus, Class of '51. According to older brother John, who is also on the Marlboro faculty, he chose Marlboro in order to spend one less year at his Toronto high school. Canadian universities, John explained, required five years of high school, rather than the four below the border. Then, also according to John, he lured father, mother, and brother to Marlboro in order that the college have sufficient faculty to stay open.

"A family friend from Toronto introduced my parents to Newfane. Robert learned that a new college was being launched here while vacationing with them," John told Jewel just before he abandoned the college for a year at MIT.

It was a good time to take the leave. Enrollment had dropped precipitously, so that the fifteen Marlboro faculty members that year had only fifteen thousand dollars to share as compensation.

"You do the math," he concluded that explanation.

Jewel and Danny are staying at his house.

Jewel is confident, however, that Robert MacArthur chose Marlboro out of love for the Vermont landscape. At seventeen hundred feet above sea level, the woods around Marlboro are southern fingers of the northern coniferous forest, to put it in terms of biomes. It was where Robert studied warblers for his dissertation, often, she learned, with John's help. Newfane and Wilmington, tiny towns short distances from Marlboro, impress Jewel by their pre-twentieth-century buildings and abundance of white clapboards, as is true of the old farm buildings making up the Marlboro campus. She felt initially as if she had returned to Old Saybrook, but with mountains and no sea.

When Robert matriculated, the school had just opened. It made the cover of *Life* magazine in 1948 by graduating the smallest class of any college in the country, one Hugh Mulligan. Hugh was a returning GI for whom the school's founder devised an instant final-year curriculum, plagued though it was by *Wings of the Dove*, which the graduate had helped the founder scrounge up in post-war Europe. Hugh described it as "the most boring book ever written." As if in compensation, he claimed the unusual benefit of not having to worry about his place in the marching order at his outdoor graduation. It was Robert Frost, Dorothy Canfield Fisher, and presidents of Harvard and Yale, along with other academic dignitaries, who jockeyed shamelessly for preferred space in line. Fisher stunned the audience by ending her speech with, "Trust in God, She'll be with you always."

"Robert's contribution was providing the school a warm body," John summed up his brother's college career as he drove Jewel to her first class.

Then a hawk swooped down to chase a sparrow in front of their windshield. John and his wife, Margaret, leaped out of the car, binoculars in hand, leaving Jewel to ponder for twenty-five minutes how she would explain her lateness to her students.

II

"WORTH it, isn't it?" Jewel asks breathlessly.

All around them are the fall colors of Vermont, maple reds, birch yellows, and stands of fir greens and dark hemlock. Danny endured a full lesson on tree identification from his Aunt Jewel on the ascent up the peak. The only indication of interest he gave her was a question on why the variety of colors.

"Pigments," Jewel had answered, wondering if she should go into a full biochemical explanation, before realizing that she did not have one.

Five needles, white, Danny repeated to himself, just like the name. Two needles, red. Why not three needles?

Jewel had no inkling that her lesson was sinking in. As far as she could tell, his adolescent mind was on some "horse opera," a term that she liked, he had watched on a neighbor's "TV," a term she did not like. But unknown to her, Danny was actually working out the difference between the flat leaves of firs and those of hemlocks. Images of trillium, trout lilies, and spring beauties are already imprinted in his mind, where there is also the truculent garlicky smell and taste of wild leek that Jewel coerced him into trying, and which he then stealthily munched on as they continued up the trail.

"I guess," answers Danny, looking around for a likely place to sit. He has gamely kept a limping pace with her all the way up the trail. The scenery holds less interest for him than the chance for a rest, although Jewel notices that he is less out of breath than she.

"What's that down there?" he asks, having chosen to sit on the ground. "That building by the road. See it?"

"Waffles and fudge," Jewel replies. "That's the Skyline Restaurant. Interested in lunch yet?"

"Yeah!"

Down they go, following a ski trail. They had started out at Marlboro after breakfast, keeping to the parts of the Molly Stark Trail that are not paved road. They were few and far between. It is a trail only by its history. Still, a path off it brought them to the top of one of the T-bar lifts at Hogback Mountain.

"So it's like sledding, only you don't have to drag your sled back up the hill," Danny says after Jewel explains the purpose of the structure to him.

Skiing was a foreign concept among New Haven children.

"Can we try skiing?" he asks.

"Why not?" she answers.

As she watches him favoring his affected leg on the short descent, though, she wonders how good an idea it will be to put him on skis. But that is months away, she counters. Perhaps the exercise regime she has put him on will continue to produce improvement. Perhaps coming to Vermont will bring him to walking normally.

The restaurant has as good a view as the top of the mountain, and the downhill hike back to Marlboro turns out to be no less easy on her over-forty knees than the uphill one had been. A momentary wish to have chanced the Hudson crosses her mind, but is quickly dismissed. The ancient heap's unreliability and the fact that John has yet to fully "bring in electricity" for his abode are the reasons that they have moved from John and Margaret MacArthur's house in South Newfane to Olive's house in Marlboro. The wood fire at John and Margaret's, already necessary in October, Jewel and Danny will miss, but reading by the light of a kerosene lamp they will not.

Olive continues to teach in the department her husband created on his retirement from the University of Toronto. After his death, she took over as the biology head and moved to a house closer to the college. She is happy to have Jewel and Danny move in with her. She knows that what the college can afford to pay can barely meet expenses, and she does not want to lose Jewel from the faculty. By not having to pay for housing or heat, and by making use of complimentary meals in the old barn of a dining hall, Olive assures Jewel that the pittance she is receiving will go far in Vermont. But she has other reasons for having Jewel move in with her. Both are fellow University of Chicago graduates. And Olive especially values Jewel's company because of her connection to Yale ecology. Jewel's presence is like having her son Robert's inspiration with her always.

Jewel minds not at all being given Olive's biology course, instead of ecology, which Olive is team-teaching with Henry Crowell, who will take over in her absence. The bio course is mostly botany and mostly labs. It is exactly what Jewel enjoyed teaching the most in Detroit.

Small class sizes are the rule at Marlboro—and a special treat for Jewel. A cute young couple, Bruce and Barbara Cole, comprise one-sixth of her class. They are newlyweds, and they moved into John and Margaret's house almost immediately on Danny and Jewel having left it.

All in all, Jewel muses, as her tired legs bring her to within view of the college, she may have found exactly the paradise that

Robert promised. Danny and Jewel head right for the Dining Hall. As with Dalrymple, the outside of the old barn has been dressed up in fresh white clapboards, and an entrance façade, Greek Revival to match the other buildings, has disguised the old barn door opening. Several large, wooden tables are set up inside for lunches and dinners. Even if half the building is no longer in use as the college's only classroom space, as it once was, it is still a multipurpose space, with a raised platform in back that can function as a stage. The wooden benches by the tables provide seating for Monday night lectures, while everything can be pushed back to the sides for dances.

Seating at meals is very informal. Jewel and Danny find seats beside a young man with a three-day beard. He is wearing army fatigues. His age and clothing give him away as a Korean War vet and GI Bill student, although the latter can be predicted of any male student with almost fifty-percent accuracy.

Danny balks at the piece of meat before him.

"It is too tough even to cut," he whines in Jewel's general direction.

"Steak tough?" their neighbor asks. "Knife too dull?"

He reaches down and pulls up the right leg of his pants and removes a twelve-inch knife from an ankle scabbard. It has a polished deer antler handle and an intricately serrated edge that looks capable of cutting through wire. He raises it above their heads and stabs down sharply. The knife's razor-sharp point sinks an inch and a half into the tabletop. Jewel and Danny watch, hypnotized by the knife's vibrations slowly coming to a stop.

"Thank the nice man," Jewel says.

With some difficulty, she removes the knife from in front of Danny's plate and hands it to him. His problem solved, he finishes his meat in small, chewable pieces.

Before returning to Olive's house, and before the light fades, they stock up with apples. The farm's old apple trees are still good bearers, but the Thursday student work program has already been charged with the task of apple picking. All the apples will be scoured from the trees by Friday to make cider for the kitchen. It is a welcome chore for the students. The ease with which the cider can be coaxed to become "hard" is a special incentive. Most Thursday afternoon workouts are much less fun. They are devoted to maintenance chores or to hauling and stacking wood. And cutting, endlessly cutting wood. Spring sugaring is the only respite from the monotony, once apple picking is done.

III

ASIDE from her still-unspecified position on the faculty, Jewel is now also the school's Assistant Librarian. The post was added to her resume by the powers that be in Marlboro to keep her from pleading poverty and leaving. Every coin added to her purse is a welcome gift. The extra money let Jewel sell the Hudson and purchase a two-year-old Volkswagen beetle, with ridiculously low mileage, for only $300, from a recently transplanted flatlander. The low mileage, the owner confessed, was a result of the car being out of action from December to May, unable to manage snow or mud season, or sometimes even the deep ruts of country roads in summer. But its beauty blinds Jewel to its faults. She was tempted to offer more than the owner asked. She felt the bug's dignity should not be insulted by so deep a discount.

Jewel's duties at the library are slight. Only Penny Wiederhold stopped in after lunch today, looking for a book about nursing. Surprisingly, there was one. It had been Olive's at one time. The rest of the afternoon, Jewel spends grading lab reports.

Grading done, dinner approaching, driven by boredom, Jewel picks up a feather duster and sets to work on the library shelves. She stops before what she recognizes as senior theses, but in the jargon of the school's curriculum, they are called Plans of Concentration. One in the row of thin, bound volumes catches her attention as the thinnest. It is Robert MacArthur's.

"Mathematical Foundations of Boundary Value Problems" is fourteen pages in all, characteristically typed on onionskin paper, making it especially thin. There are ten references, several in German. On the front page, "MacArthur" has an extra space, "Mac Arthur."

"Must have been typed by someone else," Jewel muses. "But why not corrected?"

There is no date on the cover. That is found on the binding. Even though the corner of the frontis page is marked, "Excellent

Piece of Work," over the initials, A. H. P., clearly the advisor on it, Jewel is suspicious.

"Fourteen pages," she says, unnecessarily under her breath, for had someone been there to hear, the peacocks outside would have drowned her out anyway. "It is hardly long enough for a term paper."

She has been reading MacArthur's work avidly. Reprints of articles he is getting into print show up regularly at the library while Robert is away at Oxford. Olive or John, no doubt, is responsible for that.

All that has come directly to Jewel is a photograph from England that Peter Klopfer recently pleased Jewel by sending, probably taken by Martha, of Peter, Robert, Betsy, and the first born of each couple. She enviously admired each family's youth and beauty over and over. Strangely, though, in his letter, Peter placed them on a punt on the river Cam. That kept Jewel confused until she was reminded that Cambridge and Oxford were separate places. Peter was doing a post-doctoral year at Cambridge. Robert's return from his year in England, she learned from Peter's a letter, would be to a prestigious faculty position at the University of Pennsylvania and a prize awarded to him by the Ecological Society.

Just out, MacArthur's warbler paper, from his dissertation, impresses Jewel as a significant piece of work. It is what has earned the Mercer Prize that awaits him. She likes that it is all biology and no math, although Robert does have an interesting way of presenting data using triangles. His broken stick paper she understands less and admires less, although she knows that Hutchinson transmitted it for MacArthur to the National Academy of Sciences for expedited publication in the Proceedings, as if MacArthur were concerned over priority for his idea. Maybe he was, Jewel thinks, remembering Clements's zealous defense of his complex organism. Hutch also made much of the broken stick in the paper he presented as the concluding talk of a conference. An outgrowth of discussions in the Ecology Seminar, the talk was published in the *American Naturalist*. The paper pleased her by being the first and only instance of her name being found in an ecology journal. Hutch noted that he was "very much indebted" to the participants of the seminar and listed all their names, although his inclusion of a fictitious "Dr. J. C. Foothill" detracted somewhat, Jewel thought, from the honor.

Still, "Take that, Fred Küchler!" she said aloud on seeing her name in print. It caused Anthony Cucchiaro to look at her suspiciously from his seat in the corner of the library.

MacArthur really knows his warblers, Jewel decides, and he really knows his math. His senior thesis is dense with equations. There are Lebesque integrals, Cauchy's inequality, Hermitian and Sturm-Liouville type equations, Rodrigue's formula, Legendre and Laguerre polynomials, and Bessel's inequality. Symbols, such as for partial derivatives, are neatly penciled in by hand. And symbols dominate the pages. What little text there is recedes into the background before those symbols. Two paragraphs of text, Jewel notes, barely a hundred words.

But, what a handsome man, she thinks, turning back to the photograph that Klopfer sent, before putting it away. And so devoted to Betsy. What a pity! I batted my eyes at him as best I could. Only with Küchler was I more wanton. And I got about as far as I did with Küchler, even though, this time, I was the sadder but wiser older lady, rather than the innocent ingenue.

"Robert must have been in about first grade at the time," John MacArthur recalls for Jewel the next evening at the Dining Hall. "One night my father was trying to read a bedtime story or something to him and ran into resistance from Robert."

John has just came back up from Brattleboro, where he is working as an engineer at the Esty Organ Company to supplement what little salary he is drawing from Marlboro. His "paying job" he calls it. A former student, Larimore Toye, who did his Plan of Concentration under John at that facility, is now a co-worker.

"I don't want a bedtime story, Robert insisted," John continues his recollection. "Send John up, he said. Tell him to teach me algebra."

"That must not have gone over very well," Jewel remarks with heavy irony.

Experts in schools of education have her convinced that abstractions such as algebra can't be learned until thirteen or fourteen years of age. But before she can marshal her arguments, John contradicts them all.

"Oh no," he says. "He seemed to have caught on fairly well to what I was trying to explain. He always had a talent for math."

"He must have just waltzed through here."

"Precisely," John answers. "Waltzed is exactly what he did. Who on the faculty could understand what Robert was doing or what Robert knew—or some of the other students, I imagine—from their Plans of Concentration, especially Robert's? He learned only what he wanted to. The unstructured environment we had here let him pursue exactly the things that interested him and not much more. The general comprehensive examination was put in place soon after Robert graduated."

"Because of Robert?"

"Not really. But we did need to know if our students were getting the liberal education advertised. I don't think Robert did. That sort of thing is why Roland Boyden instituted our general comprehensive examination. It would let us judge by objective criteria, in his words, whether a student achieved the minima of liberal education, again in Roland's words, in the first two years of his curriculum."

"Yeah, but," Dick Fudd, who had slipped into the seat beside Jewel and was listening surreptitiously, takes the pipe out of his mouth and interrupts, "in the absence of prescribed courses, students still can prepare in whatever fashion they choose. They can pass that exam simply by growing up bookish."

"At Chicago, we had a core curriculum," Jewel offers. "You had to take each yearlong core course before you could take the comprehensive exam on the subject. You didn't have to pass the core courses—their grades were advisory—but we all took them anyway, because we needed to know what material would be on the comps."

Fudd takes his pipe out of his mouth again.

"Big school," he says. "Marlboro could never afford to staff all the sections that would require. Not and still have the variety of course offerings we have now."

IV

OTHER than a grandmotherly woman reading a paperback book, Jewel appears to be the only non-skier in the lodge. They sneak glances at each other from opposite corners of the table they share beside a large picture window that looks out at skiers coming down the practice slope.

Jewel has put Danny completely under the tutelage of Dick Fudd. She has resigned herself to being among the ranks of watchers. The skiing craze that is sweeping the country to Vermont's benefit is leaving her untouched. She would rather be in Brattleboro watching Jimmy Stewart in a matinée of *The Spirit of St. Louis*.

Marlboro has its own ski tow, right on campus, by the music building. "Moskito," it is called, which is "Marlboro Ski Tow" said very fast. An engine removed from a small truck pulls a riotously looped rope up a small hill. Skiers hold onto the rope with both hands, one ahead and one behind, and are pulled uphill. It pulled fast enough to have Jewel fall off it twice each trip she took. Each time the second fall caused her to abandon it before reaching the top. The very short downhill parts that followed were no more auspicious. Fearful of gaining speed, but unable to maneuver her cross-country skis to a stop, she bailed out in what Danny sarcastically called "seat-of-the-pants stops." Nothing about her experience resembled anything like fun. Danny, however, took to skiing like an acrobat. When Dick Fudd walked by Moskito as he came from teaching his Saturday morning English class, he saw Jewel's distress and quickly put on skis to take over her failed role of ski instructor. Dick did both cross-country and downhill skiing expertly. Jewel left him with Danny and took her borrowed skis, home made by a former Marlboro student, out on the parking lot. Then she abandoned them entirely in favor of Danny's "flying saucer," her Christmas present to him, which he decided was for "little kids." Without even giving it a fair try, she thought.

At first, the winter took forever to come. Christmas was barely white. Then it came with a fury, the coldest and snowiest winter in recent memory. Roads closed from the Dakotas to Maine. Schools closed for days at a time. Power outages were common. New York City went almost two weeks straight without a thermometer in the city registering above freezing. Marlboro students buried themselves under thick covers at night and cut more wood in the daytime. And shoveled and shoveled. Every day was Thursday afternoon. They would have swapped their below-zero temperatures for those of New York City in an instant. Rumor went around campus that Princeton students, stranded in their dormitories by the same snowstorm, were lamenting the loss of maid services. They had to make their own beds. Jewel heard much unfit language from Marlboro students describing the "Princeton man" and his predicament.

At the height of the biggest snowstorm, another rumor began to circulate, this one about visiting lecturer John Aldritch, author of *After the Lost Generation*. He had imbibed too much hard cider or other stimulant, the rumor went, and was lost out in the snowstorm. The entire college, cooks, students, faculty, all went out into woods that were knee-high in snow — waist-high in places. Even dogs joined the search, even Babe. The author turned out to be in the cabin that Robert and Betsy MacArthur had built by South Pond. He was with a very attractive young lady and was embarrassingly in no need of rescue. Snowshoe tracks are what led rescuers to the cabin.

Then the sun came out and everyone except the author, who by then was on a bus to New York City, rushed outdoors to play. It was Dick Fudd, very impressed with Danny's progress, who suggested the trip to Hogback to Jewel, enlisting Danny's help to convince her to come along. He drove them up in his Buick, his skis sticking out an open back window. Jewel's Beetle was still under three feet of snow in Olive MacArthur's driveway. Jewel was finding it more and more difficult to turn down Dick's suggestions, but she balked at the four-dollar lift price, even when Arnold White, the owner, insisted on throwing in skis and poles for free. And she refused to let Dick pay. So Dick and Danny left her behind to nurse a hot chocolate by the picture window.

Now Jewel wishes she too had a book to read. The woman with the distinguished gray hair notices Jewel eyeing her book with envy and smiles at her.

"You don't ski?" she asks in an accent that Jewel cannot place.

"Haven't really begun yet. And you?"

"No. I came along for the view. Lovely here, isn't it? My family usually skis at Pico, but my husband claimed some sort of business here. Imagine that, having business on a ski slope! Usually it's on a golf course."

When Jewel, to whom Pico means nothing, does not answer, the woman introduces herself as Gladys.

"Don't bother learning to ski," she prods the conversation along. "It'll just lead to a bruised ego, bruised muscles, and even broken bones—or even worse. Let your son and husband deal with the aches and pains. You know—"

Jewel interrupts just as Gladys is about to share a confidence.

"Oh they're—" Jewel sets out to correct her, but decides against it.

What would be the point? They will never see each other again.

"Men seem to like putting themselves in danger," Gladys resumes. "I have a son-in-law who lost a leg in a skiing accident. He and my daughter are still avid skiers, though. He has an artificial leg, especially for skiing, that he designed himself. He's an engineer. He has all my grandchildren on skis, too."

"Edge of the Sea?" Jewel asks to change the subject.

"Yes. Rachel Carson," Gladys answers. "Are you a fan?"

"I did know a Rachel Carson once," Jewel says, as memories of Woods Hole flood over her. "It couldn't be the same person."

"Oh, my dear, she is only the best nature writer in the world."

"I have seen the book in bookstores," Jewel offers in atonement.

It troubles Jewel not at all, however, to be an ecologist and be totally unaware of popular books about the sea. But few ecologists studied oceans. After all, didn't Gordon Riley almost have to invent oceanography so he could do his research?

"My goodness! Is the book a best seller?" she adds. "Just imagine if it is the same person!"

"Indeed it is a best seller," Gladys says, handing the book to Jewel. "Take it. Read it. Rachel Carson is a neighbor of mine—"

But a toboggan coming to a stop below their window interrupts the conversation. Jewel grabs her hat and mittens and heads for the door. Danny is in the toboggan, with Dick behind it, skis and poles in his arms. A hurried trip down to an emergency room is in order. Realizing she still has the book in her hands, Jewel glances back at the window. The woman is on her feet behind it. Her face is grave. Jewel forces a smile, holds up the book, and gives her a friendly wave.

Dick is charming the entire agonizingly slow trip down. Famous for his teaching style of "question and wait," as his students call it, a tactic he inherited from Marlboro cofounder Roland

Boyden, Fudd is uncharacteristically effusive on a variety of subjects as he eases the big Buick through the winding curves of the road to Brattleboro. His banter soon has Danny laughing.

"It's just awful," Bruce Cole once prefaced a description of Dick's classroom discussion method to Jewel, to whom all things about the handsome Dick Fudd were interesting. "He'll throw out some question to the whole class that none of us are comfortable in answering, but he waits for an answer. Doesn't say another word until someone else speaks up. He looks at our faces for a volunteer. No one meets his eye. Then he looks out the window. Then he looks for his pipe. Then back at us. Then he goes over to the wastebasket and empties his pipe by banging against the side of it. Then he looks back at us. Then he takes out his tobacco and looks at us. Then he fills his pipe and looks at us. Then he looks for matches and back at us, but one face at a time. Then he lights his pipe. Finally, someone breaks down and offers an answer. But you know? All that leads to a really great discussion, because we have all been thinking about the question. It can be intimidating, though."

Danny's shoulder injury turns out to be a mild one. No broken collarbone. No dislocation. Nothing but a mild sprain. Danny is back on the slopes the next week, even though his aunt Jewel tries to keep him off longer.

She was just being like a mother, he complained to her when she tried to limit his time on the slopes. He did not tell her why he wanted to ski so much. It had to be his secret. He did not want to tell anyone that he did not feel like a cripple on skis. His polio-weakened leg stopped being a problem when he laced it tight in the high boots, strapped a ski to it, and let it glide over smooth snow. And he could glide down the slopes just as well as everybody else. Better than most. Better than anyone, he decided he would be.

Their first touch is electric. He guides her so gently through the dance steps that she feels as if she knows them all from long experience. Her glance follows him as he strays down the line in accordance with the caller's instructions. She has to endure lesser partners until he comes around again. Being touched by others suddenly is somehow distasteful. This one's touch is too sweaty, that one's too stiff. This one has clumsy feet. This one holds her too close. Dick Fudd, when he comes around, has too proprietary a hold.

His name is Jonathan, she learns between dances. He is a cook at the Skyline Restaurant. He was born in Readsboro, in a tarpaper shack, he tells her freely, in Heartwellville, as the little village near Dutch Hill, still another ski area, is called. He went to Syracuse on a football scholarship but ruined his knee and was cut from the team after his first year. He is a few inches taller than she and a number of years younger. His eyes sparkle at her when he speaks. His neck is a tree trunk and his chest a barrel. His limp is barely perceptible.

His touch on the dance floor is just right. It gently fuses with hers. She wants to know everything about him, and everything she learns makes her want to learn more. He cooks, he tells her, because he started cooking for his younger brother and sister after their mother left them during one of their father's drunken rages. She had been no less drunk. He had been nine years old. He once had a restaurant of his own in Manchester until the lid of a pressure cooker blew off and penetrated his skull. That same brother and sister ran the restaurant into the ground while he was recovering, if he ever will fully recover. He is awaiting a settlement with the manufacturer of the defective cooking device. Meanwhile he cooks wherever he is hired and lives with his grandmother in a trailer that has replaced the tarpaper shack.

He has been admiring her from a distance ever since her fall visit to the restaurant with Danny. Finding her at the dance, he tells her, is an unexpected treat, "chocolate sauce on ice cream."

She will miss Fudd's large dick, she knows, but this is the man for her. He is what she had searched for in the string of men she let take her to cheap hotel rooms at the end of the war. Jonathan is the anti-Küchler.

Danny, who has been moping around the corners of the Dining Hall, complaining about the "fiddle music," is sent home on his own to Olive's house. He is out the door even before she can finish the suggestion.

She stays with Jonathan until the last dance. They separate with a handshake and promises to be in Brattlebro for the next contra dance.

"Good dance?" Olive asks when Jewel floats in some time close to midnight.

"Good dance," Jewel answers.

She suddenly realizes that she and Danny will have to find someplace else to live now. She will no longer be satisfied with the usually one-sided furtive sexual collisions she has been having with the married Dick Fudd. Sometimes he never even takes his pipe out of his mouth. Classrooms, cars, outdoors, even the library, while still open, have been the scenes of their encounters. She wonders how no one can know. Perhaps they do.

V

DANNY could not find a barber, not in any of the five shops in Brattleboro, who could give him the Elvis Presley haircut he wanted, so he just let his hair grow long. To Jewel's further disgust, he swept it into a ducktail. As in all things sartorial or hygienic now, Jewel's opinion carried no weight with him. In almost every part of his life now, his aunt's opinion carried no weight. When Jewel mentioned liking a Patti Page song playing on the radio, Danny immediately changed the station.

What he does and what he listens to and what he reads and what he thinks, Jewel knows she can no longer control. But when, she wonders, did that transition occur? Jewel has only memories left, it seems, of the child she comforted at night and through illness. She can no longer even touch the hair she cut or make a suggestion on his wardrobe. The baby she helped her sister bathe, that miracle has transformed before her eyes into a crackly voiced, hideously pimpled monstrosity that fights and resents her every suggestion. Is it what she deserves? All these years, she has only been trying to bring him to a safe place. And now that, with relief, she finally is almost there, is she to find even that simple vision a mirage? And will he now blame her for its not being soon enough? None are questions she dare ask him.

"It's a hoodlum haircut," she complains instead, gangs and rock 'n roll tied inextricably together in her mind. "Didn't you see the Daily News I brought home today? Of course not, all you ever read is Mad magazine. Did you see anything about the gang murder of that fifteen-year old kid in New York? He had polio, the poor child. Don't you see? We left New Haven to get away from all that. Those city gangs are spreading to there too. We left just in time. Imagine! Twenty-seven defendants, some hardly older than you, too young even to stand trial, but not too young to kill."

"You're not my mother," Dan says before going into his room. "I have no mother."

I am more than your mother, Jewel wants to say, but he is already gone.

They have moved from Marlboro to a two-bedroom apartment above a store in Brattleboro. It is temporary, but it is right, Jewel knows, even though Jewel wonders how she will make it to campus in the next winter's storms. It is her next step in reaching that safe place which she has been trying to find for Danny, that she can now feel within her reach.

Danny, almost by instinct, disapproved outwardly of any change Jewel brought into their lives. Still, he did enjoy the shops in downtown Brattleboro and was fascinated by the other youths who spent their time along the streets and parks of the town. But he greatly resented the noises he could hear coming from his aunt's bedroom whenever Jonathan came to visit. Either to drown out their sound or to let them know he could hear them—which it was, he was not sure—Danny played the guitar that Jonathan had given him extra loud. And he missed his forays through the Marlboro library, especially when Aunt Jewel was not looking. *On the Road* and *Catcher in the Rye* spoke directly to him from its shelves. Both, he was certain were telling him something that he had to work out. Just solving the puzzle of the title of the Salinger book, he thought, would be a step in the right direction. But now, cut off from the library, he was cut off from its words, except in memory,

"I'd rather have gangs in the neighborhood than the hillbillies up here," he dismissed Jewel's entire argument.

He wanted to keep his cool hairstyle. He wanted to listen to Alan Freed on the radio, instead of Martin Block or the Saturday opera. Enough Patti Page and Pat Boone, already! He was disgusted with the transistor radio Jewel bought him, because he couldn't find a single New York City station on it. He nagged her to buy him a record player, instead, one of the new ones that played the new forty-fives. And he thanked his god, vaguely more Buddhist now than Episcopalian, for the record store in Brattleboro—and the Friendly's—where he could hang out to be cool.

"You're just acting like you're my mother!" he could not help shouting accusingly as his last words in any argument. "You aren't my mother. Stop trying to be my mother!"

And he slammed the door to his room. In the moment before it shut he thought he caught a glimpse of his aunt crying.

Couldn't be, he thought. Aunt Jewel never cried. Nothing ever troubled her that much.

If he only had that book, he thought. Maybe he could steal it from the bookstore, but they kept such a close eye on him whenever he wandered toward the back, where all the good stuff was.

Holden Caulfied—or the author, which was which was confused in his mind—had to have known the right words. Everyone knows that there is no such thing as a catcher in the rye. What did that mean?

And what simplicity, in comparison, is Sal Paradise and Dean Moriarty's road! No Aunt Jewel boxing them in. No teachers pulling them down. And no kids … well, mocking him? No, not mocking. Not understanding?

No grownups, no kids, really, in either book. Just them. Dean, Sal, and Holden—and a search for something. When he could not find it, he picked up Jonathan's old guitar and tried a new chord.

VI

IT is the last Sunday of the summer's festival, a special day. Director Rudolph Serkin is not listed on the hastily, but handsomely printed program. But there is a Serkin, Peter, Rudolph's son. He is to solo.

It is an all Haydn concert. An entire chamber orchestra, some two dozen musicians and a piano, have crammed together on the small Dining Hall stage, the same space occupied by three fiddlers just months before, as melting snow was threatening to create an early mud season. The wooden tables are gone, replaced by rows of folding metal chairs. Friends and students of the musicians stand along the sides of the barn to listen or sit outside on the grass beneath open windows, not because they cannot afford a ticket, but to leave more room for patrons.

The Marlboro Music Festival is the showcase of the Marlboro Music School, which would never have come into existence without Marlboro College and the coincidence of violinist Adolph Busch settling with his family in nearby Guilford and dragging his son-in-law Serkin and the Moyses family into the venture. The musicians are a mix of professionals and amateurs that come together for a summer of seclusion in music. All see themselves as students, all rehearsing hard together, all the time. They rehearse pieces of their own choosing. Chamber music always, their choices range from obscure early Baroque to obscure small-ensemble modern pieces. When a group feels it has rehearsed a piece to its satisfaction, when it has explored all of its musical possibilities, it is put on the list for a public performance. No concert is given before August, and not all pieces or musicians make the concerts. The always-appreciative audience never knows what to expect, other than something musically interesting, well performed. This late afternoon, though, starts with Haydn's Symphony No. 49.

Jewel loses focus in the middle of it's second movement and lets her glance leave the musicians to examine the audience. She looks for familiar faces near the stage, but finds only someone in an aisle seat who reminds her of the woman at Hogback who gave her Rachel Carson's book. And her mind drifted to the book and the idyllic life she imagined that fate had decreed for her former acquaintance.

Danny quickly became bored to anger by the music and glanced randomly about the hall. He noted a few younger children in the audience, but none his own age. Those on stage closer to his age were so far removed from his world that they might as well have come from Planet X.

The second piece is the Concerto in D Major. All eyes are fixed on the twelve-year-old as he takes his place at the piano and looks to Alexander Schneider, the conductor, for a signal. Some, in the front seats, can see an encouraging smile pass from conductor to boy as the baton is lifted. Both relax when the piece begins, while the audience tenses in anticipation of the piano parts. Only the occasional half-stifled cough is heard from the audience through the boy's solos. Then, as if having built to an unbearable silence, the audience explodes into a thundering standing ovation at the conclusion of the piece, punctuating its approval with bravos and whistles. Even Danny is moved to clap his hands enthusiastically.

Jewel wishes she knew enough to tell Danny something about the music as they wait awkwardly together during intermission. Maybe the performance could pique an interest in him for something besides rock and roll, she thinks, but, alas, Haydn is no less a mystery to her than Martinu was the week before. So, unlike other groupings outside the hall, Jewel and Danny observe a silent truce.

"Beautiful, wasn't it?" a voice from behind breaks their silence. It is Gladys, who immediately reintroduces herself. "Young people showing their capabilities always lifts my spirits," she says to Danny.

"The festival is a treat, isn't it?" Jewel agrees when Danny gives no indication of speaking. "I THOUGHT I recognized you near the front."

"You should have been here two summers ago, when Van Cliburn was here," Gladys says excitedly. "And there was also the cutest little Jewish boy, Levine, I think his name was. They played a duet."

"THE Van Cliburn?"

"The very one. Isn't it great the way he showed the Russians how to play Tchaikovsky?"

"I did read about that."

Danny finds the moment right to excuse himself.

"I do hope he will recover fully from that injury," Gladys says, watching him wander away. It takes a second for Jewel to realize that Gladys is referring to Danny's limp.

"Oh, no, no, no," she responds, almost startled. "That was nothing. Just a mild shoulder sprain. He walks that way because of a bout of polio when he was younger."

"Oh, dear, Jewel, that must have been trying," Gladys offers.

"Yes. Our eldest granddaughter also had polio," a male voice breaks in.

It is her husband. He appears at Gladys's side, as if conjured up, and beats her to what she was about to say. He is Gordon Landon. He is retired from running the family hardware business in Rutland. Both are big supporters of the arts, especially with

Gordon's checkbook, which is what was holding him up, he explains to Gladys.

"Yes, our granddaughter recovered completely," Gordon turns to address Jewel once more. "We were very fortunate. She had the bulbar kind. There was no paralysis."

"Danny had the bulbar kind, too. But somehow it did affect the lower muscles of that leg."

"Oh dear," says Gladys, searching without success for something more to say.

"I hardly noticed the limp," Gordon insists.

Jewel returns to her seat to discover that Danny's is empty. She knows that she will find him after the performance at Olive's house, where there always seems to be a plate of cookies awaiting him. That part of him, at least, is still a child, Jewel knows. Strange though, she thinks, how Olive has taken on the role of favorite aunt that Jewel had once tried so hard to fill in his life.

The finale is Symphonie Concertante in B flat Major, Opus 84, Hob. 1:105 (1792), as it is identified on the program, to Jewel's puzzlement. What are all those numbers? And, could "Hob." possibly stand for Hoboken? Then she laughs at herself.

During the performance, conductor Schneider picks up his violin to join the orchestra as one of the soloists. Loud, persistent applause leads to many bows at the conclusion of the piece, but no encore.

As she files out with other concertgoers, Jewel wonders if what she has heard is really as first-rate as it seems to them, although she does hear, "I think it was somewhat disjointed," from behind.

Disjointed? What does that mean?

Then once more, she finds herself next to Gladys.

"How did you like that?" Jewel asks.

"Simply loved it. A real tour de force for Haydn. Marvelously performed. Now where is that Gordon?"

She stops to look behind.

"I bet he is someplace telling the musicians how the piece should have been played."

Then, to break a sudden awkward silence when they come to a stop outside, she asks, "So, this last Vermont winter has not driven you off I see."

"I love it here," Jewel answers, "but I miss the seashore. I grew up next to the ocean in Connecticut. My friends have a cabin at the lake here that we often use when they are not there, but South Pond is nothing at all like the sea. I miss the smells and the sounds. The waves putting me to sleep. Angry sea gulls fighting one another waking me up."

"Oh, my dear, you have that exactly right. But you and your boy simply must come up to Maine for a weekend with us. It'll make you forget all about Connecticut."

"School is almost upon us, I'm afraid," Jewel turns her down politely, assuming the invitation is just out of politeness.

"Why, it's only August tenth," they hear Gordon from behind them.

And before she knows it, it is settled. They will be expecting her in a week.

Robert and Betsy are at their mother's when Jewel arrives to track down Danny, who is in the back yard, talking to Robert. The baby is now a toddler, busy with unraveling one of Olive's balls of wool. He is healthy and beautiful, a joy for both Olive and Jewel to help with, one the real grandmother, the other still the honorary WASP one. The new baby is on Olive's lap. The mother, Jewel suspects, is not the picture of health that her children are. Betsy's pretty face is drained of color. Her greetings lack a smile—or just are not given.

"It is no better in Philadelphia," Robert finally confides to Jewel in a whisper as she is leaving with Danny. "I guess we just don't like city living."

Jewel stifles the urge to wonder aloud whether it is just too soon after the babies to shake a simple postpartum thing. Danny has already crawled into the Beetle and is waiting impatiently.

"Children are what keeps her spirits up, I think," Robert answers her unasked question. "But I'm afraid I'm not getting much done professionally this summer. Betsy is happiest right here, surrounded by family and living in the cottage next door to the one she spent her childhood in. I imagine it brings back nothing but happy memories for her and she wants our children to enjoy the same."

Then he takes her even farther aside and into his confidence.

"You know," he says in his pleasing baritone, "I met her at a local dance. Not square dance, but what do you call it?"

"Contra?"

"Contra dance. She had the sweetest face. She was also just the sweetest person to match. I realized instantly that nothing could make me happier in life than to make her happy. Nothing means as much to me. Of course, I didn't know that she was being especially nice to me, because I was her brother's roommate. But she has never stopped being nice to me. And the babies have been a great joy to her."

The cabin that Robert and Betsy built, hauling things—beds, tables, refrigerator—either up the half-mile trail from Olive's house or across the lake in a canoe, becomes Betsy's summer refuge with the baby. Supplies, such as the large propane tanks needed for cooking and washing diapers, for there is no electricity, are still brought in by Robert by canoe. Still trying to get fully settled at Penn, Robert is the cabin's most frequent visitor. Jewel helps to close it up in the fall and intends to prepare it in the spring. Summers, she is sure, she will be making certain there are enough clean diapers, laundry soap, and food in its cupboards.

VII

IT is almost a day-long drive across New Hampshire down to Route One at Portsmouth and then down east through Kittery, Saco, Portland, Falmouth, Yarmouth, Freeport, Brunswick, Bath, and Wiscasset, all requiring slowing for traffic—or the worst blow of all—negotiating the perils of a traffic circle. Finally, toward nightfall, Jewel and Danny are on the road to Booth Bay, but the end of their trip is not near. Although getting to Booth Bay is a simple matter, getting to Southport first requires Jewel to miss a turn and tour a neighboring island. In the dark, the tour disappoints. Jewel finally finds what passes for a grocery store on the island and makes a call from its pay phone. Gordon orders them "not to move an inch" until he can rescue them. Ten minutes later, they are following his Volkswagen in their Volkswagen down winding roads. His Volkswagen, however, is a Karmann Ghia. The "cottage," as the Landons called it, is a low-profile modern construction that can sleep ten when the need arises, which it does much of the summer. It sits on a slab of rock that, even in the dark, has an obvious view of a sizable stretch of ocean.

It is the Landons' first summer in the just-completed house. They have been in a whirlwind of guests and grandchildren, Gladys shares. Their invitation to her, Jewel now suspects, may have been as much from pride of ownership as offer of friendship, but she does feel very warmly received, regardless.

Jewel is given her own room. It is small and spare, with bunk beds, the upper of which goes unused. Danny's sleeping bag is comfortably accommodated on a sofa in the large all-purpose room that comprises most of the house. It is one of several such sofas in the room. The grandson occupies the one next to Danny The granddaughter, the polio victim, sleeps in her preferred place, a cot in the small porch that serves as the rear entryway to the cabin.

In the morning, a spectacular view of the Dog Fish Head Light to the right and Cedarbush Island straight ahead greets Jewel through the large array of tall windows.

"Cedarbush," she remarks, "seems remarkably bereft of cedars."

Even looking at it through Gladys's binoculars, Jewel can see none.

"Perhaps there are some small, low, storm-swept specimens," Gordon suggests, but all Jewel can see on the island is what looks like a green lawn, even through binoculars.

"This is Suki," Gladys introduces a raucous seagull perched on the rail of the large deck facing the ocean. "He won't leave until he gets his daily ration of Pepperidge Farm Bread, and only if buttered."

"He smells pancakes," Gordon adds as they come out onto the deck for breakfast, "which he will get only if there are leftovers and only if buttered and with syrup."

"Vermont maple syrup," Gladys adds.

There is nothing in any memory of Fairfax gatherings to match this scene, Jewel knows, as she looks down from the deck at the waves breaking against the rocks and roiling the seaweed in the pools. A seaside cottage in the Fairfax family always came with a quarter-mile walk to the beach. Even those of the richer Smith side of the family, who once had a large, historic house at Woods Hole, could not eat their breakfast out by the sea. Who are these Landons? And where are the Smiths now? And is she what the Fairfaxes have come to? Nothing more than the struggling Michigan schoolteacher that was her grandfather, whose daughter he had thought he had set up for life through marriage to a wealthy family?

Rachel Carson is at the back door when they finish breakfast. She is with Dorothy Freeman, a friend and neighbor, and Roger Christie, Rachel's ward, who she introduces as her grandnephew. Full of energy, and under little restraint, he bursts into the house in search of Landon grandchildren. Perhaps prepped by Gordon and Gladys, Rachel pleases Jewel on greeting her by remembering her with ease.

Gordon has arranged a sail for the day for all but Gladys. Jewel suspects that, as with skiing, Gladys will be satisfied with reading, this time from her comfortable settee, close to her gulls and bird feeder and Peterson guides, and just enjoy watching others sail. Gordon starts bustling about, trying to usher everyone into his Volvo. Rachel and Dorothy, however, demur.

"I'm not very fond of boats," Rachel explains. "Someone once suggested that I really don't care much for the sea around us when I chose not to come aboard with them."

"Oh dear," Gladys says. "What an unkind remark!"

"I don't think she meant it that way. It was Marjorie Spock's mother."

"It took Stan an enormous effort to get Rachel to come out on our boat to see her cottage from the water," Dorothy began, before being interrupted.

"Then he almost ran aground and capsized!" Rachel completed the story.

"I love to watch the Lazy Bones tack across the sea past Cedarbush," Gladys says. "Why should I go out in it? I won't be able to enjoy its beauty as much if I'm on it."

"But don't tell me you have become a scuba diver?" Rachel asks, turning to Jewel.

"No," Jewel laughs, "but I'll see if I can tolerate this outing."

"But thank you ever so much for taking Roger," Rachel turns back to the Landons. "He needs to do more things like this—or just be with other children. I just can't give him the attention that children his age demand, I'm afraid. It is such a relief to have you take him. It will also give me a chance to get some work done."

Dorothy has already maneuvered her vehicle free from its tight parking space, so that Gordon can leave, but the children have already raced off to see if they can beat the car by using a low-tide shortcut across the cove. Gordon ends up driving only Jewel in his Volvo, to the relief of his two grandchildren, who fear immanent disaster from Gordon's peculiar driving habits, a fear Jewel soon adopts.

"Never ever," the granddaughter whispers to Jewel at the harbor," get into Granddad Gordon's Karmann Ghia with him."

And she gives Jewel a wink.

Danny learned to duck when "going about" and how to secure "sheets" onto "cleats, but the way the boat heeled while tacking startled him.

"Is the boat supposed to lean this much?" he asked, with poorly disguised concern, as water crept closer and closer to the edge of the deck of the speeding boat.

"Oh yeah," Roger, the youngest of the trio pipes up.

"When racing," the grandson offered authoritatively, even though he was younger than Danny by a year or two, "we tack so hard that sometimes the rail goes completely under water."

"The centerboard helps," the granddaughter competitively added to her older brother's remark. "The boat can't tip over as easy if the centerboard is down."

Gordon deliberately, Jewel suspects on seeing his mischievous smile, tries to pick up even more speed.

What a board somewhere in the middle of the boat had to do with staying afloat, Danny could not imagine, but refused to ask.

Jewel is in the cabin, carefully following Gladys's instructions on putting together lunch, even though it is only two hours after breakfast. She has hot dog rolls toasting on the tiny galley stove as she hurriedly chops celery to be added with mayonnaise and salt and pepper to the lobster meat. Gladys's method makes "the best lobster rolls in Booth Bay," according to Gordon. Her "secret ingredient," he shares, is the lobster meat Gordon bought that morning at Robinson's wharf, on the island.

The result truly is the best lobster roll Jewel has ever had. Not the least of its appeal is eating it out on the deck, as the boat rests, sails down and at anchor, in a sheltered cove of an island full of basking seals that bark at them. Unfortunately, though the boat rests, it is not still. Even in the cove, the boat rocks and Jewel's face begins to catch the green of the Atlantic. Soon, some of the best lobster roll in Booth Bay is overboard.

A smart maneuver past Cedarbush to catch Gladys's attention marks the end of the sail. Jewel, better now that the boat is moving forward, waves along with the children, even though she doubts Gladys will be able to see them.

Rachel is waiting with Gladys when they return from the sail. Gladys had telephoned to let her know that the Lazy Bones was heading into Cozy Harbor as soon as she saw it pass Cedarbush. Rachel offers tea at her house to any who want to accompany her back to it. She leads Jewel and the children down a short path through pine and cedar woods and out to Ruth Gardner's tiny beach, a small crescent of sand, hemmed in on one side by a road, and protected from heavy surf on the other by rocks forming tide pools indistinguishable from those described in *The Edge of the Sea*. Rachel stops at one to lift some bladder wrack to expose periwinkles and small, scuttling crabs.

"The big crabs usually stay down in crevices and under ledges in the daytime," she explains to everyone, "but we might come upon them now at low tide."

She steps into the deeper water in her tennis shoes. Then she gathers an entire forest of seaweed in her arms and holds it aloft. Sure enough, a large crab is exposed. It tries to scuttle back under cover.

"I have such mixed feelings about the Landon's house," Rachel confides to Jewel while the children are engaged with the capture of the crab.

"Why? It fits beautifully into the landscape. Especially as seen from the sea."

"It does. But I always had a dream that I might buy up the lots along here and preserve the land in its natural state. So much of our nation's seashore is being developed in one way or another. In our imaginings of how we might preserve it, Dorothy and I even gave a name to this forest along the coves. The Lost Woods, we called it. But the Tenngrens—Gustav, he's a children's book illustrator—wanted much more than I could possibly afford for it, although not more than Gordon could, apparently."

Crab suitably examined and released, they all slip carefully past a hedge of poison ivy and the road to the lighthouse. While the children run ahead, Rachel begins to tell Jewel all about her new project.

"I started to write about the whole ecology of man," Rachel explains, "but now I see that I need to write about the chemicals that are degrading our environment and harming our bodies. It is quite different from anything else I have ever done."

Rachel's small saltbox is amazingly modest for a successful author, Jewel thinks, especially in comparison to Gordon's architectural marvel, even with the various additions she has made to it. It stands on a ledge above an old salt pond that is now open to the Sheepscot River and has reverted to a tide pool. A deck with railing resembling that of the Landon's faces the pool.

"That is my laboratory," Rachel says, directing Jewel's gaze to it. "It has little to tell me about pollution, I'm afraid."

"I know nothing at all about pollution," Jewel says when Rachel tries to tell her about all the information a University of California scientist has, and how he might be harming his career by helping her. "Dieldrin and Heptachlor mean nothing to me."

"Fairfield Osborn told me about Robert Rudd," Rachel persists. "He is pretty far along in his book about how pesticides harm wildlife. It should be of real help to me, if he is allowed to publish it. He came by for a visit with his family last month, but you know, Momma so dominated the conversation that he and I never got to share any ideas."

Only Fred Küchler and his herbicide work come to mind when Jewel tries to think of ecologists who work with chemicals. But his work, in her opinion, is an eccentric mix of research that is flogging the dead horse of Clements's climax concept, in part, and a way of making money for Fred, in the main. Jewel could not imagine how he would be of much help to her. She does not think he is even worth mentioning.

Tea is with Maria Carson, Rachel's mother, of course. She is wheelchair bound and hard of hearing. Cat Jeffie occupies her lap.

"Are you as concerned about Sputnik and the problems with Vanguard missiles as Rachel is?" she asks, almost on introduction, in a loud voice.

"I can't say I regret their not getting off their launching pads successfully. I am not at all certain they have as much to do with space as keeping up with the Russians," Jewel answers, tentatively, but almost as loudly.

Maria smiles in agreement. Then, as Rachel carefully puts a recording of a Beethoven symphony on her new "phono," as she calls it, Maria launches into Roger's history.

"His mother, poor dear, died the winter before last. Pneumonia. She was only thirty-one, poor dear. She was never a healthy one. We were all afraid for the poor dear during her pregnancy. The doctors never thought she would make it, but she refused an abortion."

"Roger's father—?" Jewel starts to ask.

"We hardly knew him," Rachel steps in quickly.

Her glance at her mother makes it clear there is to be no more on the subject. Then she asks how Jewel came to care for Danny.

"My sister killed her husband," Jewel says, her voice steady, low, totally without emotion. "You may have read about it in the papers. He was wheelchair bound."

She specifically looked away from Maria before deciding to share that last.

"I had been caring for them all," she adds, "and my mother, who died soon after, from the scandal, I think."

Should I have shared that? Jewel wonders as she watches Maria's eyes widen in fright. Rachel has taken me into her confidence, she rationalizes, as if all the years between now and Woods Hole never were, but there are a few things it is better that no one know, aside from those few who already know.

"There was no one else to take Danny," is how she cuts off any possible confession.

"It is always that," sympathizes Rachel, "isn't it. Who else will take care of them?"

A lull follows in conversation, filled only by Beethoven's Fifth playing quietly on the phono.

The lawsuit that Danny's grandparents brought against her, she will not reveal, nor the scandals that that uncovered, which were the true final blow for her mother.

Maria gives signs of having fallen asleep. Rachel first checks to be certain that it is sleep.

"Death has been so much with me this last year," she says almost matter-of-factly, but after an audible sigh of relief. "I don't know what I would do if—"

She drops the thought and moves her chair closer to Jewel.

"I really am impressed with your accomplishments," she says, keeping her voice low.

"I am so sorry I learned no ecology at Hopkins. The closest thing to it, I guess, was in a botany course given by, ah ... Dr. Livingston, I believe it was."

Her face beams in delight.

"It was called the organography—or something like that—of plants. Only the field trips made it tolerable. And I must admit that I strayed not an inch from physiology in my Master's thesis. It was on the pronephros of fish. I never took my research to the field. Had I known about ecology back then, I never would have settled for preserved specimens. And I certainly would have finished my PhD had it been on an ecological topic." She pauses to give time for Jewel to react. "We both need to take pride from our personal lives, too," she resumes when no reaction is forthcoming, "for having stepped up to care for family and head households as single women. I know exactly what you have gone through."

Then she leans toward Jewel and takes a hand in hers.

"But can I ask something of you?" she almost whispers. "Are you interested in getting you feet wet with another area of ecology? I wasted some time already with a useless collaborator. I guess I was just always meant to write—to work, perhaps— by myself only. But I need research help. It is just too much, what with caring for Roger and my mother. I did have a Bryn Mawr senior helping me in Maryland. She was worth every penny of the two dollars an hour I paid her, but she took another job. So you see—"

Suddenly, the granddaughter interrupts to complain that the boys have locked her out of the attic.

"What on earth are they doing there?" Rachel asks, jumping from her chair. "They shouldn't even be up there."

What they were doing is more than an embarrassment to all.

"It was just an I'll show you mine, if you show me yours kind of thing," Jewel tries to defuse the situation with.

"But with males?" Rachel objects. "At that age? Your nephew is what? Thirteen? Just look at him! Look at his hair! He is an adult almost."

"Oh, they probably just need a male figure in their lives," Jewel says, hoping to gloss over the unpleasant incident. To her, it seems no different from playing "Doctor" with her cousins during her girlhood.

"I think you should go now," Rachel says with finality. It is clear that it is much more than a suggestion. It is to be the last communication between the two women.

On their return to the Landon's, the grandson admits that there had also been some touching. Initiated by Danny.

It is a very long, unpleasant night. Danny has been moved to the bunk above Jewel's. It is on the pretext that Danny might be "more comfortable with more privacy," as Gordon puts it, his voice unjudgmental. Danny retires early and is absolutely silent when Jewel comes to bed soon after. She decides not make an effort to get him to talk. Instead, she gets him up before dawn.

They leave the next day before anyone else is up, as Suki screams for breakfast. They drive in silence back down an empty Route One.

"Maine's not really all it's cracked up to be," Jewel breaks the silence on crossing the bridge into New Hampshire.

"Yeah," Danny suddenly brightens. "The ocean is nothing but sails, rocks, and cold water. I like Vermont better."

VIII

IT is on a hillside near Ames Hill. It is, in fact, on *the* Ames Hill according to the seller, whose name is Ames. The house is a once-proud Victorian, the type called vernacular that farm houses once tended toward, Queen Anne windows and porch gingerbread—decaying beyond repair—but no turrets or mansard roofs. The four hundred (more or less, according to the deed) acres of hillside adjoining the house include barns, a silo, outbuildings, orchard, pasture, woods, and even some bottom land. In short, a farm.

John MacArthur has come with Jewel and Jonathan on a final inspection. He has been deputized by Betsy's father, who is financing the venture from a combination of his daughter's prodding, avuncular feelings of responsibility toward Marlboro faculty, as one of its founders, and a sense of the deal being a good business investment. The latter is the most prominent of his reasons, he made certain that Jewel and Jonathan understood. They need his backing. Jewel has accumulated nothing but debts, it seems, and although Jonathan's court case was settled in his favor for a tidy sum, the lawyers took a third and the doctors most of the rest.

The kitchen is the first room John is brought into. Following Vermont tradition, the kitchen door is the main entranceway for guests. A mud room behind it will be the main entryway for family and friends. The kitchen is a pre-Depression era model with a wood stove and a soapstone sink. Whatever cupboards and cabinets once stood in it to make it homey are gone. Neither Jewel nor Jonathan give any sign of trepidation over having to endure the rigors of so stark a kitchen.

"The wainscoting is nice," says Jonathan.

"And the wallpaper can stay," says Jewel. "At least for a while."

The words are to reassure John. They already have details of an upgrade in mind. The kitchen to them is only a temporary space. The wallpaper will be gone with the wall for the addition already in their minds.

Heat is also primitive: steam. But beside a giant coal furnace, looking very much like a small locomotive engine, stands an almost new oil one.

"That should give you years of service," John says of the working furnace, "and many musical interludes. I hope you like that song from Pajama Game."

"You mean, pssssssssteam heat?"

"I recommend leaving the monstrosity next to it right where it is. It'll be a monster to move."

"No sign of serious water," Jonathan says, checking corners of the basement for moisture.

"Never been a problem," says the seller, "not situated the way the house is on the hillside. And you'll get unlimited hot water from the boiler. We had five of us lining up for Saturday night baths. Every one of us had hot water."

"I imagine, though," John counters, "the well might give you problems in a dry year."

"Hundred and twenty feet," Mr. Ames counters John's counter. "It would take a lot of dry years to give you problems. And there's a spring for animals behind the barn."

"Joists and beams look good. No sags or cracks."

"No plumber or electricians drilling holes all through them, either," John adds.

Then he takes out a large folding pocketknife and stabs the beam above him. The knife blade stays in the wood. The vibrating handle reminds Jewel of dinner at the college.

"Solid," John says, removing his knife. "Knob and tube wiring, though, is what has spared the holes. OK as it is, but I wouldn't trust it to carry much load. You'll need to add a new supply box if you want enough amps for modern appliances. Even a vacuum cleaner might blow fuses on these circuits."

Bathrooms are pre-turn-of-the-century: off the kitchen, a tub, sink, and potty—and not much else—and sink and potty in a closet upstairs.

"We won't need four bedrooms," Jewel says. "Can we convert one to a bath?"

"Might," John answers.

"Should be able to," Mr. Ames says, warming up to the idea of Jewel and Jonathan taking over his family home. "Pa had it all planned out to do so, but Ma would not give up her sewing room. She needed her sewing room. She kept the door closed to it and off limits to us. All we knew about it was that was where all the pins and needles we stepped on in our bare feet came from. Then we all left and the bathroom situation left with us. Pa decided things were fine the way they were."

Attic beams, too, pass the knife test.

"Let's close the deal," says John.

He takes a signed check from his pocket. It already has an amount filled in.

"Arthur Whittemore," the seller says, making a face at the check. "I guess it will do. Let's go sign some papers."

So begins Ames Hill Game Farm and Restaurant. It is Jonathan's dream to have a restaurant that serves food it produces itself. It is Whittemore's idea, however, to separate the farm and restaurant operations, thus Ames Hill Farm Restaurant is already open under the name of "Jonathan's" in a rented location in downtown Brattleboro. It is Jonathan's intent that the confusion of names be cleared up as soon as meat for the restaurant is on the hoof at the farm.

Danny went out for the Brattleboro High soccer team on Jonathan's advice. Too slight for football, the wrong season for the ski team (which Jonathan claimed would not be the right sport "to make friends and influence Vermont teens," anyway), soccer was it by default. Practice started two weeks before classes, in the sweltering heat of midsummer, it seemed. He wanted to quit almost as soon as he joined. He was by far the slowest player on the field. He could not kick well either, especially if it took any tricky footwork. Nobody laughed at him, but that was the only saving grace of the situation until fall arrived the final week of August and made exercise more bearable.

None of the high-school-age teens Danny had come to know in hanging out in Brattleboro haunts—a stoop at the mansard-roofed seediness of the Brooks House, or the statue of the soldier in the park, or by the river—were the ones he now needed to cultivate as friends, he realized once classes started. None were in his classes but for phys ed. One, a tall thin boy with dark curls that made him so handsome that it almost hurt Danny to look at him, had run away from home the first week of school and simply disappeared. None of the others were in Danny's classes, but for phys ed, where none showed any talent at anything physical. There, at least, he could fit in well. Those in his "real" classes, as he referred to academic courses, however, formed a social group that was closed to him. They were polite, as on the soccer field, but it seemed only surface politeness.

"Keep mixing it up with them on the ball field," Jonathan suggested when Danny brought him the idea of quitting the team. "Knock a few of them down in practice. They'll come around."

"Is that what you did?"

"I knocked so many of my teammates down, even in games, that they voted me captain and I got a scholarship."

Fortunately, although Brattleboro was a large school for Vermont, it perennially lacked the manpower to field as strong a team for soccer as it did for football. Soccer was an insignificant sport in an era when Ted Williams was finishing out his career nearby in Boston. Fielding a soccer team, in itself, was sometimes an issue. That made Danny welcome as another body at practice, even if he was the slowest—by far the slowest—on the team.

"If he was in a horse race, he'd be ten lengths behind the pack at the half-mile pole," Jonathan put it to Jewel as they watched the team finish laps. They had stopped by to give him a ride home after practice.

"Don't be so cruel," Jewel reprimanded him.

He gave her a confused look. He had no idea of having said anything cruel. She let him stay confused.

But kicking the ball hard with his bad leg became less of a problem for Danny than running, at least when no tricky footwork was required. In fact, if he "tee'd" the ball up, in a sense, he could use the bad leg like a club to send the ball a distance that sometimes left teammates open-mouthed. Then, in a hastily arranged junior varsity game for the benefit of those few who never got a chance to play in varsity games, Danny and the coach discovered the goal for him. No one else wanted the position, but goalie required no running, no tricky footwork, just manual dexterity, quick reflexes, no fear, and a high tolerance for boredom. Danny had all those attributes, especially quick hands. He patrolled the goal area the way the mongrel dog that had adopted their farm patrolled its perimeter, instantly springing up to fend off any intrusions that came his way. He gained confidence with every play. In the game's final minutes he stopped a penalty kick, appreciated as a supreme accomplishment by teammates, even if it only required keeping his knees together. When the starting goalie for the varsity came down with mono and was lost for the season, the coach looked down his bench, and there was only Danny. And the freshman stepped in like a champion. And he found that he liked the sport, after all. And the other boys liked him. Jonathan had been right. He made enough important plays, so that the others ignored his occasional blunders caused by bad footwork. He soon developed something like a sixth sense that let him anticipate when a ball would be kicked and which direction it would go, almost before the opposing player did. Indeed, his teammates began to take for granted that, if they let an opposing player by, Danny was behind them to close down any threat resulting from their errors. That let them take more chances. They forgave—or thought it not relevant—that he could not jump high enough to reach the crossbar. The one ball than an opponent slipped beneath it against him was nothing but pure luck in the eyes of Danny's teammates. He appreciated the pats on the rump after a good play and liked giving them in return. And after all, he reasoned during a boring stretch when the ball was at the other end of the field, didn't Kerouac play football at Columbia? Then he turned his attention to dividing in his head the number of seats in the football stands, the back of which faced the soccer pitch, by the number of spectators, which he could count in one hand if bench warmers were excluded. Then he worked out the square root of that number to three digits.

Just when the leaves start to turn and box elder bugs are drawn to the house on a sunny day, where they find the tiniest of crevices to crawl through, then wander stupidly on walls, furniture, and floors inside, the owner of the dog that has set up housekeeping under their kitchen porch comes for it. It is also just when Jon, Jewel, and Danny are working their hardest to get paint onto the north wall of the house before the weather turns bad. Jonathan is atop the ladder, painting the very top of the gable.

The dog is a large, good-natured mongrel with a black coat and floppy ears. The owner is a skinny little man with a scruffy beard and tight-fitting white Lee jeans.

"Quite some ladder," he says. "Forty-footer?"

Jewel nods affirmatively.

"Took all three of you to put it up, I bet," he adds. Then he turns to Danny. "What I don't understand, though, is why he's the one up on the ladder with the brush and you're the one all the paint is on."

From up on the ladder comes, "He gets paint all over just from opening the can."

"I'm afraid I took pity on him," Jewel apologizes for the dog, "and gave him a plate of leftover lasagna. It was Jonathan's lasagna," she feels she has to add.

"Actually, this used to be his home," the neighbor says in an accent familiar to Jewel. "It's only fair I guess. He moved in with us when I let him chase the heifers off my land. Then his family moved away, as did the heifers, so the place could be put on the market. I'm Don Mitchell."

Jonathan, who, in fact, sets and moves the ladder on his own, begins scampering down it, paint bucket in hand. He insists on it, in fact, after Danny took fright and let the ladder drop when they first tried to set it up. Now Danny is only allowed to set his feet against the bottom of the ladder when Jon needs to pull the rope to bring the ladder up or let it down.

Here I am, Jewel thinks as she watches Jon coming down, soon both to be a bride and a widow.

"Jonathan Bushey," Jon says as he steps off the ladder onto the ground. "This is Jewel Fairfax."

"Don Mitchell."

"Don't let Danny near that paint can," Jon says to Jewel.

"My nephew Danny," Jewel says.

Mitchell laughs. Danny wanders away.

"Fine looking young man," Mitchell says.

"Upper West Side?" Jewel asks.

"Huhh? Oh! Scarsdale, by way of Philadelphia. And you?"

"Connecticut, by way of Detroit. Jonathan is born and bred."

"You're Jonathan from the restaurant, aren't you? B-u-s-h-e-e?"

"With a y."

"I bet it was Boucheé when your grandparents—or whoever —came over from Canada."

"That would be whoever, but you're probably right."

The matter of the dog is settled when Don leaves without him. In the interim, they learn that Don and his wife have taken Bill and Helen Nearing's advice to heart and are almost two years into reaching their vision for a farm. They passed through the romantic stage, the confident stage, the panic stage, and are now into the painful stage of going back to the land, the Nearings' "good life" almost in their reach.

"Any way I can help you, just let me know," are his parting words.

Spring comes early after a cold, but almost snowless winter during which ski areas begin taking an interest in snowmaking. Summer progresses as if it is one long sunny day. The spring behind the barn dries up, but the well holds, if only barely. A hundred and twenty feet seemed like a deep well to Jewel, but on a Vermont hillside, it is only adequate. Grit has to be cleaned out of the old centripetal pump. There is enough water each day, however, for vegetables and animals, and the occasional bath. Don and his wife next door are less lucky. They traipse over to their new neighbors to borrow cups of water and leave with plastic jugs strapped to their bodies. Don's ninety-pound wife, needing more, perhaps, carries more. Meanwhile Don arranges for the town dowser to locate water for him to drill his own well. The dowser, using a wire coat hanger, rather than willow or birch twigs, confidently throws his cap on the spot where Don should drill a well, but is less confident about the depth he would have to drill.

"First his coat hanger bobbed a hundred and eighty times," Don explains to Jonathan as they carve out hunks of pork from the half carcass that Jonathan has been smoking on a spit over a smoldering wood fire for the past six hours. "That's a hundred eighty feet, but he can't tell how much water there will be. Next, the thing bobs four hundred twenty times. We're talking about a five thousand-dollar investment, and if it was on a slate seam, he told me, it might smell of sulfur. Finally, he recommended I wait for rain."

Two MacArthur children are underfoot, fascinated by the main course for the wedding feast. Betsy carries a third. She looks good, Jewel is pleased to tell her. She gave everyone a scare that first fall in Philadelphia when what had first seemed just moodiness sent her into a psychiatric hospital. Manic-depressive, is the term that reaches Jewel's ear.

It is Jewel and Jonathan's wedding, a small, simple, outdoor ceremony attended by Jewel's Marlboro family, Jonathan's friends, and Ames Hill neighbors. It is less like a wedding to Jewel than the house raising at Marlboro in which she took part, when everyone at the college pitched in to build the student center. It is a combination country dance and town meeting held in celebration of an existing couple that this gathering has pitched in to create, Jewel prefers to think, than a ceremony to bind them together. The profusion of fresh vegetables is from the garden—theirs or their neighbors. Alcohol in several forms appears unbidden, but welcome on tables. The wedding cake is a chocolate tree stump, complete with a marzipan tap, that Jonathan labored over the day before. Inspiration for it came as he was cutting wood for the smoke pit and snapped the chain of his saw on a spile hidden by years of growth around it. The chain took a lethal trajectory toward a gray squirrel. The maple is still standing. That the cake is a stump is simple Vermont voodoo, according to Jonathan. Dick Fudd calls it "a masterpiece of effigy." To Danny falls the task of destroying it. Jewel has refused the traditional cake-cutting honor on the basis that no chocolate stains will be allowed to besmirch her mother's wedding dress. She intends to keep it virginal for Danny's bride. It had been her grandmother's, one of the Massachusetts Kidders, before it was her mother's.

And it does rain soon after, a hurricane's worth, toppling spruces and blowing around small metal roofs like pie tins. The winds die down quickly, but the rain settles in. August becomes one long rainy day. Carpenter ants go back to getting their food from wherever they get it, instead of Jewel and Jonathan's new pantries in their expanded kitchen. (No more kitchen porch for a dog to live under.) Coy dogs yip less plaintively at night. Vegetables begin to outgrow the hunger of baby rabbits, but not the groundhogs that take advantage of the missing dog. Deer pluck off tomatoes as they ripen from the benefit of the abundant sunshine they absorbed earlier in the summer. And Jonathan and Don discover lamb.

Both know that there are reasons for sheep having disappeared from Vermont hillsides. Common sense tells them that sheep are a difficult animal to tend in Vermont, where winters can stay on into spring like bad guests, unlike the Basque regions of Spain and France or the southern San Joaquin Valley of California. Sheep need to be sheltered and fed expensive grain in Vermont in winter. That is why wool production has returned to the regions in which it makes sense, where sheep can pretty much survive on their own. Shipping wool makes more economic sense than shipping grain.

But Jonathan has added lamb to his restaurant menu in addition to the lean, stringy, grass-fed beef from the shaggy highland cattle he has set loose to wander Ames Hill. Their meat, which Jewel will not eat, considering each of the animals a personal friend, makes outstanding stew when not ground into hamburger. To his chagrin, his special dish, what keeps customers returning, has become meat loaf. And his main revenue comes from his take-out deserts and his catering, rather than his restaurant operations. Music festival sessions are a gold mine. But he thinks he can educate the citizens of Brattleboro to the marvels of lamb in their diets. Failing that, he tells Jewel, he will turn the farm into a hunting preserve, with the farmhouse turned into a guest house, where he will charge outrageous prices to cook meals out of the unfortunate critters the guest get to blow away (also at a charge.)

"Just keep all that out of my sight," Jewel commands.

Don joins him in the lamb enterprise simply because he needs an agricultural justification for his farm and he likes sheep. He does not like hens, ducks, or pigs, which he has tried and abandoned in quick succession. The sheep let him raise a peculiar cash crop that he calls "Schedule F tax credits" while he pursues a more lucrative editing and writing career from his farm retreat. Tax credit is a crop that Jonathan also quickly adds to his operation.

"How much onion should I use, Jon?" Danny asks on helping himself to a large portion of ground lamb in the restaurant's kitchen.

"What are you making?"

"A cheeseburger."

"Out of lamb?"

"Yeah. Why not?"

"Use as much as you want, I guess. You're a grown-up."

A few minutes later, Jonathan walks past the griddle again.

"Not enough," he says.

Danny makes a face.

Another pass.

"Too much!"

"You said as much as I wanted."

"Is that it? That's how much onion you wanted?"

"Yeah."

And then Danny was gone.

Jewel at first thinks, when he does not show up for supper, that he might have stayed after school in Brattleboro. He often does, helping out and catching a quick meal at the restaurant before hanging out downtown, but Jonathan comes home without him. Back into Brattleboro they go, hitting all his favorite haunts, which, approaching midnight on a chilly spring evening, are deserted. A teacher is called. No he says, audibly yawning, Danny was not in his morning class, although neither was he on the absence list.

 A terror seizes Jewel. She thought it was something she had permanently shaken at Grace-New Haven.

 Has she lost him? Nothing was missing from his room but the guitar that Jon had given him. All his books, all his clothes—his whole life, it seems to Jewel, still litters his room.

 He must not have gone far, Jon tries to assure her.

 Police are called and respond. Bus and train stations are checked. A sleepless night passes. There is no word in the morning.

 No word comes that week. Nor the summer. Nor the next.

Jewel turns her attention even more toward Jonathan, her duties at Marlboro, her reading. And she reads. And she reads. It is often to the sound of Jonathan gently snoring beside her in their bed.

 Her library duties drop a new book into her lap. And drop is the appropriate term. She picked it out of a list of publications for purchase. Then she was the first to take it out of the library and has yet to return it, picking it up and dropping it down again, almost every night.

 The author's name had caught her attention: Edith Clements. It was a memoir of her life as seen mainly through field trips with her husband. It brings up images of her own life for Jewel, real and imagined. Pranks and threats of dropping critters down ladies' necks. No night clothes on camping field trips. Coyote calls early in the evening. Each causes Jewel to drop the book back on her tummy and reminisce until sleep takes over. Dunes shimmering pale gold in the sun. Political arguments. Road kill. Road kill and low-flying hawks had always brought a stop to the Shelford caravans, too.

There is a picture that is recognizably Clements. None that are recognizably Edith, though, unless that is her at the front of the group photographed descending the cog railroad on scooters, as they were called. But then, of course, it is Edith who had been the photographer on the trips, again, as always, in the background.

And her writing, Jewel decides on another night, is as catty and overblown as her painting ... and her speech had been. She shows no sense of humor, telegraphing each joke in advance. And the prose!

"... many-hued pageantry of spring flowers ... new lands and adventures ... mysterious allure ... stark beauty ... fertile fields ... green pastures ... charming home embowered in cottonwood." Down went the book again.

But back up it came the next night. Here is a picture of Edith standing in front of Billy Buick. "Cherie," she is called and further identified as cook, photographer, mechanic, and field assistant. She looks almost human, Jewel judges, but youth does that.

Yes, youth. A whole generation went by between then and when Edith Clements usurped an office from Jewel in Urbana. Another generation has gone by since. A busy one. Science has turned upside down. Or rather, inside out. Liza and colleagues have finally delved into the insides of the inside of an atom. Ecologists, meanwhile, have rediscovered Mendell's peas. The blending aspects of inheritance that so befuddled Darwin have been pushed aside by the new synthesis of Huxley, Mayr, Fisher, and all those others who now lead the field of evolution. Clements all the while stayed at the margins of the science, trying to create new species in a Lamarckian way by transplanting plants to different life zones in his Rocky Mountain laboratory. What his team actually proved right under his nose turned out to be the exact opposite.

So much new is happening in ecology. It is so removed from the ecology of Cowles and Clements that it has to be unrecognizable to them, should they be looking down at it from somewhere. It is almost unrecognizable to me, she thinks to add.

And then the thought strikes Jewel that the tale Edith spins is what she had dreamed for herself with Fred Küchler. With Arden Forest replacing Billy Buick? Had she exchanged it all for Danny? Was it all gone now?

The assassination affects her more strongly, more than she first thought. She wishes Jon was home with her instead of at the restaurant. If that sort of thing could happen to a President, keeps going through her mind, what might not have happened to Danny? And how is he taking the event? What thoughts of the past might it be dredging up?

Jewel has had their little TV on constantly since the assassination. At the moment, it is repeating footage of Lee Harvey Oswald being shot in the stomach by someone now identified as Jack Ruby. She had seen the event as it happened live that morning.

She was at the Sub Shop when she first learned the President had been shot. She had grown to love the way they made their subs, using cabbage instead of lettuce. In secret from Jonathan, who had the item in competition on his lunch menu, she often enjoyed bringing one home for dinner. Assembly of her sub that day stopped when music on the shop's radio became the voice of Walter Cronkite.

"Someone shooting at the President?" a teenager ahead of her asked.

The young man behind the counter was frozen in silence.

"That's crazy!" a second teenager countered. "That couldn't be!"

She shuts the TV off and takes her poetry out of the small lacquered box with the cat images on it. She never did write that great beat poem, as she now thinks of it, and she knows she never will. Alan beat her to it with Howl. How can she try to write the poetry that is—or is it was—in her head after reading that? Strange, too, she thinks, how it was Alan who reproduced Walt Whitman's powerful voice a century later. Jack could not manage it. Talentless Jewel never even made a start.

She decides she should write prose now. Honest, simple prose about the joys of sitting by the fire on a crisp sunny morning after a snowstorm, dog sprawled at her feet, cat on its cushion, and … And what?

How did Rachel do it? Jewel suddenly wonders. Her glance has fallen on her copy of Silent Spring, recently read and left on the table for further reference. No PhD. No academic position. No formal training, even, in ecology. More family responsibilities than have troubled Jewel for years. And look what has come of it for her!

She and the book are on the TV news and the subject of countless magazine articles. She has taught more people ecology than Cowles, Clements, Shelford, and Hutchinson, combined. She has reached the public. They can only claim grad students.

Thankfully, hearing Jon coming home early breaks her train of thought. Emu, he tells her, which he put on the menu a month before, is no longer being ordered, except for the one flatlander tourist couple who stumbled into the restaurant this evening. And he still has pounds and pounds of it in the freezer. It may have to go into his meatloaf, he says with resignation, as she leads him upstairs to their bedroom.

The bedside phone interrupts their lovemaking. Jewel has not lost the hope that one day it will ring and Danny will be on the other end. Her hands are free and the phone is within reach. With one hand, she picks up the receiver, while with the other, she continues stroking Jon's balding head, as he wonders whether to resume what he was doing.

"Danny?" she says, suddenly pushing Jon away.

"Danny, where are you?"

IX

AN infrequent breakfast together is seasoned by an almost-friendly argument on the subject of peeling eggs. Jonathan has a huge pot of just-boiled eggs he will need for a spinach salad dish at the restaurant.

"So why is it that running cold water over hard boiled eggs makes them easier to peel? Does the egg shrink or something?"

"That may be true, but it doesn't matter what temperature the water is, actually. You're running cold water over that egg only so you don't burn your fingers. It's the water that's important, I should think. It gets under the egg's membrane and lubricates it so it comes off the white easier."

"But I'm pouring the water around the egg, not into it."

"Capillary action, Jon. The space between membrane and egg draws it in."

Jonathan says nothing, but he looks at her in a way that lets her know he is an unbeliever. Jewel is reminded of the argument they had over how best to make coffee. The water temperature should be one hundred ninety degrees, according to the sales representative for the company that sold Jonathan his coffee maker. Therefore, not boiling. And the coffee should not be ground too fine, but just the way it is sold for that coffee maker by the same company. Jonathan sees coffee making as a commercial transaction. A satisfied customer, served at a profit, denotes success. Jewel sees it as a simple extraction process, no different from the things she used to do as a lab technician or now occasionally teaches in a chemistry section. Success must only be determined by how many molecules of coffee flavor are extracted. Grind the beans as fine as you can to increase the surface contact area, she argues. That increases the rate of extraction of oils and alkaloids, which is what coffee flavors and caffeine are. But do not grind them so fine as to plug up the filter. And, since the solubility of all oils in water increases with its temperature, pour almost-boiling water (which is what it is when you take the pot off the heat) over your coffee grounds. A filter and funnel are all the equipment needed. Steam, as in an espresso maker, works best for extracting all those components that make us prize fresh, rich coffee beans, she concludes her mini-lecture, but boiling hot water will do.

"Then why keep it at a hundred ninety degrees in the pot after brewing?" Jonathan had then persisted. "Tell me that!"

"Look, let the eggs cool and then peel them under warm water," she now suggests, "if you don't believe me."

He already does not believe her, and he will not try her suggestion. A phone call, therefore, is a welcome interruption.

It is Robert MacArthur. He has moved from Penn to Princeton, finally getting his family out of the city. Princeton may be rural, but summers and vacations, he assures his Aunt Jewel, will not be affected by the move, other than by the hour less of travel time. All of their summers, MacArthur tells her, he intends to spend on South Pond.

"Great job, you got," Jewel kids. "You seem to need to work only when your family doesn't need you around."

She is repeating something that Peter Klopfer once wrote to her, also jokingly, in a letter from North Carolina, where he has settled in at Duke.

"Family always comes first, especially Betsy," Robert answers good-naturedly, but firmly. "You know that, Jewel."

Still, even given that less-than-fanatic devotion to career, reprints of papers by him keep piling up in the Marlboro library. Some are co-authored with Peter Klopfer and others with his brother John. Jewel likes that. The easy way that MacArthur invited collaboration is a far cry from the sturm und drang she remembers between Clements and Shelford.

He has gathered together several friends at his in-law's cottage above the lake, he tells her. Their intent is to "make something scientifically sensible out of ecology." They would like her company.

"Oh, you don't want me there," Jewel says.

"Larry specifically suggested we invite you," Robert persists.

"Larry Slobodkin?"

She and Slobodkin have been exchanging their thoughts—mostly his—about ecology and life in a regular correspondence. She is surprised that he had not mentioned coming to Marlboro.

"Do you know any other?"

"I'd love to see Larry again."

Jewel loads a canoe onto Jonathan's truck and drives to the small boat launch area on the opposite shore from the Whittemore cabin on South Pond. Leaving the truck unlocked, she paddles across the pond. It takes her no more than twenty minutes. She arrives just as they are about to take a mid-morning break. Instead of tea as with Hutchinson, with MacArthur it is an occasion for a hike.

"Miss Farifax," Ed Wilson, who met her previously on a visit to Yale, calls from shore.

"Just Jewel, please," she says as he helps her ashore with gallant southern politeness.

To Wilson, the meaning of life, she is sure, is something that can be learned only through the study of ants. He has spent the greater part of the last decade studying life by keeping his nose to the ground and his eye on a magnifying lens. His studies have taken him, he tells Jewel, still calling her Miss Fairfax, to Mexico, Cuba, islands in the Caribbean, New Guinea, Australia, New Caledonia, and other places that he probably deems unworthy of mention. Oh—and Ceylon on the way back. Still calling her Miss Fairfax even after further admonishment from her on it, he excitedly details descriptions of doing research in the various tropical locations, right down to the life cycle of tropical ground leeches. Only Mexico is on both Jewel's and Ed's lists of places visited, and the part of it she had been to had not been tropical.

"Why don't you try Aunt Jewel," she pauses walking to suggests, "instead of Miss Fairfax?" He simply cannot bring himself to call any woman older than himself by her first name alone, she realizes.

Issue settled, she lets Wilson talk on, enjoying his enthusiasm.

"Robert says you have great common sense when it comes to applying math to ecology," he tells her as the path strays from the lakeshore and follows a small flow out of a swampy area.

"And Robert should know," Ed thinks to add. "Just being in his company always has me reining in my wilder flights of fancy."

A snake catches the attention of both. Before Ed can find an appropriate stick with which to pin its head to the ground, Jewel snatches it up and has it coiling around her arm.

"Water snake," she announces.

"I wouldn't be so hasty, Aunt Jewel," Ed warns her, eyeing its mottled colors and mentally going over a roster of dangerous possibilities, each of which he rejects based on their normal ranges.

"Northern water snake," Jewel says firmly, letting it go. It briskly snakes off into the water.

"Oh, there's Dick Levins," Ed notices. "Reading his recent paper gives me the feeling that I am receiving secrets of the universe from a space visitor anxious to be on his way. But I have to ask him something. Excuse me."

He hurries off. She spies Dick Lewontin coming toward her. She knows Dick well. He has a vacation home in Marlboro and is a patron of the Marlboro Music festival. He is also a resource for Marlboro students. Dick's field of science is population genetics, something not within Jewel's purview. A number of times, when working with a student on a Plan of Concentration and getting stuck on some new twist or discovery in genetics, Jewel has tossed up her hands and suggested, "Why don't we go ask Dick?" And he always welcomed the opportunity to clear up any confusion. Whenever she is with him, Jewel cannot help but think fondly of the stereotype of a little fat Jewish boy with glasses and asthma who appeared in her Detroit classes from time to time. He was the one who wanted to answer her every question and who was always right and knew it.

Now she knows what happens to those boys. They are still always right and they succeed by it.

"Have you heard from Danny lately?" Dick asks, his usual easy grin set in his still-youthful face.

"Phone calls," she answers without enthusiasm.

"Still in New York?"

"Yeah. Greenwich Village. He is living in an apartment with a girl—woman, really. She's older than he is by several years."

"And?"

"Jon and I managed a visit in April. She's from Minnesota. A Norwegian bible, which she reads aloud at the drop of a hat—in Norwegian—is the only book in the apartment. Jon could not take his eyes off her. I suspect it was her combination of short skirt and no underpants."

Dick's eyebrows rise almost to his hairline. "Still the folk singer?" he changes the subject.

She nods.

"Any success?"

"What can I do?" she blurts out as both start walking toward the cabin. "He's not twenty-one, but he's past eighteen. I no longer have a hold on him. Oh, how I wish I'd been granted extra time somehow from when he first left! Or if I'd tracked him down when he first called after the assassination."

Robert has been listening to them approach from around a bend in the shoreline.

"Perhaps," he says, falling into step with them, "I should take him bird watching with me. There are allegedly wooded areas near Princeton, and I know for a fact there are birds. Danny seemed to have enjoyed our walks together. He was becoming a rather respectable birder. I think he has the makings of a quite good ecologist, too, if my brother might not have already pushed him into the harder sciences. Oh! And here we all are!"

Of the others assembling at the Whittemore cabin, Egbert Leigh is a mathematician who, Jewel suspects, sensed an opportunity in ecology and like MacArthur found it under Hutchinson. Dick Levins she has not a clue about. Somehow she missed him in the introductions.

"But where is Larry?" she asks.

"Larry is here both morally and in spirit," Robert tells her. "I just got off the phone with him when I called you. Lee Van Valen—do you know him? An evolutionary theorist, he is also with us in spirit. We've all of us sort of decided to join our minds in taking Hutch's Concluding Remarks paper to heart."

"There is a war about to begin in biology departments," Ed Wilson uses to call the group to order.

Although it is obvious to Jewel that MacArthur is their leader, he is not taking a leadership role. Wilson has stepped into that.

"James Watson," Wilson continues when he has everyone's attention, "the most unpleasant human being I have ever met, seems to be transforming biology at Harvard into a science directed at molecules and cells and rewritten in the language of physics and chemistry. When I tried to get Fred Smith for the department, Watson sarcastically shot the idea down by saying, Anyone who would hire an ecologist is out of his mind."

"Kingman Brewster at Yale seems to have the same idea," Leigh adds. "Markert, the new biology chair, has let it be known that he thinks there are too many of Hutch's old students on the faculty. Gordon Riley is leaving for Dalhousie and Ed Deevey is thinking of following him there. And Hutch has had to step down as director of graduate studies."

"We need to make ecology respectable," Wilson says. "Elso Barhoon told me recently that he didn't think we should use the expression, ecology, any more. He thinks it has become a dirty word. And we need to make evolutionary studies something more than proteins and molecular clocks."

"I think I may just call myself a biogeographer," MacArthur says, cocking his head.

"Evolutionary biology," Lewontin offers. "That's what my interest is. Isn't that what you call your course, Ed?"

"I think, whatever we are called, we can divide ecologists into two camps," MacArthur says, after the slight throat clearing and eye rolling that the others interpret as signaling the importance of what he is about to say. "One camp is so aware of the complexity of nature that it is critical of any simplifying theory. It is content to continue to just document observations, and do it at endless length. The second camp, and I count myself in it, is primarily interested in making a science of ecology. We want to arrange the ecological data as examples that test our proposed theories. We then spend most of our time patching up theories to account for as many of the data as possible. Both camps are necessary, aren't they?"

The broken stick next becomes the engine of the discussion. MacArthur is beginning to have doubts about it. Then it is the species-area curve, an old observation that Jewel thinks has mystical significance for Ed. Behind both is the very hot topic of Competitive Exclusion. Behind that is the nature of the ecological niche, Hutchinson's version of it. Robert argues convincingly that competition over niches is the key to the patterns found by ecologists. Ed agrees but insists that islands hold the key to understanding and building a true science of evolutionary ecology.

Jewel pays more attention to the people than their ideas. How Lewontin controls an audience captivates her by being exactly as Ed Wilson has described it to her during a brief pause in the proceedings. First, he raises his hands over his head like a Roman calling the Senate to order. Then, speaking in complete sentences and paragraphs, the hands float down to the tabletop. There, palms down, they hold everyone's attention as they slide apart. Then he raises them to chest height and windmills them around each other as he sews up all the loose ends of his discourse.

Robert, she notes, seems reserved with his comments, letting Ed speak for him most of the time. And only when Robert's eyes widen with interest, does Ed come to a halt.

"Bird communities," Robert suddenly tilts his head back and says.

All fall to listening. He too holds their attention with complete sentences and paragraphs.

"His ideas have been worked out considerably since the ecology seminars at Yale," Jewel whispers to Ed, who has taken a seat next to her.

"I think he has a full theory of ecology in his head that he doles out as needed," Ed whispers back to her. "And doesn't his clipped diction confer on him the wisdom of Oxford?"

"Had you spent any time in Ontario, you would have found an entire population with the same mannerisms," Jewel assures him in another whisper. "Toronto and Detroit—"

But she has lost his attention. Ed is busy recapturing the floor to urge greater focus on island communities.

"They are discrete," he points out. "They are spatially separated. And there are multiple island groups. That allows for replication. We can test ideas derived from one island against others."

That gives Levins a chance to return the conversation to the species-area curve. Robert and Ed have just published a paper in *Evolution* with their equation relating the number of species on an island to its size. Characteristically, Robert has reduced the underlying explanation for the pattern that has Wilson so intrigued to simple sketches of colonization and extinction curves.

"What great simplicity!" Levins exclaims. "It is identical to the basic supply and demand curves of economics. How clever! Equilibrium species number is just optimal price! It's like what I am working on. The math for it is all worked out for us in advance."

"Not quite all," a discomfited MacArthur says.

"Yes," Ed adds, "there's the distance effect to be taken into consideration, Dick. That puts a different gloss on the math. It also makes our paper different from Preston's."

The discussion that follows makes it clear to Jewel that Preston published almost the same ideas in *Ecology* a year before MacArthur and Wilson's *Evolution* paper. Priority again, she says under her breath, thinking back to Urbana.

"Math is very important," Levins is suddenly arguing, although no one is in disagreement. "College presidents and academic deans may not understand much math, but they do see it as something rigorous. We in ecology must use it to the utmost."

"I think you're right," MacArthur agrees, "but using math is also our problem. Remember the two kinds of ecologists that are extant? Some accept mathematical theory and our hypothetico-deductive method of doing science. Others, though, still just blindly gather data. They are the ones giving ecology a bad reputation, just as their predecessors had."

Lewontin, Jewel notes, does not miss a chance to push the conversation toward a population ecology perspective and those equations from the Ecology Seminar that Jewel disparaged almost a decade ago. They are now being combined in various ways with some from population genetics. She makes an unsuccessful effort to point out that they are not new but have been available in the literature since the nineteen thirties. Lewontin, however, turns her remark into a passionate insistence that his view of biology is primarily holistic.

Jewel has not heard that term since Australian John Phillips's summer visit to Urbana. Now holism flits lightly about the room. Closing her eyes, she can imagine Lewontin's words coming out of Phillips's mouth, incongruously so, for she knows Lewontin has made his name studying proteins found in mice, as molecular an investigation as any Jewel can imagine.

"I think the coefficients of the community matrix are the future of ecology," from Richard Levins startles her out of her imaginings. "They are highly mathematical, are governed by competition for niches, and span entire communities."

"They are numbers that can be put into generalized Lotka-Volterra equations that specify the effect of one species on another," Robert, who has replaced Wilson at her side, takes the time to explain to her as Levins continues what is becoming a soliloquy.

"Why, they sound like what Shelford tried and failed to measure with what he called coefficients of similarity," Jewel finally gets in a word to those assembled.

"Hummph," she hears from someone, but nothing else. The conversation goes on, bypassing her remark. Lewontin holds the floor with his hands parting before his face to question the holistic nature of community matrices.

The thought suddenly strikes Jewel that Robert may not have invited her for her common-sense input, as he told her, but simply to bring her up to date on ecology for her own benefit as a teacher. She should feel somehow demeaned, she knows, to be nothing more than an appreciative audience, but she cannot summon up any anger. It is Robert, after all, she would have to be angry with. Taking out her knitting needles and Olive's special wool, she silently sets to work on a sweater for the youngest MacArthur as the men around her create a new ecology.

She seeks out Robert during another break, lunch this time, to remark that, "Things seem to have come a long way from Hutch's mice are born and all is confusion assessment. Or from his review of Bio-Ecology."

"Hutch is still showing the way for us," MacArthur says. "His Homage to Santa Rosalia paper has prepared the ground for us. You have read it, haven't you?"

"Read it? I heard most of it along with you at those seminars at Yale."

"It's getting a good reception. It could set the direction of ecology for years."

His hand reaches out to tuck a strand of hair behind her ear, gently caressing her cheek as he does so.

"I like your hair this length," he says. "But is that a white strand?"

"Gray, it's called," Jewel says, enjoying his touch.

"Not for a blonde. You don't color it?"

"Why should I? I'm well into middle age. Pretty soon, you will be too."

"What about the kick in the pants we got from Rachel Carson's book?" she hears Ed Wilson ask Leigh out on the tiny sleeping porch. She turns away from Robert. "Odum is Johnny-on-the-spot with it," Wilson continues. "He's going to take that environmental slant and really run with it to the funding agencies."

"As if he's not tapping those trees enough already," Leigh observes. "The IBP seems to be all ecosystem analysis."

"I'm sorry to hear that," Levins catches up with the conversation. "Ecosystem science, with all that energy analysis and chemistry, is not what ecology should be about. Leave that for the engineering schools. There is nothing that can be said about the evolution of species by doing the equivalent of grinding up a landscape and its animals and studying the chemical composition of the soup created. How can anybody analyze that? And not with those God-awful computer models the ecosystems people keep grinding out."

"Larry Slobodkin says," Jewel suddenly cannot keep from blurting out, "that, unless mathematical modelers can show him where in their equations the prey evolves horns and escapes the predator, they are useless."

"Evolution is what ecology should be aimed at," Ed agrees. "That's what it was proposed to be by Haeckel. That's what it was for Darwin—"

"Even though he never did use the word," Lewontin has to interrupt.

Wilson turns to MacArthur. "Speaking over your silence," he says, obviously soliciting a positive response, "always makes me speak more succinctly?"

"And sensibly," MacArthur laughs.

It is Robert's reticence, Jewel decides, that makes him their leader, that gives him his surprising power over the group. What she knows is a sign of his shyness has a different meaning to them. And how different from Hutch, with his esoteric digressions. Robert comes to the point, instead of leaving the listener with puzzles to figure out.

And how lucky she is to have been party to so much in her career. Yes, it was a career, even if her only mark on her science was a footnote of appreciation in a paper by Shelford. Then, realizing she has lost her stitch count makes her lose track of the argument going on around her.

"There has to be an equilibrium species number," she hears Robert say. "Each island seems capable of only holding so many species. If there is an equilibrium of bird species on islands, then all those equations we worked out should be applicable, as are those from population genetics that Dick keeps pushing on us, and Larry's prey never get to grow horns. As islands get smaller, so do the populations on them and so does the chance of extinction."

"Primate and insect societies must have some common principles," Jewel hears Wilson announce a bit later. "Perhaps, Robert's r and K idea."

Here Jewel has to give up on her knitting and ask for an explanation. It is "r", always small letter, she is told by a gabble of voices, that is the natural rate of increase of a population, and "K", always a capital, that is the carrying capacity for it. They are part of the magic of the logistic equation that she knows so well. Robert's use of them in his "r species" and "K species" concept is building a new theory of ecology by giving them evolutionary meaning. She likes that. She can understand it. It makes sense. It is like Robert's ideas on specialist and generalist, or "jack of all trades" species, as he put it in a paper she read in the library. No math to obscure his point.

"An animal society is a population," she finds Wilson holding the floor after she has finally figured out her stitch count. "We should be able to analyze it's structure and evolution as part of population biology. My student, Stuart Altman, and I once threw around the word sociobiology for it. I haven't come up with a better name."

Lewontin throws him a dour stare, but says nothing.

"Not a term I should think would go over well," Levins steps into the silence. "Sounds too much like sociology."

Then he brightens.

"Still," he says, "I think you are on the right track, although the math you are looking for might not exist yet."

"Not r and K?"

Robert tilts his head back again, clears his throat, and swallows.

"Maybe some math for r and K can be worked out," he says, "especially in conjunction with some of the things Ed and I have been talking about in island biogeography."

"But wouldn't that require some sort of group selection?" suddenly cuts through the discussion and brings it to a halt.

It is Lewontin speaking. He is the only one in the world, Wilson had earlier whispered to Jewel, who can make Robert MacArthur sweat. He is doing it now. Robert is frowning.

In the discussion that follows, of altruism, the Allee effect, interdeme selection, Prince Kropotkin, David Lack, and Wynne-Edwards, the name "Maximin" catches Jewel's attention. George Maximin, first name arbitrary, last after a term in optimization theory, not the Roman emperor, is the group's choice for a pseudonym under which to publish the ideas they have been bandying around. They suppose that the anonymity will free them from egotistical arguments over who gets first authorship for what. They also think it will let them be as audacious and speculative as they might want to be.

This, Jewel decides, is where she will make her contribution to science. She will slay George Maximin.

"You sound like a goofy bunch of frat boys planning a prank," she says coldly.

It is the end of the day. She offers to take the group out the next morning to where she knows there to be lady slippers still in flower. The hike never happens. The group never leaves Olive's house. Jewel does not join them. She chooses to spend the second day of the "Marlboro Circle" conference, as Ed Wilson has named it, tending her garden, instead of midwifing the birth of a new science.

But she does get a promise from Robert.

"Princeton might be a reach for him," he tells her, "but I still have friends at Penn. Let me see what I can do. But he'll have to get a high school diploma first, or at least show some sort of unusual equivalent proficiency."

Fern Lake

HE bought the cabin for Jewel, or, more accurately, he had convinced her to buy it with him. Living on Ames Hill had become difficult for her after Jonathan's death. The house had begun to decay from disrepair—even the remodeled kitchen needed work. The barns and outbuildings had become liabilities. No longer in use, but for an intrepid flock of chickens who laid their eggs in its farthest reaches, the main barn had fallen into that sagging, listing condition that is so picturesque to tourists, but portends immanent collapse. Taking it off her hands became a necessity over which Dan fretted and Jewel was oblivious.

Jonathan's restaurant, never very successful, Jewel had sold immediately on his death. Surprisingly, it managed to bring enough to pay off the Whittemore heirs and leave the farm clear of debts, but with not a penny left over.

When she reached sixty, Marlboro honored her with a ceremony that essentially promoted her out to pasture and took her off the payroll. So Jon was gone, the restaurant was gone, her teaching was over, friends had died off, neighbors had moved away, and what was left of the farm threatened to collapse with her possibly underneath it. Meanwhile, Dan faced a six-hour drive every time she hiccuped, or a rafter creaked in the night, or wind blew snow or rain through a crack. But get her to move he could not, not until she looked through the windows of a cottage perched on a bluff above a cove at Fern Lake, when she instantly lost all her resistance to a move. It was not the sea, Dan knew, but it was the next best thing. There were even sails in sight out on the water that day. Small Sunfish had navigated around the island that created the secluded cove below the cottage and sailed smartly past its docks.

The cabin had a kitchen that was just the right size for Jewel. It was off a main room that had picture windows looking out into and through the wrap-around windows of a sun porch. There were twin bedrooms across the hall from each other. Jewel took over one. The other now held a washer and drier in an alcove that had been a closet. Not a very inviting guest room, but Danny told Jewel that he preferred climbing the ladder to the little sleeping loft, with its view of the morning sun to wake up with.

"No. No," Jewel had joked. "That loft is for grandchildren."

He had thought she was referring to Betsy MacArthur's grandchildren, before he realized that his aunt still had a sense of humor.

"My future grandchildren," she had tried to clear up his confusion.

Dan had winced at that, but made no remark.

Jewel was not at the lake on this day. A stroke had her in a rehab facility in Rutland. Her speech had returned completely and she was able to get about with a walker, but there was concern about being able to manage the stairs from the cottage to the water. They were wide and not steep, but there were many, and with railings meant more to support a Margarita or a glass of Scotch than someone needing to lean on or hold onto something while walking. So Danny was at Fern Lake with Merle to scope out what new modifications were needed, work a bit on his book, and enjoy a beautiful weekend of bass fishing. In June, the bass at Fern Lake were so frisky that they launched themselves two to three feet straight up out of the water when hooked.

Danny's project was still referred to as "the book," even though it was becoming no less shapeless. Still, he made discoveries and wondered how to announce them to the world. There was the matter of Rachel Carson and Fred Küchler's first exchange. He had caught up Linda Lear, whose biography of Rachel Carson he greatly admired, in a factual error. Ray Fosberg did NOT bring Carson and Küchler together. Fairfield Osborne should be given that honor. And Lear had flummoxed up the sequence of letters between Bill Brown and Rachel Carson in such a way that E. O. Wilson's advice seemed more important than Brown's. But although he found both points especially interesting, neither justified publication, not in the competitive field of environmental history. Every time he tried to invade that foreign territory, the referees tore his manuscript—and him, as an obvious non-historian—to a shredded still birth.

Why didn't he just stick to his teaching? Merle had asked. And he had had no good answer.

Now he wondered if Küchler's tussle with the Entomological Society might not make an interesting paper. But again, where could he publish it? He could not possibly make it book length. Perhaps it was Jewel's incessant prattling about Küchler after her stroke, he thought, that kept the subject on his mind.

So, having come to another dead end with the material from Arden Forest in his laptop, Dan turned again to Jewel's letters, this time in the breeze on one of the decks of the cabin. Missing an Internet connection to the Middlebury Library, the location lacked the ability to hook up instantly to its resources, but its ambiance was every bit as good as the library's.

The summer vacation is drawing to a close – It has passed so quickly! Gardening always – of course. Then I took on a biggish project of refinishing 2 corner cupboards rescued from the dump - much sanding – stain – shellac – wax – Last week we went shopping for dishes. The informed pattern we selected in Haviland is not too pretentious for our simple apartment – and is quite charming. Since nothing has been added since we moved here before the war – the place was getting pretty tacky. I also transformed a chair from maple to "walnut" – by the elbow grease method.

I haven't written to you for a long time, have I? – Yet it certainly does not reflect my real interest. You would be surprised – perhaps – but I hope not – embarrassed – by the tenderness that enfolds your image in that twilight zone between working and sleeping. Even in this glare of sunlight + hum of traffic my thoughts are often probing those experiences of childhood and youth that you have told me – seeking the harmful thing that delays your full maturing – Somehow in the strange childhood that frightened – immature – little-girl mother taught you – ineradicably to fear life. A boy must admire someone – and needs desperately to admire his father – and unconsciously copies him. Retiring father – retiring son.

I can only guess (how I wish I knew the intimate story!) at the hidden feelings of shame, the dread – that shut the adolescent Fred away from other boys and girls into a world alone. What pressing need to prove himself unafraid – or exceedingly clever – or - ? – drove him to daily tasks he now admits he did not love; to skimming over the mill pond of the world for motives he now judges inadequate.

Those wasted years – of carrying a can to kill thousands of harmless little plants on a little hill of a planet teeming with pushing unconscious life - What I wonder is the significance of this? What is Fred trying to destroy? Will he ever reach the stage of desiring to plant? What form of life for mankind does he wish to promote. – Is he capable of caring?

This went on for page after page, Dan saw, clicking and skimming ahead. He could never have imagined such prattle coming from his aunt. She had always seemed the supreme pragmatist to him. Here, though, Aunt Jewel's old phono needle was stuck in the same psychobabble groove. Nothing in the letter caught Dan's interest, nothing about either Jewel or ecology, as he scanned the offending pages almost to the end. Then came a revelation. "I want the courage to grow within you to launch out upon life," Dan read. "That is the Fred with whom I find myself increasingly in love."

Now that's more like it! What did Küchler have to say about that?

I realize now that I never did answer your note of September. Your August letter, as you might have expected, made it rather difficult for me to answer. You see, you have such faith in your religion (I mean, your Freudian psychology), you are so sure that you know more about me than I know about myself, that nothing I can say would hold water if it is not in accord with your own opinion. I am amazed at the ready facility with which you flip me into a Freudian category. And I am humorously tempted to wonder what sort of debate would ensue between you and another pro-Freudian on the interpretation of the forlorn individual concerned. You ignore so many things in my life that some other psychologically minded friend would leap upon. With it all, you appall me by the social role of tinseled mediocrity that you would have me fill. And likewise, you tell me more of yourself, by writing of myself, than you have ever said before.

And what came next? His "assoc. professorship was continued at the Univ of Connecticut," tidal marsh work, 2,4-D work in press, and acceptance of an offer from Beech-Nut.

To Washington the end of the semester, to finish a Hawaiian paper. Then to the Everglades to finish some Florida research.

"Dammit man!" Dan shouted, startling Merle, who was reading quietly beside him. "The woman has just told you she loves you!"

He was disappointed to find nothing from Jewel until January, dated as a Saturday night.

> *I picture you in your comfortable study by the big pine, cosy under a lamp – a symphony flowing around you – shutting away any inharmonious thought – as effectively as the Big Snow must shut you off from all that is irritating in the world of men. So I'd like to thank you for the Christmas greeting – and for refusing to be browbeaten – and for overlooking the spinsterly spasm of August.*
>
> *It would be funny – were life not so short – the way we keep sniping at each other – like the Martins and the Coys. You probably think I've done all the sniping – But you see I've a curious habit of identifying myself with the side of any argument not represented otherwise in the discussion, and with any human not present to defend himself – So I've a very neat collection of your shafts – probably never meant for this particular schoolmarm at all.*
>
> *Any sensible person would wonder why we persist in coming back for more – like the dog who howls at the high note of the sax. – The sharing of indignities must be an amazing bond: the lady who for lack of epidermis can not sit, the gentleman with a two day growth of beard – who needs spoon feeding.*
>
> *I'm grateful to be down off that rickety pedestal in your imagination labeled 'Very Superior Person a Lady'. High places make me very dizzy.*
>
> *To be sensible for a moment. – Honestly Fred – I've never questioned the possible values to human life of your research projects. Science has always progressed by people finding the answers to questions which interested them – regardless of remuneration – or applause. So often, tho, in your letters, you have been the angry man – sniping at people and experiences of previous years – rather than the joyful discoverer of new facts – new relationships so that I was forced to question your motivation. True creative work is always – I think – a labor of love – not hate. But I believe the old anger and resentment are fading. I think some day you will be able to view with sympathy the people who angered you most – see them as lonely, or frightened, - or crippled persons –*

hurting you more or less inadvertently in their efforts to achieve some sort of satisfaction in this necessarily complex and unsatisfactory world.

    I can understand the pleasure with which your students would cooperate with you in the preparation of the botany text. Your personal enthusiasm and charm make people all warm and glowy inside. Can you resist the temptation to gloat over the errors of the young men who were also enthusiasts – a generation ago?

    Have a wonderful time in Washington and Florida. Tell me about the Everglades – a biome I never got to experience. They fascinate me – as – just now would any place where there was no need for snow shovels, and the radiator was in no risk of freezing.

There was no response from Küchler. The next was another long letter from Jewel.

"Atta girl!" he again startled Merle. "Hang in there! It's never over till it's over!"

    A flicker has been exploring our premises for two days. No holes I'm afraid. A flock of starlings is purring and bubbling in the apple tree. Narcissus, tulips and bleeding heart are popping up around the fresh green of the lawn. Life is stretching itself mightily. Little Danny has just left. He promises to return "tomorrow." I look forward to the times that I can "steal" him back from Marjorie.

    I must ask you to be patient with me through this one bit of necessary explanation – It may be too late to repair the injury I have done our friendship but I must have a try.

    You see – and I have come to see also – that I've been carping and criticizing and doing a holier-than-thou – until; I've become – to you – a smug horror.

    A true friend would have rejoiced in your joy – and shared to the full your new wonder at the beauty of the world along your chosen road. But I was guilty of thinking – probably saying – that the inspiration of my road is truer. Instead of delighting in the ever unexpected quirks of your humor – and glorying in the fierce integrity that made you almost choke once over a term of endearment used falsely; instead of rejoicing in the many ways in which we are alike – and can speak one another's language – I have emphasized our differences and held a magnifier over your slightest *fault – and where I felt my vision was keener – held your inability to see against you. If I tell you why – the demon will be exorcised – forever lets hope. I was weaving of all this a tight shield to keep myself from being hurt by caring too much for you. Remembering how childishly disappointed I was that fall you said you would stop on your way home (from Hawaii) and didn't, I made every effort not to care and to avoid being hurt again. – And was hurt by you again, anyway—But when you were ill the cowardly fear was banished. I loved you simply and without fear of consequences. You must have known it --for once you said – "You are a Christian" – <u>not</u> a Freudian. Remember? Then you were swell again – and the old self protecting was resumed.*

I'm telling you this that I may be free to enjoy the warmth of the sun – the splendor of spring. But more than selfishness prompts the writing – I really have no axe to grind – save an open mind – and a chance to start over – and allow that friendship that was nearly pruned to death to grow again. (Had <u>you</u> been to blame I'd have said it was 2-4 D.)

Also – if one of the storms that threaten should really burst over us and our communications be terminated – I should like you to be sure that I do love you – for what you are – and want for you – above all things that inner peace which philosophers are never able to experience, Mystics call it the love of God. I cannot tell how that realization may come to you – To me it was the experience that set me thinking last week

You must not allow any thing that I have said to embarrass you, Fred, nor need you reply to it in any way when you write. Tell me about the view from the hilltop in the spring – and what you were working on in Florida – and how goes the saltmarsh project. Is your rhubarb up?

"It's over," Dan said.

Although discomfited by the remark, Merle returned only a puzzled look before going back inside. Dan watched a pair of canoes, a yellow Mad River and a green Old Town, gliding over the still water. Domestic noises coming from within the cabin suggested that a meal would soon be at hand. There was no use starting anything new. He read on.

For all I know, even if you did come East this summer you might not let me know were you not to hear from me after some Küchlerianly long period. I've been wondering whether I might get a telegram, announcing the time of your arrival. As for me, I am so pleasantly tied up with field projects that winter is now my time for travel, if at all.

The big post-Christmas blizzard did more than snow me in. It snowed me out. I stayed over in New York for a conference, attempted to leave N.Y., got no farther than the farthest reaches of the Bronx, where the car was snowed up for the day. I was most lucky tho. I was near a highway, under an elevated R.R.; shoveled out the next day; took twelve hours in driving back to Norfolk. I would much have preferred to be up here – snow-shoeing through the woods.

Both your letters made me feel both glad and sad. It is embarrassing to be taken too seriously in any way whatever. And yet two people without similar factual knowledge and without complete frankness cannot possibly hope to be mutually understood. Nor am I sure that it is desirable or necessary to be understood so. Like most of us, I think we both still retain the worship of false goals and idols. I am not sure that either of us can worship the "God" of the other – but I am having a helluva lot of fun in my present "worshipping".

I returned from Florida March 15; buckled down to writing, and made good progress. With no schedule for either eating sleeping or writing, never waiting until the thing was already well "written" in my mind, utilizing any of the 24 hours for that which was most urgent at the time, I did much before family visits began the end of May.

My annual fracas with the police has already occurred this spring, this involving most of a night spent in the woman's cell of a town jail. In this instance I am most deeply ashamed of myself, and am red-faced at the thought. Yet the story is too good to keep hidden from a few friends who can keep tight mouths. One morning in May I left Norfolk at 3 A.M. for a breakfast conference in N.Y. My headlights were defective and I was stopped 20 miles south of here. On request I gave him my operator's license. "No, that is your old 1946 license", he said. "Where is your new 48 license"? I looked. I could not remember renewing my 47 license. The officer was not impressed by the self-depreciating amusement. With car impounded,

I accepted the hospitality of a woman's cell for the rest of the night, reading a new book on electronics. The next morning (that morning) I was fined appropriately (and I had the money); took a new driver's test, received my license, and was on my way. It was a strong temptation not to tell the court how happy I was that the situation was not worse. After all, I was stopped for defective headlights at a similar hour in Boston the previous week, driving here with a friend, and the officer never noticed the 19<u>46</u> license. At least twice in Florida, officers checked my license when they caught me camping by the side of the road; and never noticed. On the way to Florida, a car delayed braking on an icy road, slid in to me. Had the matter been checked by police at the moment, they might have noticed. On the way back from Florida my 1948 plates had been sent here parcel post, and for the last two weeks of the trip I was driving, technically, without registration and without license. But the most amusing part of the whole affair I so wanted to tell the court, and could not. In the affair of July (when I went left of a center post in town, at 4 A.M., to avoid hitting an officer who had his back to me and was giving a ticket to another driver – as I wrote you), officers, clerk of the court, and judge, and who knows who else, all looked over my license, and failed to notice that it was 1946 and not 1947!

That building drama having been resolved by Küchler's deft side-stepping, Danny gently removed the laptop from atop his stomach and rose from the deckchair on which he had been sprawled for a good part of the day.

Too bad, he thought as he stretched his legs. Poor Aunt Jewel. Her one chance to escape her virginal spinsterhood. Gone. No wonder she devoted so much of herself to him. It must have been a lonely life without her one true love. Without any one love, but perhaps himself. And then...

A very lady-like card. No date. Either Dec 48 or 49.

Still Angry?
Yesterday in browsing thru the library shelves I came upon a book recommended some years ago by a good friend. I realized that it was too good to keep to myself – that you were the one person I should like to share it with –
A copy will arrive in a few days. Please give it a hearing.

How's the snow shoeing? We've had <u>one</u> day of snow this winter – when all the kids came shouting out of driveways into the street. Michigan – as you already know – is unpredictable.

The next had no date. Somehow, though, it seems to be properly in right sequence. Someone must have taken the effort to put it there. Küchler?

It was good to hear from you in September. You continue to astound me with the variety of your readings, and of your interests in people. Surely you belong in a large city, with all of its problems, solvable or not. So La Rue would prune civilization back to its roots. And do you consider that a doleful comment? I do consider that comment one of high optimism. Is the fault really with our civilization alone? Or is it with the basic nature of man? Were I capable of paring, I believe I would go farther than paring down to our Neanderthal ancestors, or even to our vertebrate forbears. I think I'd prefer to reorient the planet on a basis other than carbon chemistry. But if it is civilization that is to be pared, I am not sure we would lose much if our whole gadget civilization were swept away.

It seems wrong, almost, for me to be so happy here. Were this all to vanish, I think I would have enough memories to keep me contented the rest of my life. I refused to teach this fall. Something had to be pared off to give me more time here. Beech-Nut continues their grant for the herbicide work, and as before, I do exactly what I want. Chemical corporations supply me with all materials. My job: to produce semi-natural communities by floristic control alone, said floristic control being the killing out of certain plants by selective spraying. Beech-Nut thinks it has practical value for weed control in their peppermint field, and I do not object. The right of way people (power line corporations) are increasingly interested. Apparently various middlemen have taken the herbicides, and screamed their virtues in high pressure salesmanship – with vegetational results not expected. No one seems to have combined a bit of ecology with restricted spraying. In a weak moment at a dinner last summer I agreed to talk on the subject in New Haven in January. With no job to hold, no boss to please, no boss to tell me what to say, and not really caring whether the power companies insist on taking

Fern Lake

advantage of those money-saving ideas, I may enjoy the coming discussions. But, most satisfying, the communities have been showing up wholly new interpretations of old-field successions. Apparently I and the textbooks had been on much the wrong track.

I've found an illustrator for my ecology text, a zoologist-artist, well known, who at least has turned down similar illustrating offers on the presumption of collaborating with me. So this winter, I hole up here working on the book. For that reason, I have put up the car. Have in all my furnace oil. Plenty of food and symphony records for body and soul. Now the days are merry rounds of desk work thru a long morning, outdoors for a time in the afternoon, and evenings <u>read</u>ing all sorts of things. But botanical visitors find their way here, and make up for my present lack of traveling. Most fresh and pleasant in my mind is a 3-day visit from an Australian ecologist, making a few stops in this country between England and his home: I learned much of Australia.

Had I told you that Dr. Meier finally heraused from the Forestry College? After his retirement, his conversational ability, which he called "carrying on research", became a bit trying. He and the new dept. head finally had an agreement, to wit, HFA went home. But – the latest news, he has taken a fall-winter-spring salaried position inspecting trailer camps in New England and the Southwest. I am shocked. Such an existence (I despise trailer camps). And to so completely forsake his profession. But at least this way, he will continue to be a conversationalist. Yes, I do not forgive him for not living up to my expectations of him – and that is no fault of his.

Are you coming to New York this winter? If so, why not save a night's hotel bill and pass this way? You may have to snowshoe in the last mile, even up to the doorstep (for I wield no shovel except for a "stamping ground" on the small front porch), but to know this country in the dead of winter should not be uninteresting.

So much for any drama, he thought, but he went on to Jewel's next letter.

You have been much in my thoughts since your card came – as doubtless you intended else you would not have challenged so forcefully my basic assumption that life is not worth living – and human beings very worth serving.

You are still using poor Dr. Meier as your whipping boy. It has always seemed to me that a psychoanalyst would be very interested in your preoccupation with Dr. Meier and his affairs - I feel quite sure that you – your father – Dr. Meier and your inner necessity to avoid people and despise everyone are closely tied to a fancy subconscious knot. As a wild guess – as a <u>very</u> wild guess – your small boy's need to worship your father met with unhappiness somewhere in your growing up – you adored him – as little boys must – yet during later years your older mind found things to criticize in him – you felt guilty at your critical attitude. For a few months you worshipped Dr. M. with the same uncritical devotion you once had felt for your father – and the release of that feeling made you for the time quite happy – until he too turned out to be a mere human being. You can't stand a boss – or a critic. If you could recall <u>all</u> the tiny experiences that made up your relationship with your father – you would come to realize that many of your adult reactions to people were conditioned by your conflicting and contradictory feelings toward him. It is a relief to your feelings to castigate Dr. Meier. Lucky for him he's quite unconscious of it. When you grow a little tired of the tediousness of the routine part of your self appointed task you can give Dr. M. a good beating for deserting his profession – and return with renewed vigor to your task.

Forgive me — for sounding smart alecky. I don't want to, but I have to say that I have found the real reason for your not wanting children. It is not at all to do with overpopulation.

Good night, dear Fred, and may the new year bring you a new capacity for joy and peace. You have my love.

He really should, Dan thought, abandon this melodrama for more professionally worthy pursuits, but intellectual inertia, he found, was every bit as substantial as the Newtonian variety. Besides, he did not think there were that many letters left. He read on.

I am writing this on paper only because I thought you might need some fuel for the psychiatric flame. It is a real pleasure to start reading Liebman's book. The thoughts of a mature intellect are always a rich pleasure. It seems quite appropriate to have a volume with such a title on the table beside my favorite chair. Of the long string of guests who have passed through these doors – there has only been one – yourself – who has not had some sympatico expression. The "peace of mind" brain is so appropriate to this Forest of the Sun that it is sometimes difficult for me to realize that others are totally blind to a rural life.

You remind me very very much of my mother; and also of the Organic Gardening cult. My mother can trace every gastro-intestinal rumble and burp back to an extra egg, piece of chocolate, half glass of milk, or salted almond that was or was not eaten. The Organic Gardening chap (if you have not read their journal, you really must) can trace every extra caterpillar, every extra blossom or fruit, to the compost which they did apply or should have applied, and are implicitly content in their decision.

You have already switched from interpreting my whole life in terms of mother-complexes to interpretation in terms of father-complexes. It is really quite interesting to see how you pounce on every little phrase, and disregard other phrases, which fits into the particular jigsaw puzzle which you have fully "solved" in advance.

I find that in 1948 I left here on 35 separate trips, totaling 125 days, for purposes of field work, library work, consultations, lectures, seminars, and professional meetings, averaging one trip every ten days and totaling one third of the entire year. My! My! What a horrible record for a recluse who hates humanity because he is afraid to face it.

But I have said far more than I wanted to say.

May you have peace of mind.

Another card, but this one, strangely a negative. White writing on black background. How did they do these things in those days?

This is to remind you that it's time for your annual report.

I've been enjoying a book by one of your neighbors – Rutherford Platt –This (?) or Our Flowering World. He's managed to make a popular work out of paleobotany plus a vivid imagination and attractive style.

I've been teaching physiography until I'm almost ready for a good course in geology. Can you recommend one?

The card brought a full letter in return.

I know this comes at a time of the year which makes you think of "annual reports" and such tripe. But would you have preferred to wait until March for a letter? It has been 9 months since I received your last letter. Long time no see.

My spring time tutoring sessions cannot, I regret to say, be called a success. The fellow left me, as was originally planned, for several weeks in a New Rochelle school, with teachers of his mother's acquaintance. Then back to the Gilbert School, where he did miserably, and failed to take any advantage of opportunities I'd put in his way to discuss things with me – albeit we remain very good friends. This fall he went to a special school in Vermont. Some grades still very bad.

My next contact with this same Gilbert school was an absolute antithesis: one of their past Valedictorians, and a farmer-neighbor's son. This year a senior at Yale, I chose him last spring for recipient of a small Research Grant, to encourage his carrying on a field problem, up here. That he was a neighbor, was entirely independent of my choice. He had already been doing herbarium work at Yale, highly thought of, had originally planned to major in language, the kind of chap who studies Sanskrit and Persian as a hobby. He has developed magnificently, along many lines. Lichens his special interest. He responds in other ways: he once repeated to me a Yale professor's very adverse reactions to my comment to that professor that if that professor came to visit me on a Saturday afternoon during the opera season, I would be glad to have him listen to the broadcast with me, or he could wander around the forest by himself. Mason Hale (the student) and opera were then completely unacquainted. So one evening here I purposely mentioned the matter, suggested jokingly I play one side of one record of Die Walkure, of which I have the complete recording. I slung a libretto at him and watched his reactions. He left four hours later; listened to it from beginning to end, with his eyes glued on the libretto. I never again hope to get such a reaction – like a starved animal suddenly finding and devouring food, without having known it was hungry to begin with.

It is my herbicide work that has the biggest possibilities. I sometimes regret that I have not a business "sense", and willing to exploit the field. There is good opportunity for someone there. The amount of <u>re</u>invasion that I get, once I have killed out the unwanted shrubs and trees is so small as to defy all my old ideas on old field succession. Power and phone corporations are beginning to see some value in the work, and the first half of this season began to pepper me with visits and requests-to-visit. I got provoked with all that; stopped it most effectively by putting a high price on my time.

Just recently, I reached a long-term agreement to handle the brush-control on a 50-acre transmitter side near Boston, of a radio station owned by a big newspaper. It is being handled as a research project, in cooperation with agencies and corporations interested. Sounds like an ideal arrangement – am sole professional boss, with none of the headaches of the actual work, of the publicity, stenography, or visitors. Since I insisted that my own work here never be mentioned any closer than "northwestern Connecticut" I am reasonably sure that my privacy and this work will not conflict. Already, the opening blast has appeared in the newspaper; I cringe at this horn-tooting. It befits me ill, but I guess I can take it.

Wait! Isn't Mason Hale someone who wrote a stack of letters to Küchler, filed away by Küchler alongside clippings from the *Evening Citizen*, Winsted's local newspaper, concerning his accomplishments at Yale and Wisconsin? Dan had gone through those letters with much more discernment than he had those of Mason's twin brother, Dick. Mason obtained his PhD essentially under John T. Curtis at Wisconsin. Dick had merely followed Küchler to Syracuse Forestry, then the pesticide business. Curtis, when Mason was there, was building an empire of graduate students, all using his principal components method. Along with Whittaker, they had shattered any remnants of the idea that plant communities actually existed in any sense in nature. In doing so, they resurrected the long ignored, but unvanquished idea of Henry A. Gleason, that plants distributed themselves mainly through random factors that are independent of the identity of the other plants surrounding them. That is what had drawn Dan to the letters.

That Mason's research, encouraged by Küchler, contradicted Curtis's new dogma, at least for lichen communities, had Dan once more considering a book topic—unsuccessfully, of course.

Now Mason holds Dan's attention as one of a string of young men that Küchler befriended, helped professionally and sometimes financially, even to the point of offering living accommodations to one in the chicken coop Küchler had converted into his office at Arden Forest. That put Küchler's relationship to Jewel in a totally new light for Dan. It put an entirely new slant on Küchler's life even. Jewel could have been both right and wrong in her last letter, he thought. It might not have been only pessimism of the human condition that kept Küchler from starting a family. And it might not have been only to escape society that he had become a recluse.

But then, what about those cards and letters from all those women? And what about the braggadocio in letters to male friends over the bevy of women who chased him to his lair in Arden Forest?

What about Jewel's love for him?

Now he had to read on.

Whether conscience or coccus – something has me by the throat. I suspect it's the latter. This unexpected day off is a boon, especially with a doting mamma handy to carry trays. I'm a third of the way through Wm Vogt's 'Road to Survival' already – While none of the general ideas are new - it's a meaty sort of book – Enough biology to read it intelligently should be required of all statesmen, preachers, poets – and such formers of public opinion.

You must be busy answering letters these days – after the beautiful buildup your Boston Herald friend gave you. "Again Science Points the Way" – the plaid jacket being a nice variation on the usual white lab coat costume. Joking aside – it's a good picture. But, my dear Fred, if you insist upon building and advertising such fine money-saving mousetraps however can you expect to continue to "dwell among the untrodden ways"?

Time to reply to the insistent scolding of the cardinal about an empty feeder on a blizzardy day. They're both stuffing themselves on sunflower seeds now.

I'm taking advantage of your kind offer of reprints. – Thanks for including it. I know I should not be so lazy as to ask you – but please recommend a good not too technical reference giving an *explanation of just <u>how</u> the herbicides kill. I wasn't even aware of the 2-4,5 -T mentioned. I used a crab grass spray in the fall – next August will tell with what success.*

I got an invitation to counsel at another Jr. High Congregational Camp – in the U. P. this time. It should be geologically interesting, - but I don't want to accept until I know if it conflicts with Dunkirk, N.Y. The latter is more attractive because it brings me within reach of several friends in the East including Hoiman the Hoimet.

Getting travel and lodging expenses paid in exchange for 5 or 6 days of leading kids on hikes probably sounds like a questionable sort of vacation to you – but I'm too poor this year to look any gift horse in the mouth. It all comes of spending my substance in comfortable living. The Hudson was getting too balky in cold weather and needed to be overhauled. What with house painting last summer, some new storm windows – carpeting for 2 rooms – new washer, etc – you know how houses eat money. However if there's another war you can't <u>count</u> on being atomized at once, especially if the bomb shelter works as advertised, and until then, it's dashed inconvenient without one's gadgets. And nephew Danny always seems in need of new shoes.

The wind is howling like mad – They tell us we've had double the usual snowfall this year – all since Christmas. You must teach me to appreciate opera some time. My attention span seems only good for short exquisite bits – a Bach chorale – Liszt – shorter Tchaikovsky numbers.

I shall look for the promised letter.

Did she never suspect? Dan wondered.

In the first place, I am grieved to hear that this flu of yours is keeping you so close to your bed. 15 days! Sounds horrible. I am really extremely sorry, and so hope you get the upper hand any minute now, and slap it down.

I still do not have my car out. Gravel roads are a mire of mud right now, delightfully springy to walk upon, and the equal of quicksand to any car. Besides, I took my car out in January once, hit a bump and a stretch of glare ice on the road here on the property. Then a tree came up, whammed my bumper and fender and headlight into unrecognizable creases. I got the car into the garage, but it will take a mechanic to put it into shape even to drive for repairs into town. I had a friend bring in my mail this afternoon, which included your airmail-special delivery. I am shocked and abashed at the time it took for me to get it. I note you wrote it on April first; mailed it on the second. It arrived in Hartford on the third; in Norfolk village on the fourth. I received it today. Unfortunately, neither air nor special delivery has a terminus at Arden Forest, and this unbusiness-like individual is likely to call for mail but once a week. I sent you a night letter earlier this evening.

I am greatly appreciative, Jewel, of your good invitation to spend Easter and the weekend with you, and all that it implies. Be assured that I would enjoy it so very much. But I look at my calendar and sob out "But hoooowwww can I?" My work has gained me publicity and busy-ness, and great satisfaction (and less income by far than my first year at Syracuse). Some 50 first-class pieces of mail this afternoon, and several pounds of second-class mail. April first an herbicide visitor here. April 2, checking on herbicide work in New Milford. April 3-4 in New York for library work. April 6, 7, 8 a Yale student here (he lives 4 miles away), the one who worked up the lichens of this area last summer. Easter Day I am refusing all invitations, to stick right here at my desk and clean up correspondence. Richard (Audubon Bird Guide) Pough comes here April 15 (Amer Mus Nat Hist is interested in my soon-established Arden Forest Research Foundation); April 16 in NY for Mother's birthday party; probably 17 and 18 with Gleason for discussions at his house at Cos Cob. He and I share a kinship as the two least cited ecologists in America. A trip this month to Boston for my WHDH work. A trip to Hadlyme (Conn.) concerning a misused State Park there. I sign an agreement tonight with New England's biggest power corporation for the starting of a mile-long brush control demonstration to begin this month, wherein I train the sprayer-foreman. April 21 in Albany for three different conferences on three different subjects. Plus my herbicide work, and writing, and housekeeping here. ... I should say, also, that I am running a phenology project here (now in its third year) on over 100 plants and other phenomena, which makes it absolutely impossible for me to be away from here during the growing season for, at the very very most, three days at one time. In midsummer and fall, I've stretched it out to four days, but not more.

Glad you've been at Vogt's Road to Survival. I'm sorry that public notice of it is slacking. Did you see TIME's reaction to it? Abominable. But I have not too much hope. There are not enough Vogt's and not enough intelligence to understand it. Have you read the lead article of a recent article in the Sat Rev Lit on the Art of Persuasion? The first page of this article expresses perfectly why persuasion in any form may not work.

Yes, it is anachronous of me to try to publicize this R/W work when I do not wish to get into the business of it. Yet it does not seem right to keep to myself something that would so greatly speed up efficiency. Now I would not mind if, having candy, I would give it to children who would grab it at once, and eat it down. Instead I find myself in long and difficult problems of adult education. The industrialists are almost (but not quite) as hard to convince as the oldtime ecologists.

<u>How</u> the herbicides kill? I have no idea. I know no literature on the subject, aside from scattered references, mostly wandering speculations, based on the hormone nature of similar compounds used in much more dilute concentrations. They <u>do</u> kill. For an herbicide, need anything more be known?

And let me know when this Dunkirk position of yours materializes. For I would like to see you here for a time. (But do let me know in sufficient advance to counterbalance any wayward visits to the PO, and my visits away from here. I assume, as last year, my parents may be here the last half of each month, problem-producing in that I cannot leave here then, and in that their doctors tell me no overnight visitors or other than "picnic-meal visitors". A real handicap and a senseless one at that. But the way they live, and the things they get upset about, are such that I am a guest in my own house at such times, and a guest who submits completely to their way of life.)

As for opera – try following a full broadcast some time with libretto in hand – but follow it in the foreign language – NEVER in an English translation. Operatic English by tradition is a stilted abomination, with thees and thous and divines etc. that are ridiculous in this day or any age. And pick your opera well. Some are slapstick horseplay comedy, some the equal of Shakespeare's heaviest tragedies.

My thanks for the comment on the R/W bulletin. Strange: so many have liked its style. It is in this manner that I wrote the ms. for my textbook, and planned to illustrate it. But that format has gone cold with every professor to whom I've talked. A Wiley editor saw that bulletin in advance; I wrote him about it; then I talked a whole afternoon with him. He did not get the idea. What good does it do to please the student and the layman. One must work via publishers' editors and their botanical reviewers – and to a man they have downed their thumbs.

And for the two reviews: I fear that I fly under false colors there. I accept writing a review only when I wish that the public see its good points, or its bad points. I liked Degener's book. I liked Gilliam's approach, but in order to spotlight it, I cruelly showed the weakness of Küchler (a good friend of a good friend of mine who has been trying to get us to meet) and at the same time struck at one of the weaknesses of American ecology. But lest you think I've grown honeyed on this forest, I'm enclosing another book review. And my review of Donald Culross Peattie's new book is in the current Natural History Magazine. I have on hand a 35-page "Commentary on American Plant Ecology, based on the Textbooks of 1947-1949" which may show Fred Küchler in a new light. I am not interested here in the art of persuasion. It will be the younger minds who may take this medicine. If enough do, I stay in academic ecology. If they do not, I work on other things for the next 20 years.

Midnight now. I really regret that I cannot take advantage of your good invitation to spend Easter in Detroit.

Suddenly, Dan was not at all certain when he would examine the small number of scans remaining. It had nothing to do with the content he was reading. As their dates approached uncomfortably close to 1950 and something that he knew had had nothing to do with Küchler, a queasy feeling surprised his stomach and brought a sour taste to his mouth. A half century later, he still was cautious about opening those old childhood wounds.

Too late anyway. Time for dinner. Merle had concocted some simple croque-monsieur-type meal to be eaten out on the deck. The letters were not accessed again that evening.

Philadelphia

I

HE was late already, he was certain. And he was in charge of the event, technically at least. He had the duty of introducing Ed Muskie, the probable next President. No way Nixon could repeat, in his thinking, even with his administration's recent discovery of the environment. The phones in the Fine Arts faculty lounge, the committee's de facto headquarters, however, were still ringing off their hooks with people who wanted to participate, even if only by the equivalent of buying an ad. That had held him up, that and Bernard Birnbaum of CBS News calling him again that morning in search of a story. Phone calls kept building day by day all week to a crescendo on this, the last day, but Ed Furia made it clear that no donations would be turned down, so they hung up on the others, but those with money got full attention. After all, there would still be unpaid expenses after everything was over. Ian McHarg might be able to reach into his own pockets, but the rest of them had nothing but lint and marijuana crumbs in theirs.

Was it really my idea to have an Earth Week, he wondered, instead of Earth Day? That it was, he was afraid. Just had to put his two cents in. Now he was paying for it.

Thinking no one would come, they had invited all sorts of speakers, dozens of them. Everyone on the Committee thought the week would be spent mostly in building exhibits, handing out leaflets while wearing gas masks, or passing out clean water and surgical masks, those kind of things. Just start a dialog about ecology was the goal. Friends of the Earth promised to have an environmental handbook ready for teach-ins on Earth Day. The Sierra Club promised something similar they called "Ecotactics." Even if neither came through, there was still lots of literature for use to attract people for teach-ins, so they threw names of speakers around like items on a birthday wish list, asking for a lot while expecting very little. Many more invitations were sent out than they had venues to accommodate.

Dozens surprised them by accepting. Ralph Nader gave a speech in the light drizzle at Independence Hall the night before. The entire cast of Hair came from New York to sing "Age of

Aquarious" and "Sulfur Dioxide" after his speech. Who would have thought? Or was it after Alan Watts' speech? Nobel Prize winner George Wald flew in to proclaim surprise at the "devastated area" he saw from the air around the city, Filthydelphia. It was the industrial region of refineries and chemical plants that had caught his attention. It was the same story of pollution around other cities, he told them. Hugh Scott, the senator, and Rene Dubos and Helmet Landsberg and Kenneth Boulding of "Spaceship Earth" fame and John McHale and Paul Ehrlich and Ralph Lapp and Dieter John and Luna Leopold and Lewis Mumford and Ruth Patrick and Frank Herbert all gave talks. Allen Ginsberg read a silly poem. "Merrily, merrily, we welcome, we welcome the end of the earth." Had that been yesterday? Kenneth Watt, who was either an entomologist or a computer scientist—it was not clear which, but he was introduced as an ecologist—had to be sent off to Swarthmore with Simkin earlier in the week in order to fit him into an event needing a speaker.

"The world has been chilling sharply for about twenty years," Phil reported Watt saying. "With present trends, the world will be about four degrees colder in 1990, but eleven degrees colder in 2000. It's about twice, according to Watt, what it would take to put us into an ice age."

And the Sierra Club's David Brower, Dan wondered as he looked out a bus window, wishing it would hurry along, where did Brower end up talking? Was he another of those who were sent elsewhere? What were his words? Something about less real estate and more wilderness?

Oh yeah! We're not borrowing from our children, Brower had said, we're stealing from them. And it's not even considered a crime.

The 32 bus, which he had had to catch from the Market Street subway, finished poking its way through the side streets near the museum where, Dan heard, there had been an impromptu kazoo concert of Woody Guthrie's "This Land is Your Land," which he did not regret missing.

Hell, he cursed himself, it couldn't have taken any more time just to walk over and pick up the bus here. Or, maybe even to have walked all the way from campus to Fairmont Park.

Crowds spilling out of the park and over into the street slowed traffic even more, but to Dan, that was a good sign. And thank God for the sunshine. This day, this event, was the culmination of the whole week. He pulled the chord to signal his stop. The driver looked back at him in his mirror and opened the door in the middle of the street, certainly a violation of some SEPTA code. Dan gratefully dashed out and into the crowd gathered on the large, grassy lawn.

He was too late, though. The keynote speaker was already on the platform and—

"God damn it! It's old One Horn. What the hell is he doing up there?" Dan asked aloud.

"Ira Einhorn?" came a voice from seemingly above. "I think he's the master of ceremonies."

Dan turned to see a very tall, very skinny young man. A cute blonde half his size hung off his hip. Both looked familiar, the blonde particularly so.

"He's just doing his usual rant," Dan said. "Do you know him?"

The young man shook his head. "Only that he teaches a course in the Open University. Ira Einhorn 101. I think he does it naked."

Both the young man and his companion seemed not just familiar, but somehow out of place, he with his neatly trimmed mustache and hair and she her page-boy cut. Where could he have seen them before? There was a hint, though, of a Zapata-like dip at the ends of his mustache, Dan noted, although the button-down shirt and white chinos he wore were just as home on the Penn campus as here, but then so was the work shirt and faded blue jeans, the uniform of a social revolutionary, that Dan wore, or his own unruly brown locks that spilled onto his shoulders. What world was the couple in? Preppie, more Fifties than Sixties? Like the vets that were coming back from Viet Nam having missed the Sixties? Then the clean cut young man accepted a lit joint being passed over his shoulder, took a toke, and passed it to the blonde, who passed it on to Dan.

"Were you two Clean for Gene?" Dan asked before taking a toke and holding it in.

"What?" the young man exhaled. "Well, actually, yes, we were. We did some campaigning for McCarthy."

"Hah!" Dan said on breathing out. "I think I drove you to your polling place. You still look clean. Jim Tayoun had a fistfight with his opponent, I remember."

"Yeah," the young man said as recognition came to him. "You did, but no, that was my roommate Jimmy Hartung in South Philly. And he was hardly Clean for Gene. He was a poll watcher for the Republicans. You drove us out toward the end of Baltimore Avenue."

"Hmm," Dan thought aloud, intending that to serve as a vow of silence, but he suddenly had to burst out with, "Why the hell don't they get him off that podium? He's had nothing to do with this event. We had to bodily remove him from some of our meetings, he was so disruptive. I think he was supposed to be helping with the microphones or something today, instead of giving a speech."

He could make out Simkin and Furia at the front near the speaker's platform. Both looked bemused, if not bewildered.

"Maybe," Dan said, totally forsaking his vow, "they're just waiting for him to complete his act and then go on to the serious business of Muskie's speech."

"He's been up there ranting for what must be a half hour," the young man said as Einhorn finally did wear down to relinquish the microphone. Ed Muskie stepped up to it as if the introduction never happened.

"We have more kinds of things than we really want," Musky admonished the audience. "We have more kinds of things than we really can live with."

Then, after boring them with numbers from the federal budget, he began exhorting everyone to do something to fight pollution and to protect the environment.

"We can use the power of the people to turn the nation around," he said to cheers. "The power of the ballot box, the cash register, the courts and peaceful assembly, where we can demand redress of grievances as we are doing here today and across the land."

That's my man, Dan thought gleefully. That's the next President!

When Ian McHarg took the podium, people expected an equally uplifting message with which to close the proceedings, but it was his shouted chant of "You have no future. You have no future.

Philadelphia

You have no future. Why am I to tell you the bad news?" that rang in their ears as they left.

"I guess I should help clean up," Dan thought aloud, wondering if someone had thought to send garbage bags out for that purpose. Then another joint came his way. He fell into step with the young couple as they joined the general flow out. "Which way you walking?"

"Penn," the young man answered.

A good four-mile hike, it would take well over an hour at the pace at which they set off. Dan did not care. His time was now his own once again.

"So am I," he said. "From Penn, I mean. How are you getting across the Surekill? Down by the Museum? I'm Dan Atkins, by the way."

He extended a hand.

"And across to 30th Street Station. Is there any other way?" the young man said, accepting the handshake. "Bill," he added. "She's Jamie."

"Undergrads?" Dan guessed.

"Phew," Bill let out a breath. "Just barely."

"Draft?"

"Yep. I seem to have won the lottery big time."

"What's your number?"

"Forty-two."

"Oh yeah. They'll be calling you up."

"I thought I'd be going to medical school, but now I'm stuck. I didn't get in. So what are you? Landscape Architecture? Regional Planning?"

"Neither. I'm a physics major. A junior."

"Junior? Viet Nam?"

"Nope. Just old, but I'm also a draft counselor. You should come and see me. I can work something out for you. Cassius Clay—I mean, Muhammad Ali—is showing us the way, I think."

"Say, it's been some party."

"Doesn't the Girard Street Bridge have a pedestrian sidewalk?" Dan asked.

"Let's find out," Jamie finally spoke up.

"Huh? What party?" Dan turned to Bill.

"Earth Day!" Jamie shouted the answer.

"Yeah," Dan answered thoughtfully. "A whole week of great parties."

And soon enough, people were assembling at a little row house, one of only four in the row at the foot of the South Street Bridge. They were friends of the students Dan shared the house with, whose numbers and identities seemed to change monthly. Bill, who he learned was Bill Dritschilo, and Jamie, who was to become Jamie Dritschilo in few weeks, were the only party-goers he could claim as his own guests. Jamie positively made Dan love sick by the casual way she demonstrated affection to Bill. More and more over the alternately raucous and quietly mellow evening he wondered why Ingrid did not show up that night as she had promised.

II

HE awoke on the couch in the downstairs room. He knew it was Thursday and that he had a morning class, but he failed to stir. Instead, he daydreamed. He imagined himself combing his hair into a duckbill in a bus station mirror in Brattleboro. It had been just before boarding a bus that he thought would take him in search of the heart of Rock 'n Roll. John Kennedy had not yet been shot. All things seemed possible. He had climbed off the bus at the Port Authority Terminal in downtown Gotham and found only some jazz clubs and the sleaze of the peep shows and dance halls that dominated Times Square. And grime. He blew his nose and his handkerchief was black with soot. He carried only a guitar and a battered school briefcase. The briefcase held underwear and warm socks, extra shirts, three fat salami-and-cheese sandwiches, and two twenty-dollar bills, but no handkerchiefs. He had seven dollars and thirteen cents in his pocket—and a dirty handkerchief. A Times Square creep latched onto him right away. The center of Rock and Roll was eighty blocks to the north, in Harlem, he told Dan. That was, unless he wanted to get back on a bus and go to Memphis. He knew that, Dan said to him, trying to fend the older man off. A deft maneuver through a turnstile got him on the "A" Train and took him to Harlem, where a stunning blonde coming out of the Apollo with a tall white boy rescued him from the clutches of the same dirty old white man. After managing to follow him somehow, he had been insisting that Dan come with him. Ingrid's offer was a better proposition in every way.

Over an egg cream at a Greenwich Village diner, he told her he was an orphan, and he realized that he meant it. Tears came to his eyes. She said her friend, Eric, who had continued on his separate way, had insisted that she step in to his rescue. Dan had reminded him of someone.

She was nineteen, barely out of childhood and on her own herself. She was a knockout, the prettiest thing he had seen since his nurse in the polio ward. She had a third-floor apartment on MacDougal Street. Going up the stairs, dawdling needlessly to let him keep up, she explained that Eric, who was also from Vermont, might be there, perhaps with friends. Ingrid had opened something like a homeless shelter for young runaways in the apartment which she had briefly shared with a fellow student at Pratt Institute. The runaways had driven the roommate to lodgings elsewhere. Dan was replacing the latest runaway, who had moved on. Eric still crashed at Ingrid's place on occasion, though, sleeping in the bunk bed above her. Dan, as the shorter of the two, she explained, would have to take the lumpy couch in the other room.

Had they spotted each other walking past the Brook's House in Brattleboro, it would have meant instant recognition, but it was halfway through breakfast that he and Eric realized that they already knew each other. Eric was the tall handsome boy who had disappeared from Brattleboro even before Dan could learn his name, which he found out was Weissman, a name he remembered on a sign over a haberdashery in Brattleboro.

"You were the guy who never wanted to play that game we made up for rating women," Eric had said on recognition.

"Brazil," Dan asked, with the accent on the second syllable.

"Yeah. It made me wonder about you," Eric said.

"What?" came from Ingrid.

"Just something silly," Dan answered, face reddening.

A ringing phone, the only one in the house, brought him out of his reverie. Tired of answering phones, he first made no effort, but it kept ringing. No one was answering it and it kept ringing. Finally, afraid whoever it was might never give up, he got up and tried to step over whoever it was who was groaning on the floor beneath him.

Oops! Make that two people, he thought on stepping on a second person, a feminine one.

"Sorry!" he shouted back in haste for the phone.

"Sorry? For what?"

It was Dritschilo on the phone. He and Dan had forgotten to nail down a time to meet about draft strategy. They made an appointment for that afternoon at the South Street anti-war office. All the while Dan tried to picture Bill in his mind. When he hung up, the picture was that of Eric Weissman with Ingrid at his hip.

Eric had introduced him to a whole new musical center right outside Ingrid's apartment. Around the corner, at the Village Gaslight, kids like him, white kids, except in Mort Sahl sweaters instead of a cowboy shirt, were stepping up on a stage with a guitar and singing songs that they had learned in kindergarten. And they were picking up handfuls of change from the baskets that were passed like church collection plates during performances. They garnered more change in less time than a hat left on the ground in Washington Square, where Pete and Toshi Seeger had set up a public folk music forum with the city police. Only Rambling Jack Elliot and youngsters such as Dave Van Ronk and Mary Travers still drew crowds to the dry fountain in the center of the square—and away from the Beats who were spouting poetry in the clubs of the Village.

Eric was walking testimony that anyone could climb up on a stage with a guitar and sing at one of the basket clubs. He knew the chords to only three songs. Still, he got to sing at the Gaslight. Audiences in that basement club thought he was stuck up when, after going through his entire three-song repertoire, he refused their eager calls for an encore. He was afraid to tell them that he had played every song he knew for them, even after the baskets started returning empty. He never did learn any more chords and, failing in his musical dreams, had disappeared, probably back to his parents' home in Brattleboro, but not before teaching Dan those three chord progressions.

His third floor room, with its view of piles of rubble along the Schuykill, was empty, but not unruffled. Someone had at least tried to make his bed, for which he was grateful, even as he stripped it to take the sheets to the laundromat. A lacy black bra fell out. It could not have been Ingrid's.

What was it that Ingrid had seen in him that others had not, as she had first with Eric, and then with a scruffy college boy the three found singing Woodie Guthrie songs at a hootenanny night at the Café Wha?

Now that was a story he rarely told anyone for fear of not being believed. Dylan had also been in need of a place to sleep. He had told them that he had just that day come into the city from Gallup, New Mexico, and been given a chance to perform at the Wha? He wound up on the lumpy couch, while Dan was briefly promoted to the bunk bed. It's thin mattress lay on a hard wooden slab instead of springs, a Scandinavian design, Ingrid told him. It made it even more difficult for him to sleep, given the distracting presence of the blonde beauty below.

Everything about her—what she did with her hair, how she put on make-up, and the clothes she wore—had held a magnetic attraction for him. It still did. He thought that it had to be love, but he had not a clue how to act on it then, other than to rummage through her drawers in secret and try on her bras and panties. He wished he could do so again. He had asked her to leave her underwear her previous visit to Philadelphia. He wanted to enjoy the arousal of feeling himself that close to her, he told her, but she had laughed and refused with, "I'm not getting on the train to New York without underwear just so you can get a hard on in it!"

Dylan, who looked like Harpo Marx then with his hair dyed darker, was hardly a rival, Dan now thought, but that corduroy cap he wore, and the way he left the front button undone, that was cool, that drew attention. They didn't learn his real name until much later, when someone saw Robert Alan Zimmerman on his draft card, or that he had invented the absurd tales of what his life had been like as a circus worker, vagabond, freight train rider, prisoner, and all the other folky experiences, short of being a Negro. And that ridiculous harmonica! Dan was almost too embarrassed by it to introduce Bob to John Mitchell at the Village Gate. To Dan, a harmonica was just a miniature accordion. He feared it might have started playing a polka and gotten Dylan laughed off the stage, and Dan along with him. Still, the musicians Dylan played with liked having it in the background. That was why he soon was getting asked to sit in on more sets than Dan was.

That was about when Dan began to think that the baskets that the kitty girls passed at the end of his sets garnered more contributions because of his limp than his playing, although he had to admit now that he tended at times to exaggerate it. He had confessed it then to Dylan. In return, Dylan had shared in confidence with him that he had taken years of piano lessons.

He really was a musician. Quicker than he thought was possible, Dylan was fronting for John Lee Hooker at Gerdes.

Dan suddenly felt strange. Like the character in Kurt Vonnegut's novel, he felt unhinged in time and space. Could it be some sort of acid flashback? What had he taken last night?

A jazz piece was being played by WXPN on Dan's stereo, a system that Francis had put together for Dan at his fix-it shop in the Village. Dan would not trade it for the highest end Kenwood-Garrard-Acoustic Research combination that might be put together now. The tune was fast but catchy, jazz before Ornette Coleman and others started pushing the envelope and pushing Dan toward the Doors and Frank Zappa. He couldn't place the tune or its performers, although Coltrane with Miles Davis came to mind, probably a famous recording. It reminded him of how Dylan described Jack Kerouac's writing. "Breathless, dynamic, bop phrases," he had called writing that Dan would describe now as "disjointed." He didn't know that term then.

They had been in some bar, he remembered, all of them together, Dylan, Ingrid, Eric, Suze, and himself, when Dylan had said that. Possibly the same tune was being played. Eric, Dan remembered, was explaining why he had to grow his curly hair longer than Dylan's before he could go home. The bar had been the Kerouac connection, Dan now remembered. They were finishing the evening at the White Horse Tavern, a frequent haunt of the Beats in On the Road and still a place where Alan Ginsberg might show up. Dylan had by then had his breakthrough performance, the one that was written up in the New York Times, the one that had landed him a signed contract with Columbia. Suze Rotolo, Dan remembered, was at his side. Dan had met Suze only days before at a make-shift basement theater where Brendan Behan was putting on his play, The Hostage, One Sheridan Square, it was. Suze's mother had an apartment on the eighth floor. Suze worked on the sets, while Dan tried to make some money with a concession stand in the foyer.

Dylan couldn't seem to take his eyes off her, so he must have just introduced them. Yes, Dan thought, that was when he and Dylan had become friends, when Dylan had switched his attention from Ingrid to Suze, and Ingrid had begun taking a new interest in Dan. They were all drinking Irish whiskey with Tommy Makem that night. He, too, had just signed a contract with Columbia, with the Clancy Brothers. And his buddy, Frank McCourt, with his gummy eye and bad teeth, was with him. "We usually drink at McSorley's," McCourt had said to him in his soft Irish brogue, by way of introduction. He was teaching English at a vocational high school on Staten Island. Before he left, he had Danny, as Ingrid still called him, promise to finish high school and then go on to an engineering school. "That's where the good jobs are," he said. Later, Ingrid had followed up his advice by getting him to pull a few very tenuous strings to get Dan into the New School for Social Research. And she stopped calling him Danny.

Had Ingrid made eyes at McCourt that night in the White Horse Tavern?

Peter Yarrow and Jack Elliot, who people had taken to calling, "the son of Woodie Guthrie," just as they would soon start calling Dylan, "the son of Jack," which Dylan hated, were camped out on the floor of Ingrid's apartment when they got back to it. So the four of them left to let the sleepers sleep. After watching the roosters crow in the window of the Italian grocery at Bleecker and Thomson that dawn, they went into the Five Spot Café, possibly for no other reason than that its door had been opened to air out the evening's cigarette smoke. Thelonious Monk was sitting all alone at the piano. Dylan left Suze's side for the first time that night to go up to him to tell him that he liked jazz, but he was a folk singer. Monk said to him, "We all play folk music."

If Ingrid was not coming to Philadelphia, he came back to the present, he would just have to go to New York. He knew he should call her right then, but he was afraid that she might not be in or—worse—some man would answer her phone.

III

BILL did get draft counseling from Dan and, with the help of Clay v. United States, it did work out for him. They became fast friends over it. Each gravitated to the outdoor tables at Houston Hall for lunch or late afternoon coffee on warm, sunny days. They fit in smoothly with a variety of mostly graduate students and postdocs who adopted the location for their social headquarters. They were mostly chemists and biochemists, mostly foreign, from Iran, Pakistan, and India, Sikhs Hindus and Muslims, many of them married and lonely for families they left behind.

"Can you believe the way God made each woman so beautiful?" Liberatus DeRosa, born and bred in South Philly, espoused over the coffee and donut that constituted his lunch as he eyed the girls who passed by. Libby, as he preferred being called, was once a fellow grad student with some of the others. Now he was a suitably clean-cut medical student. "And each in her own special way? Just look at them! No painter, not the greatest genius ever, not Rembrandt, could ever create the beauty that God has with every woman."

"You are in such rapture because you are getting married next week?" Jimmie, an Iranian who insisted he was Persian, asked in his perfectly accented English, his sentence perfectly inflected to make it a question. Invariably, he was the one who showed up early to claim their favorite table and was often the last to leave. He had time on his hands. His thesis had already been written and approved. All the award of a PhD required of him was the filing of a form, which he was ready to do the moment a suitable position in astrophysics turned up. Meanwhile, he was content "sans doctorate" with comparing the various attributes of the passing parade with Libby and, according to rumor, collecting a comfortable stipend.

"It's just because I AM getting married," Libby countered. "Unlike you, I can appreciate one enough to marry her."

"So, what are your plans?" Dan ignored the other two to ask Bill. Like Jimmie's, their lives were approaching milestones requiring decisions. Bill was finishing his stint of alternate service. Dan was running out of degree requirements to fulfill. "Can you stay on at the Med School?"

"I don't know," Bill answered, his fingers in his hair, which Dan teased became longer on his becoming a conscientious objector. His mustache ends turned down more, too, a clear sign to Dan of Bill's radicalization.

"I'm sure they'd happily keep you on as long as you want," Libby broke into their conversation to suggest. "Good lab techs like you can be really valuable to a research group."

"Oh! So now that you're no longer in our lab, you can finally admit that!"

"Hey! I invited you to my wedding! Doesn't that count as approval?"

"I thought you just needed another wedding present," Bill laughed.

"What?" Libby erupted in mock anger. He jumped to his feet, trying his best to tower over the much taller-but-seated lab tech and wedding guest. "So you don't want to be a lab tech any more, do you?"

"No, not without a PhD," Bill answered in mock anguish. "I'm fed up with being the equipment wrangler. ESR, NMR, mass spec, centrifuge. I feel like their slave. Some days I wish I could just refuse to turn them on, to just spend a day using my mind instead. But not having a PhD, what my mind comes up with gets no respect from academics."

"A PhD in biochemistry?" Jimmie turned to Bill to ask. As always, he was immaculately groomed and in an expensive Italian suit, ready at all times, it seemed, for an interview. "Here?"

"No," Bill answered him in an uncertain voice. Then he turned back to Dan. "You know, that day in Fairmont Park had a real influence on me. So did marrying Jamie. Obviously, so did marrying her."

Libby nudged Jimmie's shoulder with a closed fist. "See?"

"Maybe I can do something good for society," Bill continued. "Maybe I can meld ecology with Earth Day. I keep picking up that paperback copy of Sand County Almanac you gave me that day."

"It must be because it is always on the floor," Mohammed, a Pakistani post-doc in Bill's lab, began with a smile, "that you have to keep picking it up. You should tell your wife to keep a neater apartment."

"I gave you that?" Dan asked. "I don't remember that."

"Never mind. It's just that I don't want to spend my life in laboratories, measuring unseen things with instruments whose workings I don't really understand—or want to. I want to get my hands on something real. I don't know, I just feel out of place in the slide-rule culture of engineering."

"Tell me about it," said Dan, pulling aside a loose strand of hair. His long locks now spilled over his shoulders and down to his back. He was proud to have the longest hair in the group, although what was under the Sikh's turban was a matter for serious speculation. Dan was beardless, unlike all but the Sikh, but he had a full mustache that he thought maintained a folksy image. "I'm in classrooms with younger kids. They think they're so cool. They're hippies, they claim. Hell I still think of myself as Beat."

"But, after all, in medical biochemistry you can help make life better for people," Libby suggested to Bill.

"That's true," Dan agreed before Bill could answer, "but look what I have to look forward to. Either nuclear power plants or weapons work. Not exactly in the feeling of that Earth Day is it?"

"That was some party, wasn't it?" Bill said.

"It taught you about Aldo Leopold, at least," Dan answered. "And that was some grass."

"So, I'm thinking about ecology. If I can get in some place good. Only if I can get into some place good."

"PhD in ecology?" Jimmy asked, his face contorted skeptically. "That's no more employable than astrophysics is these days. You had better find a top program. Very top."

Then he lit a Turkish cigarette. Bill lit up a Newport.

"Didn't you get an A in the ecology course we took from Ricklefs?" Dan took advantage of the pause to ask.

"Yeah, and in his seminar. He was the reason I was at Fairmont Park that day, you know. I thought he was going to give a talk."

"And that evolution course you just took?"

"Moss, Meers, and Gill? B, but you gotta hear how. I got an A the first test. The second was a take-home. We were on our honor not to look at the test before starting it and to take it all at once and not to take more than an hour on it. So, I studied until I felt comfortable with the material, then I set my alarm clock and went to work. An hour was plenty of time. I got done early. I thought I did pretty well. So I get it back and it's a D. And all around me I hear people with much better grades saying how they couldn't believe they gave a take-home test."

"Aha!" Jimmy voiced before languidly breathing smoke out through his nose. "Are you saying that Penn students are cheaters?"

"I'm saying I got a B instead of an A because of that take-home test," Bill laughed.

"Did you take anything from Martin Cody?" Dan asked.

"Hmm?"

"MacArthur student. He's at UCLA now. Might look favorably at someone from Penn."

"No. Never heard of him. Wouldn't go to Los Angeles, anyway. Who's MacArthur?"

"Hespenheide?"

"Hespenheide?" Bill repeated. "I think he filled in for Ricklefs a few times. Don't know him. You seem to know a lot of people in biology, though, for someone in physics."

"I'm sure Ricklefs will give you a good recommendation, but about that B in evolution, one grade can't matter much."

"Except that maybe had I had a three-point-oh instead of a two-nine-something, maybe I'm slicing up cadavers next to Libby in the med school."

"You want to go to medical school?" Libby tried to get back into their conversation.

"Not any more, thanks to Dan. Now that I don't need to, I no longer want it." Then Bill turned back to Dan. "So what are your plans. Grad school? Physics?"

Dan laughed. "Maybe ecology like you. You know, all the time I was involved in Earth Day, I never thought of anything related to it as a career. Ecology and physics seem an unlikely match, but actually, ecology may be in my genes. My Aunt Jewel studied it. And then there's Uncle Robert."

"Uncle Robert?"

"That's MacArthur, and he's not my uncle. We just did a lot of things together, bird walks and such, when I was growing up. The reason I'm here is because he could get me in without my ever getting a high school degree. By the time I matriculated, he was at Princeton, though. I never got to take even one class from him or just wander into his office. But that was OK. I mostly took physics and math courses."

"Why, with that background? Math talent? It's our curse."

"No, I got through the physics curriculum by the skin of my teeth," Dan admitted. "John MacArthur, Robert's brother, is a physicist. He insists that the only way to make a living is through math skills. So I set out to get them. I could never have gotten by without John's help. Every chance I got, I went running up to Vermont and parked myself in his kitchen with my math and physics books. The reading week before exams was a God send."

"So do you think I should become an ecologist and work on the nuclear power issue?" Dan turned to address the general gathering. "It may be humanity's only—"

"What the hell is going on here?" Libby interrupted. In synchrony, all eyes aligned their gaze to his.

"Yes. Highly unusual," the Sikh noted. From his standing position, he had the best view. He normally spoke very little, so little that Dan never learned his name. "Everyone is going through that one door into College Hall."

"I bet it has something to do with ROTC," Dan said. "Wasn't there some demonstration scheduled?"

"Oh yes," the Sikh said, "to remove the military from campus."

Dan looked at Bill. Bill looked at Dan.

"Let's go."

Libby had already left for a better vantage point so as not to miss any beauty in the line that was streaming past. The foreign students all held back.

"They are photographing people coming in," Mohammed called out. "That is why only the one door. They will have a picture of everyone who goes inside."

That stopped neither Dan nor Bill. Out of habit, Dan turned away from the camera as he reached the narrow entranceway. Bill smiled at it, no doubt with heart pounding.

Inside, the building's central hall was packed with people. First comers had courteously seated themselves on the floor around its edges. Others stood crowded together in what little room remained. Up toward the president's office, Dan could see what looked like things being organized.

"Doesn't it feel like we're another generation already from these kids?" Dan whispered as they looked around.

"It does. And I'm still only twenty-five."

"A quarter of a century? Makes you feel like an old man? I'm two years closer to thirty."

Someone in front stood above the crowd, exhorting it to stamp out ROTC by marching down to the ROTC building. Someone else shouted to occupy it. Another person insisted from the crowd that they should not give up the administration building now that they had seized it.

"No. No," Dan said with exasperation to Bill, but loud enough for others to hear. "He's giving up the floor."

Shushing noises were made around them.

Dan shouted, "Stick to you guns!" but the original orator had already given way to others.

Someone suggested some totally different goal. Someone else asked the assembly to split up into committees and give all potential actions due consideration. A female rose to take the floor to suggest tentatively, plaintively, delicately, that perhaps the women inside might, "you know," not feel comfortable making plans in groups, "you know," dominated by men. She suggested that her sisters meet with her at some other venue.

"They can't even focus on ROTC," Dan moaned. He wanted to stand up and lead them down Spruce Street, but something kept him back.

"Let's wait to see what they're going to do," Bill suggested.

"I think we've already missed our chance."

The assembled rabble did start to break up into organized sub-groups.

"I've got a synthesis I have to start today," Bill suddenly remembered.

Tails between legs, they slipped away.

"That's the way the establishment gets taken down nowadays," Bill said when they got outside, where photographers and FBI agents were no longer in evidence.

"I think Meyerson is going to serve afternoon tea with buttered scones, then he'll let them all go on home."

"That's more like Harnwell would have done, and he'd have to serve them in groups. Women with women. Gays with gays. Young Republicans with Young Republicans, maybe."

"We would have gotten them to march," Dan said with confidence. "We could have shut the ROTC building right down."

"You think? This isn't Kent State."

All the foreign grad students and postdocs had disappeared from the tables outside Houston Hall. Unusual, Dan thought, but then he realized that all of them were destined to disappear eventually from the classrooms and labs of the university and back into their home countries, and none wanted to rush that through any hint of involvement in a demonstration. Bill and Dan walked on past Houston Hall to Spruce street.

"Yeah, I agree," Dan said. "They are a new generation. Dylan's Nashville Skyline has calmed down too many of them. Totally undid any effect of Four Dead in Ohio."

"Lay Lady Lay?" Bill inquired.

"You got it. No more Hard Rain or Masters of War. They were already moving on to their own things. Dylan helped them along."

"Do you resent him for that?"

"Hmm. Don't know. We're all supposed to resent him for letting folk music down. As if you can't protest by singing rock and roll. Rock Around the Clock might have been the biggest protest song ever. And Dylan really couldn't carry a note, anyway.

"Don't you mean tune?" Bill asked.

"No, a note. That's why he wrote his own songs, I think. He couldn't sing the traditional stuff. Mostly, he just copied Woodie Guthrie's Talking Blues. Then that Free-Wheeling album came out with Suze Rotolo on its cover."

"Suzie? Is that how it's pronounced?"

"Yeah!" Dan laughed heartily as the light finally changed to let pedestrians cross the heavy traffic at Spruce Street. "Everyone wanted to learn about this Bobby Die-lan after that album. I think Suze on the cover—she never looked as good as on that cover—that had as much to do with its success as Dylan's singing. Did you know that Dylan thought meeting Suze Rotolo was like stepping into the Tales of 1000 Arabian Nights? I quote exactly. He said she was the most erotic thing he had ever seen, like a Rodin sculpture come to life. I quote again. He said the air was full of banana leaves when they met. That one's not an exact quote. He said a lot of stupid things then."

"You sound like you know him."

"A little."

Dan normally never discussed Dylan. It always seemed pretentious to him—"I knew Bob Dylan when"—but something was different now. He had come to a crossroad or turning point, it suddenly dawned on him, even if he had no clue what it was. Dylan and Ingrid and Earth Day and graduation were all confabulated, along with his past and future, in his head.

"You're kidding!" Bill stopped to exclaim between the Gothic towers of the men's dorms and the towering modernity of HUP.

"I met him a few times. That's all."

Bill took a moment to stare into Dan's averted eyes, then continued onto Hamilton Walk and toward the medical school. Dan followed aimlessly. "Aren't you going the wrong way?" Bill asked.

"Huh? I'm going home."

"Aren't you still going the wrong way?"

"Aren't we all? But did you know that Dylan was a closet Elvis Presley fan?" Dan continued his Dylan lore as they resumed walking. He felt relieved to talk it out with Bill, to purge himself of it for some reason. "So was I. An Elvis fan, I mean. I think we all were, whether we admitted it or not. The only reason I learned Dylan was, it was because I started an impromptu Don't Be Cruel and he joined right in. Then I switched to Why do Fools Fall in Love and he joined in with me on that, too."

"Frankie Lyman? I can't believe it."

"Believe it. He was word for word with me. Although both of us sang things lik Irene, Good Night and On Top of Old Smoky when we were kids," Dan continued to babble, "we never even knew who did those songs. We thought the Weavers were an old fogies' group until Suze explained its history. Then we began to take Pete Seeger seriously."

By then they were standing at the Gothic entrance to the medical school and its laboratories.

"Did we do the right thing?" Dan asked, holding Bill back by the elbow.

"What? Not taking over that demonstration?"

"Or anything. Sometimes I think things pass me by too much, that I keep taking Frost's untaken road. I missed out on Freedom Rides. I didn't march on Washington. No one famous ever shook my hand."

"You missed being killed with Chaney and Goodman," Bill joked.

"Did you just wish it had been me instead of Schwerner?"

"I missed the march, too," Bill said after a laugh. "I'd just gotten my learner's permit and I was damned if I would get on a bus for the weekend, but you know," Bill lowered his voice soothingly, "it's almost May. The semester is over. Nothing would have come of taking over the ROTC building today, except maybe some nights away from home."

That was true, Dan thought. And he was expecting a visit from Ingrid that evening. Why had he lost sight of that? Instead of flirting with an arrest, he would be better off in his room, cleaning it up, and whatever needed cleaning in the common areas, and the kitchen, and the bathroom. Oh God, the bathroom!

Fortunately, "Whale" was home. He was the most unusual of Dan's roommates, all of whom had been strangers to each other prior to becoming house mates, for which status four hundred dollars was paid, essentially as an entrance fee, although putatively as a one-fifth share in the house's ratty furniture. He was a football player with skills that were attracting pro scouts. He had a wife from whom he was estranged, a matter discussed only in hushed tones and out of his presence. It was rumored that an annulment was in the works. He rode a motorcycle. That, the rumor had it, had been the cause of the estrangement. When his wife went to visit him in Saigon several months into his stint in Viet Nam, it had to have been for the purpose, as far as the best that anyone could make out, of consummating their nuptials. He had insisted on keeping the motorcycle in their tiny hotel room. She had insisted that either it or she had to go.

He was technically Bill's legacy. Bill had directed him Dan's way in search of housing. Although, he and Bill had not known each other well, they had grown up as neighbors in New Jersey. He had adopted Bill as a big brother on coming to Penn.

Except for his leather jacket and rebellious mustache, he looked every bit the crew-cut Young Republican that he was, but he was also anti-war, anti-establishment, and very pro-sex-and-drugs. Standing six feet five and carrying two hundred fifty pounds of solid muscle, he found it easy to fit in almost anywhere. And he didn't mind doing chores. Half an hour of "policing the area" had it presentable in both his and Dan's opinions, after which and a beer or two, he accompanied Dan to 30th Street Station.

Ingrid, even with her hair pulled back so that it seemed to Dan to be stretching her face, was as breathtakingly beautiful as ever.

"Why, thank you," she answered Mike's complement when his words beat Dan's. Then she gave Dan a quick peck on the cheek.

"Mike Whalen," he offered when Dan did not introduce him.

It was her first visit in over a year, Dan reminded her tentatively, finally returning her peck with one of his own. It had been a disastrous visit. They had slept head to foot in his dormitory bed out of awkward deference to his roommate. At least, so he thought.

"Has it been that long?" Ingrid raised her hand to her hair to reply, causing her nipples to shift against her filmy blouse. Even though she was barely under the age at which she should no longer be trusted, according to the reigning philosophy of their generation, nothing about her, not the turned up breasts visible beneath their diaphanous covering, not the long, shapely legs emerging from her hot pants, suggested any years beyond those at which she and Dan had met.

"So, Mike, you are ..." Ingrid tried to make conversation as they walked through the station, but she suddenly lost his attention. It was fixed on a lone figure slouched with legs outstretched at a large hexagonal wooden bench. From it, he commanded the entire chamber, appearing bigger than life in a trim business suit and shiny black shoes. Two squealing girls with South Philadelphia hairdos discovered him and ran up to him with appeals for autographs as Mike and Dan watched with open mouths.

"That's—" Ingrid started to say.

"Muhammad Ali," Mike finished for her.

In those few seconds, the former champion became surrounded by more admirers until he disappeared from their sight.

"I didn't know you'd taken an interest in sports," Dan turned glumly back to Ingrid. By not being quicker, Dan realized, he had lost a chance to shake the hand of one of his heroes.

"He's more than a sports figure," she said, touching her hair again. Previously, she had shown little interest in the subject beyond trying to tell football from baseball from basketball.

"So," Ingrid began again as all three squeezed into the back seat of a waiting taxi, "Mike, are you a student?"

"Sort of."

Ingrid raised an eyebrow. Mike was very obviously trying to keep his focus on her eyes, rather than what was showing through her blouse, to which, it was true, his eyes involuntarily flitted on occasion. Dan was totally absorbed in her closeness.

"What do you mean sort of?" Ingrid flashed Mike a mischievous smile.

"I guess I'm on schedule to graduate," Mike answered. "I'm a Wharton student," he added.

Ingrid screwed her face in puzzlement.

"Business," Dan added.

"Which I don't want to go into," Mike confessed.

"No?" Ingrid showed genuine surprise. "Why not?"

"It seems more like the problem than the solution. I should do something useful after I finish here. I thought I was going to go on with football, but playing a game for a living seems stupid. Besides, given the shrapnel scar on my knee, I doubt any pro team is going to offer me much money. Penn is hardly tearing up the Ivy League with me as linebacker. Not like the basketball team. And I'm no kid anymore."

"Not a kid? Shrapnel?"

"Viet Nam," Mike answered both her questions.

The ride to South Street ended too quickly for either of Ingrid's bookends. Mike, reluctantly, was the first to relinquish closeness to her to let her out.

"This it?" she asked, staring at the white-washed brick facade of their row house, one of only four standing where the South Street Bridge began its rise over the Schuylkill. "It's cute."

A good sign, Dan thought.

"I like it," said Mike. "These houses stand like a castle on this block."

Mike, by nature a helpful sort, now had even more incentive to take over cooking duties from Dan. It was to be just the three of them at dinner. All the others in the house worked for their meals at

Houston Hall, either waiting on tables or working in the kitchen. By offering to cook, Mike technically guaranteed fifty percent of Ingrid's attention for himself. He was already back from O'Connell's grocery and had the rusty charcoal grill going before Dan and Ingrid emerged from Dan's room, the door of which, Mike had taken notice, had stayed open. Dan had spoken very little about girls with Mike. To him, Ingrid was possible unclaimed property.

When Dan and Ingrid came down from his room, it was so that Ingrid could cut Dan's hair outdoors in the postage-stamp of a back yard, where, under a heavy plastic tarp, Mike's bike, the very same one he had bought in Saigon, took up most of the space that the Weber kettle and several out-of-place chairs and a table did not. The hair cut was at Ingrid's insistence. Wielding only dissection-kit scissors, she forbade Dan from speaking so as not to cause an accident. She and Mike did all the talking.

"There," she finally said to Dan. "There's the handsome boy I fell in love with."

"I like Mike—Whale do you call him?" Ingrid remarked later from Dan's bed. After the steaks, Mike had insisted on taking her on a motorcycle ride through Philadelphia's most scenic streets. Then the roommates showed up. It was well after midnight before Mike and the others let them return to Dan's room. "I always feel like a fish out of water with your friends. They are all scientists. They are all logic and function. Mike is very different. He's all heart and emotion."

"And you're all art and music?" Dan asked, wondering what might have transpired on her after-dinner jaunt with Mike. It seemed to have taken much too much time, even for every single sight in Philadelphia.

"I just want nothing more to do with with Philadelphia," Ingrid suddenly spoke out. "It wasn't just that dorm room. I've outgrown cockroaches and cracked plaster, dirty dishes in the sink and full ashtrays everywhere. I am gentrifying along with the Village."

"So where does that leave us?"

"What do you mean?" she asked, letting her hair loose. "I love you, Dan. You're … Well, I just do."

"Yeah, I'm the only lost kitten or stray dog that's stuck around with you this long."

"Yes! Yes!" she laughed. "But hardly a stray dog. You were my neediest kitten and I fell in love with you for it. Who can tell why one loves someone? And what does it matter?"

How bad could that be? Dan thought. She said she loves me.

"And I have loved you since."

"I m-mean tonight," he said almost with a stutter. "Where does that leave us for tonight? There are no extra beds in the house. Do we sleep head to tail, like last time?"

Even though it was not much more than an hour on the train, Dan had not often been to see her in New York. Something, school mostly, draft counseling, Earth Day, always seemed to get in his way. And when he did manage, it was only a daytime visit or a quick, chaste overnight on his way to or from Vermont. Usually, she had things to do, usually in the company of others. The bunk bed was gone. Her new apartment had a guest room. She seemed more older sister than girlfriend.

"Head to tail?" Ingrid laughed. "That does offer interesting possibilities."

"How are you ... ah. Are you still on the pill?"

"I still get them mailed to me from Sweden," she answered, now lying back in bed, "even if I no longer need to. I'm a pace setter in their use, I think. One of the first."

Maybe he should just lunge at her, he thought, out of something like passion. That was just not his way, though. And how could he now? He was not even hard.

"I take them whether I need them or not," Ingrid added, looking straight into his face.

"When do you need to?"

"I don't—need them—Dan." She paused for a reaction from him at each phrase. None came. "But have I had other partners? At times. They mean nothing. It's just pleasure. Sexual gratification. Don't you?"

"Not with others."

"Sweet, sweet, Dan."

"I guess what I was asking is what do you want me to do?" he asked, sitting on the bed beside her. "About in bed?"

"Do whatever you want."

"What do you want to do?"

"Whatever you want me to," she said.

Early the next morning, she was gone. She had things to do in the city, even on a Saturday. Mike had insisted on taking her to the train station on his motorcycle to let Dan catch up on his sleep.

"Danny, I love you more than anyone," she had said on parting, "but I hate Philadelphia."

She had been no older sister, but he had failed as a lover. Fear had overcome him. Fear of rejection, fear of inability to perform, fear that he was worthlessly wasting away his life, fear, just plain fear. Even fear of the new tricks she had tried. They just made him wonder who she had learned them from. Neither relaxed, nor fully tumescent, he had never quite risen to the occasion for her.

Still, the visit let him come to some sort of decision. After waiting the precisely estimated time to catch her in her apartment, he picked up the phone and dialed her number.

"Of course," she told him when he asked if he could stay with her after graduation. But it brought him neither happiness nor peace of mind. Runaway strays were still appearing regularly in her apartment, he knew, and there was the image that Dan could not get out of his mind of Mike and Ingrid as they road off together the previous evening.

Maybe to her he was still just a stray. Maybe she just put up with him because he needed mothering. Maybe he needed too much mothering.

Ithaca

I

THE bells in the McGraw Hall tower were about to ring noon. Masses of people in winter clothes crowded the walkways that crisscrossed the spacious quadrangle. Those from eleven o'clock classes dawdled to lunch, while those with noon classes hurried to them. Snow had fallen the night before and been shoveled into waist-high banks that lined the walkways. It was over a foot deep beyond them, eliminating all hope of shortcuts, even where the banks could be scaled. Dan ignored their disapproving snarls and redoubled his efforts to force his way past the dawdlers. Then, inexplicably, the sea of students pushing against him suddenly parted. He rushed into the opening, only to collide with the reason for it: Carl Sagan.

Sagan, too, was in a hurry. They stared at each other momentarily, the younger man looking down at the older man in awe, the older one looking up at the younger with annoyance.

The Loch Ness Monster instantly crowded out everything else in Dan's mind. Just days before, he had gone to a combined presentation and panel discussion of new research on the creature. Two photographs from an underwater camera, one possibly of a fin, the other a head, had been followed by an artist's interpretation. In the murkiness of those photos, the artist had seen ET-like eyes and two worm-like antennae. Sagan, the first of the panel to speak, had bubbled up like a wealthy suburban mother finally given a chance to talk about her daughter's wedding. While the evidence was being shown, he told the large audience, he had done a paper-and-pencil, mean-free-path calculation. Based on the volume of the lake and the size and number of creatures detected by the researchers' sonar, his analysis predicted exactly the two collisions between camera and creature that had happened.

Having Sagan now before him, Dan wanted to tell him that he had been much more impressed with the analysis of the ichthyologist on the panel. That old professor had brought out a huge stuffed sturgeon from behind a curtain. Then he showed how that creature's barbels, worm-like growths that hung down from its mouth, when viewed upside-down, explained the antennae in the photos perfectly.

But the mean free paths of the two men precluded an encounter long enough for that. They continued on in opposite directions without a single word passing between them, one back to academic heights, the other, a basement in Comstock Hall, where David Pimentel's empire occupied the entire ground floor. Other than for official business, such as plumbing or telephone repair, no one from the outside world ever dared venture into that level of the turn-of-the-century building.. Pimentel's office was in one corner of it. Dan entered at the opposite corner, where the laboratories were, and hurried past the various storage rooms and offices for postdocs, graduate students, lab technicians, and research assistants—and the occasional undergraduate—before he reached his destination.

"Just in time," Cathy Woodson said to him from the small outer room that guarded the entrance to the much larger room that served as both conference room and personal office for Pimentel.

Posted outside it, Cathy functioned as a secretary-receptionist, but her job title, which no one knew or cared to know, probably had something to do with research or administration. Whatever her duties, they did not require attendance at the meetings. She was pretty and curvaceous and had fiery red hair and everyone wanted to know why she was unmarried.

"There he is," Don Nafus announced with relief as soon as he saw Dan.

Don, with whom Dan was to do that day's presentation of new research in the literature, had a trim, outdoorsy beard and an almost indiscernible blonde mustache. Dan called it a "magic mustache." The moment one looked away from him, the mustache— and most of the beard— disappeared from memory.

Pimentel sat imperiously alone across a huge wooden table from Nafus. The table filled the room and easily fit the dozen or more graduate students and postdocs in Pimentel's stable of academics. It was comprised of a number of normal-sized wooden tables pushed together, but it gave the impression of the single solid substance one might expect in a boardroom at General Motors. It was clear of all clutter, except for a small, neat pile within an arm's reach of Pimentel. His documents were always either neatly arranged close to him on his desk or filed away by a succession of very competent office assistants. Only guests, postdocs, and Cathy Woodson typically ever sat with him in his relatively sunny corner.

Aside from the walls with the windows that met at Pimentel's corner, where legs and feet of people passed outside above his head, one wall held a large slate blackboard, which had been washed clean by someone, possibly Cathy, and bookshelves. Another had specimen cabinets, atop of which was a mongoose stuffed in a fierce pose. It looked suspiciously identical to one posed on grass that Pimentel had once used as an illustration for an article on biological control.

Only about half of Pimentel's stable, which he restocked yearly, appeared to be present. Those who were finishing up usually behaved as if they had more important things to do than attend his lunch meetings, although Dan was pleased to see that Larry Hurd, the current postdoc, who had already accepted a faculty position elsewhere and would be leaving in less than a week, and Rick Whitman, a Canadian finishing up his degree in entomology, were seated in a clump of first- and second-year graduate students near the door. For them, attendance was mandatory unless classes interfered.

While they had been waiting for him, Pimentel, flashing his ready smile as always, had been holding the floor by showing off his new calculator. When he saw Dan walk in, he handed the instrument to Rick Whitman and solemnly turned to a development concerning his theory for the evolution of predators and their prey (or herbivores and plants, parasites and their hosts). Natural selection caused prey to become more resistant to predation, the theory went, which in turn limited the population size of the predators. Ultimately, a stable equilibrium of predator and prey numbers was reached, rather than predators driving prey and themselves to extinction. That was the entire gist of the theory. Everyone in the room was well versed on it.

The concern Pimentel brought up had to do with a new paper by Polish scientist Adam Lomnicki. Lomnicki had once before questioned the math behind Pimentel's theory, Pimentel explained. As he did so his lively eyes penetrated each person in the room with their gaze, even as they took in everyone around him. They were the eyes of an Air Force pilot, which he had been in Korea. He was as fit as a pilot, too. His slight body was that of an athlete who refused to let himself get out of shape. He jogged daily, without exception, even during an insurrection in the Philippines. He jogged so early in the morning there, according to him, that he had faced little danger from the sleeping insurrectionists.

He had impressed Dan early that winter by his Vermont-like ability to jack a car out of a ditch, which Dan had witnessed him doing for his college-age daughter one snowy day. Her beauty, Dan thought, owed much to the dark features she had inherited from her father, which in him were softened by a powdering of white in his hair. Dan was certain that Pimentel was also capable of cutting and splitting his own wood and Bondo-ing the rust holes in a car, the other two prerequisites to being a genuine Vermonter.

Genetic feedback was what Pimentel had named the mechanism for his theory. It had captivated Dan on his first reading. Its name, two simple self-explanatory words, connected it to cybernetics, and Dan recognized the very venerable math of the logistic growth equation combined with Mendelian genetics at its heart. He had been certain genetic feedback was to enter the vocabulary of ecology. More importantly to Dan, and probably to Pimentel, when it came to funding purposes, genetic feedback applied to agriculture, biological control in particular. It was what had brought Dan to Cornell.

Now Lomnicki was once again picking on Pimentel's vulnerable math for the genetic changes in the predator and prey populations, the preciseness of which weakened, rather than strengthened his arguments for the theory. What Lomnicki had just published in the *American Naturalist* appeared to show that the math did not give the results that the theory predicted nor that Dieter John's experiment and computer simulation had shown. It could be a heavy blow. Dieter John, already a Cornell legend, had made his reputation with that experiment. Moreover, most of the dissertations coming out of Pimentel's lab were based on the genetic feedback model in one way or another. Still, few in the room had read either of Lomnicki's papers or understood any more about the controversy than that Simon Levin, an applied mathematician in the process of converting to ecologist, was working with Pimentel on a rebuttal.

"The American Naturalist is publishing so much mathematical theory these days that I hear they are going to change its name to American Unnaturalist," Rick Whitman joked when Pimentel had finished.

"Hah! Hah!"

No one laughed but Pimentel. It was a joke they already knew. But Pimentel's research was not on Dan's mind. The scheduled topic for Don and Dan was new research on dinosaurs. Not their own, but that of Robert T. Bakker. Dinosaurs, according to Bakker, did not—like fish, amphibians, and reptiles, have their body temperature vary with that of their environment—but like mammals and birds, kept their body temperature constant by producing their own metabolic heat. Reading the evidence required Dan and Don to plunge into dinosaur anatomy, physiology, cell structure, and what could be inferred about their posture, gait, and ecology.

Dan, whose knowledge of cell structure and physiology was limited, focused on the ratios of dinosaur predators to their prey. It was ecology, after all, even if published in *Evolution*. The predator-to-prey ratios for dinosaurs, according to Bakker, were not like those for cold-blooded fish or spiders. They were more like those of wolves or—birds.

"You know," Dan suddenly extemporized based on a thought that flashed through his mind as he finished his presentation, "the idea that the Nessies might be dinosaurs that somehow survived the great extinction of their kind in Loch Ness's deep, cold waters, require a cold-blooded Nessie. So what, I wonder, might the implications be on Loch Ness lore from what Don is about to present?"

Then he collapsed with relief into his seat as Nafus took over. The giddy thought struck him that the previous month's lunchtime heresy had concluded with discussion of a monster. It had come out of the closet after Mike Whalen, a connoisseur of heresies, and Nafus (again) had presented what embryologists were learning about genetics and development. Not many genetic changes, it turned out, were required to produce large physical changes. A small change in a regulatory gene that affected early development in an embryo could create a cascading effect and a large difference in the adult, a monstrous difference even.

"Oh, evolution is still Darwinian," Mike had summarized, "The genetic step is still very small. It's non-Darwinian only by the size of its effect."

That had been when Pimentel had brought Richard Goldschmidt's "hopeful monster" out of the closet. Even when Pimentel had pressed them on it, neither Mike nor Don had chosen to defend Goldschmidt's thoroughly discredited idea that a large change in a single individual, the sort of births that breeders called "sports," could lead to some of the evolutionary changes in the fossil record.

Why not? Dan had thought then, but had kept to himself—and still thought now, as he listened to Nafus explain what Haversian canals were. Are some heresies just too heretical? What's wrong with following your speculations to their logical conclusion? Isn't that what creativity in science is all about? Isn't that how Robert MacArthur—

"It's not very sophisticated programming," Bill Dritschilo broke Dan's train of thought by whispering.

He also handed him a calculator. It was Pimentel's HP 65, programmable, with both internal memory and with a removable memory chip. It cost Pimentel over $700.

"The programming steps have to be pretty short and you can only look at a few at a time," Bill added when it was clear that Nafus had concluded his presentation. "I'll stick with the 360."

Dan was first with a suggestion for the next month's lunch meeting topic, some new work questioning whether speciation needed to take place only over long periods of time, as Darwin had professed, and only in physically separated populations of a species, as Ernst Mayr still insisted. Don Nafus (again!) immediately volunteered to lead that discussion. In fact, it began as they filed out of Pimentel's office, and it continued as they congregated in the small room that held most of the first-year students.

"Whaddaya say, there?" Don Saari asked as he passed through that room to get to his own room. A Viet Nam vet with an appropriate mustache, but not a beard, he was one of those who had skipped the lunch meeting.

"Speciation can be saltational," Mike answered as he came in on Don Saari's heels. Mike was now addressed almost universally as "Whale," to differentiate him from Mike Burgess, who had abandoned his graduate studies in microbiology under Martin Alexander to become a research technician under David Pimentel.

Saari shrugged his shoulders and walked on.

"So? Is it a great time to be an ecologist or what?" Mike exclaimed as he removed his heavy parka and unzipped his leather jacket to let his white t-shirt breathe. "Besides warm-blooded dinosaurs—hope the talk went well—how about group selection? Now there's another great controversy. Or that species themselves can be selected. And that punctuated equilibrium idea with a— Who is it?"

"Stephen J. Gould," Don Nafus said from his perch on Mike's desk.

"No! Not the guy who writes the essays in the Smithsonian's magazine. The other guy."

"Natural History?"

"Niles Eldridge?"

"Yeah! Gould and Eldridge. Their ideas fly in the face of neo-Darwinism, too. Boy, Gould's into all those things, like Steven Stanley's idea of species selection. What a super time to be in ecology!"

"But none of this is ecology," Buck Cornell said, popping through the door with lowered head right after Mike. He was the tallest in the stable and had to lower his head to avoid injury at that under-sized door. "No more so than dinosaur evolution. Sorry to have missed the talk, guys. I just got back from retrieving my beetle from the repair shop."

"Beetle?"

"VW."

"But species selection is cool!"

"It's evolutionary ecology," Dan countered. "All the intellectually exciting stuff seems to be evolutionary ecology. There are no revolutions in regular ecology."

Dan stopped before saying that none of all that excitement seemed to have anything to do with their own research topics, which they were pursuing diligently. Graduate students were supposed to work on the research of their advisors. But even though genetic feedback, too, was evolutionary ecology, no ecologists outside of Eastern Europe seemed to care much about it, and then only about the niceties of the math behind it, that no one seemed to understand, anyway. The biocontrol people in Ag schools, of course, of which Cornell was one, wished it dead. Dan was beginning to fear that it might become a non-issue in academic ecology.

"Why can't ecology have heresies?" Mike persisted.

"It does," Buck said. "Clements's superorganism is one."

"Old hat. Dead and buried, along with plant ecology, in general, I think."

"Oh, I don't know," Buck said. "Whittaker isn't dead and buried. There's a lot going on in plant ecology. It's not just describing communities any more."

"Not if you look at succession as analogous to evolution," Mike started, looking from one to another in the room to make sure he had their attention. "Early to late succession communities are stages, just like primitive to advanced species. The difference is that even though neither Wallace nor Darwin discovered evolution, what they did discover was a mechanism for it, natural selection, but neither Cowles nor Clements ever found a mechanism for succession. There is still that to be discovered."

"Not if there aren't any communities," Dan put in.

"I should have taken his course, shouldn't I?" Bill asked.

"Whose?"

"Whittaker's?"

"I found it worthwhile," Buck answered him.

"But it competed with Mammalogy."

"How about MacArthur's proof that diversity promotes stability and Robert May's assault on it?" Dan offered. "That's ecology."

"That is ecology," Buck admitted, "diversity-stability theory. Although to have a heresy, don't you need to have an entrenched dogma? We seem to have so few of those."

"Well," Mike said, "we'll always have dinosaurs."

"Hey Whale!" Bill chimed in. "How about this for an analogy: natural history is to ecology as mathematics is to physics?"

"Hmm?" Dan intoned, still lost in thought.

Why had Buck not brought up genetic feedback? Dan wondered. Was it the idea that heresies required entrenched dogma? Has Pimentel's model just not stuck? And why did no one else seem worried about Lomnicki?

Buck and Don were out the door already, heading for their own office enclave in a different part of the basement. Dan became lost in thought, again, this time about the nuclei, mitochondria, and chloroplasts of cells. They were the subjects of another evolutionary heresy. Those organelles were the products of symbiosis, that heresy went, rather than strict Darwinian evolution. It was already being widely accepted.

What a coincidence, he thought, that it had come most forcefully from Carl Sagan's former wife, Lynn Margulis.

Was this kind of excitement, he further thought, what it must have been like for Aunt Jewel when she was at Illinois? Just being at Cornell is exciting. Why didn't she—?

Then a thought struck him from deeper in his memory, perhaps from his very soul. Could Aunt Jewel have given all that up on account of him? Had she quit graduate school to take care of him?

What other sacrifices had she made for him, that he had never shown his gratitude for, only because she was not his real mother?

He really should call her, he thought. And he did. That night.

II

FLIES circled in a small, central cloud beneath the ceiling of John Gowan's house. Graduate students, some postdocs, and a few professors milled about less energetically below them. They were there by invitation to discuss the latest hot topic in ecology: how competition structured animal communities.

"Cluster flies," Bob Poole explained on noticing that Dan's attention was on them. "They're harmless."

"What are they doing here in the middle of winter?" Dan asked.

"Trying to keep warm, like all of us."

Poole was a thick-bodied, bearded man. Drifting continuously in and out of the large, main room of the old farmhouse, he had taken little part in the discussion that Richard Root and Simon Levin had organized for the evening. He had come mainly to speak with Dan Botkin about the book he was writing. Apparently, he was not getting much of a chance to do so.

"They squeeze themselves in between cracks in the clapboards of old houses like this when the weather gets cold," Poole elaborated. "They're gone again in the spring."

"How do you know so much about flies?" Dan asked.

"Why shouldn't I?"

"I thought you were some sort of mathematician."

"My specialty is the Lepidoptera," Poole said, his syntax identifying him as a taxonomist.

"I thought the title of your book is seesawing between An Introduction to Quantitative Ecology and An Introduction to Population Biology."

"It's gotten around, huh?" Poole laughed. "Does the difference seem slight to you? Or are you just surprised that a systematist can be good at math?"

"It reminds me of the manuscript of MacArthur and Wilson's book," Dan said. "I came across it in Robert's cabin in Marlboro. It had The Theory of Biogeography on the cover page, but that typing had been crossed out. The Theory of Biogeography, colon, Islands had been written below it by hand. That, too, had been struck out. Then one of them must have finally gotten it right."

"THE Theory of Island Biogeography?" Poole asked in astonishment. "The famous MacArthur and Wilson book? Did you get your degree under MacArthur?"

"Hardly. I'm just a new grad student. He was sort of an adopted uncle to me in Vermont."

"Oh my God," Poole could not contain himself. "Don't tell me you're the grad student Cornell took on based on Robert MacArthur's deathbed request!"

Dan's face turned beet red. It had been nothing like that, he knew.

"I didn't mean—" Poole hurriedly added.

"It's OK," Dan said on regaining his composure, "My Aunt Jewel and he were old friends. I hope I got in here on more than just that. But about the titles—I remember puzzling over what the differences between them could be. I was home from college hoping that either John or Robert—preferably John, Robert's brother—could explain what the point of Gauss's Law was before I took my GREs."

"I don't remember Gauss's Law being on the GREs," Poole said, seeming to pay close attention to Dan, although his eyes were straying around the room.

Dan wondered if Poole was so embarrassed by his gaff that he was looking for someone else to talk to. He also wondered how far that story had spread and in what versions.

"They WERE on the physics GREs," Dan announced firmly, having decided to aggressively ignore any gossip about himself. "I was a physics major."

"Ah, another Robert May."

Again, Dan's face crimsoned. He did not know how to interpret that remark. Robert MacArthur had taken the Australian astrophysicist under his wing, and May had just risen to a very prestigious position at Princeton's Institute for Advanced Study. It had famously been the final intellectual home of Albert Einstein—and of the man May succeeded: Robert MacArthur. Dan was also feeling sensitive at having had what he thought was his own MacArthur-style brilliancy totally and brutally shot down by Si Levin recently.

"I mean," Poole added hastily, "that you're going from physics to ecology."

"I guess," Dan answered coyly. "So—and I'm conceding that someone who is writing a book with your possible titles, even if he is actually a butterfly man, knows that a triple-integral can only be solved for a few simple shapes—I wanted to know what practical use it could be. John and Robert were both good at that. Gauss's Law, John explained to me, was taught because those approximations gave useful predictions. Infinite cylinders are good approximations for wires. And flat plates for capacitors."

Poole had already excused himself and gone off in the direction of the kitchen, leaving Dan talking to himself and puzzling over whose postdoc Poole was. He had assumed he was Levin's, even though Si supposedly had no funds left for more grad students, let alone postdocs. And Si had just moved from Applied Math or something. Poole had to be in Entomology. Dick Root was in Entomology, although he was clearly an ecologist. But then, Si Levin was now in Ecology and Systematics, although he was clearly a mathematician.

People were gathering together again. Various coinages of niche would soon be flying about beneath the cluster flies. Fundamanental niche, habitat niche, place niche, and associational and distributional niches had already had their flights. Dan awaited hypervolumetric niche, Hutchinson's mathematically precise, but unmeasurable formulation, to take off next, followed by his realized niche, which, in theory, was supposed to be measurable.

George White and Alan Hastings, Levin's students, were again sitting next to each other on the floor, where they had been before the break. Both were Ph.D. candidates in mathematics, but they were taking graduate courses along with the ecology students in the room. Most of the others present seemed to belong to Dick Root in one way or another, and most had reoccupied their former places.

The Root students occupied the higher level of the room. It had clearly once been two separate rooms, before Gowan or some previous owner had taken out a wall. One part was a step higher than the other. It almost constituted a stage. Dan was on the lower level, in the audience, as he thought of it. Buck, he saw, was seated on the higher level in a wooden chair next to Jamie Cromartie, who was in a rocking chair.

Other than Buck, on whom Root had shone his blessings for some reason, Dan was the only other Pimentel student present. He wondered why. Root had given Dan no such blessing. In fact, Dan was certain that Root pretended not to know him, giving him only the most fleeting glance of recognition when the occasion required, as on this night, but never a word of greeting. Alvan Brick, another Pimentel student, had noted the same behavior toward him. Al's theory was that Root probably avoided Pimentel students because he was afraid they might ask him to be on their graduate committees. Root was on Buck's committee, though.

So why, Dan wondered, was he in this group at all? Could it really be only because Uncle Robert had championed his candidacy just before dying? Was he Robert MacArthur's legacy to Root or Levin in some way? Penance to be paid by them, perhaps, for neither having attended MacArthur's funeral, nor been invited to the symposium at Princeton that eulogized MacArthur?

A cancer that struck him at too young an age had taken MacArthur too quickly. The funeral had been a private one. Betsy had been too distraught to deal with anyone other than family and a few close friends. The more public memorial had been the gathering of MacArthur's students and collaborators at Princeton. They praised him by praising the work that he inspired in them. All of the praise was gathered together in a book. Even though it had not yet been published, some of its chapters were already having an influence on ecology. One even crept into the evening's discussion. Written by Jared Diamond of UCLA, it set out rules for how species in bird communities, the fragment of a community consisting of birds, might be "assembled," as he put it, to give the numbers and kinds that are found on certain islands. Competition—or its avoidance—was at the heart of the rules.

Root remarked that there was a consensus building that Diamond might be the next Robert MacArthur. That had raised Dan's silent ire. Something about Diamond's work struck him as odd. Although totally free of mathematics, it was still, in its own way, as impractical as Hutchinson's niche hypervolume.

And Dan was looking for the practical. He needed it, in fact. The chance to save the world through ecology, Hutchinson's and MacArthur's ecology, was what had drawn him to Cornell. Now, he sometimes wondered if ecological theory, in general, the mathematical kind that was the subject of Bob Poole's book and Robert MacArthur's life work, could ever contribute to that. It all seemed either too primitive to have much chance to really describe how the world works, or, like Gauss's triple integral, so sophisticated that it could never be tested in the real world, except approximately.

"Theory must eventually be falsifiable," Dan remembered MacArthur having said to him. "But it does not IN ITSELF have to be directly and clearly verifiable. Look for a model's theoretical consequences, Dan, then test those. Measurements CAN be made of various approximations of niche theories. Fiddle with the equations until you find them."

It had been after his kidney cancer had been diagnosed. They were his parting words to Dan as he wished him success in ecology.

"It's heuristic," Si Levin startled Dan out of his musings by seemingly reading his thoughts. "Even a model that's wrong can teach us something about the world by being wrong."

"I'll have to remember that for the Field Exam," Mark Rausher quipped.

With his healthy long hair and beard, Rausher reminded Dan of Dave Van Ronk. White and Hastings, too, were growing beards, the former more successfully than the latter. Dan wondered which of theirs his might come out like, should he decide to grow one. Then he forced himself to refocus on the discussion at hand.

"Some models have assumptions that are so unrealistic," Dan spoke up for the first time in the evening. "There's no point to even consider them."

"Not true," Si objected.

Levin's eyes blinked in slow motion. It was almost like the eye-roll Robert MacArthur used to emphasize a point, Dan thought. But Levin's eyes, set in his round, boyish face, looked more comical than wise, even when judgmental.

"They can still be heuristic," Levin said. "Let me give you an example. Take the logistic growth equation. Useless?"

"No," Dan answered cautiously. "Not in certain cases."

"And not in general useless, either," Si persisted. "But no one ever complains about one of its basic assumptions."

"Carrying capacity?" Buck asked.

"No! Even more basic."

"Fractional individuals?" Al Hastings asked.

"You've got it!" Si applauded excitedly. "It's a continuous function! It allows for fractional individuals. No one ever complains about that."

"Maybe they should," Dan spoke up again.

Suddenly feeling the need, he rose to go off in search of a beer. For some reason, possibly because he was trapped in it, Dan Botkin, in his full, almost rabbinical beard, was receiving people in the narrow, cramped kitchen of the farmhouse. There could never be too many cooks to spoil the broth in that kitchen. There was no room for them, even had Botkin not been taking up the center part of it. Way in the back, John Gowan cheerfully waved to Dan and pointed at a beer. It was clear that he would not be able to make his way out of the kitchen with a beer for Dan unless he went out the door at which he was standing, into the cold January night, and come around and back in through the front door. Not even he was that gracious a host, Dan feared.

Botkin, then at Yale, had given a guest lecture in Ecosystem Ecology, one of four sequential courses called "core course," of which any three were mandatory for a PhD in Ecology and Evolutionary Biology. The other courses were Autecology, Population Ecology, and Community Ecology. Autecology was an old term for studies of individual organisms, usually of their physiology and behavior. Synecology, another old term that had been paired with it, had been superseded by Community Ecology. The only time Dan saw synecology in print was on the door to Robert Whittaker's office. The Field Exam of Mark Rausher's joke tested all four, however. The Ecosystems course was nominally taught by Gene Likens, but being one of the discoverers of acid rain, he was away speaking at other places more often than he was present to teach the class. Besides the normal number of guest speakers for a core course, he also had a postdoc covering for him, Charles A. S. Hall. (The unfortunate connotation that could be drawn from his initials was eagerly pounced on by some of the more cynical students in the class.) Botkin, although not a particularly dynamic speaker, either, had still been a welcome change.

Botkin's lecture had been on a computer model that simulated a forest's growth based on how the tree species in it grew. It was being used at Hubbard Brook, where Likens and Yale's Herb Bormann were carrying on an ecosystem study of an entire watershed, the area from which water collects to flow eventually through a single stream. The computer program that Botkin had helped create for Hubbard Brook had been given a name, JABOWA, based on the first two letters of the last names of the IBM researchers who produced it, BO for Botkin. It had failed to excite Dan. Dritschilo, in a whisper to him during Botkin's lecture, had called the work too much like the engineering he had come to Cornell to get away from. Just another "tool," is how he had described both model and modeler before rushing off to smoke a cigarette. "All models are wrong," Mike Whalen had continued the whisper across Bill's vacated seat, "but some are useful." Then he had shrugged his shoulders and smiled Cheshire cat like.

Dan had to return to the main room without a beer. There, he found that Ricardo Mendez had taken his chair. Mendez was physically notable for having hair that was completely gray, white almost, even though he was the same age as Dan. He wore it like a signal of his status as the program's current star student, the one whose great success was to keep alive the names and reputations of his mentors.

Jamie Cromartie, a Root student, was at the moment the one holding the floor from a rocking chair at the edge of the higher portion of the room. He was seeking some intuitive meaning in the concept of the niche when Dan felt a draft behind him then a tap on his shoulder. A beer appeared before him. Gowan was that gracious a host.

"Mouseness, for example," Jamie argued, "should apply to —"

"And NUH is the letter I use to spell Nutches, who live in small caves, known as Niches," Si Levin cut Jamie off.

It was a quote from the Dr. Seuss theory of the niche.

"What comes next?" Si tried to remember. "Wait! I remember. There are many more Nutches than Niches. Each Nutch in a Nich knows that some other Nutch would like to move into his Nich very much. And I'm afraid I forgot the rest."

"Wait, wait! I got it," Alan Hastings almost shouted. "So each Nutch in a Nich has to watch that small Nich ... Wait! Wait..."

"Or Nutches who haven't got Niches will snitch," Levin beat him to the finish. "That's the theory of community structure in a Nutchshell."

"Nutshell!"

"What did I say?"

"Nutch-shell."

"Nutchshell? I'm useless for tonight, I'm afraid. Where's my beer?"

"You drank it," said Alan.

"I'm not a believer that competition structures communities," Bob Poole whispered to Dan on his way to the door. "Bev has just had a paper accepted in the American Midland Naturalist that fails to show that stem borers compete with each other."

Bev was Bev Rathcke, a postdoc with Root. She was at his side, dragging him away and out the door.

Jamie Cromartie recovered the floor from Levin and excitedly moved the discussion of niches back to "mouseness." The marsupials of Australia, he explained, included little creatures that resembled in every way the mice of the rest of the world. That meant to him that there had to be something like "mouseness" in the world. His rocking became more and more frenetic as he became more and more excited, and it brought him ever closer and closer to where the floor dropped off.

"It had something to do with mouseness, didn't it?" Dan asked on the drive to Buck's trailer.

"It was his downfall," Buck answered.

"Did you see Gowan's jaw drop when he saw his antique chair in pieces?"

"First time I ever thought Gowan was going to lose it."

"But what was all that niche stuff? I thought they were beating the concept to death."

"Whittaker, Levin, and Root just wrote a paper about it. They're pushing for a simple definition for niche. They claim theirs has the, you know— the math what is it to satisfy Levin."

"Mathematical formality?"

"That's it. And it includes Whittaker's ideas of alpha, beta, and gamma diversity."

"I missed it somehow. Where's it published?"

"It isn't yet."

Dan gave Buck a confused look.

"Root let me read his copy."

Privilege, thought Dan jealously, but he said, "Well, at least I finally heard Ric Mendez say something. I swear, he's the dullest brilliant guy I've ever run across."

Buck did not answer. Buck and Mendez were good friends. They had started together with Pimentel before Ric switched to Bruce Wallace. Dan knew that but still could not help speaking his mind.

"Maybe it's his premature gray hair?" Dan prodded.

"It can't be solely intellect that has the faculty dazzled," Dan pushed some more.

"They do seem to be grooming him for success," Buck finally agreed.

"You think it's because he's a minority?"

"I don't know. He seems to me to be about as Hispanic as Milton Timm is Black," Buck said, referring to a very upper-middle class grad student.

"How does one become groomed for success?" Dan asked, but they had already reached Buck's trailer, and Sally Cornell had heard the car or seen its lights and was at the door to greet them.

"Hi Dan," she shouted in her always-inviting husky voice, her breath making clouds in the light from the door. "How was the evening?"

"Well, see you in lab tomorrow," Buck said.

Dan arrived home not too particularly late, but Ingrid was already asleep, as she was on most nights that Dan worked late in the library or the lab. Sometimes Dan preferred it that way.

III

IT all finally came to a head. The awful thing about it was not that she and Ric Mendez had so noticeably disappeared from the party, but that he did not seem to care enough about it. He and Ingrid were not married, after all. Ric was, though. It was his wife, Beth, Pimentel's former lab technician, who had first noticed that the two were missing, embarrassing some of the other guests into making preparations for leaving.

What obligation did Ingrid and he have to each other? Dan wondered. Loyalty? What was that now?

"Well, it is the Seventies," Buck said amid the commotion.

"I think I'd like someone to take me home," Beth demanded shrilly. Bill and Jamie offered to somehow stuff her into their Spitfire and take her back into town with them. A general departure of guests followed.

"You think she'll forgive him?" Dan asked Buck after seeing them off and looking suspiciously at a closed door on the way back.

"It is the Seventies, after all," Buck repeated, shrugging his broad shoulders from his position on the couch.

The same confusing remark.

"Sex and drugs seem all that's left from the Sixties," Dan found the need to say to Buck for some reason. "Stronger drugs. Stranger sex."

Buck said nothing. Dan suspected he would love to quit the awkward situation, too, but Sally, sleeping with her head in his lap, was keeping him there. Sally was still out cold. What could be seen of her pretty face was mashed into a Halloween mask on one of Buck's huge knees. Swedish potatoes seasoned with crushed marijuana seeds, Ingrid's contribution to the refreshments, were having their effect on her.

"...Like jazz?" Dan heard.

It was Buck's voice.

"Huh?"

"I thought you were grooving to the music."

"I was reminiscing about another life, one in which I was known as Danny Larsen."

"What?" asked Buck, his eyes no longer drooping.

"In the Village. I was under eighteen. I was passed off as Ingrid's little brother in order not to have her run afoul of the law."

"Oh!" Sally suddenly awoke. "Where is everybody?"

She needed to have the situation explained to her, which neither Dan nor Buck wanted to do. Buck started, but was cut short by noises coming from the kitchen. The small room with the closed door was off of it. The illness of a previous resident of the old farm house must have prevented him from climbing stairs and caused what was once a pantry or a mud room to be converted into a small first-floor bedroom. Dan and Ingrid had the intention, in theory, of using it as a guest room, but it had instead become storage space with a bed in it. It worked perfectly as a coatroom for parties during Ithaca's long winters. Ingrid emerged from it on this coatless evening with a sheepish grin. That and the flush on her cheeks made her face quite fetching and almost drew away Dan's attention from Ric's eyes, which were frantically searching for his missing wife. Neither he nor Ingrid had been seen for almost an hour.

Barely past thirty, Ingrid was a fully opened flower. Always tall and blonde, she was the best model for the clothes that she designed. And she still had that soft girlish smile that had been breaking men's hearts since puberty. How could Ricardo have resisted her? And how could Dan, night after night, resist her so easily?

"Any of you think you could use a walk?" Ingrid broke the silence, still standing beside Ric. "It's such a warm November night."

Sally immediately rose to join the pair. They were soon out the door, leaving Buck and Dan to stare at each other, and at the empty wine jugs. Or at the walls, in Buck's case.

"Beautiful, isn't it," Buck finally said, looking at a framed poster of Earth as seen from Apollo 17.

"Yeah," Dan said, "but to me it looks more like a fragile, antique Christmas ornament than a blue marble."

The party had turned into an awkward way for friends to part. Buck and Sally were leaving Ithaca. That had been the point of the party. Larry Hurd had helped Buck land a position with him at the University of Delaware to teach plant ecology. It had been a strange choice, Dan thought, since Buck could not tell *Taraxacum officinale* from *Solidago canadensis*, dandelion from goldenrod, at least from their scientific names, but he was happy for Buck's good fortune. Jobs in academia were becoming rare prizes.

"Whose soup can?" Buck asked of another framed picture.

"Andy Warhol."

"No. I meant yours or Ingrid's? Is it an original?"

"Yeah. Ingrid's, of course. You know, she had not been sure about the move to Ithaca," Dan surprised himself by suddenly confiding to Buck. Why not Buck? He was so imposing, seemingly so self-assured, so connected to whatever was around him. Dan had been instantly drawn to him from their first meeting.

Ingrid's fears about Ithaca had been groundless, he explained to Buck. She found that she loved Ithaca. Things should be going well between them, he told him. What he was afraid to tell Buck was that the real problem, currently, might be, could be, possibly, maybe, was sexual appetite. Hers. And, maybe, his.

"She was at Penn?" Buck asked. "I thought you both moved here from New York City."

"I was at Penn. She only visited, and not very often. Is there no more wine in that jug?"

"Bone dry," Buck said, swirling nonexistent liquid in a gallon jug of Gallo Hearty Burgundy. "Physics seems to be the right major these days for going into ecology. That and engineering. You could be another Howard Odum."

Dan winced at the remark.

"I went to North Carolina to be an Odum student," Buck continued, catching the wince, but not what had elicited it. "But Howard moved to Florida while I was doing my alternate service. I was going to be an ecosystem guy."

"You? Really? Why didn't you follow him?"

Buck scratched the beard he had started to grow.

"You know how it is," he said. "Southern schools have reputations based on what they do on the football field. Delaware is as far south as I want to let myself get and, hopefully, not for very long. Also, I wasn't as strong in math as I thought."

Buck had talent, Dan knew, if not for math, then for determining which way the ecological wind blew. He had pointedly avoided doing any of the energy studies Pimentel had started, and his dissertation work had barely touched on genetic feedback. That already had Dan wondering. Now Buck had given Dan worries about ecosystem ecology, which he until then had thought might be a better way for him to go. Other than Botkin, systems ecologists did seem to be associated with southern schools—or no schools. With the national labs instead.

It was time to clean up. Dan picked up the two bottles of Mateus that had been drunk early in the evening and led Buck into the kitchen. Ingrid and Sally were obviously in the notorious guestroom. This time, the door was open, Dan noted. A major discussion had to be under way. Cleaning up noises, Dan thought, might signify that it was time for all guests to go home.

"I learned to cook from my stepfather," he said to Buck as he rinsed out the bottles for later, decorative use.

"Chicken satay on sticks, scallops wrapped in bacon," Buck marveled, "not the usual hamburgers and hot dogs of a graduate student cookout."

"Funny that I should call him that," Dan said, turning thoughtful. "I mean Jonathan, my stepfather. I never did before. Never called him anything but Jonathan or Jon."

He fell silent again.

"He's a great cook," Dan continued. "I worked with him in his restaurant. I really enjoyed learning from him. I'm nowhere near as good a cook as he is, but I can put together and organize huge meals with the best. Got twenty people to feed at once? Count on me."

"It's become a matter of some controversy whether you or Jamie is the better cook," Buck said.

"She, too, learned her skills from a Vermonter," Dan said. "Her mother."

The friendship that had so quickly flowered between Dan and Jamie based on that mutual interest had withered as quickly on a ski trip to Vermont by Dan and Ingrid, Buck and Sally, and Bill and Jamie. It took only a moment. It was on the way up the winding, narrow dirt path that was the Chateaugauy Road. They were on the way to Jamie's artist friends, the Marikaartos, for a lutefisk supper.

"Of all things," Dan had grumbled about that prospect.

The route went over seven temporary-looking wooden bridges that had no side rails and only paired plank rails, put down over similar lateral rails. It was to guide wheel placement. The subject in the packed car had turned to Bill's fear of tipping over on the first sail he had ever taken, then to sailing, then to Maine, then Boothbay and Jamie's grandparents' house. That was when Dan suddenly recognized in Jamie the little girl whose brother he had apparently molested.

"Jonathan always said, He who cooks must be he who cleans," Dan said loudly enough to be heard in the next room. "Otherwise, according to him, the kitchen would get incredibly messy and maybe even dangerous."

"Dust dragons?"

"Yeah, these have grown way past the bunny stage. The ones under the bed could be dangerous."

The toilet and the kitchen had been cleaned, of course. They needed straightening out more than anything else. Dan had scrubbed them down prior to the party. Now he and Ingrid were frantically policing the backs of closets and other spaces up to then ignored by them, but of possible interest to Aunt Jewel. The old farmhouse they were renting had many such spaces. Their cooperation on the cleaning and straightening tasks extended in some unspoken way to their ignoring the elephant that was left over from last night's party.

Between fall colors and winter white, November was a slow month in Vermont for tourists. Jon's restaurant was doing well enough to give everyone on staff two weeks off, and himself and Jewel, one. His doctor had recommended a month for him, but that had seemed too much to Jonathan, considering all the time that the restaurant had been without him right after his heart attack. That had been too long a time, Jon had explained to Danny on arranging the trip.

"It wasn't pretty," he had told Dan over the phone. "I almost had another heart attack from it. I can't take more than a week away from the kitchen. Besides, what would the people of Brattleboro do without my Thanksgiving turkeys?"

Jonathan had just called them again, but this time from a pay phone in Cortland. Even on the phone, an hour away, Jon's excitement had been palpable. It was Jewel and Jonathan's first visit into Dan's life since their day trip to the Village back in the Sixties.

What a time it's turned out to be for a visit, though, Dan thought, as he watched Ingrid attacking cobwebs with a long-handled duster. She looked and acted as if last night had never happened. She even flashed a smile at him after chasing and squashing wraith-like, almost invisible spiders that wove cobwebs in every corner and alcove in the house.

"It wasn't the person," she said as she shut the door to the downstairs bedroom. "He means nothing. It was the opportunity, that's all."

Then there was the sound of tires on gravel. Dan went immediately to the kitchen door.

He was shocked on seeing what had become of the powerful, barrel-chested man he had known. It was hard to believe that the thin, emaciated man coming to his doorstep was the same Jonathan. Instead of the full bear hug that Dan used to fend off as a teenager, there was now a mere pat on the shoulder and a handshake that was just a formality. He even seemed shorter than on their last meeting. Only his smile was unchanged.

"Great," Jon said in response to the standard polite concern from Ingrid about his health. "I've been cleared to return to the kitchen, although not to actually cook. I just supervise. What a dream life! All the fun of a kitchen and none of the work! Never get my hands dirty and never have to clean anything up!"

"Don't listen to him," Jewel said, coming after him with their luggage. "Getting him to stop playing with food is like trying to keep a pig out of a wallow on a hot day. He says he's just supervising, but every time I go check up on him, there he is, in the kitchen, in front of a hot stove, sweating like a pig. And pigs aren't supposed to sweat."

"But you, Ingrid," Jon tried to change the subject. "You're more gorgeous than you were in Greenwich Village. How many years ago was it?"

"Too many," Ingrid answered. "Ten maybe? But we saw each other just last winter, remember?"

"Oh. Yeah," Jon said, stumbling over his words. "But. That was— I barely— I mean you were going skiing. I could barely get a good look at you."

Then Jon turned beet red, making the others fear he was unwell. They surrounded him and led him to the wingback Victorian that Ingrid had rescued from a dumpster in the East Village and had reupholstered. It was the most comfortable chair in the house.

"He's OK," Jewel said after some frightened looks from Dan and Ingrid. "I think he's just remembering the dress you wore the first time we saw you."

"I didn't think I could make that kind of impression," Ingrid laughed.

"There are new procedures that are promising," Jewel whispered to Dan later, out of Jonathan's hearing, "but I don't know, Danny. He doesn't seem to want to go through surgery. He wants to just go on the way he is. You see how he is. How long can he go on that way?"

"I don't see how he has any choice, Aunt Jewel."

"Danny, I'm so afraid of being left alone," Jewel said, almost tearfully.

"You won't be left alone, Aunt Jewel."

And for the first time that either could remember, he put his arms around her and they hugged each other. Jewel reacted almost as if unsure it was proper, but she was really unsure if it was true, if it could be true. He had abandoned her once already, but maybe, she thought, this new relationship he was building with Ingrid marked some sort of turning point. Maybe they would marry, have children. Grandchildren, she thought warmly, and something bright suddenly appeared in her vision of the future, dispelling the darkness. A grandchild! Someone to carry on, if not the Fairfax name, but what was more important, the rest of the heritage of her side of the family, their looks, their temperament, their genes. Her genes.

She brought up the matter of the stairs to break the tension both felt. One trip up and it was clear than Jon would have to stay downstairs.

"Most nights at home, he falls asleep in his easy chair by the fire," Jewel confided as she and Dan made up the single bed in the guest room, the downstairs guest room. "I've gotten used to sleeping alone."

Dan concentrated on the sheets that were coming off the bed. Would they reveal something?

"Don't worry," Jewel said, startling him.

She was referring to the dust bunny she had just kicked back under the bed.

"I have bigger ones at home," she added.

"That's not it," he began to explain.

But he went no further. What could he even tell his Aunt Jewel about it? What could she know about things like that?

When he crawled into bed at the end of the night, he was relieved that Ingrid was apparently asleep. The previous night it had been Dan who had pretended sleep when Ingrid had come to bed.

Having become completely accustomed to Vermont's tidiness and its classically proportioned architecture, Ithaca looked worn and dowdy to Jewel. She made sure to point it out. It was like going from the UVM campus in Burlington and into Winooski, Jewel whispered to Jon as they were being driven around. The whisper was loud enough for Dan and Ingrid to hear. Then she announced to all that she liked the Cornell campus much better than UVM's, but not Marlboro's or Bennington's. She agreed that there was nothing like the area's gorges in Vermont, however, even though she enjoyed them only from parking lots and scenic lookouts. Hikes into them were too much for Jon.

"Marjorie always raved about them," she said from the back seat of the old Buick Special Dan had bought used when he and Ingrid moved to Ithaca. "She insisted that I just had to see them. Well, now I have."

Their Finger Lakes sightseeing ended with a trip to a vineyard in Hammondsport. They found no one there but for an old man wandering among the vines in a worn coat. Thinking that he was some sort of caretaker for the vineyard, they asked about tours. He introduced himself as Dr. Konstantin Frank, personally gave them a tour, and invited them to taste some of the wines he produced. Having Ingrid sit on his lap while he sang to her in Russian seemed to be part of the bargain, but getting Jewel to do the same was beyond his powers. Failing that, he made her listen to why the Algerian grapes in Blue Nun wine were so bad for women and children. He bolstered his argument by producing a reprint of a scientific report linking the grapes to abnormalities in newly hatched chicks.

They skipped the obligatory hike through the Watkins Glen gorge in favor of an early return to Ithaca and a nap for Jonathan. Two cases of Finger Lakes wine rattled in the trunk of Dan's car. Jon closed his eyes in anticipation of the nap and nodded off in the back seat, his head coming to rest on Ingrid's shoulder.

"It's OK," she said to Jewel and Dan in front. "I just may close my eyes, too. We'll sleep together."

Jewel laughed at the remark. Dan did not.

"So, what's hot in ecology these days?" Jewel asked after a brief silence.

"Hubbard Brook. Acid rain. Island bio. Optimal foraging theory. Microtine cycles. Predator-mediated coexistence. Habitat patchiness and disturbance. Niche studies. Whether food resources control populations is still an issue. So is Robert MacArthur's broken stick."

"I think that warbler paper of his is still the best thing in the literature."

"Me too. And it's acquired lots of imitators. Dick Root's gnatcatcher paper is one."

"Root?"

"An ecologist here, The paper was from his dissertation at Berkeley under Pitelka."

"Frank Pitelka?"

"I think so. Why?"

"Just interesting," Jewel answered, her face showing something between joy and perplexity, "but never mind that. What about vegetation studies?"

"It's all ordination now."

"Like at Wisconsin?"

"Yeah. And biomes are synonymous with landscapes now, it seems."

"Is evolutionary ecology taking over, like it seems to me?" Jewel asked, adding to herself, like at that meeting at Robert and Betsy's cabin on South Pond.

"Yeah! There's even an Englishman, John Harper, who is doing community studies on plants that are a lot like Uncle Robert's warbler studies. He calls it Darwinian ecology for plants."

"What of Clements's superorganism? Dead and buried?"

"Dead and buried. Although there are a few holdovers like the Odums. And there's a lot of math to ecosystems. No more simple descriptive studies like you did with Shelford."

"Well, I still teach those old fashioned interactions between species and habitats in ecology. The kids love them. That and the environmental aspects of ecology. The balance of nature is big in that. I somehow can't give it up. I pretty much ignore all the theoretical stuff coming out in the journals. There seems not to be much point to it. I sometimes teach right out of that chapter in Silent Spring, you know the one. Thoreau, too."

"Never read Thoreau. What would be the point? None of his ideas can be used to generate even a single testable hypothesis."

"Oh, is that what you've become?"

"Hey!" Ingrid interrupted from the back seat. "What are you two cooking up up there?"

Jewel turned to ask Ingrid about life in Greenwich Village.

"No more folk music?" Jon asked on waking in the Victorian chair several hours later. Dan had an LP playing on his turntable.

"I guess Brubeck and the Beatles made me give up folk music," Dan answered. "Brubeck first. Take Five was all over the airways, remember? Brubeck banging on the heavy chords, keeping time while Paul Desmond flew elegant little rings of melody around them. Then Paul Morello threw Jackson Pollock musical paint at his drum canvas. The New York stations played the full five-minute version."

"I remember," Jon said. "It was almost creepy to listen to something that long, when everything else was around a minute fifty."

"Folk music just had nothing to compare. Tom Dooley? A jingle. Only Dylan could come close to the jazz musicians, but he was special. He was the only one. Jazz was full of talent, meanwhile, MJQ, Getz, Mulligan, Miles Davis, 'Trane."

"Don't forget Chet Baker," Jon interrupted.

"I knew folk wouldn't last," Dan continued without acknowledging Jon's comment. "So did Dylan. And then the Beatles showed up, and all the girls streamed to them. Then Dylan went electric."

"I remember that change the Beatles made, too," Jon said, laughing. "And all those short skirts."

"You can't credit miniskirts to the Beatles."

"I'll never forget," Jon said, shaking his head, "right around the corner from you, you know, where all the clubs and shops were and tourists crowded the streets. Jewel and I took a little walk there, for some reason. I guess we were tourists, too. There was this guy I remember, not all that much younger than I was then. He was dressed very formally in a black tie and jacket. He had a pair of high-heeled shoes in his hand and was looking for something on the sidewalk and shouting something back to someone behind him. I couldn't imagine. Looking for loose change to play the stock market? And then I saw. Following him was a beautiful young blonde in a sexy black evening dress. She was barefoot."

"Wanted to walk barefoot in the park, but not step on glass?"

"I think you got it!"

"Barefoot on Bleecker Street. She should have gone into Alan Block's sandal shop and bought some sandals, like all the Village girls did. He made you stand on a piece of cardboard so he could trace your foot on it. That was the template for your sandal."

"What was it, Dan?" Jonathan asked, suddenly serious. "Why did you run away? Was it me? Did I try too hard to be a father to you?"

Dan had no ready answer for the question. It had come at him like a sucker punch.

"Maybe I wasn't running away from anything," he said meekly. "Maybe I was running to something."

"Hmm. That I understand. Looking for something, huh?"

"I guess."

"Find it."

"No."

"Still looking?"

"I think."

"And what happened to all the posters you had on your walls then?" Jon asked. "You know, the ones with all the crazy lines that seemed to move if you looked at them too long?"

"Oh yeah, Op Art. They were Ingrid's. Still in New York, probably. Thank God for that. I got tired of feeling like I was dizzy or stoned all the time."

Jon laughed again.

"I've still got one of the lava lamps, though," Dan offered, then continued in a conspiratorial whisper. "The blue one. It's in our bedroom. The ugly orange one disappeared somehow, somewhere."

"And I always wanted to know, still wonder," Jon asked through his laughter, "whether you and Ingrid were, you know, an item, when Jewel and I visited you in the Village. Jewel had no doubt, but something didn't seem right to me. And if you don't mind my adding, I sense it's still the same."

Were they an item? Dan wondered, too. He lived with Ingrid. But so had others. Eric Weissman and Bob Dylan and Suze Rotolo and Peter Yarrow and Jack Elliot and Jean Redpath and maybe even Judy Collins, he thought—if that was who that Judy had been—and a number of others he no longer remembered or never knew, had lived with Ingrid in one way or another. Even sharing the bedroom with her meant nothing, at least until that night when he couldn't sleep and she invited him to climb down from his bunk into hers and then stayed in it with him. That should have marked a change. He could only remember it, though, as having been almost clinical. A hand on his cock, then lips until he became hard, then, awkwardly because of the low clearance from the bunk above, but expertly, it seemed to him, she lowered herself onto him. And then—did it seem now to have taken a long time? Apparently, it hadn't to her, not like it did later times. But the next morning had seemed no different than previous mornings. They were still roommates, best friends.

When did they become an item? That first night had not been it—or those that followed. Things had ended between them so seamlessly in Philadelphia that it could hardly have been called a broken relationship. And it wasn't. And it wasn't a relationship. It was only after he returned to the Village again that they became best friends and roommates and lovers all at once. Coming to Ithaca together had to have made them an item. Or had it?

Had it been weeks without sex until last Saturday, when she had closeted herself with Ricardo and planked down where Jonathan was now sleeping?

"You don't have to tell me, if you don't want to," said Jon, surprising Dan, but Dan knew he already knew.

"Ah, Jon," Dan said. "Didn't Socrates say that the unexamined life may not be worth living? I think neither may having to live through an examination of one's own life."

Dan was surprised at how interested Jewel was in all things ecological at Cornell. She had him take her around the entire campus. She poked into every lab, greenhouse, and other facility that was available to him for research.

She was suitably impressed with the elaborateness of the abandoned research facility set up in an old field that Dan and Mike Whalen wanted to take over. Then she warned him against doing thesis research on mammals, unless it was strictly taxonomic. There could never be enough time to learn anything about them in the field, she insisted. It took years just to learn how to collect them, and even then, the numbers were puny.

She thought that the Fly Lab, as the students had christened it, had a hilarious name, but that it looked every bit the way that sort of facility should. She wrinkled her nose only slightly on hurrying through it. She especially liked that it had an environmental chamber.

She insisted on barging into any ecology professor's office that was unguarded.

She liked Root for his endearing smile and eyes and the way that his students adored him, an impression the Peter Feinsinger confirmed when arrested for questioning by her in the hallway.

She adored Bill Brown. One curmudgeonly teacher recognizing another, Dan thought. Brown had not at first responded to them at his door, so absorbed he had seemed by whatever ant he had under his microscope, but Steven Handel, his graduate student, had nudged him awake, something that Handel said needed to be done more than just occasionally. Instead of talking to her about his research, Brown listened with interest to Jewel telling him about her experiences with Cowles at Chicago and the field trips she took with

Shelford to try to describe how animals fit into the biomes of North America.

She did not like Langmuir Lab, part of a research park built way out by the city's airport in the nineteen fifties to keep a General Electric facility from abandoning the area. When GE left anyway, Cornell moved its Division of Biological Sciences into it, so that now it housed the Section of Ecology and Systematics and the Section of Neurobiology and Behavior, with its member faculty, graduate students, and research facilities.

She did very much like Tom Eisner, whose office there they visited first. She liked him even before meeting him, because she used his research in her classes, especially the photos. She was impressed with the Cornell University rejection letter he had framed on his wall. She too had suffered from the crowds of GIs returning to classrooms and graduate laboratories, she told him. Eisner had then surprised Dan by inviting them into his lab and letting them peek at what Karen Hicks was doing with ants and woolly aphids and lacewing larvae. It was all about "wolf-in-sheep's-clothing" mimicry, he told them. He also promised to buy them drinks that night at the downtown restaurant where he and his close collaborator, chemist Jerry Meinwald, were to perform musically.

She kept LaMont Cole from his daily appointment with the airport bartender. It was her insistence that Elton's evidence for a four-year cycle in Arctic foxes was absolutely solid that did it. Cole insisted as vigorously that Elton had merely so impressed readers with his tales of cyclic irruptions in Ungava and Labrador that soon ecologists were believing that the tropics were stable in comparison to the Arctic, without a whit of evidence for either. Then he grumbled his way out of his office.

She disliked Paul Feeney, who had little time for them. She thought his British accent was exaggerated and his hair comb-over was ridiculous.

She was surprised that Peter Marks, a plant ecologist, seemed to her not to be doing plant ecology. It seemed to be more like ecosystem research to her. She asked him if he knew that Gene Odum had started out as a bird watcher and wrote the silliest dissertation.

She rushed right past Whittaker's office after a single glance, almost knocking over Bill Schlesinger as he came out of it, and kept right on going out of Langmuir Lab, passing by the offices of Peter Brussard, Brian Chabot, Tom Emlen, Likens, and Levin without a pause, hustling Dan all the way back to Comstock. They arrived there well in advance of the meeting Cathy Woodson had set up with Pimentel. His had been the only office Jewel had burst into, only to find it empty.

She liked Pimentel, especially his environmental research.

"But, you know, so many of the problems you're identifying with your studies are just a result of consumerism," she lectured the professor. "We knew all about that in the nineteen fifties. Have you read Kenneth Galbraith's The Affluent Society?"

Pimentel could only nod in assent before she resumed talking.

"And Murray Bookchin, or whatever the name he used in writing Our Synthetic Environment. You know Fred Küchler made it all very clear in those papers he wrote that got him censured by the Entomological Society. You surely couldn't have been a member then. Were you?"

"Fred Küchler is a good ecologist," Pimentel finally got the chance to say. "What the Ent Soc did was inexcusable. Most of us didn't even know it had happened."

Cathy Woodson's ushering in another visitor probably came as a relief to Pimentel, as it did to Dan.

She liked Cathy's red hair and asked her if she was going to go on for a PhD.

A big item on the agenda when their trip to Ithaca had been planned was a visit to Grandma Atkins. She lived at the other end of Tioga Street from Bill and Jamie. They had an apartment in a stately Victorian close to downtown and Cascadilla Gorge. Henry Miller, who had been the first graduate of Cornell's architecture school, had designed the house. Grandma Atkins' house was one of many small, nondescript ranch-style boxes at the other end of Tioga Street, where it ended in a meadow. No doubt, the meadow was zoned for future housing that was certain to come after some new war and new version of the GI Bill and new cheap building techniques. It made Dan hum Pete Seeger's Little Boxes. Visiting Grandma Atkins should have been one of the easiest items on their agenda to check off, but it became the most elusive.

Grandma Atkins could not always be reached, and Jewel kept putting off calling her, and even canceled a meeting that had been set up. Dan, although feeling an obligation to go see his grandmother, now that he lived in the same town with her, did not want to go see her by himself. He knew her not at all. They had never met. Taking Ingrid would have done little to allay his fear of the visit, so he put off going until Jewel could come with him. Now Jewel did not want to see Grandma Atkins either. Dan made no headway in learning why.

"Oh, I knew the Atkinses pretty well," she told him after some prodding. "We saw them a number of times after Marjorie married Jimmy. Even with the differences, we all got along together."

"Differences?" Dan asked, suspecting some sort of snobbery.

"Well," Jewel began, suddenly effusive, the result of the bottle of Konstantin Frank white they had opened, "your grandfather was a Yale man and Mother was a Connecticut College girl from a University of Michigan family. That put them in a kind of closed society. Marjorie and I played with Katherine Hepburn as girls, don't you know. The Atkinses were an Ithaca family, but Ithaca Guns all the way, not Cornell. I think they resented those of us with college educations. It was probably a town and gown sort of thing. Of course, Marjorie married Jimmy before she could finish high school, so that was never a problem with them. And everyone thought she was pregnant, but it was nothing of the sort. Your mom just fell completely head over heels for your Dad."

"How did they manage to meet?"

"Oh, sailing. Your Dad was quite a sailor. I think he started here, on Cayuga. It was quite a blow to him when he got hurt and had to give up the sea."

Dan waited for more. His only memory of his father was as a wheelchair-bound cripple.

"I think it was sex that kept them together," was what Jewel finally said.

What a jolt! Those nightmares again. Those horrid events that still woke him some nights. He very much wanted to know what they were, more so as they were hidden further in the past with every passing day. He had asked about it one way or another before, and she had never really given him a straight answer. He didn't expect one. But he tried once more.

"What was she like, my mother?" Dan asked, trying to make it sound innocent.

Jewel brushed him aside with "You know everything you need to know about your mother."

They never did go to see Grandma Atkins. Jewel was finally cajoled into making another phone call, and Grandma Atkins answered it. They set a time to meet on Jewel and Jon's last day in Ithaca. Then Jewel found a reason to get back to Vermont a day earlier and would not be dissuaded from leaving.

Dan had to go alone to see Grandma Atkins.

IV

THE Fly Lab was variously funded by the Ford Foundation, National Science Foundation, Rockefeller Foundation, and a few others in smaller amounts. Their goal was essentially to help feed the world and improve its environment. The Ford Foundation, for one, saw in Pimentel a way to train high-level agricultural scientists from all over the world in ecological principles. Pimentel's empire was minuscule in comparison to research institutes such as Sloan-Kettering or national laboratories such as Oak Ridge, but for a single academic scientist, it was substantial. When Earth Day caused the same expanding bubble in the ecological sciences that Sputnik had caused in the space sciences, new graduate enrollments in ecology at Cornell jumped from four to almost twenty in a single year, of which Pimentel had the funding to garner more than his fair share. He had more graduate students than any other ecology or entomology professor at Cornell, and for those crowded into his academic stable, unlike Shelford's at Illinois during Jewel's sojourn there, no one was out in the wilds of Utah or Cape Anne gathering data for a dissertation and freeing up office and lab space. Still, on this day in October, there were several prominent personalities missing from the Fly Lab.

Dan, Bill Dritschilo, and John Krummel were unsure who they were to find occupying places on returning to their little office enclaves from an early morning meeting around David Pimentel's desk. They had gathered in Pimentel's office to put the finishing touches on a study that entailed digging up and crunching numbers to tabulate the energy inputs in beef protein production. It had taken the better part of a year. It followed closely on the heels of Pimentel's previous study of energy use in agriculture. That one, now called simply, the "Corn Paper," had come out in print just days after the Arab states embargoed oil going to the US and caused rationing and lines at gas stations. Energy use in food production was suddenly a huge concern.

The meeting mostly had to do with minor changes suggested by the referees who had accepted it for Science. One change was major, though. Mark Westoby, the English postdoc who had replaced Larry Hurd, who had worked on the previous number-digging-up-and-crunching study, had asked to have his name removed from the list of authors for the new paper, by telephone, from the other side of the world, Australia. Somehow, Pimentel told them, the paper conflicted with Westoby's Marxist principles.

Westoby and Krummel had been the ones who had nicknamed the new study, "Meat," to differentiate it from the old study, "Corn." For that reason, Krummel was deferred to on the philosophical basis for Westoby's action, but he was as clueless as was Pimentel.

Besides "Meat," Krummel had so far distinguished himself by having tried to field an intra-mural basketball team. He had expected it to be formidable, given the height of several Fly Labbers. Unfortunately, only Krummel had even a modicum of basketball talent, and Krummel was not one of the tall ones. Whale assessed Krummel's skills at "Good enough to be a walk on at Wisconsin as either a shooting guard, if he could only shoot better, or a point guard, if he only could learn how to pass or dribble the ball." Buck was the tallest of the Fly Labbers, a full head taller than Dan, but he had refused to participate in team sports on some unspecified philosophical grounds. The lanky, long-armed Bill Dritschilo was tall enough, but as a former soccer goalie he preferred to position himself away from the others to grab outlet passes for easy layups or pop in fifteen-foot open jump shots which, given his three-pack-a-day cigarette habit, he was rarely open for. Whale loved the part of the game in which he knocked over both teammates and opponents to get a rebound, all the while oblivious to the referee's whistle. Postdoc Larry Hurd, another of the tall ones, had missed the first and every subsequent game. Soon, John, Don Nafus, who made a good center for Krummel's outside game, and Dan, who had been offered the position of coming off the bench as the sixth man, were the only ones showing up to play. The rest of the season had to be forfeited.

Krummel's hair was still the same dark reddish brown it had been as a student in Wisconsin's wildlife program, but it was beginning to recede on two salients from his forehead, and his red mustache was sloping downward like Elliot Gould's in M*A*S*H, which, not coincidentally, was his favorite movie and TV program.

Dritschilo was now a father and had traded in his three-pack-a-day habit for a briar pipe. Many pipes, actually, one of which was always in his mouth or in his hand. He was also growing a goatee. Dan thought it made him look like a skinny, bespectacled Pete Fountain, although with longer hair.

Dan still held on to the image that he had of himself when he came to Cornell, that of a folk singer. Other than replacing his limp with a shuffle, he was totally unchanged, he thought, from his undergraduate days at Penn.

"Well, anyway, I walk away from these meetings feeling absolved, as if I had gone to confession," Bill thought to remark as they negotiated their way through Cathy Woodson's cramped office. He had a special reason to feel absolved. Pimentel had asked him about the "C" he had earned in his Mammalogy class.

"Did you deserve it?" was how Pimentel had put it.

Yes, Bill had said. Then, maybe. Then no.

He always tried to understand general principles over details, he had defended himself. Mammalogy seemed to have none.

"So what about entomology?" Dan now asked. "You did well in Eickwort's class."

"Eickwort is a special teacher," John said.

"Hmm," Bill stopped to ponder. "I think being here in the Fly Lab surrounded with entomologists, I couldn't help learning all the details. Maybe if I'd been with the wildlife people, I'd have learned what they wanted."

"But no principles probably," Krummel said before peeling off in the direction of his office, as Dan and Bill stood at the door to the Fly Lab proper.

To get to their desks, they had to first traverse the "Great Hall of the Fly Lab." This was a miniature version of a warehouse room. Its shelves, painted a dreary grayish-green like its walls—hospital colors to Dan—held the research of graduate students studying genetic feedback through artificial systems that used vials of sugar and houseflies. The vials represented plants and the houseflies, herbivores. A plastic container with a lid in which the vials were embedded represented their world. The houseflies, honorary herbivores at best, were the only part of the system that was alive. There were various experiments underway using boxes and boxes of the plastic containers, on shelves that rose to head height. They filled up several rooms off the main one. The other rooms were smaller, but similar. In one of them was a door to what looked like a meat locker, but was in fact the walk-in environmentally controlled chamber in which Bill was currently doing an experiment with aphids on clover.

The first thing that greeted them on entering was the sight of Don Nafus's chameleon. The chameleon was not a pet, but a very important part of his research. Don had added it as a third trophic level. The chameleon was housed in a dry aquarium with flies that were shuttled in and out of fly boxes, as those vial-and-larval-media arrangements were called. The toothless chameleon sat motionless, absolutely indifferent to the flies, even those that alighted on him (maybe her), even those that did so right on his snout. No one ever saw it eat a fly. It sat the same way day after day, letting flies land on it.

The chameleon's equanimity toward flies was not shared by the graduate students in the lab. Copious amounts of flypaper hung down from the ceiling seemingly everywhere. A theory documented in the literature, that flies avoided pristine new strips of flypaper in favor of those already spotted with fly carcasses, meant that the flypaper was replaced only on reaching maximum grossness. There were also copious supplies of truly wonderful wire fly swatters close at hand in all areas for immediate resort against escapees. There was no theory, however, to predict that the flies would take to sitting on the chameleon.

Then Dan and Bill had to go through the "Troll Room." It was the Fly Lab's least desirable office location. The most desirable was in the building next door, on the third floor of Caldwell Hall, totally cut off from the Fly Lab. Its last occupants were the Two Dans, the ascetic-looking Udovic and the affable Olson. When one gave up his desk to take a faculty position in Oregon and the other to become a Woodward-Clyde consultant, the office reverted back to the Entomology Department. Alas, it was about to be given away to two students who had just moved with their newly hired professor from the University of Alabama. The current best office was a small, private room off another office off a hallway in the Comstock basement. Buck Cornell used to spend his days meditating in it. Mark Westoby had just left the separate cubicle in it. It awaited one of the missing, Elinor Terhune, the soon-to-be next postdoc. Don Nafus, whose face hair was still magic, and Mike Whalen occupied the space outside it. Whale had given up the contacts he had worn since he first donned a football uniform. He now wore granny glasses, and his hair, like Dritschilo's, was approaching shoulder length.

The Troll Room had also been named by John Krummel, who had started out as one of its denizens, as had most Fly Labbers. Its current resident was Chris Rose, who had decided to finish out the semester and return to Minnesota. Either the flies, or the smell of their larval growth media, or the mathematical intricacies of the genetic feedback model had turned out to be too much for him. Or maybe it was the poor prospect of getting a job in academia. Just that morning, he had announced to Dritschilo that he would not need any help with computer programming for his project. In order to "reproduce," the vials in the genetic feedback experiments needed the aid of a computer program based on Pimentel's mathematical model. The computer provided the concentrations of nutrients for each vial of the next generation in the experiment, based on the specifics being investigated. But it needed to be programmed to do so, something that was beyond Chris's abilities. Before Bill had left for class, Chris had whispered to him that he was not staying at Cornell. Being a Minnesotan, though, he was too polite to say why, saying only that he was going home.

Al Brick, who had one of the other desks in the room, was another of the missing. He was at the moment still in New Jersey, taking care of something having to do with the cranberry harvest at his family's farm. Tunde's desk had already been vacated.

Babatunde (no one knew his last name or even if he had a last name) was the last and most ominous of the missing He had failed to return from a visit home to Nigeria. There had been no issues, as there had been with Diane Fossey, whose failure to come to Cornell to work under Pimentel in some way was attributed to political unrest in her part of Africa. Conjecture had it that Tunde had been felled by the Field Examination. He had failed it twice. Language may have had something to do with that. It was certainly at issue for the language requirement that he also had failed to meet. According to Whittaker, who held sway over such things, a PhD in ecology from Cornell should be proficient in two foreign languages —or highly proficient in one. Proficiency was demonstrated by the ability to translate a scientific article in the chosen language with a dictionary or, for high proficiency, without one. Unfortunately for Tunde, neither Swahili nor whatever tribal language he spoke in Nigeria was acceptable for the language requirement. It had to be a language in which original research in biology was or had been published. English, perhaps as foreign to Tunde as German was to Krummel, was, of course, unacceptable. Dritschilo, who had been born speaking Russian, got through easily, while many others in the Fly Lab struggled in language classes or switched to entomology, which had no such requirement. Whale, who had also failed the Field Exam, was struggling with Portugese on the assumption that no one in Ecology and Systematics knew the language well enough to be able to judge his competence at translating it. He was troubled by rumors, however, that Whittaker was fluent in Portuguese, as he was rumored to be in all other languages. Whale suspected that a PhD in entomology might be in his future. The same fear troubled Krummel. Latin was of no help to him. He had taken it in high school, as recommended for a future science major, but it was not acceptable to the Graduate Field of Ecology and Evolutionary Biology. He was spending long hours learning Spanish, the universally acknowledged easiest language to learn of all those acceptable for the exam, to add to his high-school German. Pimentel still hoped that Tunde would return, but new people were rumored to be moving into the room. One was Mark Loye, a gregarious Coloradan who had been disowned by his thesis advisor, but picked up by Pimentel. The other was rumored to be an applied mathematician studying under Christine Shoemaker, a systems analysis and computer expert. She had no room available for him. Thus, Troll Room was an appropriate name. One never knew who was hiding in it.

Chris Rose was at the moment engrossed in his reading, so Bill and Dan went on through to their room, which had never been christened by Krummel. Nasser Zareh, recently having arrived from Iran with wife and children and a government scholarship, was at his desk. He was studying, as always. Next to him was Ida Oka, a short, stout, happy middle-aged Indonesian, soon to be leaving Cornell with his family. He jumped up from his desk to greet Dritschilo.

"It worked," he cackled excitedly. "Thank you, thank you."

He held a thesis box in his hands. Its contents, when turned in to the Registrar, meant that he would be returning to Bali with a Cornell PhD. The favor that Dritschilo had done for him was to provide a single control IBM punch card that caused the thesis materials Ida had on Cornell's main frame computer to be printed on 8 ½ by 11 paper, as required for a dissertation. Someone at the computer center had shook his head at Oka and said it could only be done by a computer expert—he had recommended himself—and for a hundred-dollar fee, at minimum.

Nasser's desk had belonged to Don Saari, whose mustache had been the best of all those that turned down in Elliot Gould-David Crosby-Frank Zappa-Emiliano Zapata fashion, which had pretty much been everyone's in the lab. Having had a jaundiced view on whether Pimentel's star was rising or falling, he had gone home to New Hampshire after failing his Field Exam. He took up antiques there. Soon after, it was noted that beards began to be added to mustaches. Dan's desk had been that of Don Saari's friend, Nelson Byers, who was similarly jaundiced, but who had managed to complete all four of the ecology core courses, pass the Field Exam, complete the language requirement, pass his qualifying exam (an oral grilling from his advisory committee), and complete and defend his dissertation, all while clean shaven. Now he was happy as an ecologist at the Patuxent Wildlife Research Center. Like Dan, Bill, and Mike, he had also been a Penn student, as had Art Shapiro, a Pimentel student from a few years before. Shapiro had also had a MacArthur pedigree, having studied under him at Penn. Coincidence?

Bill's desk had belonged to a student who had been found dead one evening with his head face down on it and an open, cyanide-filled killing jar next to it.

V

THE main entrance to Comstock Hall was up a short set of stone steps that faced Caldwell Hall, where most of the Entomology offices were, except for the few that were in Warren Hall. The other entrance was at the back of the building, into the Fly Lab. That was what gave the feel of a basement to the ground level, even with its sunny windows. It had been built to be a basement.

The indoor stairway that connected the two floors was used almost exclusively by the Fly Labbers, most often to go to and from the small meeting room that served as a gathering place in the morning and toward the end of the day. It had a coffee maker. It also dependably had someone to talk with almost any time of day.

Lee Miller was one. A former faculty member who had failed to get tenure in the department, perhaps the reason for his prematurely balding hair, Lee was technically employed by the Ecological Society of America as the managing editor of its journals. He did so out of an office in Caldwell Hall and, it seemed, the Comstock coffee room. He was a willing listener for anyone on any subject.

John Gowan was another. He supported his Dryden dairy cows and draft horses with his day job as Root's assistant, which seemed to require regular attendance in the coffee room. Besides animal husbandry and dairying, he was willing to offer an opinion on almost anything to anyone.

"I was always aware of systems in physics, such as the Periodic Table of the Elements," he had surprised Dan with that morning, his beard hairs bristling straight up on his chin in emphasis of a point, "and in astrophysics and the various classification schemes for stars and galaxies. Not to forget systems of the whole, like Gaia, the Big Bang Theory, religion, and occult cosmological systems such as Astrology and the I Ching."

John claimed active interests in cosmology, spacetime and particle physics, unified field theory, Einstein's life and work, evolutionary theory, the Earth sciences, paleontology, anthropology, human history, and, of course, ecology, entomology, and botany. John and Lee always sat on opposite sides of the room, perhaps out of fear of being trapped together in endless conversation. When Root happened to be in the coffee room, however, John put his beard hairs and coffee cup down.

Maurice Tauber was another regular. He considered himself to be next in line for the department's chair and was as open to discussion with graduate students as Gowan. His role in the morning coffee klatch seemed to be one of looking amused and asking questions, possibly in anticipation of the future.

The rest comprised a changing cast of other entomology professors and students. George Eickwort always brightened the room when he came in, which was much too infrequently for those in it, especially the ones who had taken his introductory insect biology course, which was almost all of the students. George Stockman, who kept his hair and face to military standards and preferred being called "Butch," even by students, on the other hand, brought a pall into the room with him. He was what Krummel said were called "Nozzleheads" at Wisconsin, meaning his specialty was economic entomology. He claimed an expertise in agricultural economics and accosted Pimentel students with allegations that the "Corn Paper" was rife with mathematical and factual errors, that it was a sloppy piece of work. Rumor had it that he had only been hired as a legacy in order to attract his wife from Alabama to Cornell's sociology department. Another rumor went through the male students that he had had sex on his office desk with his attractive blonde secretary.

Some, such as Pimentel and Ed Smith, the department chairman, could never be expected to make an appearance. Pimentel had Cathy Woodson making coffee downstairs. Smith took his coffee at home.

Dan and Whale were lingering over their coffee with Sandy Fiance, an entomology graduate student studying mayflies, apparently with the sole purpose of improving his success at fly-fishing. Field season was over. They could afford a leisurely coffee before going back downstairs to their research. In fact, they had already had a second coffee with that day's version of the Daily Sun at Willard Straight, after having scaled the path up through Cascadilla Gorge and under the suicide bridge. They had come from

Whale's downtown apartment, where Dan had been spending nights in a room recently vacated by a PhD student in agricultural engineering, rather than having to go home to the house in Danby, empty with Ingrid away in city again for a long stretch. Whale had vials and vials (and jars) of aphids that he had collected over the summer to study over the winter. Dan was beginning a new project having to do with fruit flies and parasitic wasps. Both projects had to do with genetic feedback. Both could be worked on after supper, when there were fewer distractions. For the time being, they were letting themselves be distracted. Since they expected to work well into the evening after dinner, they could let a particularly interesting coffee room discussion keep going until very late in the morning.

Then Mark Loye came in with Don Nafus. Miller and Gowan scattered as fast as they did when Stockman appeared.

"Hey guys," Mark greeted them warmly, a huge smile under his blonde mustache.

The mustache was neatly trimmed, as was his hair.

"How's it going?" he added, ignoring the fact that his greeting had not been returned and that Sandy Fiance was slinking toward the door. "Anybody watch the Broncos' game yesterday?"

"Mark," Dan answered him stiffly, "I gave up watching pro football when Y. A. Tittle retired."

Why Pimentel had picked up Loye was as much a mystery in the Fly Lab as why he had let Owen Sholes go a few years before. But then, the thinking in the Fly Lab went, Whittaker had picked up Owen Sholes. Maybe Pimentel was just paying back a favor to the plant ecologists. More important was that no one liked Mark Loye. Just his obsequious smile and whiny little voice, especially if punctuated by an annoying giggle, made their teeth grate.

"They should have kept John Ralston," Mark persisted. "He's totally radical. He was the coach at Stanford when I got there. And Craig Morton at quarterback? I'm afraid not! Weren't you a quarterback in college, Mike?"

"I was a linebacker at Penn," Whale grumbled with his head down.

"Oh? Penn State? Say, Joe Paterno is some kind of football coach, isn't he? Especially for linebackers."

"No, the University of Pennsylvania, Penn," Whale corrected.

"The one in Philadelphia," Dan added, rolling his eyes toward the heavens.

"Say, there's a lot of you here from that school. What's with that?"

"The admissions people still think MacArthur is at Penn," Dan remarked, then headed for the door, with Nafus behind him.

"Huh?" Mark grunted, sitting down beside Whale. "So is this Tunde guy really not coming back? Is that whole room gonna be mine?"

"Don't know," Mike said, getting up and following Dan out the door, but not back to the lab, stranding Loye like an abandoned puppy.

In fact, even with Chris Rose gone and Tunde not coming back, Loye did not have the Troll Room to himself. Alvan R. Brick was back and making his presence felt by having set up a stereo system there that was blasting out Fleetwood Mac's Rhiannon. He was James Dean in hair, dress, and mood, everything but the cigarette. He proudly proclaimed that he had been at Cornell "since the first Johnson administration." He had come for a summer program while still in high school, stayed on as an undergraduate, and now might possibly be dragging out his dissertation in order stay through several more presidential administrations. The dissertation was on swamps. Krummel thought that he might be "swamped by it." His genetic feedback research had to do with mosquito fish and mosquitoes. He did it sporadically, just enough to earn his keep with Pimentel.

Al was either up or down. Today, he was up, ready to take on the world, starting in Dan and Bill's office. Dan had to examine hundreds of fruit flies in search of ones that had been parasitized. He was finding none. All of Bill's materials—binocular microscope, specimens, pinning and dissecting implements, taxonomic works—were at his desk. Both knew that, tied to their desks, they would not be getting much work done with Al seated in the corner of the room, apparently listening to his music.

It did not take long before Loye, too lonely in the Troll Room, wandered in, too.

"So what happened between you and Marks?" Al asked him without ceremony.

Loye answered with candor, even if nervously. He spoke rapidly, smiled, laughed, and tried to joke his problems away. Dan had the impression that he really did believe his explanation that it was because Peter Marks was a liberal Democrat, while Loye was a conservative Republican, that he was changing professors. Pimentel having voted for Nixon for President in three different elections was at least consistent with that.

"Do you realize how like quicksilver Pimentel is?" Al suddenly almost shouted, as if to broadcast it throughout the Fly Lab. "The man manages to always get there first—or, at least, early. Energy in agriculture is just the latest example."

Dan looked around to see if Pimentel might not be in earshot. There seemed no other reason for Al's remark.

"Although genetic feedback was what made—and might possibly break— his reputation as an ecologist," Alvan continued.

"I think you're being a little harsh, Alvan," Bill countered, pronouncing it "Alvin." "It's true that the biocontrol people don't like it. It kind of undermines the entire basis for what they're doing."

"Huh?" Mark asked.

Bill turned away from his microscope and reached for a pamphlet atop a disorderly pile of reprints.

"Here. It's his nineteen sixty-eight paper. You should read it."

He handed the reprint to Mark, who took one glance at it and gave it back.

"Thanks," Loye said. "I don't think I need it. So, have you guys seen The Exorcist yet?"

"How about the use of the term feedback?" Al ignored Mark's question. "Perfect for its day. The debate over what regulates animal populations was already raging back then. HSS was published in nineteen sixty, wasn't it? Pimentel published his first genetic feedback paper in sixty-one. It was also right on the heels of Robert MacArthur's three influential papers. Genetic feedback was already there as a mechanism for the coevolution of species, even before Ehrlich and Raven."

"Three influential papers?'" Bill asked.

"It should be in quotes," Dan answered for Al. "You know, the ones in the fifties. Broken stick, diversity, warbler niches."

Bill decided he had had enough.

"It think I'd better go to the library," he announced as he stood up. "There's a reference there I need."

"Paul Ehrlich?" Mark asked, signaling that the name was familiar to him.

Mark had graduated from Stanford with honors, to Al's chagrin. He had also made top grades in the core courses and one of the highest scores ever on the Field Exam, both also to Al's chagrin.

"The butterfly and plant paper?" Mark persisted.

"Get me some fruit flies with parasites inside them while you're at it," Dan called after Bill, who was already into the Troll Room.

"No resistance?" Al asked. "These are the flies you got in South Jersey?"

"And from the orchards by the Gunks in New York. And what a great collecting trip that was!"

"And none show any resistance?" Al persisted.

"No, plenty did. Things were even beginning to look interesting. Maybe there is a north-south gradient. But then I mated resistant flies—they all had visible capsules with dead parasites in their abdomens—and nothing! The only flies that emerged after exposure to wasps were perfectly healthy. Not a single encapsulated fly out of thousands!"

Alvan wrinkled his brow and tugged at the sleeve of his white T-shirt, where, had he really been James Dean, a pack of cigarettes would have been rolled into it.

"That was the F1 generation," he said. "Wasn't it?"

"Yeah. So, what's your point?"

"Sometimes these things skip a generation," Al said simply. "Try the F2."

Dan slumped into his chair with a heavy sigh.

"So just breed all of these capsule-less flies and see what happens?" he asked incredulously, but Al was back on the subject of David Pimentel.

"I mean," he almost sang out to Loye, "distribution and abundance, invasive species and biocontrol, spatial effects, the interaction of trophic levels, competition and community theory, they're all there. And, of course, it actually combined population genetics and population ecology before Robert MacArthur did it

Ecologists   378

with his r and K selection. If only Pimentel had more math talent, he could have started the MacArthur revolution."

Dan swiveled nervously in his desk chair. Although he was grateful to Al for the suggestion he had just made, he still hoped that Al had not become rooted to his perch. Mark Loye, meanwhile, paced slowly, with babyish steps, but did not sit down.

"The math wasn't all that bad, Alvan," Dan said as Al caught his breath. "It's no worse than that paper that Levin made his first splash with. You know, proving that a community having fewer limiting factors than species could not be stable? Even some of Uncle—some of MacArthur's early papers had pretty primitive math in them."

"I didn't read that one by Levin."

Of course not, Dan thought. Alvan was no mathematician. Al was every bit the naturalist and scholar he described himself as.

"It was supposed to prove MacArthur's stability theorem by disproving its negation," he explained. "It's a silly piece of work, really, except for all the formalistic math. You know, lemmas and such."

"Sort of a Sophist trick?" Al asked. "But isn't that the paper that got Dr. Seuss's peregrinations on the meaning of niche into the ecological literature?"

"That it did," Dan agreed with a smile.

"You know," Al started again, "strip genetic feedback of its modern terms and you might find it in the Origin of Species. But what about that Polish devil?"

"Lomnicki?" Dan asked.

"Lomnicki?" Mark echoed. "Isn't he a linebacker for the Bears?"

"You have to be able to measure something in science," Dan said, ignoring Loye, "and testing an idea requires some sort of model to be tested. Pimentel's model was disappointing that way. Lomnicki is right, I'm afraid, although I don't see why he seems to want to make his reputation by publishing articles on the flaws in genetic feedback."

"So Levin couldn't help?"

He wouldn't let me help, Dan wanted to but did not say. Dan feared a common pattern was developing. The boisterousness had gone out of Al's voice. Soon it would be replaced by a leaden lethargy, and the world around him would be transformed as if by some conjurer's trick known only to Al into a dark, sad place, and his audience would be dragged down with him, ever deeper and deeper. Reasoning with him never worked. He was too bright for that. He could out-argue anyone. Escape was the only way out before Al's all-consuming final eruption left him purged of his despair, but at the cost of transferring it to his listener. Sharing how painfully Levin had crushed his attempt to apply fuzzy logic to genetic feedback with Al at the moment could only lead to Al spiraling down faster to his eruption point and leaving Dan smarting from a wound he had almost let heal.

"And so all the research we're doing—that Loye, here, is doing— is all a waste," Al said with finality.

"I don't think so," Dan said, unable to leave that little bombshell untended. "The projects with the fly boxes are testing the model. You and I are studying evolution between predators and their prey. Dritschilo is studying coevolution between herbivores and clover."

"And Levin can't help the others?"

"I think Levin would rather collaborate with Paine these days," Dan said. "Wouldn't you rather be out in the rocky-intertidal of the Washington coastline than the Fly Lab?"

"Amen," Al said. "But don't you notice that Loye is gone?"

He leaned back in his chair, smiling smugly. Dan breathed a sigh of relief, realizing that Alvan's entire argument had been a put-on to get rid of Loye.

"I learned that was a good way to get rid of him," Al explained. "Switch the topic to ecology. Pretty good trick, huh? But what is he doing here, I want to know, if he has no interest in ecology? He's in a PhD ecology program, for God's sake! He's not even interested in his professor's research! And while I'm at it, how can they make Levin the Chairman of Ecology and Systematics? He's a mathematician, for God's sake, not an ecologist! He doesn't know any ecology. We have to take all those core courses before we can call ourselves ecologists, not to mention two languages. Has Levin even had an ecology course? What does Levin have degrees in? Applied math!"

"What about Bill?" Dan asked, fearing that the eruption had not been averted, after all, and ashamed for possibly having goaded Alvan on.

"He's got two degrees," Al answered. "He's got one in bio. That's why he breezed through the Field Exam his first year here."

"What about me?"

"You're no mathematician. You're a special case. You were raised by MacArthur, who was also a special case. His paper on warblers was beautiful."

"It was one of my bedtime stories. So, now that Loye's gone, what IS your final word on Pimentel?"

"Don't know. How can we predict history? So, what's up between you and Ingrid?"

"I don't know, Al. If I did, I'd do something about it."

Wouldn't it be great, Dan thought, if Al would come back from New Jersey some time with a prescription for lithium? How nice would that be?

"Want me to ask Allison to find out? They seem to have hit it off pretty good."

"No," Dan said.

Al's wife had been too easily won over by the fashionable discards available to her through Ingrid to be trusted with a mission like that.

"It would take a pretty lengthy long-distance phone call, I'm afraid," he said instead.

And, as often happened when Alvan parked himself in the chair in the corner of the room, the afternoon was coming to an end. This day it was marked by an "All Souls" meeting, as Krummel called it, claiming that the only reason Pimentel had the meetings was to see who showed up. The only way he could keep up with "who was coming and who was going," according to John, was to schedule a meeting. That was why they were now always late in the afternoon. It meant no one could use a conflict with a class as an excuse not to attend.

"Cheerio!" could be heard from inside as people pressed through Cathy's room. It was followed by "Right-Oh," another British affectation with which Pimentel sometimes peppered his speech. They and others were holdovers from a sabbatical spent in England with Charles Elton some twenty years before.

Pimentel was in his usual corner, this time with a guest and Elinor Terhune, the new postdoc. The students crowded together near the door, also as usual. This time, though, they had a reason for it. A projector screen was set up in the far corner.

Dan and Al found empty seats on both sides of Judy Hough. She was a frail-looking girl from an academic family. She had the beautiful long hair that was associated with Blue Grass performers, which she was. To Dan, Blue Grass was what was left of Folk, and it was not its better part, but Judy knew that he had known Dylan and was always eager to chitchat with him about what Folk Music was back then, in his day, which always made Dan feel important.

The reason for the excess Britishisms by Pimentel was made apparent by his introduction of the day's guest speaker. Malcolm Slesser was a sturdy Englishman who was doing a book on energy in agriculture on the other side of the Atlantic. He was also famous for his mountaineering, Pimentel noted in his introduction, a nicety returned in kind by Slesser's plaudits for the "Meat" paper, which had just come out in print.

"Do you use system analysis in your studies?" Slesser asked at the beginning of his talk.

No one answered.

"Do you know system analysis?" Slesser, a PhD engineer, pressed them further.

Then he started drawing boxes, representing processes, and arrows, for inputs and outputs, on the blackboard. Bill and Dan looked sheepishly at each other from across the table. Both realized that they had been doing system analysis since their second year in college, but had never known it to have a name and rules. It was just common sense to them. What goes in must come out, unless it accumulates or is consumed somehow.

No one volunteered a question for Slesser, not even one on mountain climbing. Pimentel had to break the embarrassingly long silence at the conclusion of Slesser's talk with a question. Another from Elinor Terhune followed it, a long one, probably also out of politeness. Whale had already judged her to be "a damned sight better to look at than Westoby," even describing her face as "a fragile flower." She held the rapt attention of all the men, Slesser and Pimentel foremost, through her entire, lengthy preamble.

Ecologists

The two women around the table, soon to be joined by others, marked a turning point, unrecognized as such, in the Fly Lab. Its climate changed. Cleanliness and order improved. Language, too, was cleaned up. Girls had been, before, merely techs or secretaries. Now they were fellow grad students and postdocs. A poster, rather innocuously advertising the Cornell showing of Deep Throat, disappeared overnight, culprit never identified, after having been taped to the door of a room by one of its (male, of course) denizens.

Then, thinking that Elinor was finished, Loye, sickly smile on his face as he always, broke the spell. Apologizing for his interruption, he asked Slesser and Pimentel how their work was received. Slesser's having yet to come out, the question was clearly aimed at Pimentel, however.

"Ecologists liked the study," Pimentel answered. "Entomologists and agriculturists felt that I should stick to entomology."

Al Brick jabbed Dan in the side at Loye's next question, almost knocking Judy Hough from her chair. It was a long question about the origins of the study, made even longer by Loy's clumsy inclusion of terms such as "brilliant," "accolades," and "classic."

"Look at him!" Al whispered angrily. "He's trying to score points."

Dan had to suppress a giggle. Judy remained sitting stone-faced between them.

"That is a long story," Pimentel tried to brush Loye's question aside, as if from modesty.

Loye persisted, however, causing Pimentel to once more relate his involvement in a National Academy of Science panel in which he had suggested that energy was going to be important to agricultural research in the future. None of the other members of the committee agreed with him.

"But I was convinced that I was correct and they were incorrect."

Was it typical of successful people, it made Dan wonder, that at crucial times they decide to follow their own ideas, no matter how unsupported by "those in the know?" Mountain climbers intent on scaling unclimbable peaks came to mind. Dylan had been like that. Gene Likens, too.

He remembered Likens telling about a similar episode. It had to do with whether New Hampshire granite bedrock truly is imporous to water, as the assumption went when he and Bormann, both young professors at Dartmouth then, had initiated their Hubbard Brook watershed studies. Geologists always expected cracks and such to complicate flow, even in bedrock. Dan had wondered whether Likens had obtained advice that the geology might not be as simple as originally thought, but had ignored it. So he had posed the question to Likens at the end of the class.

"That's absolutely right!" Likens had answered, laughing his hearty Midwestern-salesman's laugh. "That was what I was told, but I went ahead anyway. That's been my view all the way along. Well, it may not work, but let's try it."

But is it also true, Dan wondered, that for every success story of someone stubbornly sticking to their guns, there is some number of much more capable, much more worthy individuals who did so in a hopeless cause and faded into obscurity? Shouldn't young researchers know that those exemplars of success through insight and hard work depend as much on pure luck and specific circumstances as on genius? What would Likens be today, if the bedrock had been so fractured that the watershed leaked all over the place like a sieve?

"Anyway," Pimentel continued, now speaking as much to Slesser as to Loye, "I set about putting together the data myself. How to go about it? How to get the manpower together? How to do all this without funding? I started a course and did not give the students a choice of topic."

The students had been mainly his own graduate students.

"Where did you get the idea for the paper in the first place?" Loye persisted.

"Had you heard about Howard Odum's remark about potatoes being made of oil?" Krummel thought to add.

"I knew about Tom Odum's book and an earlier publication," Pimentel said. "He didn't make any quantitative assessments of energy use in agriculture. Thus, his paper was of no help to us—other than providing a philosophical perspective."

And then he called an end to the meeting.

"So, how many courses is Pimentel running now?" Dan asked Bill as they headed down toward Cascadilla.

Whale, who normally walked up with them in the morning, had taken to mysteriously disappearing in the afternoons, often not returning until well after midnight—or not at all. He refused to give up even a hint as to what he was about, not even to his fellow Penn grads and Fly Labbers, but he had given Dan a key to his apartment. Bill and Dan were left with only their own wild guesses. Dan kept his to himself. It had to do with Ingrid and those times that she was away.

"A bunch," Bill said of Pimentel's new venture. "It's hard to tell, actually, because the course is broken down into groups. You never got in one?"

"I've got to get my dissertation done. Besides, I'm not sure I want to be known as an energy analyst. Nuclear power is going to make the whole energy problem go away. I came here to be an ecologist like my Uncle Robert—or Aunt Jewel."

"Pimentel's repertoire has grown. There's a study on flood control. I'm working on the one on food standards. There are others, all packed with lost-looking undergraduate students. His table has become a factory for producing studies for the pages of Science. What he's got is like a machine, well oiled with money, to spit out environmental study after environmental study. I'm going to volunteer for as many as I can. If you ask me, what we're doing is putting hard numbers on what Earth Day was all about."

"Hey," Dan said after clearing his mind of environmental issues by thinking about birds while they silently negotiated a steep set of steps. "We've already got two articles in Science in the same year."

"We do," Bill answered and stopped in his tracks.

A smile lit up Bill's face. A frown appeared on Dan's face. Birds gasping for breath in a pesticidal haze had crept into his image of warblers in coniferous forests.

"Not bad," Bill said. "Let's have a drink to celebrate. In fact, let's have several and not bother to drive back up the hill tonight. You can stay at Whale's again, can't you?"

"Depends. What have you got?"

"We better go get something."

"How about a big bottle of Lancers?"

"You're on. Sounds as good to me right now as the Lafite-Rothschild that Westoby brought to that party. Remember?"

"How could I forget? Nineteen fifty-three was a very good year for a Marxist vintage."

"Are we still Marxists?"

"Marxists?" Dan laughed.

"I don't think we're even activists any more."

"Yeah, all that has passed us by, I think. We still have a joint once in a while, though. That's something.

By then, they were well into the gorge.

"This is a lot easier going down than up."

"Tell me about it. Except when there's ice. Then downhill is just as bad. I do this every day until snow fills the gorge. Then I walk up that little winding road, whatever it's called, that goes up beside it."

"Not University Avenue?"

"Sometimes I take that. It's the longer way, so not as steep. Depends how I feel. But do you remember when we were going to occupy the ROTC building? When was that? It was some years ago."

"Seventy-one? Seventy-two?"

"Was it fall or spring?"

"Had to be spring. No one did stuff like that in the fall."

They were at the bottom of the gorge. There, the river became a concrete-lined flood control channel through the city. In spring floods, boulders rolled against its side, sounding like distant cannoning at night. Dan stopped.

"Did we do the right thing?" he asked, holding Bill by the elbow.

"What? Not taking over that demonstration?"

"No," Dan said. "I mean, coming here, to Cornell, to the Fly Lab. Are we doing any good? Everything here is so geared toward academics, even the Corn and Meat papers. Weren't you the one that Whittaker told that E and S didn't want the kind of students who wanted to work for consulting firms? Can we only succeed here by being either Robert MacArthur or Gene Odum?"

"I thought Robert MacArthur was what you wanted to be."

"I wanted to be the Bob Dylan of ecology. I thought this fuzzy logic thing would do it for me."

"Hmm?"

"I guess I didn't tell you. It was an idea I had about a new kind of computer programming. I thought it might be a way out for Pimentel with this Lomnicki problem."

"Yeah, go on."

"It's based on outcomes being neither deterministic nor fully stochastic."

"Neither real nor random. Hmm."

"It's like playing cards with a joker in the deck. I thought it was a great way to model things that can't really be solved with normal math."

"So?"

"So, Pimentel sent me off to Levin with it. Levin blew it out of the water. And me! Not only did he think my idea was stupid, but I think that he thought I was stupid, too. Try something like Dieter John did, he told me, instead of my own ideas. So much for my shaking up ecology."

"Ah, let it go. It might all have turned out like my attempt at applying dimensional analysis to food webs."

"Buckingham Pi?"

"Yeah. What a waste."

"At least you got to try it out."

"Have we done the right thing?" Bill repeated with a sigh. "You mean morally? Philosophically? Practically? I think we haven't done anything yet in our lives. It's all in the future for us. So far, I think it looks good. Don't forget that the other *Science* paper is theoretical. We'll get academic jobs. Then we can contribute to moral integrity and social progress or mathematical inexactitude or whatever you want."

"So, where the hell do you think Whale is?"

"Beats me. You were his roommate."

"Then I'd say he's somewhere releasing his pent-up aggression. Maybe he found a pickup tackle football game somewhere."

"Do they do that in the middle of the night, too?"

Their other *Science* paper was a graduate-student-only production. Pimentel had had no input to it. It was the sum of many coincidental factors, without any of which it never would have happened. Buck

Cornell had not yet left for Delaware was one. Another had been Robert Ricklefs' visit to Cornell to give a lecture in that semester's ecology core course.

Normally, ecologists who came to Cornell were sequestered away from campus at Langmuir. Dick Root, however, was not based at Langmuir. He was a bird ecologist who had been hired by the Entomology Department. His dissertation had been on the niche of the Blue-gray Gnatcatcher in the Carmel Valley. Now he was studying insects on collard greens and struggling over the ethics of having once accepted funding from a pesticide manufacturer for it and how to fit the work into mainstream ecology. He managed to make his collard patches seem non-agricultural in his papers, developing a concept of community for insects found on them, coining the term, component community, for it, but he probably emphasized agricultural implications in grant proposals.

"You used to be a pretty good ecologist," Frank Pitelka, his California mentor had once joked on a visit. "What happened to you?"

It had not struck Root as funny. He still very much considered himself a bird ecologist. Maurice Tauber, from his favorite place at the Comstock coffee table, thought it funny, though. He had had a good laugh.

It was with seeming trepidation then that Root abandoned bird ecologist Ricklefs, who he had been squiring around, to the Fly Labbers and Nozzleheads in the Comstock Hall coffee room while he attended to some business at his Caldwell Hall office. That had been another of the coincidental factors. The rising young star had immediately drawn a crowd from the ecology students, mostly Fly Labbers, who awkwardly tried to start a conversation with him. Ricklefs acted as if he were singularly uncomfortable and showed relief when Root returned to rescue him.

The crowd began to disperse.

Bill, who had been glowering at Ricklefs all the while he was there, turned to Buck and said, "Ricklefs refused to give me a recommendation to Cornell."

"What?" Buck had asked, sitting back down in acceptance of a duty to hear Bill out.

"Back when I was applying here," Bill started to explain. "He said he only gave recommendations to students who got A's in his classes. I got A's from him. He said that only applied to students he had had in something like a small seminar. I was in his ecology seminar. There were only a dozen people in it. I know that there'd been my alternate service in between, but that should not have been long enough for him not to remember me. Hell, I was in the first ecology class he ever taught and one of his first senior seminars. I think he just thought of me as an engineer and wrote me off. He kept looking over at me just now, pretending not to recognize me. He didn't say word one to me."

"Well, but you're here," Buck had said. "Now show him that he was wrong."

"Bill, you nitwit," Mike Whalen had suddenly come out of nowhere to say. "Of course, he remembers you. But how could he have agreed to write you a recommendation, when he had already written one for me, calling me the kind of student who comes along only once in a lifetime? How could he write the same thing about you?"

"Thanks, Whale," Bill had answered, his disbelief obvious.

"What else are roommates for?" Mike had smiled and said before dashing off somewhere.

It had been at the beginning of his mysterious disappearances from Ithaca.

"So, what was it you were trying to talk to Ricklefs about?" Bill had turned to Buck in another in the series of too many coincidences to continue to identify every one.

"He didn't seem to pay much attention. He must be having a bad day. I asked about Paul Opler's recent paper. He didn't know much about it."

"Opler?"

Buck explained the study. It was based on an idea by Dan Janzen that was inspired by MacArthur and Wilson's now almost sacred Theory of Island Biogeography. Reasoning that plants were very much like islands to the insects that fed on them, Janzen had hypothesized that the greater the area in which a plant was found, the more insects would be found on it. Buck wondered if the same thing could be done for birds and their parasites. Having just finished his dissertation, parasite ecology had been much on his mind.

"Not birds," Dan had suddenly appeared to suggest.

He had not yet taken the advice that Aunt Jewel had given about not working with mammals. Mammals were still very much on his mind. And the idea of adding a wrinkle to one of Uncle Robert's theories was too exciting for him not to enthusiastically push for the project, even if it turned out to involve something as unattractive as ticks.

Each suggestion was followed by another, and soon they and Don Nafus (again!) were making a trip to see Barry O'Connor, who had briefly been a Fly Labber, but had by then been studying the taxonomy of mites. After several nights of going through printed sources, measuring areas from maps, and entering data onto IBM cards for computer analysis, they had a paper to write. What the reason had been for Bill to be the first author was lost along the way, but all felt it to have been a good choice by the way he had ushered the project to completion and acceptance in Science.

John Krummel, of course, had suggested its title, "Of Mice and Mites," even before they had left the coffee room to go in search of O'Connor.

VI

THEY worked hard and they partied hard. If it wasn't at Johnny's Big Red in Collegetown on a Friday night, it was down the street at The Palms, and it was because Johnny's was too crowded to have their usual table free. Or it might be at the Chapter House, where the avuncular Bill Brown might treat them to a beer and sit down to share it with them. Or one of the downtown bars avoided by the college crowd. Or it might be up the lake shore at the Rongovian Embassy in Trumansburg, just down the street from the workshop in which Robert Moog built the music synthesizers that were sweeping through pop music. The beer there was the cheapest and the ambiance the best for talk—you did not have to shout to be heard, at least not until the bands began playing.

Or, if it was a Saturday night, they could go directly to Bill and Jamie's downtown apartment or, more rarely now, Dan and Ingrid's rented farmhouse. Buck and Sally's trailer was greatly lamented for no longer being a Saturday destination.

Krummel, whose idea it had been to drive out to Trumansburg, now that he had a car, was in a celebratory mood. He was trying to get some of the others to stay to hear the band. No one else had heard of them, however, and they were all being non-committal. John was celebrating a middle-of-the-night release from jail. Feeling a need for personal transportation, and needing a way to get to his field sites, he had gone to Wisconsin to purchase a 1961 Volkswagen Beetle. Requisitioning a truck from the Entomology Department motor pool had become impossible for him once Ed Smith, a gentlemanly southerner who was scrupulously frugal with entomology resources, had learned that John was officially an ecology graduate student. Worse still, he was studying crustaceans, not insects. That meant no truck for him. Not having the time to go through the registration procedure in Wisconsin, and reasoning that there was no need for it, since he was to be back in Ithaca the next day, John had taped a muffler receipt onto the passenger side of the windshield and set off on the interstates, without registration and without license plates.

"I can't believe I got as far as I did," he confessed. "So when I got off the Thruway, I thought I was home free."

"They got you up by Geneva, did they?" Don Nafus asked.

"No! Ovid, of all places. That's what makes it so hard to believe!"

"So what did you do?" asked David Gallahan, a likable new Fly Labber with a chin beard out of the nineteenth century.

As much as the falling status of Pimentel's genetic feedback theory darkened the outlook of the students that Dan's cohort had replaced, he noted that the rising prestige from Pimentel's environmental studies was brightening the outlooks of those replacing them. Or maybe it was just something like the enthusiasm of youth, Dan thought on considering the new students around him.

"What could I do? I went to jail! Bail was set at eighty-four dollars. I guess that was what the total of the fines would be for all the laws they claimed I broke. I had no money left after paying the Thruway toll. I couldn't think of anyone else to call but Pimentel. Can you believe that?"

"Pimentel got you out?" Gallahan asked.

"Al Brick!" John exclaimed, hands in the air.

"Al?" It was a revelation that took everyone by surprise.

"Pimentel didn't have that kind of money lying around. It was after midnight. So he called the Fly Lab. Can you believe that?"

"Al Brick had the money?" Dan asked.

"He was in the Fly Lab in the middle of the night?" Don Nafus asked simultaneously.

"Yeah. And he had some kind of bank card. But he only got twenties, and no one at the police station had change. Dunkin' Donuts was already closed, so Al had to go back home to get change. It was all in coins. I think he robbed his kid's piggy bank. I finally got out about three in the morning."

"Why was he in the lab?" Dave asked.

"You still haven't learned the ways of our Alvan R. Brick, have you?" John answered. "He'll go without sleep for days sometimes. I've left with him being the only one in the lab at night and come in the morning—"

The rest of Krummel's explanation was cut off by Bill Dritschilo pushing through the door. He was holding a copy of the Ithaca Journal in front of him like a shield.

"Wisconsin man arrested in Ovid," he cried out.

"Oh no," Krummel groaned, realizing it was describing him.

The questions that Nafus and Gallahan had in their heads about how and why Pimentel had contacted Al Brick, or why Krummel thought a muffler receipt would work in place of temporary papers—or why even a muffler receipt—stayed unasked.

"No!" Linda Jaconnetta groaned even louder.

She was another new Fly Labber. All of the lab veterans claimed that she reminded them of Tony Bellotti, a favorite of all, who had been from that part of Brooklyn that is in Staten Island, and had an accent that was identical to Linda's. Some of the women students—and there were more and more of them suddenly flooding the Fly Lab and ecology classes at Cornell—suspected other reasons for her popularity.

"Wisconsin man," Krummel groaned, reading the brief paragraph that documented his infamy. "It makes me sound so criminal. Couldn't they have said Cornell graduate student instead?"

"You're lucky it didn't say something like Fly Lab inmate," Gallahan joked.

"I'm surprised they even printed something like that," Jaconnetta said. "You have to be arrested for murder to get into the papers in Brooklyn."

"Enough of it!" John announced. "So, how was the seminar? We didn't think you'd be able to make it here in time."

It was Bill's turn to groan.

"I didn't stay through it," he told them.

"No good?" Don asked.

"Why not?" Ilse Shreiner, another new Fly Labber, asked from her seat next to Don.

"It was Paul Ehrlich, wasn't it?" Dave asked.

"Yeah," John added. "I heard him lecture at Madison. He's always good. That checkerspot butterfly work is really cool."

"Hey look, there's Whale!" Dan almost shouted. "Who's that with him?"

"Where?"

"Over by the bar."

"Wow!" Bill exclaimed. "That little slip of a girl? I almost didn't see her, even though she's standing right in front of Whale. She must be half his height and one-quarter his weight."

"That doesn't scale right," Dan corrected. "If she's half his height, she should be one-eighth his mass."

"That would make her thirty pounds. I don't think so."

By then, Whalen had spotted them in the back of the room and was bringing a pitcher of beer over to them. The tiny young lady was a step behind him.

"This is Jacki," he introduced her, "without the e. She's at Keuka College."

"Hi," Bill greeted her. "Pleased to meet you. So, what are you, about five-foot two?"

"Thank you," Jacki said uncertainly. "I'm actually closer to four eleven."

"And about ninety pounds," Dan guessed.

"That works," Bill said.

"How can you do cube roots in your head?" Dan asked.

"What?" Jacki asked.

"I don't," Bill said. "I multiply fractions instead."

"They're practicing their math on you," Ilse tried to explain.

"By the way," Mike suddenly spoke up. "We got married last night."

Stunned silence turned uneasily into a round of congratulations. That then subsided into bewildered questioning.

"So what happened at the lecture?" Dan asked, turning back to Bill after bewilderment lulled into embarassed silence.

"I got there just about when it was scheduled to start," Bill began. "I had to trade off the baby with Jamie. There weren't too many seats left. There was one next to Whittaker, but of course, well... Then I saw that Dick Root was pointing LaMont Cole my way. There's one of the authors right there, I heard Root say."

Before going on, Bill greedily took a few gulps of the beer John poured for him.

"I figured it had to be the Science paper they were talking about," he continued. "I walked over holding out my hand. I think I expected a handshake and maybe even a few words of praise. Jesus, with a wife and new baby, I need all the positive stroking I can get."

"Don't we all. So?"

"So," Bill said, "instead of a handshake, I got the kiss-off from Cole. Terrible, he blurted out when I asked him what he thought about our study. He shook his head instead of my hand. He might even have repeated himself. I didn't know what to say."

"Did he say why?" Dan asked, obvious concern in his voice.

"Ehrlich was already at the podium with whoever was about to introduce him—the behavior guy—"

"Emlen?" Dan guessed.

"Yeah. I think so. Anyway, he was making throat-clearing noises. Even though I'd been looking forward to that seminar—planned my whole week so I could go to it—I left. I slunk out the back."

"Cole's an alcoholic," Whale tried to console him as his new bride looked on with a bored expression on her face. "Don't listen to him. Loye says he's always sneaking off to have a drink at the airport. Even in the morning."

"You should take him off your committee," Nafus said to Dan.

"Still, he's a big name in ecology. But there's worse," Bill continued as John poured the rest of the beer from the pitchers at the table into Bill's glass. "Milton Timm followed me out and stopped me. He wanted to warn me that Ric Mendez had overheard Whittaker and Feeney talking about me and Dan and the paper. His news was not good. Whittaker, according to Mendez wanted to check into policies to see if something could be done about students publishing on their own. So that it doesn't happen again, Milton said."

"What did that mean?" Dan asked.

"Can he do that?" Gallahan asked.

"Who knows what Whittaker can do?" Krummel put in. "I'm sure he could control the weather around here, if he wanted to."

"Milt couldn't say," Bill answered Dan. "Or maybe I didn't ask. I just wanted to get out of there."

"Milton Timm is a pretty straight guy," John observed, "even if I'm more jive than he is."

"Mendez isn't," Dan said.

"Professional jealousy?" Ilse asked with remarkable insight for a new Fly Labber, even in missing the mark slightly, having no idea about the main reason for Dan's coldness toward Mendez.

"He seems to need to be the big cheese here," she added when she realized that everyone was looking at her.

Nafus, who never drank and never talked about it, just like he never talked about Viet Nam, now offered to buy more beer.

"Not for me," Dan said. "Ingrid's here. I've got to go to a party at some Ithaca College people she knows."

"Good luck with that," said Krummel. "Staying to hear Orleans is a much better prospect."

"Nah, I'm going home, too," said Bill.

"Us too," Whale said, getting to his feet and gallantly offering assistance to Jacki. "We have places to go."

"Nice girl," Dan said, watching them leave.

"Beautiful girl," Bill said. "Didn't talk much, though."

"Can you blame her?" Ilse chastised. "You guys almost dissected her before you even said hello."

"Was that wrong?" Bill asked.

"Intellectual curiosity," Dan said, rising from the table.

"You could have at least asked her what she was doing at Keuka," Ilse suggested.

"What could she be doing at Keuka?" Bill asked, also standing up. "Tradition has it that the goal of all Keuka women is a Cornell man. She'll have to settle for Whale."

"Do you think they're really married?" could be heard as Dan and Bill went off.

"Come on," John pleaded to the others. "Stay. Dance with Me is a really mellow song. You've gotta hear it."

Krummel was soon left with only Linda Jaconnetta. She had come with him in the VW.

"You know, Keith, my advisor at Wisconsin, said they used to shout Cole's name at babies to frighten them," John said, for want of anything else to say.

"Why would they do that?" she asked.

"Keith did a lot of the research on wildlife cycles. I guess he and a lot of other wildlife people had built their careers and reputations on it. Cole claimed that there were no rabbit or lemming cycles. He said that by just pulling playing cards out of a deck you would have, on the average, every third card being high. Like a peak. That was the three- and four-year cycle, as far as he was concerned. He said you also got a ten-year cycle from those three-year peaks."

"No. I mean, why would they want to frighten babies?"

Krummel shrugged his shoulders. Then he laughed.

"Want to stay for the band?" he asked.

She smiled.

The party Dan and Ingrid went to was at an apartment in a large downtown Ithaca Victorian. He wasn't feeling good about it—or much of anything—after what Bill had just told him, but it was so rare that he and Ingrid did things like it together that he persevered. Their hosts were a young couple. The husband, Ted, had just graduated and was working at a local bank. He was clean-cut and clean-shaven, sparkly neat and clean, as befit someone hoping to rise in the banking business. His wife was just as fresh-faced and wholesome. They were Ken and Barbie, Dan thought, as prospects for an interesting evening deflated even more. Cheryl, the Barbie of the couple, was to have finished her final requirement for her degree in marketing just before their wedding. That requirement was supposed to have been an internship in Ingrid's fashion house. Ingrid had come up to Ithaca especially for their party.

Cornell was on one hill above Ithaca. If you knew the right places—such as the Johnson Museum—you could get a dandy view of Cayuga Lake from the campus. Ithaca College was on another hill. Its campus had much better views of the lake, a fact unknown to

Cornellians. They had no reason to know. Cornellians rarely mixed with Ithacans. The total view was rosier from Cornell than from Ithaca College.

Three other couples had been invited. Two were Ted and Cheryl's former classmates, the other, an Ithaca College professor and his stringy-haired his wife. A fourth couple could not make it.

"That's really too bad," Ted said to Dan. "Greta and her husband are both Cornell professors."

"Greta?"

"Greta Lomborg. She's a sociologist. I'm afraid I don't know her husband very well, but I thought you might get along. She's this spectacular dark-haired Swedish beauty."

Dan regretted the loss. He found the other couples about as interesting as he expected Ithaca College people to be. They offered no distraction from the flap over the Science paper, and he just could not let go of the injustice of it. He wondered if it could be something personal with Whittaker. Every one of Dan's approaches to him concerning his dissertation work had been met with stony silence. No, Dan corrected himself. It had been an irritated silence. Had he offended him in some way? Was it retribution he was taking. Could he? A cold shiver passed through him.

The awkward small talk around him became more awkward when Ted passed around an album of pictures he had taken of Cheryl on their wedding day. Among them was a very well focused Polaroid of the bride naked, facing the camera in a yoga position on an undisturbed bedspread. Had it been in color, it could have been a centerfold in Playboy. Dan passed it on without comment.

"Wedding night?" the professor asked.

His wife sneaked a glance over his shoulder.

"Nice bubbies," she laughed.

"I think so," her husband agreed with an undisguised leer.

"I think it's the best picture in the album," Ted said. "I think it's the best picture I ever took."

"Go ahead and look," Cheryl urged. "I'm proud of it, too."

"Not skinny enough to make it big time as a fashion model, I'm afraid," Ingrid said on studying the photo. "Not that I wouldn't trade my business to have your breasts."

She handed it back to Dan for some reason. He examined it again, this time feeling himself under examination. Looking at a naked picture of a woman who was in his presence was unsettling compared to coming upon an actual naked woman while skinny dipping at the reservoir. That was natural, accidental. Eyes could be modestly averted after the unexpected peak. This was lurid, deliberate. There was no doubt what he was looking at. Still, he took his time.

Full breasts. Firm. Nipples high and virginal.

Innocent face. Also virginal.

Then an unexpected fear came on. Five couples—and only couples—he realized. And a naked picture of the hostess being passed around. Was that what Ingrid had come back to Ithaca for? Did she already know what was about to take place? And what would he do, if his suspicions were as well founded as his discomfort?

But the conversation in the room made it unlikely. Cheryl was describing in clinical detail how her internship had come to an end. She was supposed to have been an office assistant to Ingrid to start. Then she was to move on to helping with design. Crohn's disease had flared up, however. Every morning.

"I would have had to have the phone moved to the bathroom," she was saying. "And it wasn't just diarrhea. It was scary bloody. And no sooner than I got back to my desk, I had to run back."

"You're OK now, though aren't you?" the professor's wife asked.

"I have my pills. I like my happy pills. I took some just before the party. I am feeling no pain at all."

Then the professor began to make a persuasive argument about pain and happy pills. Until that moment, Dan had vaguely suspected that he might know him somehow. His voice and his words, more so than his appearance, now brought the incident back to mind. It had been at L'Auberge du Cochon Rouge, the area's best restaurant by agreement of the Cornell crowd, but not in the opinion of the locals, who thought the service too snooty. The Ithaca College professor had been the one who had almost ruined Dan and Ingrid's only evening there. They had had to listen to every word with which he tried to seduce some unwilling French-speaking woman. The woman kept asking for more and more of the expensive items on the menu and succeeding. He kept asking to get her to commit to the rest of the evening and failing. Egos and tempers flared. It had ended with the two storming off in opposite directions, but not without many accusations in several languages of "whore" from him and "bastard" from her.

Dan instantly wanted to leave the party, but things around him were happening too quickly. Munchies were being provided. Joints were being rolled and passed around. An assortment of pills and lines of powder appeared on the glass table in the kitchen.

Would they? Dan wondered.

He and Ingrid stayed. And they did.

Dan drove back to Danby with extra caution, keeping exactly to the speed limit, lest he be pulled over for going too slow.

Ingrid, he tried to convince himself while concentrating on his driving, was the best thing in his life still. How could they not be going in the same direction?

But he could not blink away the image of Ingrid with her mouth around the professor's red cock. Or, try as he might, not still hear the cheers of the others as they urged her on.

"Wasn't Cheryl beautiful?" Ingrid asked as they pulled into their driveway.

Her face still looked flushed to Dan, even in the weak light from the dashboard. That summoned up another image that he could not blink away. It was of Ingrid straddling one of the recent graduates, she naked above him, pumping herself up and down like a piston, he still clothed, but unzipped below her on a couch.

Cheryl *is* beautiful, Dan thought. Then he realized that the tense change meant *then*, back *there*, when she was naked before him.

"Yeah, Cheryl was beautiful, I guess," Dan answered, getting out of the car.

He had not really been aroused when Cheryl had chosen him. Ingrid, still the only one naked, had had to join them to make a trio. She undressed them like dolls—her own Barbie and Ken.

"I thought you might like it," Ingrid had defended herself over Dan's silence as they had dressed to leave. "It's every man's fantasy."

"I took you there for your benefit," she now said to Dan at their door. "I'm sorry you couldn't get to orgasm. I always feel bad when you get good and hard that way and nothing comes of it. I thought the two of us, taking turns, you know—"

She was standing under the doorway light. She looked old to him, her face harsh and almost malevolent.

"Did you at least enjoy it?" she asked. "You were hard as a rock for a while."

He had to turn away.

"I don't understand how these kids with their sleek, hard bodies could be so comfortable doing things that we couldn't do without guilt, even in the Village," he said without looking at her.

"That was almost a generation ago," she said. "Things change. We're the older generation now."

When well-wishing friends asked Dan how things were going between them, he now changed the subject. That she was in New York was always a given.

At the moment, what Ingrid was up to was less important than whether the monthly ecology discussions that Root and Levin had been hosting had stopped happening.

"No longer considered worthy?" Whale remarked as they came back to Comstock Hall after a quick dinner at a sandwich shop in Collegetown.

"It's scary," Dan replied.

Noises coming from the direction of Pimentel's office drew their curiosity. The room was open and Cathy Woodson was still in it, well past her quitting time. What they heard was her portable radio. The Red Sox were in mortal combat with the Cincinnati Reds.

"There can't ever have been a game like this," she gushed before shushing them into silence.

They smiled back and nodded at her and continued on their way to the Fly Lab.

"He did it!" she then shouted over the noise of the radio. "Fisk just hit a home run. Fisk hit a home run. The curse of the Bambino is finally lifted!"

Her shouting drew them back in from the corridor. They expected to share her joy, but instead found her in tears. Heart-wrenching spasms of heavy grief were wracking her whole body.

"What's wrong?" Dan asked, kneeling by her chair.

She continued to cry.

"Hey, the Sox won," Whale said, standing above them.

She shook her head.

"Tell us."

"It's nothing," she said, her sobs subsiding.

"It's not nothing," Whale said.

The sobbing returned. Whale lifted her out of her chair and held her against his massive chest. He let her cry that way for what seemed to Dan to be several minutes. It was enough time for Dan to have to hand her at least a half dozen of Kleenexes.

"It's just all the emotion," she managed to gasp through her sobs.

"Oh God!" she broke down again. "It's not the ball game. I'm not crying because of that."

And her head was back on Whale's chest. More Kleenexes.

"I don't know what to do," she finally calmed down to say. "I don't have anyone to turn to."

"You have us," Whale said and gave her a hug.

"Maybe you and the other students ARE the only ones I do have," she said, trying and failing to laugh as Whale eased her back into her desk chair, "even if you are just here and gone. You're right, Mike. Something did happen. I can't explain, but now I can't stay here any more. But I don't want to leave. I don't want what happened to Caroline to happen…"

Tears started flowing once more. Caroline had been Stockman's blonde secretary. She disappeared soon after the rumors had started.

Whale parked his behind on Cathy's desk, his every ounce the epitome of immovability. It did not take long before what was troubling Cathy came out in full.

"It was in his office?" Whale asked when she had finished her confession.

"I know it was stupid. I don't know what I was thinking."

"I know what he was thinking," Whale said.

"It doesn't change a thing," Dan sputtered angrily. "He still took advantage of you. He's just another predatory alpha male who thinks that all females working under him—or any females around him—are just there for him to dominate. It's genetically ingrained in some males, and academia is full of his type. I think they just act out of a need to have women submit to their wills. For some re—"

"We're the first ones you've told?" Whale cut Dan off.

Cathy nodded her head.

"Good," Whale said. "The police would have been no help at all in this. That probably would have just made it worse."

"So what can I do? I don't want to leave. I love working here. I love my job."

"Should we go to Pimentel?" Dan asked.

Whale shrugged his shoulders.

"No," Cathy said, shaking her head. "Maybe I'll talk to Pimentel myself. You were a big help, both of you. I mean it. Just having you here on my side ..."

And the tears flowed again.

"Maybe we can be of more help on this than you think," Whale said.

There was determination in his voice and a steely hardness in his face.

VII

"HE had a gas chromatograph coupled to a mass spec," Dritschilo excitedly explained as they set up. "I was a biochemist, you know. That's an impressive piece of equipment. I never had one."

"When were you ever a biochemist?" Krummel asked in disbelief. "I thought you were an engineer."

"Alternate service as a CO. The medical school at Penn hired me to do an engineering design that I finished up in six months. They didn't know what else to do with me after that, so they used me as a biochemist the rest of my stretch."

They were in on an old field where Bill had set up research plots. It was to be the climactic day of his experiment, the day on which data was to be collected. It required Nafus and Krummel to help with the equipment and Dan, for some reason, to provide a photographic record of the event, even though he had no talents with a camera.

"I got him that job," Dan proudly offered. "I was his draft counselor."

Bill's inspiration for the day was a recent lecture on the bombardier beetle that Tom Eisner had given in Paul Feeney's class on chemical ecology. Eisner had presented not just the ecology, anatomy, physiology, chemistry, and behavior of the insect, but he had also shown spectacular close-up photographs, mass chromatograms, and even electron microscope images to illustrate the lecture. For his own research, Bill hoped to have good photos, at least.

"Eisner even rigged up a little thermistor to measure the temperature of the beetle's spray as it came out," he continued. "Now that was some real engineering. And he had a sound spectrogram of the beetle's pop."

Dan's role as the official photographer left him with little to do while the others prepared equipment. Having captured all the equipment photographically from every possible angle, he amused himself by clowning with the D-Vac's hose as Bill adjusted its shoulder straps for Don who, as the only entomology student among them, was entrusted with the use of that Entomology Department's equipment. It was essentially a gasoline-powered vacuum cleaner on a backpack frame.

"As I remember it," Bill said, "you got me the job by suggesting I go down to the medical school and ask around to see if they had anything."

"I'm surprised that you can't quite see the lake from here," Dan changed the subject. "You seem to always choose your spots based on how scenic they are. What happened here?"

"The drive up was good, wasn't it?" Bill answered. "You know, I think Cornell must own more land than the Catholic Church. I had a lot of choices. I liked this. Easy drive to get to it."

"Hey," Krummel called. "Speaking of Cornell land, did you guys go to Bill Brown's Jugatae lecture?"

Krummel was feeling triumphant. He had convinced Bill that he should be the one to throw the enclosure down on the clover plants being sampled, even if it was Bill's thesis, Bill's design, and Bill's construction. Otherwise, as John put it, he wasn't going to play.

"You mean about him going down to check that land in the Amazon that Cornell was going to get?" Nafus asked.

"And that old lady who was going to buy it for Cornell turned out not to have the money," Dan continued. "But she gave him a check for it."

"Seven million dollars," John said. "Now that's a bounced check!"

"And not a drop of Ballantine to be found anywhere in the Amazon, according to Bill Brown," Dan said. "I think he mentioned that three times."

"Here we go guys," Bill announced.

Krummel immediately hoisted the cylinder over his head. It was designed to trap all the insects present on a clover plant, flying and hopping ones included. Bill had fashioned it himself out of steel bars and rings. Its sides and top were covered with mosquito netting. It was an ungainly piece of scientific equipment, four feet high and two feet in diameter. Still, Krummel had the thing over his head and was dashing with it toward where Bill had one set of his clover plantings.

"Softly! Softly!" Bill shouted, chasing after him. "Don't scare off the bugs."

"How can I run softly?" Krummel complained after throwing the cylinder down on one of the plants in the carefully tended clover patch. The cylinder wobbled two or three times before settling down.

"I think I missed it," Dan said glumly.

"Better you than me," Krummel said, breathing hard. "There'll be more. Three more plants here and three more plots."

"I know," Dan said as he snapped a picture of Bill opening up the netting so that Nafus could get the D-Vac hose into it. "But I don't want to run out of film."

With the D-Vac running, no one could hear him.

"This is a nice camera," Dan said of Jamie's Mamiya Sekor. "It was good of Jamie to let me use it."

"It was good of Jamie to let ME use it," Bill corrected, as he closed and labeled the jar they had emptied the D-Vac chamber into.

"Right. I'd better be careful. Now that she's recognized me as the pervert who pulled her brother's pants down once, I feel embarrassed to talk to her even."

"You know," Bill said, watching John make another assault, "you really should let that go. That was a long time ago, and Jamie told me it wasn't at all the way you describe it."

Don had the D-Vac running again. Dan was nervously feeling the extra roll of film in his pocket.

"An historic event," Bill said about the day.

Like great white hunters at the end of a safari, the team was taking turns posing with the equipment, their equivalent of weapons. The clover plants at their feet took the place of the hunters' trophy kills.

"With a little luck," Bill announced, "and the help you guys gave, of course, this summer's field work should give me enough to write a dissertation around. You know, a little of this, a little of that —two papers in Science—and no one will notice how paltry each little experiment that I did really was. I already have drafts of some of the chapters. I should be done by next spring."

"Are the mouse-feeding experiments going in, too?" Dan asked.

"Why not? I spent days constructing those enclosures. They were perfect quadrat-sized, escape-proof samples of natural habitat. I spent an entire winter in mighty battle with the red mites and white flies in the insectary before I finally managed to grow enough plants."

The plants were all identical except that one lot released cyanide on damage to their leaves. The other lacked the genes to do so. Cyanide, theory had it, should repulse all herbivores, mice included.

"It's not my fault that the mice did not cooperate," Bill continued, sensing interest from Don and John. "Hell, some seemed to prefer eating toxic clover. Some ate no clover at all. Some put all their energy into escaping from their enclosure—and succeeded."

"The Steve McQueens of the rodent world," John marveled.

"So much for mice in research," Bill said. "Hello six-legged creatures."

Taking over Ambrose's mouse enclosures had been an admitted disaster. So had John and Bill's idea of breeding the meadow voles that were caught there in order to have known-aged mice from which they could remove eye lenses. That was to give them a scale with which to gauge the ages of wild mice. Age structure in wild populations was still a hot topic. Unfortunately, although prairie voles bred in captivity, meadow voles would not, not even the ones they caught pregnant. They would simply give birth, then eat their litter. Aunt Jewel was right.

"My total conversion to insect herbivores has me already feeling a sheepskin in my hands," Bill said. "That D-Vac sucks 'em up by the hundreds, and you can store thousands of specimens in little jars and vials that take up very little space and study them later. What could be more fool proof?"

Dan, too, having taken Al Brick's advise about the fruit flies, was seeing a dissertation he could put together from "a little bit of this, a little bit of that."

John's switch from mice to cladocerans—honorary insects as far as the Fly Labbers were concerned, because of the ease with which large numbers could be sampled and grown in the lab—gave him hope for a dissertation that would let him pass himself off as an ecologist in the true Wisconsin tradition. After all, Gene Likens, who was on his committee, could trace his mentors back to Birge and Juday of Wisconsin.

And flies were no longer sitting on Don's chameleon. He thought the reason was genetic and saw a PhD thesis taking shape.

Al Brick, however, confessed to not making enough progress on swamps. Relevant documents were turning up in libraries faster than he could incorporate them into his dissertation. One was in Russian. It was too weighty a tome for Bill to translate, so it remained to forever haunt Al with its hidden knowledge. There was no feeling of vellum on his fingertips.

Mark Loye, too, was having difficulties, despite working with insects, the flies of the fly boxes. The consensus in the Fly Lab was that he was the exception that proved the rule, and that he would soon be gone.

Whale was gone.

"By the way," he had announced to Bill earlier that summer, "a position for a biology teacher has opened up at Freehold. Hal Schenk told me about it when he called to tell me he was retiring soon. He's going to bat for me with the Science Department."

Freehold High School was his and Bill's alma mater. Schenk was Mike's old football coach. After thirty years as head coach, he was a power at the school. Mike and Jacki were already in New Jersey, looking at houses. Someone named David Andow, rumored to drive a Porsche, a mark of merit to sports car-loving Bill, was staking a claim over Whalen's desk.

Cathy Woodson was still at her desk outside Pimentel's office. She was seriously dating a young professor in the Plant Pathology Department. Rumor had it that wedding bells were in her future.

Inexplicably, George Stockman was also still in his office, although he had stopped coming down to the coffee room after having been in some sort of mysterious accident. That had happened at about the time that Mike had decided to become a high school teacher. Rumor now had it that he was soon to be following his wife to Sweden. Or perhaps it was only she and their son who were leaving.

VIII

"LOOK at E. O. Wilson over there," Dan said to Ingrid. "It's as if he's afraid to step into something, but only with his left foot."

Wilson was walking with hunched shoulders and a slight stoop. His was head cocked to one side.

"It's from years of walking frozen in position with his head down in search of ants," Bill Brown's son, home for a leaf-peeping visit, explained it to them the way that his dad had explained it to him. "The tilt is because he has better than perfect vision in one eye, but the right one is blind."

Dan had tried to make a sophisticated joke to impress Ingrid, who had surprised him by a visit, also for leaf peeping. Wilson really had stepped into something, an incident the day before that Dan had witnessed. Creighton Brown, who had been named for the man who encouraged his father's taxonomic interest as a teenager, was sticking too close to Ingrid, however, as young men still did, to her obvious delight and Dan's annoyance.

"He lost vision in that eye from a fishing accident when he was a kid," Creighton elaborated before Dan could explain his joke. "He tugged too hard on hooking a fish and it smacked him right in the face. One of its spines caught him in the eye."

Dan knew the story and even that the offending creature was a pinfish and its scientific name, *Lagodon rhomboides*. But he kept it to himself.

Wilson was ahead of them. Tall, thin, bespectacled, he was a stork picking up ants from above. Bill Brown was low to the ground at Wilson's left elbow. Thick, squinting, Brown sniffed out his quarry like an anteater. Tom Eisner was at his right elbow. The others were young faculty and graduate students who, like Dan, had got wind of the planned hike and invited themselves along.

Instead of an ant, Wilson found a snake. It skittered away from his grasp and headed right at Dan. Ingrid shrieked girlishly. Dan deftly snatched it up with what he liked to think were the lightning-swift reflexes of a goalie. Then, snake in hand, he smiled sheepishly at the others.

"Hope it's not a rattler," he said, offering it to Wilson.

"Snakes were my first specialty," Wilson said, taking the snake from him. "It kind of made up for my small size and slight frame as a kid. Being able to handle snakes, especially poisonous ones, helped with any feelings of inferiority I may have had. This young rat snake, however, despite the blotches that might frighten you as being like that of a rattler, is harmless, like most of the snakes we are apt to find here"

"I wouldn't be so sure that there aren't any rattlesnakes out here," Dan countered. "This looks very similar to the habitat where my Aunt Jewel caught one in Vermont."

They were at Thatcher's Pinnacles, almost to the edge now. No one had brought up the geologic origin of the formation on the way and no one brought it up at the top, as interesting as it might have been. They were, after all, biologists. Trees, birds, ants, in deference to Ed, and now snakes were the topics of discussion. Ed let it go. Straightening out, he propped his hands against his sides and turned to enjoy the view. A formation of geese was catching a thermal at about the altitude of the bluff.

"Aunt Jewel, did you say?" Wilson asked with his back still to Dan. "Did you by any chance grow up in Vermont? Jewel Faifax wrote to me that she had a nephew in grad school here."

"Rattlers in Vermont sun themselves in quarries," Dan said by way of answering him. "Aunt Jewel caught hers in a marble quarry."

Bill Brown had introduced Dan to Wilson the day before. Their surnames being different, Wilson had no reason to make a connection between the young man with the slight limp and the charming woman he had shared a pleasant day with as part of the "Marlboro Circle," as he now thought of it. It had just been that one day—she had disappointed by not showing up on the following one—but she had stayed very much on his mind, so when he got a letter from her, he had encouraged her correspondence.

"Did she now?" he pressed Dan some more, wondering if he had been the teenager who had come for Jewel that day. "In Vermont? I wouldn't have thought there were rattlers so far north."

"Oh, we have 'em. They like sunning themselves in some of the old slate quarries, especially, but not in the granite ones."

"That doesn't surprise me," he said, now certain that it had been Dan. "I mean that your Aunt Jewel would go after a rattlesnake. I saw her catch a snake for Robert MacArthur in Marlboro. I remember warning her never to try to reach for a snake so blindly outside of Vermont. I guess she must have thought it had been a joke."

"Ingrid Larsen," Ingrid finally introduced herself when no one else did.

Wilson took the hand she offered with great formality.

"Maybe," Wilson said, still holding Ingrid's hand, but speaking to Dan, "she went after dangerous snakes for the same reason I had as a boy. I did it to prove myself somehow worthy of the other boys. It's a kind of southern thing."

"Why would she need to prove herself worthy of other boys?"

"Those were different times from now, I imagine, Miss Larsen. Is that a Swedish accent I detect?"

"Norwegian."

He let go of the hand.

"I was quite a snake handler," he continued as the small crowd closed him in, "until I picked up this one cottonmouth that was a bit too big for me. As soon as I grasped its neck, it surprised me by its stunningly violent reaction. I never would've thought a snake could be that strong. It didn't seem to matter that I was holding it right where I wanted. Boy! I can almost still smell the must. It started twisting its neck in my hand and showing its fangs. It was so strong that it managed to get its neck to where it might be able to clamp its jaws on my hand."

"You sound like Darlington with his crocodile," Bill Brown loudly interrupted them.

He held up some imaginary object in his hand.

"Red zone!" he shouted.

"That's his phony meter," Wilson explained. "He used it to measure passing notables at Harvard when we were both there."

"Off the scale," Brown added.

"I expected that," Wilson shouted back.

Then he returned his attention to Ingrid.

"He's referring to a story about the Harvard biogeographer's legendary tussle in the waters of a New Guinea jungle," he said softly, as if taking Dan and Ingrid into his confidence.

"What did you do?" Creighton Brown, sticking to Ingrid like glue, asked. "About the snake, I mean."

"Flung it. As far as I could into the brush. Decided right then to concentrate on ants."

Then Wilson flashed a smile at both the younger and older Brown.

Dan too smiled, but for a different reason. Some wag—could it have been Bill Brown?—had compared Simon Levin's recent tale of slipping on a rock on the Washington coast and scratching his leg on a barnacle to that of Darlington and the three-hundred-pound crocodile. The croc had pulled Darlington under water before the two-hundred-pound naturalist got loose to describe it.

"Those few seconds seemed like hours," is what Darlington was quoted as saying.

"I saw my life flashing before my eyes," is how the wag had the mathematician describe his fall.

Nope, Dan now remembered. The wag had been Al Brick.

"Why ants?" Creighton asked as Wilson turned to head toward the edge of the cliff.

He had been raised on stories of his father always looking for ants as a child in Philadelphia, of family trips to the Jersey shore interrupted to collect ants in the Pine Barrens. He was surprised, Creighton explained, that that was not a universal experience for "ant men."

"Because too many people study butterflies," Wilson answered. "I actually had decided first on Diptera, but this was nineteen forty-five, and there were absolutely no insect pins to be had. They had all been manufactured in Czechoslovakia, it turned out, and it was wartime then. Vials and alcohol were available, though, so it had to be ants."

"Is that true?" Creighton asked, looking to his dad, who was coming toward them.

"Not only true, but probably very sensible," the elder Brown answered.

In the meantime, Eisner had found a bombardier beetle underneath a log. He was explaining how the tip of its abdomen worked as a turret to direct its spray. Then he poked at it with the No. 3 watchmaker's forceps that he had taken out of a small leather holster strapped to his belt. The holster also held a brush and soft forceps. He never went outdoors without it.

"Don't let him put that thing in your mouth," Bill Brown warned Ingrid, who had crowded in to see the creature.

Ingrid made a face that was both squeamish and—to Dan—unbearably pretty.

"Feel the heat?" Eisner asked when the beetle fired at her hand.

She squealed, both in fear and delight.

Dan stepped away to leave room for the others to crowd near the cliff edge. He had seen the view before, on a botany field trip with Robert T. Clausen. After cackling in delight in the rain as the class had filed out of their school bus, Clausen had seemed almost disappointed to find the sun poking through when they reached the top of the pinnacle. He had stayed back from the edge with his Spaniel, an obviously old dog that could not understand why humans might want to stop and examine some boring plant or look out from a hillside. Clausen, missing a lung due to lung cancer, which he admitted had been caused by heavy smoking, not only had to wait for the dog to catch up with him on the hike, but even had occasion to allow his young students the same courtesy. Clausen had used the wait at the top of the pinnacle to tell Dan that he was not impressed with what was new in ecology.

"I especially don't believe in the theory of island biogeography," he had shared awkwardly.

It had been just after the paper on mice and mites had come out.

"I don't think it's true for plants," he had added.

Dan had let the remark drop the same way that Bill Dritschilo had LaMont Cole's.

To do his life's work, an exhaustive study of the genus Sedum, the stonecrops, Clausen had developed an elaborately scientific sampling system. He subdivided his study areas, which, in total constituted the entire terrestrial world, into equal-area grids. Each grid was numbered and subdivided into smaller ones, also numbered. Where he sampled in each grid was chosen at random. (Scientifically at random, using a method that Dan figured was probably as prosaic as drawing playing cards from a well-shuffled deck, but might have been some more sophisticated computer method.) Regardless of where the random number landed him, he went to that location and searched it for stonecrop, recording the location and numbers of any he found, along with all other possibly relevant data. If the grid location fell in an area where stonecrop could not possibly grow, he went to it anyway, even if it meant rowing out into the middle of a lake. His monograph on the taxonomy, distribution, and ecology of each of the four-hundred-plus species in the genus was his idea of what research in ecology should be.

"Can we count on you and Dan coming to dinner tonight?" Wilson's invitation to Ingrid surprised Dan back to the present.

"I'm sure mom and dad won't mind," Creighten added eagerly.

"I have to go back to New York City tonight," she demurred.

"No! No!" Bill Brown seconded the invitation. "You and Dan must come tonight. Wilson insists on it."

"I'll be there," Dan said, looking past Ingrid, who was being coyly non-committal. He wondered why he had not brought Jewel to see the view. Then he remembered. Jonathan. Anyway, the Finger Lakes' hillsides seemed unspectacular in comparison to his first view from Hogback. There were more oaks than maples here. Their yellows and muted reds looked brownish in comparison to Vermont's fiery oranges and reds. It made him realize for the first time what a debt he owed the MacArthurs and Aunt Jewel for having dragged him out on hikes when he would rather have spent the day indoors with his radio.

"I've never seen anything more lovely," Ingrid chose that moment to exclaim.

Having satisfied themselves with the view from the pinnacle, the group around Wilson turned back toward Michigan Hollow Road.

Bill Brown kept filling Danny's glass—and his own—with Ballantine while Wilson nursed a glass that was always half empty. Brown left it that way, knowing that his friend drank very little. He couldn't resist scolding, though.

"I always said never trust someone who doesn't like beer, Wilson. Even after all these years. At least, not completely."

"Who said I didn't like beer? I like to sip it, that's all."

Perhaps amusing himself by testing how many beers it would take for Dan to call him by his first name, every time Brown refilled Dan's glass, his face lit up with a huge Cheshire-cat grin. All students called him Bill Brown to each other, but few could call the bear-sized leprechaun anything but a deferential "Dr. Brown" in all other situations, even though he encouraged the informality of just "Bill."

"Is it true, Dr. Brown, that you know the word for beer in thirty different languages?" Dan asked.

"Who told you that? Wilson?" Brown asked, feigning anger, before adding with a smile, "Fifty, if you count dialects. Some languages—would you believe?—have no word for beer. Do we need more? I'll have to launch an expedition in search of more specimens having that easy identifiable three-ring field mark."

"I hear you have a practical bent," Wilson said to Dan "I'll have to report that back favorably to Aunt Jewel. I read that energy used for corn production paper. It was a good piece of work. I'm sure she already knows about that."

"A practical bent. Yeah," Dan answered, disappointed that Wilson praised the wrong paper. "I guess I have one."

"You go right ahead with that and the environmental work," Wilson continued as Brown came back with two beers. "More power to you for it, although I fear that, for myself, I've had as much social activism as I can take right now."

"Ah, you're only saying that because of that Science for the People stuff," Brown joined in.

A heckler from that group had confronted Wilson at the previous day's lecture, the last of his half of that year's six prestigious Messenger Lectures. Noam Chomsky gave the other three in the series without incident. Wilson had allowed the heckler to speak his brief piece before being shown away.

"I thought you handled that very gracefully, Dr. Wilson," Dan said.

"You'll be back trying to right wrongs with your books and papers in no time at all, Ed," Bill added.

"Thank you both. I seem to get more criticism than praise these days. Even as recently as the beginning of our century, people still thought of the planet as an infinite resource. The highest mountains had yet to be climbed. No one could even imagine reaching the ocean depths. And vast wilderness stretched along the equator of the continents. Now, man has poked himself into every little corner of the earth to do his damage. Species are disappearing at an unprecedented rate. How can that be argued? I can't keep quiet about it, and you shouldn't keep quiet about our profligate energy use."

"You're preaching to the choir, Ed. Do you guys think I should I build a fire? It's cold for October."

"Did you hear about this year's Anthropological Society meetings?" Ed asked instead of answering the question. "They had motions on the floor to censure sociobiology and ban two scheduled symposia. They would have, too, I understand, if Margaret Mead hadn't made an indignant little speech about book burning."

"Don't you guys feel cold? I think I'll build a fire. This almost feels like that night last winter when the furnace died, and I had to stay up all night keeping the fire going so that the pipes didn't freeze. I could barely keep my eyes open the next day. Remember that?" Bill asked, turning to Dan.

"I do," Dan answered. What he remembered was that no one had noticed. Bill Brown could give most of his lectures in his sleep, Dan was certain. He turned back to Wilson. "I'd like to be able to do both. I mean, do applied environmental work and also theoretical ecology. But I don't know. Sometimes it seems that why there are only a certain number of species of butterfly in Florida, say, but not some other, is a mystery in which there has to be some important principle waiting for a solution, but—"

"The number of butterfly species in Florida is a direct function of who the taxonomist is," Brown interrupted.

He was busily balling up pages of the entertainment section of the Sunday New York Times and tossing them into the fireplace.

"I thought that was common knowledge," he added. "Was he a lumper or a splitter is all you need to know."

"But then," Dan continued to Wilson, "I think it might instead be like wondering why a certain element has a certain number of electrons—but wait, that's not it."

By now Dan was slurring his speech. Brown was grinning.

"It might be as useless as wondering why the Boltzmann constant is one point three eight times ten to the minus twenty-third," Dan recovered his diction, "and not some other number."

Mouth open, Brown turned back to them to say, "Is that really what the Boltzman number is?"

"I'm shocked, Dan, that you can quote the Boltzmann Constant, but not the number of species of butterflies in Florida," Wilson said.

"I used to be a physicist."

"Have you recovered yet from the flap over your biogeography paper?" Wilson asked unexpectedly. "Bill's told me about it."

Dan made no answer. The remark sent his stomach into spasm.

"Yeah," Bill Brown added. "That paper was okay. It was interesting. You used taxonomic data for something that Wilson and I discovered."

He turned away to stuff a wad of newspaper into the flue. He then lit it with a cigarette lighter. Dan knew that he was one of Brown's favorites ever since the incident of the slide projector with Alan Hastings, the other teaching assistant in the course. Still, he appreciated the praise, especially in front of Wilson.

"You'd better put some wood in there, too," Wilson admonished.

"Yeah. Yeah."

"The reason why that paper may have got you boys so much painful criticism," Wilson said, putting on a southern accent, "is that you young rascals did not follow the protocols of science. Any idea a whippersnapper like you gets has to first be evaluated by some of us senior scientists. That's what I did with my taxon cycle paper. I sent it out to everyone I knew. When no one objected, I knew I could publish. LaMont Cole, I think, would certainly have told you to kill your paper."

Then he dropped the accent.

"So what organisms are you specializing in?" Wilson asked. "Mice or mites?"

"Neither," Dan answered. "I wanted to study evolutionary ecology, like you. I wanted to be an ecologist with a big E. I thought watching the Chilean condor in the Andes was just the thing for me. And I wanted to do all that while saving the earth from human civilization. Still do."

"Love the organisms for themselves first," Wilson said, "Then look for the generalizations."

"Isn't just knowing stuff enough?" Bill Brown again turned away from the now roaring fire to ask. "That's what's kept me going."

"Try ants," Wilson said to Dan.

"Yeah," Brown seconded, pouring still another round of beer, even for Wilson. "There's plenty of room for more ant people."

"I don't know," Dan said. "Taxonomy seems like such a monkish activity. Although I think I actually wouldn't mind that about it. But I don't see how it could lead to the big issues I want to tackle. I want big ideas. But how do I know what's important to study? Old fields, for example. They're important to succession. Every field course requires a trip to an old field. The instructors seem to know everything there is about them. Should I study them? How do I know?"

"The temperature is going down," Bill Brown said, looking at the fire with satisfaction, "while the price of heating oil is going up. At least we're not rationing any more. Everybody turn the thermostat down five degrees, indeed! Hell, we were already at sixty-eight."

"Only a specialist who is expert enough to immediately say, for example, Ah, that's a carabid of the genus Scarites," Wilson said, ignoring his friend, "can unlock all that is already known about it in the literature. As the Chinese say, the first step in wisdom is getting the name right."

"What would that mice and mites paper be without Barry O'Connor?" Bill Brown asked.

"Nowhere, of course," Dan answered. "Nor the rebuttal."

"That was good too," Wilson said.

"I've just finished reading your Sociobiology, Dr—"

"Ed."

"I read it the way I read novels," Dan continued with an embarrassed blush on his face. "I thought it was a great read, not just great science."

"Thank you, Dan."

Wilson looked at his glass of beer and frowned. It was still half empty. Brown was fussing at the fire again with a poker.

"I guess I never realized what a minefield the subject was. And like Caesar, I never realized my enemies would be so close to me. I dismissed the first critics. They have different worldviews than biologists, I thought. Then came the Sociobiology Study Group. These were my colleagues at Harvard. They were the ones linking Sociobiology—and me!—to racist eugenics movements and Nazi policies. Richard Lewontin, Stephen J Gould, Richard Levins, they were the ringleaders. Lewontin is my Department chair, for God's sake!"

Afraid to call Wilson either Ed or Dr. Wilson, Dan stayed silent.

"I never realized that belief in the infinite plasticity of the human mind was not just a hypothesis to be tested by scientists," Wilson continued, speaking more to the older man than to Dan, "that it was something that scientists could adopt as a moral view. Religion, not science! And I feel like an atheist in a monastery at Harvard. Mostly, I get the silent treatment at all the liberal dovecotes now."

Apparently satisfied, Bill Brown turned away from the fire and came toward Ed, still holding the poker.

"But what keeps me from total self-doubt over what might be an intellectual misstep is that none of the attacks have been substantive. My evidence has been untouched. Even my reasoning remains unimpugned. Only my premise that I could study such a thing in such a way, and then publish it. But what are you going to do with that poker, Bill? You're not going threaten us with it like Wittgenstein did Popper?"

"You're the one who spawned Dan Simberloff with all that null model stuff."

Then a huge grin broke out on Bill Brown's face.

"It didn't stop Popper, did it?" he said, putting the poker back in its stand.

"All the time I've known Dick Lewontin," Ed resumed with a sigh, "I never knew he was a Marxist. You know, Harvard did not want to have him. They thought he might be too disruptive. If Ernst Mayr and I hadn't argued against political beliefs influencing faculty appointments, his candidacy would not have gone through. Then George Kistiakowsky, the chemist, called me up to warn me that I would be sorry. So, now I'm going to study Marxism."

"And in my research," Dan confessed, "I'm putting together a pie diagram map of gene frequencies that is just like the one in the Lewontin and Hubby paper. I guess I should apologize to you, Ed"—There! Finally did it—"but I love those diagrams."

"Why apologize? Lewontin is a damned good scientist. Of course, I strongly disagree with his view on group selection. Mayr has argued very well again and again that there is more to evolution than bean bag genetics."

"It seems to be this holism and reductionism thing all over again," Bill Brown said softly.

He had slumped into his easy chair by the fire, which was now crackling satisfyingly. He looked as if he were about to fall asleep.

"By the way," he said, his eyes drooping. "It was smart of you guys not to take your idea to some of your professors, regardless of what Wilson here may have just told you. LaMont Cole would have been OK to pass the idea by. I agree that he wouldn't have liked it, given his ideas about what is strong inference in science, but he would have given you good, honest suggestions. There are some in that Ecology and Systematics Section, though, who would not be above stealing the idea from you one way or another. They might now resent that you guys never gave them a chance to do it. Good ideas come easily, but they come rarely."

He stopped in a way that made the other two lean forward to see if he was asleep.

"Wilson there," he suddenly started up again, "never had any of his ideas stolen, because they were all so hard to demonstrate in the first place, even if he did go on to demonstrate them. No one wanted them."

"Did he ever tell you," Wilson turned to Dan, "that it was his idea that the exponent in the species-area curve for islands should be point two seven?"

"Back when we were both still at Harvard," Brown said firmly. "I suggested that."

"Quit bragging, Bill. Next you'll be telling us you're the one who showed Tom Eisner what a bombardier beetle is."

"I did! When we were all at Harvard. He tried to put one of the damn things in his mouth. I was the one who told him to expect a pop and some real nasty stuff."

"Or that you gave Rachel Carson the idea for Silent Spring."

"Reading Silent Spring in college changed my life!" Dan interrupted.

"I sent her the only copy I had of my fire ant paper. The original was still at the publisher's. But did Wilson tell you that he was the one who pointed her in the direction of Charles Elton's book on animal introductions?"

"So, whose idea was character displacement?" Dan asked, getting into the swing of the kidding.

"Ah! Let me tell you about character displacement!"

"Oh, you don't want to tell him about that," Wilson stopped him. "He doesn't need to hear a couple old farts like us talk about what we did in the old days."

"Oh yes he does. He's a very smart young man, although he seems to be developing a reputation for being a loose cannon. And remember, Wilson, I can still get the poker."

"By all means, then."

"Loose cannon?" Dan asked. "You mean because of the Science paper?"

"Rumor has it," Brown said with a wink, "that you and Don Nafus showed up at Jerry Meinwald's lab asking about equipment to measure silica content in grasses."

"Why was that wrong?"

"It's someone else's turf. You're supposed to stick to genetic feedback and pest control."

"Hey go easy on him, Bill. He's part of Robert MacArthur's legacy."

"Well, then he'll want to hear how we came up with character displacement."

"Yes. Yes. By all means, then, Dr. Brown," Dan urged, "I'd love to hear about character displacement."

"Really?" Bill asked. "You want the short version or the whole thing? And you really should call me Bill. I think what you need is another Ballantine. Wilson, you've heard all this before. Why don't you see what's in the fridge?"

"I'll bring three."

"So, the success of a paper we did together on subspecies set off a train of what Wilson called megathought discussions on all sorts of evolutionary topics. Those were fun days at Harvard, when we were young. We poked into everything new in ecology. Wilson was a Harvard Fellow, so he had nothing to do but gab. I urged him to do a taxonomic revision of Lasius for his doctoral thesis, you know. We discussed his findings daily. I think one of our lunch discussions was what led to Hutchinson's one-point-three size ratio idea."

"Don't tell me! That was your idea too, Dr. Brown?"

"Bill!"

Silence.

"So, what was I saying? Oh, yeah, one of the most interesting things in the literature was that certain pairs of species were distinct morphologically and ecologically where they occurred together. And this was over wide geographical areas. But in other regions, populations that appeared to be intermediate to—or a blend of—the same two species replaced them. Sometimes, such intermediate populations were classed as hybrid swarms. We considered this as a possibility for Lasius.

"They're on the door, Wilson," he suddenly shouted into the kitchen.

"Got 'em."

"About this time," he turned back to Dan, "I came across Charles Vaurie's analysis of the rock nuthatch species Sitta neumayeri and tephronota. They differ considerably where their ranges overlap in Iran but are virtually identical outside Iran, where each species occurs alone over wide stretches of the Balkans and Central Asia. So, in nineteen fifty-four, when Wilson left for a long collecting tour in Melanesia and Australia, I kept on looking for evidence of the phenomenon in question. I began calling it character displacement."

Wilson was back from the kitchen with the three beers.

"So, on Wilson's return in nineteen fifty-five, we wrote our paper. Later redefinitions, I think, have confused the phenomenon and its causes."

"In practice," Wilson added, "the causes are often difficult or impossible to separate."

Brown gave Wilson an irritated look

"A few years ago," Brown said, "Peter Grant published a paper pointing out, quite rightly, that most of the cases we cited were incompletely analyzed."

"He completely overlooked our observations on the interaction of two fire ant species in the Florida panhandle," Wilson interrupted. "You're not going to bring up Simberloff again, are you?"

"It's interesting to note that Grant, who was an early skeptic about the existence of character displacement, is now deeply involved in producing the most detailed evidence for it with Darwin's finches in the Galapagos. Now, this Simberloff guy—"

"Can I use your poker, Bill?" Wilson asked.

"You know," Bill said, ignoring Wilson, "until a seminar in Caldwell Hall a while back, I never realized what a long time has passed since our excited discussions over noontime coffee. I mentioned a double invasion by a genus of birds on an island off Australia. An eager undergraduate sitting next to this guy right here," he indicated Dan, "patiently explained to me that what I was talking about had a name. It's character displacement, he said."

"That must have been Paul Dubowy," Dan said. "But who is this Simberloff guy?"

"One of my students," Wilson answered. "One of my best."

St. Louis

I

THE best thing about Dan's stay in St. Louis was that it came to such a rapid end. From the very beginning, things there did not seem right. The feeling of having risen in academia out of the Fly lab was missing. Barry Commoner's empire at Washington University in St. Louis (the location awkwardly appended to the name to distinguish it from the dozens of other Washington Universities in the country), it turned out, if not totally contained to a basement, everywhere, in all of its metastases of SIPI and CBNS and others, had the feel of a basement. In fact, his Center for the Biology of Natural Systems did occupy most of the basement of Rebstock Hall. It was not a good sign.

All about, too, were the earmarks of an empire in transition. The offices housing the organic farming studies, for one, were squeezed into a former apartment building, Millbrook Apartments, it was called, tucked into the corner of Big Bend Boulevard and Forest Park Parkway, almost not part of the campus. The rest of the building was occupied by married students. The arrangement did provide the advantage of a bathroom with a tub rather than institutional toilets, but that small luxury did not make up for the feeling Dan had of being an academic outcast there. Having to use—being allowed to use!—the unit's tiny library for his office needs added to that feeling. It was formerly a living room, Dan guessed, or maybe a bedroom. Could it have been the kitchen?

Had he been married, or managed to have coaxed Ingrid to come with him, Dan could have had an apartment in the other wing of the C-shaped building and been able to walk from home to office by way of a long basement without once stepping outside. Then one day, warning sirens went off and he did make use of that basement. He and the cockroaches and an Indian postdoc fresh from Minnesota took refuge in it from a potential tornado. Others were not in the office or simply ignored the sirens. To make conversation while they waited for the all clear signal, which they never heard, necessitating their rescue by the office secretary, the Indian postdoc, an agricultural economist, related how his uncle, also an agricultural economist, had died when his skull was punctured by a flying piece of straw as he hid from a tornado in a roadside ditch. Another bad sign.

Dan found housing in South St. Louis with friends of Georgia Shearer, Dan Kohl's lab tech. It was a room in a drab turn-of-the-century two-story in the middle of a long block of identical such two-story houses, all on a surprisingly steep hill for a city set in the flat plains of the Midwest. People on both sides of the block all seemed to know one another, not surprisingly so since they all either went to the same Catholic church at the top of the next block over, or drank in the same bar at the end of the street, Fairview, or both. Dan never learned whether it was Fairview Street or Avenue or Place, or Whatever. Those designations, he was told, changed from place to place along the same streets in St. Louis, so it was accepted practice not to use them. Dan did not.

For a city with a substantial black population, there was not a black face to be seen along that part of Fairview. And living there necessitated that Dan cross a large part of St. Louis in his ancient Buick to get to work, which in turn led to several breakdowns and exorbitant repair bills. More bad signs.

Dan Kohl was a plant physiologist, which technically gave him the grounds to claim to be an ecologist, which he did not. It had been Kohl, not Commoner, who Dan assumed had orchestrated the interview process. At Dan's talk, he had suggested that a teaching arrangement could be made when Dan told him that he would like to create a course in applied ecology.

"You're a good speaker," he had said, as if it was a done deal. "You're obviously well versed on the subject matter. You're, ah, presentable. Why not?"

That was the last Dan heard of that. Another bad sign?

Georgia Shearer fulfilled the same role in Dan's lab as Aunt Jewel had in Hutch's, it seemed to Dan. It was one more bad sign when she admitted to Dan that she knew little ecology.

"Isn't it just scientific natural history?" she had asked, and he had had nothing to say in answer.

By appearing temporary, Commoner's office in Rebstock Hall seemed all the more spacious. A chaise longue that looked like Plato might once have reclined on it dominated the room.

What did he use it for? Naps? Like Dan Kohl?

Kohl had taken a back problem to a doctor at Barnes Hospital who had prescribed a daily after-lunch nap. The treatment had made the back pain go away, but Kohl had never returned to that physician out of fear he would be told that he no longer needed the naps. Had Dan recommended the same for Barry?

Book cases in the office were in disarray and half full, another bad sign. The office itself seemed half full.

It was, in fact, occupied much less than half the time by Barry. Anointed the Paul Revere of ecology by *Time Magazine*, Barry spent most of his time sounding his alarm for the environment seemingly all over the world. Dan's second week on the job coincided with the first day of an all-but-dissertation research associate from Stony Brook who annoyed so many people with her arrogant superiority that Susan Sweeney, a research technician with moxie, had to call Barry in India to complain. Barry had her bring the offender, who was putatively Susan's superior, to the phone and fired her on the spot. Susan, a Nebraskan, had previously caught Dan's attention by her t-shirt with "Where the hell is North Platte, Nebraska?" on the front. The hot weather clothing that revealed her home town had left nothing unconcealed and nothing to the imagination. Her attributes aside from moxie were so small as to need little material and little imagination. Not at all a bad sign, that.

Copies of the issue of *Time* with Commoner on the cover, almost a decade old, which Dan dearly wanted to read, were stacked along one otherwise empty shelf next to Commoner's desk, as if they were gifts waiting to be proffered. Dan was not offered one. Another bad omen?

When not traveling, Commoner spent his time writing. His most famous book, *The Closing Circle*, was tied up in Dan's head with Earth Day, even though he knew it had been inspired by the event, rather than the other way around. It came out the next year. Dan did not read it until grad school and then with skepticism about its Four Laws of Ecology, skepticism not about the laws, but about whether they were in any way a foundation of the science. To Commoner, ecology was just another issue to add to the mix of pollution, war, and racial and sexual inequality. His latest book, *The Poverty of Power*, did please Dan by having included data gathered for "Corn," until he noticed that the citation was to a secondary source, rather than *Science* magazine, a hint that Commoner was little interested in Pimentel's work in general. Another bad sign. The Pimentel connection (and Dan's degree in physics), though, was probably what caught Willie Lockeretz's attention and gotten Dan hired to help with the organic farming studies. Lockeretz was a physicist who saw a career chasing pions with an accelerator as less promising than one doing the kind of research Commoner had done tracing Strontium-90 from nuclear fallout into children's teeth or in general using nuclear techniques to trace the flow of chemicals through the environment. At CBNS, Lockeretz had made himself an expert on energy in agriculture, the focus of the organic farming studies.

It had not hurt Dan at his interview to have been able to give the proper regional (Brooklyn) pronunciation of Loew's Theaters (Lowees) and the rubber ball used in stick ball (a Spaldeen) and the composition of an egg cream, which was delicious nonetheless for having neither egg nor cream in it.

"I'll give Barry a call tonight," Lockeretz had told him at the end of that interview. "He's from Brooklyn, too."

Everything about the situation in St. Louis seemed to cry out for getting off before the ship sank. His appointment was temporary, paid out of money from a large grant from a short-lived National Science Foundation program (RANN, Research Applied to National Needs). It was about to run out. The research was essentially over. Dan's role was to help tidy up loose ends (mostly sieving Midwestern farm soils in search of corn borer and corn earworm larvae) and look for further research and funding. Rumors abounded that Barry and SIPI (Science in the Public Interest) and CBNS were all soon moving, lock, stock, and perhaps staff, east. Some said to Cambridge (MIT? Harvard?) or somewhere near the Beltway around Washington, while others, probably those in the know, thought it would be back to Barry's native Brooklyn. He was apparently homesick.

It was at the very first general meeting, one which Barry attended, the only such he would attend in Dan's presence, that Dan realized that he was the lone ecologist on the staff. For all he knew, he might have been the only ecologist in St. Louis. Commoner, although a biologist, was a "hard" scientist, having made his reputation in cell physiology. That explained the naivety of his so-called Four Laws of Ecology. (And why couldn't he have stopped at three? Kepler had three. Newton had three. Both knew better than to offer a fourth. Why couldn't Barry?) The Cosing Circle is more apt to cite an economist than an ecologist. (Marx, Karl, not Groucho, makes an appearance with a comment on the ecology of the soil, while Paul Ehrlich merits attention in the book mostly because Barry disagreed with his pessimistic outlook.) Ecology to Commoner, Dan realized, was something like pollution studies.

Dan's stomach had churned in anticipation of the meeting. A first audience with Barry Commoner was a possible career maker. It could also be a career breaker. Lockeretz and Ajay Sanghi had warned Dan to make a good first impression.

"Barry makes up his mind about you at first meeting. Once he does nothing can change it," Ajay had put it.

"If you disagree with him, then as far as Barry is concerned, it can only be because you're stupid," Lockeretz warned. "So watch out."

The exciting news that Barry had brought to that meeting was that his lab had identified hamburgers from a popular chain as the most mutagenic (thus possibly cancer causing) material ever tested, more so even than dioxin, of Agent Orange and 2,4,5-T fame. He coyly refused to name the chain, even though everybody at the meeting could guess it was MacDonald's.

Ames test, organic soils, Amory Lovins, E. F. Schumacher, mutagenesis, socialism, Marxism, none of the subjects that were bandied about around the two large oak tables put side by side in a Rebstock Hall basement conference room gave Dan an opening for a witty, learned comment. Ajay, though, had a witticism. His joke that Ali Shams, another economist, as a "revisionist," would be able to slip past the Ayatollah's rabid hatred of Marxists was more than Barry's quick, playful mind could let pass.

"None of you are revisionists, Ajay," Barry quipped. "To be a revisionist, you must first understand orthodox Marxism."

Ali Shams, a balding, serious, young scholar, was as different as one could imagine from Nasser Zareh, his Cornell countryman. Shams' goal at the moment was to return to his home country to provide a Marxist perspective to the revolution brewing there. Nasser's had been to avoid returning.

"Do you think you can do any good?" Dan finally broke his silence to ask.

"I'm certain that democracy is about to overtake the chaos. There has to be fertile ground for a Marxist state now after all the years of oppression by the Shah. I can help steer it in that direction," was Sham's answer.

(A month later, Dan watched with bemusement as Ali Shams appeared on national TV as the head of the Iranian delegation to the United Nations.)

Now Dan had to say more. He had opened his mouth and had really said nothing of any substance. What kind of impression was that making? He listened with excruciating care for his next chance. It never seemed like it would come up. Then he took that chance when Commoner called most ecologists "Neo-Malthusians."

"Human population is not what ecology is all about," Dan blurted out. "That's demography. Raymond Pearl. Economics, maybe."

"The logistic curve?" Barry sneered in sharp rebuke. "Isn't that ecology?"

That made Dan's tongue refuse to work. It apparently needed his mind to untangle itself from the knot it was in from coming to grips with what that little equation really was for ecology.

"I think," Barry resumed chiding Dan over his crime, "it was a cop-out of the worst kind for Ehrlich to say that none of our pollution problems can be solved without getting at population first."

Dan walked away from the meeting feeling queasier and queasier in the stomach. An entire roll of Tums was no help. So much for a career with Commoner. So much for a career at Washington University might be added, he thought, then he did add it.

The only scientist at Washington University whose name Dan had run across in an ecology journal was Alan Templeton, a population geneticist whose mathematical models appeared in the *American Unnaturalist* alongside those of the more mathematical ecologists. He read the articles, but they had little in common with his own work, more genetics than ecology. He truly did feel all alone.

Other than that it was a job with a salary, at a university, the one saving grace to it was that some of the best college soccer games in the area were played at Francis Field, still in use after being gifted to the university for the 1904 World's Fair and that same year's Summer Olympics. Dan took any pretext at all to sneak off from work and let himself be embraced by the sport's familiar choreography and sounds. He watched Ty Keough play for the Billikens and Angelo DiBernardo score the only goal in an NCAA playoff against them. DiBernardo had taken a thirty yard pass near the midfield stripe out of the air, with one deft touch of his foot. Dan could see the indecision on his face as the ball was coming back down to where he could control it. Unfortunately, he was fully covered by his defender. What could he possibly do with it, Dan wondered, even after such a nifty bit of skill? The defender might as well have been holding him in a bear hug. No teammates were close enough to pass to. What DiBernardo did was shoot, with his back to the goal, on the volley, over his head, some seventy yards. The white sphere flew over the open-mouthed St. Louis University goalie, who was usually rock steady, and just under the crossbar. Game won.

Dan wanted to stop the clock, go back to that moment, replace the goalie, and show the crowd how it should have been done. How much simpler, how much easier it was for him to read life on a soccer pitch. He was certain he would have stopped the shot had he been in goal. He would have been ready for it. That was his secret in the goal: be bored, but be ready, then be good.

When Dan Simberloff came to campus, it was as if by the hand of God. A student organization invited him to give a presentation of his and E. O. Wilson's work with mangrove islands off the Florida coast. They had poisoned all the animals on them by fumigation and had even cut some of the islands up. The number of arthropod species equilibrated quite rapidly at the numbers predicted by the species-area curve of MacArthur and Wilson's Theory of Island Biogeography, and within the four-year period reasonable for a dissertation. As a field experiment in ecology, it was a welcome rarity. As a robust test of an ecological theory, it became an instant classic. Their paper was awarded the same Mercer Prize by the Ecological Society of America as the year's best that MacArthur's warbler studies and Root's gnatcatcher studies had, the same prize that Dieter John had won with his "Natural Population Dynamics and Genetic Feedback" paper, the same prize that Dan had day-dreamed about garnering with a paper with the pie diagrams from his thesis. The lecture hall was packed.

After his talk, Simberloff briefly and distractedly answered questions that deteriorated into undergraduates badgering him about the morality of killing myriad numbers of insects just for scientific research. Seats began to empty.

Dan held himself back from speaking up. Did he really have a right? Was he really a part of ecology any more? At the level that Simberloff was? He had not spoken in person to a bona fide ecologist in months. Did he even belong in the audience? Was he as valid a member of the university as those students with the insipid questions?

Having finally been satisfied on the matter of Simberloff's scientific ethics, the undergraduates began to file out. Simberloff was left alone to put away his slides. Dan took the moment to introduce himself.

"We have a friend in common," Simberloff surprised Dan with. "Ed Wilson spoke very highly of you."

He said he liked their mice and mite paper and had met Dritschilo at a conference in Washington—DC, not St. Louis.

"What are you doing here?" he asked.

"Studying organic farming," Dan answered, his face mildly reddening. Then he added, "Passing through, I think. Still looking for a permanent job."

"The mangroves don't really prove island biogeography, though," Simberloff said suddenly after putting all his things away and listening to Dan praise that work. "The data just showed a fit to the equation. It's like all those equations that fit something to the Boltzmann Constant. Proof needs to have turnover demonstrated. A real test needs to show that the number of species was kept at the predicted number by competition or something else biological. It has to show extinctions, real extinctions, causing the turnover. Our study showed very few. It's hardly the proof people seem to want it to be. Certain people."

Dan was aghast. Simberloff appeared to be disavowing one of the most lauded studies in ecology.

"Have you had a chance to read my latest paper on it in Science?"

Dan was ashamed to admit he was not aware of it.

"Say, why don't we meet for lunch tomorrow?" Simberloff asked, sincerity obvious in his voice. "We can talk some more about it."

"Where? When?"

"I'm being taken to the Soulard Market tomorrow for some reason. The local organic gardening club, I think. Is there a place there we could eat?"

Other than right from the farmer's stands, Dan could not think of one. The meeting never came off.

"Polish. Polish. Polish," was the advice Barry Commoner had for Dan and George Kuepper, the male version of Susan Sweeney, a strapping young man from Wisconsin who unfortunately could do nothing at the center requiring a healthy back. Couldn't bend. Couldn't lift. They were meeting with Barry to learn how to write a winning proposal for a grant, one that would let them keep their jobs.

Dan was just fine with the advice. His problem was putting something together to polish in the first place.

II

"ECOLOGY is hard," Bob Rovinsky said.

It was a sympathetic remark, generally elicited by the various travails that Fly Labbers were enduring in their quest to find the correct path to a PhD. Mark Loye, Bob's fellow Troll, was its direct recipient.

"I really admire you guys," Rovinsky continued. "You have to learn so much stuff."

Rovinsky's expertise was operations research, a mysterious subject to Fly Labbers, but his own dissertation had to do with corn, cotton, pest species, agricultural economics, insecticides, and the environmental effects that result. He was puzzled as much by them as the Fly Labbers were with Bessel functions and LaGrange multipliers.

He held up Odum's textbook. It took both hands.

"This is hard reading, You have to learn so much stuff for ecology. There's chemistry and thermodynamics and hydrology and meteorology and biology ..."

"That's the Yellow Version," Mark Loye didn't so much interrupt Bob as step in as he elegantly trailed off. "It's got a yellow cover. It's the newer edition. The previous edition had a green cover. Likens said the green version is what made him decide on ecology. He said it was easy to read, because it had a lot of white space on its pages."

"And I don't know if ecology can ever become like physics or chemistry," Rovinsky continued in an apologetic tone. "You know, full of mathematical rigor and free of mere conjecture, like some ecology theories seem to be. I can't tell what's established from what's just a guess."

Loye had come to Bob for sympathy. It was not just because he shared the Troll Room with him. People sought Rovinsky out. He was the pleasant sort who might have made a great rabbi. Being strictly a mathematician, he also always had a fresh view on things. That had even extended to Alvan Brick's campaign to remove Linda Olsvig from the Fly Lab. The slight slip of a Minnesota girl's offense had been to target her feminine wiles, of which she had few, on the newly widowed Robert Whittaker. Al had succeeded and Linda had succeeded. Al's success had come from a night spent making and hanging Christmas decorations in the room he shared with her. It was, after all, only a week to Christmas and more tasteful than the Playboy centerfolds he had first considered. She had had to press through a curious crowd of onlookers who had gathered at her office door when she came in that morning. After one look at the thousands of little vials, the kind used in the fly boxes, that Al had filled with red, blue, and green liquid and hung everywhere in the room, she took her things and stomped out of Comstock. How she succeeded with Whittaker was less clear, but Bob Rovinsky had kept the Fly Lab together and sane through all that insanity. From that aspect, Pimentel and Christine Shoemaker had been right in thinking that cross-fertilization between applied math and insect ecology, in the persons of Rovinsky and the Fly Labbers, would benefit both.

Loye's current problem was that Peter Marks had announced that not only would he not approve the dissertation Loye had turned in, but that he would approve no dissertation ever with Mark Loye's name on it. Neither would he withdraw from Loye's examining committee.

"So, what can you do?" Bob asked.

"Nothing. I'm done. You're losing a roommate. I'm going back to Denver. You can have my copy of Odum's green edition, if you'd like. It's a classic. It's smaller, so it's easier to hold in your hands to read. My dad got it for me at a used bookstore in Denver. Supposedly, it's sold more than any ecology book ever."

"Well, thank you, but I'll try to make do with this version," Bob said. "Don't give up, though, Mark. You're a bright guy. There must still be something you can do. Have you thought about having the dissertation read by someone outside of Cornell?"

"Huh? What do you mean?"

"Professors aren't infallible," Bob explained. "And they don't always agree. Your dissertation may not be good enough here, but it may be good enough somewhere else—"

"Like Colorado?" Loye interrupted, suddenly enlightened. "Could I do that?"

"It's been done."

Rovinsky went on to describe an example he knew about in math.

Temporarily back in the Troll Room, Dan Atkins listened with interest. The semester break, with its opportunity to escape St. Louis, had come none too quickly for him. He was afraid he was falling into the same trap as Mark. Whittaker had turned down Dan's thesis again, this time for a different reason—or, more accurately, a different section of it. He did not give reasons. Although replacing Cole with Bruce Wallace had been a formality, no more than a signature on a form, taking Whittaker off, he feared, would not be so easy.

"Is this really what you want to submit as part of your dissertation?" Whittaker had written in his neat script at the top of the title page to the offending section. "Maybe you might want to take some more time to think it over?"

"Are you really satisfied with these results?" he had written earlier in the same script on a previous draft. "Think about it."

Thinking about it had resulted in four more months of data massaging. The "little of this and a little of that and two papers in Science" strategy was not working for Dan the way it had for Bill Dritschilo. Of, course, Bill hadn't had Whittaker on his doctoral committee. It was as if an evil genie had attached himself to Dan's career in the form of Robert H. Whittaker.

Who could Dan turn to? Not Pimentel. Pimentel seemed as confident that Dan would overcome any problems he had with Whittaker as he had been that Mark Loye could overcome his difficulties with Peter Marks or that Al Brick would overcome the demons troubling him. Rovinsky? As much as he oozed compassion, Bob was too much of a stranger. And, Dan was ashamed to admit, even to himself, that Rovinsky for him was somehow tainted by his accommodating attitude toward Loye. Buck and Bill were gone, as were Mike and Krummel. Nafus? Nafus was in entomology. Professors from Caldwell were much saner and more reasonable than those out at Langmuir. Entomology students did not have the wealth of bad experience that the ecology students did, so not Nafus. And not Alvan. Never again Alvan. Al was too far gone on his campaign to break up the Olsvig-Whittaker love affair to be of help on anything else.

But then he did go to Alvan. And... And Alvan was being Alvan, unfortunately.

"Did you see them together at the seminar this week?" Alvan launched into as soon as he saw Dan. "They were holding hands when they walked in! Whittaker had his arm around her the entire lecture. I could see Slobodkin wince every time he looked their way. I was surprised he could finish the lecture! God! He's forty years older than that gold-digging bitch! And she has the nerve to pretend to be taking care of him and his kids. She can't even boil an egg!"

He was lighting candles on Olsvig's abandoned desk. Dan did not ask him what or who the shrine was honoring.

"God, Whittaker!" Alvan exclaimed. "It's not only Olsvig, either, you understand. He tried to date a friend of Elinor Terhune's. I forgot the name. Someone from California. Someone closer to his age. She asked him what his wife did. He thought for a bit, according to her, and said, Macramé! Now that's exactly the kind of person who needs Olsvig in his life!"

"But wait!" Dan said in confusion. "That would— Oh, never mind."

Dan had only one person in the world to turn to, he realized. Aunt Jewel.

He walked out of the Fly Lab without a word to anyone. He crossed the campus deep in thought about what he should say to Jewel. He crossed over the suicide bridge into Collegetown with a new determination to act somehow, any way he could. His car, however, was not where he had left it. It was nowhere. It was gone. It had been towed. It had to be. Who would steal it? He had to walk downtown and write a bad check that he would have to make good the next day. And Ingrid was away.

He got on the phone to Marlboro as soon as he got back to Danby. He did not even take his coat off.

"I don't know," she said about Danny's struggles, "none of these new ideas in ecology sounds very new to me or very interesting. When I was younger, I latched onto every new idea that some young ecologist—Hutch's students were rife with them, all sorts of new ideas about diversity ... and behavior ... and trophic structure—and I instantly made my decision on whether it was sheer genius or sheer gibberish. Genius was more often. And then I couldn't get enough of it or its defenders. Now I just don't seem to care. So much that is new just seems so meaningless."

"Well, I—"

"And what exactly is ecology now? We're talking about something as complex as the entire world!"

What was bringing this on? Dan wondered at the other end of the line.

"First ecologists studied dunes and prairies, then it was jungle, mammals in the Arctic, and algebra equations. Lakes and ocean fisheries, then. Differential equations. And always there were the butterflies and the birds."

"And the bees, Aunt Jewel. Don't forget the bees."

"Liza might be smirking at us somewhere, now with her eight kinds of quarks, or however many it is. We have googols of possibilities."

"Liza?"

"Never mind."

Jewel was demonstratively glad, though, that he had called. Jon was little better, she told him. It seemed that nothing short of heart surgery could save him. And Jon wasn't sure that he wanted it.

"Can you believe that?" she asked. "He prefers leaving me alone the rest of my life over the trauma of the surgery. It's just bypass surgery. It's not like it's a heart transplant."

Jon's travails made his own worries trivial. His were hardly life-and-death issues. And yet, he did feel that the world was crashing in on him. Worse yet, he had no idea what life was demanding of him. Was Whittaker really carrying on some sort of vendetta against him? It sure seemed that way. Why? Could it have something to do with MacArthur and why he was accepted at Cornell? And what did Ingrid want from him that he had not already given? What else did he have to give

Jonathan, at least, Dan concluded in gloom, knew what he was facing. It had to be easier for him, even if it was life and death.

And then shame overcame him. Then loneliness, utter, hopeless loneliness. The bridge over the gorge took on new significance to him. Fortunately, he was in Danby. Having to drive to it was more than he could muster the energy for.

It was too bad for Dan that Bill Brown was on Sabbatical. Even though Brown and Pimentel did not particularly like each other because of some ancient departmental battle, Dan hoped that he might still be able to get the two to combine against Whittaker for his sake. Bill Brown being out of the country dashed that hope.

So he decided to just redo the offending section of his thesis, even though his funding in St. Louis had run out. That month's rent on his room on the hillside had been paid and his deposit covered the month after that. No one had yet asked him to remove himself and his things from that library in the married students' building. So staying on presented little hardship beyond mental anguish, he decided. If it only took a few weeks of literature research and writing to get Whittaker to pass on the offending section, maybe he would be able to get through it.

Or maybe not. Like Al Brick, Dan was deep into despondency. He could not shake the thought that Whittaker would just raise some other objection. The only thing that he could take any solace from was that, if he had to, if he could take it, he could go back to Ithaca for another year or two. Ingrid had as much as said so.

Maybe the son of a bitch would die, he thought. There were rumors. One that came by way of Mendez was that Whittaker had complained to Gene Likens, apparently his only friend at Cornell, that radioactive tracer studies had "finally gotten me." It sounded like cancer to Dan. If so, he might well be able to wait Whittaker out for years, if necessary.

Then, almost overnight, the gloom of winter came to an end. The St. Louis snow, a record amount for that winter, melted away in torrents that sent roiling muddy waters through the Missouri and Mississippi, closing roads and bridges. Hannibal, Mark Twain's home town, was reported to be threatened, but the sun shone for days on end. Undergraduates came out on green lawns with dogs and Frisbees. Lesbians embraced in the bushy corners of the quads. Ingrid invited him to come up to glory in the redbuds that were everywhere soon to burst into flower in Ithaca. Things even seemed to have been worked out between them in bed on his last visit. As long as Ingrid was willing to let him write checks on her Ithaca account and added to it monthly, whether she used it or not, he now felt confident he could wait Whittaker out.

Things were looking up everywhere. Don Nafus had found a position for himself in Guam. John Krummel was at Oak Ridge and happily married. Dritschilo was now at Tulane, his second position in less than a year. Colorado, Dan learned from Pimentel was interested in Loye's thesis. Pimentel even discretely hinted he might be able to do something similar for Dan.

But something even better happened. Whittaker agreed to withdraw from Dan's committee on the basis of his health. He did make one condition, however. It was that someone from Ecology and Systematics replace him. It seemed perfectly appropriate.

For heaven's sake, Dan thought, where else would he look? Of course, he would choose somone from E&S!

What a glorious spring! Dan proclaimed to everyone, to Ajay and Willie and his wife Frieda and Susan and George and Diane Wanner and Rick Shea and Robert Klepper, and even Barry on one rare occasion.

It did not take long, however, before Dan realized what a Pyrrhic victory he had gained, and his spring euphoria vanished behind the gloomy clouds of a normal Ithaca spring. Whatever had soured Whittaker on Dan turned out to have permeated Langmuir. He felt truly hexed.

"I'm afraid I don't know you well enough to step up on your committee at this late date," Peter Broussard answered his request by phone.

It was for different reasons, but he got the same answer from Brian Chabot and Gene Likens. Peter Marks, he did not even try, nor Paul Feeney.

Dick Root avoided him completely, not even returning his call. It was a long-distance repeat of Root's having once bloodied his nose doing a quick turn to maneuver away from Alvan in the hallway at Comstock. Instead of the bathroom in which he had intended to seek refuge, Root had turned in the opposite direction and right into a wall.

Dan's dissertation was once more in limbo. Crazily, it seemed to Dan, Mark Loye's happened to be on the opposite trajectory. His rejected thesis, Dan learned, was going to be accepted for a PhD in ecology from the University of Colorado.

Mark Loye getting his PhD in the midst of his own struggle was a low blow. Dan soon stopped going to campus at all. He secluded himself in his room. He turned his TV on and left it on day and night. He took up smoking cigarettes again, three packs a day's worth. He took out his guitar. He strummed some chords. He put the guitar back in the closet.

Three chords no longer did it, he knew. Rock and Roll was now full of performers who actually could play their guitars. And folk music was dead. There were no more basket houses. There was no more Village. New York was a grimy, sleazy, depressing, failed city, suitable only for junkies and criminals.

Then Ingrid came into his mind. In her way, she had always been his rock, his firmament. His solace. She always had confidence in him, believed in him, whether it was folk music or science or sex. Would she feel the same way when he had no dreams left? And what would he do with his life in New York City? Or any city?

There was a knock on the door.

Georgia Shearer was at it. Her broad smile hardly hid the concern on her face. His Aunt Jewel was trying to reach him, she told him.

"She said your phone has been busy for days."

St. Louis

Dan realized that it had been off the hook.

For how many days?

He picked it up to call Jewel. Georgia stood solemn guard over him.

Jewel had bad news. Dan started getting things together to go to Marlboro.

Before leaving, he called Ingrid. She surprised him by offering to drive to Brattleboro from the city on her own. He found her BMW already waiting for him at Jewel's—how awful it was to think that it was no longer Jewel and Jonathan's—farmhouse when he arrived.

It was a simple funeral. A few words from the bible were read, "Amazing Grace" was sung, and handfuls of dirt were thrown into Jonathan's grave.

Dinner for the mourners was provided by the staff of Jonathan's Restaurant at the same old farmhouse whose soundness John MacArthur had once tested with a penknife. Jewel had sobbed her heart out at the cemetery on Ames Hill, but once back in her home, her relief became unrestrained. The bartender from the restaurant might have had a hand in that, Dan considered. He served up martinis to her non-stop. Waiting and dreading the moment for so long, Dan knew, also had something to do with it. Tears of relief sadly mixed with the tears of grief.

Uncomfortable with the endless condolences, Dan took refuge upstairs, where he and Ingrid had been installed in the master bedroom. Jewel had slept that night in his old room. But for the photographs, magazine covers and posters that had been on its walls, it was unchanged from Dan's high school years. It was probably for the better that images of Elvis, the Everly Brothers, Buddy Holly, Chuck Berry, and others now painful to remember—Fabian? Annette Funicello? Frankie Avalon?—were gone. Only a bullfighting poster advertising Manolete on the closet door had been left in place. He passed the room by.

He examined, instead, without touching them, every photo, every book, every bric-a-brac he could see as he sat on the edge of Jewel and Jonathan's bed. Little by little, Jewel had accumulated items that now crowded out the few things that Peter Klopfer and she had once moved in one trip in the Hudson. There were pictures of Robert and Betsy and their children and pictures of Jon's few relatives. Color photographs taken during the fifties and sixties, of Jewel with Marlboro students, Jewel and Jon, Jewel and Dan, Dan and Jon, were fading away into Cheshire-cat nothingness. The old black-and-white prints of grandparents, of Jewel and his mother as little girls, of Fairfaxes he barely knew, had fared much better.

But where was there a picture of his father? Why was there no picture of him with his mother and father? Why had he never seen a wedding picture? Or a baby picture of himself, except for the one in which Jewel was holding him in what looked like hospital swaddling clothes?

"Danny?" Ingrid called to him from the door. "People are leaving."

As he walked down the stairs with her, he steeled himself for what he had to do next. For the first time in his life, he felt, he would have to burden Jewel with his own problems. And at such a time. And what a way to do it. The feeling was not good.

"When your Pimentel set out with his team to document energy use in corn production," Jewel responded when Dan made his first measured mention of problems with his dissertation, "he did so in part because energy accounting is right in the mainstream of ecology. It's ecosystem analysis in the tradition of the Odums."

The mourners were gone. The bartender was gone. Flowers, cold cuts, and casseroles remained. And a bottle of Hennessy, which the bartender had left. Jewel was having at it.

"Lindeman, you know," she continued, now turning to address Ingrid, "wrote his famous ecosystem paper with Hutchinson's help while I was still chasing after biomes with Shelford."

"Who's Lindeman?" Ingrid asked.

"He died young," Jewel answered. "Hutchinson had to pull a lot of strings to get Allee to even publish the thing. We paid no attention to it at all."

"Who's Hutchinson?"

"My Lord, Dan! Have you taught her nothing?"

"I didn't really take that much interest," Ingrid defended Dan. "Until now. I can see why Dan got into ecology. It's so peacefully beautiful here, especially at the cemetery. It reminds me of Norway when I was a very little girl. The memory of the fjords has never left me. What a peaceful place Jonathan has to rest!"

"It was what he asked."

"We can't let Vermont become like New Jersey," Ingrid said.

Jewel became contemplative. It gave Dan a chance to move the conversation back to the troubles he had too subtly introduced, but he chose not take it. It seemed not the right moment to share with them his need for exorcism.

"Then Howard Odum came to work under Hutchinson," Jewel resumed, slightly slurring her words, "and things really took off. He totally infected Larry Slobodkin with his energy ideas. As he did his yokel brother. Now ecosystem ecology is all the rage. It's what the public means when it says ecology. It's the ecology of Silent Spring."

"So, why isn't Dan doing ecosystems?"

"Not my thing," Dan said, bemused at the way the conversation was going.

"How can you help the ecology then?" Ingrid persisted.

That grated on Dan's nerves. Bill Brown had browbeaten him in his nonetheless avuncular way into never using "the ecology" in that way. It was a particular irritant for Brown, like "specie" used as the singular for species. Both quickly became irritants to Dan, too.

"Dan is what you call an evolutionary ecologist," Jewel stepped in to answer over Dan's scowl. "We invented that when I was at Yale. Ecosystem ecology seems to be pushing evolutionary ecology aside. Ever since Earth Day. Ecosystems don't evolve, you see. Only the individual species in them evolve. How strange to think that the same man started both."

"Hutchinson?" Ingrid asked hopefully.

"Maybe that was the problem with your mice and mites paper," Jewel turned to Dan. "Some people, I read, have a rather jaundiced view of MacArthur's ecology."

"Are you having troubles, Dan?" Ingrid asked.

Dan chose not to answer. None of the conversation was going as he had planned. He waited instead for Jewel to jump back in.

"I like Pimentel's work," Jewel said. "Ecologists should not shy away from studying managed ecosystems. Like cornfields.

Shelford and his generation, on the other hand, preferred to study untrammeled nature only."

She stopped, as if having lost track of her narrative. She took another healthy swig of Hennessey.

"Un-tram-mel-ed," she then said, drawing the word out. "That was why they were all so keen on protecting natural areas. They needed them to study un-con-tam-in-at-ed nature. As if there is such a thing! And why should, I want to know, the subtle, cryptic forces within natural ecosystem proc-ess-es be easier to study than the overt, highly visible, and well-documented man-ip-u-la-tions that man imposes is what I want someone to explain, please. There!"

And she stopped, perhaps to catch her breath. Perhaps, Dan thought, for applause.

"What trouble?" Ingrid pressed Dan, harking back to the conversation's beginnings.

Jewel barged right back in before Dan could give his prepared-in-advance explanation.

"My friend Fred Küchler," she said, "watched himself fade out of ecology when he started doing research with herbicides. 2,4,5-T, it turns out. Just like the stuff in Viet Nam. But that's all irrelevant. There was no Viet Nam then. It was all just that his research was too far removed from what ecology should be doing, too agricultural, too applied."

"Ahhh," Dan finally turned to Ingrid. "Just dissertation problems. I can't seem to get it past Whittaker and I can't find someone to replace him."

"Whittaker?" Jewel asked, suddenly sober. "Robert H. Whittaker?"

"Yeah. Do you know him?"

"Never met him in my life," Jewel said, with a dismissive hiccup.

"He just doesn't seem to want to approve my thesis no matter what, and I can't get anyone to replace him."

"Hah!" Jewel startled them. "Could I? Maybe ... Hmm."

She fell into a contemplative silence. Dan and Ingrid looked at her in a stupefied silence.

"I can take care of it," Jewel broke the silence to coolly announce.

"What?" Ingrid asked.

"Whittaker," Jewel answered.

"How?" Dan asked. "You don't even know Whittaker."

"I have some papers," she told them. "They got mixed up with my own things when I sat at his desk—MY desk, it should have still been—at Urbana. Kendeigh just kept me waiting and I became more and more flustered by it. I think it made me realize that I no longer had any prospects for a PhD. All the men returning from the war on the GI Bill were filling up the universities, just as they did at Marlboro. So, instead of waiting for Kendeigh to finally have my interview, I got up in a fluster and left. Apparently, I picked up someone else's papers along with my own. I never realized it until we had to move back to Connecticut. You know, there were these neat stacks on the desk and nowhere to put my own things, so I put them on one of the stacks."

"What were the papers," Dan asked.

"They're very personal," Jewel answered. "More than personal. Some are of such a nature that I could neither throw them out nor attempt to return them when I found them again."

"OK. I'm curious," Dan said with a hint of condescension. "What's in them?"

"Yes," Ingrid said. "You must tell us."

"No. They were how he felt, about himself and about others, things he would never want anyone to know. Ever. Things that no one in my acquaintance could ever admit, not even to themselves. I don't know how he could have left them on his desk the way he did. It would be better Dan, if you knew nothing about it. So, let me come back with you to Ithaca and look up this Robert H. Whittaker."

Jewel wound up going to Ithaca with Ingrid in her convertible. Dan followed closely behind in his, losing them on coming down off the mountains into Bennington. Jewel knew a way around the traffic jam that always built up in the center of town. Dan missed seeing her turn off and went through town in panicky irritation at a slow-moving truck that blocked his view, seemingly on purpose. He finally caught up with Jewel and Ingrid as they parked across from the Old First Church in Old Bennington. Jewel had decided that Ingrid should see the monument.

The Buick had died on the way to Lambert Field and been abandoned by the side of the road on Kingshighway. For all Dan knew, it was still there. He had found its replacement through the Brattleboro Reformer on a farm just outside of Wilmington.

"How long has it been out here in this condition?" Dan had asked suspiciously on seeing it.

"Oh, not long. Just this spring," the owner had answered glibly. He was a farm boy, he had told Dan, on his father's farm, but he had a bouffant hairdo and a Hell's Angels leather jacket that Dan recognized as the the field marks of a musician.

He had doubted that the car had come off the roads so recently. This was Vermont, his native state, almost. This car had tires, flat, of course, that had nonetheless sunk several inches into the ground, a sure sign that it had spent several freeze and thaw cycles in the same place. Still, it was a Triumph Spitfire, a 1968 model, exactly what he had been looking for in honor, he supposed, of Bill Dritschilo, who had sold his to take a temporary position in Sacramento.

"The registration sticker is from 1977."

"Yeah, but it's mostly been garaged. I took it out only on warm, sunny days. Then Dad needed the barn space back."

Even though the car was in Vermont, Dan had found no signs of rust. It had been an Arizona car for most of its life, the farm boy had bragged. He had bought it in Los Angeles.

The wooden dashboard, Dan noted, still had all of its knobs. Even the rag top, although an easy thing to replace, made him confident by being still in one piece, working and original. Underneath, where the most exposed steel parts were, was a mystery he chose not to explore. The engine had started and come to an almost smooth rumble, but only with the smell of oil mixing with unburned gasoline. There was original rubber still on the door frame. He didn't bother to ask to drive it.

"How much?" Dan had asked. "What's your bottom price?"

"Five hundred. Or best offer."

"Two hundred?"

No deal. Dan had turned and started walking away.

"Three hundred?" had come from behind him.

"Two twenty-five?"

"I'm goin' to hate myself."

With financing from Ingrid, new tires, and surprisingly little in repairs by a British car specialist in Bennington, Dan was soon on the road with it.

Their two-car caravan fared little better in Troy, always a trial, made more so by the city's utter lack of the Vermont-like charm of Bennington. The farther into Troy they went, the more it looked like it could benefit from a wrecking ball, and the more trucks managed to intersperse themselves between Dan and the sportily driven BMW. He finally spotted two women who might have been them in a flashy new sports car that stayed on Route 7 on crossing the bridge over the Hudson River. He followed them uncertainly, thinking that the newer route along the river was far preferable and would have been taken by them. Until he caught up with them on the Northway, he was afraid he might have been following the wrong car.

They pulled off Route 20 for a picnic lunch on a hillside table somewhere in Cherry Valley. Rolling hills and fallow fields faded away in the distance in the remnants of morning fog.

"This is the old heartland of America," Jewel said, unpacking a cooler of leftovers from the day before, "baseball country. Jon and I stopped here both ways on our visit to see you guys."

"You can almost hit the Baseball Hall of Fame in Cooperstown from here with a thrown ball," Dan said to groans from the women.

"There are few places as American to me," Jewel continued. "I'm glad that your going to Cornell let me experience it. Jon, too. It was his last trip away from Vermont. We thank you for it."

They finished the contents of the picnic basket but for the deviled eggs. No one trusted the deviled eggs. Their decorative swirls stayed intact as Jewel repacked them. They returned to Ames Hill two days later, their fate undetermined.

What the two women had talked about on the ride, Dan could only guess. Probably not much. Had he heard it, though, he would not have believed it.

"Do you think you invented sex?" was what Jewel had shouted into the wind to Ingrid in the open convertible at fifty miles per hour. "Your generation just does openly what we did in secret. The sleeping around. The sex acts themselves, blow jobs and head jobs. The gays, the lesbians. It's all the same, but just no longer shameful. Just don't let bad head or—Good Heavens! Why should it?—a dick that doesn't go limp ruin an otherwise good relationship."

When Danny retraced the trip in reverse, Jewel refused to talk either about what had passed between her and Ingrid, or what had transpired with Whittaker.

"Ah, if you see Dan Atkins," Pimentel said to Dan on passing him in the hall outside the Comstock coffee room, "could you tell him I'd like to see him."

"But I'm Dan," he answered in confusion.

"Ah, right-oh," Pimentel answered, barely flustered. "I'll be in my office in a few minutes.

Aunt Jewel had come through for him. Cathy Woodson was smiling at him when he appeared at her desk and ushered him right in, where Pimentel greeted him with an even bigger smile and the news that Whittaker had dropped all his objections to Dan's dissertation. He was willing to resume his place on Dan's committee with a positive attitude toward him. He had pretty much signed off on his dissertation already.

"He apologized for not understanding some of your work," Pimentel explained happily. "Population genetics isn't his field. He said it must have been personal things that made him moody and clouded his judgment. He's not well, you know."

Whittaker even had a job prospect for Dan, Pimentel told him.

That was great news. Krummel and Nafus were set. Dritschilo had already obtained, then changed jobs, then quit to follow Whale into high school teaching, but in Jamie's home town, rather than his own. And that son of a bitch Mendez beat out Si Levin for a position at Yale, Dan had learned from Al Hastings who had gotten it from Si. But what a strange job situation it is, Dan marveled, when students compete with their faculty for jobs!

Job hunting was exactly the kind of hell it had been described to be by those who had preceded him. Endless fusillades of resumes, letters of interest, recommendations, transcripts, and reprints, even, were launched only to find rejections or—worse yet —nothing, no response, worse even than limbo. Even with the problems over his dissertation now seemingly behind him, he could not see how he could end his personal string of rejections. He took some solace, though, from Levin having bombed at New Haven. It made his own situation less of a personal failure.

"It's as a research associate at this man's private foundation," Pimentel said, telling him what he knew about the job that Whittaker had uncovered. "He has a lot of land in Connecticut that he uses as a research preserve. I think he calls it the Arden Forest Research Institute."

"You mean Fred Küchler?" Dan asked.

"Yes. Do you know him?"

"My Aunt Jewel does."

"That's right. I remember your Aunt Jewel. A spunky lady."

"I read some of Küchler's Commentaries in Ecology. He seems to be a bit of a crank, but I do agree with his stand on licensing. Too many people are getting positions in ecology who aren't ecologists."

"Right-oh," Pimentel incongruously cheered. "Küchler is a good ecologist. He did some research on herbicide use and helped Rachel Carson with her book. You know, that was when the Entomological Society censured him for what he wrote about the Ag Experiment Stations and the way they catered to the chemical manufacturers. I can't think of any other individual to be censured that way by a professional society."

"Hmm. Is that why he's not at a university?"

"No, I don't think so. I think he's always been a sort of loner and curmudgeon. He has always been very outspoken and very dogmatic in his views. LaMont Cole thinks a lot of him, though. He came to his defense over the article that had drawn the censure."

Then Pimentel changed the subject.

"You know, I thought you really should have gone and talked to Cole about that paper you guys wrote, instead of replacing him on your committee. I always found LaMont to be a reasonable man, even if an outspoken one."

"Too late, now, huh?"

"I'm afraid so. It doesn't look so good for him."

A glum silence descended over them.

"Well, cheerio!"

How strange life is, Dan thought as he drove back to Danby. First Cole and Whittaker gang up against him. Now, Whittaker, at least, is his benefactor. Both are dying.

How sweet life is.

As usual, Ingrid was in New York. As usual, there was no letter from her. The house was cold. He wished he could be spending his nights with Bill and Jamie, as he had before that trip to Vermont, then their baby coming. Or with Whale. Or haunting the Fly Lab in the middle of the night, like Al Brick. An empty house was so much easier to take in daylight, and being a grad student still was less frightening than what comes after.

Whittaker was not at Langmuir when Dan drove out to learn more about the employment opportunity. Dr. Whittaker would not be in at all that day, the secretary in the E&S office told him, or the next day, or the day after. But after Dan insisted they had an appointment and she checked the calendar, she gave him a slim package of materials. There was not the job description in it that he expected, just Küchler's professional card and a letter of recommendation to him from Whittaker, which he read immediately. It was a good one. It did not go into any great detail or extol every one of Dan's possible virtues, but it was very positive.

As soon as he got to his Spitfire, Dan took out the road maps he kept in it. A small commercial plane buzzed overhead as it came in to land at the airport. Maybe he could fly to Norfolk, he thought. It seemingly was nowhere on his Connecticut map.

At the Fly Lab, Al Brick, who for some reason having to do with his dissertation knew of every research preserve in the Northeast, was no help with Arden Forest, although he had a few choice things to say about Küchler, all typically Brickensian. Dan ignored them.

Soon, the road map was spread open on an empty table next to the "Christmas Room," as Krummel had named it before leaving.

"You better call to get directions," Don Nafus suggested, pointing to a spot on the map.

"Yeah," Rovinsky agreed. "That's nowhere I've ever been before. Colebrook, Norfolk, Winsted, Sandisfield, where is that? No! Wait! Is that Canaan over there? I've heard of Canaan!"

"I think, maybe, from the Old Testament?"

"Hmm. Why don't I just call?" Dan thought out loud, realizing that with Al and Bob competing to find strange place names on the map, he would get little chance at it himself.

"Atkins?" the voice on the phone asked after Dan had summoned the courage to make the call. He felt much more comfortable in the job hunting process when he was the one being called. Jitters always took hold of him when he had to do the calling.

"What do you want again?" the voice on the phone said.

"Robert Whittaker said that you were looking for a research assistant."

"Whittaker, huh? You're not some sort of trick of Jeff Davis's are you?"

"Jefferson Davis?"

"He's the one you'll be replacing. Whittaker, huh? How did he know I was not getting along with Jeff Davis?"

"I don't know. He gave me your card and a letter of recommendation."

"Whittaker, eh? How strange."

Küchler paused, as if making up his mind.

"All right. Come down."

And they got down to driving directions and what day and when to meet. The latter turned into a protracted negotiation. Küchler had some objection to almost every day of the week, it seemed to Dan. Finally, a late Sunday afternoon time was settled on. It was the most inconvenient to Dan of all the choices they had rejected.

Arden Forest turned out to be in the middle of nowhere, as far as Dan was concerned. It was tobacco road without the tarpaper shacks. It being Connecticut, he wondered if he might not be in the middle of tobacco farms, but then he realized that the southern Berkshire climate was unlikely to support tobacco.

A little old man came to the door when Dan finally reached it. Short, gray-haired, with a small beard, he could have been a forest gnome.

"Atkins?" he asked through the screen door.

"You're late," was his greeting when Dan nodded at his name.

Your directions were useless, Dan wanted to say, and the way you're checking out my ass reminds me too much of that pervert Ingrid once saved me from in New York City.

He had blundered around on the back roads until almost dark. If he had not found a house with a light on and been cheerfully given better directions, he would never have found Arden Forest.

"Oh yes, we know Fred!" the woman at the door had gushed.

It had seemed a good omen after Al's stories about how crazy Küchler was.

"Don't look for the sign," she had added. "You'll never see it in the dark. Just remember that it's the third driveway on the right after the pond."

Küchler led him into a small room that was off the kitchen. The table in it suggested a dining room, but it was stacked with journals, books, and manuscripts and ringed with low cabinets. It might once have been a pantry, Dan thought. A huge, framed blow-up of a photograph of Küchler on skis dominated the room from one wall.

"Joy took that," Küchler said, noting Dan's interest.

"It's very good," Dan said.

Küchler seemed to like having Dan enjoy the portrait. Joy had been his wife, he explained. She was deceased.

"Some say that she was the only one in the world who could ever manage to keep me under control. Those few years went by so fast. I just got this print back from Hal Buechner's widow. Joy had given it to him as a present. Did you know Hal Buechner?"

Dan did not.

"So, what are you," Küchler asked, pointing with a slender finger at a chair. "Are you an ordinationist or a classificationist?"

His accent suddenly struck Dan as totally manufactured. It was the Scarsdale accent of an actor in a TV spaghetti commercial he remembered.

"Huh?" was all Dan could muster in answer.

"What kind of an ecologist are you? Are you a Gleason ecologist? A Curtis ecologist? ... Or are you a Whittaker ecologist?"

"I don't think I'm any of those. I guess I'm a Pimentel ecologist, although I used to think I was a MacArthur ecologist."

"Bah! MacArthur! Just one of those virginophilous plant and animal ecologists. Billie Shoecraft, Rachel Carson, Teilhard de

Chardin, LaMont Cole, Roland Clements, Lewis Mumford, Loren Eisley, and Ian McHarg, out-ecologize the ecologists. Not those spineless ivy-towered posers."

"Cole WAS an ecologist," Dan said.

"Right. And a damn good one, too! So why do you have a recommendation from Whittaker, instead of Pimentel?"

Dan wanted to say because Whittaker was a big name in ecology, but he said, instead, "If I had my preference, I would have come here with one from him. I can get it for you easily."

"Why Whittaker, then?"

"Whittaker was the one who seemed to know you."

"Hah! Know me? I'll say. He was why I stopped submitting anything to Ecology until they got a different editor. He made NO editorial comments. He just sent back the manuscript to think over. I feel deeply sorry for his students if he shows no more constructive pedagogic ability than he has shown me. And I think also he is trying to get back at me for the criticism I gave one of his manuscripts, although he asked for it."

Küchler walked over to a filing cabinet and picked a document out of the first drawer he opened and the first file he went to. It looked to Dan as if he might have been able to do it blindfolded.

"Here, read this," he said, opening the reprint to a specific page and handing the document to Dan. "I finally got even with him."

Dan recognized it as a book review in *Ecology*.

"Here, this paragraph," Küchler urged, grabbing the document to point out the passage. "Right after Dansereau."

"Pierre Dansereau," Dan began reading when he got the reprint back, "with Gallic courtesy, restrains himself by saying, It does not seem to be the purpose assigned to me . . . to discuss the climax hypothesis. I shall—"

"No, farther down," Küchler hurried Dan. "The next sentence."

"But in the next chapter,'" Dan resumed reading, "Whittaker plows in and reaches his climax in no time flat—"

"Hah! So what do you think of your Whittaker now?"

"—or rather his climaxes," Dan finished reading the sentence.

He smiled at Küchler. He found the pun both clever and subtle. The old gnome began to resemble a leprechaun. Dan decided to no longer be discrete with him.

"Whittaker's crazy," Dan said. "His wife just died, and he's already running around with one of his grad students. She's half his age. He may be dying himself, from exposure to radiation doing tracer studies."

"Hmm." Küchler turned contemplative. "Hanford Lab? Quite possible. Whittaker had worked with radioactive phosphorus there after being fired from his teaching position. Did you know that? He got fired from Pullman State College. Deserved it, too, Buechner told me."

"Buechner?"

Küchler paused to sigh deeply.

"He died young not too many years ago," he resumed, taking back the reprint Dan was still holding. "I had him as an undergraduate at Syracuse Forestry. He was the most promising student I ever had. I got him to transfer from Syracuse Forestry. I was afraid I was influencing him too much for his own good. Damned good ecologist. Did you know his work with lek behavior in the Uganda kob?"

That Dan did. He could remember almost word for word the lecture Rob Ricklefs had given on it in his undergraduate ecology class. He repeated some of its points to Küchler. It seemed to make the old man warm up to him. He stopped in the middle of refiling the reprint of his book review.

"I strongly suspect, although, I may be wrong," Küchler said, a pall descending over his face, "that Whittaker had a touch of what made José murder Carmen—to seek to destroy what he cannot have for himself, to belittle, and even force to turn against itself, that which he would wish for himself. And so it would seem that he has satisfied his desire to move upwards, only by pushing others down."

He moved closer to Dan and said almost in a whisper, "I think he was an evil influence on my good friend Hal Buechner. They both started their careers out at Pullman State, don't you know. Daubenmire, too. I think that if not for him …"

He broke off there and changed the subject to plant ecology. He deconstructed ordination for Dan. He was brilliant. He spiced his explanations with anecdotes that were learned, to the point, and amusing. He dazzled with erudition on subject matter ranging from philosophy to sociology to music. He wove it all together artfully. Dan hung on his every word, even though his stomach was growling for food, or a coffee, at least, neither of which was offered.

I want to work with this man, he said to himself. All his previous doubts were gone.

"I liked your letter about professional licensing," Dan said.

"Thank you. I am plagued to no end by being forced to compete with these Instant Ecologists from industry, from agriculture, and especially from Organic Gardening circles. Hell, ESA membership means nothing. Anyone can join as long as they can sign their name to the annual subscription charge for the journal Ecology. I was once tempted to sign the application form with an X to see what would happen. And the ethics committee! They couldn't even define what an ecologist are. I tried to lead Nellie Stark into the higher levels of integration, but the belle did not Nell. I resigned from the committee."

Finally, Küchler apparently decided it was time to learn more about the applicant before him. He asked if Dan had family. Dan did not offer his usual reply of being an orphan.

"I'm not married," he said, "if that's what you mean," which seemed to please Küchler

Then Dan added, "Maybe you remember my Aunt Jewel?"

The smile went off Küchler's gnomish face.

"Jewel Fairfax?"

He looked Dan over carefully and silently. Dan felt that he was being inspected for some sort of visible flaw. Then the interview came quickly and politely to an end.

"I don't think I can afford to pay a PhD," Küchler said and wished Dan well as he hustled him out the door without another word.

"What a waste that was!" Dan said aloud as he negotiated the country road in the dark. "What a strange old goat!"

Fortunately, getting to New York could be done on major highways with signs to help him find his way, instead of the backwoods roads he had blundered through in Massachusetts and Connecticut to get to this crazy Arden Forest place. Still, he couldn't expect to get to Ingrid's new place in Manhattan until almost midnight.

It was a shame, he thought, that she had given up her apartment in the Village for the fancy place with a doorman she bought uptown. He liked nothing about the building, starting right with its name.

Who would name a building in New York, Dakota? Dan wondered as he eased his Spitfire through the interchanges leading to the Connecticut Turnpike. Its carburetors had become a bit balky. He hoped they wouldn't flood and start leaking again.

Los Angeles

I

DAN was surprised to find the day's mail still in the mailbox and Ingrid's BMW in the driveway when he came home to the Danby farmhouse. It was her farmhouse now. She had decided that she liked Ithaca better than New York City and on a whim bought the house and, along with it, the barns, a hundred twenty acres, and an assortment of outbuildings that were certain to be nothing more than money-sucking mini black holes, but not as a problem, because her peasant-based designs had gone international so fast that she could no longer keep up with the retail and marketing end of the business and expected it all to crash down on her as ballistically as it had risen, so she quickly sold it, lock, stock, and fabric roll, to an Indonesian businessman. That had created a need to invest the money and find some new thing to occupy her energy, as the mortgage on her east-eighties apartment was no longer enough to keep the IRS from getting their hands on too much of her income, according to her Wall Street financial advisor. The same advisor recommended the farm as a promising way to keep her money away from them. John Gowan helped her get started with a small herd of Shetland cattle, the specific breed being Ingrid's idea, which she claimed she got from Jewel, who got it from Jonathan, who saw woolly, if not shaggy, beasts as a perfect product to keep the bottom line on a 1040 Schedule F form in the red. Jonathan had doted on Schedule F farming. It had saved Jewel and Jonathan from losing their Vermont acres. Ingrid also got advice from Konstantin Frank and was now looking at land along Cayuga to plant some vines.

"Well, if producing inedible beef isn't a good enough way to keep your money out of the hands of the IRS," Dan had said of her new enterprises, "why not some undrinkable wine to boot?"

"You're such a cynic," was all she had said to him on the matter.

Dan no longer brought it up. Neither did he say anything about the new BMW she bought to replace the previous one that was barely two years old. That it was in the driveway paradoxically meant that Ingrid was not home. There were too many places and people and things in the Finger Lakes to keep her home between breakfast and dinner times, so the BMW was parked in the driveway in daytime only when she was away in New York City. It annoyed Dan that she had said nothing to him at breakfast about going back to the city.

Pulling in next to her Beemer in his rusting Spitfire was always a reminder of the chasm Dan feared was forming between them. He thought, for example, he detected a positive attitude in Ingrid toward Ronald Reagan and a negative one for Jimmy Carter, and not just over the Iranian thing. Her politics, he feared, were shifting as much as her accent and her income had. That Scandinavian lilt from their Greenwich Village days that he had found so attractive was becoming subjugated to a Manhattan nasality. Then there was Ingrid's odd fondness for quoting Vermonter Calvin Coolidge's remark that the "business of America is business." And ever since Jon's funeral, she'd been urging Dan to go into ecosystem science.

Now where had that come from? Egbert Leigh had just claimed that part of the attractiveness of the ecosystem concept was its support of the idea of unfettered capitalism. That would be bad enough a reason to have her pushing him into it. Worse still would be if what she knew about ecosystems came by way of her fellow countryman Arne Naess's Deep Ecology topped off with a bit of New Age irrationalism. Essentially, Dan feared her becoming everything he wasn't.

The mailbox held mostly things for Ingrid. There was, however, another rejection letter for him.

Wayne State.

He wouldn't have taken a job in Detroit anyway, he grumbled half aloud, but couldn't they at least have shown some interest in him? He had applied there in hope of getting more interviewing experience on realizing the disaster his initial one had been, the one in St. Louis, the only one not counting the fiasco in Arden Forest.

Couldn't Wayne State at least have put him on their short list? That would have let him salvage some pride.

Still, they did inform him of his rejection, and promptly. Some places didn't even do that. Some never even acknowledged getting his application. Dan guessed that they assumed that the applicant would eventually forget about having applied.

"Why not just stay here without pay?" Ingrid had suggested just the day before. "Maybe something will turn up. Meanwhile, you could do whatever you please with your time."

She had a male friend—Dan knew neither his field nor his name—who had finished his PhD work but then refused to leave Ithaca. He was often at the farmhouse. He claimed to have put off defending his dissertation because he did not want to quit the town softball team. When he wasn't playing softball or pretending he was still a grad student by working as a lab instructor, he was building an environmentally correct house out beyond Newfield. Meanwhile, his wife was supporting them with her job at the hospital. Somehow, though, even with all that, when Dan was with him at gatherings of Ingrid's friends, mostly grad-school dropouts from Cornell, Dan was the one who felt socially superfluous in their eyes. Even though he had his PhD, he was the one who was asked to explain his existence, it seemed to him, and who was then dismissed by being ignored.

But there was a phone call waiting for him. And Ingrid did turn out to be home. She was in the process of taking a message for him when she saw him at the door.

"Here," she said, holding the phone out to him. "It's from UCLA."

They wanted him to fly out for an interview. They were interested in having a Pimentel student join the staff of their new program. He knew little about it and had heard of none of the people he would be working with, but it was UCLA, and they wanted him for an interview.

II

UNUSUALLY for Vermont, Ames Hill Road does not go through the dooryard of Ames Hill Farm. So often, rural roads in Vermont developed from old wagon paths and even cow paths that led between farmhouse and barn. By some Vermont mystery, though, the road is several hundred feet from Jewel's doorstep. Cows must not have liked climbing up the rest of Ames Hill is Jewel's theory on it. Jonathan had held that the final ascent had been too steep for wagons. He had often parked his truck at the bottom of the driveway in winter.

Jewel does not regret the lengthy driveway. It presents a ready-made reason, six days a week, to take herself out of the house for a late morning walk to the mailbox at its bottom. It lets her work out the various muscle kinks and joint aches that develop in the night.

One morning soon after Jonathan's funeral, the mailman arrived with an offer to bring her mail up to her door in return for a cup of coffee. She refused it and he looked relieved, no doubt thinking of winter. Still, he stayed to linger over the coffee she did give him. He was a divorcee, he told her. She listened silently to his prattle. He was handy and could help her with the house, he said. It needed painting and a new porch roof, he told her. She knew that and resented him for saying it. Nothing had been done to the house since Jonathan's illness and death. She waited until his coffee had become cold then showed him out the door.

Walking to the mailbox became a distinct pleasure after that, except during mud season, when she has to walk beside the driveway instead of on it, or during a blizzard, when the pleasure of loosening the stiffness in her bones and being in the fresh air, away from the cooking smells and cat dander in the house, is lost on her, or those twenty-below mornings following a blizzard. She has to make sure to wrap her cheeks and nose in her scarf against the cold then until she can barely look down to see where she is stepping. If she does not, her cheeks and nose will be frost bit before she can get back to her kitchen.

On a morning like this, however, she has no need of a mailbox to get her outdoors. She picks up the mail on her way back from a copse of trees, where there is a stream by which she might find trailing arbutus in bloom or spot a fawn and doe taking a drink. The excitement in anticipating what is in the mailbox tops off the walk.

Jewel has become a prolific letter writer. Her correspondents less so. The letter she wrote to Grandma Atkins is still unanswered going on five years now. Bills, mostly, and cheap advertising circulars make up the mailman's droppings: Grand Union, Price Chopper, Ames, Sears, Monkey Wards, and K-Mart. Even Ace Hardware and Rite-Aide feel obligated to honor Jewel with enticements for their dreary goods.

There is a letter today in what is stuffed into the mailbox. Jewel's immediate guess is that Grandma Atkins has died, finally. But no, the envelope is too small and too full for something like that, and it is postmarked Los Angeles.

She resists the temptation to open it immediately. She fears that might jinx her anticipation of who its sender is. Her heart pounds more than it normally does going up the driveway, where her battle-scarred cat lay at his favorite spot on the edge of the lawn. He looks to Jewel like an old lion waiting for his final fight to come to him. It is good to see him outdoors. Most other months of the year, he is her constant companion near the stove, a catmometer, she calls him, useful in indicating the state of the fire. If curled up in a ball atop his cushioned chair, it needed wood. If stretched out with belly skyward, it needed damping. He rolls over on his belly in the patch of unmowed daisies on seeing her now, so she has to stop to pat him. Except for the letter, which she carries with her, she drops the mail on the kitchen table and gets a cold beer before sitting down to open it.

It is from Danny.

"I am sorry to write so infrequently," it begins. "I guess we started out all wrong when I never wrote to you at all from Greenwich Village. I am just getting the hang of this letter writing thing in general. And I'm sorry for not answering sooner, but it took your letter some time to catch up with me in Los Angeles"

He's finally learned to be polite, she thinks, but he is no more honest with her than he ever has been. Her letter to him, she suspects, has been sitting opened and unanswered for weeks.

A few more excursions into the trivialities of his new life follow. He is living temporarily with a UCLA faculty member, a former Cornellian, a Whittaker student, who has a tiny house in Santa Monica close to Venice Beach. She surely treasures the details that follow, but they make her anxious that he is not going to answer the questions she posed to him in her letter.

Then he finally does get around to them. It is only after descriptions of the bougainvillea, giant geranium bushes, and fig and olive trees of Santa Monica yards.

No, he has not managed to publish his dissertation work. Every time he submitted it somewhere, it got rejected with suggestions that require more research. Pimentel is being no help.

That makes her heart ache, but not as much as the answer to her other question, about Ingrid.

He can not say what their relationship is, because he does not know. They left it uncertain when he moved to LA and that way it still seems to be.

Oh dear. That does not sound good, Jewel sighs, but that's the way it always has been.

"Ingrid seems to hear her biological clock ticking," Danny writes further.

She can imagine, given Ingrid's age.

"I can't see how I can bring a child into this world," the letter continues. "Not my child. Not as a father. Not into this world. There are too many hungry mouths to feed already. How could I take responsibility for another? I could never be a father. I don't even know what a father is. Is it like going out on Linsley Pond with Uncle Evelyn? Or cooking with Jonathan? It has to be more, but all I remember of my father is a ghost in a wheelchair shouting something about me to my mother that I did not understand."

The ink is heavy where he put his pen down next on the paper. Jewel suspects a pause. Tears begin to fill her eyes. She can not read more.

It all seems so familiar to her. It is an echo from a letter, oh, some thirty, forty years ago. She thought she had driven it out of her mind completely.

Oh Danny! How old are you now? Thirty-five? Has it been that long? Is it too late for you?

I have to see you, Danny. She is speaking to the letter. It is lying unfinished, its last page unread, atop a Rite Aid circular.

I can't answer you in a letter. That failed so hopelessly years ago. I know I've never understood you, but I can't stop trying. I need to see you. I need to give you a hug and a kiss and just hold you in my arms for as long as I can.

III

HE could feel Liza Sheriff Little, as she likes to be called, watching them from her corner of the room. She had headed right for it when she came in, as usual, just before the seminar was scheduled to start, as usual. She then very ceremoniously sprayed the legs of a wooden desk-chair and the floor beneath it with a spray can she had taken out of her purse, also as usual.

"Fleas," she had once said to him on noticing him staring at her. "The students and their dogs, you know. They bring them everywhere. My legs are full of bites. Just look at them."

Dan had looked. What he had seen were remarkably shapely legs for an old lady, but no evidence of flea bites.

"I told you that all the castoffs and deadwood on campus rattle their way down into ES&E sooner or later," Dan whispered to Jewel, who was disoriented by having started the morning in Albany. Dan had brought her directly to UCLA from the airport.

"Like all the loose nuts and screws into southern California?" she asked in a whisper equaling Dan's. She had barely glanced behind her when Liza came in.

Liza, Dan whispered, resuming a précis on ES&E that he had started on the freeway, was with the program because she was married to the Nobel-Prize-winner who had conceived the program. Laura Lake, Dan noted as Laura slipped in and sat down next to Liza, was with ES&E because her husband, Jim, was a good bet to win a Nobel Prize. Getting her a job had apparently been part of the package used to lure him to UCLA.

Dan had already filled in Jewel on Richard Perrine, who was not present. Perrine was the head of the program. Stuart F. Little was retired and had anyway never taken much part in its day-to-day operations. Perrine had done that from the beginning. He was a good lecturer and teacher, Dan had admitted, and a tireless administrator, but he was absolutely intransigent in any disagreement, and that was driving Dan crazy.

Perrine was not in attendance because he was in court over his role in a pie-throwing incident. He had not thrown the custard at Edward Teller, but it had been at his invitation that Teller was giving the speech to the local chapter of the Society of Petroleum Engineers. So Perrine had taken it upon himself to defend Teller from the attacker. The pie-thrower, connected in some way to an anti-nuclear group calling itself Bridge the Gap, had accused Perrine with assault on him.

"He almost strangled the poor kid in taking him down," Dan added.

Paul Merifield was sitting near enough to them that he might be hearing Dan's whispers. Jewel tried with her eyes to indicate as much to Dan.

"Merifield over there does have valuable expertise for us," Dan whispered a few decibels lower. "He teaches environmental geology."

Next on Dan's list of faculty was Robert Lindberg, also not present.

"He has academic friends, but no academic experience. As far as I can tell, he spent his career at Rockwell International doing support work for weapons or missile programs of some sort."

Then there was Bart Sokolow, also missing.

"Bart is, well, he's Bart. He's a very recent graduate of the program and its first specific hire, beating me by several months. He's a DEnv, the degree the program confers, rather than a PhD. Lindberg, at least, is a biologist, but he seems to have no concept of what—"

"Who is today's speaker?" Liza interrupted Dan's whisper by calling to him from across the room. This time, Jewel did glance back, a glance that sat her up straight in her seat.

"Jared Diamond. He's with the Medical School."

"Is he talking about siting high-level nuclear waste repositories?" Liza persisted, wrinkling her brow, nose, and chin when no further information came to her from Dan.

"Island biogeography," Dan replied.

Liza grunted her displeasure.

"He's also the heir apparent to—" Dan started to whisper to Jewel.

At that moment, Diamond, a small man—Dan estimated his height at that of Carl Sagan—came walking through the door, preceded by his chin hairs. The beard was an eye-catcher, something out of the nineteenth century. His starkly white shirt and lightly complected face seemed but settings for the dark jewel on his chin.

In other respects, he was undistinguished. He was a kidney physiologist who taught his specialty to the medical students of UCLA. Dan had asked him to give the seminar mostly because he was low hanging fruit. The University of California expected its faculty to freely lend their expertise to others in the system.

Conscious that they were already five minutes into the seminar hour, Dan quickly gave him a very short but overly flattering and possibly erroneous introduction, causing a scowl to appear and stay on Diamond's face for his entire talk. It was on islands, the bird species of the Bismarck Archipelago, Darwin, and how MacArthur and Wilson's Theory of Island Biogeography applied to the conservation of species.

It had not taken long for people to parse the meaning of MacArthur and Wilson's elegant equation. If larger islands supported more species, the thinking went, then so should larger areas in general. And if the size of an existing area is reduced, then it has to support fewer species. So as natural areas decreased in size due to human encroachment, the theory predicted that they would support fewer species. That gave a scientifically credible reason to make—or keep—nature preserves, those undisturbed habitats that ecologists had prized since the days of Clements and Shelford, as large as possible.

Reasoning from species-area data, Diamond, chin raised, argued that if a habitat area were reduced to one-tenth of its former size, only half the species that were initially in it would remain once a new equilibrium was established. He admitted that small habitat islands could exchange species with each other and thus maintain species that might otherwise have gone extinct in any one fragment, but using the bird data with which he was most familiar, he argued that some "species would be doomed by a system of many small reserves, even if the aggregate area of the system were large."

He then offered some design principles. A large, circular reserve was better than a small one or an elongated one. Fragmented reserves should be avoided, but if necessary, should be close to each other, preferably in an equidistant arrangement with connecting strips.

It was at that point that Jewel began to fidget in her seat, casting glances behind her. Her face looked pale to Dan.

"Excuse me," she suddenly whispered. "I have to go."

And she slipped from her seat and was out of the room before Dan could say a word. Diamond's talk, meanwhile, appeared to Dan to have come to a natural stopping point well ahead of the time allotted to it. He jumped to his feet and started to applaud. The rest of the audience joined in as the baffled speaker looked up from his notes and shook his head.

"Using ecological theory to guide environmental decisions is just such a great idea!" Dan gushed before dismissing the students.

Although most filed right out, one pushed his way up to Diamond to ask, "So, if a new six-lane superhighway was built across the Mojave Desert, say from Death Valley to Blythe, would that be like cutting it into two smaller areas?"

"For some species, it might," Diamond answered, a suspicious look on his face.

Dan shrugged his shoulders and glanced at the door. He was still concerned by Jewel's absence.

"Salamanders, snakes, toads, and maybe possums and bunnies? Desert tortoise?" Steve Lavinger persisted. "Navigating six lanes of pavement with high speed traffic should be tougher to cross for a turtle than miles of ocean for a bird. If so, each side of the highway could be expected to have fewer species, something like twenty-five percent fewer species, you said?"

"It would need further investigation," Diamond answered. "But it is certainly possible."

Dan saw not Jewel, but Karen Shimahara, the program's administrative assistant appear at the door, signaling to him.

"Your mom is waiting for you in the office," she whispered.

"Mom?"

"She's fine," Karen explained. "She just didn't want to disrupt the talk by going back in."

She's not my mom, he wanted to say, but Karen had already turned and gone out the door, and Dan still had a duty to the speaker. He returned to the front of the room to try to insert himself back into the conversation.

"And the species to disappear might be the desert tortoise?" Steve asked Diamond.

"Island bio theory says nothing about the identity of the species," Dan cut in, "only their numbers, but the theory would predict about twenty-five percent. Might be more. I did a quick calculation."

Diamond gave him a dirty look. That the rare species would be the ones lost was exactly what he had just implied in his talk.

"Of course, the greater concern is just simple loss of habitat," he said brusquely, quickly adding, "I'm afraid I have another appointment."

And Diamond was gone.

"You can raise to powers in your head?" Lee Hannah, the only student to have stayed behind besides Lavinger, asked in astonishment.

"Noooo," Dan scowled. "It's a factor of two. It's easy to do with logarithms."

"I guess."

"Is it just me, or do you guys think Diamond looked like a miniature version of Gregory Peck in Moby Dick?" Dan asked as he led them toward the door.

"He's a lot shorter," Lee said.

"He might be as misguided as Captain Ahab," Steve said. "You must have read that exchange in Science?"

When the question evoked no answer, Steve went on: "Two smaller refuges might actually support more different species in total. Dan Simberloff's mangrove island experiments show that. Diamond never mentioned it. And that island shape bullshit is just bullshit."

"Wait!" Dan exclaimed. "What? Who?"

"It sounds like this needs to be continued over beers," Charlie Kratzer, Lee's inseparable buddy, called from the hall.

"There's a good Mexican place that's just opened. Free natchos," Steve suggested.

"And did you notice that he never once smiled?" Lee asked Steve as they followed Dan.

"Maybe you don't smile when you're searching for the great white whale."

Westwood Village, on the edge of campus, was not like any other commercial strip on any campus anywhere. It had at least a half dozen theaters, all with giant screens and Dolby sound systems, and although convenient to UCLA, it hardly catered to the students. It catered to the world. Its shops were competition for those along Rodeo Drive and drew some of the same beautiful people. Its restaurants were the trendiest, each with a potential Wolfgang Puck in its kitchen. The theaters premiered movies. Crowds of wannabe beautiful people and youths caught up in the excitement mobbed the streets from late afternoon to midnight, when the movie theaters finally let out. The group from ES&E had to navigate around lines waiting for theater showings.

"That theater," Dan said to Jewel of an Art Deco movie palace, "the Fox, has a screen so big that you have to turn your neck to see from one end of it to the other."

Jewel had totally recovered from what she described as a little panic attack. Too much time spent in the air, she thought was the cause.

"Are all those people waiting to see Star Wars again?" she asked.

"It's a sequel. And the movie across the street also stars Harrison Ford."

"This place is heaven to movie lovers," Lee Hannah added. "There's at least a half dozen theaters within a few blocks of each other."

"More than half a dozen," his friend Charlie added. "Hey! Look!"

"What?"

"Isn't that John Wooden coming our way?"

"Probably going to his office," Dan said. "It's in the John Wooden Center."

"Yeah," Charlie agreed, "even though he hasn't been the basketball coach for several years."

Greetings of "Coach" rang out. Wooden returned them with a polite smile. Jewel's attention, however, was elsewhere. She was back in her girlhood, on a first visit to New York City.

The Fox's marquee featured a fake skyscraper, also Art Deco. It gleamed with an orange tinge in the late afternoon sun and Los Angeles smog. A developer had constructed most of the buildings of the Village's shopping area in the nineteen twenties. He had followed a Mediterranean style that was jazzed up with Art Deco motifs. That was what made Jewel think she was back on Broadway in the 1920s, 1929, to be exact, with her father. Beyond the Village were the box-like glass office buildings of Wilshire Center in one direction and the post-war utilitarian brick facades of campus in the other.

Steve Lavinger was already helping himself to free hors d'oeuvres, mostly chili-hot or salty things that needed washing down with much beer. He had a degree in geology, Dan noted for Jewel, as they found an empty table. He was distinguished by having bought a house in nineteen seventy-one that sat on the Sylmar fault. He knew the recurrence interval for quakes along the fault and guessed that buying it at a rock bottom price just after the earthquake was a good investment. Charlie, Dan told Jewel, had an engineering degree, while Lee was either a bio major or a philosopher. Maybe both.

"Why is it so important to pigeonhole the students according to their educational background?" Jewel asked him as the still-growing group seated itself around them.

"Hmm," Dan paused to think for a moment. "It is how I've been introducing them, isn't it?"

"It certainly is."

"The program requires an MS in some field of science," Dan began to explain, "but I have to reach back to their undergraduate majors sometimes. A habit, I guess. It helps me keep track of their expertise. It's important when assigning tasks in our Problems Courses."

Marlene Broutman, a dark-haired beauty with smoldering eyes, sat down at their table.

"Biochemistry?" Jewel guessed.

Marlene made no answer. She had latched onto Dan on Wilshire Boulevard and was now making certain that neither he nor Jewel had to make any exertion to get beer or nachos.

"Are beautiful women in warmer climates more intelligent?" Jewel asked when Marlene went off to the buffet.

Dan laughed.

"The female students here are a far cry from those at Cornell, aren't they? These women are never without make-up. I had one on a field trip who refused to go on a hike—and get this, it was into a wilderness area—without her make-up kit. Even Ingrid, with her glamour profession, never wore make-up on a hike."

Marlene returned to put two small plates of fried wings in front of them. Steve was right behind her with a pitcher of Corona and two mugs. Charlie then showed up with a load of tortilla chips and the bar's signature guacamole dip.

"So, let me give you the background on this island bio stuff," Steve said, sitting down next to Dan.

The eyes of the others began to glaze over.

"Simberloff is the world expert on the theory of island biogeography," Steve began nonetheless, even as he realized Dan was probably his only audience, or maybe because of it. "He and ah —damn, I forgot his first name—Abele is his last name. A-b-e-l-e. Anyway they put a paper in Science pointing out that there were neither theoretical grounds nor evidence from data to justify the way that Diamond and others applied the theory to conservation. In fact, they showed that two smaller areas would support more species than a single reserve of equal area. What is more, they had data. Besides fumigating some mangrove islands to kill everything on them but the mangroves, Simberloff cut barriers through others. Fragmented islands held more species in combination than any of the fragments. That was expected, but for one set of mangroves there were four more species in total than before the island got dissected."

"Cool."

Steve looked around. It was Lee Hannah. He was standing behind him, apparently trying to hear him over the din of the other conversations.

"But wait!" Lee piped up again. "Are they saying that refuges should be fragmented?"

"Well, the wildlife conservation crew came gunning for Simberloff and Abele's scalps over that. You should read the entire exchange," Steve said, trying to get Dan's attention back as he did so.

"So these guys are recommending smaller reserves?" Lee persisted. "Why would they want to do that?"

"From what I could tell," Steve continued, "they were arguing against bad science."

"Were those the islands he worked on with E. O. Wilson?" Jewel asked, raising her voice to be heard above the music in the bar. "The ones that proved island bio theory?"

"It was until Simberloff decided that maybe it didn't," Dan answered in a louder voice. "It was the same data."

"Who is this singing?" Jewel almost shouted.

"Why?" Dan shouted back. "Is it annoying you?"

"David Bowie," Lee shouted. "And that's Freddie Mercury," he added when a second singer picked up the tune.

Los Angeles

"I like it," Jewel said. "It's interesting. I've been hearing it everywhere, but who is Freddie Mercury?"

"Lead singer with Queen!"

"Oh! Short dark hair and mustache?"

People around her made affirmative gestures and noises.

"It used to be longer, though," Marlene added. "And he didn't used to have a mustache."

"I've seen that video. Scaramouche, right?"

"Bohemian Rhapsody."

"With David Bowie. Very interesting."

"Wait a minute. Wait a minute. How do you get MTV?" Dan asked Jewel. "Did you get a satellite dish?"

"Good heavens, no! The college kids keep me up on these things when I drop by Marlboro. So do some of the musicians. Queen t-shirts were very big last summer."

"Oh, that's right. You still—"

"I volunteer one day a week."

Then, like all grad student get togethers, the good intention that brought it about, to talk shop, soon was lost in more general types of conversations. Island bio gave way to music groups arising in LA, cases of beer drunk on camping trips into the desert, good surfing areas, and classic sports cars. Dan found himself arguing the merits of a new group called the Waitresses with Lee and Marlene while Jewel was fully engrossed in discussing wedding preparations with Bart Lundblad.

The ESE&E program had space temporarily allotted to it in a number of different places on campus. The administrative office, where Karen Shimahara reigned, was on the seventh floor of the Institute of Geophysics and Planetary Physics, Stuart Little's old home and a great place, according to Dan, to ride out an earthquake. The shaking intensified with each floor. Most of the faculty were housed in the ground floor of the Engineering School's Boelter Hall in four little cubicles off a small reception room. Around a corner and down a hall, a lab abandoned by the Engineering School normally overflowed with ES&E students. It was empty, though, when Dan and Jewel looked into it, but for a grad student from Taiwan who was heavily engrossed in a thick textbook.

"No car pools to meet with like us," Dan said in explanation of the emptiness, so unlike the Fly Lab at the same time of day, "they're either still in the bar or on their way home."

Like all engineering and physics buildings, Boelter Hall's passageways were wide and tall enough to move genuinely large pieces of equipment. They were rarely crowded, even at peak passing times between classes.

At the moment, however, one Mark Eaton, a basketball player, was taking up the entire hallway ahead of them, seemingly with his broad back alone.

"What's he doing at UCLA?" Dan wondered aloud. "He's a backup player here. Why isn't he at some other school, where he could start? Or even star."

Jewel shrugged her shoulders. She was not much of a sports fan. Dan had become one. Being at UCLA, especially with Bart Sokolow feeding him basketball tickets two rows behind Al McGuire and Billy Packer whenever he couldn't attend himself, which was often, made Dan into one.

"Maybe he gets more celebrity here," Dan continued, even though he knew Jewel was barely listening. "There was some guy here who played back-up to Bill Walton, Sven Somebody-or-other, who made it in the pros. Sven Nader, I think it was. And this guy must be half a foot taller."

"You're living in Celebrity City here," Jewel said. "Who was it, Rod Stewart, you said played soccer on the field next to yours?"

Janet Ransom, the secretary for the Boelter Hall office enclave, although anxious to leave, because it was past her normal quitting time, was giving her tenuous assessment of "Alien," which she had seen the night before, to those killing time while waiting for Perrine, back from court, to finish his phone calls.

"I don't know how to describe it. So much of it was sort of gross. It had these really, really slimy scenes in it."

"Slimey?" David Tan asked.

"Oozing stuff."

Tan was there because he normally car-pooled with Perrine to Canoga Park. David had a roomy apartment in a complex at one end of Canoga Park, and Perrine had a California ranch house at the other. Unlike how he had put it in his letter to Jewel, Dan was still transient, staying where he could. This night it was to be at Tan's apartment complex with a neighbor who had an empty room. Other nights, it was on a couch in David's living room. Last night, it had been at the home of the former Cornell student. Sometimes, it was on an army cot in his office cubicle. A very few nights, it was in a pricey hotel near campus.

As were many apartment buildings in Los Angeles, Tan's was about to be condoed, basically converted from rental apartments into condominium units that needed to be purchased. It was a good deal for the building owners, who stood to capitalize well on their original investment while continuing to collect a tidy profit on management fees and such. It was not so good for the tenants.

"What do I own when I buy a condo?" David complained. "Even if I could afford it. Pool privileges and parking?"

He explained to Jewel how he and Tessie had moved with their daughter to LA from Palo Alto on getting his degree. The assumption was that they would buy a house as soon as possible, given that their family was about to grow by one. They had first rented a three-bedroom, two-bath house on Tampa Street in Reseda. They loved it. It had a yard with an olive tree and oleander shrubs. Its lanai had been converted into a room with a hanging fireplace and glass walls. It was a cozy place, but the owner, someone in the movie industry, had to sell it to afford his condo in Sherman Oaks. He had offered it to them at a reasonable price, and was willing to accept the rent they had already paid as a down payment. But Tessie heard bad things about the neighborhood school, and they moved into the apartment complex until they could find the right place to buy. Less than a year later, the same house was sold for almost double the price. They could no longer afford it or any other reasonable house. A Stanford PhD with a successful career assured, David was seriously considering giving up his tenure-track position in Civil Engineering to take Tessie and their children back to the Phillipines.

"They say we should be happy with our salaries at UCLA," he told her. "They say we get psychic pay by being UCLA professors."

Then he laughed heartily.

"I told them, in that case, I'll give them psychic work."

"So, how are we all going to fit into your little Spitfire?" Jewel asked when another car-pooler, Perrine's son appeared. He was a sturdy UCLA undergrad, well over six feet tall.

"Nah," Jeff Perrine said. "Oh, we could all fit into it, but it would never get us over the pass. We're taking my Dad's Volvo."

"What are you doing about your car?" Jewel asked Dan.

"I'm leaving it in the parking garage."

"That works," said Jeff.

"They found the pie thrower guilty," Perrine announced, finally coming out of his corner cubbyhole. "Now his lawyer is threatening to sue me."

"What on earth for?"

"Injuries!"

Aside from being necessary as the driver, Perrine completed a full carload, enough to qualify for the new HOV lanes that were slowly being introduced in California, had there been any where they were most needed, such as on the Sepulveda Pass. Perrine and Jewel, as Perrine's houseguest for the evening in his daughter's old room, were in the front of Perrine's Volvo. Jeff was in the back with Dan and David.

"I've been looking into all kinds of schemes that will let me stay at UCLA but live someplace affordable," David continued his housing travails as they inched up the pass on the freeway.

"It means someplace like Palmdale. It's a long commute, even for native southern Californians. It's at least an hour's drive and has all the amenities of living like poor desert rats."

"An hour?" Perrine, who until then had been decidedly quiet, now interrupted. "You'd be lucky to do that trip in twice that during communing hours." Then he added, "I don't see how he can sue me over a little thing like that. I barely touched him."

"He'll never get away with it, Dad."

"I thought somewhere in the southern Sierra might be nice," Tan wistfully returned to his own concerns. "Some of those Valley towns have airports."

The Volvo's catalytic converter, a new California model, was working beyond capacity on the ten-mile-an-hour climb. The smell of rotten eggs began to permeate the car. Since all were certain one of the others had farted, no one had to speak up to disavow it.

"You could do like Ernie Englebert," Perrine finally broke the silence that prevailed. "He's a political scientist who works with us on some projects. He lives in Walnut Creek and commutes to UCLA."

"Walnut Creek?" Jewel asked.

"It's in the Bay Area. He takes a plane from San Francisco, or maybe Oakland, Tuesday mornings. He says flying to Hollywood-Burbank—you know, where they filmed that last scene in Casablanca—takes him only two hours door-to-door. He teaches his classes on Tuesdays and Thursdays and keeps Wednesday open for committee meetings and things."

"So he flies back Thursday night and takes a long week-end at home?" Jewel marveled. "I think I'd love to have an academic schedule."

"He's in poli-sci, remember," Perrine said. "His expertise is in government, so he needs to be close to Sacramento. Mondays and Fridays are his research days."

"But his is not the longest commute," Dan called out from the back seat.

"No," Perrine, forgetting his own troubles, picked up from him. "There's Stanley Trimble in the Geography Department. He had a farm in Tennessee that he just hated to give up, so he never did move to UCLA. He has a two-thousand-mile commute."

Jewel slumped back into her seat. The Volvo was finally over the pass and slowly merging onto the Ventura Freeway.

"What does he do? Bunch everything together into one semester?" Jewel asked.

"Well, we have quarters here," Perrine answered as traffic came to a halt, "but you've got the idea. There's a lot of flying back and forth for holidays and things. I think both of them spend a lot of nights sleeping in cots in their offices, although Trimble did share an apartment for a while."

"Not again!" Dan whined as the traffic appeared about to come to a permanent halt.

Perrine, though, saw a space in an adjacent lane, gunned the engine as everyone else in the car held their breaths, and the Volvo was suddenly through the bottleneck and down into The Valley.

"Their trunks look so skinny that they might snap in a breeze," Jewel said of the palm trees that lined Sherman Way, "except that their leaves, bunched ridiculously atop like that, like the colored plastic on a cocktail toothpick, look like they would blow off in the first gust of wind."

"I think that's part of the adaptation that gets them through storms," Jeff said. "They're so skinny that they bend instead of break."

No one in the car, however, could name what species they were for her. Dan, however, was the only one who looked sheepish about it.

"Many more songs have been written about autos than horse carriages or surreys. Just try to think of some."

"Jingle Bells."

"Surrey with the Fringe on Top?"

"And how many of us saw our first movies at a drive-in?"

Jewel laughed politely. All the way back over the pass, now free of traffic, Perrine was charming her by recounting the various ways that autos were important in American life. What usually followed, Dan knew, was a lecture on SOx, NOx, VOCs, ozone, VHCs, PANs, and other ways autos have of begriming the air in Southern California.

"How many of us had our first sexual experience in a car?"

Jewel laughed uproariously, even wiping tears from her eyes. She had totally charmed Perrine and he was trying to charm her in return, even offering his services as a guide for the next day, which she turned down graciously, but he still insisted on driving them back to Westwood instead of letting David Tan do it. Tan, Perrine was certain, would rather spend the morning with his family. Meanwhile, Perrine added, due to his court appearance, he had work he had not finished the day before. In return, Dan promised to introduce him to a presidential candidate.

The turnout was so sparse for a Saturday appearance by a Presidential candidate that they feared they were either too late or too early. Only one of the four local news services was in evidence. Tricia Toyota was there with a cameraman, but Connie Chung was nowhere to be seen. Neither Peter Jennings nor Tom Brokaw nor Roger Mudd nor any of the nationally known newsmen were there. That Barry Commoner had been interviewed on television the night before may have had something to do with that. Bridge the Gap came out in force, however. Their placards objecting to UCLA's nuclear reactor were conspicuously in sight beside the candidate, who they assumed shared their views.

The crowd made up in enthusiasm, though, for what it lacked in size. Every one of Commoner's pronouncements from the top of the Janss Steps raised a cheer and supportive motions from hand placards below him.

"He's right in what he just said about the Texas Railroad Commission," Perrine turned to Dan to say. "It does set oil prices in this country."

"I was so happy when you went to work for him, Dan," Jewel spoke up with pride. "He was one of the very first to warn of dangers from nuclear tests."

Dan had no wish to correct Jewel on how much he had actually worked for Barry. Or with Barry. Or even seen him while in St Louis.

"Yeah," Dan said instead. "His Science in the Public Interest is older than Silent Spring."

"He's not always right, you know," Perrine then said indignantly. "I can show you some things that he's dead wrong about."

"Oh?" Jewel asked.

Dan immediately recognized in Perrine's attitude a reason to change the subject. "Dead wrong" from Perrine's lips meant absolutely, irrevocably, in disagreement with his view of things and indicated a need for some educating, which he would soon very pompously provide.

"So," Dan ventured. "Are you going to vote for Barry?"

"Why not?" Walt Westman suddenly appeared beside them to answer first. "An ecologist in the White House!"

There had been a number of people Dan had been told to look up at UCLA, people one way or another in ecology. Many had met him warmly with well intended promises to include him in future activities, but with no departmental meetings or functions in common—not even offices in the same building—the promises had come to nothing. Walt had been different. Dan had not known him at Cornell. Their times there had not overlapped. Dan gave him a call only on an off-hand suggestion by Bill Brown. "Los Angeles is such a hedonistic place," Bill had said on hearing of Dan's appointment at

UCLA, "but Walt Westman is there, so it can't be all bad." Walt had stepped in perfectly for the forgetful others, always smiling, always willing to listen. Often, it was he who called to see if they could share sandwiches together. He also went as far as offering to put Dan up for a night. Dan had accepted and enjoyed not just a comfortable bed but also a pleasant evening of conversation with Walt and his roommate. Walt made it clear that Dan could always crash with them in an emergency and Dan often did.

"I can't vote for Reagan," Perrine said. "He absolutely ruined the University of California when he was governor. I just might vote for Barry."

Westman's bookcases were stuffed with books on various liberal causes, Dan knew. All the "rights" were covered, from prisoners' to women's to animal to Chicano to gay. Perrine, meanwhile, good petroleum industry scientist that he was, was known to have voted for Nixon. Still, the two appeared to be agreeing.

"Come on," Dan urged on seeing that things were breaking up. He led them through Commoner's mostly small, mostly Angeleno retinue to the candidate himself, who impressed by remembering Dan.

"What?" Walt asked of the puzzled looks coming at him from Jewel.

"I'm sorry," she answered Walt as Dan said his farewells to the candidate, who was looking dubiously at Perrine, who held his hand in a firm grip while he instructed Barry on something and was not letting go. "It just struck me how much you look like Freddy Mercury. You could be his exact double. Also, I don't think we've been introduced."

"Thank you," Walt answered with a broad smile. Then he gave a full laugh and held out his hand. "Walt Westman. I've been told that before. But you mean how he looks now, not in his glam rock phase."

"What would you call it now? His butch phase?"

The smile left Walt's face.

"I'm Jewel Atkins, Dan's aunt," Jewel said, offering him her hand and her own smile.

"I know."

"I love that song he did with David Bowie," Dan turned away from Commoner and Perrine to say.

"Under Pressure?" Walt said, his smile back. "It's my theme song."

"That's the one I like. I hear it these days, seemingly everywhere," Jewel said. "Even on the airplane. Several times."

"Yes," Walt said. "It is ubiquitous. And it's a long flight." Then he turned to Dan "You know Dieter John, don't you?"

"I know of him, of course. Haven't met him yet."

"A former Pimentel student and you haven't met him yet?"

Dan shrugged his shoulders.

"I talked to him last night. He expects to be in San Francisco next week. You've hit it lucky. The people renting his house while on sabbatical have moved out, so it's all yours, if you want it for a few weeks."

"Where is it?"

"Woodland Hills. Right at the bottom of Topanga Canyon Road."

"I can still car pool with Dick!"

"Sure," Perrine chimed in, having freed the potential future president from his grip. "David and I would love your company on a more regular basis. Say, Barry Commoner is all right. He agreed with me completely about the oil crisis."

"Summer school?" Jewel asked, watching children being let out in small orderly groups that fell apart as soon as they were out on the sidewalk.

"No," Dan answered. "School starts in August here. Looks like it's the first day."

"How cruel. Hispanics, are they?"

"Mexicans mostly," Dan said, "but you're right to call them Hispanics. Not all are Mexican. Some are Americanos, Americans, like us. Some consider themselves still Mexicanos. I imagine there must be Cubans and Puerto Ricans in LA, but I have yet to run into one."

"Have you ever run into a Cuban?" Jewel asked.

"Hmm. Maybe. Yeah, once at a party at Penn, but he didn't look at all Hispanic."

"What about Puerto Ricans? Is Walt Puerto Rican?"

"Why do you ask?

"I guess from the way he greets—Hispanics?—in their own language. He's so accepting of them."

"Walt lived in Puerto Rico as a schoolboy."

"His name isn't Puerto Rican."

"I think he said his father was Czech."

"Westman?"

Dan shrugged his shoulders.

"Hot," Jewel said, stopping in the shade of a eucalypt. "Oppressively so. And not exactly dry air, is it?"

"All the swimming pools and watered lawns might have something to do with that."

"And smoggy, too," she said, starting off again. "Is it as bad for us as they say?"

"Yep. All these people that you see here are going to die from it, if this keeps up. Last week, I went right from my soccer game to the emergency room of the nearest Kaiser Permanente. I couldn't catch my breath. I knew I was too young for a heart attack, but I thought I was having one. They told me it was just the smog."

"Just the smog! Oh dear." Then, "Kaiser?"

"A managed care system. One of my bennies."

"How is it?"

Dan shrugged his shoulders. "It works really great for me."

The thermal inversion responsible for the current smog episode, one of the longest in years, coincided with the fire season. Dan and Jewel had to abandon the idea of driving the Angeles Crest Highway, even should the Spitfire, still at the parking deck, be brought to life. It had refused to start. Rather than haul it to a shop at Reseda, Dan had spent the rest of the day with Walt in assembling the various tools he needed to adjust the carburetors, replace a cracked distributor cap, and adjust the valves, all of which he claimed were needed for it to start.

Jewel had wished to see the high chaparral, a biome she had never experienced, and to collect Coulter pine cones—and get above the smog to look down on it from Mt. Wilson. The road was closed due to the fires blazing in the surrounding forest, anyway, Walt told her before dropping her off at his house while he and Dan went scavenging for tools. Fire-fighting aircraft, the usual method used in that rugged terrain, were also restricted from the area in the daytime, he further explained. They could only be used at night, because the inversion kept the smoke so thick that flames could not be detected to drop water or fire retardant on them in the daytime. At night, their glow gave them away.

Jewel had hid her disappointment. The high chaparral would stay another biome she regretted not getting to experience, another feather in Edith Clements's now long gone hat. She had willed herself to find something else to experience. When Walt returned with Dan, without the Spitfire, she told them she wanted to wet her feet in the Pacific Ocean. It was within walking distance of Walt's place, even if few Angelenos would have walked it.

"It's sort of like the Socialist Realism movement of the thirties," she now remarked, stopping at a Venice Boulevard wall mural. "You know, Diego Rivera, Thomas Hart Benton, Rockwell Kent. It's good."

As far as street art went, Dan only knew the soup cans and Marilyn photos of Pop Art posters glued to Greenwich Village walls and the graffiti of Chewy and Corn Bread in Philadelphia. A street mural as original art was a new concept to him.

"When do I start smelling the ocean?" Jewel wanted to know. "It seems as if we've been walking forever."

"It depends on the wind direction. Right now, it's coming off the desert. Santa Ana winds they're called. They're what fan the flames of all the fires we're having. We should be in sight of the ocean by now."

"I think I can see it." Then, as the wall murals gave way to graffiti, Jewel said unexpectedly, "So I want to know what the story is."

"What? This graffiti?"

"You and Ingrid. What's the story?"

"I don't know myself," Dan answered, picking up their walking pace in annoyance.

"What do you think that means?" Jewel asked, easily keeping up with him. "You two have been together for—what is it? Almost twenty years? What do you mean you don't know?"

"No." Dan stopped. "Can't be. No, you're right. It's almost been that long. Wow."

He started walking again. Jewel kept after him.

"She'd love to come visit you."

Dan kept walking.

"How long has it been? Over a year?"

"How can I invite her out here?" he stopped to say. "You see my situation. Big shot UCLA professor. Doesn't even own a hook to hang his hat."

"Ingrid wouldn't care. But why not fly east?"

"Money. Time," he said as he resumed walking. All those other marks of success that I'm lacking, is what he did not say.

"I think she wants to be a mother, Dan."

"Maybe," Dan said, deep in thought. They walked slowly in silence for a few moments, then Dan picked up the pace, asking, "What if I'm just someone who is handy for it?"

"Don't be silly," Jewel suggested, keeping up with him. "She wants a life with you. That's obvious to me. Why isn't it obvious to you?"

"Have you talked to her about it?" Dan asked without looking back. "Are you two planning something for me?"

"These things are obvious to a woman, Danny," Jewel caught hold of his elbow to say. "And it would be like a grandchild to me. I wish we were planning something. I—"

"Look out!"

Dan just barely managed to drag her out of the way of an onrushing skate boarder who was followed by an out-of-control roller skater. They had reached the boardwalk at the beach, or, rather, its skating path. Aunt Jewel surprised him by feeling so small, so light, so fragile in his arms when once, in her arms, she had seemed so formidably solid to him.

"I'm all right, thank you," Jewel said as he led her to a nearby bench and made room for her next to a muscled Californian. "This is better than the shade. I noticed the change in the air a few blocks ago. It smells like Old Saybrook."

"So what do you want to do tomorrow, here in Southern California, after I fix the Spitfire?" Dan asked. "Malibu?"

Jewel thought for a second.

"You always wanted to go to Disneyland when you were a kid," she said, "especially after the polio. We could never afford it. I always wanted to go to Disneyland with you."

"Well then, we'll go."

"Right now, though, staying here on this bench, under these palms, is the best thing I can think of doing."

The other occupant made no effort to move. Dan remained standing. Jewel turned to stare out to where the waves were breaking. It was full of surfers. It was the Pacific Ocean.

"Let's go," she said, leaping to her feet. "Let's do it."

Ignoring—or no longer feeling—the heat and the smog, she ran to the beach in her sandals and was in the water before Dan could catch up.

When she turned to look back at him, he looked to be dancing away from the surf as it came up on the wet sand, studiously avoiding getting his sneakers wet, rather than taking them off and wading in. She slogged up toward him.

"Did I tell you I was just out to Yale recently?" she said. "Evelyn invited me to a birthday party, so I thought, why not?"

"Anybody there that we know?" Dan asked, relieved at being away from the surf.

"Not really. They were all Yale people, I think, but not any I knew. The ecologists are all gone from Yale. The molecular biologists won that war there, I'm afraid. Margaret Davis was hired to replace Hutch. They don't seem to see her as an ecologist."

"Yeah, I sort of heard that. The guy they hired from Cornell was something like a molecular ecological geneticist."

"He has a new wife," Jewel added, as they headed to the street.

"Who? Mendez?"

"Mendez? No, Evelyn. Margaret died, you know."

"Margaret Davis?"

"No! Evelyn's Margaret. It was quite a shock to him, even though it might have been for the best. She had Alzheimer's in the end. I'm told he had been forced to scrub the kitchen floor himself, when he could get around to it. He was never very wealthy, apparently. Who's Mendez?"

"Nobody," Dan said, deep into thoughts that then flitted away as quickly as they came. "So how is the new wife?" he asked just before spotting a bus coming down Venice Boulevard. "Ooh! Let's catch that bus. Maybe we can catch it before it gets to Pacific Avenue."

He trotted ahead to stop it before she could answer his question.

"She's black," Jewel said once they were seated in the air-conditioned bus that Dan hoped would take them to within blocks of Walt's bungalow, where he had offered to put them both up for the night so that Dan could attack the leaky carburetors first thing in the morning. "Very elegant," she felt the need to add. "Much younger than Evelyn. I think she works as some sort of lab assistant in a freshman biology course at Yale and teaches at a New Haven high school."

"And?" Dan asked when Jewel was silent for a moment. "You seem to be avoiding something."

"She drinks like a fish. There's fear she's a full-blown alcoholic. Hutch will be scrubbing floors again, I'm afraid. He'll be taking care of her in his old age, instead of the other way around."

Dan made a whooshing noise.

"Yeah. Life doesn't turn out like you expect."

"**Rachel** Carson? Rachel Carson wanted you to be her assistant? I mean, wow! You could have worked on Silent Spring! How could you have ever passed that up?"

"Geography, I guess," Jewel says with a shrug after a short pause to think it over. "Neither Maine nor Maryland are very close to Vermont."

"Its impact on ecology is incredible. On the profession of ecology, I mean. We're still sorting it out." Walt is holding forth at a table at the Hungry Tiger in Westwood. There were three places set at it, but only he and Jewel remain, stretching out the meal to pass the time. Dan took off to try to balance the carburetors on the Spitfire. There were two of them, he informed them before leaving. "The exact effects of Silent Spring didn't really become clear until after NEPA was passed, but they are substantial. Wow! It's amazing to follow it through. It think it's why the International Biological Program developed as it did. We call it IBP for short."

"I know the IBP and also the IGY and I know NEPA," Jewel says. "I taught ecology. I've only been retired a few years."

She pushes about the remnants of what was a mountain of crab meat topped with shredded cheese and things that Jonathan would have identified for her, all served over a bed of cob lettuce, another thing Jonathan would have explained to her, were he still with her. She surprised Dan by ordering the cob salad instead of the twin lobster dish, as Dan and Walt both did. He must have assumed that, as a New Englander, she would enjoy having one of the lobsters that the Hungry Tiger flew in fresh from Maine every day.

"Lobster fits an ecology-friendly lifestyle," Walt claims as he cracks his one remaining claw. "It's a bottom-feeding organism. Eating it is eating on a lower trophic level than predatory fish like tuna. It makes us closer to being herbivores."

"Herbivores, eh?" Jewel says. "That means you kill innocent green creatures that can't fight and can't run. They are rooted to the ground, so to speak. Hardly sporting, if you ask me."

"They feel no pain, at least."

"I suppose, having no central nervous system like ours," Jewel replies languidly, "plants can't experience consciousness, self-doubt, and despair like we do, but who are we to say that their kind of consciousness is less worthy than ours?"

"Did you know that plants do have well-studied responses to injury, though? But you don't have to kill a plant to eat it," Walt says, his broad smile filling his face. "You can remove leaves, or eat fruits and grains."

"Yeah, right," Jewel keeps teasing. "Torture the poor insensitive plants! Could you, with a guilt-free conscious, rip the wings off chickens for Buffalo wings, then turn them back out on free range to fatten up their drumsticks? How hypocritical would that be! How cynical! And why should plants suffer to have their babies eaten by us?"

"I could never do that!" Walt says, feigning shock.

"Well, what about the air pollution impact of flying these lobsters cross-country?" Jewel presses.

"How much added weight can a lobster be on an airplane full of tourists coming to LA for fun in the sun and a visit to Disneyland?" is Walt's reply.

"Two lobsters," Jewel corrects.

Walt starts to nod his head in agreement. An uncertain smile replaces his normal all-accepting one. Both smiles annoy Jewel. They are hiding something, she is certain.

"So, Rachel Carson's book resulted in major changes to our quietly subversive science," Walt turns on his professor-in-front-of-a-class persona again.

"Yes," Jewel interrupts, "but it's an unusual view of ecology she had, wouldn't you agree? I never expected anyone to profess so much faith in the balance of nature stuff since Professor Allee died. She was almost religious about it in that chapter."

"Yeah. It is a bit problematic for us that way. It's almost Clementsian, isn't it?"

Jewel slumps away from the table and into her chair.

"I thought this salad would be something small and light. Too much for me, I'm afraid. But what comfortable chairs these are!"

"Padded leather, I think. They are comfortable. They whirl and rock and glide along the floor on invisible wheels."

"They're like some kind of genetically engineered cross between the bucket seats of one of Dan's beloved British sports cars, a good desk chair, a Lazy Boy, and something from the bridge of the Starship Enterprise," Jewel says, taking what she hopes is her last sip from her glass of Anchor Steam beer. It tastes bitter. Too bitter. It somehow fits Westman's concept of an ecologically friendly life, though. Being brewed in San Francisco seems enough for Walt to recommend it. Meanwhile, he is drinking tea.

Even with Dan's place cleared, shells of claws and tails are piled up around them. The bodies, Jewel notes with disapproval, remain untouched, however.

"Did you know that Stanley Cain was an Assistant Secretary of the Interior in the Johnson Administration?" Jewel asks, watching the last of the claw meat being dipped into butter. "That's about as high as an ecologist will ever get in government."

"What about Barry Commoner in the White House?" Walt asks. "Wouldn't that be even better?"

"Were you clean for Gene?"

"Three-piece suit." Again, the smile.

"I would have liked to have voted for Gene," Jewel says. "A poet in the White House. Can you imagine?"

Walt's typical smile is firmly in place. He stays silent.

"You couldn't have voted for Hubert, could you?" she asks him, pronouncing the name, "Huber," in true Lyndon Johnson fashion. A sly smile now forms on Jewel's lips. "I voted for Norman Thomas," she whispers.

"Why Aunt Jewel, you old radical," Walt says in mock horror.

"I felt obligated to do so. We Fairfaxes were not supposed to vote for Democrats, especially not Roosevelt, but he was going to win anyway, even without my vote, so I followed the example of someone I truly respected in all ways, who I might have been in love with, even."

"Who?" Walt is eager to know. "Did you vote for Roosevelt the next time?" he asks when Jewel demurs.

She shakes her head, almost coquettishly. "Thomas again."

"I bet you voted for Eisenhower, though," Walt teases her.

"I liked Ike," she admits. "What are the words you put into the Clean Water Act?" Jewel then takes advantage of the lull in conversation that comes while Walt wipes his fingers with a moist towelette, the kind that comes packaged. "No! I think I remember. The objective of this Act is to— How did it go Walt?"

"To maintain the chemical, physical, and biological integrity of the Nation's waters," Walt finishes for her. "It sounds like Dan told you I was a Congressional Fellow. They were actually George Woodwell's words. He's at Brookhaven National Lab. He suggested them in a letter to Ed Muskie. All I did is make sure that they got into the Act. It impressed Dan, though. He doesn't think he'll ever accomplish anything similar. Sometimes I think he's too hard on himself."

"There's still lots of time for him, isn't there?"

"Yeah! Look at Gene Odum. You can lay his success at Rachel Carson's feet. Now, the IBP had been inspired by the IGY," Walt returns to his history exposition for Jewel. "Its year turned out to be more of a year and a half. It turned geology upside down. Continental drift was rehabilitated. So, a similar program was proposed for biology. Its theme started out not as ecology, but as the Biological Basis of Human Welfare. It morphed into the Biological Basis of Productivity and Human Welfare."

"Because of Silent Spring?"

"Because of Silent Spring. The IBP might as well have stood for the International Biome Program. It had to be stretched to several years, of course. It was biota under study, after all. And with that change from human welfare to biomes, ecology became Big Science with a big budget. Ecosystem ecology was what was funded, because it had the proper image to be the basic science for solving environmental problems. It was the image that Eugene Odum had."

"It was Rachel Carson's image."

"Yes. And that textbook of his, the first ecology textbook organized around energy and ecosystems—" Walt resumes, only to be interrupted by Jewel.

"I never used a textbook for ecology," she says with disdain. "I used Great AEPPS, at one time, but only as a reference. Odum was a bomb lover."

"He was lucky to have landed close to a nuclear reactor facility," Walt continues. "They needed somebody to monitor impacts around the Savannah River Plant. He got what was a good chunk of money for those days to do the research. My research on air pollution effects on plants was made possible by NEPA, but those tracer studies with radionuclides were the start of all modern pollution studies."

"Are you studying killer trees?"

"Other way around, Jewel. The trees I study are absorbing air pollutants and dying. But hey! Reagan's going to be in the White House, even without my vote."

"You're not like my former friend Liza, Walt, are you? She thinks nuclear energy is environmentally the cleanest."

"Liza Little? I'd go for nuclear, compared to some other choices."

You couldn't, could you? Jewel wants to shout. She assumed that the Earth Day crowd was anti-nuke, but now she wonders if Danny really is. He and Walt are sort of in between generations, too young for Hiroshima to be anything but a history lesson, too old to join the new anti-technology Luddites. It is proliferation rather than radiation that Dan worries about.

"As ecologists," Walt picks up a former conversational thread, "or even just as society, what we should be doing is putting dollar figures on the air and water that nature cleans for us. Cleaning it up with technology is expensive. Nature does it for nothing. That is, as long as we don't swamp it with too much pollution or just trample it the many ways we can."

Getting no reaction, Walt shrugs his shoulders. Jewel is listening, but she also is trying to catch the fleeting thought that she can feel slipping away from her mind. It has to do with something that Walt is hiding from her behind his smile, some secret that he wants to share with her, but just keeps talking around.

"No, that's brilliant, Walt," she gives up to say. "That's also what George Perkins Marsh said about nature a hundred years ago. He read it to the Rutland County agricultural society in eighteen forty-seven, I think it was, in Vermont. Why does it take us so long to learn?"

"Why, indeed, Jewel? Should we go see how Dan is coming along?"

"Where's the check?"

"Dan already got it, and he wanted to make sure I knew that we have Gary Meunier to thank for this meal."

"I thank him. Who is he?"

"An ES&E student, an intern."

"It's like no other internship I know," Jewel says, shaking her head. "It's eighteen months of professional work at—" she pauses as if expecting a drum roll, "I have to say, professional, rather then intern pay. Apparently, ES&E does nothing to arrange those internships. The students go out and get the best job they can. The only rule that I can see is that they have to do some sort of environmental work. They do their internship after finishing a year of what they call Problems Courses, which is what Dan teaches. He says it's like running a mini-consulting firm but at less pay. So, what about this Gary—?"

"Meunier. All I know is that he caught on with a small firm started by one of the first ES&E graduates. They just won a contract having to do with the safety of certain pesticides."

"They're working as ecologists?"

"Does the term, Instant Ecologist, come instantly to mind?" Walt assays a joke.

"You know Fred Küchler?" Jewel shoots back in amazement.

"I have met him a few times, at ESA meetings mostly, although I did also once visit that forest research station he has for his very own. He's a good ecologist. His initial floristic composition is a concept brilliant in its simplicity. He tried to get me to join him on Nellie Stark's committee on licensing. How do you—?"

"Old friend."

"Hmm. I should have joined that committee, if only to keep ES&E honest. It troubles me that ES&E students only need to show that they passed an introductory ecology course. You know the level of ecology they teach in those. None of the employers seem to care whether they know any ecology. They're geologists, biologists, engineers, health scientists. The internships are mostly technocratic. They don't do any science. They just use it. Supposedly. Anyway, no one in the firm knows a thing about pesticides, so they hired Dan as a consultant. This fine food and drink was brought to us with his first check, a hundred and sixty bucks, at eighty bucks an hour. Not bad. Not bad at all. It's more than I get consulting on vegetation."

"I'm amazed by how much you know about Dan's program. Are you part of it somehow?"

"I was. For a little while. A very little while. A very small part."

That smile again. It wasn't there when he was talking about Küchler. Why is it frightening her?

"Too late for Disneyland," Jewel says after looking at her watch.

"Not at all. They're open until dark."

What Jewel wanted to do her last day shocked Dan. She wanted to see Liza Little. He was flabbergasted that they even knew each other. He could not imagine what his peacenik, anti-nuke, environmentally liberal Vermonter aunt could possibly have in common with Liza, the Reagan-supporting nuclear queen, especially right after Three Mile Island.

"Chauncy Starr," Liza had announced at the ES&E Seminar on Day Three of that crisis, "tells me the pile is only three percent uncovered. Everything really worked exactly the way it was supposed to."

Worked? Dan had kept himself from saying at the time. The plant was crippled and eastern Pennsylvania was in panic. He had wanted to offer to take her to a showing of *China Syndrome,* before thinking better of it.

"We knew each other in college," Jewel said.

"Were you friends?" Dan asked as he avoided the sort of traffic that Perrine found pleasure in conquering every morning. Dan took the Spitfire over Sepulveda Pass on a tortuous path that Steve Lavinger had told him about. It crossed the freeway by way of Mulholland Drive and descended to campus by way of the streets of Bel Air. It was twice the distance, but the same amount of time and much, much more pleasant. And if the Spitfire became cranky about going uphill, he could find a bit of shade to pull under.

"Best. Inseparable. That was why I walked out of the seminar. I didn't want it to be her."

Dan was aghast. Totally grody, from a popular song on the radio, came to mind, maybe even grody to the max.

"Her name was Liza Woods then. She married John Sheriff, the physicist. We lost track of each other while she was in seclusion building the atom bomb. After Hiroshima ... well, we lost touch. I knew nothing about her being married to Stuart Little until I thought I recognized who she was yesterday. Little's dead, isn't he?"

"They married a few years after his Nobel Prize award," Dan said. "His first wife's name was Lisa. His second wife's was Lise. Liza told me once after a few drinks that she never had to worry about him calling her by one of his other wives' names."

"You socialize with her?"

"It was at an ES&E event. She's really a very kind, friendly person."

"I didn't want to ever see her again after Hiroshima," Jewel said in a shaky voice.

No, she would not explain the remark. And no, Jewel did not want to call to make an appointment to see Liza. If they missed each other, then they missed each other.

She and Dan showed up unannounced at Liza's office in Boelter Hall. She had finally been moved from the office space that she had enjoyed sharing with Stuart Little in the Institute of Geophysics and Planetary Physics, where he had been its long-time director. Unlike Dan's office in Boelter's basement, Liza's was a room, not a cubicle, and it had a view that almost reached one of the grassy quads. It was on the fourth floor, which on that side of the building was ground level, near that of the Engineering Dean. She was in it when they stopped by, and she recognized Jewel immediately.

"Was that you? Is it you Jewel?" Liza cried out, genuinely, joyously surprised. "You looked so familiar the other day. Why didn't you introduce us, Dan? What a surprise! What an incredible surprise!"

She and Jewel were instantly chatting away like schoolgirls. "How many years has it been?" and "Is this little Danny?" and "I can't believe it!" drove Dan off after the few minutes that he had first expected the meeting to last. He excused himself to take care of some duties. "Errands, really," he told them.

Imagine, Dan thought, feeling every bit as surprised as Liza by the reunion, as he walked down the staircase to the Water Resources Library. Girlhood friends almost. With all the "uncles" he had had when growing up, there had never been a peep about an "Aunt" Liza. He had no errands, really, but he knew he could find what he wanted to read in that cozy little place

"As human destruction of remaining natural habitats accelerates," Dan read after tracking down the appropriate issue of *Science*, "biologists have felt intuitively that most wildlife refuges are too small to avert extinction of numerous species. However, because there has been no firm basis for even approximately predicting extinctions in refuges, biologists have had difficulty convincing government planners faced with conflicting land-use pressures of the need for large refuges."

Is it bad to use island bio theory to give scientific credibility to what we know intuitively is true? Isn't keeping refuges as large as possible a good thing?

Probably, Dan answered both of his own questions, but maybe not. When reread, the arguments sounded less like technical disagreements and more like a clash between competing philosophies. But ecologists are scientists, aren't we? We all follow the same methodology, don't we? The scientific method?

Dan read on. Diamond cautioned that, "because those indifferent to biological conservation"—he read that phrase over several times—"may seize on Simberloff and Abele's report as scientific evidence that large refuges are not needed"—there you have it, Dan thought—"it is important to understand the flaws in their reasoning."

Those flaws, according to Diamond, were that Simberloff and Abele had not taken into consideration that some species have poor dispersal ability, while others have low population sizes and are especially susceptible to extinction on small islands. Except for the reference to Simberloff and Abele, it was exactly what Diamond had said in the ES&E Seminar, as was his recommendation for as large a refuge as possible AND some smaller ones.

The best of all worlds, thought Dan. Diamond, though, did allow that putting your eggs in one basket might not be a good strategy. How's that for science? The Eggs in One Basket Theory!

Then Dan read John Terborgh's letter that followed Diamond's. Dan couldn't disagree "that the primary objective of a rational conservation policy should be to preserve viable populations of as many as possible of the species that inhabited the pristine landscape," or that "at least some large reserves are a necessity," but he could disagree with Terborgh's claim that "species loss is area dependent."

None of the points that Diamond and Terborgh made needed a theory of island biogeography as justification, Dan thought. If there are species that need special attention, it should be based on those species' particular ecology.

But wasn't that exactly what Simberloff and Abele had suggested? Autecological studies in place of community theory?

Then he read the letters of the wildlife types that followed Diamond's and Terborgh's.

"The preservation of entire ecological communities with all trophic levels represented requires large areas," struck him as an odd statement.

It was ecosystem ecology, not island biogeography. It sounded Clementsian.

And how, it suddenly struck Dan, could Diamond have written—what was it, exactly? He looked back for the exact phrase.

It was "… that the urgency of conservation obviates the need for scientific rigor."

The argument was not about the wildlife, that much was now clear to Dan. The conflict was good science versus bad science. He felt shame at having invited Diamond to present his ideas to the ES&E students and shame at having been so out of touch with what was going on in real ecology to have what had to be one of the most important conflicts ever in the science slip by him.

Realizing over an hour had passed, he raced back up the stairs from the basement. To keep in shape while not being a runner, he had vowed never to use elevators on campus. He paused at the fourth-floor landing to catch his breath, however, blaming it on the smog.

"So have you found the meaning to life looking inside an atom?" he heard Jewel ask. The tone coming from the room was far from the giggly one he had left. "Quarks, I guess it is now."

"I think so," Liza answered. "There is a lot of uncertainty, a lot of randomness. A lot of beauty to it, too. Have you found it in your ecosystem? I guess that's what it's called now. But who is that breathing out there."

Dan showed himself.

"Ecology," Jewel corrected Liza's previous statement. "And I have."

"We've both been lucky then."

"We have," Jewel said, glancing at Dan. "Although I suspect that you might have been, if not more lucky professionally, more persistent than I, I'm afraid. More directed, maybe?"

"But you're not unhappy?"

"No," Jewel scoffed, hesitating only briefly. "What good is being unhappy?"

And then it seemed that they had no more to say to each other. Their brief reunion came to an end with polite exchanges of invitations and promises. The moment she was away from Liza's office, however, Jewel unleashed a torrent of Anglo-Saxonisms that almost made Dan blanch.

"I don't know how you can stand to work with that woman," she growled. "She's a totally unrepentant nuclear power freak. She's become exactly everything I was afraid she'd become. Why, after Hiroshima—"

And she stopped.

They never got to Disneyland.

"Maybe next time," Jewel consoled Dan at the airport.

"Maybe the Spitfire was not such a good idea."

"Suffer the little children," she said, as what she took to be a three-generation family, the father striding forward, nose in the air, jaw set firm, leading the others out of unimaginable danger, while the mother, mousy, urging their offspring along, a dawdling girl about to enter puberty, a boy a few years younger, looking to his older sister for clues, then, behind them all, a gray-haired grandmother and a little boy, not quite a schoolboy, all in mouse ears, all hurrying to refuge on an airplane that was to take them away from southern California and back home. Kansas, maybe, she guessed.

Dan fixed her with a puzzled look.

"Something out of the Bible. A good aphorism for Vermont," she explained. "Not for LA, it seems. This is the only place I've seen children being coddled—or seen them at all, except for those school kids being let out."

Dan shrugged his shoulders.

"So, what are you going to do with your life," she failed to stop herself from blurting out again.

"I don't know, Aunt Jewel. I sometimes wonder if I'm part of the solution or the problem. Who was it who called ecology a subversive science? Was that Fred Smith?"

"Paul Sears, I think."

"I know it was somebody at Yale that I didn't really know. To tell you the truth, I don't like where my life is going. You mentioned that study on nuclear waste siting—"

"That thing you worked on with Liza?" Jewel interrupted him. "How could you work with her like that? She's biased."

"We have to work with all kinds, don't we?" Dan countered. "Just like you had to teach all kinds, whether you wanted to or not."

"I never felt that way about anyone I taught. They were all young and innocent, even the GI Bill students. None of them had been dropping bombs on Hiroshima."

"Don't think of Liza as evil. I think like the rest of the people involved in developing the bomb, she feels guilt over Hiroshima."

Jewel looked at him attentively.

"Electricity so cheap the we wouldn't have to meter it, as our President used to advertise on TV commercials. It made them feel less guilty. I remember those GE commercials still. Death Valley Days, right?"

Jewel made no response.

"And the marvels of nuclear medicine? What about the—"

"Never mention her name to me again," Jewel spat out.

"I won't."

"This alternative energy stuff in the desert you are working on sounds OK to me, though."

"Not for the desert."

There was a pause.

"I don't think you can solve these problems we set out to solve in the sixties," Dan said. "Whatever you do, it just causes some other problem. It's like trying to stuff a big floppy feather sleeping bag into too small a cover. Something somewhere bulges out anew. The only solution is population control. Not just population control, but population reduction and life style changes. Severe life style changes. It will never come to pass. I sound like Paul Ehrlich, don't I?"

Jewel said nothing. Just as she said nothing to him about her fear for him surviving through polio only to be obliterated in a Cold War nuclear error. She tried thinking no more about a Fairfax grandchild. It was not to be, that dream.

"And the only job possibility I seem to have left is something at Oak Ridge," Dan prattled on. "It's a weapons facility! Just being there, no matter what I actually work on, is more than I can stomach."

"Then don't do it," Jewel said, suddenly cheerful once more, suddenly realizing that he was on her side after all.

"If that job doesn't come through, I've got no other prospect but to try to hang on here. I think if I want to, I think I can."

"You know, Ingrid would love to come live on the West Coast."

"Yeah. She would. She's the type."

Jewel wanted to hug him to her at the moment, but she knew if she tried to reach for him, he would push her away. Like he had in Detroit, when she had come for him. Like he had in New Haven, after coming home from the hospital. Like he had in Brattleboro by running off. Oh Danny, Danny, I love you, she wanted to say.

"There's lots of room in the Ames Hill farmhouse," she said instead.

Dan did not respond.

"Or in Ingrid's," she added, looking him full in the face.

"No thank you," Dan said, exhaling deeply. "What would I do there?" A smile came to his lips. "I'm hardly a farmer," he said. "You know that."

"But imagine either house with tiny feet thumping through it. You can't imagine what joy that would bring to your heart."

"I'll try not to."

"I meant a dog," Jewel said forcing a laugh. "I have a cat."

Her smile disappeared.

"Teach," Jewel then said simply. "Both Brattleboro and Mount Anthony are looking for science teachers. I'm sure that's also true around Ithaca."

"Mount Anthony?"

"It wasn't built yet when you were in high school. Even Vermont has been growing, I'm afraid."

But his smile was gone. Her plane was ready for boarding.

IV

GEORGIE Best, rather than Rod Stewart was the big celebrity attracting attention this day on the UCLA athletic fields, coming at Dan with moves that would have still been applauded at Old Trafford, but it was another player on whom Dan's eyes were riveted: Dieter John, the Cornell legend, everyone's fair-haired boy, destined to have been the next Robert MacArthur had Diamond not beat him to it, or someone on the level of Cowles, Clements, or Elton, perhaps even Darwin. Dan had made several fruitless expeditions to the upper end of campus in search of him and made many phone calls. Now they were finally to meet. Rather than coming with the UCLA contingent, however, Dieter had surprised, as befit a hero, by being in the company of George Best.

Dan had heard the stories that had abounded about Dieter John in the Fly Lab, read his papers, stayed in his house for a weekend and rifled through his bookshelves, record collection, and anything else he came upon that tweaked his curiosity. His drapes were purple. His furniture was leather. His wine glasses were oversized long-stemmed goblets. Artful photographs of male and female forms, draped and nude, close-up and part of landscapes, eyes peeking from behind hair, teeth from lips, buttocks and backs taut with muscles, and stomachs molded into washboards decorated his walls. He liked Queen and Leonard Cohen and Bob Dylan and Mama Cass and Edith Piaf and opera apparently most of all. Dozens and dozens of vinyl LPs having full performances of Wagner and Tchaikovsky and Verdi and Puccini were stacked upright on a tall shelf. There were three different versions of La Boheme. He had duplicate cassette versions of most, indicating that he listened to them in his car. Stacks of annotated reel-to-reel tapes for a Grundig recorder suggested live performances, recorded, perhaps, by him.

And Dieter John did not just play soccer. He had been an All-American fullback at St. Louis University. He had starred at Francis Field and in the parks around South St. Louis where Dan had a few years later stopped on his way back from Washington U to watch the ends of games. He had grown up three blocks from the flat in which Dan had spent a miserable winter in St. Louis. The church at the top of the hill was the one Dieter had attended.

He was blonde, handsome, athletic, brilliant. His blonde hair curled in ringlets about his neck and his blonde mustache had handlebars that hung down like those on racing bicycles. He was not as powerful as Whale, who gave the appearance of being capable of picking up Dan with one arm to fling him over his shoulder and carry him through a snow drift or protect him in a bar fight, but Dieter John gave off the same aura of strength, of being always in charge, always in command, even as he smiled angelically at the world.

He had rocketed through Cornell in three years, totally put genetic feedback on the intellectual map of ecology with his brilliant experiment supporting it, and been hired by UCLA even before putting pen to paper on his dissertation. Early tenured, he had spent his first sabbatical in Latin America setting up forest preserves in Guatemala and the Amazon.

At the moment, he was holding back Georgie Best from taking a shot at Dan's goal. So far, all the Manchester United legend had managed was a soft, but exquisitely precise dribbler toward the far post, which Dan had parried with an outstretched foot, and a bouncer that Dan caught like a basketball pass.

Life could be no better than this, Dan was certain. No day in his life could ever be better. How lucky, he thought, this Sunday morning soccer ritual was for him. It had grown out of a softball game at an ES&E picnic. No one, Dan was certain, had expected more from him than the catcher's duties he unenthusiastically had taken on. When a soccer game suddenly erupted, though, he had parked himself in the makeshift goal and parried shot after shot from Pankaj Parekh and Ali Kashani. That, he was certain, was what earned him an invitation to take part in their Sunday matches, the only ES&E faculty member so honored.

The ES&Ers were a rag-tag crew that started playing together Sunday mornings on the crowded UCLA athletic fields. Besides Pankaj and Ali, superb soccer players both, regulars included Charlie Kratzer, Lee Hanna, and Cathy Fitzgerald, who had been on the woman's basketball team with Anne Myers that eventually won one of the first women's NCAA championships. She was there not so much for her soccer skills, but her athleticism. They rarely could field more than six-on-six sides even after cajoling friends, neighbors, and relatives. Thus, it was inevitable that they combined one day with a group on an adjoining field. Tim Considine's just-as-informal group of Hollywood types had just as much trouble filling full sides even when nieces and grandmothers were added. Combining the two groups resulted in enough players for a legitimate game.

The first time Dan participated had been at the well-manicured field at Beverly Hills High School. Entrée to it was courtesy of one of Tim Considine's group. Tim was promoting soccer in the US as his acting career was ending and the North American Soccer League was folding. One of his soccer cronies was substituting at the school. Besides giving him more time than his police job did and just enough money to scratch along while trying to market a script of a police melodrama, which he expected to take him out of the classroom and bring him fame, a common fantasy among young LA police, substituting gave him free access to the campus.

Tim had lured George Best, now playing on the West Coast in the NASL, and Mario Machado, the broadcast voice of soccer in America, out of their beds early this particular morning. Machado knew Carlos Palomino and convinced him to come along at the last minute. Palomino had just quit boxing in favor of making Miller Light commercials after his loss to Roberto Duran. Best had brought Dieter John. They had become friends in England on one of John's many long absences from UCLA.

"So, do you notice Rod Stewart anywhere today?" were the first words Dieter John said to Dan.

"Nope," Dan answered. It was during a lull while someone tracked down a mis-kicked soccer ball. "You heard about that, too?

He looked cute in his little soccer shorts. Here he was, playing in a game with full sides, team jerseys, and a uniformed referee. It's an anomaly that will always be without explanation. He's not part of Considine's circles."

"I bet he looked cute," Dieter said, standing on the goal line, smiling at Dan. "How could I have missed that?"

"I almost did," Dan said. "Cathy Fitzgerald had to point him out to me."

"That Cathy? The one playing with us?"

"Yeah."

"Do you think Palomino could ever have been a soccer player?" Dieter then asked, disapprovingly shaking his head next to Dan on the line. "All he seems to do is kick people, Pankaj, especially."

"Ah, Pankaj," Dan said. Dieter's attention made him want to talk, even if only about the first thing that popped into his head. "He's just finished his internship doing public health work in The Gambia, as he insists that everyone calls it."

"The Gambia?"

"The Gambia. Pankaj is the organizer of these games. He loves soccer and is good at it. The ball never seems to leave his feet when he dribbles until just before he shoots, which is always at close range. I can anticipate and block his shots, though."

"He is good," Dieter said. "And you're Dan Atkins, aren't you? I'm Dieter John."

Dieter John clasping his hand in Dan's caused a submissive weakness that started at Dan's knees and progressed throughout his body. He could think of nothing more to say, nothing to do, but hold onto the handshake to keep from falling to his knees and bowing his head to Dieter.

"Money?" Georgie Best could be heard from inside a group a few yards upfield. "Of course I make good money, but this is how it is: I spend ninety percent of my money on women, drink, and fast cars. The rest I waste."

"You play a good game in goal," Mario Machado said to Dan after trotting over for a corner kick. Dan couldn't have asked for a better complement from a more knowledgeable person. What could possibly be better? A kiss on the cheek from Dieter?

Why did I think that? Dan asked himself.

"GOALLLLLLLL!" someone suddenly shouted. Sure enough, there was a ball in the net.

"Not even Angel Fernandez could do that any better, Mario," Dieter said, pronouncing the "g" in Angel as an "h."

Did Mario just sneak that shot past him? Dan puzzled. No, Georgie Best was smiling modestly while Pankaj was slapping him on the back in congratulation. Well, Dan decided, there was no shame in being beaten by Georgie Best, but what happened to always being ready?

"Sorry about leaving him open like that," Dieter said, smiling again as people mulled around, the game not quite over, but not still on. "I just lost my concentration. Something distracted me. That rarely happens."

Dan made a gesture he hoped showed that it did not matter.

"So, did I remember to tell you how great it is to finally meet you?" Dieter asked. "I've heard a lot about you. I like to keep up with Dave and what's going on at Cornell."

"I guess I'm flattered," was all that Dan could say. Dieter's use of Pimentel's first name marked him, Dan thought, as being on a different academic level, in the clouds above Dan, who had not yet learned to call Pimentel "Dave."

"So, how're your living arrangements these days?" Dieter asked and the casualness of the question put Dan back at ease.

"I'm surviving. Most night's I'm at Walt Westman's."

"Ah! Walt and his domestic dreams!! He's never gotten over having to leave his commune in Danby."

"What?"

"This game is over," Dieter remarked on what was obvious. "Why don't you walk along with me? You didn't know about the commune? Oh, of course, you came along later. It was up in the hills. I was one of the members. For a while. It was as much a half-way house and a youth hostel as it was a commune."

Dan followed, trying his best to hide his limp.

"Walt invited all of his professors to the commune, but Whittaker was the only one who ever came," Dieter said. "I was there, that night. He came for dinner. Stayed after, too."

"I think Walt still thinks he lives in a commune," Dan said.

Walt was as accommodating in that way as Ingrid had been in the Village. People were always crashing at his place. All sorts of people. Ecologists, educators, artists, butchers, bakers, and candlestick makers tramped through it. They were mostly men and mostly from the Bay Area, and they arrived at all hours.

By then, Dieter and Dan had reached the parking area and Dieter's Porsche. It was a 911 model.

"Well, I guess I'll be seeing you around," Dan said. He wanted to add "Dieter" to that, but could not bring himself to do it. "Are you coming to any more of these games?"

"I don't know. My bed is the most comfortable place in the world on a Sunday morning."

Then he said, "You know, why don't you stay with me tonight? Three bedrooms is more than I ever need. We can talk. We've got a lot we can catch up on."

He moved closer. Dan could smell sweat mixed with cologne.

"Come to think of it, why don't you just move in with me?" Dieter asked, his face inches from Dan's.

"Of what few things I have, some are already at your apartment," Dan said, putting off an answer so as not to appear too eager.

"I noticed. That's why the offer."

"Sorry."

Well, why not? Dan decided with as much suddenness as Dieter in putting the question to him. Crashing that night years ago had worked out for him with Ingrid. Who knew what this could lead to? And if he stayed with Dieter, he would save himself the ordeal of finding a place on his own, only to move out on leaving UCLA, which he hoped would be soon.

"Fine with me," Dan said as Dieter turned on the ignition. "Any place I hang my hat is home now to me."

Dieter's smile lit up his face.

"Did you know that Bob Whittaker is dead?" Walt asked of Dan and Dieter. Dieter had inserted himself into Dan and Walt's custom of having sandwiches together once a week. This time, in the general relief that came after the Santa Ana winds had blown themselves out, on the lawn of the Sculpture Garden.

"No," Dan said. "When?"

"A few days ago. I just learned it today. He's really going to be missed."

Not his words, but the heaviness of face, the unsteady little crackle in his voice, the slowness of his words, gave them an idea how Walt felt.

Dan had once wished it. Now he was ashamed to have. He said nothing.

"He was a great man," Walt stopped munching on his homemade alfalfa-sprouts-and-avocado-on-Pita-bread sandwich to say. "He was really, really—I mean, exceptionally—helpful and supportive of me. He's a big loss."

"I'm sorry to hear it," Dieter said, looking far off past Jacques Lipchitz's statue, The Bather. "I knew he had cancer."

"It was in his hip. They couldn't remove it. It metastasized everywhere from there."

"Maybe it's for the best, then."

"All that work at Hanford, you think?"

"I feel like I'm losing friends left and right," Walt sighed. "My roommate moved out."

Dieter and Dan's heads were held so low it was as if they were in prayer together. Walt did not explain his last remark.

The rain that drove them indoors in February, when it never stopped raining, finally gave in to a sunny day, but not before leaving the grass too wet everywhere. Instead of eating amid the sculptures on the north end of campus, the arts and humanities end, as they usually did, they gravitated to the artificiality of the inverted fountain by the Physics Building. They sat quietly on the low stone wall surrounding it, watching people move through the square. They were no longer making sandwiches at home, but had stopped at Ackerman Union for subs.

"You didn't get the mortadella, did you?" Dieter asked. "It's just baloney with pieces of fat stuck in it."

"Cashew chicken," Dan answered.

"Cashew chicken? That's on the menu now?"

"I'm moving to Geography next week," Walt diverted that discussion. "Finally! Thanks to Dieter here, I think."

"No more Planning School, huh?"

"Geography is a better place for an ecologist," Dieter said. "It makes historical sense, too. Ecology and geography were once almost indistinguishable. My taking a job in geography let me climb the tenure ladder much faster than I would have in a biology department as an insect ecologist."

"How did either of you ever decide to apply for a job in geography in the first place?" Dan asked Dieter.

"In my case, Carl Sauer took a liking to me. I met him at a AAAS meeting. He recommended it. And recommended me."

"Who's Carl Sauer?"

"He's dead," Walt beat Dieter to the answer. "Too," he then added.

"All the more influential by it," Dieter laughed, "especially given that his son is in the department. Ah. You should be up for full professor in no time, even without Whittaker's influence. I'll help. Like Jared Diamond helped me," Dieter added. "Fortunately, he's still alive."

"He's in Geography?" Dan asked.

"Might as well be."

"David Conn read my paper about how much nature's services are worth and convinced me to come here," Walt said. "Funny, how that was it, rather than my vegetation stuff."

"I wish I could get away from planners," Dan suddenly threw up his hands and almost threw away half his sandwich. "Planners are capable of nothing but planning! I still haven't figured out, though, what that is, but they seem to have no useful skills. Environmental planners are the bane of my existence."

"The economists among them can be useful," Walt said.

"Your point being?" Dieter asked.

"My point is that Dan should not be so hard on the urban planners," Walt replied. "Their hearts are in the right place. But you're working mostly with planners from the Public Health School, aren't you?"

"Different programs?"

"Different programs."

It was a gorgeous April Day. Every spot on campus with grass on it seemed more attractive for a picnic than the others. So every one was taken. Walt, Dieter, and Dan eventually wandered into UCLA's arboretum before finding a place to have their lunch. It was just a pocket version, being urban, of a major university's arboretum, but it had a variety of plantings from the Mediterranean regions of the world. They thrived there, even in Southern California's smog.

"This tree is diseased," Walt said about the cypress they were under. "See the brown needles? It's indicative of smog damage."

"Killer trees?"

"You got it backwards, like your aunt!"

"Aunt Jewel told me you talked a bit about how ecology can be something more useful."

"Take one of those economists you complain about to lunch and find out," Walt chided Dan.

"You geographers, from your new vantage point, think it's all so easy," Dan joked, "but ecology seems to be waiting for its Einstein, when there hasn't even been a Newton. Look at this hypothesis testing flap."

"Whew!" Dieter drew in his breath. "Null models," he breathed after what seemed a very long time.

"Null models?"

"Haven't heard of it?"

"There was a long monograph about somebody's neutral theory of communities," Dieter began in answer. "Hal Caswell? Yeah, Caswell. He borrowed some math from population genetics to see how the number of species in communities might come out if only random factors were operating. So?"

"Do you read Evolution?" Walt asked of Dan.

"Yeah," Dan answered meekly. "When I have time."

"That's where you'll find most of this argument," Walt said. "There's also a back and forth on it, sort of, in something called Synthese. It's a journal you'll have to come up here to get. You won't find it down in the science libraries."

"Not in Science?"

"That's just the island bio part of it."

"Jared Diamond has brilliantly put species identities on the species in the island bio equation, that's what I think," Dieter said with a firmness meant to cut off any dissent.

"What about Diamond's thing about fragmented areas?" Dan persisted, but only tentatively, feeling he'd struck a nerve and ready to let the subject drop.

"Any way that habitat can be saved is okay with me."

"I don't know," Walt surprised Dan by saying. "I think the jury's still out on that. But let's go for a walk. Do you have time?"

Dan nodded yes. And they were up and off.

"This null model stuff to me all just sounds like things we've already hashed out in plant ecology," Walt said to Dan as they walked a few paces ahead of Dieter, who was fuming visibly. "I don't see what the big controversy is."

"It's trivia," Dieter shouted from behind, "but it can be amusing. Peter Feinsinger had something in the Bulletin the other month, I think, that showed how silly the whole thing is."

"There is some good stuff coming out of Florida State," Walt ignored Dieter to say. "My friends in Australia speak very highly of Strong and Simberloff."

"Friends in Australia?"

"I got my Masters at Macquarie, on a Fulbright Scholarship. I went back to Australia after working under Muskie. Then I was at Queensland before coming to UCLA."

"Faculty?"

"Yeah. I was a lecturer. I love the climate. I love the people. I loved it all."

"So, that's when you wrote that paper about rationing environmental impacts."

"Yeah, that one," Walt chuckled softly. "You mean the one with Roger Gifford? You read it?"

"Yeah. Great idea. Never to come about, though, is it? Was Gifford an economist?"

Walt chuckled again. "Plant ecologist."

"So, what did you study at Macquarie?" Dan asked.

"Mediterranean vegetation, of course. That's why I'm at UCLA. That's why I like it right here."

Although urban and tiny, the arboretum had spots in which the city totally disappeared from view. Walt led them to one of his favorites, one that Dieter turned out to know well. From it, the city disappeared, but not its people. Hikers and bicyclists and lovers frequented the little park. All of its benches were occupied by couples, men with women, women with women, and men with men. One couple, of indeterminate sex, was grinding hips together in a secluded grassy spot.

"You can't just assume that animal communities follow along with the plants," Dieter caught up with them to look down at the couple and said. "Biomes again, Walt?"

"I already said, we've already had that battle. That was Clements versus Gleason. Complex organism versus mere coincidence, as Gleason put it. Whittaker pretty much put the period to Gleason's argument with his Smoky Mountains data. Gleason was right. Plants adapt to their environment pretty much independently of one another." Then he cut off whatever Dieter was going to say by turning to Dan. "So what are you doing in the Santa Monica Mountains?"

"I'm trying to get data on carabid beetle communities. I had good luck with pitfall traps in Midwestern corn fields. I thought I'd try here."

"Pitfall traps?"

"Plastic coffee cups buried level with the ground. Beetles come out at night and fall into them, then can't climb up the slippery sides and get out."

"Why the Santa Monicas?"

"I like the view," Dan said. "They're close," he added.

"What do you really want to do Dan?" Dieter suddenly asked, his hand on Dan's shoulder, his face very close.

Dan stopped in his tracks. Walt looked away.

What did he really want to do? What a simple, but important question. And the hand on his shoulder felt so reassuring.

"I don't know," Dan surrendered to that feeling.

"So what are you finding in Malibu?" Walt asked when Dieter took his hand off Dan's shoulder.

"Beetles. Snail-eating carabids. Mole crickets. Tarantulas. Nude sun bathers."

"Watch out for the rattlesnakes."

"Are they more dangerous than the sunbathers?"

"Not if you wear high boots. Those protect you from nude sunbathers, too. I speak from experience. The higher the bite is, the worse the consequences."

"Are you recommending hip boots?"

"Against the sun bathers? Were they male or female?"

"Female both."

"Good looking?" Dieter asked.

"Don't know. As soon as I realized they were naked, I turned my back to them and let them get dressed before checking my traps. Might have been good looking, though."

Walt laughed. Dieter laughed louder.

"So, Whittaker didn't believe in competition?" Dan asked

"Didn't you notice? He called himself a synecologist." Walt said as they ascended the steps beside Boelter Hall. "Ecology, you know, started as plant ecology. Plant ecologists had a monopoly on the use of the term until the nineteen-fifties almost. What people like Pearl and others were doing, they didn't even call ecology. I think, like John Harper, Whittaker was trying to bring ecology into the present."

"A Darwinian approach to plant ecology?" Dan asked as he limped his way to the top.

"Yeah, but do remember that plants can't get up and move around like animals do. Meanwhile, the allelopathy war is going to peter out, I'm pretty sure."

"Allelochemics?"

"Allelopathy.

"Whittaker coined that term, didn't he?" Dieter, who had been sullenly silent, asked.

"Maybe it was Feeny. Anyway, if plants are to compete with each other, you have to have a mechanism for it. So far, all we have is something like, maybe, Leibig's Law."

Then Walt withdrew his seemingly perpetual smile.

"I think what's coming out of Tallahassee," he said as he split off in the direction of the arts quad, "is—in the end—nothing less than an attack on the legacy of Robert MacArthur and G. E. Hutchinson."

"I think what's coming out of Tallahasee is bullshit," Dieter said as Walt disappeared in the crowds of students going to and fro.

V

"COME to think of it," Fred Turner said, "you might have the right idea about the IBP data. I don't think any of them are doing anything more with it."

Dan had taken to alternating his outdoor lunches with Walt and Dieter with more formal lunches with Fred at the UCLA Faculty

Club. It rankled Dan that he had entrée to it only as the guest of a club member, which Fred was. Adjuncts were not admitted to membership, although other non-tenured ranks, such as Fred's, were. Dan would normally have laughed off the slight in a very Groucho Marxian way but for Fred. He and Fred had developed an instant friendship. Bob Lindberg, who had known Fred from their days working together at the Nevada Test Site, had introduced them one day at a seminar. Fred was a biologist with one of the national laboratories that grew out of the Manhattan Project. But it was a strange example of one. Instead of a large, gated, secure facility, it was in a modest building, Warren Hall, on the edge of campus. It was simply called "Warren Hall," instead of the "Laboratory of Nuclear Medicine and Radiation Biology," its formal name, surprisingly without the "National Laboratory" appendage. Its scientists were all UCLA employees and access to it was not restricted in any way. The lab's sole function, as far as Dan could make out, was to deal somehow with the effects of radiation released during an aboveground bomb test in Nevada in the 1950s. A rancher's dead sheep had been a particular issue then. It still was almost thirty years later.

The two almost instantly took to each other like uncle and favored nephew. Agreement on nuclear power being ecologically preferable to other energy choices, but for the proliferation problem, was a big reason for that.

What had he meant by proliferation? Fred had wanted to know during their first conversation.

"Do you mean by weapons," he had pressed, "or nuclear facilities?"

"If you have nuclear technology," Dan had answered, "you've got the weapons."

That answer had sealed their friendship. The balding man at the end of his career and the long-haired young man trying to launch his found common pleasure in talking about life, ecology, nuclear power, and the strange parties being thrown by Rock Hudson.

Fred had been late to lunch that day, causing Dan to wait for him outside of the dining room. Fred had explained apologetically that he had had to help out his ex-wife with an emergency. He had stopped in at their place—her place, he had corrected—to show her how to ease down the hammer of a revolver without having it go off.

She had thought there had been an intruder in their yard—her yard, he had repeated—and taken out and cocked the trigger, fearing she would have to defend herself. She had not yet gotten over her fear of the Hillside Strangler. When no rapist appeared, she was left with a loaded and cocked pistol.

What interested Dan about the incident was that she could call on Fred for such help. They were divorced, but they were still on good terms. It had to be some sort of California thing, he decided, like the thing with Dieter that had him so confused. He wondered why Fred and his wife had divorced and if it was really possible to end a relationship as friends. He also wondered how close what Fred and his former wife had was to what he and Ingrid, neither married nor divorced, had. It seemed like prying, though, to ask.

"I was really surprised how much data there is on insects found on those desert shrubs," Dan said instead, biting into his usual, trendily healthy cashew and chicken sandwich, "Larrea in particular. Each plant sampled has a separate computer output on the insect species found on it."

"Species, huh?" Fred marveled, putting down his own, less adventurous ham and cheese on rye. "For insects? I thought species identity didn't matter for ecosystem studies. All the IBM analysts need to know is what an organism's biomass and energy content is. And its place in the food web, whether it's a producer, consumer, or decomposer. I identified all my lizards, anyway, because I wanted to. It was important to me. It would have seemed like shoddy work if I hadn't."

"I know, but those Long Beach State people did identify all the insects, whatever the reason. As far removed as it may have been from the basic energy studies of the IBP, the desert biome has species lists. Very thorough lists. On insects, even."

"That's what comes of hiring a taxonomist to do the work, I guess," Fred said. "You should have been with me when I went to Long Beach to see the guy, whose name now escapes me. A senior moment, I'm afraid. But I remember vividly what an exquisitely cluttered office he had. There were reprints and monographs and specimen boxes covering every square inch of horizontal surface. There were three chairs in the room, but I couldn't sit down. He tried to take some of the stuff off a chair for me, but he had no place to put it down."

"A true collector."

"I think there was an MS thesis involved. Mispagel, I think was the name. Of the Masters student, I mean. I still can't remember the professor's name. You might want to look him up, though. You really might be able to do some sort of community-level analysis on that data. You could probably do a quick grant proposal on it, something like what Eric Pianka did with lizard communities. You know, MacArthur-style niche and diversity studies. Is that what you had in mind?"

"Yeah, something like that. If they'd let me submit a grant proposal from ES&E."

"Because you're an adjunct?"

"Because of everything."

And the subject was temporarily dropped. Getting no public credit for winning grants for ES&E, then not having any control over the projects, was a very sore point with Dan at the moment.

But Dan did intend to pursue his idea. He was not keen on sharing with Fred what he thought he might get out of the data, however. He wasn't sure how Fred stood on MacArthur. He wasn't really sure how Fred stood on most of modern ecology. Autecological studies on his desert lizards seemed to hold more than enough satisfaction for him.

"Say," Fred called to Dan's attention a few moments later. "See who's over there with Charles Young, the Chancellor? It's Norman Cousins."

Dan recognized the pair at a table near the center of the modestly sized, wood-paneled room.

"Yeah. And he is neither laughing nor does he look well."

"I understand he really does not have much time left. Pity. He's about my age."

A silent pall fell over their table. Fred had only recently stopped wearing the toupee he had used to cover surgical scars from the removal of a cancerous growth atop his head. He was not yet convinced that he had survived one of the occupational hazards for scientists who did field research in the desert sun.

"It needn't be a grant," Fred picked up the conversation again. "You've got the data. Maybe you could get a paper out without any funding. Then you can write a grant. All you need now is some time on the computer."

"Time is exactly what I don't have."

"You have summers."

"I wish! Moving in with Dieter John gives me a place to stay, but he has me splitting expenses with him, and his house has a huge mortgage. I had no housing expenses when I was sleeping in a cot in my cubicle. I need the money I get from the summer Problems Course. Besides, Perrine will insist I take one on. I can't do like the others, Ernie or Bob Mah, for example. They take their cut as payment for what they do during the regular academic year in the Problems Courses, which is damn little. Then they have their summers free of ES&E obligations. I actually have to work in the summer to get my summer money—and to get the projects down and written. How can I get my own research going? ES&E projects take up all my time. ES&E students and their needs never leave my side, twelve months out of the year, seemingly seven days a week. They even barge into my dreams. Worst of all is that we need to keep their stipends funded for fear that enrollment will drop and the program will be cut. I'll be cut. It's a real vicious circle. It's like we have to bribe students to enroll. Hell, it's not a scholarly PhD, it's a professional degree like an MD—or an MBA. An MBA, I think, is actually a lot closer to what a DEnv is than Stuart Little's original concept of an environmental doctor. Why should we have to recruit them into the program with the inducement of a free ride? These kids are going to make real money in their lives, more than their professor. They should pay their own way for the degree."

Fred had kept a perplexed silence through Dan's diatribe. He had heard it before.

"And I feel so isolated here from ecology," Dan added as final punctuation for it.

"But what you just said about being isolated here is nonsense," Fred countered. "There are plenty of ecologists at UCLA. Martin Cody, for example, and Henry Hespenheide. Both are MacArthur students. From Penn, too, I think."

"Ah, Hespenheide!" Dan perked up. "Listen, I tried calling his office to talk to one of his grad students. Todd Shelly. He was one of Buck Cornell's master's students at Delaware. Do you know him?"

Fred did not.

"So, Hespenheide has three grad students in this office. One is Todd Shelly. Another is Tom Sherry. The third is from Japan. Guess who answers the phone!"

"Speaking of ecologists, how about Malcolm Gordon, of course, and Park Nobel and George Bartholomew and Tom Gorman?"

"And Fred Turner?"

"Thank you."

"Isn't Gorman going to Law School or something?"

"Is he?"

"Called the other day about a study we are doing on the Salton Sea. He's thinking of leaving UCLA."

"Interesting," Fred said softly. "Very interesting."

"Well," Dan continued, "except for you and Dieter John or Walt Westman, I never see any of them."

"You just got here. Now, John, you know, is an interesting case."

As unhappy as Buck was at having landed at Delaware, the thought came into Dan's head, that Buck was at least a "player" in ecology, in the Hollywood vernacular that was creeping into Dan's speech and thought patterns, even if Fred had never heard of him. Meanwhile, Dan had landed at UCLA and apparently was anything but a "player".

"Hmm?" Dan prodded the older man, realizing just then that Fred had meant Dieter.

"His thesis, the basis of that Mercer Award paper, it's all a sham."

"Huh?"

"The data was all screwed up. His lab tech, Mendez was it? She accidentally switched two IBM cards. That's what got the famous result. When they switched them back, the populations crashed no matter how they tweaked things."

"What are you telling me?" Dan suddenly panicked. He had to believe that what Turner was telling him was true. His knowing about Beth pretty much nailed that. How?

"She was disconsolate about it," Fred continued. "Dieter John told her to just forget it."

Dan went silent. He knew that Fred would tell him only what he thought he needed to know. Prodding never helped. He had once alluded to Liza Little being a heavy drinker, as was Stuart, hinting at a tragic incident a few years back. A death in a car crash, drunken driving. As with all his hints, Fred had not continued when Dan did not press him on it, as much as he wanted to.

"So?" he asked, the moment he noticed any signs that indicated that Fred was about to speak again.

"Oh, nothing. I thought you might want to know some details I've learned about Rock Hudson's parties," Fred said, rising from the table. "Who some of his guests are."

"Someone I know?" Dan joked.

"Well," Fred hesitated is if preparing to say more, then changed his mind. "We really need to be going."

VI

"MANY biologists, when they turn to philosophical (epistemological or ontological) questions, abandon the standards of accuracy that, at least in the layman's view, ought to govern discourse as scientists. Simberloff's argument forms an unusually flagrant example of this practice."

He read the paper with that paragraph in it in order to understand the paper that followed it in sequence, but that he had read first. Paragraphs from both had been quoted in a book review he had come across in *Ecology*. It had sent him instantly to the Research Library in search of the book. The reviewer had claimed that the exchange brought "images of hand-to-hand combat or a bar-room brawl" to mind. It had turned out not to be in a book but in an issue of the journal, *Synthese*, that Walt Westman had mentioned.

"Many philosophers," that other paragraph went, "when they turn to biological questions, abandon in favor of captious logomachy the quest for epistemological or ontological enlightenment that, at least in the layman's view, ought to govern their discourse. Grene's argument forms an unusually flagrant example of this practice."

Cool, he had thought on first reading the paragraphs in the book review.

Gutsy, he thought on reading them now in the context of the journal that published them.

Marjorie Grene, of the first paragraph, apparently was a founding figure in the philosophy of biology. Dan Simberloff, was a still-young biology professor, barely older than Dan, at a southern football school.

Names blazed up from Simberloff's paper: Popper, Wiener, Barzun, Gödel, Shannon, Szilard, Pynchon, Kuhn.

Pynchon?

Dan would have to read them all. And Mayr, Lewontin, Waddington, Slobodkin, Cohen, Odum. He would have to re-read their papers as works of philosophy, rather than ecology or evolutionary biology.

In order for ecology to be a science, ecologists had to behave like scientists, Dan summed up Simberloff's argument.

Wasn't that exactly what Hutch and MacArthur were trying to do when they pushed ecologists to thinking in more deductive ways? Starting with that ecology seminar that Aunt Jewel had described to him when he had gone off to graduate school?

Their intention had been to make the science more rigorous, Dan knew, but their efforts have brought more confusion than rigor, it seemed to him as he tried to parse out the various positions of the controversy, all of which were surprisingly new to him. Fly Labbers had been sheltered from it at Cornell, isolated as they were from Ecology and Systematics. Not a hint of counterrevolution had ever entered the core courses, but for one stray remark about paradigms from Brian Chabot.

The complaints that did reach them, by way of the ecology journals, had been puzzles to Fly Labbers. First, there had been Van Valen and Pitelka, complaining about intellectual censorship. No one in the Fly Lab, not Buck Cornell and not Al Brick, had been certain who was being censored by whom. Then Canadian Robert Henry Peters had challenged all niche theories as mere tautologies. For good measure, he had also taken on the theory of natural selection on the same grounds. That had brought him castigation in print by a host of evolutionary biologists, even though the idea that the fittest survived because they were the most fit, the simplest formulation of natural selection, was obviously tautological. When Hutch had dismissed Peters' complaints in the brief final chapter of his book on population ecology, Dan had dismissed them, too.

Now, here was Simberloff, claiming the same goal of making a respectable science of ecology, but taking knocks at the very foundation that Hutchinson and MacArthur had laid down. Robert May and Richard Levins, Eugene Odum's ecosystem idea, and all of Barry Commoner ideas took the biggest knocks. As they should, Dan thought.

MacArthur, Dan mused as he crossed campus in returning to Boelter Hall, probably would have enjoyed stepping into the fray. Oscar Wilde's sentiment on not being talked about being worse than being talked about was well known to Uncle Robert. It was the intellectual chase that he had loved more than anything else in the world, except his family, of course. But on whose side would he be? He had not been as enamored of his own theories as some of his followers were.

Then, an enigmatic bit of poetry that Hutch had used to dismiss Peters and justify his own career associated itself with Dan's thoughts on the controversy. He turned to the book. It was conveniently in the earthquake-safe metal bookshelves bolted to the wall behind him. It was *An Introduction to Population Biology* by title, but it was more the kind of rambling history typical of Uncle Hutch's soliloquies than an introduction. It might more accurately have been titled *Ecology According to G. Evelyn Hutchinson*. Dan had only skimmed it previously before putting it aside.

Maybe, he thought, it would hold more meaning for him now. He went right to the end of the book. It was just like Hutch, he paused to think, to have titled that, "Aria da Capo and Quodlibet."

"My propositions are elucidatory in this way: he who understands me finally recognizes them as senseless," was the line of poetry Dan had sought, except it seemed not to be poetry. The poet was Ludwig Wittgenstein. The work was his tract on philosophy. To make things even more obscure, Hutchinson had added in a footnote that the whole thing could only be understood fully if the last phrase was read in German, "am Ende als unsinnig erkennt."

The gist of the short chapter was that, unlike Peters, who he identified as part of a "school" that was skeptical of theoretical ecology, Hutchinson believed that science could uncover important possibilities even through tautologies, and had in fact done so in evolutionary ecology. He had aimed his brief remarks at Peters, but Simberloff, not mentioned, could just as easily have been his target.

Dan turned back to the Synthese volume he had checked out of the library and read on. A chapter by Levins and Lewontin followed Marjorie Grene's.

"Simberloff's essay seems to us to embody the false debate based on three fundamental confusions," they brushed it away. "As a result of these confusions, Simberloff, in his attempt to escape from the obscurantist holism of Clements' 'superorganism,' falls into the pit of obscurantist stochasticity and indeterminism."

Then they went on to attempt "to develop implicitly a Marxist approach to the questions that have been raised."

Marxist ecology? Dan marveled. Simberloff had been ambushed by a couple of Trotsky-ites, very much as Ed Wilson had. One of them was Uncle Dick.

He had Lewontin's phone number in Marlboro, where he was a summer squire and a patron of the music festival.

"Esa Saarinen sent me the paper," Lewontin explained. "He is a fine young man. Finnish. I believe he has just received his PhD in philosophy. At twenty-four. And he is already serving as an editor for Synthese. He sent it to me based on Simberloff's suggestion."

"As referee on it?" Dan asked.

"No, I was invited by Saarinen to write a critique and discussion of Simberloff's ideas. Apparently, it had so excited the editors of the journal that they were making a special theme issue on it. I knew that Marjorie Grene was contributing, as was that Robert Peters. You know, the one who thinks natural selection is just circular reasoning. Having then read Simberloff's paper, it seemed to me appropriate that a joint paper with Levins would be a good idea, and we then collaborated on a reply to Simberloff that appeared in the special issues. The paper is Levins and Lewontin, by the way, because our joint work always uses the alphabetical order of names."

And he had not much more to say about it than that. He did, however, say that he and Levins were now working on a book together.

"The Dialectic Biologist, we're going to call it. It will be the result of our long-standing intellectual and political comradeship. In it will also be reprinted the letter to Nature from the fictitious

Isadore Nabi. I can now reveal to you that it was Richard Levins and I plus a friend, Leigh Van Valen, who were behind that. And did you know that it was Robert MacArthur who helped to create Nabi in the days before our meetings at Marlboro? Much of the biography of Nabi we put into American Men and Women of Science was Robert's invention."

Dan distinctly had not known. He was aware of the letter by Nabi, but not that it was a prank perpetrated by Trotskyites to belittle the views of E. O. Wilson and Richard Dawkins, not to mention the editors of *Nature*.

"But do you know," Lewontin continued, "after collecting our essays, we are still dissatisfied. The assembled work illustrates the dialectic method, but it does not explain what dialectics is. So we have set about to write a chapter on dialectics—only to discover that we have never discussed our views systematically!"

"I'm afraid that the Hegelian dialectic seems so simple to me that I could not possibly understand it," Dan apologized. "Didn't Bertrand Russel say that all of Hegel's doctrines were false, but that they did illustrate the important truth that the worse your logic, the more interesting are its consequences?"

"To understand the world," Lewontin began impatiently, "there are different ways to cut it up for different purposes. The hand, the fingers, the joints of those fingers, the tissues, the cells, the molecules of the cells are all appropriate units of function and levels of dissection for different questions. It is simply not true that everything is effectively connected to everything."

"But let me ask you something," Dan cut off what he feared might be a lengthy discourse. "Simberloff, being one of Wilson's most notable students, could he have himself become a target of criticism directed at his mentor?"

There was a brief silence. Dan wondered if he had posed that question too subtly.

"I wouldn't attack someone just because he was Ed's student," Lewontin replied. "As you can see from our paper, we thought Simberloff had made a number of errors and confusions. The paper really speaks for itself."

There was another pause.

"But you know, we are going to include our Synthese paper in Dialectic Biologist. Maybe we should edit it a bit. Maybe we can remove the flavor of Anti-Duhring from it. Maybe we can tie the discussion to a specific disagreement."

Dan went back to the journal issue. It was a grab bag of papers. Besides Marxist dialectic, there was a generative grammar. He skipped that chapter after a single glance. There was also a systems approach proposed to further develop the niche concept. He recognized Bernie Patten as an ecologist, but not his collaborator. He skipped it, too. British insect ecologist T. R. E. Southwood had some words to say about ecological research, and ecologist-historian Robert McIntosh gave a historical perspective. Peters repeated his familiar assertions. Then there was a paper by Donald R. Strong.

The name itself conjured up a young warrior. Had he heard it before? And the title of Strong's contribution, "Null Hypotheses in Ecology," turned on a flood of realizations for Dan. He dove into the paper. And suddenly, he saw computer jocks and engineering analysts and systems scientists in a new light. They might not just be tools, as he had previously dismissed them. Ecosystems might be the only approach to ecology left, now that all the clever mathematical models were no longer providing satisfaction. He even saw the fly boxes in a different light now. Whatever they were, they were replicable. They were smack dab in the tradition of the laboratory work of Gause and Thomas Park. And whatever happened in those boxes did happen, regardless of the inadequacies of the mathematical model for genetic feedback. It was not just conjecture or fanciful delusion.

It was actually so simple, so absolutely just common sense, scientific common sense. Systems people might just be the real ecologists, after all. The others just might be "ecopoets," he thought, adapting a term, "geopoetry," he had come across in a book by John MacPhee.

A paper Strong cited had been published in a recent *Evolution*. There was a row of volumes of the journal on one of his bookshelves, each issue received consigned after a glance for later perusal that never came. The paper had the innocent sounding title of "Tests of Community-Wide Character Displacement Against Null Hypotheses." Lee Anne Szyska's name was listed as author between the names of Strong (the first, or the senior, author, the one who would get most of the credit or handle most of the flak) and Simberloff.

Yep, absolutely sensible, he concluded on reading it. Since island birds have had all this time together for natural selection to act on their beak lengths or wing spreads and increase the differences so as to reduce competition, why not compare their measurements to those of species of mainland birds? Within similar taxonomic categories, of course, such as families. There should be less of a difference, less character displacement for the mainland birds. Especially if species of mainland birds were drawn at random into groups, three birds for this island, five birds for that, whatever the number of species a particular island had. Strong, Szyska, and Simberloff had done exactly that.

They found no differences between the species that cohabited an island and species in the same family drawn at random from the mainland. There was no character displacement. It was as simple as that.

When he rummaged forward in time through his copies of *Evolution*, he came upon another paper from Tallahassee. It's title, "Santa Rosalia Reconsidered: Size Ratios and Competition," caught his eye before its authors did. And it started with a quote from someone identified as A. D. White and dated eighteen ninety-five. The bones that had set off Hutchinson's famous discovery of the one-point-three rule, according to it, were those of a goat.

In the paper, Simberloff, with William Boecklen, had set up a null model for testing observed size ratios against ratios that might be expected by chance combination. It was a bit like MacArthur's broken stick, Dan thought. Using the technique, few of the examples used to support the idea of biologically determined size ratios could be shown to be different than what might be randomly expected. There were pages and pages of tabular analysis of almost every set of examples in the literature. Hutchinson's sacred ratio of one point three, they concluded, was "in no sense a rule of nature."

He gazed at the paper's bibliography, at the names whose work was being impugned. Jim Brown, Martin Cody of UCLA, Joe DeVita, of all people! Then, Jared Diamond, Henry Hespenheide of UCLA, MacArthur and May, of course, Jon Roughgarden, and Tom Schoener.

And Dieter John. He had done a study on ground beetles in the Andrews Forest in Oregon. That research forest had mountain slopes at various elevations and various stages of recovery from logging, and even virgin, never-logged stands. The paper John wrote on it gave indisputable evidence in favor of Diamond's community assembly theory. John's beetles demonstrated all of its elements: forbidden species combinations, checkerboard patterns, high S to tramp to supertramp species. Dan wondered fearfully if he might be in the wrong place at the wrong time.

So how could he jump into the fray? Uncle Robert, had he still been alive, would surely have found some way for Dan to contribute, even if it was not clear to Dan for which side. After all, Uncle Robert's acolytes were at the center of the controversy. He was their ecopoet laureate, exalted by untimely death.

Ed Wilson, he wondered? Could Aunt Jewel's effect on Wilson lead to him pulling some strings with Simberloff? But Wilson still seemed to be busy fighting another battle, the one over his Sociobiology. And how much sway could a hike and a pleasant evening with Dan have over Wilson? And were there still strings tying Wilson and Simberloff together? Would Wilson put Dan into the enemy camp on showing interest in Simberloff's ideas?

And was that really the side of the fray for Dan to join? Could Simberloff, who Dan envisioned as a Byronic hero, mesmerizing by his brilliance, just be flitting through his science only to eventually be brought down by the weight of his own ideas? Where would that leave Dan?

Dieter, too?

VII

"THIS is the kind of project I like," Paul Merifield announced as he leaned back against a small boulder. His hair was neatly combed, as always. His face was without stubble, other than a neat mustache that looked circa nineteen sixty.

He, Dan, and ESE&E student Michael Weinstein were at an off-road campsite somewhere in the Mojave Desert—only the latter knew exactly where—trying to put away two six packs of beer. They were there as part of a study commissioned by Southern California Edison that covered a mishmash of technologies that the utility planned for the state's southern deserts. It was a hot, dry, thirst-making desert, and they had neither ice nor a cooler. Dan and Paul were the ones trying to drink the beer. Weinstein was not much of a drinker. The other students had taken off right after their dinner of camp beans and coffee. There was a gambling casino nearby at the Nevada state line.

Part of the ES&E group had just visited the "Barstow Turkey," as the pilot plant for a proposed larger version of the solar-thermal technology had already been scornfully named. It was an array of 4774 sun-tracking parabolic mirrors aimed at a central tower that held molten sodium. That, in turn, boiled water for steam to turn a turbine. The full facility for which the Barstow Turkey was the precursor was to generate 100 Megawatts of electricity and take up a square mile of desert.

The rest of the group had examined the flowering of wind turbines on the desert foothills of the Tehachapis. Wind prospectors had beaten SCE to the windiest sites, where they had set up a panoply of devices to harness wind energy. Of the variety of designs, the ES&Ers were fondest of an incongruously original concept that did not involve a propeller of any kind. It had a sail traversing before the wind on what looked like two clothes lines that each spun bicycle-wheel-like pulleys.

SCE had had to set up their turbines on the flats outside of Palm Springs. One was a giant structure that looked like it had come off a large airplane. It was "off-line," meaning not running. That was its usual condition: under repair. The egg-beater-like turbine blades of the structure beside it were gone, blown apart in a windstorm.

Southern California Edison worried about an exclusion zone to prevent injury and damage around their structures. The prospectors in the hills worried about cows chewing on their wiring.

"Weinstein, here," Merifield said from his position at the boulder, "tells me he's almost done with his part of the project."

"Kristen Berry of the BLM pretty much has it all done already," Mike explained. "I just have to rewrite it."

"She's going to let you do that?" Dan asked from his perch atop a deteriorating picnic table, where he was safe from snakes and scorpions.

Weinstein had led them to the campsite. It had the picnic table and a stand of mesquite and not much else. The mesquite signified water somewhere below the sand, but more importantly for them, it gave them some homey-looking shade for their assorted tents.

"As long as it helps protect the desert tortoise," Mike elaborated. "She grew up near China Lake. Her back yard was desert. Her father kept desert tortoises there in a pen. She loves the creatures. I think she knows every one of them by name."

"So, what are we going to do with you now?"

"Oh, I'm going to do a lot of rewriting. I mean a lot of rewriting."

He went off to his tent to rummage through his pack.

"I wish we could do more stuff like this," Dan said to Paul.

"You and me both. It's fun, isn't it?"

"Better than writing and editing and rewriting," Dan answered. "And having to convince the contract people how good the study is. That's the worst."

"So where did they finally put you?" Dan asked when Mike came back.

"Huh?"

"I mean which of the student offices?"

"Oh, the big one in Health Sciences. With Rita O'Connell, Harlan Hashimoto, and Michael Simpson. Duane Van der Pluym, too, I think. And some interns. Janet Nakamura and that blonde girl."

"Heidi?"

"What's her name? West?"

"Davis, I think. But it seems to change yearly."

"Yeah. And the guy with the Triumph. Burgess?"

"Ken Berger."

"Yeah."

"What a character," Paul said.

"How about Jerry Wilson?" Dan asked. "Wasn't he supposed to be on this trip?"

"He couldn't make it for some reason having to do with his job," Paul said.

"Hah! He probably didn't want to leave his Porsche behind but didn't want to take it off road."

"It must be pretty crowded in that office," Dan said to Mike.

Weinstein looked nothing like a future consulting technocrat, not the kind who could be envisioned behind the wheel of a Porsche. He was in his element right there in the desert. His unruly hair and beard, his worn clothes, and the general, indefinable air of slovenliness about him made him look more like a desert hermit. Hair and beard were already peppered with gray, so that he looked closer to Merifield's age than Dan's. Dan liked Mike for the way he looked and his degrees in ecology, BS and MS. They were about the same age and the same height. They had started their careers at about the same time and with the same style and the same intentions.

Unlike Mike, Dan had let a barber trim his locks, though, bringing his looks closer to the consulting firm conformity of ES&E interns. Shorter hair was now the mode. His beard, which never had approached the length of Weinstein's, he had long ago shaved off, leaving just a neatly-trimmed mustache that resembled—Dieter John's new mustache, he realized. Handlebars were no longer trendy in the Dieter John-Walt Westman set.

Mike was amusing himself by lining up sunflower seeds in the sand. With dusk descending, they were barely visible.

"The room in Boelter Hall is even more crowded," Mike said, crouching on the ground.

"Yeah, but Conrad and Barry Schuyler are probably never around," Dan said. "Empty desks don't crowd as much as full ones."

"Is Conrad a college professor of some kind?" Mike asked.

"Conrad Newberry?" Paul answered. "He teaches engineering at Cal Poly Pomona. A lot of engineers got faculty positions right after the war without a PhD, even at places like Berkeley and UCLA. They needed teachers. I guess Conrad decided to finally get his doctorate with us."

"Is that why Schuyler's here?" Mike asked.

"I don't know," Paul said. "He's chairman of his department at Santa Barbara."

"Environmental Studies?"

"Yeah. He replaced Garret Hardin when he retired," Dan added. "I understand they're bringing Dan Botkin in to take over for him. Schuyler must be ready to retire, too. I don't know why he thinks he needs a PhD, but it's a feather in our cap to have him in our program."

"It's not a PhD," Mike reminded.

"It's at the same level," Paul said. "It's a doctoral degree. As long as the degree is at that level, it doesn't matter whether it's a PhD or an MD or a DEnv."

"How do you feel about that, Paul?" Dan asked.

"How do you mean?"

"There is a difference. PhDs do dissertations."

Paul shrugged his shoulders.

"Schuyler probably always wanted a doctorate," Dan speculated, "and figures he can finally get it from ES&E. Why not take the easiest path, if he won't need it? It's probably what Conrad is doing, too. They only have to spend two years, at most, on campus."

"Easiest way to one in the environmental field," Mike said. "I read where Stanly Auerbach called NEPA an ecological Magna Carta. D'you think ES&E is part of all that?"

"Yeah," Dan said, thinking that over. "A legal analyst at Oak Ridge told me that the courts have, in effect, legitimized ecology based on NEPA."

"They had you see a lawyer?" Paul asked.

"They had me meet with everybody. I think they all felt sorry for me, knowing that the Hunsackers were going to be hired instead."

The Hunsackers were a husband-and-wife couple about to be awarded their DEnvs from the ES&E program.

"You know," Dan said above the forced silence that followed, "I think Auerbach has always had a bone to pick with ecology. Academic ecology. I read the article you mentioned. The purists that Shelford fought against when he started the Nature Conservancy are still in charge of the society, even if Auerbach was voted in as its president."

"Society?" Merifield asked.

"Ecological Society," Mike said, laying out another seed.

"He did complain to me about the"—Dan made quotation symbols in the air with his fingers—"aloofness of ecologists who insisted on staying within the confines of their"—more air quotes—"pure research."

"That's me right there, all right," said Mike. "At least, I wish."

A kangaroo rat appeared at the end of Mike's trail of seeds. The reflections from its large black eyes flickered from one direction to another. It picked up a seed and eyed Mike. The seed disappeared. The rat remained.

"Auerbach also stressed in that article how he had not been a traditional president," Dan continued. "He was an administrator, rather than researcher or professor, and what he administered was applied science, outside of academia."

"Oops! There goes another one!" Merifield shouted from his position against the boulder.

He jumped to his feet. A large, hairy spider was stopped beside the boulder. It was the season for tarantulas to migrate from one part of the desert to another. This one raised its hindquarters when Merifield blocked its way with a boot.

"See it?"

"The hind end isn't exactly the business end of a tarantula, is it?"

"He's acting more like a stink bug. A tenebrionid."

"What does he know that we don't know?"

"That behavior doesn't always help the stink bug," Mike said. "There's a mouse that can grab it and stick its hind end in the sand so that it can't be sprayed. Then it eats it from the front end right down to the tip of the abdomen, which it leaves in the sand. Tom Eisner has great pictures on it."

Mike was now laying seeds on the bench and the tabletop. Merifield stepped aside to let the spider pass. It skittered off, abdomen still conspicuously in the air.

"Auerbach always felt as if he was an atypical student, I understand," Dan continued. "He didn't turn to ecology until after military service in World War Two."

Could he have been one of those GI Bill war vets who had crowded Aunt Jewel out of ecology? Dan suddenly wondered of the coincidence of Auerbach starting at Illinois as she was leaving.

"He said he might even have been doubly atypical on becoming a master's student under Shelford, coming as he did from an urban milieu and a culture that did not send students into the field of ecology."

"Culture?" Paul asked.

"He's Jewish," Mike answered. "Not many of us go into something as impractical as ecology. The provenance of the ecologist is through WASPY old men in tweed jackets. Although NEPA may have changed that too."

"Anyway, Auerbach thought the typical culture in ecology," Dan continued, "was an Ivy League one."

"There you go," said Mike. "That certainly does it for me. I should be in that other room with Ken Jennings and Miguel Monroy. Are they our token minorities?"

"Jennings is from Yale," Dan objected.

The kangaroo rat was now on the table, taking seeds from Mike's fingers and stuffing its cheek pouches full. It's tail, pale brown on top, immaculately white below, stretched out more than a full body length behind him, where it ended in a magnificent white tuft.

"I'm impressed," Dan said, not moving from his perch.

"I didn't know they were that easy to train," Paul said.

"I camped here when I worked for BLM," Mike said. "They dropped me off and left me here for a week at a time. This is one of my old friends. He remembers me."

The chubby-cheeked rodent jumped off the table and was gone.

"He'll be right back. He's got a stash some place nearby he's taking it to."

"What's the species?"

"Dipodomus deserti."

"So let me ask you Mike," Dan prefaced a question. "What exactly is an ecologist? That's the post-Earth Day issue, isn't it? NEPA has made ecology something of a profession. ES&Eers are not ecologists."

"Thanks a lot. But wasn't there an exchange in the ESA Bulletin about that? Some cranky guy from someplace called Arden Forest wrote that ecology needed to be a profession and ecologists should be licensed."

"Arden Forest? You mean Fred Küchler?"

"Yeah, that's the guy. On the other side was some guy from Harvard, I think. Bossert?"

"It was Ed Deevey," Dan said. "I'm not sure that he was at Harvard, though."

Uncle Ed, Dan mused to himself. Where would all his other uncles be on the licensing issue? Deevey had written that an ecologist was no more qualified to manage the environment than a physicist was to build a bridge.

"Was he the guy who described himself as a biologist first, ecologist second, activist third?" Mike asked.

"No. That was someone else," Dan said. "It's on the tip of my tongue, but I can't think of his name either. At the opposite end, there's Richard Levins arguing for theoretical research over engineering systems-type ecology. He claims it's more useful in solving applied problems and more worthy of funding."

"Did you know that Levins's little mathematical model on island bio theory is being used in the snowy owl fracas," Mike asked.

"Spotted owl?"

"You guys are as clear as mud to me, I'm afraid," Merifield said.

"You're an interesting case, Mike," Dan said. "Wildlife ecology from Davis, right?"

"Yep."

"You might be able to get licensed at the Senior Ecologist level."

"Like I would want to. What I want is a job. Are you licensed in geology, Dr. Merifield?"

"Certainly am," Merifield answered. "But I don't need a license to teach or do research. Only to consult."

The rat, now almost invisible in the moonlight, was back on the table.

"Why don't we continue this tomorrow while we search for that elusive desert tortoise?" Dan suggested.

"John Baldwin," Dan suddenly spat out as he headed toward a tent with Merifield. "Remember him?"

"Yeah," Merifield said. "Of course. He was the ecologist from Wisconsin who worked with David Conn in the Planning School. Nice guy. Where is he now?"

"Well, he was no ecologist. Didn't know squat about ecology. He got his degree in something like environmental studies. Now he's at the University of Oregon. I couldn't get that job, and I'm an ecologist."

"He's still a nice guy, though."

"Well, he gave me great advice before he left," Dan said. "Close the door to ES&E, he said, and don't look back."

"Cold morning," Dan said.

He was looking out at the water from a parking area near the wildlife refuge at the southern end of the Salton Sea. An Israeli firm had a proposal to create a solar salt pond by sequestering that part of the sea and letting its salinity increase to the point that the highly saline, greater density water could be used to trap the sun's heat at its bottom. That, they claimed, could provide 600 Megawatts of electricity and, in a way that Dan found hard to believe, stabilize the sea's salinity.

The Salton Sea had started out the century as the Salton Sink, an alkaline depression two hundred and fifty feet below sea level that was not good for anything. A storm in 1905 breached a levee and sent Colorado River water through irrigation canals to fill it. It was left as a thirty-five-mile-long, fifteen-mile-wide permanent feature. A productive fishery was established in it and seaside communities were built and proposed around it. Migrating water birds discovered it, using it as an important stop on the Pacific Flyway.

Marinas and homes built on the shoreline were soon engulfed by rising water. Guy Lombardo no longer came to race his boat at Date Palm Beach. Frank Sinatra and Jerry Lewis no longer came to cheer him on. Its yacht club was under water.

All the while that irrigation runoff into it raised its depth, evaporation left behind dissolved solids. Salt concentrations pushing past that of ocean water were now threatening the fishery. Only birds were benefiting from the changes.

"The water dish I left out for my animal friends was frozen when I got up," Mike said. "Temperature must have dropped down to thirty degrees, at least."

"Not necessarily," Paul said. "You can get a skim of ice on still water out here, even if the temperature is above freezing."

"It's like frost," Dan stepped in to explain. "Radiation goes directly into outer space in dry air. Add evaporative cooling and the water is freezing faster than it can thaw. But what animal friends are you talking about? Coyotes? Those rodents of yours don't drink water, do they?"

"They might."

"We could have left the beer out."

"Then you would have had to drink it in the morning."

"It would have been nice and cold about the time Lee and Charlie were getting in."

"What are those birds?" Paul asked as he leaned against his Grand Cherokee and looked out over the vast expanse of shallow water. From the parking area, all that could be seen were little white specs.

"I'm not sure," Dan said. "Egrets?"

"Herons, maybe," Mike guessed. "What do you think, Dr. Merifield?"

Towering above them with his high-school-basketball-center height and the team's only binoculars, he had the best perspective on the birds.

"I think it's really great to have two ecologists with me," Merifield joked in response, handing the binoculars over to Mike.

"I'm an insect ecologist," Dan said. "Mike's the wildlife ecologist. Besides, you're the one who couldn't tell me if that cone-shaped mountain on our way out here was volcanic or not."

"Well, I'm not a vulcanologist."

"Hah! And I'm no longer an insect ecologist," Dan laughed. "I'm calling myself a systems ecologist now. I don't need to be able to tell the bugs from the bunnies. They're all just herbivores to me."

"The ones in flight are pelicans," Mike announced from behind the field glasses.

"That many?"

"The place is lousy with them."

"Systems ecology?" Paul asked.

"Yup! Systems ecology. That's the future of ecology according to Gene Odum. I'm hopping aboard his bandwagon. I was hoping to do something on the Arabian Gulf in the other Problems Course, but maybe I'll try the Salton Sea, instead."

"The Saudi course?" Paul asked. "How's that going?"

Saudi Arabia, through the beneficence of a member of the royal family who had graduated from UCLA, had given the university a $50,000 gift, but it came with strange strings. It had to be used on unspecified planning work on two new towns Saudi Arabia was having built, Jubail and Yanbu. One string was that the UCLA planning team was not to be given any specifics on the two projects. Another was that they were not allowed to visit the building sites. That was almost on a par with the task an unfortunate

ES&E intern had with trying to identify the environmental impacts of the MX missile, given that all the information he needed was classified.

"Other than Steve Lavinger, that Problems Course is loaded up with planning students from the Public Health School."

"They could probably stand to learn some ecology," Paul said.

"Whoof! Yeah, except that Climis Davos thinks he's in charge of the thing and wants to do something using Delphi methods for decision making."

"It's his specialty."

"I know, except that Climis isn't around for very many of the meetings to decide what we could do Delphi on. Ernie Englebert shows up even more rarely. Poor Steve and I have to make something out of it all and neither of us has a clue what."

"Lavinger told me it has to be the worst Problems Course ever."

Dan was hurt by the remark, but he said, "I try my best, Mike. It's a project we never should have taken on. And have you seen the proposed report cover?"

Mike shook his head.

"It's a map of the Arabian Peninsula. Except Israel is not on it. Paul Smokler insisted on it. He worked for the Saudis before."

"You guys seen enough?" Paul asked.

"Yeah, let's move on."

They got back into Paul's Cherokee and headed north. Their intent was to circumnavigate the sea, then meet up with the others in Westmoreland, which had suffered an earthquake just days before.

"Don't forget what Hutchinson said about MacArthur," Mike said when the view of sea and desert began to bore him. "Can you say that about Odum?"

"He really knew his warblers?" Dan asked.

"What are you guys talking about now?" came from Merifield.

"I'm impressed with your knowledge of the lore of Prince MacArthur and the Knights the Yale Table," Mike said. "But Odum did start out as a birder when he was a kid."

"Didn't they all?" Dan noted. "Howard Odum really knew his circuits, too."

"This all has to do with licensing, I take it," Merifield said in frustration.

The other two looked at him, then at each other.

"You know," Dan said, "I doubt that either of them are licensed."

"You can say the same thing about pretty much everyone else in academia," Mike said.

"And here I am, turning out unqualified ES&E graduates to compete with qualified ecologists," Dan lamented.

"Oh, you're being a bit hard on them," Merifield said. "Some of our students are very capable."

"Yeah! Like me," came from behind.

The highway sign at the intersection they approached pointed to Palm Springs. They went in the opposite direction,

"They're not PhD ecologists," Dan insisted as Paul negotiated the turn.

"What do you think Mike?" Merifield asked turning his head briefly toward the back seat.

"I think Dr. Atkins is ticked because some consulting firm in Beverly Hills just hired an ES&E student, instead of him. It's the one Jerry Wilson works for."

"Is that true?" Merifield asked Dan.

"I don't want to talk about it."

"He thought they might triple his salary," Mike called from the back seat.

"Hey!" Dan barked back at Mike.

"But you should be able to get consulting work," Paul said. "I do it to make enough money to live on. Most UCLA faculty do."

"I tried that," Dan said. "Eighty bucks an hour I was supposed to be getting by helping Gary Meunier."

"That's not bad money,"

"Yeah, except that Mustafa got it all. He chewed up all the consulting money that should have gone to me. I only got two hour's worth. Meunier claimed he could handle the ecological effects himself, but I think that was mostly because they couldn't pay me. Mustafa kept claiming he needed more time to look into the health effects of the pesticide. He claimed the data was not as clear-cut as had been represented, and that meant more billable hours and more money for him. I've seen it, and it didn't seem that unclear to me. I think he just smelled money. He got eighty dollars an hour, in essence, to study up on the subject."

"How's that for a building lot?" Paul asked as he pulled off the main road.

He stopped the jeep on a side road along a flat part of the shore. Dirt roads crisscrossed in front of them in a rectangular grid of streets. Road cuts suggestive of driveways could be seen here and there. One had a mailbox. None had a house on it. Creosote bush had invaded most of the lots.

"How about it, Dan?" Paul laughed. "You've been looking for affordable housing. Want to invest in some seaside real estate?"

"How long do you think it's been like this?" Dan asked.

"I bet since the fifties," Mike answered.

"There are probably people that still own each lot. They buy it sight unseen then never build on it," Paul said.

"I bet some of these lots have multiple owners. There were some major real-estate shenanigans out here. Still are," Mike added.

Paul drove the vehicle onward as Dan and Mike threw names about faster than he could take them in. Cowles, Darwin, Clements, Curtis, Whittaker, Allee, Emerson, MacArthur, Hutchinson, Pearl, C. C. Adams, Simberloff, Connor, Paine, Grant, Connell, Nicholson, Bailey, Lotka, Gause, Park, Huffaker, Margalef, Watt, Woodwell, Golley, O'Neill, Elton, Lack, Slobodkin, the Odums, Likens, Watt again, the other one, LaMont Cole. Often, those names were combined with others and with a date, like MacArthur and MacArthur in 1961. Paul lost track quickly.

They recited a history they had never been taught. There were no history of ecology courses.

"I resent having to pick up the history of ecology," Dan directed at Paul, "my chosen science, in the streets, like I did about sex."

Paul's attention, however, had by then turned to the geological effects before him. Small rubbles of brick from former chimneys and collapsed porches could be seen through the car's windows. They were in Westmoreland.

"DDT accumulating through food chains, for example," Mike took over the history lesson as they got out of the car. "It's so important to the message of Silent Spring, but Rachel Carson would never have known about it had there not first been studies of the bioaccumulation of radioactive materials."

Dan was totally uninterested in earthquake damage. Paul scanned nearby buildings for more signs of it. Dan scanned the streets for a tan van.

"Where's the rest of the crew?" Dan complained. "It's past noon. I told Terry Sciarrotta we'd meet him at the Brawley geothermal plant at one."

The rest of their party, those who had come in late from Nevada, had chosen not to participate in their circumnavigation of the Salton Sea. The gas station at Main and Center in Westmoreland was that day's rendezvous point. It was a brief drive on a straight desert road from almost any direction and had ample places for a quick lunch.

"Ah! They're probably just late getting up," Mike answered. "I think the Casino treated them to drinks."

"They'll be along," Paul said.

"Computers are important, too," Mike picked up his previous conversation with Dan as Paul filled up with gas.

"Ecological data is collected very slowly," Mike continued, pretending to address Merifield, "tree by tree, leaf by leaf, beetle by beetle, rat by rat. The bookkeeping needed for ecosystem studies—or most other studies in ecology—would simply be impossible without high-speed computers with large memories. And data is important. Any kind of data. Other people's data. I bet Dr. Atkins will have to make a model of the Salton Sea ecosystem without any data."

"That's no bar to a model," Dan said.

"Model?" Paul asked. "You don't mean like F equals m a, or E equals m c squared?"

"How about S equals k A to the z power?" Mike put in.

"Perhaps those two geniuses, Newton and Einstein, took all of the best letters for themselves," Dan said. "Such elegant simplicity is not easily found in ecology. Mine's going to take a whole page of ugly difference equations."

"This is where systems science comes in," Mike said, still to Merifield, who was once more leaning against his Jeep. "There's input and there's output and they're connected. Quite simply, too much salt, too little reproduction. As long as he has those, Dr. Atkins doesn't need to know the identity of the fish."

"Given that big fish eat little fish is enough," Dan laughed. "But where are those guys? We've got to meet Terry Sciarrotta in half an hour."

"They'll be along soon," Merifield said again.

"What's alarming" Mike said, still talking to Merifield, "is that he doesn't need to deal with any real fish at all. The Odum brothers may have known their birds, but they could not identify most of the species of coral at Eniwetok, their most famous study. Boxes and arrows—stand-ins for numbers, actually—are all that's needed. And numbers. That goes without saying."

By then, they had been waiting for almost an hour. Even Merifield became concerned. Dan called the geothermal plant from a pay phone. They decided to get back into the Jeep and retrace the route from the camping area after first picking up something for lunch. Merifield emerged from the gas station store with a large brown paper bag in his hands.

"What have you got?" Dan asked.

"Sandwiches! They had lots of stuff. They even have cashew chicken!"

"Oh, God," Mike complained.

"You don't like cashew chicken?" Dan asked.

"It's become so trendy. Every place seems to have it," Mike said. "Pretty soon I bet, Macdonald's is going to put it on its menu."

"That will take care of the carcinogens issue," Dan said.

"Huh?"

They did not have to go far before they found the rental van by the side of the road. Someone had had to pee. Joe DeVita, a levelheaded sort, had been driving. He was an ecologist who already had a PhD and a faculty position, but he no longer wanted to be an ecologist. He was being retrained in ES&E, once more a graduate student. Unfortunately, where he had pulled off the road there had only been soft desert sand for a shoulder.

Judy Liedle, half of a husband-and-wife ES&E team, flagged them down. Steve, her husband, and the other male students were trying to push the van out, but they were only getting it stuck in more sand. Their various imprecations suggested that she was the one who had needed the stop. Merifield, the geologist, and Dan, the one-time physicist, took it upon themselves to devise a method to get the van out. Mike insisted on calling it a model of a method. It required driving into Brawley in the Cherokee and getting a tow-truck.

VIII

LUCK was finally going Dan's way in housing. Two of Walt Westman's friends had a falling out and were simultaneously abandoning their tiny rented house in Malibu for separate accommodations in San Francisco. They had four months left on their lease. The gay couple's dour demeanors and the strange blotches on their faces struck Dan as possibly having to do with something in the media having to do with some sort of disease gay men were getting, but the healthy discount they gave him on the rent kept him from asking any prying questions. It was so much below what he was contributing to Dieter that Dan could see not needing any summer pay. He could devote that time fully to research. Their medical issues, he thought smugly, were none of his business. The disease needed intimate contact, the kind only gay men have.

So, he was out from under that situation with Dieter, whatever it was, but only at the loss of car-pooling companions. Still that would have been true, even had he stayed with Dieter. David Tan was leaving UCLA, throwing away his academic career, to return to Manila; Perrine was being driven by developments with ES&E to the point of being unpleasant company; and Dieter, who Dan should have been car pooling with, drove to campus on a schedule that suited him—and only him—perfectly. The Spitfire was barely trustworthy, even if it now would no longer have to climb the pass ten times a week, but Westman, who could ease the burden on the Spitfire by driving him part of the way, was giving indications, too, of moving. He was quietly, but hardly secretly, negotiating for a position with NASA that would let him continue to do research on the effects of air pollution on California vegetation, but from its Ames Research Center in Sunnyvale.

What was that all about? Dan wondered. It would be a big step down for Walt. Could the disappearance of his ubiquitous smile have anything to do with wanting to follow his two friends to the

Bay Area? Mixed up with those questions in Dan's head was an uneasy question about Dieter. What had really happened that day?

These were the thoughts that occupied his mind as he sat in traffic on the short segment of West Ninety-sixth Street that he had to negotiate to get to the airport, just a few miles away. Maybe it was not even a mile, but he was very glad that he had an hour still before Ingrid's flight landed, given the traffic.

And what did that thing with Dieter John really mean? Dan simply could not put down the thought. His cock, usually so slow to arouse, had gone rock hard instantly. And instead of interminably laboring toward climax in a semi-hard state, it had swelled even more unbearably and exploded as soon as Dieter freed it from his blue jeans and held it in his hands and to his lips.

Sure, Dieter is gay, but does that mean that I'm gay? After all, if I like getting a blow job, what difference does it make if it is by a man or a woman? That's what Dieter said before that second time. A man knew just how a man would want it. Women just struggle in the dark with a penis. And he was right.

Instead of reciprocating, he had let Dieter go on to release himself on him. True, when asked, he had squeezed the base of Dieter's cock and held his balls while he came, but what was that? It was no more than playing "I'll show you mine if you show me yours" with the girls in Brattleboro, down where the Whetstone Brook went under the Main Street Bridge, except that the girls did not cooperate once dongs were out for viewing. Circle jerks had followed, instead. True, there had been some cross handling of cocks, but it had had nothing to do with sexuality. All that had just been kids learning what a penis was for, Dan was certain.

None of that is enough to make me gay. And what I did with Dieter was hardly enough to put me at risk of the gay disease.

Dan negotiated the right turn onto World Way and started inching visibly closer to LA's futuristic control tower and the airport parking lot. With luck, he would be seeing Ingrid in only minutes.

What a world away from each other he and Ingrid were now!

And there she was, only moments later, coming out of the corridor from the airplane!

She ran to hug him like a little girl on seeing her daddy after a separation. He could not bring himself to let go of her.

What was going on with him? Loneliness? Longing for the familiar? Did he just wipe away a tear?

"Hey, who's been cutting your hair?" she asked almost first thing, even though he had just that week visited the Rodeo Drive salon patronized by Dieter John. "Don't you own scissors? Why don't I do it for you?"

Yes, do take care of me. I need being cared for.

Dan started in earnest on the shwarma he had picked up from the Felafel King on the edge of campus. Once it was in his hands, he would not be able to put it down again without a mess. He was lunching with Walt by the Lipschitz statue, this time with Ingrid along. Handling an identical sandwich with dainty bites, she listened with rapture to Walt's tales of working with Congressmen.

"Boy," Walt teased, "I could tell you some stuff about some of our congressmen that you'd never believe!"

"Maybe you shouldn't," Ingrid said, laughing, flirting coquettishly with Walt.

Dan thought so, too. There were things that he did not want Ingrid to get into with Walt. Just days before, a similar question had brought out a shocker from him about Jonathan Roughgarden.

"Does that mean he's gay?" Dan had asked. "Don't be so quick with labels," Walt had said. "Sexuality is not so simple. Are you gay?"

Dan had not had an answer. Walt had hit a hidden target.

Dan could relax and go on dealing with his pita, though. Ingrid led Walt off into other areas of conversation: fashion, New York City, Greenwich Village, the Stonewall Inn, at which, incongruously, she had been in attendance during a police sweep.

"Not THE night?" Walt erupted.

"No. Much earlier that summer. Several weeks at least."

"What were you doing there, if I might ask?"

"I was accompanying one of my street kids, I guess they were called."

"She used to take in all sorts of homeless strays," Dan explained.

"I felt sorry for them. I felt like I needed to take care of them. No one else seemed to."

"Gay?" Walt asked.

"Some of them were. This one wasn't sure. He was afraid to go in alone, so I went with him. I think I helped him figure it out."

"What?" Dan asked, his last bite of sandwich still in his mouth.

"So what happened on that night?" Walt pressed. "Did you get arrested?"

"No. The police officer was very nice after he'd grabbed me by the crotch. I think he called it a search. They let us both go. He was under age, but they let him leave in my custody, so to speak."

"No harassment?" Walt asked.

"Not me. Well ..." She smiled mischievously.

"I can't imagine why," Walt laughed. In Ingrid, he had found a kindred spirit.

"So, what are your plans for the afternoon?" Walt asked, angling for an invitation to join them.

"Stay in Malibu?" Dan assayed. "The beach is beautiful, as always, although there's nothing standing in some places but brick chimneys after the fires last fall. Or, see if the Spitfire can make it up Angeles Crest?"

"How about Mulholland?" Walt asked playfully, turning to Ingrid.

"Yes! Yes! Yes!" she shrieked excitedly. "Mulholland Drive. Definitely."

"You aren't thinking of a threesome up there, are you?" Walt laughed. "That would have to wait until after dark."

Before Dan could think of anything to say, Ingrid said, "Why not?"

Ingrid, too, got the full Hungry Tiger experience. Except, unlike Jewel, she went for and finished off the twin lobsters, claws, tails, and body meat.

"How can you do that and not gain weight?" Dan asked.

Ingrid just shrugged her bare shoulders.

When Dan excused himself to relieve his bladder of three pints of Anchor Steam Beer, Walt followed him to the men's room. He and Ingrid had kept up with Dan beer-for-beer.

"I took the offer from Moffett Field," Walt said matter-of-factly from the urinal next to Dan's.

"The Bay Area is where I have to be now," he added, stepping away to the wash basins. "There are very bad things happening. People are dropping like flies. They say it's being spread through the bathhouses in San Francisco."

Dan was speechless.

"It never would have worked between Dieter and me, anyway," Walt said. "We just aren't right for each other. You should watch out, though. Dieter is unable to pass up a conquest of any kind. He sort of always gets his own way."

Dieter and Walt? "Walt, you're—you're my best friend, Walt," Dan stuttered. Walt is gay? "You'll always—always be my best friend."

It was true. Spending time with Walt was as pleasant as going bird watching with Robert MacArthur or going with Hutch to Linsley Pond. It was always the high point of Dan's day. With Dieter, however, it was something else entirely.

"By the way," Walt said as he headed for the door. "You should watch out for yourself. I frequented those bathhouses. So did Dieter."

His face was as grave as Dan had ever seen it.

"I don't know how any of this is going to work out for any of us, but I want to feel like I'm helping solve things. Being a part of the gay community there, I think I can. What can I do here in La La Land? Also, I have friends there I can depend on for support should I come to need it."

"You know, you should be concentrating on getting something published for that evaluation that's coming up," Dieter suggested—no, insisted—to Dan, his tone that of an older brother giving stern advice. "Malcolm Gordon told me he'd love to put you into a tenure-track position."

It was Sunday. Ingrid had been put on a plane at the ungodly hour of five that morning. Dieter had insisted that Dan come directly from the airport to his place for breakfast before the Sunday soccer game. Dan had, as he always did with Dieter, obeyed.

"If one ever comes up," Dan said wearily from his position slumped on the couch in the adjoining room.

"The eight-year review of ES&E is ready, I hear."

"Two to the third power. How appropriate!"

"What I hear is not encouraging," Dieter dismissed the joke. "Get some data together. Have something to show for your time here other than ES&E reports."

He started making breakfast noises before Dan could answer. He had the griddle out. Vermont maple syrup was on the counter. It was a gift from Jewel, delivered to Dan by Ingrid. He, in turn, brought it to Dieter's as a peace offering for closing him out of Ingrid's visit.

"I think those carabids I've been collecting are ready for analysis," Dan said drowsily.

"What?" Dieter shouted.

"The carbids!"

"That Malibu stuff? Don't even bother!"

Dan was too dumbstruck and sleepy to ask why, although he was sure that Dieter was about to tell him without any prodding.

"That study would be so derivative," Dieter continued in a steady voice that was easily heard above the kitchen fan. "No one in ecology ever tries to confirm someone else's findings exactly. It can't be done anyway."

Dan raised the ends of his mouth into a defeated smile. Dieter turned the fan off.

"You know," he said, "if I have to referee whatever paper you write out of that study, I'll turn it down."

Some advice, Dan thought. Some friend!

"So, you moved out so your old girlfriend could visit?" Dieter asked when Dan, following the smell of pancakes, appeared at the kitchen table.

Dan waited for more, but all that was heard was the noise of the swamp cooler outside the kitchen window as it strained to take away the heat generated by the griddle.

"No," Dan said when his plate was empty but for a slick of syrup. "My moving out has nothing to do with you or me or Ingrid or Walt, even. Maybe I'm not gay. Or maybe I've been gay all along, but didn't want to admit it."

Maybe Walt knew that, Dan kept to himself, but waited for me to come out on my own, rather than impose himself on me the way you did.

"But maybe it's just because I can't afford to stay here," he said instead. "Maybe it's something just that mundane."

"You know how expensive this place is," Dieter stopped him. "Just like you and everyone else who came out here a few years too late, I can barely keep up this laid back LA life style."

"The expenses I shared with you really added up, Dieter. And unlike you, I may not have a job soon. There's that to consider."

Dieter did not answer. Did you sleep with her? his face seemed to ask instead.

Yes, Dan tried to say telepathically. I did.

When he stood to clear his breakfast dishes, Dan realized he was aroused in a way he could not hide from Dieter. He was not certain he wanted to.

Did you have sex? Dieter's face now asked.

Yes, the urgency of his cock straining inside his pants made him want Dieter to know.

Yes. Out on the sand in Malibu, and I enjoyed it and she enjoyed it, even if I didn't get completely hard and couldn't come and she tried and tried to get me to come inside her, but then she gave up disappointed and gave me the blow job that I want now from you.

Dieter's eyes were on his condition.

Please, please do it. Touch me there. But just touch.

IX

CHANGES were afoot at ES&E. Perrine's notorious obstinacy had saved the program from the threat of "disestablishment," as the complete dismantling of a program was called, but it was at a personal price. He was relieved of his leadership duties and given a testimonial dinner. Bob Lindberg became the interim director. A search for a permanent home with a permanent director was under way. Lindberg thought he was in the running. Meanwhile, the engineering school, which wanted no part of the program but still had Perrine, began to recover its space with avidity. The office over which Janet Ransom had presided was taken back. All but Perrine were evicted from the cubicles within. The suite of rooms that had housed the ES&E students, Perrine's former laboratory, had its residents on notice to remove their things. People were adrift. Laura Lake found no place to settle that was better than at home with an adopted baby. Only Liza seemed unaffected.

Dan settled into very spacious, very unwanted, very unmoved-in-looking quarters in the basement of the Geology Building. They had been in the possession of Don Brown, an overage geology undergraduate. They still looked the way he had left them. In his years working part time for Dick Perrine and some of the geology faculty, Brown had garnered more resources than any ES&E student or adjunct. Files and files of papers and reports that he had amassed filled the two basement rooms. Like Al Brick, however, he had accidentally completed his degree requirements and had had to move on.

Al had not only completed, submitted, and defended his dissertation but had also been given an award for it as the most creative dissertation of its year. His pride was not diminished at all by the monetary part of the prize being confiscated to pay his overdue library fines, even if some wag—could it have been Krummel?—suggested the award had been bestowed on him only as a way for Mann Library to collect Al's fines.

Dan's new office had to be entered through a large room that looked to have been a lab at one time. Besides Brown's leavings, it now held a row of file cabinets in its center, an obviously temporary arrangement. They stored the history of the ES&E Program, as constituted by its paperwork, all the way back to its 1970 inception, appropriately during the year of the first Earth Day. The smaller, book-lined (mostly Don Brown's), but windowless den of a room at the far end of the lab could only be reached by passing the file cabinets. In fact, it still looked like Don had not left the office but had just cleaned out a desk and some space for Dan's much less extensive files. Dan organized his books and papers around the large metal desk and added a cot, a hot plate, and a few dishes to the working refrigerator, easy chair, and reading lamp Don Brown had abandoned. Dan's problems in finding temporary housing had a new solution. Unwanted glassware in some of the cabinets was replaced with clothing, Dan's.

The file cabinets in the outer room were unlocked, Dan discovered. Besides the usual bureaucratic detritus that academic programs create, he found certain personnel files of interest to him, such as those of the applicants with whom he had competed for his worthless position. The quality of the field he had risen above shocked him. Robert Costanza, in particular, was a name that caught his eye. He was already a rising star, with a clever publication in Science that argued persuasively for the use of embodied energy in economic accounting. He seemed to be pioneering the ecological method of accounting that Walt Westman had dreamt of creating on his postdoctoral sojourn in Australia. Of course, Costanza had not yet published his paper when he had applied for the ES&E position. Of course, Dan already had two papers in Science.

PhD from University of Florida, Dan noted from Costanza's cv. Had he been a Howard Odum student?

And there were others, equally impressive. There was ... Dieter John? Wait. No. Yes! There it was, a cv and an application letter and ...

And other things in other cabinets. And in the last one, a field notebook of sorts and files of computer output. Deter John's.

Dieter, Dan was surprised to learn with a little more snooping, had officially been an ES&E hire, even though he had never participated in any meaningful way in the program. ES&E had in essence subsidized his postdoctoral years under Jared Diamond. There were receipts in that file cabinet. The field trips resulting in the notebook, as was the computer output, as were the publication costs of the paper John wrote, were all paid out of the ES&E budget.

Why didn't Dan know that? Why hadn't Dieter ever said anything to him about it?

He picked up the small, bound notebook. It had elaborate map sketches of sampling positions in the Andrews Forest. It had to be Dieter's carabid data. The computer programs were rather cryptic, but to Dan did have the superficial appearance of that same study. What circuitous series of events had landed it here among ES&E detritus?

Dan left the application material where he found it, but for some future contingency he could not at the moment conjure up, he moved the ecological data to someplace more convenient: his own meager files. As basic ecology, they seemed out of place among the bureaucratic minutia of ES&E.

Dan suddenly felt good—more than good—about having his home and office in Don Brown's former lair. He was energized. He plunged into his research and his Problems Courses. The IBP data was soon whirring on the magnetic tape and leaping through the binary circuits of UCLA's IBM computer, where Dan subjected it to multiple analytical attacks. The result of that labor was lots of tables, lots of statistics, but nothing that resembled the assembly rules that Diamond had dreamed up for his island birds.

Which were the vagabond species? Dan wondered as he scanned the output data for patterns. Where were the forbidden combinations? Where was the size structure?

Based on his statistical analysis, the size ratio between co-occurring species of insects feeding in the same way on creosote bush could be Hutchinson's golden 1.3, statistically, or it could be as high as 5.2—or less than zero. Clearly the data were not normally distributed. Analysis was ludicrous.

Other than for some species being generalists and others specialists, which could be looked up in the literature without recourse to sampling and analysis, it all just looked random to Dan. The data set was useless. There was no way he could make the kind of nice story out of it that Diamond or Dieter John had made out of their observations.

Maybe, he thought, he should see how Dieter had done his analysis. Maybe he had some tricks that Dan hadn't thought of, some ideas he could use, something that would have his numbers suddenly fall out with the expected answers instead of the random garbage that the IBP data was giving him.

But the Salton Sea distracted him before he could get around to it. Charlie Kratzer, Lee Hannah, and Marlene Broutman developed data from which they could predict the salinity changes the sea would face, given the various energy development scenarios in the area. Others in the course turned up data on the effect of salinity on the life table properties of its sport fish. All that was needed was a sharp mathematician—Dan nominated himself—to put the two together. He greedily jumped into the task.

There was no need for Dan to invent equations. Those he needed already existed, he was certain. From the start, he intended to avoid the logistic equation in its many forms. Yes, it was a true friend of ecologists. Its concepts of r and K were obvious in the real world, intuitive almost. However, it had never successfully modeled anything but Gause's paramecium populations. Having data on fish species, Dan turned to the fisheries literature instead. Ricker-type equations, named for the scientist who developed them, looked promising in their practicality. Their aim was to allow an optimal harvest of fish. Maximum sustained yield it was called in the current jargon. As he delved deeper into the equations, however, he recognized in them, too, that little logistic curve. He followed the fisheries' literature forward in time, nevertheless. They did, after all, work reasonably well for fish. His search brought him to a name that surprised him. Robert May was dabbling in fisheries models. The article by him that Dan thought he absolutely most needed could not be found in the UCLA libraries, however, necessitating Dan to send him a brief letter requesting a reprint. May responded to the request with relevant reprints and an offer to meet with Dan. He would be visiting UCLA in the very near future for some purpose he described vaguely as having to do with editorial duties. Could Dan find time in his schedule to meet with him?

Could he? A date and time to stop by to see Dan in his out-of-the-way corner of the Geology Building was soon arranged.

Anticipation of the meeting electrified him with excitement. This, he knew, was his opportunity to become a player in ecology. He needed moral support, something to encourage him to be at his best when he saw May. He called Walt. Walt was pleased to hear Dan's changing attitude from the usual despair he had over his career, but Walt had more weighty matters on his mind.

"It seems as if a week doesn't go by that I don't lose a friend," Walt said. "I'll go to a get-together and someone who was there a week before is missing. Dead or dying. Soon to be dead. And all alone, except for his lover, or maybe a friend, and he might not be well, either. It's brutal."

Dan could find nothing to say to that.

"The flower of a whole generation is being lost," Walt said. "And all the while, priority is being given to protecting the blood supply rather than prevention and cure. It's not right."

Dan had thought little about it. It all seemed so much like someone else's problem. Still, the disease's newly conferred official name, AIDS, sent an icy stab through him.

"Even getting enough research subjects to conduct good experiments is a problem," Walt continued. "Gay men don't want to be identified. They're scared to come out of the closet. They don't want to lose their jobs. Even in California, there's no real job protection for us."

Los Angeles

"How about you, Walt?" Dan asked the question that he knew would elicit the stab again. "How are you?"

"OK, so far. I may have dodged that bullet. I still have energy. I'm starting an organization to represent individual gay and lesbian scientists. I want it to speak out against homophobia in science and research funding."

"What are you calling it?"

"The National Organization for Gay and Lesbian Scientists and Technical Professionals."

Not exactly a catchy name, Dan thought.

"Technical professionals?" he asked. "I think I may have a few for you in the ES&E program."

"Any way I can do it," Walt continued, ignoring or not understanding the joke, "I want to help other people. Let's face it, if this disease affected anyone but gays, there would be massive, very well publicized prevention efforts. But the federal government is afraid the Christian right will accuse it of providing instructions about how to have safe sex. I want to change that. All of that."

And I want to model the Salton Sea, Dan thought.

Then, after a pause, Walt said, "I'm OK, really, but it might just be a matter of time. But I refuse to be fatalistic about it."

Dan didn't ask for further explanation. He called Jewel. He wanted to lose himself in his research the way Walt was losing himself—perishing even—in his new cause. Dieter was no longer a person to talk to. Neither was Dritschilo, now teaching high school in Vermont. Buck? Krummel? Nafus? Would any of them really understand his situation? He called Jewel. No, she had not read that literature. No, she only knew what May had published with Robert MacArthur.

It was mud season, she told him. She had to park her car at the bottom of the hill in order to be able to go into Brattleboro to buy groceries. Current research in ecology did not have the same immediacy to her.

He called Ingrid. She was cheered by his news. He was cheered by her.

"What is it?" she asked. "Do you need another haircut? I thought you were going to a barber."

"I do," he laughed.

No, she would not be able to come to LA, she told him firmly. There were calves being dropped all over the pastures. Why didn't he come out to see her? She offered to send him tickets. More exactly, she offered to have her travel agent send him tickets.

"I really would like to see you," she said in closing the conversation. "I'd love to cut your hair again. It'll remind me of the boy I fell in love with."

He put the phone receiver down. He wandered over to the Health Sciences complex looking for someone to talk to. It was a huge structure that connected to the UCLA hospital. The Environmental Health Department was housed on its fifth floor, along an endless, hospital-like corridor. He walked past John Froines's room. Froines was one of the Chicago Seven, a defendant in the most famous political trial of the century. Now he was a health chemist. For some reason, he and Dan never hit it off. Froines was too perfectly conventional now, while Dan still thought of himself as a social radical. Next was Climis Davos's office, followed by Mustafa's. He walked with silent, careful steps past them, feeling as if he was behind enemy lines, even though one of the moves afoot was to place ES&E into the School of Public Health. Finally, he came to the tiny office that housed—desk upon desk, it seemed—Mike Weinstein, along with Duane Van der Pluyme, and the Liedles. The Liedles could be depended on being upbeat, but they were disappointingly elsewhere. His trip was wasted.

When the day came, Bob May showed no surprise at the extra audience as he was introduced to Mike Weinstein and Fred Turner, who had come early to swap desert tortoise stories with each other while waiting for the great man's entrance. They sat in chairs that were the product of Don Brown's masterful scrounging.

"Interesting office space," May said, trying to give no hint of condescension as his eyes stopped at the dress shirts on wire hangers that hung from a coat rack in a corner.

Dan suspected his demeanor might have been due less to where the shirts were, than their quality. Perfectly coifed, May was also perfectly tailored in what Dan took to be an Italian suit and a French shirt. It all made him look bigger than life.

Moving to his hot plate, Dan offered tea.

May frowned.

"How about a pint of Fosters?" Dan asked, taking a motor-oil-like can from the refrigerator.

"I guess I will have one," May laughed, "if only out of patriotic duty."

Dan opened another can for himself. He had long ago learned that Mike and Fred would not imbibe and would not be offended at not being offered any. The beer did have the wanted effect on May of taking him out of his suit and making him the affable Australian he really was. Still, there was little small talk. The discussion quickly settled on to the mathematical model Dan had worked out. He brought out the large-format computer printout that the Liedles had given him that morning. It was complete with graphical output, although, to Dan's regret, not in color. That was an option available only to the privileged few at UCLA, Nobel Prize winners, medical researchers, and such.

"Of course, you have to expect that these equations will converge on extinction under these conditions," May said, looking again at the equations of Dan's model after a glance at the graphs.

Fred and Mike looked on in silence, rooted to their chairs.

"But you really shouldn't try to be so explicit with your models," May advised with a frown. "Why don't you take a more general approach. Don't try for specific numerical solutions. See if you can develop equations that model the intrinsic features that govern the system. Analyze their behavior. Don't try to solve them numerically as you have."

Then, judging that he could accomplish no more good, May excused himself and was gone.

"Wow! I can't believe he solved those equations in his head," Dan marveled after having seen May out.

"Oh, he's probably seen so many equation like those so many times that he can recall from memory what the solutions are," Fred said, adjusting his toupee.

Another melanoma had been removed.

"You think so?" Dan asked, deflating.

Mike agreed with Fred.

"Still," Dan defended himself against May by proxy with them, "Isn't an exact solution what this situation requires? Wouldn't an environmental manager having to make a decision rather see concrete numerical results than vague mathematical boundaries? We're doing exactly what we need."

With each word, Dan's confidence rose until he was again ready to take on the world of academic ecology. His base at UCLA now seemed perfect for it. He became more certain as the days went by that it had been less criticism that May had given him than helpful suggestion, pointing Dan in a direction that he thought would lead to academic success. After all, May was known to suggest that many computer models could benefit from the addition of an on-line incinerator. Dan even scheduled himself for an ES&E Seminar, then was shocked to find the room full for him. The seminar normally only attracted those few students who were actually enrolled in the course.

There were politics afoot around ES&E, he knew. FTEs (full time equivalents, shorthand for a position budgeted on the salary scale for professors and usually held by professors, what Dieter John had managed from ES&E and Dan had not) were being moved from department to department, as if on a chessboard. One of them could be his. He smiled at Liza, who stood at the back of the room, her usual seat taken, and launched into his presentation of his Salton Sea fisheries model.

Minutes later, the door opened and Dieter John made a show of entering. He stood next to Liza, even though there were one or two seats still empty. Dan nodded and went on with his talk. He loved having the audience. Next time he looked up, however, Dieter was gone. Someone else was standing next to Liza.

"What did Dieter say to you?" he asked Liza at the end of his talk, rushing straight to her before she could leave and ignoring the hands raised for questions from the audience.

"Who?"

"Dieter John. He didn't say anything to you?"

Liza looked at him with some alarm.

"Why, I never saw him," she said. "Isn't he in San Francisco?"

"I saw him standing right—"

He stopped. Had he imagined it? Could she have not recognized him?

Dan's new mood lasted for less than another week. It was not the shock of the apparition at the seminar that ended it. It was another, totally unexpected shock.

"I can't go on with this anymore," he groaned aloud in Don Brown's old desk chair.

He was alone. He was about to hold his head in his hands. He would have, had he not been holding a letter in one of them. It was from Manila, from Tessie Tan.

He could not keep the news to himself, but he could not think of someone to share it with. He left his basement lair in Geology and found himself staring at Boelter Hall. He went in. It was through the entrance at the top of the steps, on the same level as the Dean's office, rather than Perrine's basement level. He walked past David Tan's old office. The door was closed, the new occupant unknown to him, but the door to the departmental office was open. He went in. Two men in white shirts inside one of the cubicles looked up at him.

"Did you know that David Tan is dead?" Dan asked.

"Of course," one of them answered. "It's sad."

He turned his attention back to his colleague.

Of course. Dan thought, I'm one of the last to find out.

He wandered off. He stopped at Liza Little's open door. He looked in.

"You look terrible," Liza said to him looking up from her desk. "What's the matter? Is it Jewel? You've been acting so strangely recently."

"No, but I think I could use something from the flask you must keep in your desk," he said.

"I don't understand."

He repeated his request. She repeated her confusion.

"I really could use a drink," he finally said.

She pointed with her eyes to a chair beside her desk. He collapsed into it.

"David Tan is dead," he said.

The name meant nothing to her. Her office had been in the Geology Building when David had been at UCLA. They had never had a chance to meet.

He explained how Tan had moved back to Manila when his apartment went condo. Fed up with the meager benefits UCLA provided young faculty so that they could lavish them instead on senior faculty they stole away from other universities, Tan had gone back to work in his family business. His death deprived two small children of a father.

"I'm really sorry to hear that," she said. "He must have been a good friend."

"Briefly," Dan said and left.

He walked slowly down the stairs to the basement, to Perrine's office, still in the same enclave they had shared as ES&E faculty. Janet Ransom's absence, though, made it feel very foreign. Perrine, now emeritus, had been moved from his old cubicle with the corner windows to a windowless one beside Dan's old one. It was larger, but Perrine had to share it with an engineering postdoc.

Perrine, too, had already heard Dan's news, but not its circumstances.

"It happened all at once," Dan elaborated for him. "Tessie said it was leukemia. They noticed a black and blue on his back that could not be explained and immediately went to the doctor's. Six months later, he was dead."

Perrine whistled through his teeth.

"Tessie asked about the reactor in her letter," Dan continued.

"What?"

"The UCLA reactor."

Dan waited for more.

"She said that David suspected it as the cause," Dan said when Perrine said nothing. "She's coming to the US and wants to talk to me about it. As an environmental scientist."

"Ionizing radiation is one of the few definite causes of leukemia that's known," Perrine said.

"Yeah. And his office was really close to the reactor. He even usually kept his window open."

It was a small teaching reactor in the basement of Boelter Hall. Some enterprising UCLA undergraduate with the Committee to Bridge the Gap had discovered it had accidentally released radiation on several occasions. It had become a cause celebré for them. It had only been very small amounts that were released, but it nonetheless should not have happened. The release had been during the time that David Tan had sat at his desk in his office, two stories below, by the open window downwind from the reactor's exhaust stack, wondering what he should do with his life.

"What can I tell her?" Dan despaired. "In theory, any amount of radiation can cause cancer."

"Realistically," Perrine said, "that amount is very unlikely to have done so. Maybe less so than their flight back to Manila. It could have been anything. It could have been a glow-in-the-dark key chain or a watch face."

"Maybe. Or maybe there is now a widow with two young children, all because someone could not keep that thing from releasing radiation."

"You sound like you're from Bridge the Gap."

"Wow," Dan said. "You know, with all my high Earth Day ideals, I have no way to confront this. Nothing but the cold, mathematical reasoning. We're so inculcated with it. We reduce David Tan to just a number, a mere uncertainty in the scheme of things. Anywhere I can—"

Dan stopped in mid-sentence.

"No," he continued, now with calm determination. "I'm not going to do this anymore. I'm not taking a job like this again. I want nothing to do with weapons or nuclear plants or pesticides."

Each sighed at the other.

"What can I do Dan? I can't change the world for you."

"I just know I can't go on here," Dan said. "This is all such a sham. I'm not doing any good here. I'm just training well-paid businessmen to work in subverting any goals for a healthy—an equitably healthy—environment. I've got no guts. I should just tell Tessie that, in my opinion as a UCLA faculty member in the Environmental Science and Engineering Program, that student reactor gave Dave leukemia."

A knock on his door ended the conversation. It was Liza.

"I thought you might have come here," she said. To cheer him up, she brought with her a can of caviar from Trader Joe's. "It's the bottom of the barrel, I'm afraid" she said, "but it's still very good. It's the bottom of the barrel of the highest grade. I always keep a can in my desk."

Maidstone

... had there been more students like you, I might feel differently. All joking aside, I hope you do not have me all wound up in certain ideals. That is a grand idea as long as it lasts; but the awakening can be orrfully rough.

Those were pretty much Küchler's words at Arden Forest, Dan thought, before resuming his reading.

... I find most of my intense objection to winter was from Syracuse city life – the dirty streets, the icy sidewalks, the run-down car battery, the futile aim of keeping a polished pair of shoes, the bus-waiting on blustery street corners, the filthy ash and garbage on the snow. But out here all is as clean and white as the day the snow first fell, and paper birch, mt. Laurel, pine and hemlock take on new meaning. I suppose that human failing of "profession" plays a big role, for these forests and fields I can save from destruction, and I have long plans for research on them, much outlasting my life.

He was looking for a passage he thought he remembered in which Hal Buechner might have mentioned symptoms resembling what was now well known as post-traumatic stress syndrome. It was probably a final straw he clutched at before having to abandon the project. He was losing all confidence in being able to get anything at all publishable out of the letters. This last was part of an attempt to write up something about ecologists in World War II. Unsurprisingly, it had changed their world views. And DDT had come out of it. That was a thread he could follow. Buechner's post traumatic stress syndrome, however, he feared had little to do with DDT.

A loon surfaced within his sight. He watched it until it dove out of sight again. There was no predicting, he knew, when or where it would resurface. It might come up by the other shore of the lake.

He was at the lake not so much to find that passage, but to get a start on a different project. The Champion Paper Company was ceasing its logging operations in Vermont's Northeast Kingdom, a wedge of land that abutted Canada at its north and the Connecticut

Lakes country of New Hampshire at its east. Champion had just sold 132,000 acres to various state and federal agencies and private foundations, notably the Nature Conservancy, for $26.5 million. Plans for it called for wildlife preserves, wilderness areas, recreational areas, and preservation of the logging and hunting lifestyles of those who lived or enjoyed the area.

It was being folded into something larger called the "Northern Forest," which as far as Dan could make out referred to the biome, for lack of a better term, that stretched from the Adirondacks, across Lake Champlain, through northern Vermont and New Hampshire, and into Maine. Bill McKibben had suggested he look into it. Bill Dritschilo suggested the accursed lean-to on Maidstone Lake. It may have been paradise for Bill's family in August, but it was cursed by mosquitoes at the present.

Slapping one, he returned to his laptop and the letters.

I suspect my god parents, and perhaps many friends, feel that I am locally loco for living alone. However, I'm alone because no one else that I know is either freeto, or will dare a winter up here.

This second typo brought him up short, as did two more mosquitoes. He was not certain if either typo had been his mistake or in the original. What he had came from his first perusal of Küchler's letters, before he had brought along his scanner. When he did have the scanner, he had not bothered to scan those letters he had already read and partially transcribed, of which this was one.

Damn. Now what? Should he just go ahead and correct the errors, even though they might very well have been in the original? What was the accepted convention? A lot of "[*sic*]s?" What did Strunk and White have to say?

He didn't have Strunk and White with him. This was all a bad idea, he despaired. He was already a year past Buechner's release from service and was finding nothing. Still, he might as well finish this particular letter.

...Strangely, the gentle sex is the one to have first invaded these precincts of Adam. She came from a distance of several hundred miles. I am not sure yet whether her chief interest was

husband-catching, curiosity about the eccentric Dr. Küchler, or the desire to tell friends, boastingly, that she actually survived a visit to this bluebeard's den. At least I am sure that a few people in nearby Norfolk are buzzing, for the same taxi man who brought her, took her away again, another day. She is still a good friend of mine, at least she has no cause to object to anything. I find that loneliness is just a disease which may sometimes follow the real disease, super-sociability. Although I have no intention whatever of becoming a recluse, nor of being surrounded by mobs every waking moment, if I had to choose between the two, I would certainly turn hermit. The company of music, books, plants, and animals makes the world seem far more rational than otherwise. I have two neighbors within a mile. One is a World War I veteran, who leaves his wife working in the city while he lives out here, alone. Sounds strange, but actually he is quite fine. The other is Roy Chapman Andrews, at present very busy writing a book. We see mighty little of each other, altho it is a standing "law of the wild" that each can call on the other for any help at any time or for any thing. So the chapters of "Vegetation Science" peel off.

"The gentle sex" caught his attention, but it disappeared from Küchler's mental maze wanderings as quickly as it had appeared. Could it have been Jewel?

Nah, he decided, and shut down his computer. Camping out gave him little chance to recharge its battery, which seemed to have considerably less than the four-hour life it was advertised to have.

He slapped another mosquito. The Northern Forest was wilderness mainly in its mosquitoes, he complained to himself. Much of it had been logged within the last fifty years. Some appeared to him to have been logged within the decade.

He slapped another mosquito after crawling into his sleeping bag. Maybe he could zip his head inside?

So far, the best part of the day had been the bstilla he had for lunch at the Rainbow Sweets bakery in Marshfield. The worst part had been finding an old envelope with a Noe address on it just as he was gathering materials together to leave. It had somehow found its way into and fallen out of the folder labeled "Buechner." He took it out now while there was still light. It looked as if it had never been opened. It unsealed easily, though, without tearing, but something yellowish appeared to flit out of it on a gust of wind. A moth? Unlikely. Whatever it was, the sudden wind took it away into the flickering darkness.

Dear Dan,

Thanks for your recent note, as well as all the attention you've showered on me from your busy post at Oak Ridge in the past few months. I have appreciated it. Isn't it strange how life works?

I did have a wonderful nine days in Maui. A beautiful place, and it was good to have a total break from work and a change in venue.

I'm still working full time, but am not sure how long that will last. My energy has been fading in the last couple of months; the DDI has held my T-cells constant, but they are low -- in the range where many are much sicker than me. Next week I have an appointment to see a second doctor about trying Compound Q—a rather harsh chemotherapy that has had good results in people with a higher T-cell range than me. Whether such a treatment is too risky for me is a judgment call, but this doctor has been high on Q for others, so we'll see. I do feel very lucky with my health so far, but I need only look around me to see that DDI alone is probably not enough.

My dispute with LBL and Prudential over my disability payments last year continues. This week I authorized a lawyer to send a letter to try to move the process along. She seemed chafing at the bit to do so, so we'll see.

If I do start taking Q, and the side effects are as severe as expected, I will probably go on disability, at least for a time. The Q-treatment side effects are supposed to lessen after 4-5 months.

Walt

What a strange, frightening world that had been all those years ago! He turned off the lantern and slipped the letter under it, unfolded, apparently for mosquitoes to read, for no more bothered him that night.

Oak Ridge

I

DEAR Danny,
   Did you know that your Aunt Jewel writes poetry? Well she does. Here is my latest. You may not like it. I am not sure I like it. Quite a dilemma, isn't it?
Love,
As always
Your Aunt Jewel

   The poem was separate from her letter. It was typed on a white half-sheet of plain paper, rather than in the neat longhand on the colored and perfumed thank-you-note stationary so characteristic of her letters. It was titled, "Dilemma."
   He sat down for a more careful reading after his initial glance at it. What was she saying to him?

>*I have lived to see the gazelle and springbok.*
>*I have camped beneath the elephant's trumpet.*
>
>*Will my grandchildren see the graceful leaps?*
>*Will my grandchildren hear the trumpeting?*
>
>*If I have any!*
>
>*No, for I fear they will say,*
>*Just think of all those lovely animals*
>*That were alive in Granny's day.*
>
>*Lions and tigers and bears.*
>*It must have been wonderful.*
>*Have you not lived among the desert poor of Somalia?*
>*Have you not lived among the slum poor of Rio?*
>*Have you not lived among the desperate poor of Calcutta?*

> *Have you not lived among the silent poor of Appalachia?*
>
> *Would you not feed their starving children*
> *The gazelle and springbok you now bequeath*
> *Live to the unborn?*
>
> *Or convert to grain*
> *The grass they eat?*

II

"WHEN I set out from graduate school to fix the world," Glen Suter began his lament. "I thought NEPA gave us a chance to combine modern ecological thought with political activism."

Lanky, like too many ecologists, in Dan's opinion, Suter had his legs stretched out parallel to his desk. His light brown curly hair was neatly trimmed, as was his mustache. He spoke with a bit of a drawl that was hard to place. Maybe he had just been infected with the accent in Tennessee. At any rate, what he was voicing were thoughts filling Dan's head.

"Five years and over twenty NEPA documents down the road," Suter continued, "that part of my baggage has yet to be unpacked. My ecosystem coveralls are definitely still in my luggage, and I didn't just forget them. I get regular reminders to use the ecosystem approach, but ecosystem theory, as far as I'm concerned, is useless for NEPA."

Oak Ridge was still trumpeting the ecosystem modeling that had brought Dan there despite his qualms, but its scientists had been caught by surprise while trying to assess environmental impacts from nuclear power plants proposed for the Indian Point facility in New York. They found themselves studying the autecology of striped bass, rather than the ecosystem in which it was found. The questions they needed to answer required little knowledge of the place the fish had in the Hudson River ecosystem. What did merit study was bass being trapped against intake screens, bass eggs and larvae being entrained with cooling water and perishing within the plant, and the temperature of that water when released back into the river.

"I don't agree with everything Glen says, but I will defend to the point of personal discomfort his right to say it," Robert O'Neill laughed off Suter's complaints. "But you just can't depend on a piece-meal approach to provide predictive capability within a useful time scale. You need to look at the bigger picture. You need to look through your macroscope, as Tom Odum would say."

Dan's main duties at Oak Ridge were as a contract manager, overseeing research contracted out to investigators at other facilities. It was very bureaucratic. It also required more diplomacy than Dan could tolerate. The small role he was also given as liaison between the theoretical ecologists and those more recently hired to do environmental assessment must have been a sop to keep him from going crazy and quitting. It was the only part of his job that required any knowledge of ecology.

Suter was with Oak Ridge's Environmental Impact Program. O'Neill was with the Terrestrial Ecology Section. They were housed in different parts of the recently built Environmental Sciences Laboratory. The two groups seemed to Dan to also exist in two different intellectual worlds.

O'Neill was was an official ecosystem computer model guru in the theoretical group. He had been at Oak Ridge since before the Radiation Ecology Section began to grow into the Environmental Sciences Division. He very much believed in the usefulness of the ecosystem concept. Chubby, always smiling, even with his eyes through his thick, dark-rimmed glasses, clean shaven, although always seeming in need of a visit to a barber, he exemplified in general to Dan how Oak Ridgers appeared neither as well coiffed as Angelenos, not a surprise, for they were computer jockeys rather than butterfly chasers, nor as physically fit, as was expected for those working at desks instead of hiking to field sites.

How strange, Dan now marveled, was the chain of events that had brought him to where Stuart Little's gaseous diffusion process was put to use to make the bombs that fell on Hiroshima and Nagasaki. First had been the idea he had gotten into his head from Stanley Trimble that Tennessee could be a fine place for an ecologist to live, Next had been the strings he could pull through John Krummel to get himself invited to Oak Ridge to explore mutual suitability. He had had to concoct some sort of reason to make the trip an ES&E function. Fortunately, David Guzzetta, a Viet Nam vet who had not yet abandoned his mustache, was at the Batelle Institute, analyzing the effectiveness of the IBP Biome Program compared to that of the Hubbard Brook ecosystem studies. Guzzetta had been clamoring for someone from ES&E to come out and put the official stamp of approval on the internship. From a West Coast perspective, Columbus might as well have been next door to Oak Ridge, so Dan had discretely put together an itinerary for an intern visit. Out of guilt, he had eschewed a food and lodging allowance, choosing to accept invitations to stay with Guzzetta in Columbus and Krummel in his home outside of Knoxville. Everything had been set for his escape from LA.

"No way I'm going to be hired there," had been the first words out of Dan's mouth when Walt picked him up at the Hollywood-Burbank Airport.

He had shared not a word with Walt about how comfortable the flight, only half-full, as were most red-eye flights, had been or how impressive the Grand Canyon was from forty thousand feet at dawn when powdered with snow.

"He thinks I want to be a butterfly collector."

"Who?"

"Auerbach. Stanley Auerbach."

"Well, wouldn't you and I both rather be out collecting butterflies?"

With little early-morning traffic, they had quickly scaled the pass and were within sight of the Getty Museum.

"I have the Hunsackers to compete with," Dan had complained.

"What?"

"We're competing for the same position, although two against one doesn't seem fair. Can you believe that? Krummel wasn't supposed to tell me that, but he let it slip out just before I left. One Phidie to another. He's looking to move, too."

"Phidie?"

"Phidie is Krummel's take on the concept of Okie. He has this image of young families, father with PhD in hand, loading all their things and themselves into the family car and setting off for Academe in search of work. Any work. Post-doc, adjunct, lecturer, instructor, research associate, any kind of position, as long as it is in academia. They're the new Okies. Bill Dritschilo is his exemplar. He made three cross-country moves in one year and never got a job he liked. It's like Levin and Mendez at Yale."

"Huh?" Walt had asked, trying to maintain his smile through his confusion.

"But there's no way they should get the job instead of me. They're not even PhDs."

"Of course you'll get the job, Dan."

"Believe me, don't bet against them. Don has a MS in physics. I only have a BA. That makes him a harder scientist. And Carolyn—well, she's a wife."

"Maybe they want to add a woman.".

"Yeah. They'll find something for her. And I've already gone down in flames."

"Maybe it's her they want, and the husband is the one they'll find something for."

"Shit! I thought I had the job all wrapped up when their company doctor fingered my prostate."

"Ouch! Felt raped, did you?"

"I thought they would never submit me to that unless they'd already made up their mind to hire me."

"So, what exactly happened?"

Walt had already turned off the Freeway and was on Santa Monica Boulevard.

"I gave a seminar in order to show my stuff. It looked like the entire research staff of the Environmental Sciences Division showed up for it. Michael Browman, who I knew from St. Louis, sat right in the front row. We'd played a few pickup soccer games together. That made me feel pretty relaxed. My first slide was that beautiful photo of the Klamath River. You know, with the blue sky and the clear water and the old pine tree framing the scene. California's Wild and Scenic Rivers were the kind of environment I would have happily spent my life studying, I told them. For contrast, my second slide was a big manure pile in Iowa. I said that was the kind of environment that my career would more likely turn out to consist of studying. It was supposed to be a joke."

"You gave your talk on energy in agriculture, rather than wild and scenic rivers, right?"

"Yeah," Dan had continued in the rapid-fire mumble that some New Jerseyites use when excited or distraught and that he had picked up in his years in Greenwich Village, where he had often been distraught. "Meat. Son of Meat, actually. That's what Krummel calls it. I just couldn't come up with anything ES&E related, in the end. And I already had that lecture in the can—slides and all. I tried to stretch the joke by saying that manure is very big on Midwestern farms—organic or otherwise. I mean this manure pile was huge. But I felt something cold from Auerbach at our interview. I started out by saying that Bob Lindberg sent his greetings. All he said was, Who? I dropped that tactic immediately. So much for what kind of connections Lindberg has. So, instead of chitchat over joint acquaintances, our conversation quickly turned to the issue of the manure pile. I still avowed, when given a chance by him to retract, a preference for scenic vistas along the Klamath River over the useful countenance of the manure pile. That was no joke."

Then he had stopped, as if needing to take a breath. Walt had already pulled into his driveway.

"We need more ecologists willing to study a manure pile, was what Auerbach had to say at the end of our interview. He ushered me not just out of his office, but out of any future at the lab, I'm sure. According to Krummel, Auerbach has always been afraid that the physical scientists at the labs saw ecologists as not much more than a bunch of butterfly chasers. Too late! Now he tells me! Auerbach already had me pegged as a butterfly chaser. No way he's giving me a job."

"Don't be so sure," Walt had said, turning off the engine, but not getting out. "But you're right that Auerbach is afraid of butterfly collectors. That was why he chose to focus on the ecosystem level. Ecosystem ecology is the closest thing in ecology to physical science. That was what let the ecosystem approach and ecological research flourish at Oak Ridge. He had kept out the butterfly chasers."

"I wish I knew that before my visit to Dr. Coldfinger."

Westman's broad smile had grown into a laugh. "That must have been the defining moment of that trip for you," he shared. "Well, it's going to be two against one now, I'm afraid, you against the Hunsackers." He had laughed again. "They sound like characters from the Ring Trilogy."

"Does that make me Siegfried?"

"Be glad you're not Alberich."

No, Oak Ridge had not hired Dan instead of one of the Hunsackers. Carolyn was one of those Dan had to liase with. He had most definitely not convinced Auerbach that he felt out of place around only ecologists. His proclamation at his interview that he had since childhood wanted to be like the MacArthurs, Robert, the mathematician, and John, the physicist, rather than just any old butterfly-chasing ecologist, had fallen on deaf ears. So had kindly Fred Turner's recommendation. So had Liza Little having "put in a good word" for him at Jewel's request with some friends in the Department of Energy and the Nuclear Regulatory Commission. Liza had not meant to let Dan know that, but she had.

Liza had some kind of friends, Dan knew. Edward Teller she counted as a personal friend. Others were less well known, but probably more powerful. None seemed powerful enough to dissuade Auerbach from his decision.

What had happened to bring Dan to stand leaning against Bob O'Neill's desk is that Auerbach retired. Liza's "good word" had currency there again. It had to have been because of her in the end, he was certain. The phone call with an immediate offer to come to Oak Ridge had come through the UCLA physics department. What might have necessitated Dan's hire, temporary as it was, though, was Krummel moving to Argonne National Laboratory, near Chicago, and nearer to his hometown of Milwaukee.

"Now, why would anyone want to teach undergraduates?" Bob O'Neill was asking with feigned shock on hearing Dan express such a desire during one of their putative "liasons."

"I still believe I have a shot at getting a faculty position somewhere in some university or college."

"Using Oak Ridge as a jumping board?"

Dan made a confessional shrug of his shoulders. "My resume is short on classroom teaching," he said. "Nothing I did at UCLA was anything like teaching a class. I need something on my cv that shows a desire to teach. I'm no longer aiming at a research university position. That dream is gone. I'll be satisfied with any second rate school calling itself a university or even a third-tier teaching but non-learning college that caters to the great unwashed, as Krummel calls them."

"Ah, Krummel! He'll be missed!" Then, realizing his gaffe, O'Neill quickly turned to dissuading Dan from his goal. "But talking to students is like talking to stone walls. Even with graduate students, you feel the same way sometimes. If I could, I'd let someone take over my course at UT completely. It's not at all like working with a graduate student on his PhD research."

Dan then shocked O'Neill by volunteering to do just that. O'Neill immediately agreed. He handed Dan a stack of computer printouts and a stack of floppy disks, the newest 5¼-inch versions. They represented the final products of the students in the systems ecology course O'Neill taught at the University of Tennessee. It had been started, the first of its kind, by Bernie Patten and George Van Dyne.

"Grade these," he said. "If that doesn't turn you off, maybe you can take over my lectures in the fall semester."

Both thought they got much the better part in the transaction. O'Neill preferred to occupy his time with an analog computer model that simulated the workings of a river system. It was not necessarily the Hudson or even any real river. Modeling at Oak Ridge was no longer aimed at environmental management, like Botkin's JABOWA model. Modeling at Oak Ridge had become a tool for theoretical insights, in both ecology and systems science, and it was being done on analog computers. In effect, they were following the advice that Dan had refused from Robert May.

The modern analog computer was a way of ratiocination, as Uncle Hutch would have put it. Calculus had provided a new way of looking at the mechanical part of nature through math, but almost as soon as Newton and Liebniz had gifted mathematicians with the tool, they found calculus equations that could not easily be solved. In fact, some were proven by strict mathematical logic to be unsolvable. Often, the best that could be done was to make approximate solutions for them.

"Calculus equations govern current and voltage in electrical circuits," is how O'Neill explained analog computing to Dan. "Equations for capacitors are integrals."

"Current is differential," Dan jumped ahead of him.

"Right," O'Neill said with only a hint of impatience. "You catch on quick. So some genius came up with the bright idea of building circuits to represent the equations needed to be solved and then just read off the voltages and currents with a meter. Tom

Odum's first simulation was assembled with batteries, capacitors, and wiring."

"Was that for Silver Springs?"

"Yeah. Current represented the flow of energy or materials. Batteries and capacitors represented storage and release."

He paused to let Dan give some sign of being suitably impressed. When none was forthcoming, he said, "You should have seen the computer model he had set up at North Carolina State. It was of a tropical rain forest. Twice a day, there was a simulated rainstorm. That was during the rainy season. The world, according to Tom, was a huge analog system based on material and energy flow."

O'Neill's new generation of analog minicomputer, as far as Dan could understand, did away with visible batteries and wires. It had a simulated mini telephone operator's switchboard to patch together the needed circuitry. At first glance, it looked every bit the toy circuit board he had used in his undergraduate physics course.

"So how did you get to be a computer guru?" Dan asked "Were you an engineer?"

"I started out in every respect a biologist," O'Neill sternly corrected him. "I was doing my PhD on the energetics of millipede populations at Illinois. I learned systems science from the mathematical models of radioisotope behavior developed here by David Reichle and Jerry Olson. I needed it for the millipede study. When I was offered half a postdoc to come to here, I jumped on it, even before my dissertation was finished. Before I knew it, I was the model coordinator for IBP's Eastern Deciduous Forest Biome study."

"For which Auerbach was the director."

"Well, yeah."

III

DEAR Dan,

Health alert: I tested positive in December. I probably contracted it years before. Dieter tested positive in January. In February, I came down with pneumocystus [?] pneumonia (PCP) (the #1 killer for people with AIDS). I had been taking dextran sulphate, one of the many drugs proved useless. I started AZT, acyclovir, and aerosol pentamidine in March. AZT is an HIV anti-

viral; acyclovir fights certain other viruses; aeropent supposedly prevents new outbreaks of PCP. In January I switched from AZT to DDI. DDI stabilized T cells at 45-50. In May I considered Cpd Q. To qualify I needed various tests done. Among these was a chest x-ray. The x-ray turned up abnormal. I'm on anti-biotics currently to see if they help (the lung infection has not been diagnosed yet). I'll have to get it cleared up, however, if I am to qualify for Cpd Q. In my state, there's an 11% chance of inducing coma with Cpd Q, so it's not exactly a benign drug. I should know later this month whether I am eligible to proceed with Q. Right now, it's about my only hope for improvement. Did you really want to hear this?

I've just spent the last two weeks preparing an NSF proposal on exotic tree invasions in Puerto Rican rainforests and, while it was fun preparing for the most part, I am skeptical of its chances. Did you see the latest on the crunch at NSF in the May 4 Science?

All the best,
Walt

Dan put the letter down. It was the bombshell he had been awaiting and fearing.

IV

DAN was very aware that he was now a part of Big Science. Just the sheer immensity of the Oak Ridge National Laboratory cried out that it was Big Science, with security around the facility accentuating its importance. Somewhere behind the fences, gates, and guards that barred his access to various areas, Uranium-235 was probably still being separated from Uranium-238.

According to Liza, that had been Stuart Little's proudest accomplishment. His only regret about it, according to her, was that he couldn't get any patents on it. It was all classified. It was used by nuclear facilities all over the country, but he never made a penny from it.

Without it, to Dan's alternate point of view, it would not have been possible to bomb the people of Hiroshima and Nagasaki. The bomb would not have been ready. Neither did the excuse that the weapon had been developed to use against the Nazis, as if no women or children would have been hurt had the bomb been dropped instead on Hitler's eyrie in Bavaria, hold any moral substance for him.

When the call from Oak Ridge came, though, he had answered it without qualms. In fact, changes in ES&E were apt to leave no place for him, as was already the case with Bart Sokolow. And technically, none of the projects at Oak Ridge in which Krummel had been involved were related to weapons work in any way. So, when thoughts of nukes or radiation releases drifted into his head, he kept them very much to himself. How others at Oak Ridge dealt with their personal ethical quandaries, Dan did not know. And he did not ask.

Yet here he sat, with Liza's help, in front of a computer terminal possibly connected to one of the massive parallel-processing computers used for weapons work, some IBM-numbered successor to the laboratory's ORACLE computer, the world's largest and fastest when it was installed, also for weapons work, in 1954, the same year, coincidentally, that Auerbach had started the ecology program. Having dispatched the final projects O'Neill had given him, he was at the moment attempting to remake himself, finishing the transformation he had started at UCLA, and he was not doing well at it. Ecosystem modeling was losing its appeal and making him lose his concentration. But O'Neill had shown as little interest in Dan's MacArthur-style ideas about ecology as Robert May had about his Salton Sea model. As impressively theoretical as community matrices and alpha coefficients sounded, they were the tools of another army, as far as O'Neill and others at Oak Ridge were concerned. They were systems ecologists at Oak Ridge. They studied Odum's ecosystems, rather than Hutchinson and MacArthur's communities. They had their own parameters of interest. Others were a waste of time.

"All these ground beetles are but a minuscule compartment of an ecosystem," O'Neill had dismissively responded to Dan's ideas, "of little more relevance to an ecosystem than its particular bird communities. Probably, in total, less than one percent of its energy budget. You won't find any real ecology in it."

As far as the null model debate was concerned, ecologists at Oak Ridge watched it from the sidelines. They had their own battle to fight.

Still, Dan kept inserting his particular numbers into an Oak Ridge ecosystem model. Each time, though, the computer crashed. In the past, Dan would have eagerly tried to puzzle out where the math had blown up, hoping to find something like Einstein's cosmological constant fix for his unruly equations, maybe multiply everything by ten and see what happens. Now, however, the situation merely caused him to turn off his console and return to his office. That required walking past O'Neill's office, where a chair seemed to call to him.

"There is no one way of doing science," another Oak Ridge scientist, who had just come into the room, retorted on hearing Dan once more speak respectfully of null models. He had the unlikely name of Carlos, "Carlo," for short, Marx. He kept his dark, curly hair in a huge Isro. A magnificent mustache, with waxed tips so wide it threatened to flap away and take flight, adorned his face. Marx had both an analog minicomputer and a personal desktop computer in his office.

An Apple instead of an IBM and for a researcher rather than teacher, Dan thought. Gone was the slide rule which, like a policeman's revolver or woodsman's buck knife, was sure to be holstered on the belt of any self-respecting engineer well into the 1970s. Pocket calculators and personal computers had made slide rules obsolete in less than the span of a decade.

"Especially not that of Peters," Marx punctuated his remark.

Their issue was holism, re-christened now as "emergent ecosystem properties." Without unexpected properties appearing at the ecosystem level, the abstract models coming out of Oak Ridge and the other lairs of systems ecology have no reason to be.

"But aren't the properties you point to as emerging at the ecosystem level," Dan fended off Marx, "productivity-to-respiration ratios, diversity, or stability, in its many forms, aren't they just the additive result of well understood properties of individuals and populations?"

"Every plant and animal is involved in the metabolism of the ecosystem," O'Neill spoke up. "That was Dave Reichle's advice to me. It set the course for my career. You should take it too. Look at joules, not species."

O'Neill even had some good things to say about Clements's superorganism.

"Not that it should be taken literally, of course, but the idea of an ecosystem tending toward a stable climax was—and still is—an attractive one."

"But doesn't that require a system to be in equilibrium?" Dan objected. "Nature in balance?"

"Read my lips," O'Neill responded. "Stable equilibrium, just like for a nuclear reactor, is an absolute necessity for ecological models. Without it, there is only chaos. So there has to be an equilibrium point for an ecosystem, even if it is only being approached and might never be reached."

That sent Dan back to a computer console. Every free minute he had, he "played" with or "tweaked"—no known word seemed to describe it for him—the model that had first been developed by Phillip Goodyear and—of all people!—Charles Hall. And every time, the same result. It blew up on him.

Charles A. S. Hall, he sat back from the console to think. That model was why Charlie Hall had taught parts of the ecosystem course at Cornell. Likens' modeling output had consisted of little more than an unsophisticated diagram of the Hubbard Brook watershed abstracted into its components. It was a childishly drawn cartoon that had jokingly been called his "udder model," based on its shape. It was Botkin and crew who put the sophisticated programming on Hubbard Brook's trees.

But for all its lack of modeling sophistication, the Hubbard Brook work had discovered acid rain and set the direction of forest practices in the northeast for years to come. The little science of Hubbard Brook had trumped the Big Science of the IBP in every measure. Dave Guzzetta, on Dan's visit, had shown him a preliminary copy of a report that attested to that. The report was still causing consternation at Oak Ridge and more gray hairs to fall out of Auerbach's now-retired scalp.

Strange, Dan could not get out of his head, that a mushroom cloud rising over white sands in New Mexico could promote the growth of Clements's superorganism. And that he would be in this place to help it. Strange, too, to think that community ecology was born around a pond and on an easy chair on the top floor of Osborn.

Unable any longer to force himself to concentrate on putting numbers into a computer model that was not his own and run on a computer system that gave priority, no doubt, and better results to bomb designers, Dan once more abandoned his computer terminal and returned to his office. It was after five, though. No one else was around. Nothing in his office drew itself to him but the telephone. Dan picked it up and dialed a San Francisco number.

"Feeling pretty good," Walt reported. "The KS lesion has responded and no new lesions. I'm kind of hopeful that I'll avoid any further KS difficulties."

"KS?"

"Kaposi Sarcoma. Two of my closest friends have died of KS complications and it is painful."

"Sorry to hear that," was all Dan could say.

"I haven't yet made any moves at work. I'm still working full time, but the KS news did puncture motivation to worry about things at work. I don't care at times. Coworkers are stealing resources and obscuring my existence. I try not to get involved, too tired to fight, I guess. The noose is tightening, but I am feeling more in control having gotten treatment "

"Hang in there," was all Dan could think to say. "How's James?"

"James has been out of town since Thursday visiting his folks. I'm getting wonderful support from friends, though. I even went on a hike and out to dinner with old friends. They just bought a new house. James will be back on Thursday. I missed him the first few days. I had to draw on my own resources. I can handle it."

V

HE was lucky to be here instead of Paterson, New Jersey, he thought as he looked away from his mail and out on campus through his office window. He thanked whatever gods had landed him in Palo Alto.

He knew himself to be the kind of mousy looking young man who could be expected to come out of that city only by being the brightest kid on any of its blocks. Clark Kent looked back at him through dark-rimmed glasses whenever he looked at himself in a mirror.

He wished he were not Clark Kent. In a convoluted way, he too had a secret, one that he could never allow to be known about him. His career depended on the reputation he had built as Jonathan Roughgarden. He could never jeopardize that success by revealing his true self.

He was a professor at Stanford. Academically, that made him a super hero. A whiz at math, he wrote and analyzed ecological equations—models, he called them, for their math was not new—based on the ideas of Robert MacArthur. As a theoretician, he knew that he was every bit the equal of Robert MacArthur. His models were much more complex, much more elegant, much prettier, he could say to himself, than the primitive things MacArthur had managed to produce.

But hell, he thought, MacArthur had been the only theoretician on the block. He had been the king—was still the king—but now there was a slew of imitators to compete with for his title and challengers to fend off.

Some of them were making fun of Clark Kent. One of his papers was being ridiculed. His offense to them was having used differences in covariance to argue for the presence of competition. Oh, it had all been perfectly valid mathematical reasoning. No one had denied that—could deny that—but they were still making fun of him.

The Tallahassee group had to be behind it. If they were only to use their null models to test for the effects of chance events, such as climatic influences, dispersal issues, or extinction, they might be onto something. As it was, they just didn't understand the concept of irrelevancy.

He would have to respond and do it aggressively, he decided, briefly taking off his glasses. It was, of course, to rest his eyes.

Being aggressive was the guy sort of thing to do, he knew. He would have to hit them and hit them hard. The invitation from George Salt that he held in one hand might be the opportunity. Diamond was apparently now refusing to be in the same journal issue with Simberloff. He would have to take it up himself. He hoped he could use it to stem the extreme antagonism to theory in their rhetoric. It was reinforcing—

How would he put it in print? The inherent disinclination people going into biology have toward learning all the math that is so necessary in the study of ecology? Was that the way to put it?

And he was not aware of a single finding that emerged from what Simberloff and his colleagues had written. He was aware, though, of a lot of bitterness it had caused.

"It's clear I'm never going to figure out this guy thing," he suddenly said aloud to his office walls.

Then he turned his thoughts to the task ahead of him. He put the letter aside, put his glasses back on. He would bone up on some philosophy, he decided. That would be the thing. He suspected that whatever one philosopher might say, there would be a dozen others contradicting him. He would make use of that. It was a guy thing, too.

But how do you set out to be a man, he suddenly found himself wondering, to learn how to live as a man? It was like asking a fish to fly.

Like at the faculty meeting the day before. There were all these guys around this table, staking out their territories and going at one another. They were male birds in breeding season, fighting over some piece of sod or a twig on which to perch. It was not a battle he wanted to win. He didn't want to be like them.

The thing about competition and null models was the same phenomenon, wasn't it?

But, for Dr. Jonathan Roughgarden, such behavior should work well in the male-dominated world of theoretical ecology. He had the talent to back it up. He was at the top of his game and was universally regarded, he knew, as being the quintessential macho academic. He was aggressive, abrasive, and competitive.

Aggressiveness he found to be the easiest male trait to emulate. It was so easy to duplicate it without really feeling it. He would take no pride from it, but he would do it.

VI

"ECOSYSTEM theory is useless."

Suter again. His usual diatribe.

"Guys like O'Neill criticize impact analyses for not using ecosystem theory. They trot out MacArthur's diversity-stability theory like it's some sort of holy grail. Well, after twenty years, all there is to this theory is a sad tale full of semantic confusion, wishful thinking, and selective use of evidence."

"You're flogging a dead horse there," Dan said. "Dan Goodman has put away the idea that diversity promotes stability for good."

"It needs flogging still. Then there's Westman, saying that scientists should publish their data on the resilience of ecosystems in standard ways. He's confusing assessment with monitoring."

The name, coming so unexpectedly, was a spike to the heart. Poor Walt.

"Not to mention that there is no real agreement on how resilience might be measured," Carlo Marx, about whom it was commonly joked that he wandered the halls in hope of overhearing an open-door conversation to drop into, dropped into this one.

"Yeah," Suter agreed. "Ecosystem ecologists typically discuss the effects of disturbance in terms of the general and vague-sounding concept of ecosystem stability. I hate that. It just has the sound of environmental advocacy to me. I mean, can every ecosystem be fragile?"

"It's like a religion," Carlo Marx put in. "Have you heard of Deep Ecology?"

"Is that the guy who went out on a fjord and had an epiphany? Let me guess what it was. Everything is connected, right?"

"Sort of circular reasoning, isn't that?" Marx suggested. "Or a chicken-and-egg thing?"

"The idea of Gaia is almost religious, too," Dan said. "It's very important to Deep Ecology. So are the old ideas of Tielhard de Chardin."

"And diversity and stability are right at the heart of the philosophy, although maybe not with those exact terms," Marx said. "It is very attractive even in this day, Clements's idea that self-regulating mechanisms evolved within the ecosystem superorganism."

"On Earth Day," Dan began something of a confession, "I stood in front of a small classroom. Actually, I think it was a day before Earth Day. We had Earth Week in Philadelphia. There I was, warning against carelessly messing with something that has evolved to a steady state. A climax community, I told them, like the human body, can withstand only so much disturbance before it loses its self-regulatory properties, at least in the short term. Lower body temperature too much, I said, and death, rather than shivering, ensues. The same should be true for the metabolism of a superorganism. If an indicator of superorganism health could be identified for our ecosystems, like body temperature or heartbeat or blood pressure in humans, then it could be closely watched in our forests and lakes. I promised those people that I would devote myself to finding just such an indicator at Cornell."

"Did you?"

"I tried. It's still an attractive idea to me, but few bright ideas are incorporated into scientific thinking simply because they seem to make sense. Usually they need a champion. I'm not it."

"Westman also says that it's important to consider ecosystem inertia and resilience in planning a pipeline," Suter stabbed Dan again with Walt's name, "but in the most important such case, it simply wasn't true. The critical ecological issues were blocked caribou migration routes, disturbed falcon eyries, thawed permafrost, and spilled oil in salmon streams. General indices of system stability or holistic properties were of little use."

Carabid beetles, Dan suddenly thought. They might just provide such an index.

"Yeah, but," Marx butted in again, "that analogy of ecological systems to reactor systems is what pays all of our salaries. We would never get funding—or even exist as a division at Oak Ridge—if all we wanted to do was study reindeer and falcons."

"Bernie Patten actually condemns the consideration of specific issues," Suter said, "even endangered species. He says they were made to go extinct. So cranes and falcons are nothing more than nodes in a food web or gates in an energy model or rows and columns in a community matrix."

"Patten? He worked here for a time, didn't he?"

"Yep," Marx answered proudly for Suter. "One of the original systems ecologists."

"He's one of those who insist that ecosystems are cybernetic. Isn't he also the one who looks on ecosystems as though they're some sort of super particles. Isn't he the one who invented all those crazy terms, crayons and genons and environs and holons?"

"Craeons. C-r-a-e-o-n-s," Marx corrected. "And a holon is a quite respectable term. Arthur Koestler coined it in Ghost in the Machine. For Patten, it includes creaons and genons."

"What the IBP has demonstrated is that simulation models are too demanding of time, not to mention money—and data—to use in NEPA assessments," Suter returned the conversation and Marx to the original topic. "That Eastern Deciduous Forest model that you personally worked on showed that in particular. As does the Hudson River model that is getting so complicated in your hands, but is no more predictive than it was when Goodyear and—"

"So what exactly then is your take on the value of using holistic properties?" Dan interrupted, carabid community structure once more on his mind, specifically, whether there might be some simple equation to rank community properties, something as elegant as the species-area equation, that could then be a measure of ecosystem health.

"Bah! The most highly touted ones, such as CO_2 efflux and net primary production, don't emerge, they just aggregate."

"Maybe that's why people like O'Neill and me are being kept separate," Marx said, "even physically, from you assessment people. Production-to-respiration is strictly a result of the interaction of the organisms in the system. It's not just a simple sum."

Suter had essentially hit Marx verbally on the head with his last statement. Like a bad dog having been disciplined with a rolled up magazine, he gave that one yip then subsided into aggrieved silence. But he did not slink away with his tail between his legs.

"I like what Westman wrote about nature's services," Dan said, addressing Suter only.

"Oh, we can point out the loss of nature's services such as erosion control, pollution assimilation, and climate regulation," Suter said, "but these are all vague concepts. More work needs to be done like that done by Odum on the value of tidal marshes. Have you seen that?"

Neither Marx nor Dan admitted not to have, but their silence was answer enough for Suter.

"It was with the Center for Wetland Resources in Louisiana. I forget where they published it. They actually put some dollar figures, as imprecise as they might have been, on tidal marshes. Those particular results are regularly used in assessments of coastal developments. So, Tom Odum wants us to reduce all these services to terms of energy flow. That may be conceptually elegant, but it's practically meaningless to me, although maybe not if energy units can actually be given dollar values, but that's a big if. For example, vegetation can act as both a source and sink of air pollutants. How do you value that? And different plants retard erosion in ways that can't be measured in joules. So how do you put dollars on them?"

"So, what do you suggest?" Dan asked.

"I'm an experimentalist and practitioner. I'm not a theoretician. It's not up to me to teach another person his craft."

"I think the key to understanding the universe lies entirely in knowledge of Tarot cards," Carlo Marx spoke up again. "Bob O'Neill and I are doing a statistical analysis of the iconography of various Tarot decks. The Fool, for example, is clearly associated with zero, but the numbers three and seven are also related to him."

"You're into numerology?" Dan asked, trying with effort to keep derision out of his voice.

"As much as the Odums are into God," Marx replied. Getting no comments, he continued. "Without the ecosystem concept—any of them, Clements's, Tansley's Lindeman's, Forbes', Mobius's, Odum's, Likens', Naess's, Tielhard's, whatever—there would be no separate science of ecology. So what if an ecosystem can't evolve? It gave ecology a chance to study nature the way the other sciences study it. Take Robert Whittaker at Hanford and George Woodwell at Brookhaven and Auerbach here, they all got their professional starts by tracing the movement of radiation through ecosystems and its effects on those ecosystems. All were employees of the Atomic Energy Commission. The AEC it was then called. Now it's the Department of Energy. Of course, the IBP funding didn't hurt us here at all. How does any of that make more sense than numerology?"

An answer was on both Glen's and Dan's lips. Instead, Dan tried to find something conciliatory to say. He had grown to like this volatile systems scientist.

"Howard Odum came from Hutchinson's laboratory just after radioactive phosphorus, ac-cid-ent-ally, was spilled there by the kindly Englishman," Dan shared. "Hutch emphasized accidentally the same way I just did. It helped him trace the flow of phosphorus in our little pond, as he had called it."

"That was as fortuitous an accident for Hutchinson's career," Marx took over again, "as having Vernadsky's son, George, and the son of Vernadsky's closest friend both at hand at Yale to translate the father's ideas from Russian. I knew them both. The younger Vernadsky would have been my godfather, if Jews had godfathers. This was about at the same time that Howard Odum did his dissertation on strontium, a key element in radioactive fallout. That was right when your kindly English friend was trying to fit the science of cybernetics to Lindeman's trophic-dynamic concept of the ecosystem. Tom did not just run with the idea, he took it to the next level, taking his brother Gene along with him."

Neither Dan nor Glen seemed to want him to stop, so Marx went on.

"It was the Big Science that came out of nuclear testing that helped ecology overcome its tarnished reputation. Why, in the past —in fact, right around when Rachel Carson may have been learning it at Johns Hopkins or Woods Hole, I understand—ecology was held in ill repute by other scientists. The best and brightest of a scientific generation saw ecology as soft. It lacked rigor compared to the hard sciences. Science being rigorous, after all, to this day is still related to the density of the haze of mathematical symbols that cloak its fundamental principles. The mathematical haze around nuclear physics, for example, is well nigh impenetrable. Thus, the familiar phrase, it's rocket science. Alvin Weinberg wanted Big Science projects for Oak Ridge. He wanted ecology to be rocket science. Ecology was not rocket science. Ecology was but a point of view."

Marx paused. He looked from one to the other. Then he resumed his sermon.

"The ecosystem also had systems science behind it, something that engineers used. It let ecology sneak in through the back door here. Stan Auerbach, remember, was hired to assist in health physics. By Earth Day he had created all this, one of the largest ecological research programs in the world. He's my idol. So is Tom Odum. So is George Van Dyne. And according to Van Dyne, ecosystem ecology is the end of a continuum in science that begins with physics."

"Particle physics, probably," Dan felt the need to contribute.

Marx now noticed that Suter was missing and Dan was paying little attention. He snorted through his nostrils twice and walked back out into the hall.

Dan was alone with nothing to do but tweak the Hall and Goodyear model. His output appeared on the screen almost before he could input data. He punched the print key and headed for the printer..

No wonder the Liedles had been such a cheerful couple! Dan marveled. Not only did they have no cards to punch, but spelling and syntax were checked immediately before a job was submitted. Even better now for statistics, canned programs, like SAS, eliminated the need for programming at all. One only had to input the data in proper form.

There was no reason any more to spend long nights correcting typos one at a time, he thought as he picked up his printout. Neither was there any reason for the Dungeons and Dragons sessions that had grown up everywhere in computer labs as people waited to retrieve their programming results or to puzzle over errors in logic that needed correcting, all the while following the imaginings of their dungeon master. That, too, was soon to be obsolete. Type out a few lines now, make a few corrections, and go home before dinner to an evening free of programming and dungeon masters, or, like Dan, stay in the office and continue to work, knowing that each step was a giant leap, rather than a timid little shuffle. Given that computational power and convenience, how could Dan not find the specific tweak he needed? But he couldn't. And each time he couldn't, the idea of using SAS to analyze data relating to how carabid communities might be assembled became more attractive.

Why not do it? Maybe some simple equation will fall out of the analysis of variance.

How?

Hawaiian ground beetles, Dan knew, were unusual in their number of flightless species. He could take a look at them using SAS. Flightlessness was something common to islands, after all. For birds, it was supposed to result from lack of predation. Could the same be true for ground beetles? It seemed less likely. How to find out? Could the three species of ground beetles known to have invaded the Hawaiian Islands be of help? Diamond's assembly rules were for island birds, and, according to Diamond—or maybe not, according to the doubters—for a single guild of the birds. Hawaiian ground beetles, now, were a guild if there ever was any such thing. Dieter John had pretty much established a guild for ground beetles in general in his Andrews Forest paper. Even better, in Hawaii they were spread out over a real island chain. True, they were insects, not birds, but taxonomically and geographically, they had much that was similar to island birds. It was Dieter John's study, Dan realized, that he was about to replicate, but with real islands, a clever idea with exciting prospects. He plunged into the task confidently.

And eagerly. Suddenly, the full scope of evolutionary ecology become crystal clear in his head. Ever since its inception, both competition and islands have held exhalted places in ecology. Both were important to Darwin's theory of evolution. Competition through natural selection between different types of the same species was what drove evolution. It was the mechanism that had produced the variety of finches, Darwin's finches, as they were now known, on the Galapagos Islands. A century after Darwin's voyage, Englishman David Lack presented careful measurements supporting in detail Darwin's speculations on the birds, which fit very nicely into Ernst Mayr's theory of allopatric speciation. Gause's laboratory experiments with microorganisms, showing that two species could not coexist on a single resource without somehow partitioning it, presented an explanatory mechanism. Garrett Hardin codified it, very pithily, Dan thought, as the Competitive Exclusion Principle, "Complete competitors cannot coexist." Things began to accelerate then. Hutchinson had already looked into that pool in Sicily near where the bones of Santa Rosalia had been found and had an epiphany about the water beetles there. It led to a rule about the ratio of size differences between coexisting closely related species. Brown and Wilson discovered character displacement about the same time and Robert MacArthur mentally broke a stick and helped Hutchinson to formalize the idea of a species' niche by adding competition and multiple dimensions to Shelford's Law of Tolerance. Everywhere everyone looked, there was evidence of competition.

Now, Daniel F. Atkins was finally and forcefully throwing himself into the fracas. In truth, however, he cared not a whit whether he found evidence of competition or predation or something else causing the differences in distribution or morphology in the ground beetles he set out to examine. What he first hoped to do was develop a suitable null model to let him determine if whatever he found was real or mere chimera and then write a grant that would let him go to Hawaii to test it by direct observation and experimentation, if, of course, Oak Ridge let him do such, and if not, why he might dream up other ways to do so.

First, though, Dan had to develop data. He needed a universe of carabid species from which he could populate his null samples, the randomly generated communities he would compare to the communities actually found in Hawaii. This he gleaned from musty old publications from Hawaii's Bishop Museum and the somewhat more recent publications of Harvard's Museum of Comparative Zoology by P. J. Darlington, he of the tussle with the crocodile.

Dan had started by lining off cells in a notebook. Into them he had intended to enter each species' habitat, location, population density, seasonal activity, morphology, and any other attributes that might be valuable for analysis. Each attribute was to be assigned a number that he could then enter into a computer for analysis.

"P. J. Darlington, Jr. 1971. The Carabid Beetles of New Guinea. Part IV. Bull Mus Comp Zool," was his first entry, which he numbered "1." Number "2" on his literature list would be "Part III," published in 1968, he learned from the bibliography in "Part IV." It was backwards, he knew, but he had to purchase the older monographs directly from Harvard before he could see that data. How Dan numbered them, though, had no ecological significance, but then, scanning the bibliography further, he found that "Part I" had been published in 1962 and "Part 2" in 1952. That was really backwards.

Already a snag, he groaned inwardly. What the hell did that mean? Press on anyway, he decided.

But instead of the ecological data he was looking for, what he mostly got was location and size. And location was usually just the island or islands on which a particular species was present. There was no way to tell if two species occupied the same habitats—or even the same general areas of the islands. So now, instead of too much data, he was facing not enough data. Still, size and location were data. He entered them into his notebook. It was still going to be giant number crunching, even without all the information he had been hoping for. There were a lot of beetles in the world, an inordinate number of which were carabids.

When his pen ran out of ink, at about the time his eyes began to unfocus and his shoulders began to ache from hunching over to read small print, he began to think about maybe just entering the data directly into the computer instead of the notebook. He also noted that it was three o'clock in the morning. Saturday morning. Enough, he said, but he did not stop, even though the printouts all kept saying the same thing to him as dawn approached: no statistical evidence for anything but a random placement of beetles on the islands.

But wait! An idea came to him. What if it wasn't the data, but his analysis? He could not reject the null hypothesis with his Malibu carabids. He could not reject it with his even bigger data set of Hawaiian carabids. But he knew someone who had! Dieter John in that paper that was up there in the constellation of stars around that of Jared Diamond. And Dan had Dieter's data. Unable to leave it behind or return it, Dan had taken the printouts with him. It would be an easy thing for him to redo Dieter's analysis.

He thought to run that idea past Walt, who would not be judgmental. Letters had stopped coming from him, however. Dan dialed the San Francisco number.

"I see a doctor once a month," Walt reported by phone. "I continue to explore possibilities of DDC, but it has neuropathy as a side effect. Not cheap, either. I can get it on the underground."

"Underground?"

"Underground medicine, I guess. My doctor is used to it. People come in with ideas from the underground all the time."

The KS lesions, at least, were under control.

"The hardest thing has been cutting loose from work. I felt wonderful on Thursday evening after my talk at Cal, but on Friday and Saturday, I was wiped out. It's awkward. I have the ability intellectually, but I have to keep down the stress. That's the challenge. If could design a job for myself, I know how I would do it. When I have all my energy, I can absorb a lot. Right now, though, my resilience is weak."

"What about the community ecologist position at Berkeley?"

"I'll see next week if I can sell them on a part-time position. James said, Well, the issue is if you have something of value to offer, the department will be interested in having you for as long as available. That's good."

"How about the grants?"

"I've lost hope with EPA. I write a grant and then they tell me I have to change its focus. It's like playing ball on a football field with the goal line being moved all over the place."

"We all face that, Walt."

"Yeah."

Walt fell into a brief silence.

"James is starting AZT," he changed the subject, "even though we practiced safe sex from the beginning."

Dan had nothing he could say.

"It makes you feel miserable for six weeks until you adjust," Walt said.

"How did that go with you?"

"I did dextron sulphate first, but it was ineffective. It put me into the hospital with pneumonia and my T-cell count at 300. It fell to 90 by the time I left. I then started AZT in March and my T-cell count dropped from 90 to 50. I took AZT until December, when side effects made me stop. I developed anemia. It's better to do combinations. They're ecologically sounder."

Dan let him talk. He should, he thought, know all the ins and outs of T-cell counts, if for no other reason than to be able to speak on it intelligently with Walt, but he refused to learn them. And, he realized, he had no business bothering Walt about whether he should reanalyze Dieter John's data. He set off to do so without anybody's blessing.

Again and again, the analysis came back no different for John's data than for his own. What was going on?

He looked up John's paper in the *American Naturalist*. All the statistics pointed to ... But wait a minute!

Dan rechecked the particular data he was looking at against John's printouts. Not the same. The data in the paper did not match the data in the printout. He checked the notebooks.

He slumped down in his seat, totally defeated by life and science and hope. Some of the data in the printouts did not exist in the field notes. Dieter had not just changed some of his data to get the results he wanted, he had fabricated some of it wholesale.

VII

"WELCOME to the Tallahassee Mafia," Don Strong greeted him.

Instead of the looks of the warrior Dan had expected, Strong had the blonde hair and soft good looks of a surfer.

"I really don't have anything right now," Strong said about prospects for him. "You really should talk to Dan. I don't think that he has anything in the pipeline, though."

Dan asked about Washburn.

"Would you want to talk to him?" Strong asked, seemingly with relief.

After swatting a cockroach on his desk with a copy of the *American Naturalist*, Strong accompanied him to a room down the hall where Jan occupied one of the "veal stalls," as Strong put it without explanation. It was a room with desks and chairs crowded against one another and too many bodies for Dan to try to count.

"The way you get any kind of position around here, I think," Strong said, "is if you come in and say something like, Mah Daddy is the president of Foley Lumber. He owns half a million acres roun' heah, so y'all need to hah me raht now. Other than that, I don't know what advice I can give you."

Jan seemed glum. He gave no indication of being happy to see Dan again.

"I'll tell Dan you're here," Strong said, then left.

Jan said he would rather talk to Dan after his interview.

"Reading the ecology literature my first graduate year," Simberloff recalled for Dan, "I recognized that a lot of the quantitative work was basically models that more or less fit some data, without considering other models. I'm probabilistically inclined, and I quickly began to think of what various—random—patterns might look like. After I read Popper—soon after—I learned the right terminology. I'm not a rampant and unrepentant Popperian. I believe Popper is right in general, that you should try very hard to refute hypotheses. If a hypothesis can't be refuted, you shouldn't look for confirmation of it. But it's clear that it's very hard to devise testable hypotheses in ecology. Hard, but not impossible."

Simberloff hardly looked as Byronic as he had become in Dan's mind. He was casually, but neatly dressed in a button-down shirt and khakis. His hair was parted on the side and neatly trimmed. His glasses looked like ones he had put on as a child: dark frames above, and clear frames below the lenses, as if to hide their presence. Was that how he had looked in St. Louis?

"What did you make of Levins' and Lewontin's piece?" Dan asked

"I was a bit taken aback by the vitriol and dismissive tone adopted by them in that paper, particularly since some of what they said was junk," Simberloff said.

"How do you like the view?" Simberloff then asked him.

Dan was having trouble maintaining eye contact against Simberloff's penetrating stare and had been stealing glances out the window.

"Even if I can barely see the motel from here," Simberloff continued, "it's not much of a view. The grad students face a nice lawn and Stozier Library from their side."

In fact, eucalyptus-like trees blocked the view of the Tallahassee Travelodge. Dan had tried and failed to identify them on his way over from it.

"But it must come in handy, though," Dan replied without revealing that he had booked a room in it.

He was still sweating, even though the building was air conditioned and his only exertion had been crossing Dewey Street to get to Conradi. The hottest, most humid day in New York City—the one that had brought down Con Edison and blacked out most of the Northeast—was nothing in comparison to what awaited him outside. LA could be hotter, he decided, but not even in the sweatiest corners of the Valley was it more humid.

"That it does," Simberloff said. "We put Southwood up there when he came to give a seminar." He gave Dan a genuine smile, as if remembering that he had not yet done so. "I'm flattered to have you stop by," he added.

"Burlington, Ithaca, New York City, Oak Ridge," Dan replied, "Tallahassee is hardly out of the way in that lineup."

Dan did not want to tell him that the others were actually the side destinations on his itinerary. Ingrid was paying the airfare to

Ithaca as a birthday gift. She had no idea that Dan had decided to use it to make this direct approach to the Tallahassee Mafia.

Dan had, however, shared his plan with Buck, who informed him that he had just sent his most promising MS student to work under Strong at Tallahassee, instead of keeping him at Delaware for a PhD. Of course, Jan would put in a good word for Dan, Buck had assured him.

"We're a bit marginalized by the Department here, I'm afraid," Simberloff said, taking on a friendly tone that made Dan fear that the interview was coming to an end. "Ecology, evolution, zoology, and botany are squeezed into this building along with the departmental offices. Most of the molecular types—geneticists and physiologists—are in Biology Unit One, commonly known simply as Unit 1, numbered. And note that it's Biological Science not Biological Sciences. There's significance to that. We're just not set up for a postdoc. I'm lucky to have the space that I have in this prematurely decrepit building. I'd be happy to have you here, based on what you tell me of your interests, should some sort of funding be figured out, but have you seen that rabbit warren of offices the grad students have? It's all the space there is for us. I probably couldn't even find a desk for you."

"By the way," Dan began, not knowing why or whether he should, but desperate not to have the interview come to end. "By the way, have you seen that thing Peter Feinsinger put into the ESA Bulletin? About them being unable to find any evidence of music in Bach using a null model?"

He immediately wished to take that back, but then he noticed Simberloff's reassuring smile.

"Yeah, funny," Simberloff said. "Maybe they should have tried Beethoven, too." Then he turned and rummaged briefly through a file drawer. "Hmm," he frowned on taking out a single, thin booklet. "I guess I'll have to make you a copy. Come along."

Simberloff removed its corner staple with a handy tool he found by the copy machine. Then he cursed under his breath at the peculiarities of the machine when the first copy came out blank.

"Finally!" he proudly announced after several more bungled attempts then hurriedly stapled pages together before handing them to Dan. "This may amuse you."

The cover page had a drawing of two Triceratops facing each other across the word, Eidema. Dan tucked it away into the elegantly slim briefcase that Ingrid had bought him on his successful thesis defense. The exchange of reprints was a ceremony that traditionally ended an interview. Dan was embarrassed to have nothing to exchange.

He walked out Conradi's front entrance totally deflated. Jan was missing from his veal stall when Dan checked back. One of the female grad students offered her chair for Dan's use while he waited, but he turned it down and walked out into the Florida sun and heat on Academic Way, which was more walkway than street.

He could not miss seeing his motel from that position. He could also see the golden arches across the street from it. He turned away. West Tennessee Street paralleled Academic Way on his campus map. In reality, it looked more like an interstate highway than a street. In fact, it was an interstate, I-10, he realized. If he so chose, he could take it all the way to LA, by way of Pensacola, Mobile, Biloxi, New Orleans, and Baton Rouge, then west from Lake Charles by greater steps through Houston, San Antonio, El Paso, Tucson, Phoenix, and the southern California smog. His Spitfire could never make a trip like that any longer, he thought sadly.

His eyes drifted over Conradi. It was too new, he thought, to have so shabby an air about it. And the rabbit warren of grad student offices would not be out of place in the Fly Lab. Conradi's first floor sat directly on the ground, giving it a basement feel.

Architecturally, however, the two could not be any more different. Conradi had the same nondescript, post-war utilitarian style as the motel, but without the obligatory balconies, which the architect did seem to suggest, using a wide line of stucco to highlight the upper two floors of brick facade. The business school next to it sported the same motif.

Southern chic, Dan thought. Southern California chic, too. Boelter Hall would fit right in on this campus. It was probably built at around the same time.

Instead of returning to the air-conditioned comfort of the Travelodge and staring at the walls or a television until it was time to catch his plane, he decided to walk west, through campus. He had no hat. Sweat dripped from his armpits as if they were leaky faucets.

He crossed Antarctic Way. It was followed by Atomic Way. He took it. Love and Unit One were followed by Keene. Instead of the motel-style architecture of the others, Keene's façade was broken up to suggest the individual balconies of a hotel at a luxury resort. It also rose above the others like a mushroom cloud. It was recognizably a physics building.

He got an idea. He went inside.

He walked out of Keen and back into Conradi. Simberloff agreed to see him again.

"I think the refuge design literature is not very instructive. It has lots of irrelevant papers in it, such as on corridors, and some piss poor science," Simberloff concluded a surprisingly long discussion, given that it was their second of the day. "It's more political than scientific."

He added that the whole business depressed him. He was giving that fight up.

"Anyone arguing against even the most cockamamie idea, so long as that idea is supposed to benefit conservation, is viewed with suspicion. And Larry and I didn't at all enjoy being cast as the betes noires of conservation just because we stuck to our principles. If I had the right angry graduate student or postdoc, though, I might change my mind."

The "right" postdoc stuck in Dan's mind as he walked out of Conradi the second time.

VIII

DEAR Jewel,

I offer you, instead of a Christmas card, the following. It is something I did not want to throw out in my moving activities. (Be pleased I am not sending you any of the other things in this category.) I thought it would amuse you. I am busy busy packing and very happy.
Dan

Dan's present is a poorly reproduced copy of a journal entitled *EIDEMA*. Two staples in a corner hold its pages together. The name gives no clue to its purpose. Neither does the logo, "AN INTERNATIONAL JOURNAL OF ADAPTIVE STRATEGIES OF FIELD BIOLOGISTS PUBLISHED IRREGULARLY BY THE EIDEMA SOCIETY."

At the bottom of the page, the copyright sign is X-ed off by hand. Its articles in whole or part "can be freely copied mechanically, electrically, photographically, by hand, by laser, or by any reasonable method," is announced, presumably by the editorial board, next to the canceled copyright sign. All efforts to distribute its contents "are highly appreciated."

Jewel has never heard of any such society. She turns over the title page. Then she has to rotate the document. "On the Trail of Quarks," catches her attention as she flips through. Except that, as she reads, she realizes it is not at all about quarks.

On the Trail of Quacks: The Death of Apollo, by Donald R. Strong and Bernard C. Patten. *Academic Press, 1983, cmlxii + 572 pp., $87.00. ISBN 0 23 6421148.*

This remarkable tome arises from the collaboration of two leaders in the movement to assuage ecologists' "physics envy" (Cohen 1971). Strong and Patten have had distinguished careers coining physical metaphors for ecological phenomena, In this slim volume they report a truly astounding discovery, one that unifies and systematizes a hitherto bewildering mass of tropes and thus catapults ecology to the forefront of the exact physical sciences and, incidentally, the authors to the head of the Nobel queue.

Patten in 1981 and 1982 demonstrated that ecological systems consist of holons, each of which in turn comprises a craeon and a genon. Strong concurrently discovered a pervasive pink noise in all ecosystems, and a disturbing apparent random component that results in a universal density-vague population dynamics. A serendipitous meeting of these workers at the Thomasville Rose Festival led to the collaborative effort that unified these apparently unrelated observations. In Quacks, Strong and Patten synthesize results from environmental accelerator experiments that show that holons are but a subset of a much more diverse group, the putons. It appears that each puton consists of one or more nuclear hardons surrounded by a cloud of carryons. The genon is only one of at least six distinct, charming, and colorful hardons, while there are at least two other carryons in addition to craeons. Further, a puton may have many hardons and carryons. Clearly, a

Here Jewels turns the page, then turns the "journal" again. The pages that follow have been stapled upside down.

holon is a very simple puton, and more complex putons will be presented in the future. The accelerator experiments also suggest that all ecological interactions fall into four fundamental classes and are mediated by partial exchanges of various sorts. "Strong" interactions rest on exchanges of hardons, "weak" interactions involve carryons, "colorful" interactions are mediated by craeons, and "transposable" interactions involve jumping genons.

Strong and Patten, using the 100 bev environmental accelerator at Oak Ridge, fired thousands of particles at enormous velocities into various environuclei and photographed the resulting ejects. All particle traces were accompanied by pink radiation, accounting for the prevalence of pink noise in the environment. The authors suggest, but have not yet proved, that the hardons each consist of combinations of three quacks—red, white, and blue—and particle interactions always cause the emission of one red and one white quack. Even more illuminating are traces resulting from the quintessential reductionist experiment: firing a simple craeon (a Winchester .458) into a simple holon (<u>Oryctolagus cuniculus</u>). An abundance of pink material was always seen when this experiment was run (red and white quacks?), but the remarkable result was that, in 100 identical trials, the trajectories of resulting particles were never repeated. Apparently there is an ecological indeterminacy at the particle level, as was adumbrated by Mayr (1961). Can one doubt that this particular indeterminacy underlies density-vague dynamics and effects the Dionysian cast that so pervades ecological communities? It is clear that in this unified ecological theory Strong and Patten have broken the artificial barrier between the stochastic and the deterministic forces in ecology.

This book thus obviates a large part of ecological literature —for example, all attempts at purely deterministic or purely stochastic descriptions of ecological dynamics—and simultaneously should set ecologists on the proper path: completing the catalog of putons and their component particles, proving the existence of quacks (and antiquacks), and, now that ecological indeterminacy has been rigorously established, understanding its deterministic basis. The applied benefits of what Strong and Patten have already accomplished are enormous. One can, of course, immediately understand and solve all problems of introduced pests and endangered species, while acid rain is reduced to a trivial special case of an unsuitable craeon.

The final chapter of the book will be the most controversial. Here Strong and Patten present some untested corollaries of their general theory. Not only do they predict the existence of a monospecies (a nongeneric species with infinite heterozygosity, but an N_e of 0; that simultaneously occupies all trophic positions in an ecosystem), but they deny emphatically the existence of armadillos. The task of testing these brave new predictions will fall to a generation of ecologists trained not only in biology, but also in physics, pathology, and Restoration drama.

In sum, <u>On the Trail of Quack</u> should be a mandatory addition to every ecological bookshelf, and Academic Press is to be congratulated for putting its price within reach of the most impecunious graduate student.

> *Daniel Simberloff and Joseph Travis*
> *Department of Biological Science*
> *Florida State University*
> *Tallahassee, Florida 32306 USA*

Well, thank you, Danny, for a few smiles, Jewel thinks to herself. Then her smile disappears. She sinks into thoughtful silence.

Tallahassee

I

"Y'ALL goin' to the parade?" Susan Mopper asked in general of those in the basement of the Conradi Building. She was a willowy, sun-bleached blonde who had to have been a Florida State coed. She had been the first to welcome Dan "to our little prairie dog colony," as she had put it. The southern accent now startled him. After expecting to be surrounded by southern voices, Dan was now accustomed to rarely hearing more than just a hint of one from grad students and professors.

"So, what does the paper say is happening now?" Nick Gotelli asked, directing his question at Dan, who held that day's newspaper.

Dan had gravitated toward Nick on arriving at FSU. Jan Washburn, who Dan had counted on for a familiar face, had disappeared, gone to parts unknown. Dan suspected some drama, for no one mentioned him.

"According to the paper, the ACLU has worked out an agreement," Dan looked up from it to say.

Two weeks before, the school had elected one "Billie Dahling" as Homecoming Princess. He was a seventeen-year-old freshman named William Wade. The Florida Flambeau had been headlining the story ever since.

"This is the South," Don Strong joined in.

No one had noticed him coming into their warren of basement offices. Dan suspected he was trying to get away from his bird.

"Buffon's Macaw, Ara ambiguous," Don had gotten technical about it when Dan had asked its name at their first meeting, "also known as the Great Military Macaw."

He had then explained that someone had pinioned the bird, so that it could not fly. He was proud that it had so quickly learned to talk and could sing the Marseillaise.

"I looped an eight track tape with the signature phrase from it," Don had continued then. "He learned it within one afternoon. He just loves to scream it out my window."

The interminable screeches that Macho the macaw loved to make went more than just out the window. They were heard throughout their wing of the building, along with Don's screams for it to "Shut the fuck up!" The bird became especially psychotic whenever Don's wife, Karin, showed up to go home at the end of the day. They made an attractive couple, the Santa Barbara surfer and his tennis player wife. Macho was jealous. He thought he should be the one going home with Don, instead of Karin.

"This high ground we're on," Strong now said, addressing Dan, "used to be called Gallows Hill. You can imagine for yourself who the gallows had been for and who they might want them for now."

"Apparently," Dan further reported from his paper, "they're going to crown him at the pep rally tonight, instead of at half-time, but he still gets—"

"The Pow Wow?" Nick interrupted.

"—to be the Princess. And they're not going to let him be in the parade."

"Of course!" Strong added. "The famous Marching Chiefs, proudest symbol of the university, will refuse to march unless Wade is given the boot! We'll soon see if anything is as powerful as football on this campus."

"I hear someone wrote fag death on his door with shaving cream and someone else carved die fag on it," Gotelli said.

"According to the paper," Dan read on, "Wade didn't expect people in a university atmosphere to be this immature. That's a quote. In order to be tolerant of people who are different than you are, it goes on, you have to have maturity, intelligence, and self-awareness, and that's what this campus lacks."

"Doesn't he realize that he's talking about college kids?" Don asked with a laugh.

"SOUTHERN college kids," was heard from the other room.

Dan recognized the voice and clipped Midwestern diction as Stan Faeth's. Usually he disguised it when zinging comments from the other room. He also did a good imitation of Strong yelling at his bird. And of the bird, which he now did, startling Strong.

"Did you know that the screeches and screams caused the classroom next door to be permanently abandoned by the English Department?" Stan asked, coming in as Don exited.

"It let us grab some extra space for lab," Nick said. "We can thank Macho for that, at least."

"What I can't understand is how, for all of Simberloff's growing fame and prestige," Dan said, "he has almost no lab space assigned to him."

"The bird's screams no longer annoy me," Nick said to Stan, "but I could do with less of yours."

"It surprises me," Dan continued without getting anyone's attention.

"Ha!" Stan said at Nick and followed Strong out the door.

Faeth was one of the crew studying insects on oak trees. Unlike Buck Cornell, who was studying gall-forming wasps on oaks, they studied oak leaf miners. The situation fit what was almost a tradition in ecology. Ecologists avoid studying habitats or communities that others studied. In this case, the habitat was the same, but the communities differed. That was so unlike in the physical sciences, where any important result was soon repeated with exactitude in several other labs. Dan first thought that avoidance of others' research subjects by ecologists might have been left over from times when ecological data was mostly taxonomic. Given taxonomists' goal of describing every species on earth, they understandably avoided duplicative effort and had not the competitive instincts of other scientists. But his first impression had been wrong. Ecological observations, he had quickly learned, were inherently difficult to repeat. Conditions varied from place to place and year to year. Some of ecology's most important observations and experiments were never replicated exactly. They couldn't be.

Dan had sought safe harbor with the Tallahassee Mafia to pursue a suspicion that baser human failings were at work, too, in the world of ecologists. Sloppiness? Laziness? Dishonesty? *Science* magazine repeatedly headlined new scandals in biomedical research. How could one tell in ecology, unless ... Well, unless one had field notes that could be checked.

So here, Dan thought, in the very heart of the south, was the right place for him. Here, a threat had already been launched against that tradition in ecology of gentlemanly honor and was spreading like the kudzu that threatened to strangle and swallow up any small structure in the course of a single growing season. It threatened ecology's most entrenched and revered ideas, and that it was coming from the south was no paradox, for it was not being launched by race- and football-obsessed southerners. It was no coincidence that southern accents did not permeate Conradi's halls like Macho's screams did. Everyone who was drawn to Conradi was very intense about their science. Even the transplanted Californians, Strong and Gotelli, gave no signs of having merely exchanged laid-back California ways for the laziness of the South. Each would have stood out among ES&Ers by their intense devotion to their science. In general, the work ethic in Conradi amazed Dan when he compared it to that in the cold, sunless clime at Cornell. For one thing, there was less angst around the Conradi basement than there had been in the Fly Lab. No one seemed ready to give up science for the antique business, for example, or disappear overnight back into Minnesota.

And these Florida Staters, unlike any of the Fly Labbers, were not just bitching about something. They were out to change it. Given that, Dan could live with the peculiarities that had kept him away for so long from the Deep South, never tempted by even a brief Mardi Gras trip or spring break in Ft. Lauderdale.

Yet Peter Klopfer, the social activist, had taken a job at Duke. That had been more than a generation before. Little Rock Central was just being desegregated. From that southern base, though, and at that time, he had helped create ethology, as Europeans called the new science of behavioral ecology. And he was still at Duke. And he was happy. But then, maybe like Oak Ridge, Durham was something of an enclave of the north.

"Well?"

Dan looked up on hearing Susan's voice.

"Y'all comin'?"

Why not?

There was no Homecoming Princess in the parade, but there was a float carrying a sign that read "Vive Le Billie." There were students carrying a large sign down Monroe Street with Mickey Mouse making an obscene gesture at the float. There were also students on the back of pick-up trucks shouting various obscenities about Wade to the crowd.

"Do y'all think," Dan asked Susan in almost a whisper, "that all these parents with their children in hand find the obscenities being shouted less offensive than a male princess?"

Even though he had learned not to think "cracker" or "redneck," on seeing white men in pickup trucks with fading paint, and even though he no longer noticed that every menial service job was held by someone with black skin, he was reminded, as Susan shrugged her shoulders, that he was no longer in the realm of the Ivies or the West Coast universities.

"F-L-O-R-I-D-A"
"S-T-A-T-E"
"FLORIDA STATE, FLORIDA STATE!"

Definitely a football school, Dan decided on hearing the cheer from across campus, and nothing but a football school. He was wandering about it aimlessly, looking hopefully into faces he came across. It was Saturday. He did not want to go back to Conradi, and he did not want to go to the football game.

Bobby Bowden, still relatively new as coach, was obviously turning the school into a winner. The football stadium was adding seating capacity almost yearly. Still, Dan thought he could hear "half-ass U" being chanted instead of "FSU."

As he walked, Dan imagined fall colors peaking in the crisp air of Ithaca and southern Vermont. There was no such phenomenon in the Florida Panhandle. Here, cool, dry winds from inland replaced the heat and humidity at the end of the rainy season, but the splash and whir of lawn sprinklers overwhelmed any rustle of dry leaves. Besides watering, fall yard work around Tallahassee seemed to Dan to consist mostly of raking up pine "straw," as fallen needles were called.

Like LA, the place had no fall and no winter. He could only go on faith that there would be a spring, even if only something like the hills above LA briefly turning from straw yellow to green. Having no winter was sad. It meant no ice-skating, no ice fishing, and no snow skiing.

Now that was something else he resented, having to add that adjective to the latter term. Snow skiing, instead of water skiing? What they did here while being dragged behind a boat on water was nothing at all like skiing. There was not the sense of triumph from hurtling at speed down a steep, narrow trail lined with trees and boulders and with nothing but one's own devices to keep limbs intact. On the water, all you had to do was let go of the rope if things got dicey. How lazily southern?

Tennessee, at least, did have mountains. So had LA, to be exact. And bigger ones. Poor David Tan had replaced a professor who had disappeared while skiing the backside of Mt. Waterman. His body was never found, but his FTE was filled. Here, he would have to have been swallowed by a 'gator to release his FTE.

Another cheer arose from the stadium. It was a loud one, almost a thunderclap.

Has to be a touchdown, Dan thought, feeling lonelier and sorrier for himself. The closest he had been before to seeing big-time college football was when Cornell brought Ed Marinaro to Franklin Field or Yale, Brian Dowling and Calvin Hill. Like most of his cronies in the anti-war movement, he had haughtily passed up those opportunities as being overly militaristic.

So, Florida for intellectual climate? Hemingway had blown his brains out in Florida, hadn't he? Football instead of bullfighting must have been the reason.

Another cheer went up. PAT, it had to be.

At UCLA, at least, the madness was sequestered in another city.

The drama that day, what had brought Dan outdoors and drawn him toward Doak-Campbell Stadium, was still to come, and it would have nothing to do with tackles or touchdowns.

Why didn't they play soccer down here in the south? They had the climate for it.

And why, Dan now asked himself, was it a Homecoming Princess? Queen was more appropriate.

But before he could fully relish his cleverness or feel shame for his lack of sensitivity, a trio of coeds with identical pairs of legs coming out of tight shorts distracted him. They were going in the direction of the stadium. Their hands held Seminole pennants.

"Can you imagine—" was all Dan caught of their conversation before it faded away with a mass of hysteric giggles.

Landis Green, at the entrance to the campus suddenly looked as exotically foreign to him as Italy might, should he ever go there. Then, as an ecologist, he corrected himself. Italy, having a Mediterranean climate, had to be more like LA than subtropical Florida. The flowering shrubs live oaks, scrubby looking pines, saw palmettos, and palm trees that had temporarily misled him were universal, he realized, to urban areas in warm climates. The vines here, though, needed a stifling hot and moist climate to proliferate. They would dry up over an LA summer.

He was standing midway between Wescott, the most prominent structure on campus, and the fountain at the center of the circular drive that represented a gateway of sorts to the campus. It was a perfect picture postcard image, more so than anything on the UCLA campus, and so unlike his childhood memories of the tight, urban spaces of Yale or the rustic ones at Marlboro.

It was strange, Dan now mused, that, like Marlboro College, FSU had mushroomed after World War Two because of the GI Bill. However, instead of from a farm, it had arisen from a lonely few buildings of a woman's seminary on Gallows Hill (a name to ponder, he agreed)—and into an instant university. There was nothing here like the old barn that was Marlboro's Dining Hall or the sugarhouse that became the Pottery Shed. That remnants of the Tallahassee gallows had not been preserved was, of course, for the better.

What could he possibly have thought to find here?

II

DAN was the Florida State ecology group's first postdoc. At least, he was accepted as a postdoc, even though he was being paid through the physics department as a lab instructor. It was not much money, but it left him time for research and kept him from starving.

Unfortunately, there were no desks to spare in that rabbit warren of grad student offices to which he was assigned. Nor was there space to add another. Even the addition of another chair was an issue. There was no way he could even imagine himself as a Larry Hurd or Mark Westoby.

There was so little room in the office that Gary Graves stored his cushy stuffed chair on top of his desk to keep it out of the way of others when he was not using it. Despite his need for the comfy chair, Gary was universally acknowledged to be the most physically fit of the grad students crammed into the two rooms, always pressing ahead faster and farther when in the field.

Dan had a chair pulled up to Gary's desk, the only space available for him that day, when Gary came in late in the afternoon. Instead of asking Dan to move, Gary climbed up onto the desk and into the comfy chair, leaving Dan to continue reading beneath him.

"You look like a king on your throne," Nick remarked.

"Or possibly, he's just trying to get away from the cockroaches," Bill Boecklen, one of Simberloff's master's students, joked.

"Gator cheerleaders," Lee Ann Szyska offered.

"Phew," put in Don Strong.

He was trying to get a group together for a Friday beer, even if the ecology seminar had been canceled for that day. He was having no trouble getting cooperation, except for Lee Ann, who was a devout Mormon.

"*Pariplanata americana*," Don added, before Gary, whose ability to identify almost any plant or animal at a glance was becoming legendary, could do so. "I can't stand the way they leave these wonderful brown commas on each and every non-protected book in the building. I hate them!"

"We call them palmetto beetles," Joel Trexler, a fish biologist, fresh from the University of South Carolina, said.

"In St. Louis," Dan said, "they're called water beetles or, maybe, water bugs."

"You're from St. Louis?" Trexler asked.

"Spent a year working with Barry Commoner," Dan answered with what he thought sounded more impressive than what the reality had been. "I also have personal experience with California cockroaches."

"*Blatta orientalis*?" Don asked, casting a quick glance at Gary.

"I don't know," Dan said. "Huge dark ones with no self respect at all. They stopped and waited for you to come over to squash them, instead of running away."

"Too much weed," someone said. "Just like all Californians."

"Hey, this place isn't exactly free of weed, or even other substances."

"They're more afraid of black widows than of people."

"They should be afraid. I once had an outdoor closet that was full of black widows. We must have killed seven of them one day."

"Now, is that bottom-up or top-down population regulation?"

"What is that you've got there," Strong asked, wending his way over to Nick. "Is that John Terborgh's paper on bird biogeography?"

"Larry gave it to me my first day here," Nick answered. "He just said, This paper has been pissing me off for a couple of years now. Do something about it! I've got a draft of a paper on it, but I'm afraid to go in and talk to Larry. Every time I go up to the lab, Felgenhauer frowns and shakes his head."

"Right!" Strong said. "No one knows Larry's moods better than Bruce. It's good that his desk is near the door. But let me see what you've written."

With some trepidation, Nick handed Strong the hand-written document.

"Hmm," Strong grunted as he looked it over quickly. "Mind if I take this home?"

Of course not, Dan answered under his breath for Nick. What else can he say?

The bird started to screech.

"Karin must be waiting for you," someone said.

People drifted away until Dan was alone. He would have liked to have joined his new colleagues for beers, but worry about the way his meager savings were being depleted held him back. It was all part of his fall in status. No salary. No office. Only a desk in a room crowded with grad students. No desk, in actuality. No graduate assistants assigned to him. He had to do all his own work. And there had been no moving allowance for him, of course. He had had to drive down on his own, leaving most of his things behind in Ithaca, where he had taken refuge after quitting Oak Ridge before funding for his position ran out. The Spitfire had died, fully and finally, with a rattle of piston rods and a cloud of black smoke outside of Waycross, Georgia. On its death, Dan had had to impose on Ingrid to do some tricky things with her American Express card. It let him rent a car to go the last hundred fifty miles.

Fortunately, he had had little to move. He had left Oak Ridge with only the proverbial clothes on his back (and a few suitcases). Most of those things he still thought of as his in the Danby farmhouse were actually Ingrid's. And as long as he was staying at the Travelodge, he had no need for a car. Its weekly rates were almost affordable in comparison to buying and maintaining an automobile. Grits were cheap. He was developing a fondness for them, especially drowned in Karo syrup.

Although there were no research funds for him and no office, he had some computer time at FSU's brand new satellite computer labs—dumb terminals and line printers, almost as good a setup as at Oak Ridge. And he had not just the "floating" desk in with the grad students, but also places he could park his butt in the physics lab and the computer labs and the libraries. He could make do with that. So, he set to working on his own contribution to the null model controversy. He needed, he now thought, only to impugn Dieter's data, that is, the data that he had published. There was no need to discredit Dieter's integrity. Knowledge of Dieter's actual data and how it had come into his hands, he feared, might put his own reputation more at risk than Dieter's. Rifling through confidential material in filing cabinets, albeit unlocked ones, in a secure room was not a mark of integrity. Dieter could then just deny everything.

So what Dan was doing was meticulous reanalysis of Dieter's published data, using whatever uncertainties he could discern from it. His own data on carabids, he used as a template for analysis. It was tedious work, mostly mindless, relentlessly never ending, and more difficult than what Simberloff and colleagues had done with Diamond's island data. Dieter's beetles lived in habitat types, virtual islands at best, like mice ranges had been for mites. Dieter had cavalierly thrown up estimates, guesses for habitat acreage, really, but guesses that gave him the results he wanted for his "islands." That was what Dan attacked. Every evening.

When he next looked at his watch, it was three o'clock in the morning. Saturday morning. Enough, he said. He had Dieter John right where he wanted him. By the short hairs.

On his way out, he had to step around a sleeping bag in the hallway. Beer bottles were all around it. Two heads were inside it. Was it someone from the lab who had lost his or her keys? Or been thrown out of his apartment? Only the tops of the heads were visible until one body stirred and he caught a glimpse of a girl's face.

"I don't know how much you've absorbed about what I've been up to here," suddenly came into his head.

It was how he had started his explanation to Ingrid about why he was not coming back to her. They had been in a sleeping bag in a tent in the middle of a field in the Adirondacks that was bursting with huge, high bush blueberries.

"You're helping to improve the environment," he remembered her answer being. "I'm proud of that. But I'm afraid I can't tell one equation from another and I don't know genetic feedback from genetic engineering. But I like all those field trips and nature walks you've taken me on. I like finding out all the little things you've learn about plants and insects and small, furry mammals."

So do I, Dan now thought.

"Did they teach you in school about how science works?" he had asked her. "You know, hypothesis testing?"

"Sure, you do an experiment. You make a prediction and see if it comes out."

"Absolutely, but in biology, seeing how it comes out is not so simple. Do you remember those rodent enclosures Bill had put so much effort into making?"

"Sure. He wanted to see if the mice ate the clover with the cyanide."

"Well, he learned nothing from them. Each mouse approached the problem its own way. Some ate no clover at all. One actually did avoid the cyanogenic clover. So what did he have? To do an experiment in biology, you need a null hypothesis for comparison."

"Null?"

"That nothing happened. Bill couldn't just take the results of the one mouse, because he had the other enclosures. Even if it was three mice that avoided the plants, say, and one that didn't, and none dug their way out or were eaten by owls, he would not have verified his hypothesis. Even that might just have happened by chance, like flipping a penny and getting heads three out of four times."

"So Bill had a lousy experiment?"

"Not really. What he got let him know not to go on in that direction, but even if it had been three to one, he would have to calculate whether he could have expected to get that strictly by chance. That's the null hypothesis. We accept a result only if it has less than a one-in-twenty chance of having happened anyway. It's pretty standard in most sciences where you can't control every variable in your experiment."

Ingrid had waited for more.

"In ecology, you're lucky if you can even do an experiment, as Bill found out. The best you can hope for is to let nature do the experiments for you, then look for patterns."

"Like in the stars?"

"Very much! Some ecologists do exactly that. It's ecopoetry, a good story, like Cassiopea in a chair, but hardly what is really going on. That's what these people in Florida are trying to eliminate from ecology."

"But I like the little stories that Professor Eisner tells about things," had been the last word on scientific method before Dan changed the topic to their impending separation, how he could not expect her to follow him to Florida and would not ask that of her. He made no mention of Dieter John.

Other than Ingrid reminding him that it was easier to travel between Florida and Ithaca than it had been between Ithaca and Los Angeles, they had parted without recrimination.

"You've got to do what you have to do," she had said.

And she had slipped two hundred-dollar bills into his shirt pocket. It made him feel as if he was still a teenager in Brattleboro, and Jewel had just slipped him five dollars to go downtown so she could have time alone with Jonathan. He would need the money, he and she both knew, so he had taken it.

The couple cocooned together in the sleeping bag stirred again. The girl's face was very pretty in sleep. Her eyebrows were blonde, like Ingrid's. Her skin was the same translucent paleness. The face next to her was Bill Boecklen's.

Cockroaches, Dan noticed as he left, had already set up housekeeping in several of the beer bottles that were lying around in the hallway.

The next morning, Nick's manuscript was waiting on his desk underneath a stack of books and reprints. It was covered with comments.

"Wow," Nick said on looking over what Strong had left. "Each of these has something to do with this topic. I guess I'll have to read and cite all of them now. When did he have the time to do this?"

"He's a specialist in community ecology," Dan said. "He probably had all this material at hand. Still, I'm impressed that he would make the effort for you."

"So am I. And grateful."

A few days later, Nick had a fresh version of his manuscript. It was fully vetted by Larry. That was important. Having a faculty member as a co-author meant that he could give it to Anne Thistle, the head typist. She had a PhD in linguistics and typed manuscripts only for the faculty. The newly typed manuscript came back to Nick the same day, with a blue sheet attached to it listing all the grammatical and typographical errors Anne had corrected. She also suggested a few references and ideas for him to include in a new version.

"Congratulations," Dan said. "You've taken the first step to becoming a published ecologist."

"Hmm. I'm not sure about this particular comma," Nick said, looking at the blue sheet. "She's probably right, though. Only Simberloff dares to challenge her on points of grammar."

"When you get back a paper from her that says something like, not bad," said Bill Boecklen, who had just come in with a huge mug of black coffee, "or, only a few small errors, that means you're ready for your PhD. The thesis defense is only a formality."

"Were you guys out celebrating something last night?" Dan asked, knowing full well the significance of Bill's over-large mug.

"Since Friday night. Thank God for drive-through liquor stores," Boecklen said, then he commenced to scribble furiously on a legal pad of paper.

"We started at the Thai place," Nick answered, "then moved to a Greek restaurant. I forgot where we ended up. Maybe it was the drive-through. And that had to be Friday, didn't it? Not last night."

A small car in a driveway with "4 sale" written in lipstick on its window caught his eye on the way back to his apartment. Kudzu and trumpet vine climbing over magnolia and oleander hid all but the front door of the house beyond it.

Dan knocked on the door. The car was a Datsun, five years old. The man wanted what amounted to less than two month's rent for it, and that was not at Travelodge rates. Dan had abandoned the Travelodge, finding it much more economical to move to a new efficiency apartment. Eating out, he quickly realized, was either too expensive or unhealthy. The Travelodge did have a kitchenette unit, but the apartment was cheaper.

The door to the cottage did not open, but he did hear groaning noises within. He knocked again.

Dan's apartment complex, an extended version of the Travelodge, looked much like every other apartment he had seen in California and Florida. Two stories. Inner courtyards with balconies around them. But the simplicity of the plantings at the apartments was not to last long, he knew. Withholding water controlled plant growth in dry LA, but water came from the sky in copious amounts in Tallahassee. Vines and shrubs would soon overwhelm balconies and courtyards both, as they had the rest of the street. As they had the cottage where he was knocking at the door.

His apartment was midway between the campus and Frenchtown, from which there often came sounds of jazz. That was like it had been in Harlem, he thought, except that things had since changed between the races, shamefully so. When once it was Louis Armstrong and Jackie Robinson, now it was Huey Newton and Eldridge Cleaver who seemed to populate the streets. Even Mohammed Ali, chocolate-skinned, instead of black, a hero to Dan by his stand on the draft, would seem somehow more threatening than the jazz musicians of Harlem and the Village two decades before, should Dan run into him now in Frenchtown.

Finally, an old man opened the door.

"Dey's nothin' wrong wid it, 'cept id's old. A baht it fo' mah wahf. She don' need id no mo'," he finished his sales pitch, sadness tingeing his voice.

"Japanese," Dan remarked.

"Yeah. Some roun' heah don't work on Jap veh'cles. Claim deys all put tagether backwads. Some was in the wa' an' wan' no truck wid anythin' Japanese. Are y'all handy?"

"I reckon I can handle this," Dan said, surprising himself at his choice of words.

His mind went back to the near-zero-degree day in Ithaca when he had almost had to pull the engine out of John Krummel's VW to get at the alternator to remove a brush clip that had fallen into its armature. Their original task had been to replace the brush. Sure, he was handy with cars. The episode had become as much a

Fly Lab legend as Bill Dritschilo's taking apart his Spitfire's engine out on the street the day before Jamie went into labor pains. Needless to say, both Spitfire and Beetle were never the same.

As Dan looked the little car over, he saw the solution to all of his current problems. Although the upholstery was stained and worn —Dan could not believe for a second it had been driven only by the old man's wife—there was not a speck of rust on the car, and the engine had barely reached the hundred-thousand-mile break-in point of Japanese cars.

Ezra Cornell's Western Union Company got the money needed into Dan's hands the next day, gratis Ingrid, as always. And he almost hated her for it at the time. Three days later, though, not having any lab duties, Dan set off in the Datsun with maps and a compass, a canteen, a sandwich, and gratitude for Ingrid's largesse, but with no fresh orange to cap off the lunch. Inexplicably, given the wealth of orange groves in Florida, there had been none at the grocery that morning. He had to settle for a Dr. Pepper. It was that or a Twinkie.

He was off in search of—he did not know. Adventure maybe. Anything that beat the monkish preparation of the perfect scientific indictment of Dieter John. The most annoyingly difficult part of that task was figuring out how to cryptically present Dieter John's data as essentially phony. Readers had to come to that conclusion by themselves, yet time after time, Dan would catch himself giving more than just a hint of how he would interpret the data. Once he had Dieter in his gun sight, he couldn't help squeezing the trigger just a little bit, it seemed, just enough to make readers wonder, he would then realize, whether he was hiding something more.

What Dan found on the sand roads off the highways was pines. Everywhere, there were pines. He suspected they were all long leaf pines, although he had not brought any field guides to check against. Some may have been loblolly. How long the needles had to be to make them long leaf was not knowledge parked in his subconscious. He could tell one from the other only when he had both sets of needles in hand, which he soon did, wondering why he had not thought of keeping representative specimens at the outset. He did not let coming upon only one species at a time excuse his stupidity. He simply blamed it on wasted years at UCLA and Oak Ridge. And the year in St. Louis as well.

Elsewhere, live oaks, their leaves as tough as holly, were festooned with Spanish moss, about which Dan fancied himself to be one of the privileged few to know it was a pineapple relative. It's picturesque sprigs made up for there being not much in flower other than the roadside plants, clover and ragweed, mostly, that were common up north and boring to find here.

"Quality control?" suddenly came into his head as he drove along without anything catching his attention. It was Peter Broussard he was remembering, the opinion Brussard expressed on the issue of Whittaker's perfect attendance at core courses. Someone else—he no longer remembered who—had suggested that Whittaker attended every lecture as a way of gathering material for a textbook. Would the null model controversy have made its way into it? Dan doubted it.

Then as Dan consciously tried to find things through his windshield to push aside those thoughts, what he began to see were islands. Everywhere, there were islands. Marshes, a cypress swamp in the low ground along a river, the river itself, a field of goldenrod filling a clearing, stands of saw palmetto, an individual cypress, an individual palmetto leaf. But that was a path that had already been well trod in ecology and to not much valuable purpose.

He tried not, however, to let himself see the plant communities that Aunt Jewel had studied before she had thrown her career over and moved with him to Ithaca. Those communities, Dan knew, were no more than mental constructs at best or figments of unbridled imaginings at worse. Each plant found its space according to its own biological necessities. Dan knew all that. He could look at a plant and imagine the thousand different circumstances that had caused it to grow where it was.

But Dan nonetheless did see plant and animal communities, those patches everywhere that were virtual islands when looked at a certain way. And he could not stop looking at them that certain way. It was almost as if he had been hypnotized into seeing them.

Was the rest of ecology, he wondered, was all of MacArthur's and Hutchinson's theorizing, was it all really little more than mental or mathematical constructs? Something we were genetically predisposed into believing?

He pulled over to the side of the road, being careful not to run into the borrow ditch. He got out and looked up among the pines. The same turkey vultures cruised the sky as up north, except that one seemed to be circling directly above him. Warblers, Dan realized, were in the shrubs, on their way, perhaps, to South America. Never capable of identifying more than a few of the commoner species up north, Dan did not attempt to do so through their drab winter plumage here.

How long, he wondered, would it be before he, like the MacArthurs, would be capable of telling warblers apart merely by their song? Or was it already too late for him? The best naturalists seemed to start in childhood, like Bill Brown imposing on his family's summer trips to the shore. Should he have gone on more nature walks with Aunt Jewel or Uncle Robert and paid more attention? The various warbles and whistles and buzzes were no better imprinted in his subconscious than the length of pine leaves.

The goldenrod he saw appeared to be the same species that confused him up north. He had never felt shame for that confusion. He knew goldenrod hybridized too easily even for botanists to identify confidently. He thought he recognized one stand as the tall goldenrod that was common around Ithaca. It was the one species he was fairly certain about, but it seemed somehow different. The leaves were a bit too smooth and the stems too green. Perhaps the plant—for all the stems were assuredly vegetative outgrowths of a single plant from a single seed—was a hybrid or maybe those anomalous characters were no more than something like a southern drawl played out in vegetative terms, characteristics of the place more than the species. It had the same stem galls, it appeared, that it had up north, however.

An ichneumonid wasp, instantly recognizable by its long abdomen and ovipositor, cruised by in flight on its way to parasitize whatever caterpillar it specialized in. Parasitoid, that lifestyle was now called, not parasite.

With that, Dan climbed back into the car and drove on. When the country became too hilly and the soil too red to still be Florida, he stopped to eat lunch on an old cypress stump near the edge of a swamp. Then he turned away from Georgia and headed back south. The bluffs along the Apalachicola River became less steep, the timber less like second growth, and the land more flat. Stopping by the river to take a closer look at a conifer whose strange shape caught his eye, he discovered it was not a conifer at all. He guessed it was a yew, but its leaves were twice ranked and, instead of finding the small, fleshy, red fruit he expected, he found a dark fruit that looked like an olive. He cut off a small bough with fruit on it and threw it alongside the pine boughs on the back seat of the Datsun. A few miles down the road, a sign announced Torreya State Park. Mystery solved.

Rather than continue south to get his first view of the Gulf, he decided that he really should return to Tallahassee in time for that day's seminar. There would be other weeks, he thought happily, to have a day like this, now that he had the Datsun.

Charles Sibley of Yale, the Peabody Museum's bird man, was that afternoon's speaker, making this ecology seminar something of a special occasion. Guest speakers were not common. The FSU ecologists had no money to bring in speakers, so they had to capture whoever passed through for whatever reason. Usually, it was someone invited to give some other expense-paid lecture who agreed to give an additional one for the Conradi crew. Dick Southwood, the highly honored English zoologist was collaborating with Strong on a book on insect ecology when he had obliged. Sibley's DNA hybridization studies of hominids were of great interest (and a matter of controversy) to the denizens of Unit 1, the molecular biologists. They had brought him in for a seminar on the topic. Fran James had diverted him to also present his work on birds at Conradi.

Although Sibley was reputed to have an acid tongue and could cruelly mimic his critics, Dan expected no fireworks at this seminar. That carnage, preceded by a ritual cattle call through the grad student offices, why Don Strong called them veal stalls instead of rabbit warrens, was usually reserved for the home grown speakers. That carnage went both ways. Sloppy thinking, whether in presentation or in questioning, was always punished by pointed, almost vicious questions. Neither would silence help. Opinions to be slapped down were sometimes solicited from the silent.

Strong's knife was the sharpest. He must have felt duty-bound, Dan thought, to outwit, out-analyze, and out-quip everyone else. He was always ready to take the world on, any part of it that was handy, any chance he got. This day, he was unusually sedate, however.

Simberloff was also capable of over-exuberant testing of PhDs-in-training. He swatted down loose ideas the way Fly Labbers dispatched stray flies. Simberloff, though, would sometimes draw a line at which he would stop. From then on, he fed whispered requests to whoever was around him.

"Ask him this question," Simberloff had nudged Dan during a seminar by Jonathan Roughgarden a month before. Its topic, competition in Caribbean Anolis lizards, was a red flag waved before the Conradi bull. "I've already asked him too many embarrassing questions," Simberloff had explained in a whisper, tapping his finger on a page full of doodles.

Dan had recognized MacArthur's "Q", a quadratic term that MacArthur claimed was minimized by competition, among Simberloff's doodles. In his Synthese article, Simberloff had equated it to Darwin's gemmules and Adam Smith's Invisible Hand. "Metaphysical entities," he had called them, a term that had stuck in Dan's mind. The feisty Roughgarden had been exuding an attitude that shouted "I am right, so just try to show me where I'm wrong!" He had avoided commenting on the null model controversy to that point, however. Fur was about to fly.

"Wait!" Larry Abele had suddenly interrupted Dan before he could interrupt Roughgarden. "Go back three slides. I don't believe you can support what you just claimed."

Now, Dan again was waiting for Simberloff's nudge as Sibley put up slide after slide that alternated between pictures of birds, graphs of percent hybridization, and diagrams of phylogenetic trees. He waited, but no interruption came. Sibley was not arousing the group's carnal instincts.

"Maybe we should have started a buzzword bingo pool, like they did with me at McGill for my seminar there," Simberloff finally whispered to Dan.

"Was the word null?" Dan asked back in a whisper.

"Not likely," Simberloff whispered in answer. "That would have been one of the first words out of my mouth."

Strong and Simberloff assayed no tests of Sibley's presentation. Sibley went on without interruption. And on and on. At about five o'clock, some at the back of the room slinked away.

When it reached five-thirty with Sibley still droning on, a general exodus began. It was Friday. That meant "getting happy hours" of recovery at the Pastime Tavern. These could be as brutally happy as the seminars were terrifying. Graduate students, in particular, held their breaths as the end of a seminar neared, in hope of exhaling again at the Pastime. "OK," was the prompt they awaited. It did not matter from whom. When it did not come, as with Sibley, they followed an inner prompt.

The Pastime was a short stumble from Conradi, just a few steps past the Travelodge. "PASTIME TA ERN" was posted in moveable letters, one of which had moved away, on the kind of inexpensive signboard that was typically used to announce events or specials. "Joe and Nelly Snopes wedding," might be seen on a similar sign in front of a church. "Kitchenette units available" was seen on one at the Travelodge. A smaller sign attached above the Pastime's signboard had pictures of a beer mug, a burger, and an eight ball.

Larry Abele, on a first-name basis with the staff seemingly from his undergraduate days, was already at the pool table when Dan, who had stayed to the end of Sibley's lecture, arrived.

"Y'all want a game?" he asked Dan. "How about for a buck?"

The southern accent was strictly a part of his act to goad Dan into playing.

"Watch it," Joe Travis warned Dan. Joe was a Penn graduate who had just joined the faculty. His PhD was from Duke. So far, he was showing promise as a worthy match to Strong and Simberloff in the use of irony and sarcasm to crush sloppy ideas.

"Don't make any bets or he'll clean you out," Joe further warned. "I still owe him vigorish."

"Which arm do you want me not to break?" Larry asked as Dan chose a cue.

The evenings Dan had spent in all-night, walk-up pool halls in lower Manhattan were no match for Larry's years at the Pastime's table, even though Larry was obviously holding back. He was just too competitive to hold back enough, though, to make it a closer contest.

"Two out of three?" he asked after soundly drubbing Dan.

"I need to eat," Dan answered, dropping a dollar on the green felt.

"Oh, y'all will be able to eat," Larry said, laying on the accent a bit thicker. "Right here. Ther're oysters and shrimp here fo' ten cents a piece. A buck will get you a mahty fine mess of shrimp on your plate. And Ah'll buy you the beer."

At that moment, however, the bartender was calling Larry away to the phone.

"That's from Ira Rubinoff, the director of the Smithsonian's Tropical Research Institute. He knows he can always find Larry here on a Friday after five PM," Gotelli said with a smirk as he took over Larry's pool cue. "It's the same every Friday. There's always a call."

Instead of embarrassing himself further at the pool table, Dan sat down at a table with Bill Boecklen and Simberloff, who rarely joined the Friday festivities and drank little when he did. The table was cigarette-scarred and ring-stained. Boecklen and Simberloff were its only occupants. Dan stared silently at an untouched plate of shrimp.

"Have some," he heard Simberloff offering.

Dan dug in hungrily. His diet currently consisted of rice casseroles—especially tuna and rice. It left him perpetually hungry.

Shrimp and oysters turned out to be cheap in Tallahassee's bars. At ten cents each, Dan could have easily wolfed down several dollars' worth of shrimp, except that he didn't have even that in his pockets. It was the end of the month.

"We are SO lucky that Tallahassee isn't dry," Boecklen announced. He had several sweaty bottles of Budweiser in front of him. Most were empty, but he would not let them be taken away, lest one wasn't.

"Are there dry counties?" Dan asked.

"Are there?" Boecklen answered. "Too many."

"Worse though, Danny, are the places that drop a moldy, green sandwich in front of you when you order a beer," Gotelli said, having also abandoned the pool table. "Some are still in the plastic they were originally wrapped in years ago. You have to look at the disgusting thing while drinking."

"Huh?" Danny asked.

He was Danny again now. It was out of deference to Simberloff, the other Dan in the group.

"Illegal to serve alcohol without food in this state," Nick explained. "There technically are no bars."

"So what's this?"

"Billiard room?" Boecklen suggested, shrugging his shoulders. "Shrimp stand?"

Compared to how expansive Simberloff had been on that crazy, flying visit Danny had made from Oak Ridge, he was almost morose at the moment.

"Are you going to have a paper ready for our conference?" he asked Dan.

"I don't know. It's a bit delicate." For a brief second, he thought of revealing everything. "So, how did you ever get into this business?" he then asked instead. "Didn't you start out as a mathematician."

"You started out as a physicist," Simberloff deflected the question back to him, "didn't you?"

"Yeah, but I was from an ecology family," Danny said. "I guess like Bill Odum."

"Bill Odum?" Boecklen asked.

"Howard Odum's son?"

"Gene Odum's, I think," Simberloff said. He said it as if it was his last word for the evening, but then he suddenly smiled. "I've always loved insects and herps and birds," he shared, "even as a little boy, but I'd never thought of the possibility of a career in biology."

"And?"

"I guess around the end of my junior year," he recalled, "I began to realize that I didn't want to be a mathematician for the rest of my life. I was bemoaning my situation at dinner with classmates, and one of them noted that I seemed to be liking a nonmajors bio course I was taking. It was with George Wald."

"Were you in the class when he got his Nobel Prize?" Danny asked excitedly.

"That was later."

"I had a friend who was. He said that Wald opened up a bottle of champagne and sipped from it while he talked about the research that had won him the prize."

"That's Harvard, isn't it?" Joe Travis, standing by the table, hoping someone would make room for him, joined in. "Only at Harvard might you never even see some of those illustrious scholars the institution employs, yet still have your freshman science course taught by a Nobel Prize winner."

"Could have a great influence on you, an incident like that," Dan agreed. "What did your friend do?"

"Medical school," Danny answered. "Like his dad."

"Anyway, I said I loved that class," Simberloff continued. "When I talked to Wald about it, he told me that you could a major in bio at Harvard without any real bio courses, as long as you had a lot of other science courses, which I did. I checked it out the next day."

"But why math first?"

"Where I grew in Pennsylvania there were farms and woodlots and some serious forest. I spent an inordinate amount of time as a kid in woods and on farm fields, and very early on I collected insects, especially beetles."

"Inordinate?" Joe Travis interrupted. "Are you being Haldane?"

Travis had dragged over a chair and was crowding in.

"I told him the story about Haldane having dinner with a group of clerics," Simberloff said, giving a quick glance toward Travis.

"So, what part of Pennsylvania was this?" Danny asked.

"Hah!" Simberloff suddenly erupted with a memory. "When I was four, with two neighborhood friends, I founded the famed Society of Entymologists—I spelled it with a Y. Oh yeah, Wilson Borough, the place was called. It was just outside of Easton."

"Near Lafayette?"

"Yes. My parents were friends with a geneticist there. Jim Rasmussen was his name. Looking back, although my parents had little formal education, they were very erudite—but that's a long story. When I was very young, Rasmussen gave me some guppies to rear. He worked with guppies. They bred—well, like guppies. And although I can't remember what it was at the moment—maybe I never really understood it—my guppies did something that his guppies in his lab never did. And he wanted to have his guppies do it. So he asked to trade his guppies for mine. I, of course, refused. Eventually my parents talked me into it. Then my new guppies did something his guppies wouldn't, and we went through the same drill. Anyway, this whole experience led to a long-term relationship with poeciliids, which didn't end until I went off to grad school. I kept large numbers of them. Hmm. I also remember thinking a fair amount, even in Pennsylvania, about which species I could keep together and which I could not."

"Aha!" Travis stopped him. "On what basis? Were you a competitionist then?"

"Hardly," Simberloff said, smiled, then continued his life's story. "When I was eleven, we moved—Alas!—to Elizabeth, New Jersey."

"Exit Eleven on the Turnpike," Michael Auerbach offered.

He had taken over Travis's former position above their table. Auerbach was another northerner, although not a real Yankee, like Dan considered himself to be. Real Yankees to Dan were from northern New England, Vermont, New Hampshire, and Maine, specifically. Auerbach had done his undergraduate work at Stony Brook, on Long Island.

"You got it," Simberloff responded. "An ugly industrial city that had four EPA Superfund clean-up sites. There was, however, a rather nice woods where we lived. It was the only one within miles. I spent an awful lot of time in those woods, collecting insects and garter snakes. It was also at this time that I became intrigued by conservation, even before Rachel Carson. I thought that what happened around New York City should never have been allowed to happen."

"You still haven't explained the math major," Danny persisted.

"Probably what influenced me in that direction was that, although my parents and their siblings on both sides grew up very poor, my father's youngest sister actually went to college. Teacher's college. And she married a brilliant chemist who eventually became an executive vice president at Hoffman-Laroche. This was considered quite remarkable for a Jew in those days. This was my Uncle Leo. He was extremely encouraging to me. He took me to popular talks they had there. He challenged me with lots of math puzzles, too. He gave me books. He was a general inspiration. He was both a success and had a good understanding of what graduate school and scientific life consisted of. I was quite influenced by him."

"So the math major," Danny preempted him.

"So, inspired by Wald, I wound up seeking advice from Frank Carpenter, who was E. O. Wilson's mentor at the time."

"And that was it for math?"

"Carpenter was very encouraging," Simberloff continued. "He said of course I could get a bio major even at that late date by just taking a couple of bio courses and organic chemistry and that many areas of ecology and evolution were exciting fields where people with math backgrounds could do interesting work and were badly needed. I took the courses in the summer,"

By this time, he, Auerbach, and Danny were being abandoned by the rest of the crowd, which judged them as too sober. Most headed down the street to another bar or for a change in food. West Tennessee Street was lined with choices.

"I was pretty naïve about science when I dove into it my senior year and in grad school," Simberloff went on for the smaller audience. "In math, most of the papers are proofs, so there's not too much bullshit."

He paused, possibly to let someone else speak, but neither Danny nor Mike took the opportunity. Both thought it more important to take advantage of the beer remaining in the pitcher on the table. Simberloff ordered another.

"I guess I assumed at first it was the same in ecology," he resumed. "My first couple of years I was so busy catching up in bio and getting my dissertation under way that I didn't do much reading outside of what I needed for that and my courses. I was really a novice. However, by the end of my second year I was reading a lot of community ecology. It didn't take long to recognize that there was a lot of theory being published that couldn't be tested, because parameters couldn't be estimated and variables couldn't be measured, and that might be right, might be wrong, but didn't, at least to my mind, seem to be guiding the field. Up until that point, I had been quite reverent regarding what science was and how it was done. But from then on I became much more skeptical. Have you read Amyan MacFadyen's article? Where he assesses ecology? I think it was in the Journal of Animal Ecology."

"No," Auerbach admitted.

Simberloff gave him a dirty look.

"That's when you hit on null models?" Danny asked. "In grad school?"

Danny had not read the article, either, but he knew better than to admit ignorance of the literature in his field. He already had his PhD. Auerbach was just starting.

"No," Simberloff replied. "I didn't really undergo an epiphany about WHY there was so much crap until early on here. Then I realized that people desperately wanted to publish just to publish. Truly, before this, I didn't know much about status in science, how it is achieved, etc. I had thought everyone did science in order to do science. I know that sounds foolish, but as I said, I was naïve. After my first two years here, we hired Don Strong, and he was much more sophisticated than I, equally skeptical about a lot of publications, and we spent a lot of time talking about these issues."

"What did you make of Robert MacArthur?" Danny asked.

"I barely knew him. When I first met him in person, he seemed nice enough but very distant, a little cold. Not expressive. He was more than cordial then and later at another time, but a little stiff, I would say. We corresponded some, and he seemed to appreciate my comments on the island biogeography monograph he was writing with Wilson. They asked me to criticize it, including the math, which I did. My dealings with him were two personal meetings, I think, and some correspondence. I read a whole lot of what he wrote, but I wasn't too enthusiastic about versions of the Lotka-Volterra equations, so we didn't talk much about that area of his work, which was most of it at that time. But you were like one of his protégés, weren't you?"

"I called him Uncle Robert," Danny admitted, wondering what Simberloff had meant by "not expressive."

"Uncle Robert? Not Uncle Bob?"

"No one called him Bob. It was always Robert, even in his family." Danny now decided to share his secret. Even Auerbach had wandered off, leaving him alone with Simberloff. "I have Dieter John's field notes," he said.

"And?"

"And there's absolutely no correspondence between them and the numbers in his paper." Dan slowly drew out his words so that there would be no misunderstanding. "Some of the data in the paper isn't even in his notes. Couldn't have been, for they were for places he never even sampled."

"Made up?"

"What do I do?" Dan asked after an affirmative nod.

Simberloff made a pained face. "I think the ethical thing to do is to call him on it. Let John know what you think. How did you ever get his field notes?"

Instead of going home by way of Frenchtown from the Pastime, which he did not like doing in the dark, Dan went by way of the library, were he found and copied the paper Simberloff had mentioned. Not knowing the journal's issue or the correct spelling of the author's name, it took him a large chunk of the remains of the evening, closing time for the library approaching all the while. He had to skim backwards chronologically through tables of contents, guessing at the date of the heavy bound volume he needed to start with and fearing with each journey back for another heavy volume that he had guessed wrong.

It was an address given by its president to the British Ecological Society a few years after Earth Day. It was, he guessed, what must have introduced the ideas of Karl Popper and T. S. Kuhn to Simberloff and others in ecology.

"The assumptions, methods and activities of ecologists have from time to time been subjected to some quite strong criticism and I do not think these criticisms," Amyan MacFadyen had written, "should be quietly forgotten in the way that seems to happen so often."

What criticisms, Dan wondered, have been leveled from time to time? Could MacFadyen have been thinking about Clements still?

"There are those who argue that ecology," Dan read further, "like human history, is concerned with unique events and that these are not supposed to be open to the 'scientific method.' Is this true and does 'scientific method' referred to in this context differ from its meaning in other sciences?"

Nope, not Clements. MacFadyen had clearly fixed his aim on the current state of ecology. He was troubled by its lack of introspection over its methods, Dan learned on further reading. To MacFadyen, ecologists seemed to have developed too thick a skin. Criticism of their science was just so much water rolling off a duck's back.

"Many colleagues have little time for philosophy of science," Dan read on, "but I believe this to be an arrogant attitude in a subject which has been split by semantic schisms and methodological muddles, an attitude which we cannot afford."

And he brought up Kuhn's contention that a science in its early stages lacks paradigms, causing every publication to start from first principles. To MacFadyen, Kuhn hit "uncomfortably close to home."

Anyone who could gather an audience of an editor and sympathetic reviewers could set about defining basic ecological principles, according to MacFadyen. Although he identified four outstanding men (one of whom was Hutchinson) who successfully used the hypothetico-deductive system, he feared that their example encouraged "lesser mortals" to overly hasty generalizations.

"These usually come to the scientist in the form of 'bright ideas,'" Dan continued reading, "and they are an essential and exciting element in scientific work. But they can become destructive tyrants also. Apart from psychological difficulties deriving from protective attitudes to people's 'own' bright ideas, they set limits to the kind of questions which can be asked. There are plenty of examples from other fields of biology of the tyranny of bright ideas."

"Yeah, after reading that," Simberloff agreed when Dan saw him the next day, "I began to think, is it really this bad? And I concluded that it was. Ecology is a sick science, awash with all manner of untested, and often untestable, models, most claiming to be heuristic."

"So, it was Macfadyen who got you started?" Danny asked.

"It was not that simple. I hadn't met the man. Actually, it was reading a paper by Lewontin that inspired me to finally write down ideas I had been mulling over for a number of years. I sent it off to a journal little known to most biologists."

"Synthese?" Danny prodded.

The paper was Simberloff's intellectual ramble through Darwinism, theoretical physics, Greek philosophy, and of course, ecology. It was exactly the paper that a scientist having broad reading habits and interests could be expected to write about his field of study and science in general. Usually they did so toward the close of their careers. The state of ecology apparently kept Simberloff from waiting until then. It was that paper that had caused Danny to present himself at Simberloff's door to offer his services.

As soon as he left Simberloff's office, his cheeks still flushed from having to admit that he had not yet contacted Dieter John, Dan immediately did something he knew he had been putting off too long. He got his hands on books by Popper and Kuhn. It was an easy task. Their works were readily available on almost any bookshelf on the bottom floor of Conradi. It was better in all respects than talking to Dieter John.

He started with Popper. Popper assaulted him by too many words draped around simple equations that seemed to Dan to be either trivially true or totally inscrutable in their context. He was reminded that he had given up on Kant almost two hundred pages into *Critique of Pure Reason*. He had until then not realized that Kant had spent all those pages defining "to be."

He put Popper aside.

Kuhn's *The Structure of Scientific Revolutions* was as different from Popper's *The Logic of Scientific Discovery* as night was from day. It was more like physics to Dan than philosophy. It should be, Dan thought, grateful that Kuhn was a PhD physicist.

Dan raced through the slim paperback. He started reading during the slow periods of the introductory physics lab he taught, and he finished it while eating dinner. As he put it away, the image of Chabot in a lecture, years before, looking up into the seats at Robert Whittaker on mentioning Kuhn, rattled down from his cluttered memory. Whittaker's usual scowl had remained typically inscrutable as Chabot had gazed up at him. Neither he nor Bill Dritschilo, sitting next to him, had bothered to write Kuhn or paradigm in their notes, assuming it was an anecdote that would never find its way into an exam.

He called Aunt Jewel to share his excitement.

"Why, that's nothing new," she said, after listening to his lengthy explanation. "Oh you know, that old kook you laughed at, Fred Küchler, had the same ideas some thirty years ago. He published them in Ecology. Some time around 1950, I think. You can read them for yourself."

"You are coming up soon, aren't you?" she persisted when he started making hanging up excuses. "I know Ingrid wants to throw you a birthday party. She tells me the Dritschilos have invited you two to stay with them, too. Can you all visit with me? Maybe you can do the Sunday matinee at Marlboro?"

Yes, he thought, he had to accept that invitation. He could no longer use transportation as an excuse.

Crestfallen that his aunt might somehow have one-upped him, given that he was the one who was supposedly current in his field, Dan went back to the library. Again, it took some digging to find the article. It turned out to be a book review of some sort. "A Commentary on American Plant Ecology, Based on the Textbooks of 1947-1949," was its title.

Dan started to read. He came instantly to a stop.

Incredibly florid prose, he thought. Painfully florid prose.

His paper was not intended, Küchler had written, "for those men not yet dead." Küchler called the story of ecology a drama "with plots and subplots as well as intrigue." He described Cowles' University of Chicago as "young and lusty." The first half-century of ecology's history, he wrote, was being "ushered out by a succession of four resounding chords, a climactic finale summarizing almost ideally the four principal themes of the plot."

After some puzzling, Dan realized that Küchler was referring to the four textbooks he was putatively reviewing. The writing was almost as bad, in its own way, as Popper's, but it did hold some entertainment value. And how did "descendents" get past the editor?

He kept reading. He came upon something unexpected. Jewel was right.

"There is a period of accretion and assimilation," Küchler wrote about the development of a science, "during which the body increases in the weight of its constituents and begins to strain at its non-elastic chitinous enclosure. Then comes a sudden breaking and splitting. A new insect emerges, different in fundamental respects. The story is repeated."

And then, there it was.

"Then suddenly, there is a revolution, an upheaval."

And, "We are university-bred scientists, but rarely are we subjected to a formal course in scientific methodology, or in the philosophy of science."

Scientists should realize that they are just human, Küchler wrote. "The resistance to change, the 'close-mindedness,' the 'die-hard' qualities, the inability of most men past middle age to question the traditional, to welcome innovations or to grasp new ideas, are all recognized qualities that create the conservative forces in human civilization."

Finally, there was, "The solution of the problem lies in the next half century."

It was Kuhn's thesis in a nutshell, presented a generation in advance of Kuhn. And by that crazy old hermit of Arden Forest.

Before he could call Dieter, he had to call Walt. He dialed San Francisco. Walt reported that his health was not great. He had a low-grade fever. Strep throat was involved, and he had to take antibiotics. He had been feeling drugged out and edgy.

"I'll see the doctor again in a week. I will press to take DDC."

On the mental side, he was still struggling with feelings of frustration at not finding a job that could use his talents or that would allow him to express his full self. At LBL, he had never raised enough money. He needed to bring in $500K a year, impossible in ecology.

"I haven't had a lot to offer. I can't travel. It really boils down to finding the opportunities to communicate with the world shrinking fast. I have notes for letters, but also have too much anger."

"What sort of anger?"

"Some is me. Some is directed at the institutions that I was trying to deal with. When I first came up to the Bay area, there were geography jobs at Davis and Berkeley. I was told not to apply because my degree was not in geography. I'm angry about that. And at Lawrence Berkeley, I can point to much that was promised or implied when I was hired that became hot air."

Dan was not finding an opportune moment to bring up Dieter. He let Walt go on.

"More than forty friends have died of AIDS. Surprised? The two parts of my life are far apart, too far apart still. Most of the people I know with HIV are not academic. They do not feel in their hearts the loss of a career. Almost everyone I know in academia is straight. I needed to leave UCLA to explore myself, rather than continue doing what I had been channeled into doing."

Dan could almost see Walt shaking his head and maybe giving a little chuckle. And smiling, still.

"Academia is so competitive. There's something to be said for being more cooperative and friendly. At NASA, too, I found a competitive beehive. I did have a small group of friends there, though. I helped them rather than their helping me."

Dan continued to let Walt ramble on.

"During the last nine days, I've had a high fever—at a hundred and two. On Monday, I'm going for a Gallium scan. It goes to any site of infection or any tumor. The injection was on Friday."

Walt laughed.

"James and I were disappointed that I didn't glow in the dark. I feel something is up and needs checking into. I've had a fever since early October. I have a very good doctor, fortunately. He is thorough and anticipating. He gives a lot of personal attention, even though he has a large AIDS practice. I don't know how he does it."

Then he asked Dan to call back later, maybe next week.

"Um," Dan stumbled for words. "There is one other thing. It's about Dieter."

"Oh, are you thinking about getting together again? He has AIDS, you know, but it's not too bad, not as ba—"

"No," Dan interrupted. "It's something else."

Fortunately, Walt seemed too tired to probe into reasons. He gave Dan Dieter's newest phone number and wished him luck.

Yes, Dan thought, staring at his phone, then listening to the ring on the other side of the country.

"Hullo," came an unmistakable voice.

"Hi Dieter? This is Dan."

"Stan! How have you been? I was just—"

"No. Dan. Dan Atkins."

Dan could imagine hearing the air coming out of Dieter as he deflated during the pause that followed.

"Yeah."

Dan didn't know how to start.

"I hear you're going to give a paper for this conference coming up on null models," Dieter began for him. "Where is it? Tallahassee?"

"Wakulla Springs."

"Yeah. That's it. And you claim the opposite of what I published on Oregon carabids? You're going to say you can find no real evidence of community structure?"

"It's more than that, Dieter. But how are you?"

"Huh? Terminal. What do you think? And what do you mean by more?"

It was painful to imagine how that sculpted perfect athletic body might be wasting away, as painful for Dan as doing what he had to do next.

"Dieter, can I ask you something first?"

"Yeah, go ahead."

"I want an honest answer. Did you tell Beth not to tell anyone about the misplaced IBM card in your thesis work?"

"Honestly? Yeah, sure I did. What's the big secret? Most people know that. It was an accident and what difference does it all make now? So what if the genes transmitted backwards in time? Lomnicki pretty much made that paper irrelevant when he blew away the math behind genetic feedback, anyway. That stuff is so passé now."

What difference does it make? Dan repeated to himself. "I have your Oregon field notebooks and preliminary computer printouts."

"What? I—"

"They were in with ES&E stuff in the basement of the Geology Building. I'm going to use them at Wakulla."

There was nothing from the other end of the line. Then, "That's my property. I want it back."

"Be happy to oblige. Give me an address."

"Just send it to UCLA. It'll get to me. And you won't get away with this."

There was a click.

"Dieter? Dieter?"

III

THE gathering in Vermont was almost a Fly Lab reunion. It started in Proctor, where Buck and Sally stayed with Bill and Jamie at the old Victorian house they were rehabbing. It was to end at Marlboro, where everyone was to meet at the Marlboro Music Festival, at

Buck's insistence. They were then all, children included, to spend the night at Ames Hill, at Jewel's insistence. Ingrid promised to join them there.

Jamie arranged a picnic along a Vermont mountain stream for the group. It was reached by a rutted Forest Service road that split off the Brandon Gap road just as the landscape was opening into the peaceful green meadows of a broad glacial valley. The road slowly climbed through miles of steep forested hillside, past sparsely placed primitive camps, and over much more substantial, federally maintained bridges than the locally maintained ones on the Chateaugauy Road that Dan remembered from a previous Fly Lab outing in Vermont more than a decade ago. The picnic spot was just before the road came to a glade with flower beds and the large manicured lawn of a well tended Morgan horse farm.

"What is this place?" Buck asked, after parking behind Jamie's Subaru, filling the pull off,

"We've always just called it Bingo," Jamie said. "That's what my parents call it."

"I think it's the Bingo Branch of the White River," Bill added, taking out picnic equipment.

Jamie laid out a checkered tablecloth on a streamside gravel bed and set out wineglasses on it. While the children scrambled over rock ledges and slid down a chute into the cold water of a pool there, pate, Brie, Italian salami, two kinds of bread (one home baked), and fruit (cantaloupe and watermelon scoops, strawberries and blueberries) appeared on plastic Dansk plates on the tablecloth.

"What is this place?" Dan asked from the top of the river bank, having finally found the spot in his rental car. He parked it as far off the road and out of the way of the occasional logging truck as he could and as near to the edge of the eight foot drop down to the stream as he dared.

"Bingo!" came a chorus from below.

From above, his perplexed voice asked, "Did I win something? What was the word? Or is it just because I'm the birthday boy?"

"I think there used to be a town out here called Bingo," Jamie said.

"Back by the cemetery?" Bill asked.

"Had to be."

Always the great Earth mother, Dan thought, looking admiringly at Jamie. Now she has children to tend, rather than just us. And Bill seemed happy, too. They still had academic summers, meaning lots of family outings like this one. And although he admitted to finding no friends among his fellow teachers, Bill felt not at all like he was in an intellectual wasteland.

"That's the thing in Vermont," he explained to Dan as he attempted to make a sandwich seemingly using every ingredient Jamie had set out. "The waitress serving your pancakes in the morning might also be doing summer stock at the Weston Playhouse. The guy manning gas pumps at night might be working on a novel."

But Dan noticed that every time there was a lull in conversation, Bill tried to steer it in the direction of ecology. And every time, either Gordon, his happy but asthmatic kid, or Buck and Sally's son, Christopher, tagging along after the older boy, or Christina, the youngest, chasing after both and being excluded by them, disrupted the conversation with matters important only to them. Bill finally gave up and turned to stringing his fly rod and was soon off, children trailing after him, Jamie and Sally after them.

"So, you're doing well at Delaware," Dan reached for the last deviled egg and said to Buck, who was finishing the olives. "I come across your stuff in journals all the time."

"I hate it still," Buck said with a finality that cut of further discussion.

"By the way, how do you like the new American Naturalist?" Dan tried again.

"I liked it better the sedate scholarly gray it's always been," Buck answered.

"Actually, I think the sort of a gravy color it is now is like dog excrement," Dan laughed. "Glossy dog excrement. Maybe it's some sort of modernistic thing."

"But I like what George Salt is doing with those round table issues," Buck said.

"Issues? There's more than the one?" Dan asked with surprise. "I only saw the emergent property one."

"Ah, yeah," Buck responded, seemingly holding something back. "That one is what I meant."

"None of those ecosystem properties ever emerge," Dan said, having been trained on the topic at Oak Ridge. "And they don't tell us anything in particular, like Odum would like us to believe. Not without other information."

"There's going to be another round table," Buck then announced, almost sheepishly. "One on null models."

Before Dan could say anything, Sally and Jamie were back with the kids, who again dominated things, as kids do. Dan was grateful for it, though. He had not yet decided how much he wanted to tell Buck about what he was up to at Tallahassee.

"Did you tell him about how you set fire to the Hastings Reservation?" Bill asked Buck on his return.

"What?" Dan asked. He guessed Bill let the question deflect notice of his lack of trout.

"I'll never live that down," Buck said with a groan.

"It all had to do with his study of gall wasps on the various California oak species," Bill further prodded Buck.

"Yeah," Buck finally resigned himself to telling the story. "I'd been real nervous about making a good impression on the people at Hastings. I'd brought along Sally and Christopher—"

"He was just a little tiny baby," Sally interrupted.

"Hastings is all hilly grasslands and oak woodlands."

"It was where Dick Root studied gnatcatchers," Bill had to add.

"They let you back in again, didn't they?" Dan asked jokingly.

"I felt so ashamed," Buck said. "They had to call out helicopters and fire fighting aircraft to put it out. I don't know how many acres were burnt, but it was pretty embarrassing. I kept a low profile while there, I'll tell you."

"How'd you—" Dan started to ask.

"I'd parked my rental car over some grass. They'd warned me not to, because those new State-of-California-required catalytic converters could ignite grass. I didn't think about that at all, though. It did no harm to the car, but spread through the grass from beneath it and into grassland so quickly that Todd and I could do little more than stand there with mouths agape."

"Todd?" Bill asked.

"Todd Shelly," Dan answered for Buck.

"No one probably even remembers the fire any more," Dan said as things were being packed up. "They have grass fires in California all the time. But I'm so jealous. I wish I could have done some cool ecology like you when I was out there."

"I think that there IS competition structuring communities out there," Buck said, turning back from the path and bounding quickly up the bank. "I think the Tallahassee group is too rigid on that."

"Are you coming back with us?" Jamie called to Dan from her open car window.

"Naw," Dan shouted back. "I'm staying with my aunt again."

"You better back out of this space, instead of trying to go forward," Bill then warned.

Dan turned to see Buck already in his car and driving off.

The concert was a matinée composed entirely of small ensemble pieces. Gone was the chamber orchestra. Gone was the conductor. Everyone on stage, Jewel explained to the others, teachers and students, were just musicians, learning together by playing together. The program, made up only days before, as was the custom, promised a Busch sextet followed by a Haydn trio followed by a Mozart divertimento, written when he was ten. Each piece was unfamiliar to Jewel, but each had a Serkin listed as a performer, Irene, Rudolf, or Judith. It was held in the same old barn of a cafeteria.

"I'm impressed with the quality of the programs and the musicians" Jewel shared. "It gets better every year. The seating hasn't, though. I think they're using the same folding metal monstrosities I sat in more than twenty years ago."

There was a picnic before the concert, again provided by Jamie, much of it left over from Bingo, although Bill added to it by cooking up hot dogs and hamburgers, almost one at a time, on a tiny portable grill. They sat on park benches in a corner of the campus next to a decorative pond as they ate. They remained there to leisurely await the 2:30 start while the children darted about, wearing off excess energy before it, a strategy that was not entirely successful. One mother or the other—or Jewel, claiming honorary grandmother privileges—wound up outdoors with one or another child—or all of them—to listen to the concert through open windows. All the while, Dan fought with himself over revealing all his secrets, but every time an opportunity came up, a wife or a child or a fellow Fly Labber interrupted it.

After the performance, they repaired to Ames Hill, where Jewel served ravioli stuffed with squash. She had made in advance by hand. It had become her signature dish, a prized remnant of her life with Jon.

How that had seemed like such a lifetime to her! How it now seemed only a brief episode in an eternity of loneliness.

Sleeping arrangements at Ames Hill were tight. Over the years, Jewel had removed beds from some of the bedrooms. They were now storerooms, piled high with various items, the fate of which Jewel had not yet determined. Boxes of shellac 78-rpm records mingled with pieces of furniture, some in need of repair, some whole. One room held a considerable collection of pots and pans and other cooking utensils. They were sacrosanct. They had been Jonathan's.

Fortunately, everyone was in a spirit of make do. Dan and Ingrid agreed to share a single bed in a small attic room with a dormer window that looked down on the meadows. It was the room Dan always used on his visits and Ingrid on hers. It was the first night they would use it together. It would be the first bed they had shared since LA and the first single bed since that bottom bunk in the Village.

The bed was pushed up against the wall, so, of course, they'd be able to sleep in it together, Jewel insisted. Ingrid instantly concurred.

Jewel came downstairs with snifters of brandy after helping put the children to bed. "I hope you're not just going to talk ecology all night," she scolded them as she poured from her favorite grade of Hennessy.

Again, for Dan it was another interruption. Again, he felt he was about to bare his soul to his friends, but for …

"If you are, you'd better have some of this. Ecology's all abstract now, isn't it? It bores me. And yet, I once devoted my life to it. Well, I'll be in the parlor with the girls."

The living room was the room with couches and a television. The little room off the unused front entrance that Jewel called a parlor was now more like a library. It might once have been the parlor, although farm houses in Vermont rarely had such rooms.

"But Jewel, there are still ecosystem studies," Bill countered before she could get away.

"Not like in my day," she scoffed. "It all seems to be chemistry now, instead of ecology."

"Yeah, but that's what seems to be needed for environmental work," Buck said after a respectful sniff from his goblet. "This is good cognac."

"Thank you. V. S. O. P. But is all that ecosystem analysis and modeling really going to solve our problems? People are the problem, aren't they? But we can't have a world without them, no matter what some in this room might think."

She glanced in Dan's direction.

"We can't give up on our own kind," she continued. "You haven't," she said, looking first at Bill then at Buck. "You two have children. That's the compact we have with life. We get—a precious gift—then life takes it away. That part we don't learn until well into our lives, until we're totally used to and pleased with ourselves. Then it hits us. But it's the grandchild—not the child—that guarantees our immortality. Isn't that how natural selection works?"

Dan saw no hint of apology in her glance.

"Well, I'll go sit with the girls," she said and took the Hennessey with her.

Their conversation turned to reminiscences. Pimentel, Mark Loye, Al Brick, Dick Root, Si Levin, and Al Brick, again, were evaluated for comedic value. All were judged comical in some way. Art Shapiro, Dan Udovic, Bernie Soames, Dieter John, and others who had preceded them were judged without comedic value. So was genetic feedback.

"But you know," Dan said, "when you take away MacArthur-style ecology like genetic feedback, what's left of ecology?"

"Natural history."

"Math, chemistry, biology."

"Evolution."

"Now we're back to MacArthur."

"And genetic feedback?"

"What about all this top down and bottom up stuff I see in the literature these days?" Bill asked. "What's that all about?"

"You're still keeping up?" Dan asked.

"Trying. I still feel like I'm an ecologist, even if I am teaching physics."

"It's all about driving convertibles while drinking scotch."

"It's really just that HSS argument all over again," Buck gently corrected. "You know, do plants control insect populations or the other way around."

"Didn't Roughgarden publish an important paper with MacArthur?" Bill suddenly thought he remembered.

"Did he? What made you ask that?"

"I read somewhere where I think Roughgarden said that those who complain about MacArthur-style ecology are just spouting sour grapes because they're disinclined to learn math is how I think he put it. Wow! This brandy's got a kick!"

"He's got some things to say about your colleagues at Florida State, too," Buck added, speaking to Dan.

"I bet," Dan said, his stomach contracting. How much was he going to say? "I don't think that one-time math major Simberloff is disinclined to learn math. And I thought statistics WAS a mathematical science."

"True," said Bill as Jewel returned with what looked like a newly opened bottle of Hennessy, "and, of course, scientists don't go about their work with the dispassionate objectivity we would hope them to have. T. S. Kuhn has shown that."

"And Fred Küchler," Jewel interrupted.

"Scientists do sometimes hold on to their pet ideas to their death," Buck took over, "even in the face of overwhelming evidence. There are still people in geology departments everywhere who don't believe in continental drift."

"But nowhere has Kuhn or others said that abandoning proper controls is anything but fraud or charlatanism," Dan said.

"Fred Küchler?" Bill asked.

"Roughgarden cites F. Suppe's The Structure of Scientific Theories to support the statement Bill quoted," Buck said before Jewel could get a word out about Küchler.

"Suppay? Is that how it's pronounced?" Bill asked. "Like the guy who wrote the Light Cavalry Overture?"

"I don't know," Buck answered.

"How's it spelled?"

Jewel topped up Dan's glass a second time.

"What else could it be?" Bill asked on hearing the spelling. "Soup? Sup? Suppee?"

"I don't know either, but Jared Diamond cited him to try to discredit Popper in a recent paper."

"Yeah, he did," Buck said. "So did our very own Dieter John. According to Suppe—however it's pronounced—Diamond claims that modern philosophers of science rarely cite Popper's work on falsification. When they do it's only to explain why they have discarded it. Didn't we just go over all this?"

"Dieter John?" Dan asked in delayed reaction, dread in his voice.

"He sent me a manuscript to read."

"And?"

"Actually, I just remembered he asked me specifically not to discuss it with you."

"He did? Why?"

"I don't know. Something about being on the same program."

Dan's face went red.

"So, who is this soup guy?" Bill asked.

"So you have been reading and thinking about null model stuff," Dan said to Buck. "What did John say about me?"

"How do you guys remember all this shit?" Bill demanded.

"I just do. Don't you?"

"So, is this Suppe an ecologist?"

Bill pronounced the name to rhyme with "pup."

"Well," Dan said. "At least we've reached agreement over how to pronounce the name."

"Last call," Jewel announced. She poured the rest of the bottle into Dan's snifter. "Everyone else is in bed."

"How late is it?"

"Oh, it must be eleven or so."

"I've got to catch a flight out of Manchester tomorrow morning," Dan jumped up both in panic and relief. "I'd better turn in."

"Watch yourself on the stairs," Jewel called after him.

"Oh, don't worry, Aunt Jewel," he called back, not quite slurring his words. "I've only had two glasses of brandy."

"Yes," Jewel whispered to no one in particular. " Just enough."

"Happy birthday," was called up the staircase.

Ingrid was in bed with her eyes closed, but not yet asleep. She had a large candle lit on the windowsill.

"Good discussion?" she asked.

The candlelight against her cheeks was very kind to her.

"Yeah," he said, wondering if he should undress in the bathroom. He was unclear about what their current level of intimacy —or informality—was.

The nearest bathroom was all the way down the stairs. A light was on in it. Someone seemed to be using it. It was too far, anyway, and he was too tired. Or was it too drunk?

"Let me help," Ingrid said as he fumbled with his belt.

She slid his blue jeans and briefs off his hips almost imperceptibly. Shoes and socks disappeared from his feet. Although Ingrid always slept in the nude, she had on some sort of lacy black negligee. She looked good. What he had on, with her help, was a full erection.

"No. I don't— We shouldn't."

"Yes we should."

And she guided him down on the bed and glided over him like that night so long ago in the Village.

"We really should use a condom," Dan said in panic.

It was too late to tell her, but he had to tell her. His hard cock was already inside her, and she was maneuvering him to be on top. He should have said something before.

"I may have AIDS," he finally blurted out, the incongruous image of Dieter John arranged in a casket before his eyes.

But it was too late. He exploded inside her. Prematurely. Uncontrollably.

"Yes. Yes. Yes," came from Ingrid.

She held in her screams so as not to be heard throughout the house, each yes falling off in volume, rather than rising. Dan stayed hard, even after the spasms subsided, even her spasms.

"I should have told—" Dan tried to speak, but she covered his mouth with her hand.

Her hips quivered slightly. She was feeling his hardness still. She began to thrust once more against him. He moved in concert.

What have I done? Dan wondered as he felt his urgency building once more.

And then he could think no more. Ingrid subsided into unconsciousness along with him. A single thought stayed in his mind as he drifted into oblivion. Jewel had put it there.

Immortality.

Jewel turns off the light in the upstairs bathroom and returns to her bedroom, leaving the door open. She hears children sleeping. She hears Buck, too large for any of her beds, breathing in his sleep on the divan. She hears no more noises from the attic.

Just like Liza and I managed to set it up all those many years ago, on that single bed in Liza's old bedroom in LaGrange. It had been at the end of the war, when nothing seemed to be making any sense. Fred had been running from coast to coast on war work. Of course, he would love to meet the famous Liza and see me again, if he could. And he could. We saw to it. Even if he was as queer as a three-dollar bill.

"The sword of Damocles," she remembers promising, "hanging over us will keep us apart."

It's exactly the right time of the month for Ingrid, she thinks with satisfaction. What could go wrong?

Dan woke up soon after and found himself alone in the kitchen with a telephone receiver in his hand. He dialed a San Francisco number. It was barely ten o'clock there. He needed to talk to someone who could understand his new predicament. Only one person came to mind.

"I've been sick with a fever since June," Walt told him. "That's why no letters. They finally now just got a diagnosis. I have MAI, a form of tuberculosis. It's common in late-stage AIDS patients. I started treatment on Wednesday at an Infusion Center at a nearby hospital."

He paused. Dan waited.

"I go each day for that. I also have pills for three drugs to take at home. The treatment involves four drugs during the first month and, if successful, drops to three drugs in subsequent months. It just deals with the symptoms. It'll work reasonably well if the disease is caught early enough. The first month is crucial. One just hopes that the organism responds. I'm just lying around at home popping pills."

There was a weak laugh.

"My T-cell count was down to five in late July. So I was wide open for the organism to invade. It's a mycobacteria. It's very common. Pigeons carry it and you can catch it just by the flap of a pigeon wing. It's a slow growing organism. It can take three months to show up in a blood culture. That's why it took so long to diagnose."

Another pause.

"If MAI gets out of control, it causes a wasting syndrome. The body loses its ability to absorb food. It spreads from the lungs to the kidneys and liver. It kills by starvation. It may be the leading killer of AIDS patients in places like Texas. I'm fortunate to be in San Francisco."

"What's this Infusion Center?" Dan asked.

"Let me tell you a joke. One of my friends described it as being full of gay men but run by a dripping bitch. Bad joke, huh? Well, she deserves a medal. The doctor she works for has a large practice and all his patients are in crisis mode. Most of the men he sees in the Infusion Center are in his care."

A pause.

"He's gay. He set up practice as an internist. Now specializes in HIV patients. Over half of doctors will not take AIDS patients. Some even want them to be quarantined. Living in San Francisco certainly makes it easier for me."

A cough. A wrenching conversation-stopping cough.

"Are you OK Walt?"

"OK? No, I'm far from OK. But I'm OK now. So did you have something you wanted to tell me?"

"No. Nothing."

"My NSF grant was turned down," Walt said. "As far as I can see, no one read the proposal. The panel comments were more or less quotes from reviewers who could not have read it. All the answers to their complaints were in the proposal."

Pause.

"I'm writing up a set of guidelines to young investigators on how to write reviews of proposals without reading them."

And then, he had to excuse himself. He was exhausted.

IV

VIEWS of scrubby stands of slash pine and turkey oak interspersed with stumps of larger pines caught Dan's eye through the windshield of his Datsun. Every so often, he spotted crude shanties set on foundations consisting only of a cinder block at each corner. Some were clearly abandoned. Some had laundry hung out on bushes in their dooryard. They were still inhabited. Clothesline apparently was a luxury for its denizens.

What an existence! Dan thought glumly. It had to be why so many southern blacks moved into the ghettos of northern cities after the war.

Susan Mopper was beside him in front. She must have been reading his face.

"Moonshine and teppentine, Danny," she said.

He was Danny again in this group.

"That and in the paper industry is about how people made their livings out here," she added. "Some still do."

"Now you can add drug smugglers," Nick Gotelli added from the back seat.

"There are places I go to sample oak leaf miners, I just have to take a gun along," Susan said.

"Teppentine?" Danny asked.

"Turpentine," she answered. "It's collected kinda like maple sap is where you grew up, I imagine. Except that here, they don't just puncture the bark, they hack it away to get the rosin to flow. Metal gutters and boxes collect the pine pitch. They use'ta distill it right on site into teppentine and gum for ship sealing. Naval stores, they called that. Facing, they used to call what they did to the bark."

"Sounds like girdling," Danny said.

"It is girdling. Ten years, tops, and they had to move on. Had to pick up their little village and go somewhere else. The trees were dead."

"Now they have big tractors to process the stumps, too, I understand," Hector Quinteros suddenly spoke up.

Hector was a surprise to Danny. Hector was the only Puerto Rican Dan knew of in ecology—or had even ever met in grad school, in general. Or ever. He knew of them only from West Side Story.

"The black people I meet still warn about messing with teppentine folk," Susan said. "I carry a gun as much for that reason as for the drug dealers."

And they suddenly were out of the scrub and into park land. They had arrived. Unlike some of the speakers who were staying at the lodge for the three-day conference, Danny was driving the short distance in his Datsun. Nick, Hector, and Susan car-pooled with him that first morning.

"Faux Mediterranean," Danny sniffed dismissingly on first view of the Wakulla Springs Lodge.

It had simple white stucco walls and a red tiled roof. Classically simple arches led into its portico. The deep fresh-water spring near the lodge, complete with manatees in its waters and alligators on its banks, caught Dan's attention more than the architecture did. Ibises and anhingas posed against a background of cypresses draped with Spanish moss. They warily eyed a few small alligators. The alligators were still protected by law, even though they seemed more endangering than endangered.

Ed Connor, hair neatly trimmed and face clean shaven, as befit a new professor at the University of Virginia, greeted them in the parking lot. He proudly announced to them that he had had his wedding there the previous June.

"Can I help?" Danny asked Don Strong, who met them at the conference room entrance.

He was soon setting up folding chairs in the long, narrow room. It gave the impression of having been a porch that was now closed in. With the windows open to air out its mustiness, it still had the feel of a porch.

"Ah. The scent of flowers and birds singing their evensong in the shrubbery," Don waxed poetic. "Makes me shudder to think of it."

Small beads of sweat tracked down his face. The armpits of his shirt were dark with it.

"P. G. Wodehouse," he said. "Do you know him?"

"Of course."

"This place," Don said, glancing all about, "needs Billie Holliday's voice wafting from the wings to complete its World War Two ambiance. I think the people that run it all came from Pensacola."

"Well, this is the big one," Ed Connor said. "A big conference."

"A big day," Strong agreed.

"Did you know that J. B. S. Haldane discovered he had cancer while here?" Dan Simberloff's voice suddenly came from behind to say.

"What?" Danny asked, almost in fright.

"Actually, he noticed he had rectal bleeding here. He learned it was cancer on his way back to India. He wrote a great poem about it."

"You wouldn't have memorized it, by chance?" Strong asked jokingly.

"So pausing on my homeward way," Simberloff began to recite. "From Tallahassee to Bombay, I asked a doctor now my friend, to peer inside my hither end, some of it went. It's quite good. I don't remember the rest."

There had been an envelope with a Noe Street, San Francisco, address in his Conradi mailbox that morning. The thought of it now stabbed through Dan. He had left the letter in his mailbox, rather than bring it with him to read at the conference.

The Tallahassee group—Danny no longer wanted to think of them as Mafia—had carefully chosen the location. They thought it would be conducive to bringing into the open, once and for all, the controversial issues that had surfaced in community ecology. Strong and Simberloff had less successfully tried to do something similar a few years before over how island biogeography theory was being applied and misapplied. That had been at an Entomological Society meeting in Washington, DC. Dritschilo had attended that one, but could give no impression at all on it when he got back to Cornell, other than that he was flattered to have been asked to attend.

This time, things were more formal, with invited papers and a promise by Robert May to publish them in book form, a greater incentive even than an honorarium in attracting participants. May was one of the editors of Princeton University Press. In fact, he was in charge of the imprint that Robert MacArthur had started at Princeton with his and Wilson's book. The editorial duties had come to May on taking over MacArthur's chair at Princeton. He was also coauthor with Jared Diamond on papers having to do with island biogeography theory and conservation.

"Demonic intrusion" burst through Danny's mind, shaking free from it thoughts of AIDS.

"YOU MIGHT HAVE AIDS," is what he first thought he had heard, in Ingrid's voice.

"Demonic intrusion," Danny repeated in a whisper.

It was the last item on a list of experimental and statistical errors in one of Stuart Hurlbert's slides. It was an example of what Hurlbert was calling "pseudoreplication" in ecology. It had a good ring to it, demonic intrusion. Danny tried to think about Dritschilo and his mouse enclosures to keep the voices out of his mind. Surely some of those mice had been possessed.

"That was a good talk," Danny heard Ed Connor from behind him. "It's useful to anybody in biology."

"Might be the best one we'll have here," Simberloff agreed. "Even though it doesn't really fit in with the rest, I'm glad we asked him to give it."

As was their habit on Friday seminars, they were at the back of the room. Only Larry Abele was at the front, discharging the duty of introducing speakers. Some fifty people were in the audience, Danny guessed, presenters apparently in the majority. Dieter John was not among them. People from Tallahassee seemed to comprise a second majority. Strong, Simberloff, Abele, and Travis, of the faculty, were all giving talks. Jorge Rey, Connor, Boecklen, Faeth, Auerbach, and a few others that Danny may not have recognized as having gone through FSU were also listed as contributors in the conference's program. Danny, too, of course, was on the program, its last speaker, right after Dieter John.

So was Bev Rathke on the program, Danny noticed. That explained the person who looked very much like Bob Poole in the crowd.

Of the opposition, bird men Peter Grant and Tom Schoener were there. Jared Diamond had pointedly refused to attend. He had let it be known that he no longer wanted to be in the same room with Simberloff. May, though, had persuaded Diamond to provide a written contribution to the published volume. Diamond had agreed to co-author something with the more mathematically inclined Michael Gilpin of UC San Diego. And, of course, Dieter John would be present to defend his patron.

"I can't believe he insulted Rob Colwell like that!" Don Strong said in disbelief at the end of the question-and-answer part of Hurlbert's presentation.

Danny's dark thoughts had made him miss the exchange. Strong flitted away before explaining himself.

"Do you know what he meant by that?" Danny asked Ed Connor.

"Not sure," Ed answered. "What I dislike the most about these kinds of arguments is having to explain and re-explain null models over and over again. The models were intended to test for independence between species, not whether nature was random. I'd like to just get away from the whole fracas and actually do some experiments."

He looked to Danny like he was about to spit on the floor, but changed his mind.

"Diamond's more-than-hundred-page tome in the memorial volume for MacArthur was to me the most egregious example of fuzzy thinking in the competitionist camp. Everyone in the lab back then agreed on that. We had preprints of most of the chapters in the book before the volume was published, and Diamond's paper was read and ridiculed by all of us."

"It hasn't gone away, though, has it?" Danny pointed out.

"Dan says that the debate is primarily for protecting and building reputations. A lot of people want to be famous. It's easy in a young science like ecology. Hutchinson sees some goat bones in a shrine in Palermo and has an epiphany about why there are so many species and comes up with his one-point-three ratio. Hutch didn't do his research. We looked it up."

Tallahassee

"I know," said Danny. "No one stopped believing in the power of the bones, though."

V

THE conference began to blur past Danny the way he thought a sleep-walker's world might.

"I conclude that we need to know the exact ecological relationship to a degree that is unlikely to be attained for this or most other guilds," Nelson Hairston, Sr., was concluding at the podium, "or that this and many other claimed examples of guilds are products of an imagination."

Danny was pondering not his words, but his insistence on being introduced that his name be pronounced "Hahrston." He wondered if Hairston was being just playful, like Dick Lewontin, who was known to correct "Lewontin" to "LeVONtin" and vice versa.

Twenty years before, Hairston had teamed with Larry Slobodkin and Fred Smith, all at Michigan at the time, to write a paper questioning what regulated population size, density-dependent versus density-independent factors, as the argument over competition played itself out back then. Now the lines were drawn as competitive effects (density-dependent) versus environmental (density-independent.) The paper had become known simply as HSS, after the authors' initials.

"To have to make use of all such factors in delimiting a guild would make the delimitation pointless and remove any hope that we have a scientifically valid field," Hairston continued to conclude several minutes later.

Guild was a concept invented by Dick Root. For him, as far as Dan could make out, it consisted of five bird species that gleaned insects from leaves in the oak woodlands of the Hastings Reserve. It was very much in the tradition of MacArthur and Hutchinson and their niche theories. Had MacArthur done his thesis after Root's, he mused, he would have defined the guild he studied as those warblers found in northern coniferous forests. Guild was a plastic concept at best, though, that excused ignoring all manner of other creatures, dragonflies, frogs, and various parasites, for example, that consumed the same insects as Root's and MacArthur's birds. Of course, that then could be justified by the niche concept. Dragonflies and birds in no way of reckoning could possibly occupy similar niches. After coming to Cornell, though, Root had defined a guild of insects that fed on collard greens for his students and himself to study, but he called it a "component community" instead of a guild. He and Levin and Whittaker then teamed to try to standardize the usage of such terms, with only partial success.

Another speaker was already at the podium and well into his talk. Essentially, Danny concluded, a guild seemed to mean nothing more than that group of animals that the investigator assumed were competing with each other for some resource and that could be identified by the variations in size, place, or time, that evolved to avoid that competition.

"AND YOU MIGHT NOT HAVE AIDS," Ingrid's voice suddenly echoed through his head again.

"Isn't it sad about Whittaker," Bob Poole said to Danny when the two ran into each other at a break. "What a great guy to have lost! He was the only one at Cornell who was willing to give me any help while I was there."

"Yeah," Danny said unenthusiastically. "So what is Beth's talk about?"

"Methodological. She and I published a paper using her data showing that flowers bloom at random, rather than having flowering times staggered because of competition for pollinators. They got really excited about that down here."

Like a politician, Bob May smiled his way over to Poole to pump his arm.

"Isn't it paradoxical," he asked rhetorically, "that those who are most sensitively aware of the need to keep sight of alternative explanation for observed patterns in community structure seem, at the same time, to insist that there is only one true way to do science?"

He gave no sign that he recognized Danny.

"That's Ole Joe," Strong said of the very large stuffed alligator in a glass case in the hall. "I knew him well."

They were on their way back from lunch.

"A relative?" Danny asked.

"Did you notice that there are no Mexican cooks or waiters?" Don asked.

"Is that why the food is so bland?"

"Must be. You know, it's like Civil Rights hasn't happened here yet. Everyone is expected to still know their place."

"In Connell's apt and descriptive phrase," Englishman John Lawton was saying, "the key to understanding the structure of bracken herbivore communities may be with the ghost of competition past."

"Ghost of competition past" was a phrase Danny was hearing a lot. It meant that, just because there was no evidence of competition in an animal community or guild, it did not mean that competition might not have occurred in the past. Put more simply, if two bird species, two of Darwin's finches on the same island, for example, the two that Brown and Wilson had used in their character displacement paper, did not, in fact, compete, it was just a logical outcome of having evolved differences through past competition to avoid competition in the present. It was a lovely explanation. If natural selection caused the evolution of characters that reduced competition, then one should observe it as being absent or reduced. The problem that the Tallahassee group had brought up, as had a few others before them, is that the differences could have arisen while the two birds were separate populations of a single species on two different islands. The differences might already have been present when the two species came to cohabit the same island. How could one tell? That was one of the worms that the Tallahassee group was pulling out of the corpus of the sick science they saw to be animal community ecology.

Australian Tony Underwood, Danny noted, was the first speaker to use the term, paradigm, in his talk. It caught his attention at once. He had expected it to be sooner. Underwood was also the first to mention a philosopher's name, in fact, several. Feyerabend had come from his lips, then Lakatos and Kuhn, but not Popper. This was significant, for there was a pool among the FSU grad students on who would be the first to mention Popper. Don Strong had promised not to at their urging and had kept his word. Danny, an honorary grad student for the purposes of the bet, had expected it to be Larry Abele, but Larry had disappointed him. Gary Graves had bet on the Australian. Nick Gotelli had chosen the Finn, who had gone right before the Australian. Not even so much as a "pop" had come from the Finn. Danny held his breath.

"This is a statement," he heard from the podium a moment later, "of our acceptance of Popper's view of falsifiability and validity of hypotheses."

The Australian was also the first one to speak kindly of Canadian Robert Henry Peters. Danny suspected that he would be the only one to do that. Peters' name, like LaMont Cole's among wildlife people, was used to frighten babies and impressionable graduate students among evolutionary biologists. The Australian, however, lauded him for attempting to "introduce reason into the emotional appeals of neo-Darwinist metaphysics."

Not wanting to pay off the bet, Danny pushed his way out through the crowd and into the sunshine at the next break, all the while fearing that Dieter John might have arrived. Eventually, though, he did bump into Nick Gotelli who, like a true Californian, was out catching some rays from the afternoon sun.

"You'll have to pass that on to Gary," Danny said, glumly handing him a five-dollar bill. Gotelli had been entrusted with managing the betting pool.

"Oh, I thought you'd already paid," Nick said, handing it back. "It was too easy, actually. We convinced Larry not to mention Popper."

Tom Schoener, from UC Davis, was up next. He was famous for having made his reputation with a paper he wrote when he was still an undergraduate student at Harvard. It, of course, had to do with differences in bill sizes and evolution. The massive data set presented in his talk on hawks gave pretty solid statistical support for Hutchinson's 1.3 rule. In his soft-spoken way, he also managed a dig at the Tallahassee group.

"The novitiate reading the recent literature," he said, "might get the impression that ecology has just discovered the null hypothesis."

"It seems to me," he ended his talk, "that the real difference now lies not in stating or testing null hypotheses, but in the nature of the appropriate procedure. What set of statistical and biological information is most acceptable? What data should be included in a single test? What alternative hypotheses AND what null hypotheses are most appropriate. What I've tried to show is that how these questions are answered can make a difference."

"I MIGHT GET PREGNANT FROM THIS," Danny heard Ingrid say, as she had that night.

"So how did you come to be influenced by MacArthur?" Danny asked, sidling up to Peter Grant, who was standing alone with a drink. The day's session had ended. Attendees were assembling in the lodge's smoke-filled bar, where FSU grad students were accosting various personages in hope of scoring points that could lead to a favorable review of a paper or grant proposal, a possible recommendation, or even a job. Conversely, some of the personages were seen as the enemy and avoided. The tall, thin Englishman had the appearance of one of those. The athletic silhouette of Dieter John that Danny had been fearing to find was still among the missing, even though his talk was coming up the next day.

From what he understood, Peter Grant had vowed to devote himself to be the data collector on the most famous natural experiment in biology, the colonization of the Galapagos Islands by South American finches. They will always be Darwin's finches, but for a while, they were also David Lack's finches. Lack, another Englishman, on visiting the Galapagos and re-examining the birds, reasoned that they could not have diverged on different islands, because all the Galapagos were so similar. He invoked competition on the same island for the differences in bill structures. It was a good story. He had not bothered to test it, however. Grant was doing that. Since nineteen seventy-three, he had gone yearly to the Galapagos Islands to make observations and collect data on its wildlife, birds in particular, finches especially. It had become a family affair. Not just his wife, an accomplished biologist in her own right, but both his daughters, too, had published on Galapagos birds with him. The Grants were on their way to becoming the gurus of Darwin's finches.

"Actually, it was Evelyn Hutchinson," Grant said affably in answer to his question.

"Ah, Uncle Hutch."

"Beg pardon?"

Danny decided against an explanation. "You were his grad student?" he asked instead.

"No, I had a postdoctoral fellowship to Yale. I'd taken my degrees at Cambridge and British Columbia. I'd gone to Vancouver on a sojourn through Canada and decided to stay. I fell in love with the waters and the mountains in the background. It turned out to be remarkably easy to get into a graduate program there."

Danny waited through Grant's pause.

"Evelyn was my last teacher," Grant concluded, scratching his beard a bit as if suspicious about whose side Danny was on.

Grant was not about to admit that David Lack's famous patterns might be nothing more than the image of the man on the moon, the continents or animals that cumulus clouds take on, or the faces in an inkblot, as those from Tallahassee implied.

"To do science is to search for repeated patterns, not simply to accumulate facts," Grant had read at the beginning of his lecture that day. It was a much-quoted statement by Robert MacArthur. "This is exactly what I did and what Diamond has done, using the idea of interspecific competition both in guidance in the search for patterns and as an explanation for them." But later, he had admitted that, "Some check on theory is needed. The patterns themselves, like beauty, may exist more in the eyes of the beholder than in reality, and the explanations for patterns may be simply ingenious contrivances that are completely wrong."

Beards seemed to be replacing mustaches among ecologists, Danny thought as he admired Grant's trim beard. Buck Cornell had one. Bill Dritschilo now had a goatee. He wondered if maybe he should not have shaved his off. Beards gave a hint of exotic places with rugged field sites, ones without razors or Ballantine.

"I credit Hutchinson with furthering my intellectual development," Grant now said to Danny. "He embodied my ideal values of the academic scholar. From him I learned not to be afraid of creative speculation when it can enlighten."

"My Aunt Jewel, who adopted me, was his technician for a number of years. It was in the fifties."

"Oh really? Is that why you just called him Uncle Hutch?"

"He and I spent a lot of time together at Linsley Pond when I needed an older male in my life, I guess."

"The fifties, you say? That was an interesting collection of intellects that passed through his lab. Were you acquainted?"

"Yeah. Uncle Robert and Uncle Larry and Uncle Peter and ... I had a lab full of uncles after I came down with polio."

"Uncle Robert? Robert MacArthur?"

"Yeah."

That decided Grant to stand Danny a scotch and open up about his life. He talked about his first summer in the Galapagos. He and his wife soon realized that Daphne Major's small size could provide a safe, if not ideal, environment for their two children, Nicola and Thalia, even as it had perturbed both sets of grandparents back in England.

Working only with the six Geospiza species, Grant had applied sophisticated statistical tests on food sources and randomness of occurrence. He spoke of principal component analysis and Euclidian distances, the sort of analysis that Wisconsin ecologists had used to reject a different hypothesis about different communities, that of Clements on plant communities. In this case, Grant's analysis supported the hypothesis that species assemblages were non-random, and in the direction predicted by competition.

It was sophisticated analysis that Grant had given in his talk. For one thing, it did not just depend on presence or absence data, as was true for most bird communities. And for each test he made, he posed several alternate hypothesized explanations to compare to his data. The word null never entered into his talk until the conclusion, when Tallahassee work was discussed and rejected by him.

It had been at about then in Grant's presentation that Danny had begun to lose his concentration on Grant's arguments, even as he judged them to be very compelling. The sensation of pressure from contact with Susan Mopper's knee was more compelling. She had filled the empty seat next to him during the talk.

"Our overall conclusion," Grant had summed up as Danny forced himself not to move his leg, "is that competition has been partially responsible for present-day properties of Darwin's finch communities. We further suggest it has been important in other guilds, including those of birds everywhere."

What had Susan meant by that knee contact? Danny still wondered now.

"BUT I MIGHT NOT GET PREGNANT," Ingrid's voice was in his head again.

"The island takes less than an hour to traverse end-to-end by foot," Grant was explaining, bringing Danny's thoughts back to the present. "Camping with a family held no special perils, and our daughters accompanied us after our first trip. It has continued every year since. I hope they benefit from it as much as you have from your time at Linsley Pond."

Maybe Grant was the person who might be able to set him on his feet again. Maybe he could join Grant in the Galapagos. Maybe—

Don Strong suddenly shouldered his way between them. Grant downed his drink and left without another word.

"Did I just see him sneer at you?" Danny asked.

"Won't drink whiskey with me, huh?" Strong laughed. "I think he's mad that I made fun of him this morning."

"What?"

"Did you hear Stan Faith calling out, Hey sailor, to people coming in?"

"That was him? It sounded like a woman's voice."

"Yeah. Perfect mimicry. He was in the room above the entrance, hiding behind the window curtain. He really got Grant."

And Strong flitted off again, leaving Danny alone with his thoughts.

For some reason, Danny pondered over his cadged drink, Simberloff rising to give the next talk had required him to be very circumspect about contact—or sight of—Susan's tan knee. He had crossed his legs and twisted them away from her, his eyes fixed on the podium.

"We have attempted to be scrupulous in not claiming that our results indicate either random colonization or absence of competition," Simberloff had stressed at the outset of his presentation, "only that certain patterns adduced in support of community-wide character displacement support a non-competitive alternative just as strongly."

Danny, although concentrating on Simberloff's words to the point that he now remembered them word for word, had nonetheless thrown a glance at Susan. Her eyes had stared straight ahead.

"I WON'T LET YOU KNOW IF I GET PREGNANT," the voice came back into his head.

"I would have viewed the efforts as successful," Simberloff had continued, "if they had simply fostered the practice of formulating null and alternative hypotheses and stating what observations would NOT be taken as supporting a particular view."

Maybe I shouldn't have pulled my knee away, Danny had thought.

"None of this says that island species are but random subsets," Simberloff had made certain to say after presenting an analysis using different statistical assumptions that mostly disagreed with Grant's. "Nor does this say that competition is not occurring." He had even been admitting that his new analysis did agree with some of Grant's. "On balance, there ARE aspects of Galapagos finches that are consistent with simple models of randomness and independence, and are consistent with competitive hypotheses. So we appear to agree that Galapagos ground finches are not random subsets, that interspecific competition is likely at least partially responsible for this, and that the strongest evidence resides in bill features of coexisting races and species."

Then Simberloff had conceded that "statistical analysis of various hypotheses is becoming increasingly difficult. Which returns me to my earlier suggestion, along with Grant and Abbott, that an experimental approach, if at all possible, is worth a major effort."

That had brought Danny's full attention back to the talk.

"Finally," Simberloff had said, "I wish to note that Peter Grant and Ian Abbott have scrupulously published most data on which they based their analysis, and have provided much relevant unpublished data."

Ian Abbott had been a postdoc on Grant's first summer on the Galapagos. He also worked and published in tandem with his wife. Danny did not know whether she had been a postdoc, too.

Jim Brown had piqued the island biogeograpers at Cornell, meaning those who worked on the mice and mites paper, with his study that used island biogeography theory to analyze small mammals on mountain tops out west. Danny had especially anticipated his talk from his first glance through the conference schedule. It turned out to be mostly on hummingbirds, instead.

"Why is there only one species in the Northeast," he whispered into Susan's ear. She had sat down beside him again. "Is it a better competitor than all other species that might otherwise survive that climate?"

Susan smiled and shrugged her shoulders. It was more fun to whisper in her ear, he thought, than listen to the lecture.

"If they specialize and compete on flowers," he tried again, "why aren't there other species in Vermont? Subdividing the resource?"

Again, a smile and a shrug.

"Perhaps the lack of immediate success should not be surprising," they heard Brown saying at the podium. "Ecological communities are perhaps the most complex of biological systems. Who ever thought it would be easy to find why there are so many species?"

"BUT I REALLY WANT TO KNOW IF SHE IS PREGNANT," he heard his own voice in his head.

Then Brown launched a full recap and defense of the MacArthurians.

"He gave us the complete MacArthur hagiography in his talk, didn't he?" Don Strong said as they filed out of the room.

Robert Colwell's presentation bowled Danny over. Colwell, with another Berkeley ecologist, David Winkler, had put together a computer simulation of island evolution. It was a game really, that they had created. It allowed them "to seed a series of virgin, replicate earths with primordial life and set the interspecific competition differently in each," in Colwell's words, "to see if we could tell them apart three billion years later by looking at biogeographical patterns."

It demonstrated—rather conclusively to Dan—that formulating null models that were free of any effects of competition or other biological factors was very difficult. But that was not what had caught his attention. He knew that already from his own work.

They called their program GOD. It had a subroutine to distribute species among islands. They called that WALLACE. The outcome of competition was determined by a subroutine named GAUSE. HENNIG determined the number of nodes in the evolutionary branches.

"Who's Hennig," Susan whispered in his ear with sweet, warm breath.

"A taxonomist. A taxonomy theoretician, in fact."

Their geography consisted of the Lack Archipelago, the Tallahassee Archipelago, the Kropotkin Archipelago—

"Kropotkin?"

It was another sweet whisper.

"Russian anarchist. Believed in altruism in nature."

—the Icarus Archipelago, and the Lack-Icarus and Icarus-Tallahassee Archipelagos. The names were almost descriptive. In the Lack Archipelago, "the ravages of competition," were tuned experimentally by Colwell and Winkler. The Tallahassee Archipelago had species that were reshuffled from the Lack Archipelago.

"I'D SAY WE WERE EVEN," Ingrid's voice came into his head again. "LET'S JUST GO OUR SEPARATE WAYS. I DON'T WANT TO KNOW IF YOU HAVE AIDS."

When Colwell got to the Linnean Quadrille, he had already lost Danny. He was by then totally absorbed in a reverie on a youthful attempt to simulate baseball statistics with a deck of playing cards. It had been just after he and Jewel had moved to Brattleboro. Shyness and loneliness had had him up in his room for hours.

Spades were base hits, he remembered, but for the deuce, which was an error. The spade face cards were doubles, the ace a home run, the ten a triple. Club face cards were walks, but the other clubs were fly balls, except for the ace, which sometimes was a home run and sometimes a fly ball, depending on the respective hitter and pitcher. And so on. If he used two decks and threw out some cards, he found he got a better match to the actual statistics of a baseball game. Many baseball games, in fact, but not to any actual players. So what did it say about baseball?

He wanted very much to play GOD. He would ask no more of it than entertainment.

"The problem is that Hutchinson and MacArthur never really took ecology away from the realm of natural history observations," Danny said to Michael Auerbach as they came together with Ed Connor in the courtyard at the next break. "They just dressed it up in sophisticated-sounding theory and impractical math."

"What finally got to you?" Mike asked.

"Hurlburt, I guess. Right at the start. He's the first Cornell PhD I've heard to question Hutchinson's ratio."

Don Strong came up excitedly to them with Dan Simberloff following close behind.

"Wait till you see this!" Don shouted, even though he was now abreast of them.

He waved a copy of *Oecologia* at them. It was a commercial journal. It was published completely for profit, which to Danny and others meant it lacked the same high standards of journals put out by the ESA and the American Society of Naturalists.

"Apparently, this is the about the same as what they are going to submit to our Proceedings," Strong groaned.

"What?"

"It's a paper by Gilpin and Diamond," Simberloff, by far the calmer of the two, came up from behind Strong to explain.

"I never read anything Diamond writes anymore, anyway," Ed Connor said to Danny as Auerbach huddled around the journal with the other two. "I have serious doubts about his work. I wrote him a letter in nineteen seventy-six asking for the species occurrences matrix for the Bismarck birds. He refused, saying that they were all in marginal notes and would be too difficult to compile for me. He had been publishing on that data for almost ten years by then, but somehow the data were in marginal notes."

"Something personal?" Danny asked.

"It's a bunch of bullshit!" Strong suddenly broke into a rant. "They claim again that we incorporate hidden effects of competition. That's total crap! That's just logically and statistically bullshit!"

He poked a finger at the offending passage in the journal.

"And listen to this!" he shouted, preparatory to reading from the paper. "We shall place the word null in quotes throughout this paper, lest the reader be lulled into accepting its implication of primacy for their particular hypothesis. What gall!"

"You're the one who argues for logical primacy," Simberloff said.

"And this stuff about checkerboard patterns!" Strong began another rant. "And look! He's accusing us of calling him a degenerate!"

"Degenerate?" Aurbach asked. "I don't remember that."

"A simplified case of a more complicated distribution," Simberloff tried to explain."

"A point is a degenerate line," Danny added.

"Oh yeah. That."

Strong threw his hands into the air, along with the journal, and went inside.

"I'm beginning to feel like Br'er Rabbit enmeshed in the Tar Baby," Simberloff stepped in for Don. "Every one of our attempts to clear things up seem only to elicit a mass of obfuscatory goo. I guess I can't get inside Diamond's head and know how he really feels about me personally, but my guess is he hates me. His response to Ed and my paper in nineteen seventy-nine—remember that Ed?"

"How could I not?"

"Plus some of his writings that led up to that paper," he said, sounding as if he were working out a puzzle. "It makes me think, quite frankly, he isn't much of a scientist. He just basically tells coherent stories. But I really don't know him. He no longer answers my letters. He probably doesn't even read them. With no briar patch in sight, our best option might just be to hope that ecologists read all the papers very carefully."

"Would you call him an ecopoet?" Danny offered.

"What?"

"Would you call Diamond an ecopoet? You know, like geologists use geopoetry for a good story that fits the facts but can never be proven."

Simberloff laughed.

"Interesting term," he said. "From things I heard about him from other people, I imagine he has really hated me from the outset. I guess I don't feel much about him personally, but I do think he's a poor scientist."

"Might that not have gotten back to him?"

"Yeah," said Simberloff, looking a bit suspiciously at him. "People do talk. Let's go in."

Then Simberloff stopped in mid-stride.

"You know Dan, I'm secure that whether my reputation is besmirched or not on specific points," he said, "that we are having a big effect on the way graduate research is done. The number of papers coming out that reflect our approach shows the impact we are having. And I hope you really let Dieter John have it tomorrow."

Danny said he guessed he would. When he went to his room, he went right to the phone. An unexpected male voice answered on Noe Street.

"Dan, I have some very bad news to tell you," James said. "Didn't you read the note I sent you?"

Oh, yeah, That. "Note?" Dan asked.

"It was on a post-it with the letter from Walt I sent on to you. Never mind. On Thursday, Walt became very sick and had to go to the hospital. His condition is deteriorating fast. They have him on a morphine drip and are giving him some oxygen to try to keep him comfortable. They only expect that he has two or three days and will only be lucid through tonight. His brother is flying in today. I have been calling his family and am exhausted."

He did not bother opening the envelope waiting for him.

Danny listened carefully to Bev Rathcke's presentation for no other reason than that one time she had breezed past him at John Gowan's farmhouse. And he was trying to get his mind off other things. The end of the conference, meaning his and Dieter John's talks, was only a few hours away.

Bev, too, started with MacArthur's quote about science being a search for repeated patterns. "In community ecology," she continued from that, "competition has been invoked as an explanation for patterns to such a degree that it is in danger of becoming a panchreston, a concept that can explain everything."

"A what?" came with warm breath into his ear.

"Panchreston. It's like a Danish. Garrett Hardin cooks them in Santa Barbara, I understand."

"He does not," Susan said aloud.

It drew glances from those around them. He felt good about the glances in the same way he had felt good when Ingrid used to squire him around Manhattan.

"AMEN," he heard himself saying to Ingrid in Jewel's attic room.

"When a theory can explain everything," Bev was continuing, "it loses its power and value because it is removed from the possibility of falsification." She acknowledged Popper on that, but, as was typical of the Tallahassee crew, she too made no mention of Robert Henry Peters.

That troubled Danny. Peters had laid out his ideas for ecology in that *Synthese* volume beside those of Simberloff and Strong. Why had the establishment in ecology entered into combat with Simberloff and Strong, but simply ignored Peters after an initial rash of rebuttals? Could it be because he was Canadian? Then he decided that was unlikely. American ecologists were apt to ignore European ecology, but they generally treated Canadians as their own. There was that common border to go with the common language. Was it, then, because Peters had scorned all of ecology's favorite scientific tenets and marginalized entire careers? Maybe that was why Simberloff had made it so very clear that he did not, in fact, reject the existence of competition or its ability to structure certain communities. It was just the evidence offered for it that he thought needed reexamining.

The model that Poole had developed for Bev's analysis, and that they had published in *Science*, depended on the ratio of the variances in the data. He knew the statistical term well, but he had trouble putting a meaning to it in the reality of nature. Poole and others, Jonathan Roughgarden, he thought, for example, seemed to use statistical error not to guide them in finding limits to data, but as some substantiated property of reality.

Stuart Pimm was a former Brit who went from Oxford to the University of New Mexico, much as Mark Westoby had gone to Utah State, to be able to study grasslands and deserts. He was currently in transition from Texas Tech to the University of Tennessee, according to gossip Danny had overheard at Oak Ridge. Pimm had published a ton of material on niche overlap at first, but had recently switched to food webs. He defined his communities vertically, instead of laterally.

And why not? Danny thought and prepared to listen.

But Pimm's talk deteriorated into analysis of mathematical models based on the logistic equation, as infirm ground in Danny's opinion as the fog of error that is statistical variance. Pimm's conclusion was that perturbing densities, rather than carrying capacities modeled stochastic effects on birds better. It held little meaning for Danny. He guessed that the result argued against competition, which was normally interpreted as being part of the carrying capacity, the K, of the logistic growth equation. And that tie to K was enough to his mind to condemn Pimm's entire analysis to oblivion.

Mike Auerbach's presentation followed. He had done the study entirely on his own, entirley outside of his thesis work. What was more remarkable, though, was the reception it got from someone at the back of the room. It began right from the start of the talk, when Auerbach dismissed Lyapunov analysis, which pretty much dismissed all of stability analysis. Lyapunov functions and functionals, Dan knew from a graduate reactor design course he had suffered through with Bill at Penn, were what nuclear reactor design was all about.

The mumbled griping continued throughout Auerbach's talk. Danny could not recognize a Tallahassee voice from it.

"Why is he going on and on with this?" was something that did reach his ears.

Danny finally turned around to look, fearing to find Dieter John glaring back at him. Instead, it was Bob May who was fussing and fuming.

"Why is he spending so much time on this?"

Had a promising career, Auerbach's, just come to an end?

John Wiens stared out a window, waiting for his talk to begin. He was from Colorado State, a convert to the Tallahassee way of thinking. He was a bird man with sad eyes and a happy smile.

"They look so small to me," he said to Fran James about the redwing blackbirds that were monopolizing the bird feeder at the window. "They're almost like a separate species."

"Yes," she agreed. "that is what I keep saying. In many species, the birds are smaller in Florida than elsewhere in the US."

Arid climate birds of the same species were supposed to be larger than humid climate ones, Danny knew, but he kept it to himself. The phenomenon had a name, he remembered, maybe Gloger's Rule. It had to do with water loss somehow, he seemed to remember from one of Chabot's classes—or had it been Ricklefs'?

He wandered toward the back again. His eyes flitted from place to place, looking for Susan Mopper's and hoping not to come across Dieter John's, now that the time for their confrontation was finally at hand.

There's not much Susan could want from a failed Cornell PhD known to have been exposed to AIDS, he decided. Who would? He sat down all alone and listened as the unassuming Wiens shocked him with what only months before, he would have seen as character assassination.

"MacArthur's definition of a community as any set of organisms currently living near each other, and about which it is interesting to talk, may be operationally useful, but it is biologically sterile," is how Wiens put it.

A comment by another Australian, Peter Sale, also struck a chord. It had to do with how the Odums' study of Eniwetak assumed it to be at equilibrium. Of course, that was right in keeping with the superorganism.

Instead of a break after Wiens' talk, Fran James announced that she had arranged for everyone to have the opportunity to go on Wakulla Spring's famous "jungle cruise." An extra-long break had been scheduled, seemingly hastily and pushing Dan's talk back an hour, so that everyone would be able to take a guided boat tour of the spring and the surrounding swamp forest.

"It's really worthwhile," Fran urged. "It's a glass-bottomed boat. It has a canopy to keep you in the shade."

Everyone filed out almost immediately and headed toward the dock. Danny happened to climb into the tour boat next to Stuart Hurlburt.

"I can't believe what I just overheard," Hurlburt surprised him by speaking to him without any preliminaries, even though they were not acquainted. "A group of graduate students were pondering aloud how many faculty positions in community ecology would be opened up by a well-placed bomb at this meeting."

"How many?" Danny pondered aloud.

Hurlburt laughed heartily. They found seats together.

"Are you a grad student, too?" Hurlburt asked midway through the tour.

"Worse. Homeless former faculty."

"Where?"

"UCLA."

Hurlburt was suitably impressed, as had everyone Danny had ever met outside of UCLA been on his answer to the same question. Meanwhile, the boat's operator, an elderly black man also acting as tour guide, was making announcements in a magnificently stentorian southern voice.

"And ovah yondah on the bank you got yer big ol' alliGATOR," he pointed out a basking creature late in the tour. "Dat deah is a li'l blue heron. Dey build dey nests out of sticks in trees an' such. See? Dey look like dey's sitting on platforms. Deah nesting colonies also have great blue herons in them. Dey can coexist with the great blue heron only 'cause their beaks are in a ratio of one to one-point-three."

A titter went through the crowd in the boat. The tour guide pretended confusion. They were almost back to the dock.

"Y'all may be wondrin' why it is dat da limkin can coexist wid da white ibis. Wahl, da ratio of da limpkin beak be one point four!"

Pandemonium broke out on the boat and from the dock. Danny rose from his seat, threw his hands into the air, shouted "Arggh!" and did a backwards belly-whopper into the water as several of the other passengers barely held on to avoid a similar dunking.

"There you have it," he said on climbing onto the dock. "Controversy settled! I don't float, so I must not be a witch."

Fran James watched with a Cheshire cat grin. Both birds were about the same size and had similar conspicuously curved long beaks. She winked at the tour passengers as they marched past her. Until that wink, no one knew that she had arranged it all with the tour guide. After the many tours she had sent his way, he said it was the least he could do when she had handed him her revision of his scripted talk that morning.

Instead of Dieter John, Don Strong was in front of what was left of the crowd.

"I have some sad—very sad—news to—to share with you, I'm afraid," he announced from the podium. "I've been trying all morning and yesterday to find out what was delaying Dieter John. Now, I have the sad duty of telling you that Dieter will not be here. We are canceling his talk and the talk by Dan Atkins that follows. I'm sure all of you, especially Danny—are you out there? OK?—will understand."

He took a deep breath like it was a slug of whiskey.

"According to the California Highway Patrol, Dieter John crashed his Maserati yesterday on Highway 46 near Paso Robles. It was daylight, morning, in fact. He had had to swerve to avoid a truck that had pulled out in front of him and crashed into a trailer at one hundred thirty miles per hour. He died instantly, or almost so in the ensuing fire."

It was James Dean's death repeated. Dan was not listening. He was heading to the parking lot in his wet clothes. He thought he would drive north. Just drive.

VI

DEAR Jewel,

It pleases me to try to let you know "What Danny might have gotten himself into in Tallahassee," as you put it. I have been giving much thought to writing a paper on the matter. Consider this a rough first draft on which I would like your comments.

The substantive, superficially simple issue is whether and to what degree interspecific competition occurs in nature and how important it may be in determining which sets of species occupy particular regions. No one denies that intersp comp occurs at least in some places and some times. No one denies that it might partially determine the presence or absence of particular species in particular localities. This, of course, has been assumed for the past hundred years at least. It has also been apparent, at least since Darwin, that ecological niche requirements, the tolerance limits of your mentor, Professor Shelford, predation, intraspecific comp, and historical accident all must be considered, along with interspecific comp, in accounting for the distribution of kinds of organisms. What is also at issue here is whether or not the assertions that have been made about the importance of intersp comp in nature stand up to criteria of significance derived from the works of certain philosophers of science. The issues are therefore of importance beyond the boundaries of biogeography and ecology.

This so fascinated me 30 yr ago that I chose ecology as a career over philosophy, which was a very real alternative for me at that time. My choice was aided by the unpleasant air of conviction and argumentativeness that seemed to characterize philosophers, which contrasted with the gentler and more imaginative attitudes of biologists. The situation has now changed. Some ecologists see themselves as warriors against complacent illusion and in that sense seem more concerned with philosophical issues than they are with biology. There is an ongoing strong exchange on the statistical evaluation of island zoogeography data.

I am uncomfortable when polemics occur in science. What prompted it, and how can we extricate ourselves so that we can get on with our central business?

As you know, theoretical mathematical modeling in ecology and evolution has a history of more than a century. Starting in the early 1960s there was an effulgence of speculative mathematical modeling of intersp comp, encouraged by Hutch and influenced strongly by his students, especially Robert MacArthur, and by the curious attitude exemplified by Richard Levins, who stated that mathematical models could not simultaneously maximize precision, generality, and "reality," as he put it. Models were seen as ways of aiding the development of intuition, not necessarily as ways of generating testable predictions. Robert's theoretical models were expected to conform to facts in a general way, but it was assumed that he left out large bits of world, in the interest of mathematical tractability, and in exchange would gain in insight. The potential difficulties of this approach, in which esthetics was at least as important as predictive power, was immediately obvious. I pointed out back in 1960 that Gause's axiom was untestable. Other theoretical problems were inherent in MacArthur's excessively freewheeling approach to theory construction.

Nevertheless, his work and that of his circle was enormously stimulating. Reasonably formal theories were constructed about a nonexistent simulacrum of the ecological world. That is, formality was possible, but the relation to nature was unclear. Given the rather loose ground rules for acceptability of theoretical constructs, there was a rapid development of mathematical models purporting to predict, within loose limits, how many species would occupy a particular island, how niche characteristics should change as a consequence of how many species co-occurred, and so on. The style of optimistic theorization spread widely, and the sixties and seventies saw an explosion of speculative ecology. By the late seventies, however, it had become much more difficult to develop *charming speculations about ecology. Too many bright young assistant professors and their students had walked over the grounds.*

Others and I had been dubious about this approach for several decades, thus my absence from Marlboro that time you often write to me about, but these complaints focused on theoretical problems rather than empirical examples and in this sense were more fulminations. I must say that the role of fulminator was lonely and unpleasant. By the mid-seventies most of us turned to other things. In addition, many papers had appeared in which the promise of enhanced insight seemed to be fulfilled. For example, the MacArthur memorial volume contained papers on insular distributions which implied that results were forthcoming, despite methodological flaws. These results were not usually intended to be tests of theory but were investigations of natural history suggested by the theories, during which the investigators would become fascinated by biological peculiarities rather than staying on the path of rigorous hypothesis testing. Simberloff and his colleagues have been the most recent and articulate opponents to such speculative theory. They have been extremely valuable in analyzing the empirical data more carefully. They have, however, gone well beyond, as you will see.

I must now turn from ecology. In the early 1970s, two books, one on the history and the other on the philosophy of science, became popular reading for biologists. Kuhn's on scientific "revolutions" and Popper's on the relation between science and testability not only were widely read but generated groups of converts. Conversions of many kinds have been part of the Zeitgeist of the past decade. Kuhn presented historical evidence that science has progressed in a stepwise fashion, with relatively long "paradigmatic" periods punctuated by "revolutions during which old paradigms are rejected and radically new questions, methodologies, and answers become the center of the discipline. Popper's central concern was the role and meaning of testability in science. In brief, scientific discourse was superior to nonscientific discourse because of this testability. This assertion is neither invalid nor novel, nor can it be simplistically applied. Just as the long and complex arguments of Darwin and Wallace were taken out into the world as a set of mottoes about natural selection resulting in survival of the fittest, Popper's "true believers" have their mottoes.

"Science consists of refutation of hypotheses," "If assumptions are not being tested we are talking tautologies," and so on. Once these are accepted in all their simplicity, it is an easy matter to undertake bellicose destructive criticism of even the most significant biological advances.

The position of Popper in British philosophy of science is that of a late exponent of the analytical school of philosophy characterized by its concern for language and formalism. Unfortunately, formalism never worked well for biology. Biometry, for example, is highly formal but has no biological content in its own right. Biological systems must be "simplified" before they can be formalized. Mere narrative or anecdote, the kind of thing that fills the pages of Darwin, is not really in shape for philosophical analysis until it is stripped of ambiguity and can be stated in language so pure and mathematics-like that it deserves the name of "formal" but has lost a great deal of its theoretical impact. Attempts to avoid simplification when dealing formally with biological subject matter may become so abstruse as to be predictively sterile. Population dynamics and population genetics do contain central theories which are highly formal and mathematically concise, at the cost of requiring extreme simplifying assumption. Perhaps discussions of general questions of ecology and evolution cannot be highly formal without simplifying assumptions, but as we shall see, even the meaning of "assumption" as used in ecology and evolution is often misunderstood.

Some of the arguments arise when critics insist on what they believe to be proper biometric standards being applied to other people's data. This insistence is in itself commendable, but there is no clear consensus on the meaning of the word "proper" in this situation. Moreover, much of the polemic seems to arise from attempting verbally to fill the gap between narrow mathematical theory and the richness of the natural world—as if verbalizations could extend a formal theory beyond the domain delimited by its assumptions and boundary conditions. Often the precise meanings and derivations have been forgotten in the process.

Many recently published evolutionary and ecological polemics tend to be so informal as to resemble medieval theological disputes, arguments in courts of law, or discussions between rival schools of psychoanalysis more than they resemble physics or *mathematics. The opinions of philosophers are often invoked, but it should be recalled that philosophers of science have primarily functioned as analysts, describing scientific history, rather than as authorities of the path science ought to take. The use of philosophy of science as an assay for scientific fineness therefore deserves careful thought. Is there a scientific standard for choosing Popper over Feyerabend?*

Obviously, the questioning of empirical, or philosophical, paradigms and the refusal to accept traditional doctrines slavishly is a healthy sign. Unfortunately, while I am impressed by the cleverness and combativeness of the arguments and counterarguments, I do not have the sense that I am learning very much about plants and animals.

I can now turn to an analysis of the actual arguments. A focal concept is whether or not "hypotheses" are being properly tested. In the history of science the term "hypothesis" has been successfully used in several different ways. It is sometimes used in the term "null hypothesis" so familiar even to undergraduate bio majors and sometimes as in "one of the hypotheses of evolutionary theory is that . . . ." In the second usage, the term "hypothesis" melts into the term "assumption" and, to further complicate the problem, in biology the word "assumption" is used in at least two contradictory senses. We may "assume" things whose existence is not at all certain, or we may "assume" things that are completely obvious. Mendel did the first, "assuming" the existence of hereditary factors, Darwin and Wallace did the second, "assuming" the whole pool of data of natural history and zoogeography, as known at the time, as a starting point. Confusion between the two is a wonderful starting point for erudite nonsense.

It is Mendel's kind of theory that is taken as a model by Popper. If experimentation showed that no such hereditary entities exist, Mendel's theory is falsified. To falsify Darwin's theory requires that some counterexample be found—an organism or structure or function which is inexplicable by evolutionary mechanisms, but was explicable on the assumption that evolutionary mechanisms either did not occur at all or were irrelevant in the case at issue. A large share of evolutionary literature since then has been concerned with examinations of possible cases, and so far none have survived careful examination.

In the Mendelian type of theory, there are a small number of clear theoretical steps leading from an undemonstrated set of assumptions to a set of empirical conclusions. Falsification of these conclusions would falsify the assumptions. In the Darwin-Wallace type of theory, the assumptions are known to be empirically valid before theory construction commences. When conclusions of this type of theory are falsified, it is not the initial assumptions which are being denied, but rather the logical procedure of going from these assumptions to the conclusions. Treating these two types of theory as if they were the same thing or, worse, jumping between meanings of the term "assumption" several times during an argument, can lead to confusion, which can hardly avoid generating polemic.

The Mendelian type of theory and the Darwinian type of theory differ in the epistemological status of the assumptions that act as the beginning points for the construction of the theory. There is a third kind of assumption, the assumption of working "null hypotheses."

As you probably already know, there are at least two kinds of ambiguity in drawing conclusions from statistical significance tests. First, a small probability of being wrong does not correspond to a certainty of being correct, so that all conclusions are contingent ones. Also, while one may assign a probability that some particular null hypothesis may be discarded as invalid, this provides no information at all about the wisdom of discarding any of the infinite number of hypotheses that will fit the data as well as, or better than, the hypothesis that was being tested. These ambiguities permitted no one less authoritative than Sir Ronald Fisher to denigrate data purporting to show the unhealthy effects of tobacco smoking, and is why the early warnings on cigarette packages said that they "may" be dangerous to health.

The meaning and usefulness of null hypotheses has become a more serious problem since the development of cheap, rapid computer technology. Prior to this the only null hypothesis distributions available were those calculated from analytically tractable models. Now, Monte Carlo procedures permit arithmetical derivations of distributions from almost any tractable model. In particular, it is possible to generate distributions of numbers from what might be called "biological null models," that is, from stochastic models which roughly mimic a biological theory but in which one or more biological suppositions have been replaced by an alternative or antithetical one. Data which an author may have considered to strengthen his belief in some theoretical argument, on the basis of a routine biometric significance test, may then be shown not to be significantly different from the expectations of some other null hypothesis, based on more or less biological assumptions.

What I believe in all this confusion, Jewel, is that theories or models may be said to be "competitive" if they make similar kinds of assertions about the same empirical phenomena, but these assertions are not the same. For example, two theories may differ in their form and in their boundary conditions and yet both make assertions about, say, the number and location of hydra. In these cases there are several ways of deciding which is the "better" theory.

A possible conclusion from the arguments I have presented is that null hypothesis testing, while an eminently useful procedure, is not a simple guide to scientific advance or to the choice between competing theories. I think you might agree with me that if there were strong economic or, better yet, military consequences hinging on the scientific community's consensus as to the role of interspecific competition, the issue would be less contentious. There would be funds for extremely careful field studies on many more systems. Lacking this, we must find other ways through the morass.

If competing theories are sufficiently formal, it is possible to examine the logical consistency of the set of initial assumptions. For example, any theory with mutually contradictory assumptions can be discarded, since mutually contradictory assumptions imply all conclusions, and in that sense disqualify the theory from scientific discourse. Theories in biology, as contrasted with those in mathematics or pure logic, are often so informal that there is no way of even listing explicitly all of the assumptions made, let alone testing their mutual consistency, so that this criterion may not be useful. The usual understanding of what has been accomplished by comparing the conclusions of some particular theory with those of a null hypothesis is that failure to reject the null hypothesis is equivalent to asserting the irrelevance of that theory to the particular situation. This is not equivalent to asserting that the theory which generated the null hypothesis ought to be substituted for the theory in question. However, a modification of this understanding has become the basis for polemic argument.

An alternative criterion of the relative value of two competing theories is their relative "richness." If two theories are statistically equivalent in their predictions in one overlapping portion of their domains, but one of them can be shown to have a much larger predictive domain, this one is a richer, and therefore preferable, theory. Consider the possibility that ad hoc randomized models designed to fit, say, the zoogeographic data from a single archipelago, and not making predictions about anything else, work very well. In fact, they may fit the data better than theories based on natural selection or competition. Nevertheless, their domain of prediction may be so narrow that while they may be useful, they cannot be accepted as disproofs of richer theories, unless and until their domains can be expanded in a formal way to match those of their competitors. Notice that this standard differs from that of an elementary statistics course, in which the only consideration is the fit of very specific quantitative null hypotheses to very narrowly defined data sets.

Extremely important issues have been raised around the relation between working scientists and their chroniclers, the philosophers and historians of science. Much is, to my mind, based on misconstruction of philosophy. My fundamental complaint, Jewel, is not that it contains some childish philosophy, but rather that it exemplifies a kind of argument which is likely to stand in the way of more interesting research. It may represent an irremediable decay of ecology to the level of factionalism that has impeded the advance of psychiatry and some of the social sciences. If polemic becomes the norm for ecology, as it may have done already, there is no reason why bright students such as your nephew should elect to join us. Enough said for that.

Then I wonder whether it is possible that such questions as, "What determines the number of species in one locality?" or "How do higher taxa evolve?" are simply too large to be amenable to theoretical formulation. Is it possible that the big questions of ecology and evolution are simply too big to be answered? Might not the insights to be derived from an extremely careful analysis of the distribution of a particular group of organisms permit the construction of a richer theory than attempting to deal with all *organisms at once? But whether a question is of the right size to be answered is easier to determine in the past of science than in its future.*

The primary value of polemic is that it encourages very careful reading of published work. The primary danger of polemic is that science melts into rhetoric, and public approbation is taken as a sign of victory, even in ecology. Natural resource management, pollution studies, care of endangered species, pest control, and other areas of applied ecology, all seem capable of proceeding without resolving the quarrels between the opposing camps, just as medicine proceeded without ever knowing the meaning of life.

In short, Popperism, like early Puritanism, has been refreshing in certain ways but has not been completely salubrious. How necessary is it for scientists consciously to live within externally imposed canons? I believe that we can continue to walk forward, guided by an intellectual fascination with organisms and by the fact that false conclusions in science have the marvelous property that eventually they are found out if they deal with real problems and are forgotten if they do not. We can progress like the metaphoric centipede, and let philosophers marvel at how we do it.

I hope this can be of help to you. As for the personalities involved, I am afraid that I may be no better judge than you or your nephew.

Please, Jewel, keep writing to me with your questions. Your thoughts help me crystallize my own.
Yours,
Larry S

VII

LARRY Abele happened to be the one called to the Pastime Tavern's phone. Everyone thought it was his weekly call from the Smithsonian. Being heavily invested in a billiards game, as he called it, Larry passed the phone to Nick Gotelli.

"Atkins! Geez! It's been some time. Almost a semester?"

"Something like that."

"What happened? You left so abruptly."

"Well, one thing that's happened is that I've just gotten around to reading the round table issue of the Naturalist on null models. I have some ideas about Roughgarden's article I just had to share."

"You can imagine the reaction here," Nick broke in. "People are still arguing about it. The day it came out, there were people out in the hall shouting."

"Let me guess what," Dan said. "How could they publish such bullshit? Right?"

"Something like that. Where are you calling from?"

"A rest stop on Interstate Ninety-One. So who is the Suppie guy?"

"Soupay, I think it is. A philosopher. We know little about him. He's no Thomas Kuhn. Ninety-one? Are you in New Hampshire?"

"Vermont."

"Ah! Very mysterious. Quite like you, too. So let me give you my take on Suppe. He claims that philosophers other than Popper are no longer concerned with an objective scientific method. They are trying to make sense of reality through a haze of text deconstruction, semiotics, and moral relativism. Science to them is no different than any other human activity, poetry, for example. Lakatos is who we're reading right now. He generally agrees with Popper but thinks that young sciences should be given some leeway on strict falsification. You've missed some great discussions we've had late nights at the Pastime. Are you coming back?"

"Nope!" Dan replied in a way he hoped would make it clear that no more in explanation was forthcoming. "The way I see the Roughgarden article is that he makes these four basic complaints about criticisms coming out of Tallahassee. I see them as, One, Damn that referee! That's what you just pointed out. He claims there is no scientific method. No rules. Point two is, My star player is better than yours. Three, That rule doesn't make any sense, anyway. And four, My team has a better record than yours. That's just like losing a soccer game but still claiming to be a better team, even given the score."

"Hmm. Funny."

"What about Ludwig Wittgenstein? He's point two of my analogy."

"A strange choice." Nick said. "Wittgenstein may have been the giant of twentieth century philosophy, as Roughgarden describes him, but Wittgenstein never made any serious inquiries into scientific method. Wittgenstein and Popper were on opposite ends of a philosophical spectrum. Wittgenstein's was the end that was totally bereft of modern science. To Wittgenstein, language—in particular puzzles posed by language, not science or mathematics—was the only material suited for philosophical studies. His opinions on science are therefore immaterial. Besides Roughgarden's choice of Wittgenstein as an authority on method in science being an odd one, so was that quotation from Wittgenstein in the article. It had everything to do with language and nothing with science."

"Science has in the past made actual progress through flights of fancy, though," Dan said. "How about Kekule's dream of a snake biting its tail? He wakes up next morning with the mystery of the structure of benzene solved."

"But how common are such conceptual leaps? And the ones that do succeed are most often launched from a solid platform of data. Don't forget MacFadyen's tyranny of bright ideas, Danny."

"Yeah. It's probably fortunate that the nightmares suffered by scores of other chemists all over the world were left to remain dreams. Those of ecologists, however, seem to flood the pages of our journals."

Dan heard some sort of commotion.

"Atkins!" Don Strong then shouted into the phone. "You bastard! You have to come back! You have to protect me from Skip Livingston. He attacked me in the hall. He would never attack you. He tore the shirt off my back, like physically. You can ask Anne Thistle! Did I deserve that?"

"What Skip is doing along the Apalachicola River for a cleaner Gulf shames me in comparison to what little good for the environment I've ever accomplished," Dan said. "I'm glad to hear Ann Thistle is still fulfilling her primary role of bearing witness to his proclamations, even though they were loud enough to be heard all the way down the hall into the veal stalls. And for some reason, they were repeated, sometimes three or four times. Only your bird was louder."

"So, have you heard the bad news?"

"The parrot died?"

"No. Macho's fine, but there's a funereal gloom enveloping the ground floor of Conradi because Larry Abele's grant was shot down. Devout MacArthurians are all in powerful positions in powerful universities. Larry's is not the only one that's happened to. Yet they're the ones who complain the loudest that they are being discriminated against."

"Nick must be disconsolate," Dan said. "And I know how Larry feels. As painful as the process was, I felt cheated at never having been allowed to go through the NSF tragedy beyond the production of a proposal."

"Writing a proposal is an accomplishment in its own right. One page per thousand dollars is the current rule of thumb. Sometimes I think they take up as much time to prepare as to actually do the research."

"As an interdepartmental appointee, my NSF proposal died at UCLA just before deadline when the Dean of Engineering decided he could not formally commit any of the school's resources, as he put it. He was talking about the desk and office I was already occupying. Can you imagine that?"

"You may have been fortunate. At least that saved you a midnight trip to have the material postmarked ahead of the deadline."

The grant, Dan knew, had been intended as much for Nick to do his thesis work as for Larry. Without the grant, there not only was no money for equipment, supplies, or travel, there also was no money for a stipend. That was an issue of not paying his rent, or running his car, or eating, even.

"This is the second time NSF has turned Larry down," Nick came back on the phone to say. "I really, really wanted to study that epifauna. There is a big community of sponges and other invertebrates that occurs on mangrove prop roots in the tropics, but we don't really have the money to do that, now. What is really upsetting are the reviewer's comments, though. Larry showed them to me. We got vicious, vicious grant reviews again. I mean some really nasty, unbelievable stuff. In fact, Larry told me that he is kind of considering retooling and basically leaving community ecology and focusing all of his effort on systematics."

"Ah, the National Science Foundation," Dan said. "Why is it such a preferred source of funding for ecologists, particularly untenured ones? NSF grants are as important as publications.

They're like seals of approval, as much a badge of being a player in the scientific academy as an Oscar is in the movie academy."

"And it's a vicious circle," Nick added. "Without publications, you can't get an NSF grant. Without a grant, you can't do research to publish."

"Did I ever tell you that Pimentel used to apply for funds for research that he had already mostly done, so he could then use that funding to start on entirely new research?"

"I'm not surprised. I hear that NSF reviewers rejected a proposal on the basis that it could never possibly work," Nick added. "Well, it turns out that the chemist had already done the synthesis he proposed."

"And as important as grant funding is to us, it's just as important to the universities."

"Yeah, they take a cut off the top. Overhead costs at FSU add almost fifty percent to the funding requested."

"Sort of non-profit profit, huh?" Then Danny asked suddenly, "Could you put Dan on the phone?"

"Not sure he's here. I'll go take a look. You're on a pay phone? Give me the number and I'll call you back."

"It's long distance either way."

"Yeah, but we don't have to put quarters in."

Program officers, Dan mused as he turned toward the relieved faces of others waiting to use the phone, can make or break a proposal. They are the ones who choose reviewers for the grant application. The reviewers duties are to grade each proposal based on criteria that constantly changes due to Congressional directives, but generally includes the perceived ability of the researcher (a track record of successful research is de rigueur), the quality and importance of the research proposed, the sufficiency of the funds allotted to it, and the quality of the proposal itself. Supposedly. On the other hand, Stuart Little once told Dan that when he judged whether a proposal should be funded, he looked only at who was asking for the money and how much it was.

Only one person was now at the phone, but to Dan's annoyance, she seemed to be settling in for a long conversation.

On advice from Fred Turner, Dan had sent copies of his NSF proposal for pre-review to Dan Cody and Jared Diamond. Their comments became irrelevancies through the action of the Dean, but he now wondered if he had sent it to the right people. The most valuable opinion, he knew, was from colleagues who understood the research fully because they were involved in it themselves. In other words, competitors. But that could lead to having ideas—and full proposals—stolen or turned down or both. Or simply being given bad advice. It was all known to have happened, even though the stories of specific cases that went around sounded more like legends in their vagaries than real events. They were often told by someone who knew someone who knew the actual details. But not always.

The phone was now free. Would it ring? Or had Nick not found Simberloff? Or had, but been discouraged by busy signals?

Much more prevalent in the grant business was the situation in which a reviewer turned out to be an intellectual and personal enemy who used his anonymity to cloak himself from retribution. That was what had happened to Larry's proposal.

The pay phone rang. Don Strong's voice came from it. He had a university phone credit card, Dan remembered.

"So much of the problem with ecology and evolution is that it's so incestuous," Don said almost before Dan could get in a greeting. "Theory suigenerisly repeats and compounds mathematics borrowed from physical sciences. And they're all deterministic. How's that? I don't think Dan is here, but you should know that I can make statements that are just as pithy as his, if that's what you're looking for."

"But nature's stochastic," Dan laughed.

"Obversely," Don started again, "just as much of the problem is phenomenological empiricism, which goes on its own taxonomic or habitat-centered way, blithe with narrative accounts, and assiduously avoids the testing of hypotheses. That's just the kind of research they want to fund."

"I want to keep doing community ecology," Gotelli came back on the phone as Dan was still parsing Strong's words. "Did I tell you I'm switching to Simberloff for my PhD? I can just work on the population dynamics of a couple of subtidal marine invertebrates here in the Gulf. Drive to my research sites."

Disappointment in his voice belied the hopeful words.

"So, how are you doing?" Nick then asked.

"Well, I've escaped the yoke of the physics labs I had to teach. That's good. I hated them. Having to think about physics took away from thinking about ecology. And it's great to no longer have to face those questions from undergrads. You know, why is an ecology PhD and former UCLA prof like me doing teaching their lab? I hated that. It was absolutely demeaning."

"Yeah, I guess it's good to be out from under that. So how are your prospects now?"

"You know, Nick, I was just thinking about Strong's remark about MacArthurians being in powerful positions," Dan said, ignoring the question. "Gene Odum is at Georgia and Howard at the University of Florida, hardly powerful positions, but they are hardly MacArthurians. Hutchinson is still technically at Yale. MacArthur had been at Penn and Princeton. May is at Princeton. Richard Levins is at Harvard. Jared Diamond is at UCLA. Jonathan Roughgarden is at Stanford. Is it something like Ivy League versus you guys in a southern university?"

"Absolutely," Nick said. "That's exactly how we all see it."

"It should make it easy for a biased program officer to choose who to send the proposal out to for review." When Nick made no comment, Dan asked, "But didn't you choose Florida State to get into a good intellectual fight?"

"I wanted to do marine biology," Nick disagreed. "When I visited Florida State I had never even heard of Dan Simberloff. He was not mentioned in any Berkeley classes, even though Rob Colwell was busily at work at the time trying to find a way to bring down the whole idea of null models. He was one of my professors."

"Not a word about null models had come to your ears?"

"Not a word. I was finally told by the person who had suggested I go to Florida State that there is this island biogeography nut out of Florida, Dan Simberloff, and he's an interesting person. So, when I got here, I had not seen or heard of null models, or any of this work. There is a sense, you know, that Florida State is very different and distinct from all the other American universities. In fact, it seems that the people who think the most like us are actually all outside of the US. You must have felt that at the conference."

"So, what about Roughgarden's point that null hypotheses are not easily and reliably developed?" Dan returned to his point three. "Fabricating random communities has itself never been tested, according to him. There is little to guide an investigator in the nuances of choosing a null model. Given those difficulties, why use them?"

"Are you reading right from the article? Do you have the Naturalist in your hands?"

"Yeah."

"In the phone booth?"

"Actually, it's a little more than a phone booth, but back to the point, why use null models if good ones are so hard to make?"

"There is another point of view about what to do when the going gets tough, Atkins," Strong's voice shocked Dan, who thought Gotelli was still on the phone. "Community ecology is challenging. Those who accept the challenge have no excuse for complaining about its difficulty. I forgot who said that. It might have been me. And long distance rates are pretty steep!"

"Is that why the whole thing has been described as a barroom brawl?"

"Barroom brawl? Hell no! It's more like Br'er Rabbit and the Tar Baby. Every—"

"Hey, that's my line, and you did deserve it from Skip," Simberloff said, now on the phone, but talking to Strong. "He accused me of turning you against him."

"Your line?" Strong could be heard in the background.

Then there were muffled noises, perhaps violent.

"But listen to this," Dan continued undistracted, "I think Roughgarden was confused by the frictionless pulley he invoked in his defense of mathematical ecology. He must have been inspired by Robert May and his perfect crystal, but you know, had May used a pendulum instead, his analogy would have broken down. In theory, you don't need anything more than a string for pendulum motion, but in the real world, if a string doesn't weigh enough to push through the air, there is no pendulum. Friction with air becomes critical. That's why the bob. Ecology theorists, meanwhile, are doing away with the pendulum bob because it's too difficult to model."

"Some might say that a bobless pendulum demonstrates the necessity of a bob for motion," Simberloff said. "Without a mathematical model, we supposedly would not have known. Anyway, that's what the modelers always say!"

"I heard Si Levin say something like that once." But Danny knew he was losing Simberloff's attention. "I have heard you call him He of the Hundred Thousand Fish Stomachs," Danny could hear someone, possibly Simberloff, shouting in the background. Gotelli was back on the phone.

"Oh, my field site is on the coast near Alligator Point," Nick ignored the commotion to say. "You've been there. Once the small number of tourists leave at the end of summer, I can walk for miles in either direction on pristine sand beaches without another soul around. But I do have to watch out for drug dealers. Don found bales of marijuana piled up on one of his experimental Spartina islands. And when the authorities make drug busts in those tiny coastal villages, they often arrest the most prominent citizens. Mayor and chief of police once."

"I like how Simberloff answered Roughgarden's contention that May's discovery of chaos in Lotka-Volterra equations was enhancing the stature of ecology, as he put it," Dan tried to get back to his four points.

"You mean in the Naturalist issue? About how it might exist only in the impression that ecologists were speaking the language of mathematics, even if ill applied, rather than Latin? That was clever."

Yeah, and physics envy is not limited to ecology, Dan thought, angry at himself for not having thought that while Simberloff was still on the line. Neither should physics envy be a curse. Newton may not have been so remarkably more intelligent than Darwin. The physicists just solved all of the easy problems first, the ones that actually were suited to their Cartesian methods. Ecologists have harder problems to solve. Dan thought all that, but kept it to himself.

"I still have no lab space," Nick continued over Dan's silence. "Once a month, I have to process my formalin-preserved ascidian samples with a borrowed dissecting scope at my desk. It doesn't make me very popular with my office mates."

"Tell them all hello for me," Dan, realizing he had nothing more to say nor any reason to say it, ended the conversation.

Lincoln Vt

JEWEL was gone. She had not even had the opportunity to see the farmhouse he had purchased in the mountains above Bristol. It had a bedroom downstairs and room at the kitchen door for a wheelchair ramp, but more importantly for Aunt Jewel, Dan thought, it stood on a high meadow with a view like the one from Ames Hill. Now it was up to him to make a home of it.

He would keep the lake house, he thought. It remained furnished with Jewel's things, most of which she had bought with Jonathan for Ames Hill. They would keep her presence there always.

After her funeral was finished, after her affairs had been put in order, after a suitable period of mourning to unburden his grief, Dan sat down at his laptop for a final duty. She had left no will, no final words to him. But there were letters that he had not yet read.

On turning on the laptop, he clicked on the token for his Internet browser—a daily habit he had accidentally not suppressed. He chose to click through the headlines on the *Science* site that he used as his home page.

It was Sir Robert McCredie May now, Dan noted. He had been knighted and had just been given a life peerage. He was Baron May of Oxford. He was also a fellow of Merton College, Oxford, Dan read, and President of The Royal Society.

May had gone from MacArthur's chair in Princeton to Newton's chair in London, Dan mused. None of the honors seemed to have resulted from his involvement in the Wakulla Conference, Dan was certain.

That all seemed now to have been so little a part of his life, Dan thought as he clicked on the icon to the Küchler letters. He opened one from Jewel that seemed to be the next in the sequence to the last one he had read.

I've checked my temp. and it's normal – I take that as an indication that this is a lucid interval – so I'll send you the gleanings of the morning.

♥

Letter follows ... will write soon ... more later ... too much going on now ... too much to straighten out in my head just yet. You might already have the lurid details — a murder and a suicide are hard to keep out of the press — especially if the suicide was a crippled war hero and the murderer his attractive wife — and an orphan — and a family name that still commands interest. The Chicago tabloids — especially the Sun or whatever it calls itself now — have been full of it. I imagine the New York Daily News reaches the environs of Arden Forest. If the way the Atkinses have characterized me as the "Whore of Detroit" gets into the papers, it may just lose me my job.

Mother is taking it very hard — doesn't get out of bed — and complains about chest pains when she does. I have engaged a Chicago lawyer to watch over my Detroit lawyer. We have physical custody of Danny, so that should keep us in good stead should Grandma Atkins go ahead with the custody fight.

Danny doesn't understand what happened — he clings to mother and me.

You must believe what I told you over the telephone — Jimmy was physically incapable of fathering a child. The Atkinses have no blood ties to him, genetically or emotionally. A horrid affair!!! What a silly ploy it had been to try to involve you.

"Whore of Detroit?"

No blood ties?

Catching him without defenses up, the phrases stabbed him like cold assassins. He slumped unresisting into his chair, as if the wound were mortal.

His mind was both blank and occupied with images and ideas that swirled in and out and around. Afraid of what he might now find, he nonetheless turned his attention back to the letter.

But Darling, don't you think it's time you stopped working for at least 24 hours, sat down on a mat facing Somewhere, and while serenely contemplating your navel, came to a definite conclusion about what's keeping us apart?

I have the distinct impression of being the only woman on earth whose tough heart was won by annotated bibliographies, ecological reprints and digests. Likewise you are the only ecologist of such unique literary appeal.

Ecologists

Because of the heightened powers of perception resulting from my queer circumstances, I've graduated from Grade B to a Grade A person – right in your class. Eighteen years is a longish time – but I think each of us had more growing to do than most people <u>ever</u> accomplish.

When I last wrote, the Good Lord had just picked me out of the smug complacency of my little nest – set me on a road heading toward Connecticut, given me a smart smack on the fanny and said "There young lady – <u>that's</u> where you belong. – What are you waiting for?" – Meekly I replied, "Please Sir, just Fred.

♥

I told you the reason I couldn't see life in the woods was that there wasn't a book in me awaiting writing. Now there are not one, but three - 2 of which cry for your collaboration, one of which you have already collaborated upon – or perhaps inspired is more correct.

I. Songs Before Dawn – verse already over eighteen years.

II. Traveling Toward Light – autobiographical – describing stages in metamorphosis of 2 individuals – parallel accounts of ♂ and ♀

III. Copulation and Generation.
So That's That.

Now Lord, you can stop bothering me – and about me — and go concentrate on <u>him</u> for a while.

There were only a few more tokens representing unread letters in the file. Two of the letters were long ones, multiple scanned pages. They would be in Jewel's spinsterish hand, he knew. Another he found, just as long, would be in Küchler's typescript. He wanted to leave them—delete them out of his life! He would burn the originals in Arden Forest, if he could. But one of the letters, a short one, was already on his screen.

Your good letter came just after I'd mailed the enthusiastic number. I meant it – but please understand – for some convenient future. Your new work demands full attention now. I'll see you somehow next summer.

Above all <u>don't</u> tell your mother. I'm sure it would upset her – And I really believe she is mentally ill – to the degree that she *would upset your work plans or anything else – to keep you at hand. – You must be careful not to argue with her. – Flatter her and pay her the attention she needs – or there'll be one of those drastic illnesses that would tear your work all to pieces. Believe, my dear, you can't afford to anger or upset her now. So tell her if she asks about me – that you haven't heard lately. More power to the good work – and tell me about the Research Foundation idea. Sounds wonderful.*

It was as if what was in the previous letter had been imagined. His mind in confusion, he closed that note and clicked on the icon of the first page of the next letter in chronological sequence, dated a day after the note. Eight more icons with that date followed it.

I should explain my hasty second note of last week – There is not time to do so in person — and it is a matter too delicate to even mention over the phone. I put my faith in the US Postal Service's ability to safely put my thoughts into your hands.

First, about your mother — I understand her now and that makes me love you even more strongly. Your letter had told of the absurd Doctor's orders regarding visitors at Arden ... My hunch: When your mother was in her late teens she suffered a severe psychic blow – probably some unhappy love affair. Later after her marriage to a kindly older man and the birth of 2 sons she was extremely nervous and had spells of being temporarily at least – the young girl before the tragic incident. She was not mature enough to enjoy her children – and worried about them and at them. You rebelled – and by eight had to be sent to the country to save your life.

You had an unusual capacity for affection & tenderness and felt the unhappiness of your mother very kindly – as you grew older. When you came to see her after college – you were a young man. There must have been times during those vague spells when she was the young gal again that you filled for her the position of some young man she had cared for long ago. It was in such a role I saw her – the night — that absurd, magical night — after the dinner at the Japanese restaurant when we returned to your house – and your Guatemalan friends came. Little mannerisms – interest in makeup –

Ecologists

choice of dress, shoes, sitting on the floor – rather than occupying a comfortable chair – even the manner of her good night to you – were all the acts of an eighteen year old – of a generation ago. Then another problem seemed to my mind to solve itself. I got out your letters from 1935 to 45 – and wrote down a chronological outline of the Küchlerian peregrinations and discovered that the records show you were recalled from Florida by your mother's illness in Aug. 1942. In Dec 1942 – after Christmas – called to Washington on a mysterious charge – In 1944 were refused a passport because of an anonymous letter in 1942 accusing you of draft evasion.

    Now any person who had seen the spectacles that you wore would have known the army would reject you – So the motive of <u>fanatical patriotism is out</u>. There is the possibility of a vicious trouble causing enemy who could cause you much inconvenience and remain anonymous. But botanists just don't make that kind of enemies. There remains – someone who loved you and wanted you safe inside the country in time of war – knowing the army would never send you off to fight. Such was your mother. Remember – she was very ill that summer. Your uncle took care of her. The temperature one runs when under mental strain can simulate very closely a virus disease symptom. ... Your uncle's fear of her developing a conspicuously upset or obviously insane state would be enough to make your Uncle Fred her slave – she announces what she wants – and he makes it a doctor's prescription. It might have been better for the entire family if her condition had become acute years ago – so separation from the family would have been necessary. <u>You</u> certainly would have been less confused. Her husband would have gone out more – had more sunshine.

    Did you once tell me her father was definitely insane? I hope so - for that would relieve the family of a lot of worry. If, as I suspect, there's a psychotic gene involved – it would appear to be a simple Mendelean <u>dominant</u> trait – or <u>incomplete dominant</u> depending on environmental accident to bring it out. She got the bad gene. Your uncle didn't. You didn't. Under degrees of strain many times over any her sheltered life are likely to have given her – you become better adjusted to life and the world every year – as you grow farther away from your <u>unhealthy</u> childhood.

    And should you make a decision in favor of a wife – for instance – you would better understand how to cushion the blow for *her. – If she were confronted with a fait accompli and the calm alternative of accepting it & friendly relations within it – or of <u>having</u> to be hospitalized at the hands of <u>strangers</u> – her hold on reality is strong enough, I think, to make her choose sanity. The other way there is nothing to gain. Enough! – too much!*

So threatening are the clouds over Europe – so sure am I of what I want – that I'm taking the long chance that it's what you want too – but would be years getting at without my help. If I'm wrong – and the whole idea gives you horrors – you have only to say so – there is nothing to lose.

The <u>how</u> could be fitted into your schedule. A train out of Albany 1 ½ hours after midnight on May 18 or 25 – You arrive Fri. noon, - last details are arranged – a quiet ceremony in my home Fri evening – mother will clear out and leave us the place for the weekend.

Saturday there are some people in Lansing & Ann Arbor – U of M – I'd like to have you meet - & show your m.s.s. of the ecology text.

I take you to the train Sun. PM – and you are at Arden Monday. – A little worse for sleep – but with a devoted wife and housekeeper all sewed up for the summer. [For several reasons – financial familial – etc. I think I should teach here next winter – after that – sufficient unto the day – are the decisions thereof.]

If you could arrive on Sat. noon June 24 I'd like to have an open house where 50 or 100 friends & relatives might meet you. Sunday – we could drive home to Arden together.

After that you are responsible for seeing that I never again have an opportunity for being a "managing" woman.

As for the missing word – I shall let the verse speak it.

What verse?
Was something missing?
And what a strange letter! He could make no sense out of it. The next, again, was dated a day after the previous.

What a beating you've taken this month! ...I'm still trying to understand what just happened – I can't lay it all to horrid things in the past — and present. Suffice it to say that I liked and still like the idea that somehow you can come by the courage to face yourself before your life – goes utterly to pieces – all twisted around by a false idea of sexual propriety and legal responsibilities. I confused and challenged you apparently. – Alone – I should not have had the courage. With you as my knight-in-shining-armor to back me up – I could speak seriously without disgust of anger. So you have served a useful purpose – no matter how shocked you may have been to find yourself so enlisted, even back those many years ago when Liza and I plied you with sloe gin after a Japanese supper. Perhaps when a lady is pushed overboard she can be forgiven if her yell for help lacks something of the well modulated tone.

So you now know what a flighty creature I can be – and you can see why I never stayed longer at Arden Forest.

Friday most of us went to schoolmasters club in Ann Arbor. As usual I skipped the dullest sounding lecture to go see C. D. La Rue – The poor old boy is going to seed, - simply reeking with self pity. Lord! I'm glad that my mother taught me to be conscious of that fatal fault – and fight it while still a child. He's been teaching such ecology as they gave (his real interest is hormone studies and tissue culture) – but they are getting a man from Montreal U. – one Pierre Dansereau – "big shot ecologist" — publishes a lot – getting him they think for a reasonable figure – so that's that. At least you can be assured ecol. is looking up – in this part of the country.

Another puzzle, Dan thought. Just more to confuse him. He opened the final letter, Küchler's. It was his last chance to solve the riddle of his life. His hand trembled on his mouse. He switched to keyboard controls.

I am deeply grateful and sincerely appreciative of the trust, the love, and the respect that you have seen fit to confer upon me; and I am especially deeply disturbed, ashamed and horrified that I had not seen fit to tell you more of myself before this time.

Years ago (between the time we first met, and the time you visited me in Syracuse) I loved – and lost – and, as a youth would, foreswore marriage. It was lucky for me, and for her, for it gave me the time to develop as I would have developed anyway, and eliminated what would have been on my part as cold a leaving of one's family as that of the Buddha.

I am married to my profession now, for the good or not of society, and in a way that suits the needs of my nature for not seeing that society at close range. To be married to a woman seems like a gross selfishness, a personal luxury in which I have no right to indulge. Besides, (if I recall my Francis Bacon correctly) "he that hath wife and children hath given hostages to fortune, for they are impediments to great enterprises" – "either of virtue or mischief" he adds. My freedom and my liberty are now the keystones of my entire life. I can not take on the responsibility for the child, even as I admit to the possibility you allude to having happened that night. You cannot deny that the "opportunity" of which you speak was little more than forcible rape on your part. You must also admit that your tardiness is not credible with fact. But there is more I must tell you.

You would never tolerate my anti-sociability. I am used to, and prefer, to pass whole days and even weeks without speaking a word, or even seeing anyone. The thought of talking to the same person, even only mealtime after mealtime ... well... I can think of no author, no genius, no person, with whom I would wish to chatter for every future mealtime, no one, nothing – except possibly my Encyclopedia Britannica. The situation of having a child nattering away at me ...

You would never tolerate my refusal to eat and sleep on schedule. I scorn the person who chops up the real things of life, and plops them into the intervals between scheduled meals and sleeping times. Eating and sleeping for me are fitted into what odd intervals may be found during the 24 hours, or acceded to when the body will no longer act without them.

You would never tolerate my attitude toward sex. Basically, I am not a man that one woman can hold. I see no reason (even tho I now live in a country where Christian monogamy not only dominates the lives of most people, but stamps even our psychology and psychiatry in the form of a nationalist science) to change that attitude. I have had, and hope to continue to have, friendships with women both platonic and un-platonic. As for the latter, I doubt that we would find each other compatible: I recall blinking up at you from a hospital bed in a strange city and commenting that the very women who might have spoken for me at that time were ones whom

I would not ask to speak out. Do you remember how you literally stiffened in moral indignation?

You would never tolerate the way I would sail into you for your inordinate interest in popular psychology, in looking backward at people's personalities, in adding to insufficient facts the wildest assumptions. (Not so: There has been no insanity in my family. I did not get sent to the country at the age of 8, but at 16. I began directing my own life at the end of my senior high school year, if anything, later rather than earlier than normal. "Absurd doctor's orders regarding visitors at Arden Forest" when my parents are here. It happens to be my suggestion, seconded by the doctor. What is so unusual in a mother who has for years been mistress and hostess of a country home, wanting to outdo her strength in continuing that role when her housekeeperless son, who now runs and owns the house, has a visitor? The passport-refusal draft-evasion incident: I know 98 percent of the details. You have guessed quite wrong, nor should you guess better, for it concerns certain interests of which I have never passed a hint to you.) You would never tolerate my criticism of you for manipulating your frail evidence until they accorded with one of the stereotyped case histories of which you have read, and you sit back with your Cheshire-cat contentedness. But what does it accomplish or change? The ancients could still be kindly and sympathetic with suffering personalities, even tho they had none of the sacred cow abracadabra the we mumble these days.

And where would I get the money to support a wife? With a child? And whose child? I am making less than when an Asst. Professor at Syracuse – and the dollar has changed in value. Sure, I could get a fulltime job – and leave Arden Forest to do so, leaving the intellectual freedom which is the very spring of my professional creativeness –if there is any.

Perhaps I have no heart. At least, I have known no individual for whom I would sacrifice my last coat, my last loaf of bread, my last penny, my life. I have not that much respect for any individual human being, nor for myself and my personal happiness. But humanity – they did not ask to be here. I would destroy it with one violent gesture if I could; and since I can not, I shall try to ease the sorrow.

Don't you see, Jewel – you are fundamentally an optimist, and must work directly, immediately, with people, among people, and be surrounded by people. (Have you ever really lived alone, for days on end?) – I am fundamentally a pessimist, and must stay away from people, surrounding myself with non-human nature, and with those artistic and intellectual effluvia of civilization which kid me into thinking that the whole of humanity is worth the effort of my endeavors.

I wish you the happiness, Jewel, that you had thought we could create together, but it is not to be found in my direction. I owe more to society than I owe to myself or to you; and you owe it to yourself to realize that I am not what you would wish me to be. It is best that our ways part. I should have parted them long ago. May you continue your "travels toward light", and when they appear in print, know that one copy will be read by your erstwhile.

But what does it all mean? Dan wondered, staring at Küchler's signature. That it was without salutation stayed in his mind after he turned the image off.

Then he noticed another icon in the Fairfax file. It was a postcard that Jewel had sent after they had moved to New Haven. He remembered seeing nothing of any significance in it at his first glance at it at Arden Forest.

He never should have read the letters, he decided. He would forget the entire Küchler project. He clicked to delete the file and shut down his computer.

Had he opened that last image back then, he would have seen the following:

Greetings and thank you for the adv. on the Brush Control film. I hope to see it – I think we can use it as a tie-in on our conservation unit.

A mild winter so the roses survived – It's a <u>good</u> year for lilacs – (why can't they do equally well <u>every</u> year) and just now we have <u>hundreds</u> of starry narcissi.

Hows Salome? Best luck to the laurel - & the learned research associate.

PS. Danny is healthy and happy and looks more and more like you.

Should Dan ever open all the cartons of Jewel's things, packed at Ames Hill for eventual arrival at Lincoln, he might stumble upon a framed photo that had stood on her kitchen table. Mother and child. Blue-eyed. Blond-haired. Beautiful. Fjords are visible in soft focus in the background.

Behind them in the Madonna-and-child pose is the paternal grandmother, trying, it appears, to keep her severe visage so as not to break into weeping.

Slipped into the frame are two other baby pictures. One is of Jewel. The other is of Danny. The three babies, if posed together through some trickery with Adobe Photoshop, might be mistaken for triplets.

Afterword

Ecologists caught my attention in manuscript form when Bill sent it to me to review. He had incorporated writings and phone conversations with Walter Westman, my Swarthmore classmate and fellow botanist. They came from a self-published booklet that I produced in memory of Walt, who died of AIDS in January 1991. With the ms in Word, I used the Find function to dial up Walt's name and was taken into the latter third of the text where he appears while embedded in one of several layers of subplots within the book. His initial appearances were brief and at rallies at UCLA, where Walt was once a professor in Geography. But then suddenly I was reading familiar prose only slightly edited with Walt addressing his friend, the fictional character Danny, almost exactly as he had once written to me. It was a bit disconcerting to say the least but also satisfying. Here was Walt alive again with a light shining on this hidden tender side of him. Walt had been a pioneer among scientists in coming out and in exploring ways for gay and lesbian scientists to become leaders. He unfortunately contacted AIDS before effective antiviral drugs and cocktails were developed. The passages about him in the book tell of his failing health as one drug after another becomes ineffective. It's a poignant view of the AIDS scene in the 1980s.

The passages about Walt illustrate how this is a book of fiction in the midst of nonfiction. Many characters are real people who lived lives as ecologists much or somewhat as depicted. By representing their interactions with the protagonists, the book affords a personal view of many of the key developments in ecology in the US from the 1930s into the 1980s—a fertile time for the field as it rose from an obscure science into the front lines of conservation and environmental battles. Rachel Carson played a role in this development and she appears in the book.

Bill writes a history of ecology without its being a history, because scenes are imagined and both real and made-up characters populate them. What is refreshing is that the book's two main characters—themselves fictional but based in part on real people—provide a point-of-view (POV) sense of what transpired, rather than a third person telling in a strictly chronological order. A reader gains some sense of what it was like to be on a field trip with Shelford in forests and high plains in the 1930s or to be part of a large over-spilling lab at Cornell in the early 1970s. Many of the leading ecologists during these times are seen in action as they work with their lab groups and focus on classic problems. By listening in as the participants wrestle with ideas and how to gain the data to support them, a reader finds out how scientists work and how broad a range of ideas get introduced and discussed. Some of the issues of being a woman in science whether in physics or ecology are also revealed by two of the fictional characters. The largely unspoken subject in those years of being gay also plays a role in the story's unfolding.

It's a fascinating read.

Thompson Webb III
Providence, Rhode Island
January 21, 2015

Made in the USA
Lexington, KY
12 June 2016